Critical

MOREVI

The Chronicles of Rafe and Askana

"A magical, sensual, swashbuckling adventure! The lively cast of characters and the exotic setting -- the age of England's Henry VIII meets, courtesy of a dimensional rift, a fabulous fantasy world -- mix with action, scheming, and intrigue for an engrossing story.

And given that it is billed as 'The Chronicles of Rafe and Askana', we can hope to see the adventure continue in many books yet to come."

-- Christine Morgan, *Sabledrake Magazine*.

"Buckle your seat belts and keep your hands inside your armchair for this journey; it's a wild one.

Morevi was well written and fast paced. The characters leapt off the page and provided a great deal of entertainment, (as well as an occasional well timed chuckle to lighten the tension)."

-- Tina Morgan, FictionFactor.com

"This fantastic fantasy novel, the debut offering for both Lisa Lee and Tee Morris, creeps up on the reader like a dream: there is no escape, nor is there the desire for one.

From the very start the characterization and the action are a constant draw on your attention and all you can possibly want is more, not because the story is lacking, but because it is addictive. With a variety of vividly portrayed settings you enter a world that is like no other you have ever seen, meeting there characters that you either love or love to loath."

-- Danielle Ackley-McPhail, author of *Yesterday's Dreams*

"*Morevi* is jam packed with intrigue and excitement every time you turn the page. This epic novel is fast paced and filled with characters that emerge from the written words to delight the reader's imagination as you join them on their fantastical journey. Through Tee Morris and Lisa Lee's gifted prose, they take you on a wild voyage through time to an entirely new world that will keep you in awe at every new discovery."

-- Tony Ruggiero, author of *Team of Darkness*

MOREVI

The Chronicles of Rafe and Askana

by

Lisa Lee & Tee Morris

www.dragonmoonpress.com

w w w . m o r e v i . c o m

MOREVI

The Chronicles of Rafe and Askana

by

Lisa Lee & Tee Morris

www.dragonmoonpress.com

w w w . m o r e v i . c o m

Acknowledgements

Who would have believed a random January morning on the Webchat Broadcast System would lead to this? Since beginning this adventure in 1999, we have learned that creating an epic adventure would have been a lot harder without the love and support of family and friends.

From Lisa & Tee — A huge thank you to Danielle Ackley-McPhail, Gabrielle Harbowy, and Tina Morgan for making MOREVI sharper than a shirai. And to Gwen Gades of Dragon Moon Press who dared to cross The Rift and take this leap of faith. Without you, we wouldn't be here.

From Lisa — A special thank you to my mother, for instilling in me a love of books. To Lina, a source of inspiration and support. To Lee, who makes all my days brighter. And finally, to Tee. We made it all this way together. Thank you.

From Tee — Thank you, Mom and Dad, for always being that pillar of support in my life. (Dad, you were right about the writing.) To Natalie, for all your patience, wisdom, ideas, and love. VickieMom, for your time, critical eye, and available ear. To goldsmith Robert E. Piland and artist Anne Moya, for contributing their talents simply out of belief in the story Lisa and I penned. Uta and Naser, thank you for your "namesakes". To Kim Headlee, Tony Ruggiero, Jacqueline Carey, and Julie Czerneda, for your guidance and acceptance. To the Internet Fantasy Writers Association, a fount of knowledge, trivia, and answers. And to everyone of Wargo's Martial Arts, for keeping my path straight, my goals clear, and my perserverence strong.

However, this adventure would have never begun without the townspeople of Revel Grove. To Mary Anne Jung and Paula "Queen Schnookie-Face" Peterka for your endless knowledge and expertise on Tudor History. A huge thank you to Artistic Director Carolyn Spedden and General Manager Jules Smith for their permission, support, and blessing for taking Rafe Rafton one step beyond. And to the cast and crew of the Maryland Renaissance Festival for seven unforgettable seasons of swordfights, swashbuckling, and scotch-tastings. Thank you, everyone!

And finally, to Lisa, my Writing Muse and Partner of the Pen. It started with an idea, fifteen minutes in a chat room, and a single e-mail. Thank you for inviting me into your world of Naruihm. Thank you for your trust. Thank you for everything.

So, what's next? Let's make it happen.

Dedication

The writers dedicate this book
to the loving memory of William G. Huttel,
the Man Who Would Be King.

Thank you, Bill, for your contribution to this work
and for touching our lives.

God bless the King.

"Where there is a sea, there are pirates."

Greek Proverb

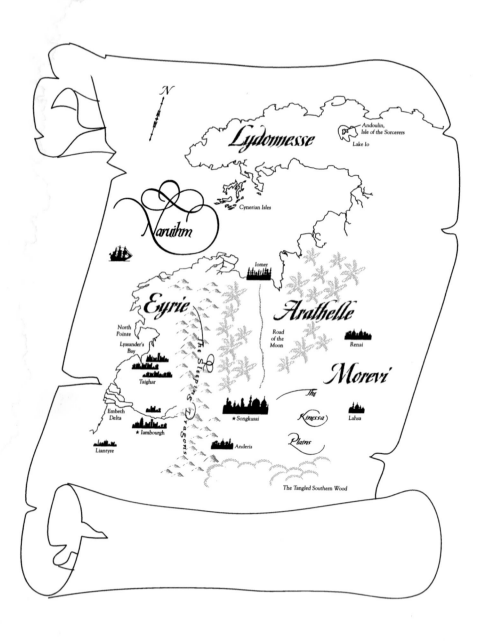

Table of Contents

A Leap of Faith

The Captain could hear the roar of powder kegs in his ears, but he could not move from where he fell. He wondered how long he had been there. He tried to remember if it was the sudden lurch the vessel took that sent him to the deck. He was having a problem recalling anything. His mind was jumbled, lacking focus. He lost track of time. The deck shuddered underneath him. *That was a well-placed volley,* he thought as he worked harder to catch a breath. It was taking the same effort to hoist a sail, to breathe. *My ship,* he repeated silently, *my beautiful ship. Please forgive me, my King. I have failed you.* The Captain closed his eyes. It was just too much of an effort to keep them open. Suddenly he found his awareness peak. It was an apex of all sensations at once. It did not overwhelm him. It did not hurt him. There was a strange comforting feeling in this place of sound, and slowly the thunder of cannons grew farther off.

Farther off than they were in truth.

"The Captain is dead!" cried one of the privateers over the fire raging below decks, "The Captain is dead!"

"The First Mate is down as well!" another sailor bellowed as he passed a full water bucket to another.

"Mind the fire!" shouted a third from the top deck, "If them powder kegs catch fire, we will have done the Spanish a good service! Keep them buckets comin'."

It was in 1492 when "The New World" was discovered. From this land of legends, legends that included cities of pure gold, mountains of gemstones, and exotic delicacies not found even in the travels of Marco Polo, explorers of the land mass called Europe launched brave and bold expeditions to bring back treasures for royalty. Some of these men sailed around the world. Some never returned. Still, Man was embracing the arts and sciences with a new-found passion, instilling fear in the religious leaders of this world. It was an age of enlightenment, a new dawn of humanity that was being dubbed as "The Renaissance."

Part of The Renaissance was an ingenious new tactic of reaping the New World's treasures without hazarding costly voyages across the Atlantic. Rival nations called it "common piracy" but the King of one particular realm called it by a different, more civilised trade—*privateering.*

King Henry the VIII of England looked upon the open seas as just that—open. Open to all nations. Open to opportunity. As privateers, these "common pirates" were agents loyal to and pardoned by King Henry. They possessed Letters of Mark that specified what ships they were allowed to engage and which were free to navigate the oceans of the Atlantic. The latter were usually King Henry's own. This "gentleman's piracy" came with a price. If privateers were captured, there would be no rescue, no ransom, or no return voyage home. The "Letters of Mark" were worth less than the rope used to hang privateers for crimes of piracy.

This is why the Captain filled a good portion of his hold with powder kegs and cannon balls. He always wanted to assure escape if under fire. Now the English faced the added challenge that their advantage did not turn against them and blow the *King's Calling* out from under their feet.

Sanders watched the men heed his earlier advice and now they tamed the fire for the time being. The Spanish warships were still closing. In his eyes, there was little to be gained from this voyage. "We should abandon ship! We've lost the Captain! The First Officer is dead!"

"No, we will not leave the ship, Mister Sanders!" a deep voice sounded over the chaos of the deck. It was distinguishable for two reasons. It carried with it a bass deep as a thunder clap. It also carried a sharp-edged accent, thick and not of the usual dialects found in England. "The Captain would have wanted us to stand and fight! It would also grant the wishes of Allah to send these Spaniards to a fiery death for firing on His children!"

He was a Moor. He towered over most of the Englishmen within the ship's complement, but his size coupled with his powerful voice did nothing to elevate his standing. The Moor's ebony skin and his beliefs made his status as "outcast" and "heathen" amongst the crew apparent.

"I think, Moor, your brain's been cooked after too much time a' sea!" snapped Liam Sanders.

Sanders stood eye-to-eye with him, his own height equal to the Moor's. The man was far from any lofty position of leadership on the *King's Calling*, but his stature, sunken eyes, and gaunt-like features gave him an intimidating look apart from the other Englishmen. Many times he was asked to "speak for the crew" although the Moor hardly felt this man spoke his mind. He could never share his opinions with the others, but he suspected the man to be nothing less than a coward. For a "heathen," his instincts were quite accurate.

The main sail turned sharply, its massive form suddenly billowing to its full shape as the wind trapped itself within the weave of the fabric. The crew siding with Sanders watched in amazement as the second sail shifted to catch the same breeze. They could feel the ship's hull shift forward as their course changed abruptly.

"Again, lads, heave!" a voice rang out over the thunder of cannons and volley of fire that slammed against their starboard side. "I did promise my sister, Serena, I would be present for dinner two days from now. I will be damned if I keep her waiting!"

The small band of privateers tugged against an array of thick, heavy ropes while another secured the cables to hold fast the sails. The self-appointed leader then assumed the Captain's Podium of the *King's Calling*, wiping away the blood from the maps with the cuff of his shirt. He muttered co-ordinates to himself as he made light charcoal marks against the charts. His actions were hurried as another volley of cannon fire came from the pursuing ships. A smile crossed his face as he could hear the cannonballs splash into the water, showering the deck harmlessly with water and foam.

"And jus' what do you think you're doin', *Snotty?*"

Sanders hated being challenged on what he considered was *his* ship. This young whelp seemed to relish in doing just that. "Snotty" was the nickname Sanders dubbed him as he carried himself a little better than the rest of the crew. Snotty's first month on board bought him a few floggings from Sanders that left his face and parts of his body black-and-blue. Still, the boy stood up to him. He became untouchable when he was promoted to the position of Ship's Navigator. Now that the Captain and First Mate were dead, nothing could keep Sanders from openly challenging him, as well as calling him "Snotty."

"Ensuring our return home to England, or are you so blinded by fear you did not notice that?" The navigator shoved him against the deck and drew a modest foil from his side, the tip resting against Sanders' neck. "We have no captain. No boatswain. I, for one, do not wish to live out the prime of my life in a Spanish prison, provided we are not executed for piracy! Now stand down and let me plot this course!"

"They have matched our course and draw close!" the Moor shouted as he saw the Spanish ships catch their breeze.

"We have a course plotted." The navigator stomped hard on the planks underneath his feet and shouted down to the whip staff's crewmen sharp commands that eventually led to the ship's rudder. Once more the *King's Calling* shifted as the navigator sheathed his sword. "Now let us hope the Spanish are not as mad as we are!"

Sanders followed the light marks against the navigation chart, his eyes widening upon their destination, "You have plotted a course for the Graveyard of Lost Ships!" The lumbering man grabbed the navigator by the cuff of his doublet and tossed him aside. "You there!" his voice boomed, freezing two young sailors in their tracks. "Fetch us a white banner! We're surren—"

The chill of the iron barrel pressing against the back of his neck cut his orders short. Sanders turned slowly to find the giant Moor aiming the ornate rifle at his head. The Moor's training in the weapon was merely a formality. He was never permitted to handle it in combat. A lack of trust that neither the Captain nor First Mate would acknowledge openly. He would have never thought his first chance would be used in an act of mutiny. Or was it mutiny? They had no one in command.

Only this navigator, still very green in his time spent upon this vessel, seemed to have a direction they all needed. It would be a direction that would get them home.

"Master Navigator has a plan I think would work better than facing a death sentence in Spain!"

"You savage!" Sanders snapped, "Lower that rifle before I whip you soundly."

"I crave a pardon, Mister Sanders, but I am on the better end of this rifle."

Over the sounds of deck fires and Spanish cannons, the successive *"click-click"* of the rifle's hammer pulling back to a firing position sounded clear in their ears.

"You wouldn't dare, Moor," he spat.

"I have made my peace with Allah." The Moor slipped his finger around the trigger, "Have you?"

The collection of privateers, their faces bloody or blackened by the smoke of battle, had gathered on either side of the gangway at the sight of Sanders held at gunpoint by the ship's outcast and young navigator. The mighty sea breeze that pushed them across the waters widened small tears in the sails but still they managed to keep a lead from the closing ships. A few ears caught what words were exchanged at the Captain's Podium, and these words were quickly passed from crewmember to crewmember. They were tired, they were afraid, and they waited for an order. Now only the wind catching the torn sails sounded in their ears.

"Our navigator means to take us to the Graveyard of Lost Ships!" Sanders announced, "This is madness, to be certain, for the Moor sides with 'im! If we surrender with no fight, we might find mercy in the hands of the Spanish!"

"I doubt that!" the navigator snapped. "Do you forget what we do for King and country?"

The enemy ships were closing. Fast. It was clear they did not intend to take them back to Spain to face a trial. It was the Laws of the Sea they would answer to with three Spanish captains serving as judge, jury, and executioner.

There was a hint of uncertainty as the navigator walked onto the gangway, his eyes looking at the crew and then at the closing ships. Then, in a moment, the fear and doubt were gone. In their wake, resolve and determination.

"Lads, we have not known one another long enough to build a trust, but the Captain trusted my talents in navigation. I know where we head may unleash more dangers upon us. Rest assured. You have the word of your navigator, Rafe Rafton, that I shall get you all home." His blood coursed through his veins. The excitement in his tone gave his words an edge that made them appear hasty and erratic. "If we dare the Graveyard, the Spaniards will break off from pursuit. This is a leap of faith I ask of you all. If you grant me this boon, I promise you all a round of good English ale at the Anchor. Come along, lads, what say you?"

They could not hide their apprehension. What did this lad know of strategy upon the ocean? He did not even have a proper beard upon his young, fresh face. Still, without a captain, it was this bravado upstart that rallied a handful of the crew to fix the sails. Now they sailed into an area of the North Atlantic Ocean that no one would dare to chart. It was off Ireland's Emerald Coast, where arctic winds would send ships into a patch of sea that opened up and swallowed them whole, so the legends told. Any ship seen heading in The Graveyard was never seen again. Be it rocks, fog, or sea monsters, no one would ever know for certain what claimed them.

The privateers looked to one another with knowing grins. No better time to find out what secrets were in the Graveyard than now.

The Moor lowered the rifle and smiled, "Guess we are following you, Master Rafton."

The *King's Calling* had taken a pounding from the Spaniards but she still managed to float. Yet their speed was decreasing as the sail's numerous tears were widening from the wind's force. The crewmen made ready weapons in case of another attack, but once more the powder made their situation dire. In fighting the fire, many of the kegs were now wet, rendering the powder unreliable. They had to keep their distance and hope to lose the Spanish in this daring, dangerous escape ploy of Rafe's.

"Master Rafton, we draw near the Graveyard." The Moor said, keeping the rifle close. His Persian accent sounded harder now, cut and sharp in its enunciation. "There is a smell in the air not like the sea."

Rafe nodded, his eyes peering forward, "I would agree...forgive me, man, but your name?"

The Moor gave Rafe a friendly smile and said proudly, "I am Nassir A'Lass Jalhammad, Master Rafton."

"Nassir." Rafe smiled back, "Good to have an ally in someone as *large* as you. Do me this service, and watch my back. I cannot tell if this crew—Sanders, in particular—would trust me in what lies ahead."

"You see trouble in the Graveyard?"

"If I am fortunate, no. If I am wrong," Rafe looked back at the closing Spanish ships, "at least I enjoyed a taste of leadership before passing into the next world."

"Snotty!" Sanders barked as he peered at the compass, "Look a' this."

North. Southwest. Northeast. The dial bobbed and spun wildly. Sanders glared at Rafe as the compass became less and less reliable, finally giving no bearing whatsoever. They were now in the Graveyard of Lost Ships.

Rafe snatched up a telescope and stood at the aftercastle, focusing on their pursuers. "Good." Rafe smiled, speaking to Sanders over his shoulder, "It seems our Spanish friends are also having problems with their compass."

The billowed sails of the lead Spanish vessel collapsed into a wrinkled mass of cloth, its sisters doing the same. Rafe's smile broadened as the ships abandoned their pursuit, the space between them widening with each passing moment.

"Looks like I will be making good on my word in buying everyone a round, eh, Mister Sanders?" Rafe's answer was nothing more than the sound of rushing water within his ears, perhaps coming from their speed as the wind remained strong. "Mister Sanders?"

Rafe turned to see what kept Nassir's and Sanders' attentions. The boundary rose high above the *King's Calling* and continued to grow in diameter as they approached it. A circular barrier of water and light. Solid, yet not an obstacle such as coral reef or crags. They could see jagged rocks shimmering behind it, but they knew whatever towered before them was no illusion. Despite the calm oceans surrounding it, a strong current rushed towards this wall of liquid brilliance only to disappear inside a canvas of ripples. *No*, Rafe thought, *not a wall. A portal.* A gateway. And perhaps, a means of escape.

He did not know where the voice originated from inside him, but it reached the crew to their basic instinct upon the sea. "Secure the ship and hold on to something!" Rafe shouted.

"Now I know you are mad, Rafton!" Sanders grabbed the rifle from Nassir's loose grasp and held them both at bay. The fuse was still lit and the hammer pulled back. He screamed over the growing thunder of water and air now surrounding the ship, "I am assuming command of this ship!"

"And where shall we go, Sanders?" Rafe stepped forward, his chest pressing against the barrel of the gun, "Go on and pull the trigger. Perhaps the crew shall back you in your order to surrender to the Spanish."

An invitation. Lovely. "Suit yourself, Snotty!" he said with a dry, hard smile as he pulled the trigger.

Rafe's own smile widened as he followed Sanders' eyes to the pan. The wind from the portal had blown it clean of powder. Nothing remained to ignite the chamber. Sanders lurched forward suddenly. He fought to stand but then realised he could not as he was being lifted off the deck. A stinging sensation removed itself from his back, returning his feet to the wooden planks. He turned to see Nassir behind him, the dagger in his grasp now decorated with his blood. He fell to his knees before the Moor, his laugh a grotesque gurgle before falling face down on the deck.

Was this to be an option for them? Turning on one another? Taking their own lives? It was either death by their own blades or the Spanish rope, or challenging this rift reaching from the depths of the Atlantic before them.

No, Rafe thought as he looked to the crew, *today is not their day to die.*

"I said secure the ship and hold fast to something!" he called again. "Steady the whip staff! I would rather chance what resides here than face the Spanish magistrates!"

The bowsprit of the *King's Calling* was an impressive carving of Poseidon that bore a striking resemblance to King Henry. It was majestically pointing forward into the unknown horizon and was first to pierce the doorway of water and light. Ripples extended outward, a site hypnotic and mysterious, from the point of entry as they continued to slip forward. Some of the crew ran for the lower decks while others held tight to masts and secured fixtures of the ship, their curiosity overriding their fears. Rafe could hear the twisted hemp stretch as the sails billowed full, the tears now gaping holes. Still they moved forward, faster than they ever sailed before across the open waters.

Hold fast, Rafe thought as the ship continued to disappear in the void, *hold your course until we reach the other side*.

His skin tingled lightly as he felt himself pass through the portal. The roar of air and water surrendered to an abrupt silence. It was not marred by any other outside noise or echoes, not even the natural sounds of wood creaking or sails catching an Atlantic breeze entered his ears. Total, complete silence. Rafe then realised he was holding his breath, his eyes lost in a brilliance that did not hurt to look straight into as sunlight would. The white light surrounding him grew in its intensity, washing over everything around him. Perhaps this was a final destination for him and his frightened crew. Could this rift be a gateway to Heaven itself?

He remembered uttering the place by name, shattering the silence. "Heaven," he said with a smile.

Then, an abrupt darkness and Hell erupted around him.

Lightning tore through the grey and black cover above them and the ship leaned sharply. A mighty wave struck the *King's Calling* as if it were Poseidon's very hand itself, his fingers of water and foam slamming hard against the deck. Rafe heard a snap behind him and saw the bonaventure mast topple towards him. A strong hand reached out from the darkness and he felt himself in Nassir's embrace as they slid along the water-drenched top deck. The crew cried out for mercy but the storm refused their pleas as it twisted the seas underneath them.

Deep in the ship's hold, a crew of ten struggled to keep the whip staff steady. That was their order. They could not see what was happening topside. From what they heard, they did not want to know.

"Master Rafton," Nassir bellowed, "where do you think we are?"

"Wherever we are, we are on the right path! Note the sails. They are not struggling against the wind. We must stay on this course!"

Another wave swept over the deck, and Rafe could feel himself pulled from Nassir's arms and towards the dark waters below him. Then came a stinging sensation around Rafe's wrist as a dark hand wrapped around it. With a growl rivalling the storm's voice, Nassir pulled Rafe back on to the ship. He could not help but laugh. It was reassuring to know that even if his decisions in navigation were questioned, his taste in allies never would be.

They both watched the bow of their ship disappear into a darkness, a wall of shadow. Another portal. As the *King's Calling* had slipped into a shimmering brilliance it now vanished within an inky blanket and Rafe could feel the undercurrents against the rudder subside. A similar chill passed across his skin and then another brilliance surrounded him for a moment. This light had sound. Within Rafe's ears played a symphony of waves, the occasional seagull, and the comforting sounds of the ship's hull creaking lightly. The chill passed and now there was a heavy, humid warmth. Rafe and Nassir rose to their feet and looked around them, taking in a deep breath of the sweet sea air.

Behind the *King's Calling* was the portal they had passed through. Following the tide and currents, the oceans carried the ship farther and farther away from this rift. High above their heads, birds cawed to them as if offering to be their guides to land. There were no other ships in sight.

"He has done it!" Nassir trumpeted, his massive arm wrapping around the navigator's shoulders, "We have survived the Graveyard!"

The crew coming from the belly of the ship raised voices with their comrades as Nassir supported Rafe Rafton to the rail overlooking the main deck. "Hip hip huzzah!" resounded. Rafe remained pensive. He looked about their lone ship. There was no sign of the Spanish. The breeze was a touch warmer than off the Ireland coast. It would not be challenged that they lived to fight another day for King Henry Tudor, but a new challenge presented itself.

Where the hell were they?

The fear he denied before crossing the strange portal now consumed him like a fire.

"Someone man the topcastle," Rafe snapped. "We need to know where the coast is."

The men silenced abruptly and one young, eager sailor leapt to the thick rope netting leading to a small outpost high above the ship's deck. He had just taken his place up in the watch when suddenly he cried out, pointing off into the horizon.

"Ship ahoy!" the watch called, "Ship to starboard!"

Through the telescope, the details of the ship told Rafe they were no longer in the North Sea. The modest vessel resembled "junk" trade ships from China. The sails were a series of rectangles linked together, far less attractive or intimidating than one of King Henry's warships. This ship had a more interesting enhancement unlike its sister ships of the Far East – rowers. Arms of wood extended from the sides of the ship, giving a hint of assistance to the warm sea wind. It bore colours of brilliant green and white. The insignia in the centre of its banner was not of any king or country Rafe knew. He studied this ship's banner for a long moment, quietly committing himself to discover the holder of this strange crest. Any ship bearing such an impressive banner could only come from a house of nobility or influence.

"Captain, shall we fly the colours of King Henry?"

Rafe continued to watch the ship through the spyglass. The junk stayed its course, the oars still keeping a steady pace.

"Master Rafton." Even at a light whisper, the Moor's voice was powerful and ominous. Rafe turned sharply to the sound of his voice and was eye to eye with Nassir. The grin worn by this Moor, a *seasoned* privateer, was obvious. Rafe was in need of some coaching in his new position. "The men are turning to you. We go nowhere without your word."

Rafe looked about himself nervously. *I am a navigator,* he thought quickly, *not a captain.* Then he saw the crew assembled on the main deck, all eyes on him. Waiting on his word, as Nassir said. Whether he was ready for it or not, Rafe was the victim of a sudden field promotion.

Captain Rafe Rafton, the navigator thought to himself. *What will Serena think of this?*

"No, we fly the signal for distress." Rafe looked across the deck, the once fine wood and ornate carvings of the *King's Calling* now blackened with soot and chipped by explosions of the Spaniard's attack. "Not a far cry from our current state." Laughter. It was a delightful sound. "Set fires on the deck. The rest of you, prepare the cannons. If we are not welcomed to where we are properly, then we shall make our presence known by more aggressive means."

"Well done, my Captain," Nassir whispered.

"I hope you approve." Rafe smiled, a sense of relief washing over him, "It would be an ill sight if my First Officer questioned his Captain's initial order."

It took a moment for Rafe's words to register in Nassir's mind. Another promotion granted from actions in battle. The Moor straightened his posture proudly by Rafe's side, adding another foot to his height. Now with a First Officer, Rafe could begin his first command. Hopefully, it would hold long enough for him to find out where they were in the world.

Banners snapped against the strong breeze pushing them closer to the foreign ship still a good distance from them. Warm winds carried off their deck plumes of dark smoke from two small, contained fires. The semblance of distress, a tactic that had served them well in the past. It would be a common practice of ships to aid others in distress. It was maritime code. Sailor's ethics. Nautical courtesy. Yet this foreign ship was, in Rafe's brief time at sea, the most discourteous vessel he ever met on open waters.

"We are closing on them," Nassir stated, the telescope lowering slowly from his eye, "but the rowers are only quickening their pace."

Rafe's eyebrows raised slightly as he looked ahead to the other ship, "Most ill-mannered, would you not agree, Nassir?"

"Indeed, my Captain," Nassir said, shaking his head ruefully, "Allah blesses those who help others. It would seem these children of His have lost their way."

"Well as Mercury failed to be an efficient messenger, perhaps Mars will do better." Rafe motioned to Gunner Williams, "Fire a volley to get their attention."

Three cannons sounded. Only three of the eight, simply as a warning that splashed their decks harmlessly. At their closer distance, Rafe no longer needed a spyglass to see the hurried activity on the junk. By the reaction of the crew, cannon fire was not customary in their travels.

The oars halted and withdrew. The odd sails slowly lowered.

"Well, that etiquette lesson went well received, " Rafe said with a grin. "Master Gunner, reload those cannons and await my word. We shall see if this crew is in earnest."

As they neared the vessel, Rafe grabbed the doublet of his dead captain. Fortunately, the bloodstains would not be visible within its finery and dark colours. While wearing the clothes of a dead man unsettled him, the doublet would give Rafe a more authoritative look aside from the rest of his crew. Regardless, the garment would make him hard to miss on deck.

"Ahoy, Captain," Rafe called. "Surrender your vessel in the name of King Henry the VIII of England." He saw only ten rowers and the Captain, none of these men with a "seafaring" look about them. They looked as he did when first joining the *King's Calling*. Green. Seasick. They also looked terrified. Not *of* Rafe so much as *for* Rafe. "Mon Capitán, parlez-vous anglais?" Still nothing. "Señor Capitán, se habla ingles?"

As Rafe attempted to recall his Latin, the archers appeared. Their movements were as swift as a fox on the hunt. Rafe managed to dive for cover as the first wave of arrows sailed through the air. Arrowheads poked through the hull of the *King's Calling*. The bows must have been of amazing tautness and quality, matched only by their archers. A few sailors were lifted off their feet, landing hard on the deck. Their bodies convulsed sharply as blood, mixed with saliva and spittle, gushed from their mouths.

"Poisoned arrows. Just lovely." Rafe sighed, shaking his head as the second volley of arrows pounded rhythmically against the side of the ship. "Williams, send them a proper English greeting!"

The line of archers disappeared with a roar of flame and smoke as cannon fire ripped away part of the junk's side. With a single gunshot from Rafe's pistol, the first boarding party threw grappling hooks into the air and heaved, bringing the two ships closer together. The air filled with howls and cries. The second boarding party's charge was answered by the shrill piercing cry of birds. Feathered creatures of metal, leather, and fabric were appearing from thin air, wrapping themselves around their attackers. Death for these privateers was swift. The first party, safely on deck of the junk, took full advantage of their entrenchment and picked the supernatural harbingers of death out of the air with rifle and pistol fire. Rafe led the third team as they swung from ship to ship, a barrage of pistol fire preceding them. A high-pitched whistle cut through the battle. Rafe called for his men to drop to the deck. Another privateer fell. This time, instead of an arrow, a large disc-shaped blade had buried itself in the man's chest.

"All right, lads," he called over the cries of battle, "Have a care! Make your aim true and your blade swift. God save King Henry!"

Rafe and several other privateers fired reserve pistols into the fray while the remaining party drew swords and charged. There were sounds of metal striking metal. Screams of agony. The shrill cries of hawks and falcons. Rafe motioned for the rest of the party to go on while he attempted to raid the Captain's Quarters. His rapier extended from his left hand while a dagger resided in the tight grip of his right. The young privateer ran into the darkness of smoke and black powder, his eyes fixed on the largest cabin above the hold.

Then it appeared. A feathered creature of metal, red leather armour, and silk, brandishing an odd weapon similar to a halberd. The blade of this staff appeared much longer and far deadlier, though. Rafe continued to knock away the blade with the dagger, his rapier useless at his distance from the assailant. He could feel himself pushed back into the battle, losing ground quickly. The soldier thrust the weapon forward, but Rafe leaned sharply to one side, his dagger and rapier catching the staff and binding it down to the deck. With a powerful axe kick of his leg, he snapped the staff in two and slipped around his feathered opponent, holding the attacker on point.

"Remove your helm, good sir," Rafe huffed. "I prefer to look you in the eye before running you through."

The helmet was off in a moment and Rafe stepped back, his sword's tip dropping slightly. She was a striking, exotic beauty. Dark eyes slightly tilted as he had seen women of far-off realms of silk, tea, and a Great Wall that spanned across a nation. *Did this rift take us to the other side of the world?* Rafe pondered as he looked upon this breathtaking maid.

The kick lifted Rafe off his feet and was followed up by a hard strike across his back from the remaining staff left in her hand. She moved in to kick him hard in the ribs, but Rafe brought his foot around in a low sweep that caught her ankles and knocked her to the ground. The savage merely lifted herself up with a light push off the ship's deck. Rafe fought to keep his balance, his back still pounding from her attack. She spun on her feet, sending him flying across the deck again with a powerful sidekick. He felt himself crash through a door and slide across wooden planks.

Rafe glanced up. He was inside the Captain's Quarters.

"How fortune smiles on me," he groaned.

His humour was short lived as the woman charged at him, a small dagger now in her hand. This time, the privateer was prepared. He quickly pivoted to her side and blocked the incoming blade with his rapier. She could not pull back fast enough as he drove his own dagger deep into her belly. Her knife fell. Rafe did not hesitate to pull his dagger back and then slowly drag it across her delicate throat. There was a slight hint of satisfaction in knowing she would feel her death for a time. The men in his company were not dying gracefully. Why should this savage?

As he reloaded his pistol, his eyes searched wildly for anything that would hold charts. Across from a modest bed was a small chest with a lock hanging and swaying open with the motions of the ship. He quickly threw open the chest and released a sight of relief. Its contents were a sight more welcome than a ship's hold full of gold or spices from the New World. Charts. Books of letters. Maps of foreign lands. He had found what he needed, but this raid was not a success yet. They were still on board a foreign vessel, fighting an unknown foe.

As he thought of an escape, he froze. Only the creaking of the ship, the sounds of the ocean, and wind filling the sails of the *King's Calling* could be heard. Rafe pulled back the hammer of his pistol as footsteps resounded on the opposite side of the door. The hatch flew open as a shadow pointed a rifle at Rafe's primed pistol.

"Nassir!" Rafe snapped and then gave a delighted sigh to his comrade, "My God, you are a more beautiful sight than Aphrodite herself!"

"If that is so then you are in need of some shore leave, my Captain," chuckled Nassir as his own rifle lowered. "The ship is ours."

"We are most fortunate, Nassir." Rafe smiled, handing him the books. "A different kind of bounty—knowledge. We have here what appears to be several books of letters as well as a Ship's Journal. We can at least attempt to familiarise ourselves with this realm. And charts, Nassir! Blessed charts! At a glance, we have much to discover."

Nassir's face went blank suddenly, "Charts and maps are not needed for that, my Captain." Nassir motioned behind him, "You will know we are in a foreign land when you see the prisoners."

The smoke cleared to reveal some of his own crewmates covering the deck of this strange vessel. From the number of dead savages to dead English, it was merely surprise and number, not their skill or prowess, that had won them this junk. It was not his dead crew that made his eyes grow wide. It was the regiment of soldiers, all decked in armour of red leather, silk, and brilliant silver. They stared at him, committing his face to memory, silently cursing him for the death of their comrades, and promising swift retribution. Rafe looked back at the green and white banner flying high overhead. Then he returned his eyes to the soldiers. His eyes went right to left over each of them, still refusing to believe what they saw.

"Nassir," Rafe whispered, "where are all the men?"

Meeting of the Minds

The morning crowd at The Barrier Reef was a good size today. Not too large, not too small. Most talked quietly about politics and new arrivals to this haven between realms, or bent over the bar closer to what mattered. No fighting today, fortunately for the bartender. Osgood had already replaced countless broken chairs and tables, and mended numerous holes in the roof *and* the walls in this past week. He was a big, beefy fellow with his remaining black hair tied back with a leather thong and a rotund waist resting incongruously over a stained, yellowed apron. The tavern master and innkeeper already faced a robust day as newly vacated rooms were in need of tidying up and the more aristocratic patrons were demanding personal attention. It was enough to keep Osgood and his three barmaids exceedingly busy.

The burly man wondered for a moment as he wiped a mug clean of dishwater if he was growing too old for this business. The daily duties, it just seemed of late, were growing beyond his control. Just as one of his customers reached a point of bliss and satisfaction, two others would find something wrong with their rooms or their afternoon tea cakes. Perhaps it was time to sell The Barrier Reef and settle for an easier life. The passing thought made him chuckle to himself as he looked around him. They were all explorers, swords-for-hire, sailors, and rogues. From different realms. Different worlds. Different ages.

Since when has time ever mattered here?

The tavern's comforting mix of candle and firelight was suddenly pierced by the brilliance of afternoon sunlight. Osgood recognised the silhouetted figure in the doorway before the door closed behind him and with a smile he watched the approach of the rogue's hat adorned with peacock feathers and a black leather rose in its band. The hat's wearer tossed his cloak to one of the barmaids, exchanging with her a glance too warm to be appropriate. Osgood's serving maids smiled for him as women always did for a ladies' man, but today only one other was expecting his arrival.

A bottle was placed on the bar for the newcomer. White wine, still covered with frost droplets. An aged vintage from the Royal Vineyards of Anderis. The man was dressed in burgundy and black, a fine ivory handled rapier by his side and a duelling dagger sheathed in the small of his back. He smiled widely as his eyes studied the wine bottle's seal. It was a reminder of a chance meeting two days prior. It was a token of interest for his particular talents. It was, more importantly, her olive branch. In her realm, the price on his head was steep. She would know as she was the one who continued to raise it an additional one hundred gold sovereigns for every ship of hers he claimed on the open seas.

The bartender smirked, motioning to the bottle. "Your class of lady has improved, Captain."

"Nothing at all amiss with your lovely barmaids, Osgood," he replied brightly. "This lady, much like this wine, is exceptional. She is truly unique. Worthy of my special attentions and talents."

"Well, you must've made quite the impression on this one. The Lady is waiting upstairs, Captain," he said with a surreptitious wink as he provided trysting places in the tavern for enamoured couples. This time, however, the Lady had taken the initiative in reserving the room.

Osgood motioned to one of his barmaids, removing her from the lap of a potential customer. The shapely tavern wench led the pirate down one of the inn's dimly lit hallways to a heavy oak door. Crudely made, but stout and protection enough from prying eyes and ears. It opened on hinges that cried out for a lubricant's touch, its creaks ripping through ambient tavern talk. The barmaid gave the rogue another inviting look, touched perhaps with a hint of jealousy towards the awaiting woman. She knew this Privateer Captain's abilities and always held her breath when he would first enter The Barrier Reef. He paused and gently stroked the wench's cheek with a gloved hand. She tipped her head towards his touch, her smile widening at the gentle gesture. Opening her eyes for one last look at him, she gave a soft sigh and then slowly shut the wooden hatch behind him.

At the far end of the room, the lady knelt, her court robes gathered around her waist. The Pirate Captain could not help but be impressed not only by the lack of modesty from this queen, but also for the faith in her abilities to sit so confidently with her bare back to the door.

"Well met, Askana Moldarin, Bla—"

"A moment, privateer," the woman snapped, neither her head nor her figure moving from its position.

Her pale skin stood out against the shadows of the room. As she had her back to him, the privateer was deprived of a more provocative view. Her back still granted an impressive display of muscles and sinew rising and falling through the soft, supple casing of a woman's flesh. Beginning at the centre and working its way down her back was a magnificent tattoo of a serpentine dragon, intertwining through a collection of Morevian characters, a brilliant white tiger, and a bird surrounded by flame clutching a delicate flower. This, he surmised, was her family crest. The canvas for this particular picture was far from perfect, marred by the scarring souvenirs of her bloody ascent to the throne. The Morevian characters reminded him somewhat of Chinese writings he had seen in his travels across Portugal and Italy. He did recognise with some difficulty the characters were her family name and title.

Askana of House Moldarin, First Queen of Morevi.

Such beautiful strokes, he thought as he surrendered to their hypnotic movement on living flesh. He supposed that was the attraction of tattoos: living art. The Queen's title writhed on her back as she performed the movements of prayer. The Captain peered around her to catch sight of a small statue, three female forms merging into one, a flame cradled in its centre. He could not hear what she whispered but was certain her words were Morevian.

Slowly her head bowed and a single motion of her arms slipped the robes back over her shoulders. The Queen secured the fine silks around her body and took one final, deep breath before rising from the tasselled cushion on the floor. She turned to face him, her tilted black eyes looking him up and down boldly with a coldness he was not used to receiving from women. Her eyes were unmistakable, unforgettable.

She had caught his attention days before dressed in simple battle armour, a beautiful woman adorned in armaments as ladies of his realm would wear gold bracelets, bejewelled necklaces, and pearl pendants. The fierceness of her attire then matched her natural radiance. She now appeared so different that, for a split second, the Sea

Captain wondered if he had entered the correct room. Now she wore the traditional court-dress of flowing green and white robes embroidered with the Turi flower, a key ingredient in the making of fine perfumes in his and the *other* realm. The embroidery matched the flower in the tattoo and the wine label.

And, of course, the emblem matched the banners of ships he attacked in open waters.

The Captain had grown familiar with this sigil and now chance had brought him before the woman it represented. Her hair was piled high on her head behind a stiff, winged creation of green and gold brocade, her eyes lined with black paint, her mouth a shimmer of red in her face. Not the full regalia of "court-paint" he had caught glimpses of in his covert visits to her cities, but just enough make-up to accent her grace and beauty. The Captain smiled with approval for she was a breath-taking woman, just as unique as the perfume she wore. An unseen signature of sandalwood, jasmine, and lily with a touch of blue tea.

She remained, however, an adversary not to be underestimated. An adversary that called for his head on a pike. A bottle of wine and a business arrangement were far cries from making an enemy into an ally.

"I hope you find the wine pleasing to your taste." The tone of the Queen was very different now from when he had entered. It was as if she was quashing down impatience to make herself more approachable.

"I am quite fond of your realm's vineyards. Morevian vintages have complex but pleasing characteristics. This one, in particular, is one of my favourites." He considered the bottle as he spoke, "Yes, this particular label pulls a fine price for me on the black markets. Always a banner day when I pillage this particular vintage from your ships."

Askana remained motionless, no trace of a reaction to his obvious insult. Assessing this privateer, if he continued to prim with this heavy dose of arrogance, pomp, and bravado, would be far easier than she anticipated. He was transparent as men were by nature. Brash. Overbearing. Revealing their intent and agenda clumsily in their posturing to be the dominant male of the pack. These traits would also make him easy to manipulate.

Nothing in her face betrayed these thoughts, even when her eyes turned to the delicate porcelain cup and saucer on the table. She had hoped a relaxing cup of *chocha*, one of Morevi's prized natural resources, would calm her nerves before this interview. It had done little to blunt her edge. For that she had prayed to Nadinath, the Supreme Goddess.

"Please, sit." She sank down onto the red cushion behind the table into a posture that would prove impossible for most, gesturing to the green cushion she had occupied earlier in prayer. With a cordial nod, the man removed his hat and placed it by the offered seat. Long nails tapped on the table's surface as the Captain knelt in a manner similar to the Queen's. "I requested this meeting because I have a proposition for you. One that will pay well, have no fear."

A fan snapped open. The privateer did not flinch, but merely enjoyed its lovely artwork depicting the Palace of a Thousand Suns, a place he knew only from a distance. Perhaps one day he would actually summon the courage to see this place *from the inside*.

"But first a matter of trust." The Queen's tone returned to its sharpness from their first meeting. "I must be able to expect a certain degree of loyalty from those who take pay from me. Of course, I am not fool enough to expect total loyalty from a man—in particular, one of your base station. If I am to employ your services, however, you will agree to my terms." The fan shut gently, and she caressed it with her fingertips for a moment before letting it fall by her waist. "No more raiding ships bearing the Morevian marks. As you know, Morevi is landlocked. It has only been in recent years that we have invested into trading ships and ports from the neighbouring lands of Arathelle. While they are not sworn allies but merely benefactors in open trade, they do respect that these ships residing in their ports belong to the occupant of the Throne of the Thousand Suns. This is recognition you lack but must adopt before we are to do business together." Her voice turned wry. "As long as you are receiving monetary compensation from me, I think it would be awkward if you—how do outlaws in your trade put this— 'take a share' of my land's trade as well.

"I have a task for you, one that should not be too onerous. Our neighbour to the west, Eyrie, has a new king on their throne, a young whelp of the Goradan line. According to my contacts there, King Cedric wishes to claim Morevi for his own. I understand that Eyriener lords have approached you to take arms against me. I do not doubt in their offer you discovered names, positions, perhaps even plans. And no doubt, Cedric is massing this conquest as he has established contacts of his own, high in my regime. I want this information. Therefore, pirate, I have a course of action for you to take."

Her dark eyes narrowed slightly, the hint of a devious smile appearing across her face.

"My spies inform me that you have declined their offer, but I desire you to arrange one last business transaction with them. Present to these Eyriener merchants a shipload of Morevian tea presumably hauled off in one of your frequent raids upon my trade ships. You will sell it to them for half your price. Then proceed to tell them the reason you declined their earlier offer is that you received a similar offer from a higher bidder within Morevi. However, the nameless bidder abruptly withdrew their offer. Now you fear civil war, revolt, or a sudden change that will affect Morevi's shipping trade. With this cargo as a sweetener they will assuredly drink down the tale. I will expect spies in my court a few weeks later—Eyriener ambassadors and emissaries approaching nobles whom they believe likely to oppose me." Abruptly, she laughed. "Then shall the Black Widow set her traps and reveal the traitors, Eyriener and Morevian, to our New Age."

The Black Widow. The name, if he remembered correctly, had been given in sarcasm to a woman who had never married and yet was always "in mourning" over the deaths of her lovers. There had been many culminating in the death of a king and, it was whispered, half a nation. Her mourning attire then had been armour stained black with blood, hence the name.

Sitting there before him, she looked deceptively fragile in her heavy robes, the high headdress making her face seem small. Many men had thought that of Askana Moldarin. That she was a precious doll to be owned and displayed for all to see. And from the stories he had heard of her, precious few lived to remember or regret such a thought.

This should have been a warning to the Pirate Captain, but he did so love a challenge.

She awaited his answer, her long pale fingers returning to the folded fan. "As for the price, you shall tell me what you think is worthy pay for this task."

Now it was his turn.

The man's carriage and poise might have deceived her into believing him to be well-born, one who possessed all the answers to The Great Game, or so he wished the Queen to believe. Something in him reminded her of the many "potential suitors" from far-off lands she had once received with puffed-out chests and inflated opinions of self-worth. Such men believed a capital city and a queen would offer themselves without question or resistance. A smile crept across her face in fleeting memory of one suitor who dared to take her hand in a bold gesture, trying to convince her of the status and strength he would bring to Morevi if she accepted him as her king. He returned to his homeland minus a hand.

This man, however, was no gentleman of high breeding, regardless of his outward polish and refinement. *"Maritime Opportunist"* he had called himself when they first met. A pirate was nothing more than a common thief of the open waters, no matter how much he would try to disguise himself in gentleman's fashions. This particular pirate was above the common thief, perhaps considered exceptional by some as he was a thorn stubbornly stuck in her side for many moons. He remained out of the Queen's reach, her spies and assassins always returning in disgrace at their inability to capture this man possessing the cunning and ferocity of a wolf that prowled the oceans of Naruihm.

And this is what had earned him a moniker of his own—*The Sea Wolf.*

Deep hazel eyes and dirty blonde hair gave sharp contrast against his pale English skin. His reckless arrogance suited him too. This man seemed to revel in his audacity, looking at her directly as if he were her equal, not even averting his eyes when he had greeted her in that chance meeting days before. The Privateer Captain was obviously a believer in his own fables of invulnerability.

Brash and overconfident enough to get himself killed, the Queen thought with some amusement.

"Your Grace." His voice was pleasant to her ear, a deep baritone hinting at a purr similar to the felines who had the run of the Temple of Nadinath. There was, however, a touch of darkness in his smug words. "You have placed me in a very delicate situation. I have developed strong ties with the Eyriener lords. In their eyes, I am what your people would call a *kasam-de-nim* in the privateering business."

Askana's eyebrow arched sharply as he spoke the Morevian words for "hero of great renown." A *"living legend."*

"Perhaps King Cedric would not care to acknowledge my popularity, but I have brought them prosperity since my arrival to your realm." His eyes seemed to twinkle with a hint of mischief as he smiled wickedly. "But worry not, I pillage their ships as well as yours."

"Indeed." The chill in her voice softened his over-confident smile a bit, "You show a certain foolhardy courage, pirate, that may prove useful. Or it may hasten you to your death. Perhaps from your benefactor. Keep in mind, this covert action I charge you with in no way pardons you for your crimes. Do know that my decree still stands— if you ever set foot upon Morevian soil, I will have you killed upon the spot." Her steady hands cradled the cup of chocha as she took a sip. "Nothing would please me more, knowing of your indignities against Morevi, than to skin your carcass myself."

"But, Your Grace, what good would that do you at present? You are in need of a servant with particular talents. I am in a constant need for a tidy profit. So as we are in need from one another, we can do business." The rogue reached into a small pouch attached to his belt and produced a small, slim tobacco stick from the "New World" of his realm—she had heard someone call it a "cigar"—and dragged it slowly underneath his nose. He had retained his kneeling position for a time that would have most Morevian men squirming in discomfort, but his discipline appeared strong enough despite his rash nature. He had passed every test presented to him so far. "I will do

Your Grace's bidding and sell this Morevian tea to plant the seed of deception for you, possibly at the cost of my most profitable Eyriener connections. If the folklore is true, I am most certain you will take full advantage of what your intriguing scheme reveals. But I digress..."

The Captain's eyes searched about the room until the flicker from the small statue's tiny, steady flame caught his attention. No larger than a man's forearm, this triple-faceted figurine was the Goddess Nadinath, the focus of the religion of her people. The tiny shrine with its 'eternal flame' signifying woman's inner light had been burning faithfully throughout their entire conversation.

The Queen's breath ceased for a moment as he gently tilted the statue in his direction and used its flame to light his cigar. As the High Priestess of Nadinath's Order it took effort not to react to this intentional slight. *Indeed,* Askana's words echoed in her mind, *nothing would please me more than to skin your carcass myself.*

The rogue leaned back, savouring the first puff with delight. "We were discussing payment."

She recognised this for the baiting game it was, each taking turns to force the other's patience. What stoked her anger was his pure brazenness. A man of his station should not presume the right to test a queen. It was a true miracle that Askana found her voice. Miraculous to them both was how calm it sounded as she spoke. "Very well," she stated in a flat, business-like tone. "I believe two thousand in gold for your services in this—"

"I crave a pardon, Your Grace," he said, cutting her off in mid-speech, "but did you say two thousand?" Askana could feel her demeanour slipping by degrees as he continued, obviously caring very little that he had interrupted her. "I would not piss in King Henry's chamber pot for two thousand." He leaned forward, the cigar smouldering between his fingers as he spoke. "I can make twice that from *one* of your ships! For my talents and personal sacrifices to your crown, my price is ten thousand. Two thousand now, and payment of eight thousand in gold once my transactions with the Eyrieners have concluded and I deliver to you what your plans have yielded."

"Ten thousand?!" The Queen's sharp, incredulous laughter filled the private chambers of the tavern. "You confess to pillaging my ships, you eye me like some paramour with no regard to my standing, and now you dare make such a financial demand upon the Morevian treasury? You insult me with such an offer!"

"Perhaps I do, your Majesty," Effortlessly, the Captain stood from the cushion with hat in hand. "But my price is non-negotiable. Therefore, as we cannot seem to agree on this presently, I will no longer pillage from your personal cargo hold the precious bounty of time. I am certain you will find someone better suited for this task."

"There is no one better suited for the task," Askana conceded with unusual honesty.

Placing the cigar in between the crossed weapons carved at the little idol's feet, he sighed in rapture, "Oh, such sweet music those words are to my ears. Especially when uttered by the fairer sex." He donned his hat and spoke over his shoulder, "Best of luck to you, Your Majesty."

The unending disregard. His flippant attitude. The flowery speech. And now, departing without leave. Askana Moldarin had endured enough.

The dagger sailed by him and embedded itself firmly into the door his hand was about to open, the hilt vibrating slightly from the force of its journey's end. The Privateer Captain calmly turned to face her, his smile obviously reflecting pleasure taken from breaking her control. He expected to see her face twisted with a rage that could mottle even the noble visage of King Henry, but he would find no such satisfaction. The dagger might have been a rose thrown at a favourite from the blank expression on her face.

"I was told you were the only mercenary who refused the Eyriener lords." She said, tucking silk folds closer around her as she spoke. An unhurried woman, as if nothing out of the ordinary had just happened.

"I know ladies. Call it a character flaw of mine," he stated with a hint of pride as he returned to the cushion before her. "And I recognise powerful allies. To not acknowledge a powerful woman such as you would be a true crime against God. I am no fool, Your Grace." The Captain reached for the cigar wedged between Nadinath's weapons and gingerly wiped the statue free of any trace of ash. Askana's stare hardly softened as he lowered his eyes in a silent apology before the tiny statue. After a moment, he continued. "I know I am most fortunate to have lived this long out of reach of your trained assassins. I know that this is a mission for profit, not pardon, but any effort to win the favour of the Black Widow of Morevi will hopefully be taken into royal consideration. And I also know," he said, taking a final puff from the cigar and then crushing it under his boot, "with a healthy financial investment in my particular talents, your plan will yield an economic windfall."

Askana's head tilted slightly, her ornate headdress catching a glint of sunlight as she studied the man who now poured himself a cup of chocha. Again, without leave. In an unexpected move, the pirate refreshed her own cup as she asked, "And what do you mean by that?"

"The men of Eyrie who conspire against you are no doubt rooted within The Merchants' Circle. I do not know if you are aware of this syndicate, Your Grace. They are comprised of traders and select noblemen, and are said to be the true keepers of power in Eyrie, the crown merely a figurehead who answers to them." The Captain blew lightly at the chocha and took a deep sip of the sweet liquid. His eyebrows raised slightly at its delightful taste, a bittersweet flavour much like the New World's chocolate, only much smoother. "Once you discover who in the Merchants' Circle plots against you, I am most certain the 'persuasive demeanour' that you are renowned for will most assuredly bring a benefit to your treasury by whatever influence you hold over them. Be it a ransom for their lives, depending on who is involved, or if you decide to use the involved parties from within to divert profits or trade from Eyrie to your own realm. Whatever the outcome, Morevi will prosper. Rest assured."

It grew quiet in the room save for the flickering of Nadinath's tiny flame. This privateer's services carried a price much higher than Askana had anticipated and there would be opposition from the Council of a Hundred Turi given the state her forebears had left the Treasury. He was correct as to how she would use 'persuasion' to funnel the gains from this intrigue back into Morevi. But could she truly trust him in this? He was a known enemy of the state. An outlaw. Unpredictable. The last person expected to come to the aid of Morevi.

He was perfect.

"Two thousand now." Askana stated with finality, motioning to a small chest to the right of the table where they sat. "Another thirteen thousand when I have this Merchants' Circle kneeling before me in my Grand Hall."

"Fifteen thousand for the delivery of the Merchants' Circle?" The Captain was caught off guard by this unexpected bonus in his fee. He smiled brightly, "For fifteen thousand, I would trade in every favour I have with my realm's nobility to gain you an audience with King Henry the VIII himself!"

"With one slight change in your plan." Askana picked herself up off the cushion and stood over the Privateer Captain, "I will accompany you upon this journey."

"Excuse me, Your Grace?" His cup was set down so firmly its saucer split. He quickly brought himself to his feet, "You will what?"

"Listen to me, pirate," her voice cut through the silence with an edge as sharp as her dagger's. "You are, as you said, Morevi's financial investment in this gamble. I merely intend to keep an eye upon my investment in case a more lucrative opportunity should attempt to present itself."

It was as if she had struck the man in the back. Askana almost smiled at his sudden flush. All part of The Great Game and no one was better at it than she. Victory over a man was always sweet, capable of wiping out years of memories under their dominance. She noted the light in his eyes dim for a moment, but a moment was all he spared for her as he removed from his finger a signet ring. With a polished bow, the privateer presented it to Askana. She noted the details of the sigil—a sword criss-crossing a black rose under a playing card. An Ace of Spades, if she remembered correctly. She had always preferred games of skill and strategy as cards and dice were too reliant on chance for her liking.

"You have the word of Captain Rafael Stringfellow Rafton," he proclaimed. "True, I am a pirate. A rogue by every account, but I never go back upon my word." He looked honest, sincere, but so could the best of liars. "You have my services—and my loyalty—for fifteen thousand, as agreed."

It was a noble and heart-felt pledge. Regardless, as he could see in the Queen's face, there would be no compromise.

"Very well, Your Grace," he resigned. His voice then sharpened, matching the tone she had taken earlier with him. "If you are to accompany me on this voyage, take to heart these steadfast rules: I am captain of my ship and I have the last say. Anything you do to jeopardise the outcome of this venture will rest solely on you and have no bearing on my cost to the Morevian crown. Be expected to dirty those delicate hands of yours for this will not be an easy journey before us."

She was beyond surprise. This pirate's presumption appeared to have no limits. He behaved as if his word was actually worth something; and because of this proud display, it actually might be. She could have laughed at his words portraying her as some doll that would shatter at the most delicate touch. Did he have any inkling as to how much blood had directly 'dirtied her delicate hands' in the past? It was clear he was knowledgeable of Morevi, its culture, and its history, but only enough to hold her interest through this meeting. He knew nothing of her life, her history.

He stepped back, perhaps to give Askana a better look at him. "Keep that ring as collateral. It is my banner and my promise to Your Grace."

"A strange sigil," she said, pulling up a fine cord from around her neck. As the ring was far too large for any of her slender fingers, she slipped it into a small silk pouch at the cord's end. Her eyes continued to stare into the privateer's own as she returned the pouch under her collar, back to its resting-place against her skin. "One day I will have you tell me the story behind it."

The Captain could not help but smile, envious of where his signet ring now rested.

She turned away from him, sending a whiff of perfume wafting through the air. Her hand reached into her sleeve to feel for the amulet. The artefact, upon touching her palm, triggered a memory. She was uncertain as to why, in all times, this particular memory returned to her. It had been many years since she recalled the old witch, but her face appeared so vividly that she would have sworn she could reach out and touch the Caillech. "I know you must have some way of reaching my world. A Rift, if my people tell me rightly. But once across it, can you reach Morevi, and more importantly, me?"

"I have my ways," he assured her with a smile.

"Privateer—"

"Please," the Captain purred with a charming smile, "call me Rafe."

Askana looked at Rafe afresh, musing. The Morevian Queen knew how to use flirtation as a weapon, a means to achieve what she wanted, and to size up her target. It was a game Askana excelled at, part of protocol in her position as queen. And it was always easier to play opposite handsome men. He was taller and heavier in build than the men of her realm. Yellow hair was rare among Morevians, and highly prized in slaves. *Yes, pleasing to the eye,* Askana mused, *but since when does trust rest in beauty?*

"Privateer, you surprise me with your vow. Your profession—a profession of choice, I should add, and one that has cost my country dearly—is based on deception and duplicity." Words could be used to subtly slap a man in the face so that he felt ashamed of himself. Something else she excelled at. Rafe, this time, never faltered. She continued, "I do not know how familiar you are with my realm but there is a forest south of my nation."

Rafe nodded, "I know of it. I know talk from the tradesmen and sailors who say that particular area of your realm is best avoided."

"And they are wise who avoid it. But, privateer, days will come when children must cease their fear of darkness." She produced from her sleeve the amulet, a smooth, brush-polished silver pendant with a brilliant green stone suspended above its criss-cross knot-work pattern. "I went to find the Caillech of the Tangled Southern Wood. This amulet of her making grants me and another passage between realms. She is half-mad and will not allow most to seek her out. If you need the means to reach me, I will take you to her now for an amulet of your own." Askana's tone changed slightly, "Otherwise, the death sentence I passed upon you may prove to be a hindrance."

"Rest assured. I am a resourceful lad."

Askana nodded, her fingertips gently tracing the pattern in the amulet. Behind her, the walls and floor of the room appeared to fold into themselves until the fold spread apart to reveal a dark void of black, violet, and grey.

Rafe gripped the handle of his signature rapier tightly. He knew sorcery was practised in and across The Rift and was accepted as part of nature, but it always unnerved him.

Noting the pirate's sudden uneasiness to the magic, Askana smiled mockingly. "We will see, privateer, exactly how resourceful you are in this venture." And with another long look over her shoulder, she stepped into the dark void.

As Askana disappeared through the portal, Rafe considered her final words. It was challenge after challenge with this dangerous woman. He continued to stare at the space where the portal had been, already charting in his head their course across The Rift and then across the lands of Naruihm to Morevi. A shipment of tea, as well as one of the riskiest endeavours he had ever agreed to undertake, awaited him. He wondered if his crew, knowing the price on his head in her kingdom as well as her reputation, would think he was truly insane. The payment of fifteen thousand in gold, though, justified any dangers he or his crew would face.

As far as Askana Moldarin's reputation and hatred for men, it was no matter to him. *She is a woman like any other,* he thought flippantly.

He never could lie to himself well.

Rafe also knew he would have to tread lightly with this fine lady as she was not an easy one to read. The dagger had surprised him. It was a sign that Askana, manipulative and commanding as she appeared to be, had a low tolerance for defiance, particularly from men. Something to commit to memory and live by as one of God's Ten Commandments.

Rafe dislodged the dagger from the heavy oak door. The blade was stronger but much lighter than any other he had the pleasure of possessing. Its engraving was in Morevian of which he knew very little, enough to survive in the streets, deal with select merchants, and sack her ships. Perhaps this was her family motto. He would have someone translate it for him. The blade's handle was not ornate like most weapons of royalty, the handle a dark redwood that twisted between the crown pommel and the dagger's hilt. Rafe knelt by the cushion she had once occupied and rested the dagger's pommel gently against his lips. A dangerous smile crept across his face.

She was as beautiful as a fine rapier, and just as lethal, too.

"And what do you think, old girl?" Rafe smirked, addressing the tiny statue of Nadinath who still nursed the flame in Her basin. "Have I stepped in over my head this time?"

Rafe had always been a God-fearing man. He knew God existed from the numerous close calls he lived to tell about. There were moments he should have clasped hands with Death only to have it averted by some Divine Intervention. As for the Goddess Nadinath, he knew only this—it was a woman's religion and the beliefs of its sovereign Queen. He gave it no credence whatsoever.

Still, there was a sense of foreboding when the flame, as if posing an answer for Rafe's question, snuffed itself out of existence.

A knock sounded from the heavy door giving Rafe a start. The thick oak hatch swung open and his First Mate breathed a sigh a relief, lowering his primed pistol.

"My Captain," Nassir said. "I was worried for a moment." Rafe could tell his Moorish friend was agitated as his speech was quick and sharp, thickening his Persian accent so much that he was almost unintelligible. "I did not see the Queen leave and I was afraid you had been taken by—"

"Calm, Nassir, and ease that hammer back into place before you pull the trigger and shoot your foot off!" The privateer motioned to where the portal had been. "She left through the back way."

"But, my Captain," Nassir said, much slower and more deliberately now. "There is no back way."

"Exactly, Nassir," Rafe said with a wink. "Best to keep Askana's exit a secret. Now back to the *Defiant* with you. We set sail across The Rift."

The dark giant began to relax finally, his words better than before but still given by his accent a sharp lilt contrasted by his deep bass voice. "Are we returning to England?"

"No," Rafe smiled clasping the giant Moor's shoulder. "We must ready the ship for a crossing not into our realm but Queen Askana's. We have been hired for a particular job. I shall explain the details once we are away. Now go, my friend, go. Your Captain is well and right behind you."

From the doorway of the room, Rafe watched Nassir motion to his fellow crewmates at one table. They had seen Queen Askana arrive, pay for the room, and then they waited with pistols primed as their Captain conducted business behind closed doors. They were the Captain's Watch and always kept a close eye on Rafe, especially when his business involved those who wanted him dead. He could overhear Nassir assuring them the Queen had left through a "back passage." It was difficult enough getting his crew to accept The Rift. Rafe's ability to navigate it like any other stretch of ocean gave them the confidence it was not "magic" but "God's Work." No need to stir superstitions telling them about Askana's unorthodox exit. Her amulet and use of it stayed with him.

The privateer slipped Askana's dagger into his belt pouch and tried to recall if in this seaport there would be a craftsman who could sell him a proper wrist-sheath for it. He was about to leave when his eye caught something by the window. A long scarf of fine silk, a deep green as that of a grove upon the eve of night contrasted by various Morevian characters in a brilliant white. Embroidered in the centre of this beautiful, sheer material was the Turi flower, the signature flower of Askana Moldarin. The fabric still carried a trace of her perfume.

Rafe felt reassured as he tied the silk scarf around his calf, physically binding his new commission to him. A gleam flashed in his eyes as he looked about the room one last time, reflecting on this pact between himself and the First Queen of Morevi.

This, Rafe thought with a smile, *is going to be an unforgettable adventure.*

Escape from Morevi

A heavy mist hovered over the Palace of a Thousand Suns as a veil. In the chambers of Queen Askana, attendants moved silent and sylph-like as they perfumed her skin and dressed her in morning robes. Lulled by their ministrations Askana allowed her eyes to close gently. Her mind would wander in times like these to trivial, unimportant matters. These thoughts would assist her in a dreamlike escape, pleasant diversions before returning to the day's reality. This morning however, her thoughts lingered on the bargain struck with the English privateer.

Oddly enough her instinct had been to trust the man, dangerous as he was. This move might gain her an unexpected and thus useful ally, as well as cut down losses to piracy by more than half. The question though was why was he willing to forego his ties to Eyrie? Unless, of course, the "ties" he claimed to keep with this Merchants' Circle were wearing down to the point of worthlessness already.

Her eyelids slowly opened to the majestic view of the Sleeping Dragons, the impressive mountain range marking the border between her kingdom and Eyrie. Askana rose from her chair as attendants bowed in reverence. Her thoughts now turned to King Cedric. He wished to extend his own realm beyond these mountains before her. He was young and headstrong, but he was also quite wary. To take Morevi, he would need an ally high in the Council to usher his forces into the Great Hall. He would leave direct attack to last, if at all.

Askana knew she could not afford to sit back and wait. Border patrols were growing bolder and increasingly antagonistic. The stream of Eyriener women stealing into Morevi in search of a better, more liberating life was slow but steady. Then came the news from her spies of Cedric hiring mercenaries, building his armies.

And her thoughts returned once more to the one sword-for-hire that rejected Eyrie's offer only to accept Morevi's.

These matters, though, would wait. It was time for her morning ritual.

The sword, an elegant, crescent blade that came alive in her two-handed grasp, could cut through the hardest steel armour. It had served her well in the past when she fought to gain the throne. Now it served as a tool for her training. She had always scorned the balance of wooden practice swords and thus abandoned them in her lessons. This element of danger, using real weapons, did not taper the intensity of her Blademaster's attacks. If the strikes were ideal, the weapons' ring would startle white doves from their perches and return them to the sky. The morning sunlight illuminated the courtyard, reflecting off the waters of fountains and the edges of swords with a curious, surreal beauty that belied the swiftness of the fight. This beauty was essential. There was no place for anger or emotion here. The mind needed to be clear, action coupling with reaction. Her blade was not a weapon but her cunning and agility taken to solid form, moving in a fluid infinity of attacks and defences. In this discipline Askana's skills were unparalleled even by her teacher's standards.

Though today, her reactions were not as precise as they had been in the past.

"You move as a pregnant yak, Your Majesty," Blademaster Kubi-Sogi snapped, pulling back his blade. "Continue this mockery of my teachings and I will give you a good scar to remember me by in your winter years."

From behind the protective mask she wore, Askana's eyes darkened at the grey-beard's challenge. Granted, that was his duty—to push her. And similar to a court jester, her weapons trainer was allowed an occasional insolence to the crown. However, this morning's customary slight was not received kindly. She quickly straightened to full posture and ripped off her mask, signifying a halt in their lesson.

"Drink," she snapped in a chilly tone, tearing the training gloves free of her hands. A young girl filled a large goblet with exotic fruit juice, a favourite of the Queen's during her training. Askana spoke over her shoulder to the old man, "Forgive me, Master Kubi-Sogi, but I am distracted by affairs of state."

Removing his own mask, Kubi-Sogi laughed as Askana drank deeply from the silver chalice. "Your Grace, I have spent my life mastering the blade, both in war and in peace. In that time, I have grown to respect how it is merely an extension of the warrior's soul. Try as you might, Askana Moldarin, you cannot hide yourself from the sword. I have seen a tiger's rage in you during battle and joy as pure as light when your heart is easy. The way you fight today—apprehensive, distracted." Kubi-Sogi shook his head ruefully, clicking his tongue. "Something troubles you."

"Are you my trainer?" Askana refused to look at him, afraid of what he would read in her eyes. Even she could see the trepidation in her own shimmering image in the reflecting pool dedicated to Nadinath. A few strands of her long, dark hair fell loosely across her face, a face that barely contained the expressions of random thought. "Or are you my counsellor?" Askana slipped the training mask on before turning to Kubi-Sogi, his own mask replaced and his sword held ready. They resumed their morning exercise as she spoke. "I have made a pact with a devil of a man. This gentleman—and I use the term loosely—seems well-suited to the task. However, I wonder if he is as talented as he claims to be, or if he is as insubstantial as a breeze that fails to fill a ship's sails."

"Good, Your Majesty." His voice softened for only a moment, "Now attack!" The old man blocked the potentially lethal blows of Askana's blade, his body effortlessly changing from attack to defensive postures. "Indeed, Your Grace, men who boast of bravery and thrive in the light of notoriety are often cowards at heart, playing at the pretence of manhood."

Blademaster Kubi-Sogi was deceptive in his appearance. Small and aged with a kind, almost monkey-like, face. Upon meeting him, his manner was always benevolent with perhaps a touch of playful abrasion. He was the storyteller bathed in the glow of firelight, telling fanciful yarns to delight and entertain. A sweet and gentle soul.

This was his advantage in battle.

She deflected his blade, catching it in a quick bind. The morning sunlight caught the flat of her own, blinding them in a swift moment as her blade slid along the length of his. Their fine edges' ring reverberated in the courtyard but was quickly drowned out by the sound of Askana's weapon bearing down on the Blademaster. This would be the crucial "killing" blow, the intent of Kubi-Sogi's lesson, and the end of their morning practise.

It would have been had the cut not been suddenly blocked by a third blade.

This was not a familiar weapon. It was heavier and not as graceful as the Morevian sword but sturdy enough in its make to stop her attack.

The Queen went to remove her mask but found herself unable to move. There was another body behind her, pressing against her own form in a familiar, intimate fashion. She could see the one hand from behind her keeping the blade still while she felt the other slip underneath her training mask and place a dagger across her neck. Askana saw her Blademaster caught between a tall, dark-skinned giant and a fair skinned man. The larger of the two intruders gingerly removed the sword from Kubi-Sogi's grip. She could also see behind them a third man nervously wielding a strange weapon longer than his own arm, her two handmaids kept prisoner on the opposite end of it. The two smaller men appeared as beasts of burden with haversacks across their backs, but their baggage did not hinder their movement. Otherwise someone would have heard them.

Askana looked closer at the strange weapon through the screen of her training mask. He had the staff-like weapon braced against his shoulder, occasionally blowing against a piece of cord that burned slowly at one end. This was the weapon of pirates! Her anger was now growing to a fever pitch. Four pirates had intruded the palace and now desecrated her courtyard!

Only one person held her. Whoever it was made no overture to disarm her.

Then she heard a familiar voice speak from behind her.

"And then there are some," Rafe purred as he removed the mask from Askana's head, her dark eyes ablaze with anger, "who boast merely to mask their true talents. A most pleasant 'Good Morning' to you, Your Grace."

He crossed in front of her with a severely over-confident grin, appearing in his garb of black as a shadow walking free in a brilliant world of marble and sunlight. Silverwork made a pattern of roses that ran inside the lining of his doublet and crept down his breeches. His footsteps were silent from the soft deerhide boots reaching up to his knees. Obviously the man appreciated fine clothing. Perhaps it was this foppish demeanour that made him so unlearned in the ways of her world. The Moor exchanged with Rafe Kubi-Sogi's confiscated sword for the Captain's heavier blade. With practised ease, he swept the sword through the air, a delighted smile crossing his face at the feel of its balance. "Absolutely glorious. Like swords of the Orient I saw in Portugal, but much lighter. What do you call this weapon again, Your Majesty?"

Askana seethed, her grip tightening on the hilt of her own sword. "It is called the *ru-yilei.*"

"The ru-yilei. I should learn more of your tongue, Your Majesty," Rafe said, giving the curved sword another pass across his body. "Nothing like Morevian craftsmanship, but I do admit to lacking knowledge in ru-yilei etiquette. Care to give me a lesson?"

The Queen's eyes darted quickly around her. Her Royal Guards were unconscious, apparently caught by surprise and subdued quietly. The Captain's skill in stealth was apparent and extended to the men under his command. She had chosen her outlaw well; but he remained, for the time being, ignorant to her faith. Sacrilege had been committed. This pompous ass and his men would pay. The Queen's eyes returned to the Captain, his ru-yilei extending to her as he took a challenger's stance. Her eyes narrowed as she also slipped into a combat posture.

"A lesson you shall have," she hissed.

Askana could not be certain, but from the corner of her eye the statue of the Goddess seemed to smile.

There was something playful in Rafe's eyes as he tested her with simple, elementary attacks, touching her blade mockingly. The contempt in his parries was his continuing challenge. His goading did not unnerve Askana so much as unleash all her skill upon him. She fought not with rage but with a controlled passion that the swordsman in him acknowledged as the mark of a master. She had precision and seemingly endless control. He wondered for a moment how far he might have to push to discover her limit.

Askana recognised this hesitation as an opening and her blade slipped underneath Rafe's defence, reaching for his throat. With dexterity unexpected from her opponent, he arched back and slipped around her weapon. His own blade quickly rotated along the length of Askana's, creating a cascade of perfect rings that echoed lightly as his bind narrowly averted the lethal attack. His body snaked around her lunge and he pirouetted back into a full stance before the Queen. With a flourish from his ru-yilei, he bowed quickly and winked at her.

It was clear to his men and the Morevians that Rafe was having the time of his life.

He dropped down suddenly, cutting at her ankles with a blow true enough to sever bone. His target disappeared with a rush of silk. He looked up to catch sight of Askana back-flipping high into the air and then landing silently across from him. Without hesitation she charged with a cut directly to his head. Rafe quickly turned on his feet, deflecting the attack with his blade laid across his back. He then pushed against her weapon, turning to face Askana as their swords remained locked in this bind. With the flat of his ru-yilei across the nape of his neck, Rafe summoned a final parry. Her blade was free of him and his own blade was continuing an arch towards her head. She turned into his body, stopping the attack abruptly with a single-handed parry. With the Privateer Captain behind her, she pulled him close with her free hand, wrenching the fine fabric of his collar unmercifully.

It was time to bring this little game to a halt. With the hand still gripping his collar, she quickly bent it back. A small and deadly poisoned blade extended from her wrist gauntlet and rested against Rafe's neck.

For a moment, no one moved. A tense silence fell across the courtyard. Even the sounds of the jungle seemed to cease during the stalemate.

"Your Grace," Rafe smiled, "you asked me if I had means to reach you. Question asked and answered. Now then, I believe you have some tea for me to sell in your name." Feeling Askana's wrist-blade press deeper against his skin, he slowly lowered his sword. Nassir took a step towards him but Rafe carefully shook his head, keeping the Moor where he stood. Both blades fell to the ground as he continued, "While we smooth out details of this agreed venture, I would be delighted to suggest some improvements you might make in your security. For starters, your city walls could use a few more guards. And your royal courtyard is far too accessible."

Askana's eyes narrowed. She turned quickly to face Rafe, the wrist-blade remaining at his neck. Rage. A boiling rage of humiliation grew in her at being caught unaware in her own private courtyard. Then she turned to the matter of their desecration. As was the case with her manor house in the country, only women were permitted to enter the consecrated courtyard she used for her practice. Kubi-Sogi was the exception since taking a vow of celibacy to enhance his concentration as a master of the sword. He had also gelded himself to keep that vow.

"Be silent!" she hissed. It maddened Askana further that Rafe was so much taller than her, forcing her to look up at him. "You pride yourself in being knowledgeable of my realm and its customs yet you blunder into this courtyard like a new-born calf, committing a grievous error in coming here. The ground you befoul with your feet is dedicated to Nadinath, Lady of the Night. Any man who desecrates this ground must pay the Goddess in blood. Are you not familiar with this sacred edict, *man?*"

Rafe's smile faded as he kept his gaze on hers. The way she emphasised *"man"* implied a vast divide between not only the two of them, but over all the people of this realm. With that single word he knew there would be no bridging of religion and gender, no crossing of the classes. Her eyes, dark and hard in the tranquillity of her face, told him so. Finding this realisation in Rafe's expression, it was her turn to smile. Rafe usually appreciated the smile of a beautiful woman, sweet and delightful with promises of later entertainment. Never had he seen a smile so deadly and chilling.

"Even in the days when men ruled, the worship of the Goddess existed, feared by all save her Maidens. Men tried to suppress the faith with fire, sword, and punishment. Still, the Maidens of Nadinath continued to pay homage in the cover of night. Now we no longer hide the rites of the Goddess behind shrouds of half-truths. I was a Maiden of the Night. Now, I am High Priestess of the Temple." She brought him closer and her voice sank to the volume of a cold whisper, "I am the one who will give sacrifice."

Her eyes flickered, Rafe's sole warning before a high, keening cry came from her like the scream of a falcon sighting prey. His ears were still ringing with the sound when the blade moved an inch to the right, away from the artery, to gash his skin. The sting came an instant after and his eyes widened with shock.

Fool, Askana thought with a strange trace of regret. *You thought it was a game, didn't you? That I would never cut you.*

The blade's toxin began its work instantly. Everything slowed down for him, becoming a surreal, living dream. Sounds grew unintelligible and his men moved lethargically in his alternating vision of intense, flowing clarity and frightening blurs of rushing colour. Rafe stumbled free of Askana's embrace to see through glazed eyes the seemingly harmless handmaids suddenly move against the distracted privateers.

One handmaid, using the same agile hand-to-hand martial art Askana had shown in her swordfight, disarmed the pirate by striking underneath the rifle to flip the weapon out of his grasp. She now held it by the barrel and swung it against him as if it were a mace, catching him to the side of his head. In a unison that resembled military precision, both girls detached the large head of plumes from their peacock-feather fans revealing the blade of the *shirai*, the signature weapon of the Maidens of Nadinath. The remaining two privateers flanking Kubi-Sogi recognised the weapons instantly from their initial crossing of The Rift. The old Blademaster, all too familiar with the Queen's training of her devotees, remained perfectly still. A pistol pointed in the direction of the rustle of silk, but the handmaids slipped out of sight. Then came the attacks. The hardwood staffs rushed through the air, and the pistol dropped from the smaller privateer. Nassir turned to see a maid next to him, then found himself groaning on the ground, clutching his crotch in agony. His shipmate soon joined him, gasping for air as the shirai-shaft attack against his chest left him with severely bruised, if not broken, ribs. Kubi-Sogi merely smiled. The shirai never touched him.

Rafe sank to the ground. His legs were nothing more than thick jelly unable to support him. His vision began to melt into a grey film punctuated by flashes of light. All semblance of time was lost as he struggled against the poison in his body. His eyes could not hide the overwhelming sense of betrayal as the blurring form of Askana knelt over him. Her words returned to him, words she uttered in warning at The Barrier Reef. *"I will have you killed upon the spot."* He could not tell if these were the words she said to him now or if they were merely from a memory.

"The light is leaving his eyes." Askana's warm palm touched Rafe's cheek as his eyes slowly rolled upward into his head, "Quick, the tray!"

The servant had not even set the ceremonial tray in place before Askana took the gold dagger from it, pulling back her sleeve to nick the tender flesh on the inside of her elbow. Blood splattered across his face as she and the handmaid next to her chanted words in the ancient Morevian tongue, a dialect from several millennia ago now used only in rituals such as this. She snatched from the tray the large, green-grey goose egg and cracked it neatly into a bowl holding incense, flower petals, and other powdered herbs. The brilliant yellow yolk mixed with the myriad of flowers and herbs, congealing to a thick paste Askana smeared across his face. The whole creation streaked fearsomely with her blood resembled a death mask.

Raising the gold dagger still decorated with her own blood above her head, Askana's eyes closed as she quickly whispered, "O Mistress of the Night, Mother and Destroyer of all, take the blood of this man who dares to desecrate Your ground. Take his death unto Yourself and turn Your anger away from Your daughters."

The rhythm of his chest had already ceased its valiant effort to continue pumping life in his lungs. With great haste Askana cut the inside of his muscled right arm, the gush of red that followed caught in a fine porcelain bowl.

"Swiftly, Your Majesty!" Master Kubi-Sogi's voice came from somewhere behind her. "The potency of your poison is unrivalled. Look, the breath slows and he dies!"

"He will die only if I wish it," she stated, grabbing from the tray a porcelain bottle.

Drawing the cork with her teeth, she forced his lips apart and emptied the antidote down his throat. Even before the tiny bottle was drained, the remedy had already begun its work as his body suddenly tensed. The poison meaning to steal the Captain's life was one she had brewed herself, and its cure also worked with equal swiftness.

The corridors leading from the Arboretum to the Palace now echoed with the cries of the Queen's subjects. The remaining three privateers were now awakening to the sight of reinforcements: a dozen soldiers—all women—brandishing either shirai or small, razor-edged discus weapons in answer to the commotion.

It was the appearance of these reinforcements however, that snapped the pirates back to consciousness.

The Morevian guards evidently had been disturbed while bathing for not one of them wore full armour. Some wore only deerhide tunics and loincloths with wet hair trailing down their backs. All of them, in their various stages of dress, gripped their weapons of choice, confident in their application.

"Handmaids!" Kubi-Sogi snapped. Yes, he was a man but he was also the Blademaster and Askana's military mentor. His words carried as much weight and authority in the Royal Guard as Askana's. These women were now about to discover just how much weight and authority this old man carried. "The Queen was forced to fend for herself in her private courtyard, rescued in the end by *handmaids!* The shirai and *atriah* you all brandish are useless if these savage Otherworlders can slip by you so effortlessly! By the Goddess, the least you could have done was *smell* them coming! I want to know who was holding the watch! I want those respon—"

Kubi-Sogi's tirade was cut short by the commotion behind him. The newly-arrived Royal Guard watched with morbid fascination as Askana and her handmaids held Rafe as his spasms increased. Even the conditioned Morevian warriors struggled against the chemically-fuelled strength of his fits as the antidote counter-acted the poison. Against human restraints, he arched his back like a bow with only his heels and shoulders resting on the ground. Rafe strained for long, tense seconds, his mouth opening in a silent scream. Only a tight gurgle came from his throat. Then, as a final breath expelled from him in a rushing sigh, his taut body sagged and returned to the ground with a hard thud. The handmaids slowly withdrew, wiping away sweat even though the morning sun as yet barely gave any heat.

Rafe's eyes flicked open as he took in a deep breath.

"You have died the Little Death." Askana seemed as composed as ever, but there was a tightness about her eyes. She did not even flinch as a handmaid tended to her own self-inflicted wound as she spoke. "Be grateful that I knew of a pardon instead of sacrificing you to Nadinath." These were harsh, sharp words from a queen, but at least her rage was appeased. For now. Rafe wondered if the Little Death was more for Askana's benefit than for her Goddess. He opened his mouth as if to speak, but Askana merely placed a gentle finger to his lips to stop him. "You will not be able to speak or move for a few minutes, but do not fear. That will pass and your body will slowly come into your command. Within the hour, you should be normal again, save for a slight dizziness." Askana stood over him, a satisfied smile flicking over her face almost lazily, "And perhaps a slight headache."

Kubi-Sogi shook his head at Rafe and chuckled, "Is this the 'devil' you spoke of, Your Majesty? A fine lad, skilled in stealth and combat. But no better than a foolish boy anxious to prove himself in battle by dying quickly." His gaze narrowed slightly on Rafe's face, certain he had seen an artist's rendering of it somewhere. "Who is he, Your Majesty?"

Ignoring Kubi-Sogi's question, Askana turned to her Royal Guard. "Maidens, escort these criminals to the Palace Temple. Handmaids, I desire a litter for my fallen guest here."

The Royal Guard took hold of the remaining privateers. Nassir offered the pirate he called "Williams" support as he held his sides where the bruised ribs no doubt were. The third pirate, still reeling from the rifle-butt to the head, was picked up by two of the shirai-wielding Maidens. As handmaids brought out a litter for Rafe and two remaining Royal Guards tended to the gash in his arm, Askana took Kubi-Sogi aside. From around her neck, she removed a brilliant pendant of white and yellow gold. The ornament's design was the unmistakable sign of her house.

"Blademaster, for many years you have served as my teacher of the sword but have also served as my adviser." Askana smiled, reflecting on some of his lessons outside of the art of war, "Whether I have wished it or not. You have also become regarded by your Queen as a second father." Kubi-Sogi was unable to answer at this sudden outpouring of emotion. He merely listened, his pride swelling beyond measure, as Askana continued, "You have more than the Queen's trust, but the love of a daughter. You know my heart better than any. Therefore, I give to you the voice of your Queen." She opened his hand and placed the Royal Seal in his palm, gently closing his fingers around it. "If I should disappear for a time, I grant you the right to speak on my behalf in Council. I also ask of you to protect the future of Morevi if I cannot."

"Your Majesty!" he protested, his voice dry. It was a storm of emotions in which he found himself. The feel of the cool metal pendant in his hand did little to give him focus. "What do mean by this act?"

"In due time, Master Kubi-Sogi," spoke Askana in the soft but authoritative tone proclaiming that this unexpected action from her and his new-found responsibilities were closed to discussion or debate.

Askana now turned to her handmaids who, with the help of two additional Royal Guards, lifted Rafe onto the litter. "Take him to my chambers. I shall attend to the privateer." Her subjects paused for a moment, looking at their regent in surprise. Her mouth firmed in the way they knew well. "Is there some peril I am unaware of? Perhaps you wish to question the Queen's wishes?"

"No, Your Majesty," quickly came a chorus of responses overlapping one another.

"Very well then." Askana walked alongside the litter as she methodically removed her gloves and sparring armour, leaving only the silk robe with its wide sash. "Servants, attend."

Kubi-Sogi watched Askana and her entourage intently as they bore the pirate into the main corridors of the Palace. He returned his eyes to the Seal of Moldarin filling his palm. The sunlight caught the curve of the pendant. He had always been in her confidence. Now he could only study the seal of power in his hand and wonder, as did many of Askana's opponents, what she was planning.

Rafe marvelled at the magnificent, imperial corridors of colour, angles, and arches through which they carried him. These were the hallowed halls of the Palace of a Thousand Suns, the very centre of the Silken Box. While he had visited palaces before, both as a loyal subject to the King of England and as a "welcomed guest" to the court ladies, none could touch the splendour surrounding him now. A union of fine white, green, and black marble accented with gold. Impressive portraits of warriors— all women—reached high to the ceiling. He was carried into a small chamber beautifully furnished with fine rugs, recliners, tapestries and hangings as well as exquisite ebony tables inlaid with mother-of-pearl. On one side, the chamber opened to a fine view of a charming garden planted with jasmine bushes and flowering orange trees. Songbirds fluted in large cages. A fountain sprayed arcs of water across the surface of a pool full of fantailed goldfish.

The attendants lifted Rafe, his arms and legs still limp from the poison, to rest him on a plush divan. A tray offering tea, choca, sweets, and also a variety of herbs and medicines, was set before them. It was as if the Queen was entertaining an ambassador instead of a paralysed and somewhat disgruntled pirate captain.

"Leave us," Askana said.

The handmaids and Royal Guard paused again as they had in the courtyard, and then bowed to their regent before leaving her alone with Rafe.

Her gaze mocked the fallen privateer as she poured the steaming, fragrant brew into porcelain cups. "It would not harm you, privateer, to know the brew you will be peddling. The tea also has a healing ingredient that will quicken the blood. It will return you to your senses more swiftly."

Askana took a dry cloth and dipped it lightly into a bowl of perfumed water. Gently, almost fastidiously, she applied it to his face removing the dried paste. Once he was clean of the death mask, her hand slipped behind his head and lifted him to the cup.

He stared at her with wide eyes, not relishing his inability to fend for himself. A part of her enjoyed his helplessness. The divide between the male and the female, for her, remained a harrowing gash in the burnt earth of her memory.

"It is not in my nature to poison someone twice. Once is sufficient to make my point known." Askana smirked, "Now drink."

Reluctantly the Captain took a deep sip of the tea. It had a lovely taste of sharp hickory sweetened with some sort of berry-honey. As Askana had promised, Rafe's ability to speak returned, perhaps from the tea's quality or from the time that passed since his Little Death. His first question sounded guttural and grating. "What have you done with my men?" It hurt Rafe to hear himself speak.

"They have trespassed and therefore must endure the Little Death as you did, unless they wish to lay down their lives to appease Nadinath," she replied calmly.

"Heathen." Rafe snapped, wincing at the effort and pain in speaking.

Askana merely smiled at the insult, apparently more painful upon the dealer than on its intended. "Indeed. Well, this *heathen* and her Maidens, upon satisfying the Goddess, will tend to their wounds as my Royal Guard did with you. We are not without mercy, privateer," she stated, lightly tapping the field dressing around the gash in Rafe's arm. "When you and your men are ready to travel, you may leave for Eyrie with the shipment of tea. For the future, take this advice—think twice before you intrude on me again, or at least before you step on consecrated ground."

After a moment, Rafe spoke easily, his voice gathering courage with each word. "Well, perhaps I did act clumsily this time. I pride myself on my finesse, so you must forgive my debacle." Rafe said, casting his gaze up to the mural upon the chamber ceiling. "Next time I will succeed perfectly."

Askana's posture straightened slightly. Even the Little Death refused to blunt his brash arrogance that made him deserve nothing less than a short, sharp slap to the face.

"You are very good with a blade." Rafe smiled, his eyes returning to her.

"The ru-yilei is not my weapon of choice." She chose to let the comment pass, barely. "While some find satisfaction in the atriah, the Maidens of Nadinath prefer the shirai. If I had been wielding one, you would not be here in my sitting room but in our burial pits outside the city with other expelled criminals of state." It was no boast she made, merely the statement of fact.

She leaned over to give him the tea again, the gesture curious in itself. The hand shot up suddenly, catching her by the collar of her robe and jerking her down on top of him. The cup fell to the floor, shattering and spilling tea across the tiles. Before Askana could react she felt the cold kiss of a blade under her chin. If she moved, the dagger would draw blood. If she called for help, the blade would slit her throat before any sound could reach the Royal Guard. The tip pushed close to a point where Askana winced from its light sting. Rafe's expression never faltered, even after he released her robes but kept her close with his knife. She waited, wondering if this was his revenge spawned from a delicate ego for besting him in the eyes of his men.

His lips formed words in a luscious, seductive whisper, as if speaking to a lover. "Be...still."

Slowly his right arm came up and the pistol discharged, the shot echoing through the royal chambers as the powder exploded. Two Royal Guards burst into the room with shirai poised for attack. His blade lowered from Askana's neck and she turned around in time to see a woman, a serrated dagger still tight in her grasp, collapse upon the marble floor, her blood slowly creeping away from her.

Rafe's eyes rolled back into his head as he groaned, "Oh God, that was loud." The Guards lowered their weapons as the spent pistol fell out of his hand. "Normally, Your Grace, I would demand a kiss of the lady whose life I saved," He returned the dagger back to the concealed scabbard attached inside his boot. "But right now I would settle for anything to stop the pounding in my head!"

Askana, impressed by Rafe's control and cunning, smiled thinly as she prepared a fresh cup of strong Morevian tea. "You were relying on my training to keep me still by placing a blade to my neck?"

"As well as giving your would-be assassin a moment's hesitation. I find no profit in revenge, Your Grace."

From the collection of powders and herbs next to the teapot, she took a few pinches of a gold powder and sprinkled it into the steaming brew, "This should ease your head, privateer. I find it impressive that you know of the ways of our training."

"I have no inkling of your training methods, Your Grace." With a great deal of concentration, Rafe took the cup into his hands and took a deep drink of the tea. "But you can learn a great deal about an opponent's discipline when you fight, provided you pay attention." And he smiled with a wink, "And, Your Grace, you do hold my attention."

The Guards, their eyes watching Rafe carefully, crouched over the assailant whose head was now surrounded by a dark crimson pool. Askana knelt over the dead woman and gently turned her chin, revealing a small tattoo underneath the right ear. It was as large as a thumbprint and just as distinctive to the Queen's eyes.

"This is the mark of my House. This woman has pledged her life to me in rituals as old as our civilisation itself." She turned the face back to get a better look at her attacker. "Tekira." The one word broke her still surface, but Askana's voice quickly returned to its even, controlled state. "This is Tekira, my most trusted servant. She has been in my family since I was a child. " Her voice grew distant as she gently stroked the dead girl's hair. "She was always by my side. In our ascension years, we never held secrets from one another. We were sisters, of sorts. Many thought we were."

"Really?" Rafe said with a sudden piqued interest. "The resemblance is that strong?"

"Yes," Askana whispered.

"Secure the room." Rafe ordered, attempting to stand.

Askana, unaccustomed to *taking* orders, turned her eyes to Rafe, "What?"

"I said secure the room!" he snapped as he stumbled for the chamber doors, his legs still uncertain on how they were supposed to work. "Let no one enter!"

"Just what are you doing, privateer?" she asked, refusing to help Rafe as he in his weakened state struggled with the door latch.

"Doing what I do best," he grunted while fighting the after-effects of the Little Death. "Improvising." If it were another place and another time, Rafe would find being locked in a room with three beautiful women quite promising but his mind was focused on the task at hand. "Her wrists, Your Grace. Check her wrists."

Askana pulled back the sleeves of Tekira's blouse, revealing on the left wrist a smaller tattoo, definitely written in Morevian calligraphy. It was a deep violet colour and the character was just one word—*xeing*. A shadow.

"I do not understand." Askana stared at the Morevian character. "This is not a marking of my house, nor of those loyal to me."

"No, it is not," Rafe said, getting a better look at the tattoo. "As I said before, I know very little Morevian, but I do recognise this symbol — xeing, a common mark found in Morevi's underground world of smugglers, thieves, and informants. This is the symbol of someone who has been turned in their loyalty, willingly or unwillingly, becoming a mere shadow of their former selves. Usually xeings serve as spies or accomplices to crimes committed from inside a royal manor. This one was intended to be a royal assassin."

Rafe slowly lifted himself to his feet and awkwardly made his way to the balcony, looking down to the jungles and rocks below him. These particular chambers extended over a cliff, the craggy stone serving as solid foundation for the Morevian palace. "You wanted to discover the opposition to the Throne? Then we shall by making them believe you are dead. Only myself, my men, and these Royal Guards will know otherwise."

"I see." Her eyes returned to Tekira's wrist marking. Even in her hard life of cruelty under Lord Norisht, she had always been of noble blood with all its privileges. Kept far from Morevi's darker side. This traitor to the throne was truly dangerous to have such connections. Askana motioned for the Guard to pick up the body and carry it to the changing room, "So you are suggesting we dress her as me and me as her, proceeding with the original plan of spreading in Eyrie the rumour of civil unrest. With my death, the conspirators may hasten their move for the throne and grow careless." Askana nodded. "A well-devised plan of which I approve."

The privateer tipped his head to one side with a smirk, "So happy to have the Royal Blessing." Askana tensed as Rafe made himself familiar with her private quarters, checking the walls for peepholes and secret passages common in royal domiciles. "And playing the part of Tekira will also justify your presence at the meeting with the Merchants' Circle. Have one of your Guard fetch my men."

"Know your place, pirate!" Askana snapped. "I am queen of this realm and you do not order me or my Royal Guard about as if you were on board your ship. You may request a boon from the Crown of a Thousand Suns, but you may never order."

Rafe turned to face her, his mouth open as if ready to spar with Askana once more, only this time with words instead of weapons. Instead, he quietly took in the picture before him. The Queen stood with her hands upon her hips, all the power of a monarch behind her. The two Guards with her also stood proudly, their shirai glinting brightly in the sunlight streaming into her chambers. Rafe thought how tragic it was a court artisan could not capture this sight before him onto a canvas.

He lowered himself to one knee, devouring his Captain's pride in order to speak to her as a humble servant to the Crown. "Your Majesty, if you would be so kind as to release my men and bring them here." He then rose to his full height to look directly at her. "We can then proceed with my plan."

Nassir and his two shipmates, quite hot for the taste of blood following their Little Death rituals, now found themselves hastily ushered through the lesser-used corridors of the Palace. Even though it was a single guard that escorted them, Nassir dared not try anything. He could still remember their initial crossing of The Rift. These women were of *that* complexion. He also knew what was at stake. Fifteen thousand in gold rested on this venture and Nassir was determined to follow Captain Rafton's orders to the letter.

He felt a sinking suspicion other surprises were in store for them but his own apprehensions were immaterial now. In Rafe's absence, the crew was his responsibility. *Keep them safe, my Moorish friend,* echoed the orders of his Captain. If the Morevian Queen had indeed dispatched Rafe, his priority would be to get the crew back to the *Defiant.* Provided he did so, a heavy reckoning would fall on her realm. On sea and on land.

The pirates entered the Royal Chambers to another surprise. A second Guard standing by Askana was wearing the simple clothes of peasant-servants while the proud warrior-queen wore a simple handmaid's outfit of white silk. Both paid no attention to them as they were checking supplies and packing bare essentials. Their escort was tossed a small bundle of clothes similar to those of her comrade. The young maiden did not shy in changing into them before the wide-eyed pirates.

Before Nassir could speak, his eyes fell on the body of a woman who could have passed for Askana's reflection apart from the lethal bullet wound in her forehead. The corpse was dressed in the Queen's morning robes and laid across a fine divan. By her hand were the remains of a fine teacup and spilt tea now drying into a thin crust across the marble floor. Nassir went to ask any of the growing amount of questions in his head but was tossed his own haversack before a word left his lips.

"Quickly, Nassir," Rafe said as he took another large coil of rope in his arms. With the rope were their packs and weapons brought from the *Defiant* that were confiscated from them in the courtyard. "You still have that henna in your supplies?"

"Yes, my Captain." his deep, booming voice said as he continued looking back and forth between Askana and Rafe, trying to adapt to this sudden paradigm shift with the Morevians.

"I need you to give Askana a marking on her left wrist," Rafe said, motioning for Askana to sit. "The Morevian character for 'shadow.' The character must appear in the colour of deep violet. Do it, Nassir."

The Moor bent to one knee opposite of Askana and produced from his bag an assortment of small jars and brushes. He gingerly took Askana's wrist, but the wrist quickly jerked away from him. Her dark eyes stared down Nassir, silently condemning him for his indiscretion. The Royal Guard quickly flanked their Queen, one watching Rafe, the other watching Nassir.

"He will apply to your wrist a substance called henna." Rafe assured Askana and her nervous guards, "It will appear as a simple tattoo but disappears with time. Before the henna fades away completely, The Merchants' Circle and your conspirators will be standing before you awaiting judgement and we will be long gone with our payment for services rendered."

Rafe and the remaining two privateers resumed securing ropes descending from the Grand Balcony overlooking the Cliffs of Markuna. As they were to stage a monarch's death, this escape was their only option in order to avoid contact with any servant or spy moving through the network of secret passages in the Palace. Luck had favoured Rafe so far as those passages connecting with Askana's chambers were clear for the moment. His plan could still work provided they left the Palace undetected.

Nassir finished the last stroke of the tattoo upon her wrist and then added to her left cheek a small black beauty mark to match Tekira's.

"Now then," Rafe said as he motioned to the ropes, "shall we depart?"

With haversacks across their backs, the small band of seven descended into the open abyss underneath the Grand Balcony, the windowless wall of the palace far from them. Rafe and Askana shared one rope while Nassir and one of Askana's Maidens shared another. Williams served as "anchor" for his companions, another crewmate and Askana's second guard, on the third rope. Only open space surrounded them as they progressed down the length of the rope, their bodies taut human knots as their hands, knees, and ankles worked together to keep their ropes stable. The fair-haired Maiden sharing a rope with Nassir lacked training at any form of climbing as her efforts caused them to sway precariously. She looked down, growing pale from both the sight of the chasm underneath them and Nassir's dark, warning face.

With a quick hiss from their Captain, the descent paused. Rafe, Nassir, and Williams, as the anchors of their respective ropes, began a gentle momentum that caused them to swing. Askana's grip tightened as her eyes looked past Rafe to the sharp rocks hundreds of feet below them. The powerful waterfall pounding hard against the rock surface created a fresh, cool mist that gently blanketed their skin with tiny water droplets. Their momentum eventually brought them to the cliff's edge. Solid ground never felt so pleasing to Rafe. Once in a strong foothold, the three men gently leaned back to steady the ropes for their companions still hanging over the ravine.

Rafe smiled as the last of them reached earth. "Excellent. Well done, all."

They proceeded into the jungles with the roar of Markuna Falls subsiding behind them. Moving quietly along the city's perimeter, Rafe whispered over his shoulder, "Your Grace, we now must procure the tea."

"The crates are in storehouses near Songkusai's main gates. But there are at least fifteen crates awaiting us there. Do you know exactly how many pack mules we would need to carry them all?"

"I am well aware of this, Your Grace," Rafe nodded. "We will have to simply change our story to The Merchants' Circle. Nothing to be concerned over."

"But privateer, we will need more than a few crates to give this story merit."

"Your Majesty," Rafe snapped, his voice raising slightly above a whisper tone. "Right now, I am focusing on the matter at hand. We are currently outside Songkusai's city walls and we must now steal back into the city only to escape once more before word spreads that you are dead." Rafe leaned in closer to the Queen, his voice as sharp as her shirai. "All this in an extremely minuscule amount of time."

"And now we waste time while you formulate this untried plan instead of setting off with a clear strategy in place," Askana answered, her voice well above a whisper.

"Question not the Cap'n's plan," Williams barked, his voice louder than both of theirs combined. "We 'ave seen worse times, I tell you now, savage!"

"Enough!" Rafe whispered. "For God's sake, Williams, your voice would herald the second coming of the Messiah!" His face reddening with anger, Rafe looked to the Queen. "You will just have to trust me, Your Grace. Come."

In times of peace, Songkusai's battlements were usually vacant, save for an occasional guard making the rounds. Rafe silently watched the one lone sentry on duty for the Western Wall pass. With a nod to his men, he pointed upwards, raised four fingers, and then drew his downward-facing palm slowly across his chest. The privateers then pulled from their belt pouches a smaller set of grappling hooks and ropes, much lighter than the ones used in their escape from the Palace Chambers. With a final cautionary glance, they hurled their ropes upward, catching soundly deep inside the thick Morevian stone battlements. The four pirates, even with the haversacks adding weight and bulk to their bodies, scaled the wall with a stealth and agility impressive even by the Maidens' standards. It was now very clear to Askana how these men had infiltrated her city so easily. Once the women joined them at the top, Rafe motioned for them all to stay low as they quickly crept to a small lookout post at the city's west corner. He gave a deep sigh of relief as they gathered at the west tower's base, its doorway leading into the city streets.

Still no sound of the alarm. So far, the improvisation was unfolding well.

"You mentioned a storehouse where this Morevian tea awaits us," Rafe said.

"That is the storehouse." Askana pointed to a large building flanked by guards who watched travellers closely as they passed. "Now comes your next test, pirate."

Rafe studied the distant warehouse as he spoke, "Three guards in sight and if they are guarding a warehouse, they are either quite fresh or not the sharpest blades of their regiment." The Captain removed his finer black doublet and shirt as Nassir tossed him a tattered vest from his own pack. "Your guards will act as trade emissaries for the Crown and we will play the part of their servants. Your Grace, remain in shadow while we attempt to get the tea. We cannot risk your being discovered. Meet us at the city entrance once we are on the move."

"Privateer," Askana snapped. "I doubt if I shall be so easily recognised since I am not in my proper court attire or make-up. I will aid in this deception."

"Your Majesty, may I remind you—"

"That we are in my city, not upon your ship." The discussion was closed.

Being called "pirate" and "privateer" and not by his properly earned title or even his first name was beginning to grow tiresome along with her constant countermanding of his orders, but class structures had to be recognised. A queen in any realm was still a queen. *Recognised and honoured,* Rafe chided himself as he looked at Askana.

"Very well, Your Majesty. Nassir and I will acquire pack mules while you and your Maidens get us four crates of Morevian tea." Rafe motioned to his own men, "Williams, O'Donnell, you are with the Queen."

"Four crates?" Askana scoffed, "Do you think four crates will be enough to bait the trap?"

"Yes, I do, Your Grace," Rafe said wearily. "Four crates will be all I need for this plan." They turned to leave the confines of the tower. Rafe paused in the doorway, fixing his gaze with Askana's. "And if you continue to call us to a meeting of Council to question my every decision, I doubt we shall discover the instruments of conspiracy before the end of the Moldarin Dynasty. Now if you please, follow my orders."

The Captain and First Mate disappeared into the nearby alleyway. The Royal Guard looked to Askana uncertainly, perhaps feeding off her own doubt. It was not the Captain's abilities that she held in question. It was relying upon him—this Otherworlder —to be her ally, but with a simple nod the Captain's commands were given equal merit to her own. She held close the promise to herself never to grow dependent upon anyone else. Now she was having to surrender this sacred vow to this man.

He made it too easy. This frightened her most of all.

Askana, her Guards, and the two pirates emerged from the surrounding buildings and bowed respectfully to the head Palace Guard in charge of this warehouse. She began the Captain's ruse of servants to the Throne, crates of tea, and journeying to Arathelle. When her story went into their destination across the Naruihm sea, Askana caught quick glimpses of the remaining storehouse guards. They were watching the privateers intently with their hands tightly grasping the handles of short swords. Askana silently prayed to Nadinath that the deception would take. Her intrigue could reach an end here and now if they were discovered. It would only be a matter of time before the ram's-horn trumpets would sound her death and then Songkusai's gates would close. No one in or out. Rafe was correct in the importance of leaving with no commotion. Whether or not they did rested on this one Palace Guard.

The storehouse sentries then heard the call of a mule. Slowly approaching the warehouse were the Pirate Captain and First Mate with beasts in tow. Askana could not help but smile for Rafe's shoulders were already turning pink from the sun's rays, his fair skin too delicate for the Morevian climate. The warehouse guards bowed quickly to the ladies as the privateers hastily loaded four large crates of tea. The mules were surprisingly agreeable this particular day. Once again, luck had blessed Rafe Rafton and his crew as they led the two mules, their backs laden with Morevian tea, personal effects, and supplies, beyond the city walls without incident. Before them stretched the Road of the Moon that would lead to the ports of Arathelle.

Outside the city walls, the path disappeared in a cloak of shadow broken by sunlight stealing through the tangle of trees and tropical plants. Once deep in foliage cover, they would begin their hike through the Sleeping Dragons. The small party crossed this natural barrier of cool shade, one by one, disappearing from the sight of the city. All save one. Askana stopped for a moment and turned back to look at Songkusai. In the distance, the Palace of a Thousand Suns appeared to shimmer through the unseen shroud of noonday heat.

Rafe brought the party to a halt and called back to the Queen, "Your Grace, unless you have forgotten something frightfully important, we should continue on to Eyrie."

Insensitive beast, Askana thought sharply.

"We continue," she stated, resolute in her decisions.

For Morevi, she assured herself silently as they disappeared into the jungle. *For my beloved Morevi.*

The ground, still soft from the tropical rains of the day before, sank under their feet with each step. Rafe and his men led their pack mules through heavy brush and vegetation while Askana and her Royal Guard followed a few paces behind them. They descended a small incline, their jungle trail defined by trees and spacious mud puddles fresh with rainwater. It was evident from Williams' and O'Donnell's occasional groan that they wished to pause, but Rafe wanted as much distance between them and Songkusai as their endurance allowed.

Suddenly audible over the jungles of The Sleeping Dragons were the distant hollow echoes of ram's-horn trumpets. One blast, joined by another. Then two more sounding, all high pitched in their tones. The four hollow blares brought the Morevians to a sudden halt. A hint of surprise crossed Askana's face. Joining the horns, a single bell tolled slowly.

"Stop!" Her voice broke the silence that hung over the party. "There have been other deaths in the Palace."

Rafe looked back, his face beginning to show signs of fatigue. "And just how do you know this, Your Grace?"

"They have sounded the alarm. Had it just been my death, only two horns would have sounded but this call was different. The higher pitched horns sound for the deaths of other Councilwomen. These deaths can only mean the conspirators are working faster than I had earlier presumed."

Rafe turned his weary eyes forward to the thick jungles and mountain range that lay ahead. It had been an eventful morning followed by a taxing afternoon, and their journey had just begun. "Well then, time is short. We must press onward to the sea ports of Eyrie. Once there, we can proceed with your counter-intrigue, Your Majesty."

"A moment, pirate," Askana said, her dark eyes still looking back towards the echoes of the alarm. "I think these drastic measures have reached far beyond your clever improvisation. We require the services of the Caillech of the Southern Wood. Perhaps she can give us an edge against this treacherous blade in my House. Her path leads south, not west."

"Now just a moment!" Rafe struggled clumsily through the heavy, thick mud to Askana. "You hired me to unearth a conspiracy against your crown and now you wish to enlist the services of some witch? Perhaps I failed to mention a small clause within our contract—no witchcraft. No sorcery. No magic. No spells. *Whatsoever!*"

"You forget yourself again, pirate. I am Queen of Morevi and you will do as I command." Askana stepped forward, expecting Rafe to back down. "This is your final reminder."

"And may I remind *you*, Your Majesty," Rafe also stepped forward, towering over her strong, slender figure, "That we are no longer within the city walls. Therefore, as Captain and the final authority on this venture, you will obey my commands regardless if they go against your wishes."

"Very true. We are no longer in the city walls." Askana said, "But until we pass over the Sleeping Dragons, we are still in Morevi where I still rule as Queen."

Rafe knew she had him on that argument. With yet another silent reminder to himself on honouring the class structures as ordained by God, he employed another tactic.

"Forgive me, Your Grace, I do forget myself. Perhaps it is my current state of fatigue. Perhaps it is being accustomed to giving orders as I am a *captain*." Rafe said, stressing the final word as a reminder of his title to her. Then, once more before Askana, he bent down to one knee. He noticed her shoulders relaxing as he spoke in a more gentle tone. "Do grant me this audience, Your Majesty. Moving southerly anywhere in these cursed jungles will add time upon our journey. Time is a luxury we do not possess. Whoever the traitor to the crown is will demand to see your body. Once it is discovered that it is merely a servant and not you, word will spread like wildfire. You must trust me, Your Majesty. You hired me to take care of this problem."

"That was when I wished to leave it in your care. Now greater forces must intervene." She motioned to the tiny silk pouch hanging from her neck, "This signet of yours may be a solemn promise in your world, but to me it is simply silver with an enigmatic crest. Nothing more."

Bugger the class structures and bugger this savage queen! Rafe thought sharply, *I have endured quite enough!*

"Your Majesty!" Rafe manoeuvred around her, blocking her southerly path and standing toe-to-toe with her. "You have hired me to do a job—so please, by the Grace of God and His angels of Heaven, *let me do it!* I cannot answer your charge if you choose to challenge me at every turn. Or does it bother you that I, being a man in a lady's realm, find your challenges too elementary?"

"Remove yourself from my path, privateer," Askana warned with an even tone to her voice, "or I will have you removed from it."

The Royal Guard gripped their shirai harder but Rafe did not notice. His men, however, watched them intensely, their own hands gripping concealed daggers resting against the small of their backs.

"I cannot help but be amazed!" Rafe's voice grew as his temperament lessened, "A land as rich in culture and resources such as Morevi has found its true sovereign in a self-centred brat—" He then placed his own hands on his hips, taking the identical pose Askana took with him in her Royal Chambers. "—such as Your Grace!"

The Royal Guard glanced at one another in horror. No one would dare speak to Askana Moldarin in such a fashion unless they desired a swift, quick death. One of the Guard went to move to her side; but Askana's hand raised upward, stopping her before the step was completed.

"You have earned this, privateer," said Askana.

Her fist struck squarely in the centre of Rafe's chest, sending him back into a large puddle behind him. Mud splattered everywhere as his body splashed into the thick earth. Rafe's men were held at bay with a single look from the Royal Guard while Askana made her way around to the other side of the puddle.

The smile on her face said it all. *That felt wonderful,* she thought with a cruel smile.

"We move south." Askana looked to each of Rafe's men with a silent promise of retribution if challenged. Her gaze finally turned down at her feet to Rafe, his fine skin and blonde hair now speckled with dark black mud. "You," she hissed, "get up."

Rafe nodded in surrender, much to the surprise of everyone save Askana. She had suspected this man's bravado was merely boastful promises of action. Pure vanity. Nothing more.

Rafe's hand suddenly wrapped around her ankle and gave it a sharp tug. The jungle ground underneath Askana slipped away easily causing her to topple backwards into the other half of the puddle. Her white robes, previously bunched up and tucked into her tight sash to keep out of her way, were now decorated as was her face and other exposed parts of her body—with dark splotches of mud. Rafe's men backed away slightly, exchanging knowing grins with one another.

For a moment Askana did not move. Her mind was trying to comprehend how she had been pulled into a mud puddle.

"But of course," Rafe said with a satisfied grin.

He pulled himself out of the mud, the suction of his posterior removing itself from the earth making a rather obscene slurp. Both the Royal Guard and Rafe's men struggled to contain laughter at the sound coupled with his muddy appearance. Not an easy task.

Rafe extended a hand to Askana in order to help her up. "May Nadinath bless you." Askana smiled sweetly as she took his hand.

Her other hand shot out from the mud, grabbing Rafe's doublet and with the momentum of the pull he was lifted into the air and sent over her shoulder to land with a splash behind her. This got a giggle out of the Royal Guard and a polite snicker from Rafe's men.

Askana slowly returned to her feet, mud seeping into her shoes as she stood over Rafe. "If you are finished, we proceed south."

She turned her back on him to take lead point of their party. She still held her chin high with all the pride of a monarch demanding respect whether clean and pristine or soiled with mud.

The clump of earth, moss, and slime sailed through the air and struck against the back of her head with a nauseating slap, knocking Askana off balance and returning her to the mud puddle. Face first.

"Now I am finished," Rafe seethed. "And so we move *west* to the Eyriener ports."

Askana raised herself up, her once pale golden skin now a dark chocolate brown. She felt the mud ooze down her cheeks, her chest, and in between her breasts. A cold, sickening feeling. She turned to face Rafe. The morning's events had brought down the wrath of Nadinath on him and therefore she had to carry out the Little Death. She could overlook his ignorance for he was simply a verbose man posturing like the peacocks in her courtyard. This current slight was a blatant disregard for her position as the head of House Moldarin, as High Priestess, and as First Queen of Morevi. Her family and history was one of honour and of pride. Centuries of valour in battle and loyalty to the realm were now openly insulted by this common criminal of the sea.

And then he did the worst thing he could have done at that moment. Rafe stuck his tongue out at her.

The air was filled with that same piercing cry heard in Askana's courtyard, only this time it mingled with Rafe's own guttural yell. The two charged and tackled one another in the mud. Like two wild animals struggling for domination, they splashed and thrashed in the shallow puddle, shouting curses at each other. Rafe's in English, Askana's in Morevian. Clumps of mud flew through the air as they fought. Askana threw herself on top of Rafe, burying his face in the muddy water, trying to drown him or at least make him suffer. With a surprisingly powerful upward thrust, he bucked her free. Before she could push him down once more, Rafe managed to fling a large handful of mud that blinded her for an instant.

As this battle raged and piqued in its fury, O'Donnell tapped the fair-haired Maiden's shoulder. "Two shillings that Captain Rafton bests your Queen."

Her name was Elunear, a young, lovely creature, still naïve to the world outside of Morevi. She turned in a blink, ready to cut down anyone who challenged her. The escape from Morevi had been traumatic enough with the descent into Markuna Falls. Now she watched her Queen in a juvenile mudfight. The pirate merely smirked as he held the two coins firmly in his hand. Her eyes flashed for an instant matching the gleam of her rare shade of long blonde hair as she gripped her shirai tightly. "Infidel. You dare?" She then caught sight of Askana clipping Rafe hard, returning them both into the murky depths of the puddle. "Five coins Her Majesty defeats the insolent pirate."

"Done," O'Donnell smiled as he rubbed his hands together.

Rafe and Askana were now barely recognisable. They were covered from head to toe with the deep brown and reddish Morevian mud. And then, without any warning, they stopped. It was not out of fatigue. It was not in order to formulate a new plan of attack. They just stopped. Their muddied faces were frozen in a twisted rage. Askana's arm was raised high, a large handful of mud ready to be thrown at him now seeped through her fingers and ran down the length of her arm. Rafe suddenly burst out into a hearty, belly-deep laugh. His white teeth were the only other colour visible as he guffawed and bellowed while Askana's arm slowly lowered, pure disbelief slowly coming into her dirtied face.

"You immature sot!" Askana screamed, hurling at him what mud was remaining in her hand. "You will stop this instant! Stop your infernal laughter! You have insulted the First Queen of Morevi!" Rafe laughed even harder, tears welling up in his eyes.

She could feel a smile creeping across her lips. "There is nothing amusing—" The harder she fought to contain it, the more pronounced it became. "—in desecrating the Throne of a Thousand Suns! Years of tradition—" She fell back into the mud puddle, finding it difficult to speak or breathe as she chortled. Yet she was determined to finish her thought, "My family is honoured and revered throughout the land!"

Both exploded in gaiety as Rafe crawled over to her. "I suppose this disrespect to the Crown carries a harsh punishment?"

"Death by disembowelling!"

Of course, they both found this hilarious.

Pirates and Royal Guard guffawed and chuckled at the sight of their masters. Rafe grasped onto his sides while Askana wiped a layer of mud from her face, flicking it in Rafe's direction. Reluctantly, O'Donnell paid the five shillings to Elunear, more fascinated by the look of the coins than happy in her winning. The Queen tried to catch her breath in the middle of her amusement when Rafe, now back on his feet, offered her a hand in earnest. Their laughter eventually subsided, the sounds of the jungle replacing their own private comedy. Rafe pulled Askana free of the earth and the diversion was done.

"We shall rest for a moment, to clean ourselves of this good Morevian earth and then decide where to go." Rafe smiled, "Agreed?"

"Agreed, privateer." Askana nodded, her smile as brilliant against the dark mud as his own.

The mud started to dry in her hair and against her skin as it did for Captain Rafton. They were quite the sight, but no one cared to share a thought on their appearance. Both women and men had resumed taking careful stock of each other while pretending to ignore each other's existence. In this silence a soft sound that had reached their ears on entering the jungle grew. It was the sound of water, and Askana was leading them right to it.

As she trudged up a small hillock, her nondescript robes sagged with the weight of mud. Askana wondered if her sudden uplift of mood and her equally sudden return to reality could have been due to hysteria. She had always carried a hearty dislike of hysterics. To her they were signs of weakness and vulnerability. Even when she was a little girl, she knew the true key to power was to contain emotion, be it rage, joy, or suspicion, so as to present a blank face and relinquish no clues to one's opponent. Biting sarcasm, a quick wit, and a ready hand had always been her weapons. After her ascension, courtly decorum alternating with bouts of unpredictable temper had been her shield. It was always good to keep people guessing.

Yet now, when everything she held dear hung in the balance, she had thrown all this discipline to the winds and indulged in a roll in the mud with the most infuriating person she had ever met in her life.

Doubtless, it had been fun.

She wondered what her father might be thinking as he watched her from beyond the Gates of Tián'ba.

A frond threatened to slap her in the face as she broke through a tangle of vines into a clearing. Here was the wide pool fed by shallow little streams that she remembered well. These waterways merged into a larger river two hundred feet above their heads that emptied down an enormous slab of rock in a grand, majestic waterfall, ferns and lush tropical greenery caressing its banks. Exotic flowers grew here, snatching life from the sparse, precious sunlight that filtered down through the gap in the jungle canopy. Immense trees towered around the area, their arms stretching overhead as if in attempt to embrace one another, concealing the spectacle from above. Birdsong could be heard in snatches, buried in the sound of rushing water.

"Here," Askana beckoned to the others. "We have little time. Captain Rafton and I were careless enough to waste some of it." It was a blunt acknowledgement of fault that would have been startling coming from any other noble, but her Maidens were accustomed to it. Equal in the eyes of the Goddess, she would shoulder her share of the blame as she did her share of the pack-weight.

Askana knew it. She was a laughable sight. There might have been some remainder of humour in her eyes as she turned to the privateers.

"We look like mud-skippers," she jested lightly. "And I do not think coats of mud are going to serve us well as disguises. A bath, a hasty one, is in order. You do have some knowledge of this procedure, yes?"

"Truth be told, I encourage it," Rafe called as he and his men moved closer to the small shore of this oasis. "But if it is fancy perfumes and fine musks you expect from us, we are not courtiers. Our time is well-spent on more profitable, rather than sweet-smelling, activities."

"Speak for yourself," grunted Nassir. "In my opinion, I always smell like a rose."

Privateers guffawed and mimicked courtiers and nobles demanding perfumes and powders while the Morevians took privacy afforded by a large Khoi tree. Rafe peeled mud-soaked garments away from his body, good-naturedly tolerating his men's jibes, as on the other side, Askana quickly shed her sullied robes with distaste.

"The man has no respect, Your Majesty," Jailene said suddenly. The tall, copper-skinned Maiden was a trusted soldier in Askana's Royal Guard, older and more seasoned than her counterpart. She had pulled back her mahogany hair with a leather thong and was preparing fresh clothes for her Queen when she began this outpouring of emotion. Her discipline had trained her to keep such impulses under control but she could no longer contain them in light of the Pirate Captain's outward demeanour. "Such men are not to be trusted. They have respect for nothing and no one. Not even a queen."

Askana paused in the act of unfastening pins and combs from her hair. Her voice was hard as steel when she spoke. "Tekira had as much respect as any. Perhaps more. Yet she tried to kill me."

It actually caught Askana by surprise how detached she was from the memory of her once-friend's treachery, but the reaction that followed her words was even more surprising.

"We knew none of it, my Queen!" Elunear protested, dropping to her knees against the cool, damp rocks. "We are sworn to you and would protect you with our lives."

"There is no place in the worship of Nadinath for oath breakers," Jailene added grimly. A thin film of sweat formed across her skin. "I ask to be punished for the laxness in guarding your safety, High Priestess."

"The arrogance of youth," Askana scoffed gently. "Do you think all the wrongs in the world lie on your shoulders, Jailene? Do not be foolish. This is not the Sacred Temple and we have no time to tend to unnecessary wounds. You would better serve me in finding the ones who have brought down the honour of the Sisterhood."

The little throb of hurt in accusing her Guard came and went. That they could threaten all she had done for them. For their freedom. As Maidens, they were tried and true as warriors. To be selected for the Royal Guard, they were the elite. But they were, after all, children still. Small, rounded Elunear with the remnants of puppy fat in her face. Jailene, tall, glossily dark and overly serious, the insecurity of her ascension years channelled through her shirai.

Elunear's dark brown eyes flamed. "Would that Lubria was here! She would stand for none of this."

The mention of the Fae-woman gave Askana pause. In her mind stared back the unearthly emerald eyes that always knew the countenance of her soul. Her blood sister and faithful companion, lost in her rise to the throne.

Sickened by the cloying stench of jungle mud and now stripped down to a short deerskin tunic, Askana stepped down into the cool water, dismissing the men's avid glances. O'Donnell, the youngest of the pirates, shuffled uncomfortably, not knowing whether to glance away as was proper for his realm or join his shipmates in watching these savages bathe. Wearing only breeches, Rafe tossed away his muddy shirt and strode down to the water. The Royal Guard watched the pirate closely as he followed the submerged image of Askana slowly moving underwater. She stopped. Her eyes obviously seeing him standing on the edge of the small rock extending over the pool. She finally broke the surface of the water. The slime and mud were gone from her face and hair.

"Your Majesty," he said, one hand lightly scratching his nape as he softly laughed. "How shall I put this? In my realm it is not customary for men and women to bathe together. In fact, the customs of my world are extremely stringent on the subject of the body. My men are bold, as all in our trade must be, and I fear I cannot stop them from gawking at your most Royal Nakedness if they so desire."

Royal Nakedness? As she went to reply to his ridiculous words, Askana suddenly realised just how tired she was. Tired of treachery, of bickering, of having to constantly banter over everything. And fast growing tired of his bombastic manner. She was not going to forego what was probably the last bath she would have for days just because these men lacked control over their lower extremities. *Far be it from me to suffer due to their inabilities*, Askana thought bitterly.

Swirls of mud floated away as she scrubbed her long black hair. "Unlike your men, Captain, I am not bothered at all," she replied coolly. "In Morevi, women and men share the bath-houses." Deliberately, she unfastened her tunic and tossed the wet deerskin up to his feet. "And they do so without the tunics."

Recognising her challenge, Rafe did not hesitate though he privately congratulated her. "I said my world is extremely stringent on the subject of the body." And with a bright, devilish smile, his breeches slipped free of him. Obscene cheers erupted from the privateers as Rafe stood proudly with hands resting on his hips. "I did not say these were my beliefs!"

He dove into the water of the small lake, splashing the Queen so she was momentarily blinded, gasping, and spluttering. He broke the surface with a small explosion of water and breath. His laughter goaded her into action. Lunging backward, she kicked a swell right into his face as she backstroked strongly to the waterfall. He immediately gave chase, taking strong strokes as the clear, cold water sliced away the mud. At the edge of the low, shimmering curtain of water she paused as if uncertain whether to duck under into the darkness of the grotto or turn and flee. In that instant Rafe had successfully cornered her in order to give her and her recovering snobbish sensibilities a good dunking.

Underwater, in a swirl of bubbles and shadows, Rafe felt her grip his wrist with surprising tenacity, but her fingers only managed to wrap halfway around the strong bones. She succeeded in pulling him under for a moment, and that was enough for her to transfer her grip to his head of yellow hair. With a kick and an unmerciful tug, she towed him behind the waterfall.

They broke the surface under the great natural stone basin at the same instant. The sunlight coming through the water gave their bodies and the small cave a strange, glimmering glow. There were only a few feet of air and rock above the water, its level reaching as high as their necks.

In the tight confines of the grotto, she was merely a foot away from him coloured in the eerie silver ripples of light and water. His fingers tangled in the trailing black hair, ostensibly to repay her for the stinging in his scalp, but she silenced him with a finger to his lips. Her eyes were not on him. She searched through the curtain of water, assuring herself no one could see or hear them through it. Rafe followed her gaze and then returned his eyes to Askana as he gently released her hair from his grasp.

"I wanted to speak with you privately, Captain." She spoke softly, bobbing up and down as she treaded water, "Away from even my own Guard. Though my heart bleeds to believe them, caution is essential until they prove their loyalty."

"Will they not suspect something," Rafe asked, "with the two of us disappearing in such a fashion?"

"No. They will think that I have decided to indulge in a dalliance and kick themselves in envy. Though now society grudgingly permits a woman to have her lovers, Maidens must be celibate until they have finished their time of service." Askana barked a laugh. "Jailene has half a year left, Elunear two."

"Poor lasses," Rafe said. "So, Your Grace, why have you suddenly decided to trust me with your confidence?"

"You have nothing to gain by giving away these secrets."

"Are you certain of this, Your Grace? I would think such privy information could provide a profitable windfall for someone in my profession."

Askana knew this to be a dare, and shook her head in frustration. "Even if you managed somehow to ally yourself with those in my Court who plot against me, they would not hesitate to send you to an untimely death once you have served your purpose. Perhaps a convenient 'loss at sea'," she said dispassionately.

Askana gently rested her palm against his cheek. "With my disappearance, governance will fall to the Council and to an elected leader since I have no female Heirs to act as Regent. The closest individual to the Throne who could serve as a temporary Regent would be Jermal, my Consort. Only after the ceremonial adoption into the Royal Family will he be regarded as a 'rightful heir' and under the protection of my Royal Guard." Her voice deepened slightly, "Blademaster Kubi-Sogi has a commission upon the event of my death or disappearance to guard the Royal Consort. Even if I do discover those against me, simply returning to Morevi armed with knowledge may not be enough. If this traitor does have ties to Eyrie, I cannot fight them merely armed with a shirai." She sighed heavily, eyes impatient at first but becoming affable when returning to the Captain's gaze. "That weapon you used on the traitor. You did not touch nor throw a weapon at her. There was a loud noise and a puff of smoke, and somehow you killed her. If you have such a distrust in magic, then what is that weapon you use?" she mused, lightly biting her lower lip.

The hand on his cheek. Soft eyes. A sign of concern. Years of practice had taught her the art of manipulating men. And it never hurt to shock them a little. Attention of this sort from a powerful ruler, especially one of her reputation, had never failed to unbalance them.

"I need powerful allies. Would your King be averse to an alliance?" Her black eyes turned shrewd. "Morevi may have much to offer England in the way of trade."

She awaited his answer. Only the waterfall disturbed the silence. Rafe truly believed this queen could not throw any new challenges before him following their diversion in the jungle. Yet here he was, nonetheless, facing the challenge of his own impulses. The body floating in the illuminated water before him was the body of a queen, but certainly first and foremost the body of a woman. Her behaviour on the banks of the lake had a sobering tinge of contempt to it, but now her tone seemed intimate. Much like the feel of her hand against his cheek. He could not help but savour it. Askana Moldarin captivated him beyond any woman who ever crossed paths—or blades—with him. Truly, she was the most beautiful woman he had ever met in body and spirit, making her all the more dangerous, concealed weapons and Little Death rituals aside.

"Your Grace," Rafe smiled, playing along with her flirtation by softly kissing the palm now resting against his cheek. "Are you aware of the unending loyalty that you engender? I cannot speak for good King Henry. That is not my place. However, I will, as I boasted to you once before, call in my favours at Court and gain you an audience with His Majesty. Then, you may ask a boon of the Crown, from Queen to King." Rafe removed her hand from his face, his tone stern and serious. "As for the pistol, allow me to teach you the art of shooting. It is not something taken lightly. Unlike magic, pistols are very real and far more dangerous than the work of witches and wizards. But for now, we should return to the others."

"Indeed," Askana remarked with her customary coolness as she glanced towards the curtain of water. "By now, both our parties should be ready to continue. We shall proceed west to Eyrie."

Askana disappeared under the water below Rafe, quickly swimming back to the outer lake. He remained in the concealment of the grotto for a moment. Any intimate urges present earlier were now distant. His own past taught him a few hard lessons on the insincerity of nobility.

The coolness of the water helped, too.

The fresh clothes waiting for him were of a similar flamboyant fashion as the ruined black garments but in dark earth colours of brown, burgundy, and red accented with traces of gold. Perhaps he was vain, but his vanity had opened doors for him that remained firmly closed to others of his trade and station. An audience with King Henry, for example. Not an easy task, but not impossible for him. It would cost him in favours and currency, but the fifteen thousand in gold would make the sacrifice worthwhile.

As Rafe laced his fine deerskin boots, O'Donnell nudged him playfully, "So tell me, Cap'n, 'ow was 'er Royal 'ighness? Does royalty 'ave a different feel than your dockside whore?"

Rafe's elbow connected with O'Donnell's obscene smile causing everyone to freeze. All eyes were on Rafe, silent with surprise at his sudden change. The young pirate covered his mouth, a trickle of blood running over his fingers as he towered over him.

"Damn your Irish heart, O'Donnell! You just bought a week's worth of watch in the topcastle." Rafe strapped on his belt, his movements mirroring the sharpness of his rage, "And any of my crew who dares to speak of the Queen in such a fashion will spend watch with O'Donnell. Is that understood?"

Askana continued to replace the pins in her hair, Captain Rafton's words bringing a small, purely female smile to her lips that went unseen by the others. She noted out of habit the large duelling dagger Rafe slipped into a sheath hidden beneath the doublet, just in the small of his back. A second, smaller throwing dagger rested in a leather gauntlet around his right wrist. Her eyes fixed on that small blade. There was something strangely familiar about it.

"We proceed west." Rafe ordered, taking Askana's attention from his variety of weapons. "We have little daylight remaining and we still have as yet to reach the mountains. Come."

Moonlight broke through occasional grey clouds that crept slowly across a star-filled sky as Rafe, Askana, and their company reached a summit of the Sleeping Dragons. The group had at least another two days' travel before reaching the docks of Eyrie. Already they were high in the mountains of the Morevian-Eyriener border overlooking both realms, the lights of both Morevi and Eyrie visible from their encampment. Seeing the fires of Morevi's towers provided a hint of comfort for Askana and her Royal Guard. Even in the distance and nested in night, Morevi could still bestow a sense of wonder and awe to anyone who looked upon it.

"Well done, everyone," Rafe said with pride. "Perhaps we have earned a rest here."

"I concur," Askana nodded. "We sleep here tonight. Jailene, you stand first watch."

"Nassir, join her. Two sets of eyes would not hurt." Rafe smiled, giving Askana a confident wink.

She merely returned a blank stare to him. His intentions were honourable, but a waste of time and effort. The Maidens were young, their upbringing deep in the fervour and heat of the female uprising. These girl-children nursed in them the flavour of the revolution. She would not expect any bonds of trust to form so quickly between Royal Guard and English privateer. Rafe, noting her disdain, quietly set up a bedroll and assembled a small canvas tent.

The evening cloud cover dissipated to reveal a vast array of stars accompanying the twin moons of this world. O'Donnell prepared a fire and a small dinner for everyone, hoping to lessen his sentence in the topcastle. Williams, exhausted from the day he endured while nursing bruised ribs, snored loudly much to the disgust of Elunear who sharpened her shirai with a flat stone.

With a small book in his hand serving as a map across this foreign sky, Rafe's eyes jumped from its pages to the stars above. His whispers of who or what the unfamiliar constellation represented were barely audible. Askana recognised the book as one authored by the Morevian Priests of El-Baz. Sea captains under her commission would use such books to navigate the Naruihm oceans. Perhaps it was a prize taken in one of his many raids upon her ships. Wishing not to cloud her mind with the past transgressions of her ally, Askana studied the temporary tattoo upon her wrist, allowing herself a distant memory of Tekira. She wondered what extremes could have been used against her devoted friend to turn her against the Crown. What could break such loyalty and intensive training? She mourned silently, a shiver passing through her at the agony and pain Tekira must have endured before finally surrendering to her tormentor's will.

Her lament abruptly halted as a small bronze coin suddenly landed in her lap.

"For your thoughts, Your Majesty," Rafe smiled.

"My thoughts are no concern of yours," Askana replied, tossing the coin back to him.

"Well then, join me in a drink," he said, producing from his tent a small jug of mead. "You say I am ignorant to the ways of your realm, so teach me, Your Grace." He took a deep swig from the bottle before asking, "Tell me what kind of people would want their reigning monarch and 'saviour' dead? From what I have seen and heard, Morevi has prospered under your rule."

"Change, whether for better or worse, angers people. Every system in motion resists change. The systems of society and culture are no different." She softened a little. It was not often men wished to speak about governance with her. They seemed to prefer chattering about irrelevant things, trivial and materialistic in nature. Askana smiled to herself at this reversal of power and influence.

Rafe shrugged, "I suppose I would understand if you were a tyrant of some kind, but I believe you to be more of an iron fist adorned in delicate lace." He offered her the bottle only to receive a withering look which—think as he might—he could not identify its cause. "Do you think for a moment that it could be someone in whom you or your women have placed a misguided trust?"

"The thought had crossed my mind, pirate," Askana snapped, her voice sharpened by his "iron fist clad in lace" comment. "There are some who prefer the rule of men, but some who have ascended to power with me would oppose me if it furthered their own interests. My thoughts lean to one in Court named Dirare. She is a good woman, but strong willed and ambitious. Too long a time holding the reins of power may turn that ambition into a vicious driving force."

"Strong willed and ambitious." Rafe raised an eyebrow, taking another drink of the honey-wine. "Not unlike yourself, Your Grace?"

Askana gave a smile in light of his comment, "My ambition is very different. It is a desire for a better world where My Sisters have a voice. Men underestimate what the 'fairer sex,' as you would call us, are capable of when driven. Women calculate. Plan in shadow. And when we strike, it is unexpected, unanticipated. We can execute cunning unparalleled. This cunning can be most lethal against our own sisters. I have found this out first-hand."

She did not speak of Tekira or Dirare. Askana spoke openly of another time. He caught a trace of loss and revenge in her face as she went silent, her dark eyes hypnotised by the dance of the campfire.

"It's fascinating, don't you think?" Rafe asked suddenly, breaking Askana's trance.

"What do you find so fascinating, privateer?"

"You have the final voice over a realm, Your Grace. The power to give or take life. To rule over all you see. And now you revel in this authority by sleeping high in the mountains of your realm with a group of outlaws. You are a queen, and you celebrate this honour every waking moment by trying to *remain* Queen." Rafe offered her the mead again. "I do hope you have good reasons for wanting such a life and such a regime."

Askana did not know whether to laugh in his face or vomit. Pirate. Criminal. And now, Philosopher. She snatched the bottle from his hand. Her eyes might have been made of glass, nothing in them save his reflection. "I have my reasons. And mine alone." With that, she took a drink of the mead. Her pupils widened a bit with utter distaste at the flavour of the homemade brew, but her face remained smooth as she swallowed the liquid warmth.

"Remind me never to play opposite of you in cards, Your Grace," Rafe said, removing the bottle from her grasp.

The fire continued to bathe them both in a soft, golden light. A natural silence now fell over them as the fire's crackle mixed with the sounds of night creatures. It did not need filling. They were two fighters who had taken stock of one another and who now sat together with the ease of mutual understanding, perhaps even companionability.

From his post, Nassir watched them in their silent stand off. *They make a pretty picture*, he thought amusingly. He returned his gaze out into the night as Jailene sat motionless beside him, also peering into the inky darkness. The Moor chose to break the tension by opened a small, bulbous bottle of mead filled from the same batch his Captain enjoyed. "Something to take the chill away, miss?" his deep voice rung in her ear.

Jailene merely flinched away from the pirate. "Infidel," she hissed.

"That as may be," he chuckled as he took a swig. "But my soul will be a touch warmer with this in it."

"I am of the Sisterhood and have made a pledge of purity," Jailene spat, her voice dripping with contempt. "I must be pure in body, spirit, and blood."

"As am I, miss." Nassir smiled brightly, his teeth almost shining in the night against his dark skin. "As am I. My faith forbids me to drink of the fermented grain or fruit. And that is why Allah grants to his children the sweet honey for mead! So maybe your Nadinath would not mind so much. Mead might make your blood that much purer."

Jailene turned to him, his eyes warm with the mead he drank as well as with a disarming sincerity. Her strict exterior would not bend so easily. Her earlier words shared at the riverbank with her Queen still resounded in her own ears.

"You are not like the others," she stated quite plainly. "Is this England not your native land?"

"No, Miss. My home is far from England," Nassir said. "A land of endless dunes, glorious sunsets, and brilliant white palaces, that oftentimes I do miss."

"Then why leave it?"

His laugh sounded within his chest as the soft rumble of thunder, "Because I have been there and back again with Captain Rafton and never has my Captain let time pass slowly. We have sailed the coast of Madagascar, the Spice Channels of the Atlantic, and we even dared the Rift."

"Ah yes, this cursed Rift between our realms," Jailene scoffed as she returned her gaze to the night. "This Rift that brings pirates such as you across to sack our ships, kill our Sisters, and take what they wish."

"Now, my lady, do not pass judgement so hastily on my Captain." He glanced again over his shoulder. Askana appeared to be meditating by the fire, her breathing imperceptible. Rafe slept, only his crossed legs extending from the small folds of his tent were visible. "He does what he must only to survive."

"Only to survive." Jailene nodded, brazenly taking the bottle from Nassir. "Perhaps I understand you better, infidel, than I earlier thought. We all do what we must to survive." She took a swig of the mead and coughed harshly. "In the name of the Goddess, what is this swill?"

A guffaw erupted from the Moor, "A taste of my realm." As his eyes returned to the watch, his smile melted away and his laugh grew softer. "Mistress!" he whispered sharply, checking his rifle to assure it was primed.

A trail of six lights paused, then appeared to move in a serpentine fashion through the jungle. By the pace these tiny fire-spheres kept, they ran with ease through the thick foliage. The lights gathered in the vicinity of Askana's hidden lake and paused.

"Not a sound, pirate," Jailene warned as she gripped the shirai close to her breast, watching the lights intently. "Please, turn back." she whispered. "Turn back."

The line of torchlight moved back and forth for a moment, then turned sharply back to the left and moved rapidly towards their encampment.

And then it ripped through the ambient noise of the Sleeping Dragons somewhere between the lights and their post. It was a howl, but Nassir could not place the cry with a beast that would make it. It was neither wolf, bear, nor any animal he knew. The sound was unmistakably from a wild beast of some kind. Its scream caused the hairs on the back of his neck to stand.

"Cover the fire!" she whispered, running quickly for the campsite.

Nassir did not question the Guard's words. The tone in her voice was motivation enough. He quickly lit a torch and smothered the campfire with dirt as he called to Rafe's tent. "Captain! Time to leave!"

Rafe shook away the fatigue and disorientation of his sleep. Askana broke her meditation and lifted herself to her feet. Only random torchlight and the twin moons now illuminated their small camp as the beast's howl sounded again, only much closer this time. Williams finally awoke to the terrified pleas of O'Donnell, the young boy's face half-lit by the torch in his hand. The Royal Guard hastily secured supplies on their pack mules. Jailene's quick words were spoken in a tongue only her Queen and Elunear fully understood.

"How many, Nassir?" asked Rafe.

Before his First Mate could answer, Askana shouted, "We move, pirate! Do not question me on this." She then took his wrist firmly, forcing his eyes to lock with her own. "Please, Rafe."

It was hard to deduce what frightened him more. The fear Askana was failing to conceal or the fact she had called him "Rafe."

As he pulled from his haversack two pistols and a small pouch of black powder, the Captain spoke over his shoulder, "Who are they, Your Majesty?"

"They are called the Morev'ar," Askana said, unsheathing her own shirai from the now-secured supplies. "They are trained to track, and their forte is hunting their prey in darkness."

"Their prey?" Rafe asked incredulously. "You mean that cry we heard—"

"—is the cry of the Morev'ar, calling to their Order. A full hunting party numbers twelve. They use stealth tactics specifically designed for night combat. The six torches Jailene saw were merely the second team following in the tracks of a stronger lead team."

Rafe shook his head, "And I was so looking forward to a good night's sleep! Right then, six incoming and six bringing up the rear. We split up from here to rendezvous in Eyrie." He took the still-primed rifle from Nassir and handed it to Williams. "But you, Williams, I want back on the *Defiant*. Not much light tonight," Rafe said. "You think you know the path we took well enough?"

"Aye, sir, I know it well enough to get back to th' ship," said Williams.

"Excellent. We'll meet you there in two night's time. Are we clear on this, Williams?"

Williams gave a smile with what few teeth he had left and a quick wink, "As clear as a summer's day, Cap'n." He took a final check for powder in the chamber and blew softly on the fuse to ensure its light, then continued west on his own.

Rafe collected the reins of the pack mules, passing them to O'Donnell whose hands trembled as he attempted to load a pistol. "O'Donnell, take the pack mules and meet us at our tavern in Eyrie. Take one of Her Majesty's Guards with you and hasten your steps."

"Your Majesty," Jailene stood at attention before her Queen, her head bowed reverently. "I shall go if you so desire."

"Do so, Jailene." Askana placed a hand upon her soldier's cheek, "May Nadinath protect you."

"She will watch over me in all I do for Morevi." Jailene stated proudly.

"Cap'n?" O'Donnell had finally loaded the gun but he was not certain if he should prime it or simply keep it close.

"Come on, lad. We have been in far worse scrapes than this. You and Jailene go on to Eyrie. If we do not meet you within two days, get yourself back to the *Defiant*. Williams will know what to do." Rafe gave O'Donnell's cheek a playful slap with his fingertips, sending him on his way before turning to the Moor by his side. "Nassir, you are with me."

Securing the lit torch in the split of a mammoth tree, Rafe primed a set of pistols by its light, pulling their hammers back and setting them by a large rock. As he did so, he could hear behind him Askana and Elunear muttering softly in the Morevian tongue. A prayer, perhaps? A petition to this bloodthirsty Goddess of theirs?

"Let us hope the old girl hears them," he whispered, standing back-to-back with Nassir, swords drawn. "Four against twelve. Does this bring back any memories?"

The Moor nodded with a wicked smile, "Aye, that it does. That seaport in France when you were caught with the Magistrate's daughter. Which of his daughters was it then?"

"Both of them, Nassir." Rafe quipped, proud of his accomplishments.

The laughter felt good as the jungle surrounding them sank deeper and deeper into silence. "Ah yes, my Captain. I believed the Magistrate was so concerned with his reputation being sullied, he would have burned the city down just to protect his name!"

Suddenly, Rafe straightened upright, inspiration taking hold as he went for the two remaining haversacks lying by the primed pistols.

Askana and Elunear, shirai tight in their grasp, crouched by Nassir. Their breath was slow and even, displaying total control. In their eyes was a distant, dark stare.

"They are here." Askana whispered, her voice almost carrying an echo. "They are watching us, trying to find which of us is the strongest. They will first concentrate on the best warrior and work their way down to the weakest."

"So why have they not attacked?" Nassir asked, his eyes trying to make out shapes within the shadows around them.

"It seems that by sight, we are evenly matched in strength. They will test us based on our cunning." Askana spoke over her shoulder, "Prepare yourself, pirate."

No answer.

She turned quickly to see Rafe grabbing his bedroll and casting it over a nearby tree. The cream-coloured muslin material was soon dotted with the dark oil from tiny lamps Nassir and he had carried in their haversacks. Holding his breath and saying a quiet prayer, Rafe touched the still-lit torch to the fabric that ignited quickly and made its way up along to the branches.

The scream of the Morev'ar slave sounded over the crackling of flames as he plummeted to the ground. The fire quickly consumed the ceremonial oils covering his skin. He charged for Rafe who swung the torch into the man's belly, knocking him back into the tree, now fully engulfed by the fire.

Askana grabbed the pirate and spun him about, "Is burning us alive in the jungles of Morevi part of your improvising, privateer?"

"I would say my improvising has just improved our chances!" Rafe said with a smile as the growing fire began to illuminate the area around them. "Your Morev'ar are skilled at night tracking, therefore I have shed a little light over their advantage. At least we will see them coming. It is a desperate act, but one with merits!"

No sooner had the words left Rafe's lips when the night was filled with the death cry of the Morev'ar.

Askana gripped her shirai as two shadows leapt from the jungle wielding enormous curved scymitars. While the shirai handled like a quarterstaff, its discipline and attack forms capitalised on the natural lightness and agility born in women. The combination of firelight and the flow of the robes Askana wore made it difficult for her Morev'ar opponents to anticipate her next move. With a powerful leap, she took flight. One Morev'ar looked up to see the blade of the shirai extend outward from the night space and cut through his neck. The second Morev'ar fighting by his side was already bearing down on Askana before she touched ground, but the Queen dipped at the waist, her leg coming up in a crescent motion. The blade of her foot struck the Morev'ar in the temple, stunning him long enough for Askana to pull the blade free of the dead man's neck and thrusting behind her. The instant she felt her shirai blade hit muscle, Askana gave the weapon a hard series of twists. She then pulled the blade free and swung it around her, removing the Morev'ar's head with one cut.

Rafe, with duelling dagger and rapier ready, took account of the battles around him. Elunear, displaying movements as precise as her Queen's, faced off with a third Morev'ar, swinging the shirai around her waist and repelling her attacker with continuous shaft strikes and powerful kicks to his chest. The heavier sword of the Morev'ar could not get past Nassir's twin sabres that cut through the air with a deadly foreboding. The Persian blades easily worked past the man's singular defence, leaving deep, elegant cuts across his oiled muscles.

Askana had said there would be six. Where was the last Morev'ar?

The high-pitched whistle came from behind Rafe. He parried to his left, quickly bringing both rapier and dagger upward to deflect the atriah hurtling at him. With a resounding ring, the weapon bounced away from Rafe and embedded itself into a thick tree trunk. Before he could take another breath, the titanic slave leapt through the wall of flames, slamming into Rafe and knocking his weapons clear. The pirate had managed to wedge his legs between the Morev'ar and himself, his feet square against his attacker's chest and keeping him at bay for the moment. The Morev'ar, his face a canvas of Morevian characters painted in dark red, gave a howl that nearly shattered the Captain's eardrums. Rafe could just feel the pommel of his dagger with his fingertips, but to reach for its handle also meant getting closer to his assailant. His other free hand was bracing himself in the mud and dirt, keeping him from losing ground to this Morev'ar's girth.

The wild man continued to push forward and Rafe could feel his legs weakening. *Allright then*, he thought to himself, *now or never.*

Rafe bent upward and pushed hard against the boot dagger's pommel, tearing through the leather scabbard and burying it deep into the Morev'ar's belly. The man staggered back, feeling the sting of the weapon in his stomach and the warmth of his own blood across his fingers. He looked at the pirate with surprise as he dropped to his knees, blood dripping from his mouth.

Rafe breathed a heavy sigh of relief and then looked down at his ruined boot scabbard with a groan of disgust. *First my breeches, then my Silver Rose doublet, and now this!* He thought bitterly, *My washerwoman in London will love me for this.*

A grunt caught his attention and he looked up to see a horror found only in one's nightmares. The Morev'ar was on his feet once more. The dark slave regained his footing as blood continued to run from his stomach wound and from between his lips. A second life came to him, granting him more strength than his previous one provided. He unsheathed a menacing scymitar from his belt, his laughter ebbing as a tide coming into shore.

Rafe scrambled for the stone where he had left the pistols. Only one remained. The privateer aimed for the Morev'ar and pulled the trigger. The simple click of the hammer and the empty silence of a misfire had never sounded so deafening.

A cry, deep and guttural, again exploded into the night as the Morev'ar charged at him with his dying breath, the massive Morevian blade held high above his head.

The gunshot could be heard over the battle cry, the flames, and the ringing of blade on blade. The bullet picked him up off the ground by sheer force of impact. Rafe looked to his right to find Askana bent upon one knee with the foreign weapon in hand. The fire of the trees danced in her dark eyes, her arm steady as the rock Rafe collapsed against in relief. A grin formed across her face as she stared at the dead Morev'ar until the cold emptiness of her action struck her. She had taken a life of a subject loyal to Morevi.

The weapon lowered slowly as Rafe crawled over to her. "You have just passed your first shooting lesson, Your Majesty," he shouted above the roar of the flames.

Nassir, weary of fighting an opponent that refused to die, mercilessly brought one sabre across the Morev'ar's chest, following this up by burying his second blade into his opponent's back. He turned to see Elunear cornering her Morev'ar against a massive tree. He went to help, but froze at what he saw. The Morev'ar suddenly reached out to grab the shirai and pull its long blade into himself. In this lethal strike, the fire caught the still-fresh sheen in the warpaint accenting his tattoos. The red colour was unique in its shade, and Elunear recognised it right away, her eyes widening with shock. She could only stare into his lifeless eyes as he pulled himself towards her, plunging the weapon deeper into his body. She was too terrified to cry out as he was completely unaffected by the blade now protruding through his back. Nassir gave his own bellowing cry and grasped the shaft of the weapon, tossing the Morev'ar into the fire as if he were a log intended to fuel it.

Then, apart from the flames now rising high behind them, a stillness fell over them. A strange scent of blood, earth, and burning flesh now permeated the air around them. No one spoke. No one moved. Shirai and swords finally lowered.

Clasping hands firmly, Rafe and Nassir gave each other congratulatory laughs as they had cheated Death once again, but their celebration was silenced at the sight of Elunear. Her voice trembled wildly as she spoke to Askana in Morevian. She made motions across her skin similar to the painted characters the Morev'ar had across their chests and arms. Askana took the young girl into a comforting embrace, her own face was pale and sorrowful as she looked at the dead Morev'ar around them while gently stroking the young girl's hair. Askana ushered Elunear to Nassir. The Moor was stunned that this mighty warrior in his embrace was shaking. Silently, Askana led Rafe to a fallen Morev'ar and pulled him down with her to look closer at the ornate designs covering his body.

"Captain Rafton, I want you to see this. Note the warpaint along the tattoos." Rafe reached as if to touch their skin, but Askana's hand shot out and held Rafe's in a firm grasp. "Do not touch it!"

Along with a sharp, musk oil covering his muscled body, the ornate tattoos of the Morev'ar were accentuated with a deep crimson paint. "They appear to be covered with some kind of ink."

"Not ink. Blood. It is a toxin I banned from use in my discoveries with poisons." Askana sighed heavily, closing her eyes as she whispered a blessing over the condemned soul. He was cold inside, empty. Beyond her own prayers to Nadinath.

"You say these men were poisoned before battle?"

"This particular toxin is found in the blood of a *Kir'shia*, a breed of wolf indigenous to the Southern Wood. It can enter the body through one's skin and grants a heightened sense of being. You feel no pain, only great strength. Everything—heartbeat, agility, reflexes, resistance—is elevated."

"So why ban it?"

"Once touched by the blood of a Kir'shia, addiction is instantaneous. The hunger becomes more ravenous with each satisfaction. If the hunger is not satisfied, madness. Then death. It only takes a small amount—a mere thimbleful—to achieve this heightened state." Askana looked around her at the Morev'ar corpses covered in the Kir'shia. "Any more than that and the body becomes a flame that burns twice as bright, but only half as long."

"They were dead before we even drew a blade," Rafe uttered dryly. "What kind of men would do this to themselves?"

"The Morev'ar are a faction of the military dating back to the beginning of the Morevian dynasties. They are comprised only of male birth-slaves and bred to fight to the death in a fanatical love for Morevi. Their loyalty is only to Morevi. It does not always extend to the reigning monarch, as you have seen tonight."

A cry of the Morev'ar sounded over the fire, still distant but close enough to cause them to all start.

"Come, Your Grace." Rafe said, grabbing his haversack, "We have a long night of travel ahead of us."

The fire now spread like a great barrier before them. It would be enough to hold the Morev'ar at bay, granting them time to escape into the darkness of the Sleeping Dragons and the neighbouring territories of Eyrie. Elunear steadied herself with a few swigs from Nassir's mead bottle. Askana could not blame the girl for her loss of composure. The sight of Morev'ar anointed with the blood of the Kir'Shia was a true horror for anyone, even for a queen.

With weapons at the ready, they continued west. Only the light of the twin moons served as their torch.

CHAPTER THREE
The Great Game

"The Queen is missing."

This news had already begun to worm its way through the halls of the Palace of a Thousand Suns. The present disturbance still remained in the scope of her control. The woman, unable to sleep for well over two nights, was silently hoping this was all some hideous nightmare brought about by the current tensions in the Council of a Hundred Turi. The pinching of her headdress against her temples was a continuous reminder that she was very much awake and in the heart of a political maelstrom.

The reports from her attendants, familiar with the passageways of the Palace's concealed catacombs, repeated again and again in her mind. For the Lady Adion of House Charmar, it was customary in the early morning hours that their four-year old son would slip between she and her husband as they slept. This particular morning, it had been a cobra joining them. It wasted no time in striking them both. Lady Inoe of House Talis had been observed enjoying her morning breakfast on the quaint terrace overlooking Songkusai. It had been a breathtaking sunrise. It had also been her last. The *if'jassa* poison was discovered in her teacup, giving off a sharp, pungent smell as it did in undisturbed liquid. The most horrific of these deaths was Lady Yurana of House Cresal as she witnessed her own assassination. The hairdresser had parted Yurana's hair down the middle, letting it fall its entire length to the small of her back as was customary in this morning routine. As the Lady's eyes shut, she lost herself in the hairdresser's slow brush strokes. The servant elegantly wrapped the long, black hair around her Lady's neck. It was sound of jewellery boxes, perfume bottles, and brushes being hastily swept from a vanity that alerted the Palace Guard. They rushed in to see the Councilwoman strangled before her own horrified reflection. Before the soldiers could reach the young servant, she threw herself from the balcony. Dirare's attendant, watching from the spyhole behind a black marble statue of Nadinath, noted the servant's face was void of all emotion. She appeared as if in a trance.

Dirare's other two attendants noted the same qualities in their observed assassins. Adion's traitorous servant handled the deadly serpent as would a trained member of the Assassins' Guild, even rapping the cobra hard against the back of its head and hood to agitate it. Once it struck Lady Adion and her husband, she went to grab the snake, making no evasive gestures as it turned on her. It bit her twice but she showed no recognition of its lethal strikes. She was able to snap its neck before the venom coursed through her and stopped her heart. Lady Inoe's servant, regarded as the daughter she always longed to have, held her Lady's hand affectionately as the sun rose in a beautiful display before them. Inoe thrashed and convulsed in her chair while the servant stood motionless. She then gently arranged her Lady in the chair, assuring her of the grandest view of Sonkusai now coloured in a shade of cinnamon with a hint of yellow. She placed a soft kiss on her Lady's forehead, took one of the sapphire pins from Inoe's hair and drove it deep into her wrist. Her face remained still and constant as she pulled the pin up the length of her arm. She died by her mistress' side.

All three attacks happened within minutes of one another. Unthinkable.

Her attendants were rapt with guilt in not intervening. Their Lady lovingly promised them absolution by the blessings of El'Baz, her True God and Divinity. While spying on one another was practised between the Noble Ladies, it was not tolerated if the spies were caught, the punishments severe. It was also law in the Palace that if any were caught spying on the Queen, the agent would be put to death along with the Councilwoman or Councilwomen to whom the spy swore allegiance. This particular morning demanded such a risk. Dirare sent two servants, one of them armed with a pair of atriah, to the passageways connecting with the private chambers of Queen Askana.

The truth of her own words still shook her, even when uttered where only she herself and the woman affectionately regarded as a surrogate mother could hear them.

Lady Dirare of House Jarahd snapped her fan shut with a resounding click. Two successive sleepless nights still could not rob her of her resolute features. To her, control was as natural as breathing. Resplendent in her signature red robes, she had been called handsome by many, but never gentle. Dirare had not chosen to be a political adversary to the First Queen of Morevi, but everything she believed in seemed to slant her that way.

Perhaps theology provided the basis for their rivalry. Askana led the movement and Order of Nadinath, a religion Dirare found too dark, too violent. It ran to extremes in its casting out of men. Worst of all, it was implied through its blood rituals that willingly losing control was right and proper. Even so, she could not say why she so venomously disagreed to its principles. It could have simply been that its time was past. While the worship of the Goddess had been the perfect vehicle for inciting rebellion, it would not provide the spiritual guidance essential at this vital phase of peace and rebuilding. She knew, regardless of her personal bias, that her own religion of El'Baz, the God of Wisdom, would be more suited to the role. Instead of turning outside the borders of Morevi to either ally or antagonise cultures alien to their own, El'Baz taught to "look inward" which, as interpreted by Dirare, would shut their city gates to the outside realms. Morevi would become a world unto itself, steeped in self-reliance. She smiled at a strange, sudden realisation that Nadinath—the Order that promotes an infallible independence from its Sisters—would promote such open acceptance in the welcoming of refugees from outside kingdoms.

Such is religion—the eternal paradox.

Nadinath. The acceptance of refugee women from neighbouring lands. The Queen's constant fraternisation with the outside world taking corporal form in such creatures as the Beast, the Elf, and now the Consort. Dirare never lacked issues with which to question the Throne. Sometimes her own logic warned her that it would not be long before the Queen's scant patience wore out.

Women leading Morevi to a brighter future was something they shared in common. Their respective visions for the realm were very different. True, Askana had the cunning and the strength of youth. It was Askana Moldarin, with great personal sacrifice, who had led an overnight revolution. Dirare would never question that. However, time had blessed Dirare with a weapon sharper than any shirai. Influence.

The death of Lady Adion dealt a severe blow to that influence. It was House Charmar who always supported the thoughts and desires of House Jarahd. For centuries, even during the rule of men, their Houses stood together as the strongest of allies. In the dawn of the New Age, they stood confidently against some of Askana's wishes for their realm, assuring her that one dictatorship would not be substituted for another.

The Queen had also gained powerful friends in her ascent to the throne. The Houses of Talis and Cresal were dedicated to the Order of Nadinath. Many times, the Council of a Hundred Turi would revolve around their four houses. House Moldarin was usually the centre of the political melee. Dirare had heard rumour, though, of an epiphany Lady Adion had experienced over the Order of Nadinath. Regrettably, Dirare ordered her attendants to keep watch over her friend's chambers.

Then, in one morning, Dirare's long-time ally and Askana's most influential advocates were eliminated. There had also been an attempt on the Queen, it appeared, but it had been a ruse. The assassin played the part of the intended, and Askana was nowhere to be found. That morning had been an aggressive move from this traitor to the Crown, but it was a hollow victory with the body of Askana Moldarin unaccounted for.

Brilliantly played, Askana, Dirare thought with a smile of approval. *I would not have anticipated such a counter-move as this.*

Strands of grey stood out against the deep brown of her hair, drawn back tight within the headdress. Dirare was the embodiment of discipline and direction. It was not that Askana failed to possess these attributes. They were found in the Queen in slightly different forms. Ironically, it was this difference that made opposing Askana in the Great Game so addictive.

The Great Game was the understood title given to the game of Morevian politics played by the Ladies of the Blood. In Court, references to the strategy game of *par-stern* were rife. It was a game rooted in the ancient traditions of Morevi, redefined by the First Queen after the War of the Fan and Slipper, and the preferred game of the Palace. The comments nobility would make in casual conversations, however, were merely polite metaphors to a more deadly and very real game played between Councilwomen. It was understood that no one played the Great Game better than Askana and Dirare. It was also understood that when they played against one another, the repercussions would be felt beyond the city walls. Rarely would their moves surprise one another. No stratagem or tactic was made without considering an attendant web of options and smaller intrigues.

Disappearing was not Askana's style. She would have fought, fortified her position and worked ruthlessly, but brilliantly, to find those responsible. Dirare long suspected that the young Queen's unpredictable bouts of temper were but a sham to keep them all off-balance. When it came to war, intrigue, and decision-making, she was rarely impulsive. The staged scene with the dead servant girl, the strange wound to the forehead, and the ropes reaching to the abyss below the Great Balcony showed the influence of another hand. Impetuous. Chaotic.

This was what gave Dirare pause.

Two days had passed and the Council was about to call itself to order, presumably to decide what would be the next course of action in this state of urgency and uncertainty. The Queen was no longer on her throne, but neither was she in the Royal Crypt awaiting proper ceremony before The Passing. The instigators of this coup could easily take the throne if allied with the right Houses, but only at an unimaginable risk to themselves and their allies if Askana were to reappear. And although Dirare was currently imbalanced, she was not lame. The challenge in getting her way was just more difficult now.

Pieces were now shifting. With the *Samsagi* moving from Fire to Earth, the Game would grow intense as the Temple would be challenged for their place on the board.

"What do you think of this?" Dirare asked her mentor, the fan lightly tapping her chin.

The old woman was as slight and as small as a withered bird. Her hair and eyes were almost bleached of colour by the relentless passing of the years. Arnese had dutifully served Dirare first as nursemaid, then as a valuable and insightful spy in the rebellion. She had watched the precocious girl grow into a formidable woman, suffer under the tyranny of man, and rise to power, becoming the adversary against the First Queen of Morevi. She was released from her charge as servant when Dirare came to her seat in the Council of a Hundred Turi and now officially served as adviser, but the bond ran far deeper than the title indicated.

Arnese had seen a great deal in her time. Her mind had only sharpened with the years, as was evident by her reply. "I think of where the balance of power will shift, and how we can move so as not to be crushed by it."

Dirare gave one of her rare smiles to the old adviser.

She always enjoyed breaking down that stern, controlled exterior of her protégé. "As the acknowledged leader of the Council, the weight of authority will now rest on your shoulders. Even those who ally themselves with House Moldarin will turn their eyes upon you for only you could hold the throne successfully against Askana. For Morevi, and your own well-being, you must discover those who grapple for power." The old woman crossed to the game of par-stern still in play, the smooth pieces of red and black marble silently crying out to continue their struggle for victory. Her less-lavish but nonetheless richly embroidered layers of court robes gave her the appearance of an old tortoise with a beautiful shell as she moved. She studied the ornate playing pieces scattered across the Four Elements as she spoke, "And while Askana's opponent has made a most aggressive move, their objective of capturing the Black Queen was bungled. They dare not move as she has slipped into Wind and will choose to move when she so desires. Therefore the Red *Morev'ar* will wait in Fire until the Queen steps back into his own element. Therein lies your challenge—find the bold opponent in hiding." Arnese nodded, moving her Red Samsagi from Wind to Water, catching the unsuspecting Black *Ajassa*. An expendable piece and perhaps not as important as capturing the Black Samsagi. The move now placed her opponent on the defence. "You have always possessed a sharp mind. Remember, the enemy who can kill is the ally whose dagger is within reach of your heart."

"The Council is in itself a nest of vipers," Dirare said in disgust. She quickly went silent as a palace servant entered with a tray of tea and *sze-rine* buns, delicate sweetbreads filled with a black-bean paste. He set the tray down on the table and bowed deeply as she motioned him out with a flick of her fan. She waited for the doors to close and the rattle of bead curtains to cease before continuing. "Establishing the Council was a wise move from the Queen. But these women have been used to working behind the curtains of male command. With this new freedom and the heady power of ruling, they're turning everything into a political play. If we don't do something about it soon this new government will grind to a halt as Councilwomen play each other into stalemate over the tax rate for beans!

"Too many have forgotten it was this pettiness that brought the downfall of men. Now they see an empty throne. The murmurs about Askana's right to establish her house as the Royal Line begin once more. The danger will come from the strongest: the Lady Miarad of House Harlin, the Ladies Pira and Pura of the House Charmar, and the Lady Radna of House Nishien. Pira and Pura, most notably, as they have the spur of their mother's death to drive them. They have felt the mortality of their House shake through them. If the rumours of their mother turning to that savage faith of Askana's prove true, I cannot count on their loyalty."

"And yourself, of course," Arnese added. "You stand too close to the Throne for the comfort of many. The Queen herself was growing wary."

She conceded with a nod. "I am the sole blood survivor of House Jarahd. Survival is not an option but a necessity."

"And survival would be less a risk if you ascended the Throne? You are wrong there, Mistress. As you have noted, the new government is too young, the way still rocky and uncertain. One of the main reasons why our Queen managed to live so long was due to her unconventional skills. You can make no pretence towards being a warrior, Mistress."

"I would not know poison from remedy," Dirare said, her brows furrowed. "The fact remains whoever the traitor—or traitors—to the Crown are, they believe themselves prepared to face the Black Widow. Askana is now on the defensive, wherever in Naruihm that may be."

Arnese clicked her tongue. "You underestimate your opponent. Do you think Askana Moldarin such easy sport? This is not a retreat, but merely a regrouping. I believe the Queen has found herself an ally. A most powerful and cunning one at that. Only El'Baz alone knows what she plans."

Dirare moved to where her adviser sat. Her eyes studied the old woman's expression. That Arnese would invoke the name of the God of Wisdom carried weight. "So what would you propose? How should we move to block the others without seeming traitorous if the Queen returns?"

Arnese did not answer at once. Her knotted old fingers reached for a sze-rine bun. She had always been fond of sweets. "To the men, this would seem like an opportunity. Granted, there are few of them left to do any harm. Askana's witch-spawn Lubria saw to that. The resentment of their reversed positions in society runs deep. If they do see this as their sign from El'Baz to reclaim their dominance, Eyrie would make powerful allies in such an uprising. Their system of government would suit the men better than the current Morevian regime."

"The Eyrieners have no foothold here," Dirare said with a cutting motion of her fan, eyes flashing. "And they will not attempt open warfare to conquer. It would cost them too much and perhaps bring down the wrath of the Fellowship of the Jewels."

"But what if they do find a foothold? Someone close enough to the throne, yet not loyal to Morevi or the new system."

Dirare's eyes widened. "He has not been formally raised to office! It has only been of late he was recognised by Council as Royal Consort." An eyebrow arched sharply as shee traced the outline of the fallen pawn piece outside the board. "He is barely a Consort. Closer to another ajassa under Askana's command."

Arnese smiled widely. Even deep in contemplation of this delicate situation, Dirare always kept her eye on the game at hand.

"The Queen made her favour plain. He lives in the Consort's quarters, you know. Even though it is no longer frowned upon for women to have their fair share of lovers, Askana has taken none save for him." Arnese's grin widened a bit, a dark, mischievous gleam passing quickly across her eyes as she said, "And the Elf."

Dirare looked up from the par-stern board sharply, a reflex action. It was still a sensitive matter and proclaimed by the Queen not to be spoken of, either in Court or private chambers. Askana's only lover since being crowned First Queen had not been human. Their affair began trade negotiations, opening the door between Morevi and Arathelle. To the Council, the affair was a necessary evil. If Morevi ever needed neutral neighbours, none could have been more important than the Elves.

Now, at least the Queen's interests were in a human consort who to some extent resembled a Morevian.

"It was told to me that Askana saw shades of her dead brother in him. I met Lord Markuna once and that whelp of a consort is nothing like him," Arnese scoffed. "He is weak. The men could seize him, or he could even support their cause being a man himself. It would be easy enough for them and the Eyrieners to put him on the Throne of the Thousand Suns. The people would not protest too much. Many are still uncomfortable with the New Order and might prefer a reversion to the Old Regime. And consider various members of Council probably at this very moment hiring assassins to slit his throat."

"What difference will it make if he dies—" Dirare began to say, then fell silent for a long minute.

The old woman merely sipped her tea primly as she studied the board's four playing fields. North, South, East, West. Earth, Fire, Wind, Water. How she enjoyed taking Dirare by surprise.

"Arnese, you wily old fox. You're not considering that I—"

"In light of the Queen's favour, Askana would not be angry *if* she returned to find him temporarily ruling in her absence." Arnese emphasised the 'if' in her reply to Dirare's broken thought. "However, she would be upset to find him dead. The Royal Guard will not protect him, not before the Raising. If you take him under Jarahd protection, not only will everyone be forced to admit the righteousness of that action, but naturally the bewildered young foreigner will need a Regent to familiarise him with Morevian government, not to mention defend him from the hostile Ladies. And, most naturally, who else would he pick if not for the Lady responsible for protecting his life?"

Dirare picked up her cup, taking a sip of the fine Morevian tea. "An excellent suggestion, little old mother."

The term of affection never ceased to make Arnese smile, "Better to ally yourself with the ruling house, be it present or no. For it is always the strongest ally that makes for the most formidable opponent."

"I agree."

Without a glance to the position of the pieces, Dirare moved her Temple along an angle of five squares. Arnese's eyes widened as she studied the board intently. The Red Sword could not defend its Queen. There was nowhere to flee.

"I had this game won three days ago," Dirare smiled wickedly, forgoing the customary declaration of checkmate. "I enjoyed watching your strategy."

Arnese shook her head in wonder at her apt pupil, "Indeed. Another game then?"

"Perhaps later." Dirare's eyes turned to the window that looked outward to the east wing of the Palace. The Consort would be there. She knew the Queen's Samsagi would be devising an escape route presently. It was time to bring her own Ajassa and Morev'ar into action. "I have another Queen to place in check. If you are not engaged tonight, would you care to be my second in this game?"

"I shall attend on you." Arnese replied warmly.

As the purple-red hue of dusk covered the sky, the twin moons of Naruihm slowly came into view. A caravan of a shuttered carriage, baggage cart, and an armed escort moved quietly through Songkusai. It could have been taken for the entourage of a Lady returning late to an estate just outside the city. It was hard to tell what standing this Lady held as none of the vehicles or escort bore house colours or a sigil. It was a nondescript party, perhaps belonging to a Lady of the lowest rank, newly raised. It could have been an ambassador's coach, flying no colours to communicate their neutrality within the city walls. Many of the storekeepers paid no mind or mention to the small procession as it passed by their shops. Some aggressive merchants tried hawking their wares in hopes of a last-minute sale, but with only the occasional warning from the soldiers who kept careful watch over the carriage, the convoy pressed on silently and undisturbed through the streets and beyond the gates.

The man hidden within the lacquered carriage worriedly peered out through a crack between the closed panels. He had not bargained for this.

First, news came to him that she was dead. Then it was told to him a few hours later that she had disappeared. His relief that she had not been killed along with the others now faded into alarm. Servants were continuously in and out of his quarters at all hours, never leaving his side. They were full of gossip. It was becoming clear through all the information peppered with far-fetched fantasy that she had dumped him in the middle of a colossal mess! Finally, after two days of waiting and wondering, the servant named Kubi-Sogi arrived, telling him only that he would be taken to a safe haven in the country until her return. He gave orders to be ready to move at a moment's notice, then disappeared in the endless corridors of the Palace.

His only allies, besides a mysterious queen, were servants that he knew remotely and an old man who would be his last line of defence against a collection of women just recently granted power over a nation. He was alone in a place where being a man and being alone were two things one wished not to be. Askana Moldarin herself was an endless enigma: a queen, a warrior, and a priestess of Nadinath's temple.

He had been there once, catching a glimpse of her latter facet. He did not care to repeat the experience.

He felt a surge of reassurance as retainers collected him, just as the Blademaster had promised. "There," he was told while hurriedly ushered through the Palace to an awaiting coach, "everything will be made clear to you." This proved that she had anticipated, perhaps even planned, for the disaster. And that she had thought of him.

As he rode deeper into the denser jungle that the Morevians referred to as the "country", his mind wandered. In the past he had done this while crouching on rooftops or clinging to drainpipes to take his mind off the cramping pains that plagued the thieves' existence. Lately, his mind seemed only to circle around his Lady, the circumstances in which he had met her, and the current title he held in her Court.

Consort. How he loathed that title. It was effectively the male equivalent of "mistress". It brought with it the constant threat of the Court but none of the power. Then again it also meant he was privy to the most intimate parts of the Queen's life. He had her fondness, that he was certain of, but not her love. Her treatment of him was far better than what others in his position endured. After months in her Court he had grown used to the sight of ruling ladies marching in with perhaps two or three gilded, submissive youths in their wake.

There was only one word to describe it—emasculating.

Emasculation had been her indirect plan from the start. As she had explained to him, Morevian rulers must be siblings, never lovers, to ensure power lay wholly in the hands of the Royal Family itself. In words he understood better, to be King, he had to keep his legs crossed demurely. Like an addle-brained lover, he had chosen to be Consort instead. Powerless, and now with her gone, defenceless.

Had he known all this before trying to lift her purse in The Barrier Reef, he would have let her pass without a second glance. He had been fool enough to notice her pretty eyes rather than the knife at his throat raising him to his feet. *"Markuna,"* she had said in that split second, before amazement diminished to the tarnish of disappointment. He had not known it then but his profile and almond eyes had fooled her for an instant into remembering the spectre of a dearly beloved brother, and in so doing, saved his life.

He had come with her thinking that association with royalty would bring a windfall with it. He had been fool enough to lose his head and his heart.

The coach came to an abrupt halt. His visions of Askana disappeared as the armed escort opened the door to reveal a Morevian estate secluded by a grove of trees. Rows of torches threw dancing light over the pathway, right up to the massive doors. With every sense acutely aware of where he was, he followed the guard up the path. Then he paused for a moment. The banners flying outside the estate and high above were not Askana's. He could not place their insignia nor could he identify the signature colours of the household.

Still, the Blademaster's message had been that he would meet him here with news of Askana. Their walk felt as if it would last an eternity, the silence broken occasionally by the rush of a torch flame or the soft but insistent music of cicadas. The escort led him into a grand room decorated in the traditional Morevian style and motioned to a pair of low chairs set before an inviting fireplace. Steeling himself, he walked over and settled into one of them, folding his legs in front of him and thanking his stars for natural flexibility. The guard then cast a quick glance behind Jermal, bowed deeply, and left the Consort in the lavish chambers.

"I am sure you have many questions," the familiar, icy voice echoed in the chambers. "And I hope you will open your heart to me as you once did to her."

He watched the colours of the fire steadily. His blank expression concealed the thudding of his heart in his chest, refusing to look as Lady Dirare took a seat close by him. She wore the casual robes favoured by the Ladies when in private, fastened with a gold-worked sash, her dark brown hair long and loose on her shoulders and breasts. The firelight seemed to only harden her features more and catch the streaks of grey interwoven within her hair. Cold as her voice sounded, there was still a haunting loveliness about her. Whereas Askana's grace was vivid and lithe, Dirare's was almost classical and contemplative. Perhaps even calculating.

Askana's many tearless periods of mourning for one used master or another in her youth earned her the mocking moniker of "The Black Widow". In some circles it was held that Dirare had never shed a tear in her life, not of mourning, sadness, or compassion.

"Lady Dirare," Jermal said respectfully, averting his eyes from her. "I thank you for offering your home to me. Askana will be most pleased when I inform her of your loyalty to the—"

"You may dispense with the formalities, Jermal," Dirare smiled, patting his knee affectionately. He gave a slight start that only caused her smile to widen. She pulled her hand away and rested it against her cheek as she studied him in the firelight. "There is no delegation here of the Crown or of the Council. Tonight, there is only you, myself, and the guards within my estate who will ensure your safety."

"*Your* estate?" Jermal asked, his voice disguising the hammering of his heart that increased tenfold. The cause of his suspicions, his sense of unease, was now confirmed.

She reached for the small bowl of assorted fruits and helped herself to one of the larger *reccaberries*. Giving it a quick dip in the chocha sauce, Dirare held it before her and studied the way the sauce slowly wrapped itself around the berry. "I was hoping we could talk. Get to know one another better."

Jermal watched her pop the chocha-kissed berry into her mouth and knew that she had him in her hands, whatever her plans were. He knew even with his short range of experience that Lady Dirare was never without a plan. "And you are implying?"

"Rest assured," said Dirare, her voice very condescending in its tone. "I have no interest in you that way."

"Then why use the same words that Her Majesty used with me?" Jermal said curtly, recalling his first night with Askana. *I do not intend to poison your meal, thief,* she said to him with a disarming smile. *I desire to talk with you. Get to know you better.* He had been called far worse, but Askana addressing him that way had cut his pride, almost in a professional way.

Hearing Dirare speak those same words to him was a touch unsettling. Jermal had never back-talked any of the Council, even socially — the only time men were drawn into the conversation. However, he was fully aware of Dirare's ambitious means.

"I see why you hold Her Majesty's attentions," Dirare nodded as she cleaned her fingertips of the chocha sauce with a delicate smacking of her lips. "No, my sweet, this time I simply state facts. Her Majesty, Askana Moldarin, has disappeared. Rumours have reached me, reporting that she absconded in the company of a fair-haired man, identity unknown. His description sounds similar to those matching an outlaw that carries a death sentence on his head. The rumours concerning him is he comes from across The Rift. Aren't you also from a realm on the other side of The Rift, Jermal?"

It seemed far away and alien now, but he could see The Barrier Reef so crisp and sharp in his mind. A place where deals were struck and people died as a consequence. Battles were fought and friendships were made between the noble, the downright evil, and all in-between. The Reef played host to all kinds. Himself, he had enjoyed the variety of scores he could come across there, and the equally varied accessible women. But had Askana returned to The Reef? Why?

Then he paused, reflecting on his thoughts. A bitter taste formed in his mouth.

"We know they were en route to Eyrie," Dirare continued. A hint of satisfaction crossed her face at Jermal's distractions of jealousy. "She has left Morevi—and you—in a state of turmoil, mourning, and chaos."

"And so you have taken it upon yourself to take charge and imprison me in your estate?"

Her laugh was sharp, mocking. "Is this what Her Majesty's affections and your short time in our Court have turned you into? A jealous, suspicious lover? Come, come, Jermal, these attributes do not suit a man of your stature. Nor are they quality attributes of a king. Better the ingénue you once were."

A sudden silence fell over them both. Jermal knew he needed to keep his wits about him and choose his next words very carefully. He could not tell what her intentions were or how sincere she was in her protection of him. But the word "king" seemed to ring in the chambers well after Dirare had spoken it.

He would serve as Consort. His choice was final, at least according to Askana. There would be little chance of a Consort raised to the position of King unless he wished to remain celibate, chaste. He was not going to allow himself to be castrated, literally or figuratively, for any crown. Yet something in Dirare's eyes told him she was not intending anything of the kind for him.

"How do you know so much about Askana's flight?"

"I am most certain Askana has enlightened you on the various influences I possess in court. I must keep hold of this influence through a complex network of loyal subjects."

"You mean spies," Jermal spoke dryly.

Dirare paused in her speech for a moment, unaccustomed to being interrupted. For a second her face darkened at his defiance, but it soon returned to its former expression which if not soft, was at least not threatening, "Call them by whatever title pleases you. They serve me well. I have been monitoring her progress for some time, just to assure myself and my associates that Askana is not blindly leading her people into an uncertain future."

"And by this, do you mean forcing her hand in banishing Lubria? Or do you refer to the current tensions between Eyrie and Morevi along the borders? I remember how adamant she was about not allowing the ambassador permanent residence in the city." Jermal could feel his posture straightening as he intended Dirare to see he was not the meek, quiet man Councilwomen assumed he was. He had a mind and an opinion, and he had a voice. "I must admit, I agreed with her upon that issue. Why invite the enemy within your city walls to spy upon you?"

"So we may discover the spies he employs in his service." His posturing for her was endearing. She sighed heavily, shaking her head, "It is all part of the Great Game. Many ladies of Council and Court, Askana Moldarin included, may think the Great Game is played only within the Kingdom's borders. I assure you, it is played with zeal in many other regions as well."

For a moment, only the crackling of the fire filled the chambers. Dirare sat back in the chair and stretched lazily. Her demeanour was very relaxed, as if she were throwing caution to the four winds. Jermal only knew her from her appearances at Court and Askana's mention. He remembered the long searching look he caught her giving him at the formal gathering of the Council to recognise him as Royal Consort. Discovered, she made no pretence to avert her gaze. There was no trusting this woman, not now or ever.

Watching the shadows play across her body, the smile accompanying her piercing gaze, he could not help but stare. A very different beauty from Askana, but still as dangerous. But if she wanted him dead, he would be already.

She had called him King.

"I am afraid you have me at a disadvantage, Lady Dirare." One look at her told him she knew that. Jermal could feel the dryness in his throat as he spoke, "You are Askana's political rival and I am well aware how deep the rivalry extends. Now, in her absence, you wish to make me King. Something I know is impossible."

"What I wish," Dirare said factually, "is what is best for Morevi. With her new regime, I believe Askana has found that. But in this tumultuous time of her disappearance, I believe we must reassure the Morevian people that her ideals and her wishes are to be fulfilled. And these wishes will be best embodied through you, Jermal."

This was definitely not the Dirare that Askana had depicted to him. "What do you mean?"

"Save for yourself, Askana has not taken a lover. You were to be raised to the position of Royal Consort, the vessel from which Askana would bring forth, carry, and bless unto Morevi an heir apparent." Again, Dirare reached across the space between their seats and placed a gentle hand on top of Jermal's own. This time, he did not flinch. She then spoke with comforting assurance, "In this time when the people must know Askana still rules even while absent, perhaps you should assume a more authoritative role. You should rule as King of Morevi, in place of Askana Moldarin, until her return."

Jermal's mind raced at the prospects. Askana had already told him what it meant to be King. Had she deliberately misled him? From thief to consort to king — *was it possible?*

"But how can the Ceremony of the Thousand Suns take place without my Queen present? And how will my voice be heard in the Council? Surely she—"

Dirare placed a finger to his lips, "Shhh, my dear Jermal. I know you are teeming with questions. Think on this, where do your loyalties lie? With a queen who disappears at a time when all she holds dear hangs in the balance? To a woman who, at a time when you need her guidance and strength the most, abandons you for some unknown journey into the heart of our sworn enemy? Or to a land that would call you King? To subjects that place their reputations and rites of passage and power in jeopardy for your safety?" Again, silence filled the vast chambers, save for the conversation of the hearth's flames. Dirare rose from her chair, "These are your chambers, Your Majesty. Rest well, and think on what I offer you." She bowed in reverence and smiled, "We shall speak again."

Jermal watched her with amazement as she floated silently across the hall. She moved like a ghostly apparition, her feet never appearing from underneath the folds of her robes. The door shut behind her followed by the resonating sound of latches being slid into place, ensuring his security. Only the sounds of the jungle, the fireplace, and the wind chimes suspended outside on the balcony remained with the man left behind.

"And you call me the wily old fox? The bow was an exquisite touch." Arnese said approvingly as she stood before the two-way mirror that spied into Jermal's chambers. "So tell me, how did you find out about this unknown ally of the Queen's? Much has happened between our afternoon tea and tonight's Game."

"My dear mentor," Dirare smiled, watching the Consort wrestle with his thoughts, heart, and the voice of Instinct. "Are you telling me that age has finally got the better of you? You cannot tell when I am bluffing?"

"Oh my dear," she chuckled, softly clapping in applause. "You are the master storyteller. To hear you tell the tale, I would have believed that Askana had defected to the sworn enemy of Morevi."

"Take care in what you speak, lest it may evoke the Fates to have it come true." Her eyes never left Jermal as he paced back and forth much like a trapped animal. She could see his keen instinct trying to tell him he was not the "guest" she had so eloquently described him as. "As in any good bluff, there is some fact woven into the fiction."

Arnese let escape a tiny gasp as she took Dirare's arm, "Are you telling me that Askana has, in fact, run off to Eyrie with some fair-haired man?"

Dirare smiled wryly. For all her wiliness, Arnese was an unabashed gossip.

"What I am saying, dear mentor, is that I am merely taking what I know and embellishing upon the facts." Dirare closed the mirror's drapes and led Arnese through the catacombs of her country estate. A solitary candle in her hand illuminated the alcove's darkness. "I only know there was an altercation two days ago in the Royal Courtyard during the Queen's morning constitution. According to my attendants, the man entered the Palace undetected. He was neither Morevian nor Eyriener, and was far too human in appearance to be Elven. He was of fair complexion, golden haired, and wore clothes that can be best described as odd."

They reached a dead end passage where Arnese pulled back the latch embedded in the west wall. A soft click activated counter-weights and latches that slid back the concealed stone door. Both ladies stepped into the larger open corridor that led to their chambers. The mustiness of the tight stone passageways surrendered to the delightful scent of flowers and fresh vegetation. Dirare extinguished the candle and passed it to the attendant waiting alongside the guards of her household.

"Thank you, Kinysa. You may retire for the night." The servant bowed deeply and bid her mistress sweet dreams, leaving Dirare and Arnese to their private conversation. "The stranger had attendants, three of them. They were described as vile, offensive, and repulsive in their appearance. I merely played upon the current politics of the past few days and Jermal's weakness for Askana."

"A well-played strategy, my Lady."

"Yes, I have placed my Ajassa well. Now we will see whether he shall fortify his Samsagi, or sacrifice his Queen."

Arnese turned to face Dirare, "Do you think this bold move will ensure your victory?"

"I do." Dirare smiled, the image of the par-stern board vivid in her mind. "I have placed Jermal in a very thought-provoking situation. But I need to know more of what Askana is planning. In particular, what she is planning with this new ally in her company. Whoever this man is, he is a dangerous sort if he has won the trust of Askana Moldarin and plays the part of the Queen's Black Sword. A stranger not of Eyrie, not of Arathelle."

"From across The Rift?"

Dirare froze at Arnese's suggestion. Mentioning The Rift had been part of her bluff, but now Arnese brought forward an alarming possibility to this unknown scheme of Askana's. Had she truly sought help from across The Rift? It was the cause of much heated debate, especially in light of the unknown assailants looting Morevian ships and sending many brave Maidens to their deaths. It was rumoured the Queen had been slipping between worlds and no one was certain as to why.

Dirare kept her own far more accurate suspicion to herself. Askana was in search of the creature. The creature Dirare herself insisted be either put to death or banished from Morevi. That abomination of nature. Why was it that her Queen had this unerring ability to pick out the oddest, most dangerous outcasts as her most trusted allies?

"We should watch how the scales tip within Council. As you say, they are delicate," Dirare said evenly. "This unique strategy of Askana's may very well tip them dangerously out of balance."

"And while we try to unravel this tangled intrigue, we watch the Consort under this guise of protection?"

"This is no guise, Arnese. We shall ensure his safety." Dirare's eyes narrowed as through a window she watched Jermal on the balcony outside his chambers. "And what comes of his trust in me we shall see. Askana intended him to be a figurehead. I can promise him more, but still keep a control over him and the affairs of state."

"Indeed, Dirare," Arnese said. "But what of this fair-haired warrior? If she does indeed return and her 'Black Sword' is from across The Rift, what do you think the repercussions would be?"

"That remains to be seen," Dirare stated with a slow nod. "But it is this weakness of Jermal—his infatuation with Askana—that will be my move to win the Game."

"Provided you have the Consort in check."

"We shall see, my friend. We shall see."

"How could you lose him?" the Blademaster snapped, pacing the confines of his study angrily. The screen doors were wide open to the coolness of the night. Torchlight washed over the company of soldiers standing at attention on the stones of his courtyard. Kubi-Sogi shook his head in disgust at this regiment of the Palace Guard. This was their second failure in the week. First the intruders, and now the Consort. The Captain stood before him, head bowed and eyes to the ground with the helm of his office tight in his grasp.

"Were your orders not explicit enough?" barked the old man, waving a crooked finger under the Captain's nose. Though his title did not proclaim it, Kubi-Sogi was more than the Queen's Blademaster. He was also a general in his own right, personally in charge of the Palace Guard and several divisions of the Morevian military.

Kubi-Sogi had known Askana since she was a young girl and was one of the first entrusted with her plans for the War of the Fan and Slipper. Without his help, she could not have ascended to the Throne and usher in the New Regime. This was something he personally believed Morevi needed as it had fallen so deep into the corruption of the Old. He was proud of all she had achieved, but damned if he was going to be outwitted by her Noble Ladies! He did not care for their shadow-games.

His Captain was now learning firsthand exactly how devious these women could be. His orders had been clear and precise—escort the Royal Consort to Askana's country estate. More of a training facility for the Royal Guard than a country retreat, the manor was virtually impregnable. The greenest of recruits could have carried out the Blademaster's orders, yet the Palace Guard was answering for another blunder in their abilities.

The Captain knew it was his good fortune that he was answering to Kubi-Sogi and not the Queen. His fellow Captain in charge of the morning watch had answered to her. He now hanged at the end of a noose for his incompetence.

"We obeyed orders, my Lord." The Captain did not raise his eyes from the ground out of respect for the old Blademaster. "When we arrived, there was no one in the Consort's Quarters. The servants said the man had left with others."

Kubi-Sogi stopped in mid-pace, white beard bristling. "Others? Who?"

"They did not know, my Lord. Men dressed in unmarked armour. The servants told us the escort introduced itself as 'The Right Hand of Morevi' offering protection for the Consort."

"The Right Hand of Morevi?" scoffed a female voice from behind the guard. "This does, indeed, put a new twist upon events."

The Captain's eyes, still turned downward, darted in the direction from where the voice came. The sight of her shin guards stepping into the light of the study only confirmed her identity. His body did not shudder, but his mind came close to it. He could feel a cold sweat creep up from the small of his back. It was debasing enough to be answering for this failure before Blademaster Kubi-Sogi, but now he would have to suffer this reprimand before Kalea Desminar, The Anjara—Captain of the Royal Guard. There was no love lost between the Palace Guard and the Royal Guard, and the rivalry between them was fierce.

The Queen had first formed the Royal Guard, an all-female regiment, in the early days of her rise to the throne. They had fought alongside her in the War of the Fan and Slipper. By contrast, the Palace Guard were from the Old Regime, still present in order to appease those of the Council of a Hundred Turi who voraciously clung to tradition. There had been vehement competition as to who would protect the First Queen of Morevi—her own elite female Royal Guard, the traditional male Palace Guard, or the Morev'ar if their support inclined to the New Regime and its monarch. To prevent overt animosity the Queen had distributed the responsibility evenly across these three factions of the Morevi military.

The Captain felt a further flush of shame in what this debacle had cost the Palace Guard in the eyes of their competitors.

The Anjara eyed the man standing before Kubi-Sogi, noting the tension in his outline. It was the same as the stony faces of his men ranged in neat rows outside the study. Much as she disliked admitting to the fact, the Palace Guard had grown more disciplined and proper since coming under Kubi-Sogi's authority. They were still a relic in her eyes, but had returned to their heritage of honour and valour under the Blademaster's command. Pale in comparison to her Royal Guard, though commendable in their intentions. Her sense of justice told her that this failing was not the fault of the men. The fault fell on the tacticians.

Kalea arranged herself cross-legged on the cushions by the low table the servants had set for them, interested in how Kubi-Sogi would react to this. "Who would want anything to do with the Queen's lover?" she mused aloud.

"Too many people for me to count on the fingers of one hand," said Kubi-Sogi grimly. "If only we could have brought him safely here!"

There was a clatter of enamelled plate against stone as the Captain dropped to his knees. "I have failed. I ask my Lord's permission to pay penance."

The Anjara's eyes flickered briefly towards the man. "By all means."

"No!" The Blademaster held up a restraining hand. "Failure is disgrace enough. Such severe punishment would be self-indulgent. You are a good soldier, Golan, and are needed by your country, now more than ever. Take your men back to the barracks."

The Captain pulled himself up to his feet and bowed deeply, glad of the reprieve and praise. For a few moments, only the men's armour marching away in precision against courtyard stone sounded in the night. Slowly, the nocturnal music of myriad insects and night birds returned. Kubi-Sogi gazed after his men long after the regiment had gone. His mind clouded with questions.

One question actually found his voice. "Who would call themselves by a title as pretentious as The Right Hand of Morevi?"

"Too many people for me to count on the fingers of one hand," mocked the Anjara using Kubi-Sogi's own words. "You should have let the fool have his punishment."

"Ah," he nodded, turning to face her. "And what would I gain from that? A well-trained soldier losing his self-confidence and the respect of his men. Nothing more. No, Golan has gone back humiliated yet vigilant, determined to do better by a commander who holds his loyalty. I am not so foolish to waste good men, Kalea. There *are* such things as good men, you know."

Kalea gave him a sour look and poured herself more chocha. The Blademaster watched her pour a cup for him and realised suddenly that they had both grown older. Not that he cared much about his own age, but even though a hint of muscle still showed under Kalea's skin when she moved, the slender litheness was almost gone. She was still a handsome woman more by dint of strength than smoothness of feature. She was now middle aged. Strange that he had never noticed until now.

"Two of these *good men*, as you call them, will remain hanging in the courtyard of the Palace Guard for three more days as a warning to the others. We do not look upon incompetence lightly." Her eyes glittered as she returned the chochapot to its setting. "As I have noted in the past, the only *good men* of Morevi are the emasculated ones."

"I will take that as a compliment," Kubi-Sogi smiled as he returned to his desk.

"You know," Kalea said as she watched him rummage through his clutter, "I'm beginning to wonder if you know more about this matter than you are telling."

"Why?" the old man asked, still concentrating on his search as he answered her. "You have always mistrusted me," he sighed, affecting the complaint of an elderly man ill-used. "You just do not care for me being able to walk the consecrated grounds or my avuncular watching over the Queen, do you?"

"Your 'influence' was not enough to stop us from moving the soldiers' barracks outside the estate." Kalea smiled, not fooled by his performance. With an exasperated sigh, she rose from her cushions and walked over to a modest dresser opposite the desk. "You exaggerate your importance, old teacher. The truth is I have been wary of you since the day you threw me into the pond during training."

His eyes widened, peaked white eyebrows giving him an almost comical expression. "That was years ago, Kalea! You were still a girl then, training in secret with a handful of others. Besides, there was not much else the soldiers could do since you women consecrated the whole of the main house to Nadinath, which is why I had to move my quarters out here. I need to be close to my men in order to lead them."

"If I was a girl then, what am I now?" she asked with good humour as she held up his favourite pipe. "I think you know that Askana is alive, don't you?"

"I know as much as you do, my dear Anjara. I will say that her behaviour the day she disappeared was more peculiar than usual."

"How so?"

Without so much as a "thank you" for finding his pipe, the Blademaster took it from her grasp. The smirk on her face melted away as he then placed in her hand the Royal Seal of Moldarin. Kalea held it up, catching the light of the paper lanterns.

"I was told that in her absence I was to speak with the voice of the Queen. She knew she would be leaving, but to where she kept secret." He removed the Royal Seal from Kalea's hand and replaced it back in the wide sash around his portly waist. She was still staring at him in amazement, not noticing he had removed her tobacco pouch from her belt. He gave a soft chortle, "Isn't it strange she chose a man instead of a Maiden of the Night to carry this responsibility?"

The comment intended to rankle her did just that, snapping Kalea out of her speechless state. She produced from her own haversack a small pipe before joining him outside in his courtyard. "Remember the day I first met you? I was a mud-covered peasant, fresh from working in a rice-field, tagging awkwardly behind a seventeen-year-old minor lady who marched me in and demanded you train me as you were training her. At that time a woman could still be condemned to death for learning to use a weapon."

"What I remember most was your swollen eye and two broken ribs. Tokens from your husband the night before, still fresh. What happened to that man anyway?" he asked casually.

"Oh, did I never tell you? I went back years later and found him with a girl half his age, who was no doubt receiving the same tender loving care I'd experienced. I resolved the issue. He is dead, and she is my Second."

Kubi-Sogi leaned back for a moment, looking at the Anjara thoughtfully as he stretched the muscles in his back. Kalea was a woman at peace inside, unlike most of the women he saw every day. Apart from the dead husband just mentioned in passing, there had been no other. There was no need in her mind. She had found a place within the Sisterhood and satisfaction in her Royal Guard. Her sharpness kept many at a distance, but Kubi-Sogi could see the tranquillity in her soul. She was a unique woman in every right.

"Who do you think has the Consort?" he continued, dipping his fingers into the black tobacco paste.

"Those girls who hero-worship the Queen might have taken him as a trophy, or he might be in the hands of a more dangerous player. Eyriener spies. The Morev'ar. Anyone in the Council of a Hundred Turi. Since he was taken by soldiers in Morevian armour, the Morev'ar can be ruled out. They would have just taken him in broad daylight, although they are conceited enough to identify themselves as The Right Hand of Morevi. I have long told the Queen that we must do something about the self-proclaimed Servants of the Kingdom," said the Anjara, frowning in distaste.

She could feel a tension rise between them suddenly, perhaps coming from her disdain of the Morev'ar. Relations between the different factions of the Morevi military had always been a source of debate between the Queen, Kubi-Sogi, and herself. A debate that, to this day, still had no resolution.

"Did you know the Council has been called to order?" Kalea asked in order to change the direction of their conversation. "Probably to decide who is to take the Queen's place. They dare not openly bid for the Crown, so there will be a few more meetings yet before anything is done."

He caught the unspoken thought. "We have little time to act. We must prevent the Council from electing a new ruler."

"The Royal Guard will have something to say about it if they do. We guard only true Morevian Queens of the bloodline. Any Noble Lady would think twice before she allows herself to be surrounded by guards who might just slit her throat."

"Isn't that a touch hasty, Kalea Desminar, Honourable Anjara to the First Queen?" Kubi-Sogi raised a bushy white eyebrow quizzically. "I shall handle the Council, I think."

"Then I shall handle the Eyrieners," she nodded, filling the bowl of her pipe with a few fingertips' worth of tobacco.

"You believe the Eyrieners have a hand in this, do you?"

"It stands to reason. Since his coronation, King Cedric has made his desires for a larger empire clear. He has made equally clear that the Silken Box will be the first prize in his campaign." Kalea stared thoughtfully into the night sky, formulating her plan as she spoke, "As the intruders appeared to be pirates, I will start in Taighar. A day in the port city will be all I need."

"A full day?" Kubi-Sogi laughed, "You are getting old, Anjara."

The trees surrounding his courtyard shielded them from the outside world, allowing only the cool night air and star-filled sky to spy on them. Removing a single twig from a bowl of dry sticks used for this indulgence, he lit it with an open flame of a courtyard torch, passing the flame to his pipe. Kalea soon joined him, taking deep drags as he lit the weed-paste packed neatly inside her smaller pipe. The night teemed with a relaxing symphony of creatures. Their songs called to one another and provided the two warriors a moment of serenity following a tumultuous few days.

Kalea finally broke the silence between them, "You think the Queen's judgement is right in this case? You think the man can be trusted?"

"I cannot say for sure, but I feel he is her best option." Kubi-Sogi puffed on his pipe for a moment or two before continuing, "Not that I think she trusts him. She lost the ability to trust since the day Lubria left, though I cannot say I wanted the Fae creature to stay."

"She refuses to confide in any, fearing they will disappear on the wishes of the Council. It will take time before she can truly exercise her priviledges as Queen."

They both nodded wisely as if reaching some conclusion about a favourite niece. There was little talk after, as tobacco smoke rose lazily into the air, each of them engaged with his or her own worries.

Enlightenment

The ocean appeared as wrinkled parchment, early morning sunlight casting yellow and white brilliance over a blue-green canvas. They stood for a moment at the top of the rise overlooking the port city of Taighar. Already three ships were coming into port. A few hours distant, two other cargo vessels, their shadows stretching behind them to the watery horizon far west, slowly made their way to this place of commerce. The sight of the approaching ships, the ocean, and the distant activity of the busy port city gave Askana and Elunear a moment's pause. They were now far from the safety of home, deep in the lands of Eyrie.

Askana could feel a tension creep over her body. She did not care to be this close to an enemy's harbour. She did not care to be this close to the ocean. It reminded her too much of *him*. Of rare moments of innocence. Of riding ahead of her train and catching the trace of salt in the wind, an indication that she was nearing the Elven Ports of Arathelle.

Now the smell of the sea made her ill.

"Good morning, Mother Ocean," Rafe said brightly, savouring the scent of salt mingling with the crisp morning air. A strong breeze pushed his hair aside. He took in a deep breath, his eyes closing in delight as a rapt smile crossed his face. He watched the grand sailing ships slowly glide across the water. Their silent grace never ceased to fill him with a child-like wonder. "Be it my world or here, nothing is so pleasing as the smell of the open sea. Do you not agree, Your Grace?"

"I try not to notice," Askana said evenly.

It was a controlled response that made Rafe turn to look at her. The Queen's face gave him nothing, no indication as to what she might be feeling. Her silence and blank expression, however, told him a chord had been struck.

Morning pleasantries were done. Time to focus on the task at hand.

"Remember, everyone, from here we refer to Her Majesty as 'Tekira'. If Eyrie did in fact have a hand in this conspiracy, it is by now common knowledge to the Merchants' Circle that the Queen is dead from an assassin's hand. They will most likely know Tekira by name. By playing the part of an assassin on the run from both sides of a civil war, it may reveal much in who is involved. Come."

While Iambourgh was the official capital city of Eyrie, Taighar was considered Eyrie's capital city of commerce. The money generated from its trade and shipping business— at least the profits that the Merchants' Circle agreed to part with to the Crown— would be taken to Iambourgh where the Royal Treasurers distributed the wealth as they saw fit. This authority over a nation made Taighar not only an influential place, but very fashionable in the eyes of society. It had grown so fashionable that the newly-crowned King Cedric Ballir Goradan the IV chose to take permanent residence there. This was under much protest from his very traditional mother who still resided in the capital city.

Although far more advanced in commerce and industry than their Morevian neighbours, sanitation was a problem. Upon entering the city, the crisp salt air mingled with a stale, musty stench. The buildings and houses were darkened by mud from ill-kept roads, soot from coal and wood smoke, and a repulsive combination of animal and human waste haphazardly tossed from high-up windows and back doors. Some vendors and citizens hung herbs and burned incense to cover the scent, but these gallant efforts were few and far between.

Under the guise of a travelling merchant from the Uncharted Lands, Rafe had visited Renai, the second largest city of Morevi, in order to find out more about this mysterious queen and her people. Renai was a very different place from Taighar. Stone streets leading to buildings and main squares of rough-cut, but still lovely, grey and white marble. As the centre for processing Turi oil into fine perfumes, Renai smelled like the gardens of Heaven. What he had seen of Songkusai was much the same in its brilliance and splendour.

Rafe cast a curious glance at the Morevians, wondering how a place such as Taighar appeared in their eyes. Askana easily concealed her abhorrence, but young Elunear's face was turning green with nausea. Although her skills as a warrior had elevated her to the ranks of Royal Guard, her experiences had apparently not extended beyond the borders of Morevi.

They did receive a few glances in passing as two Morevians, a fair-haired man too short to be Eyriener, and a dark-skinned giant were hard to dismiss. The sight of Askana and Elunear, even though they appeared in their current state more like outcasts than sworn enemies of their King, caused many of the Eyrieners to huff. One zealous citizen called out to them as they passed, "Why, look! The hallowed Maidens of Morevi in all their glory! So proud! So powerful! Not good enough for your all high and mighty Queen, eh? You're not even worth the shit on your skin!"

Had this heckler summoned up courage to move in closer, the darker stains covering them could not have been mistaken for anything other than dried blood.

They reached the rendezvous set with O'Donnell and Jailene, a small inn called "Sanctuary from the Sea." Rafe's business carried him here many times and he knew the innkeeper well. He was always assured a safe haven from unwelcome guests here. Rafe looked for O'Donnell in the pub attached to the inn. It was the same collection of fur-clad ruffians swearing at one another in a drunken mix of affection and anger. Serving wenches kept their bodices tight, lifting their already ample bosoms another inch or two upward thereby acquiring a few more crowns when attending to patrons. He noted a few sailors from other parts of the realm in search of work or a meal. Nearby, gossipmongers nursed warm ales as they indulged in news of port and Court.

O'Donnell was nowhere to be found.

"Damn his Irish heart!" Rafe whispered. "The young pup is probably deep at the bottom of a cask somewhere."

"I doubt that, privateer," Askana said, her eyes moving swiftly from patron to patron. "For Jailene would not allow him to miss a rendezvous."

Rafe looked to the Queen, an eyebrow raised slightly as he noted the complete confidence in her tone, "That efficient, is she?"

"No, Captain," Askana said plainly. "Missing you would also mean missing me. Discipline is one of many traits that elevate the Royal Guard from the Maidens of Nadinath. Unlike their Sisters, they answer first and foremost to me."

"Keep your voice low," Rafe whispered. "We cannot risk a passing ear to catch you. No one answers to you as you are a servant."

Askana turned to answer Rafe, caring little as to who would overhear her, but Nassir's returning from the upper levels of the Sanctuary stopped her reply.

"My Captain, our room awaits us and I could see the pack mules in the tavern stables. Everything is as it should be." The Moor's thick Persian accent sharpened as he glanced at the Morevians. "Except for the yeoman and Lady Jailene. They left no word to where they are. It appears they left on their own will, not to return for some time."

"Really?" Rafe crossed his arms as Askana turned to him. "So much for Morevian efficiency."

"Privateer, is it a custom in your land to make accusations without proper investigation?" She replied sweetly, then cursed herself for rising to his bait. Setting foot on Eyriener soil unsettled her more than she cared to admit. Her stomach still roiled from the stench in the streets. Overlying that was her surprise in Jailene's absence. Of the two young Guards she had brought with her, Jailene had been the older and more experienced. Something must have happened for the girl to leave her post in this manner.

As if sensing her irritation, Rafe smiled.

"Nassir, find Tekira clothes that will fit her. Be it a mix of my clothes, yours, or O'Donnell's. Make her look like a pirate. A new addition to the *Defiant*." Rafe looked at Askana approvingly, noting her fine golden skin already stained with smoke and blood from the previous evening's battle, "Refrain from bathing. The look you have now is..." He hesitated as she raised an eyebrow at him, "...appropriate. And Tekira, I suggest your sister stay behind, in case O'Donnell and Jailene appear."

The queasiness in Askana's stomach only worsened as she was called by the name of the traitor, her beloved friend. She wanted to merely denounce Tekira as a clumsy assassin, but she could only see her as they had grown up together. She recalled Tekira's smile, her sweet smile accompanying the most gentle of touches when she would attend her. Even after Askana ascended to the throne, their trust and friendship had endured.

Seeing Elunear move closer gave Askana focus, bringing her out of the silent lament for her fallen friend. The shirai's tell-tale blade had been removed, making her weapon nothing more than a large walking staff, but the young girl's eyes warned the Privateer Captain she could still break bones with it if necessary. Askana gave her guard a subtle look of assurance and lifted her chin slightly as she looked back to Rafe with an edge of amusement.

"Agreed, privateer," Askana nodded. "My life will be in your keeping."

"Excellent." Rafe gave Askana a quick wink to rankle her, then leaned closer to Elunear. "If all goes well, sweet lass, we will come back to meet you. If you see my signal, however, hurry to the back of the Sanctuary and wait for Nassir. He shall take you to safety."

"And what will this signal be?" Elunear asked.

Rafe's grin widened, "Trust me. You will know if I send it. As for your sister here, no need to worry. I will perform my office as protector to the best of my abilities."

"I should hope so," said Askana so softly that only he and Elunear could hear her. "For it would be extremely unfortunate for you if we are harmed under your care."

"Regardless of what infidels may think, the Sisterhood protect their own," Elunear added, the staff remaining poised and ready.

Rafe just stared at them both. Scylla and Charybdis. There was simply no pleasing these women, and Rafe prided himself being unparalleled at pleasing women.

Satisfied that the last word belonged to her, Askana turned and disappeared upstairs with Elunear at her side. Nassir could not help but give his Captain a look of sympathy and a soft laugh. The Morevians, it would seem, would continue to be a handful on this little endeavour. If the Captain ever needed a drink, now was the time.

Rafe worked his way through the patrons to the bar, Askana's warning still echoing in his ear. It amazed him that she could make a threat sound like an indecent proposal of pleasure. *Perhaps it would bring her a bit of pleasure*, he mused silently to himself, *my slow, agonising death*. He took his seat at the thick wooden bar, exchanging nods and glances with the other sailors. While many of the Eyrieners were strangers to him, the bartender was a familiar face, one glad to see him as indicated by the snifter of fine scotch presented to him.

"I keep your bot'l under lock an' key, Cap'n," said the Eyriener. Rafe merely closed his eyes and took in the scent of the single malt as he had taken in the scent of the ocean earlier that morning. The bartender paused in his duties, watching the pirate intensely. "Now jus' a moment here. I doubt you are the true Captain Rafton. You are far too serious for the Captain Rafton I am accustomed to servin'!!"

"That's simply the smoke staining my face, Drakkan." Rafe took a glance at himself in the grand mirror behind the bar. "I should wash up before my meeting tonight."

"Business, my friend?" he asked as he spit-cleaned a glass.

"I sincerely hope so." Rafe slid him a few gold coins. "This should pay for my room in case anything happens." Watching Drakkan give another glass a vigorous spitting, Rafe slid him another gold coin. "This is so that you use water when cleaning my scotch glass."

He gave a good chortle as he took up the gold. "Rest assured you are taken good care of here, Cap'n. Especially when business is good." He leaned in, his voice dropping low, "And by the looks a' the company O'Donnell was keepin', never been better. Quite a lass 'e 'ad on 'is arm."

Rafe froze, but managed a leering smile before Drakkan looked up again, "Really? What was she like?"

"Comely lass. Mighty friendly, but I would ratha' 'ave an adder in m'bed." He shook his head as he mopped up a bit of spilt ale from the bar. "Golden skin, black hair, eyes tha' bore through ya'. I'd wager eye-teeth she was Morevian. Wearin' those silk robes made in those parts. Morevian clothes were popular a' Court for a time, but tha' was before King Cedric coming to the throne. Soon put a stop ta' tha', now didn' he?" he smiled, exposing teeth no one would have accepted as winnings, eye-teeth or not. "Must've been a deserter. We get a few, sometimes, banished. But with the way things are, Morevians don't stay long, not welcome here. Even if some of 'em are whoring themselves out for a few coins."

"What makes you think she's a deserter?" Rafe asked as he gently swirled the contents of the glass underneath his nose. It never failed. The unmistakable aroma of scotch always managed to clear his mind.

"She wasn't the *normal* savage from those parts, ya' know? Not picking a fight with anything male is wha' I mean. When I say *friendly*, I mean it, Cap'n. O'Donnell and she was enjoyin' one another's company."

"Is that so? Most interesting, indeed," he nodded before taking a deep dram of his scotch.

A deep gold light from windows cast a warm, gentle glow from building to building. The once hard and coarse port city now appeared inviting and hospitable. The scent of burning wood from numerous hearths permeated the air, masking more offensive odours. The streets were still busy but it was not with the haggling of cargo prices or the transfer of goods from ship to store. Now it was neighbour greeting neighbour in a friendly embrace, inviting them into the closest pub for a round. Only pleasantries would be shared between countrymen and visitors. In this soft nocturnal light all were welcome and everyone would be regarded as "friend".

The night, however, was still young.

Soon after finishing his scotch in the Sanctuary, Rafe had sent word through his trade connections that he had returned to Eyrie and wished to have a meeting with a representative from its economic aristocracy, The Merchants' Circle. He hoped there would still be an interest in meeting with him following the state they were left in over a month ago. Rafe had been approached by The Merchants' Circle to take arms against Askana. It was evident by their reaction to his rejection that they were counting on employing the only mercenary to remain out of reach of Askana's assassin network. Rafe was convinced that he had severed his Merchants' Circle ties for good. He held their attention as he was an Otherworlder and a profitable one at that. Now, in light of this disappointment, he wondered if his request would be honoured. He needed only to meet with one of them to put Askana's plans into motion.

Within the hour of sending word to The Merchants' Circle, an apprentice of the Messengers' Guild brought a response that not one but a collection of delegates would meet with him. Following the sunset, some well-earned rest, and a change of clothes, the Queen's counter-strategy to discover her nobles' true loyalties would finally begin.

Rafe appeared better suited for a night of social engagements rather than business appointments as he looked very much the fashionable gentleman. Washed free of dirt and wearing his freshly laundered burgundy and black doublet and breeches, accented with fine gold and silver trim, he walked confidently with a gleam in his eye and surety in his step. Nassir, also freshly bathed and wearing clothes of dark, rough-cut leather and suede, walked alongside his Captain, keeping a watchful eye out for trouble. They appeared less the Captain and First Mate and more of a wealthy merchant and his retainer.

Askana was dressed in tattered trousers, a dingy, frayed shirt and a large bandanna covering her hair. She wore a simple leather belt across her waist, a dagger and a small pistol secured there. She walked a pace behind Rafe and Nassir as was customary for servants or slaves in the presence of their masters. She looked every bit the part of a pirate, her face stained with mud, dirt, and blood, a hint of evil temper smouldering in her eyes.

She had never felt more idiotic than she did now.

She was on the brink of telling him that his position of leadership here was nothing but a ploy of hers, to let her newest hound have his head for the time being. Instead she chose her words carefully as they entered Taighar's town centre, "So tell me, privateer, what will my enduring yesterday's stench achieve? Why is it that you and your servant here are allowed to bathe and put on fresh clothing whereas I am not?"

"Very simple, Tekira—rank." Rafe then gave her a vicious wink, enjoying the evidence of her very female indignation. "Pardon the pun. You see, Nassir is not my servant. He is my First Mate. Therefore, he is entitled to certain privileges that you, a mere crewmember, are not. Note though. Nassir's clothes do not outshine my own."

The look on her face could have stopped an army dead in its tracks. Askana mumbled an epithet in her own tongue, one Rafe recognised when shouted at him by the Morevian guards of the ships he sacked in open waters.

"I will take that warning to heart, Tekira," Rafe smiled cordially as he glanced over his shoulder. He could not help but appreciate, even in her current guise, the simple beauty about her, more to do with charm than anything else. *She would make an excellent addition to my crew*, Rafe thought with just the slightest hint of wistfulness.

Askana turned her face away to ignore his goading. She had looked worse. In the thick of a battle, appearance did not count for much. The smell of blood, earth, and death were no strangers to her. While other young ladies of noble birth had their *ingmari*—their 'coming out'—as a grand function of dance, delicate aromas of flowers and perfume, and courtly formalities, she had been formally introduced to the world through war.

So why did these clothes and this grime make her skin crawl? She silently thought about this as they continued through the streets of Eyrie. It could only be that her appearance was now dictated by the privateer and not herself. It smacked too much of the time when her life had been dictated by one man or another.

There was also a sneaking suspicion that he was enjoying this. Immensely.

Her thoughts halted abruptly as she bumped against a minor nobleman who had stepped in between her and the privateers. The classes were easy to differentiate, exaggerated by the extremes of filth and cleanliness. The common people lived along crooked little streets, tossed their waste out of the windows, and from the looks of the few she had seen, probably washed once a week. By contrast, the richer merchants and nobility were clean, dressed in all manner of finery, and talked boisterously of palatial estates both in the city and the country. Those few privileged enough to rise above the common people, however, demanded respect, earned or not.

Rafe and Nassir had only walked a few paces farther before noticing the nobleman between them and Askana. Nassir's hand quickly slipped around Rafe's arm, holding the Captain back as he went for his weapon. The Eyriener waited, his head held high, looking down at Askana from the tip of his long nose. It was obvious by his extravagant blue and silver adornments and the overly rich velvet of his clothes that he had been recently appointed some office in Court. Still this Eyriener was making it clear by his manner and clothes his advancement in society.

Continuing the deception, she kept her eyes cast downward and bowed quickly, softly muttering an apology in the local dialect.

"Clumsy bitch!" the nobleman snorted before continuing on his way.

Rafe and Nassir both let out a heavy sigh of relief.

Askana could feel the gauntlet about her wrist, an array of poisoned darts and a tiny throwing dagger concealed under the sleeve of her shirt. Did that pompous ass, so secure and safe in his station, know how close he had come to death? She could not resist a petty little smile to herself at the thought of how vulnerable these privileged Eyrieners truly were.

They finally stopped in front of a modest shop across from a small tavern called The Miller's Daughter. The large window that would allow light for the craftsman to work and passers-by to observe him at his trade revealed nothing as its shutters and curtains were closed.

"This is where we are to meet," Rafe said with a nod. "A tinker's workshop. Clever choice."

"The most powerful and wealthiest of Eyrie are to meet at the humble shop of a common man?" Askana looked up and down the street, "Very modest in its location. Much of the din is elsewhere. I must admit, they are quite ingenious, these Eyrieners."

"The educated ones, anyway. They are also the most cautious. This workshop is in plain sight from across the street." Rafe peered to the darkened windows above the pub, "I assure you, at least three crossbows are taking aim on us."

"Captain," Nassir whispered, his voice catching deep in his throat. "The alleyway."

A hand and one leg extended from behind a stack of barrels across the street. The sprawled form might have been a drunk from The Miller's Daughter bedding down in the alley after indulging in too much ale, but Nassir's sharp eyes had caught sight of a dark, irregular patch on the pale skin of an exposed ankle. A party of drunken sailors stumbled out into the street, their voices rising in a grating chorus of maritime shanties that had no set key or aspect of harmony. This provided enough of a distraction for Rafe, Nassir, and Askana to cross unnoticed to the alleyway adjoining the pub. Behind barrels of ale and wine, O'Donnell's horrified, unblinking eyes stared lifelessly upwards to the rooftops above him. Nassir made a sound, either of rage or sorrow, and turned away, ostensibly to keep watch on the street. Somehow, it was the birthmark more than the slit neck or staring eyes that seemed most poignant. Askana tugged the ragged pant-leg down over the thumb-shaped mark as Rafe gently closed the dead pirate's eyes.

"This was not to be your time, lad." He tipped the head back gingerly for a closer look at the fatal wound across the corpse's neck. Rafe pulled back slightly, his eyes never leaving the cut as he spoke to the Queen, his voice cold and sharp. "I know this wound, Tekira. I have seen enough of them in my time. This is a wound dealt from a shirai."

Askana studied the cut. "Possibly, Captain, but a trained assassin or a common thief could do the same on a good day with a sharp edge." She felt about O'Donnell's waist and nodded, "As I thought. He has been robbed."

"Then why not take this?" Rafe reached into the front of the man's shirt and lifted out a gold amulet on a fine chain, large enough for an experienced thief to see, small enough for others to miss. "O'Donnell's first souvenir. Pure gold. And his boots?" Rafe motioned to O'Donnell's bare feet, "His boots were taken from a French officer and cut of a different fashion from those found in Eyrie. Wearing them would make a killer easy to find. No, they were stolen to keep O'Donnell as anonymous as any street beggar," Rafe tapped lightly against the dead sailor's ankle, "provided you did not recognise his birthmark."

The words of the barkeep repeated in Rafe's mind. Now a crewmate was dead and Askana's trusted guard was still missing. Too much blood had been spilt on this venture already, enough to question if it was worth the risks. It had seemed a simple enough task when he agreed to it, far easier than sacking one of Askana's ships. All he needed to do was spin a tale about growing civil unrest in Morevi. He stared at the tinker's shop across the street. Inside, the delegates of The Merchants' Circle awaited his arrival. It was a simple enough task, and that was what concerned him.

"Perhaps, Tekira, in light of my loss," Rafe said, "I think it would be opportune to invest in some insurance. Follow me."

Returning to the storefront where tonight's business would take place, Rafe and Askana slipped down the alley adjacent to the tinker's shop while from its shadows Nassir continued his watch on the main street. The alley connected with several other alleyways, a network of narrow passages and storerooms for supplies and cargo. Rafe gently pressed a finger to his lips and leaned slightly around a corner. Assured there were no guards present, he carefully inspected each door directly across from the tinker's shop, stopping at one in particular. The door read in Eyriener a single word: *Danger*. From his belt pouch he produced a tiny cigar and lit the vice with the flame of an alleyway torch. The privateer lifted the cigar to his lips, drew deeply on the pungent fragrance of its smoke, and disappeared into the small storage room.

Askana looked upwards to the windows of the adjacent buildings, only two of which overlooked their position. If what Rafe said was true about The Merchants' Circle, they would leave nothing to chance. She peered into each window, lanterns burning bright on their windowsills that cast a warm yellow light in their respective rooms. No properly trained soldier would keep watch from such a place. The shadows would reveal their presence in a moment.

Rafe reappeared moments later, the cigar notably absent.

"What did you do in there?"

"I obtained a bit of insurance for us." Rafe produced a small hourglass from his satchel and slipped it into Askana's belt. "Do not lose that. There is thirty minutes of time in that glass. I will need to reference it at a moment's notice. Now then, to the meeting."

Nassir straightened Rafe's doublet. The two of them were still visibly carrying the image of their fallen crewmate in their minds. They paused for a moment, sharing a silent reassurance that they were ready to begin tonight's deception. With a final nod and a hard rap to his First Mate's broad chest, Rafe took in a deep breath and proceeded inside with Nassir and Askana following.

A modest, cast iron chandelier dimly lit the room. Its tiny flames appeared as "Will o' the Wisps" that hovered over the large rectangular table underneath it. They could make out across the wall closest to the door tools of various edges, shapes, and applications, the equipage of this common man's trade being the only decorations present. The room was full of people. Quite a few people. In fact, it was a full attendance of all fourteen members of Eyrie's Merchants' Circle. Quite unexpected. They sat or stood about the room, closely protected by a regiment of ten guards. The bolder of the company lounged at ease around the table of thick, rough wood while some wishing to remain anonymous stood in shadow. In a strange, surreal gesture, they all slowly turned to watch the three newcomers enter the workshop.

Askana's eyes immediately recognised the merchant-lord at the head of the table as Kergagi, an influential merchant who had personally sworn an oath to her to serve as emissary in possible trade agreements. He had been a trusted contact, keeping Askana's spies well informed on the economy of Eyrie. *You will die first*, Askana silently promised him.

"Dear Rafe." The woman was a full foot taller than Askana and dressed in a tight-bodiced green velvet gown. The height would have made her appear freakish among the tall men of Eyrie had she not confidence, wealth, and striking beauty about her. Long straight locks of blonde hair fell across her shoulders as she smiled warmly at the privateer. She wasted no time in taking him into her arms, kissing him fiercely and deeply. He returned the greeting with equal fervour. She finally grabbed Rafe's hair and pulled him free of her lips with a delightful gasp, "How I have missed those delicious lips of yours, Captain."

"And what about the rest of me, my Lady Yonella?" he laughed wickedly, pressing his lips to her neck, causing the woman to throw her head back in glee.

This gaudy show of lust sickened Askana as she fought the urge to shake her head at their actions. *I suppose all her wealth could not purchase a sense of decorum,* Askana spat silently. *Eyriener slut.*

"Business first, my dear Otherworlder," she said, her grey eyes flashing with a mischievous smile.

Rafe tipped his peacock-ostrich feathered hat to the entirety of the Merchants' Circle. "My most gracious lords, you honour me with your attendance."

No one moved. One merchant coughed nervously as Kergagi, his eyes never leaving Rafe, motioned for a servant to bring him drink. An ornate silver goblet filled with a dark imported wine. Askana recognised the bottle's label from a vineyard of Anderis. It was considered one of the finest wines from her realm and contraband by King Cedric, perhaps making it taste all the more sweet to those able to obtain it.

"I do not recall a Morevian being part of your crew." The goblet was placed gently into Kergagi's waiting hand as he spoke, "Who is she?"

"She's new to the *Defiant.* An outcast possessing certain skills that will benefit me, I have no doubt." Rafe turned to Askana and smiled, "Tekira, show them."

Askana revealed the tattoo Nassir had painted upon her wrist. Eyes stared for a moment at the marking while others cast nervous glances to one another. The name "Tekira" was whispered back and forth between them. She never hinted at her quickened heartbeat. Her face remained even and still as a pond in the morning.

The Moor's unseen hand slipped away from the hilt of his dagger. Their first test had been a success.

"You are brave, indeed, Captain," Kergagi said, his triple-chin vibrating grotesquely as he took a large gulp from the wine, his mouth making a vulgar slurp as he did. From where he sat, he appeared toad-like in carriage and girth. The buttons in his narrow-cut coat and trousers of an atrocious maroon colour struggled for their hold on the fabric. "Shouldn't you be wary of recruiting anyone of Morevian origins, traitor or not, knowing how the Sea Wolf has taken advantage of its Queen's bounty?"

"No, my friend, I only take advantage of *Morevi's* bounty." Rafe smiled, "Believe me, if I were to take advantage of the Queen's bounty, she would know."

The room burst into laughter. Nassir gave a booming chuckle as well, but his laughter fell as his eyes turned to Askana. She stood there, emotionless. Her face still wore "Tekira's" surly, suspicious expression under a layer of grime.

"You should take care though." Another merchant leaned into the conversation as wine was offered to him, "It is well known how deceptive those Morevians are. After all, it is rumoured the Queen claimed her throne after whoring herself to every nobleman in her realm. How does that verse children recite go again? They sing it when skipping rope...

> *'Beware the Black Widow, Morevi men said.*
> *For it's you, poor soul, she intends to wed.*
> *And then such joy in the wedding bed —*
> *How many nights 'til you are dead?'*

"And then they count each skip until they are done. My littlest gave one of Askana's lovers thirty-eight nights!"

She thanked Nadinath silently for the dim, yellow light of the candles for she could feel the burning in her skin. *Calm. You are among the enemy but they do not know you are among them. To them, you are merely a shadow. This weakness of theirs will keep you alive.* But her mantra provided little comfort in the sea of mocking laughter.

"Then if I am to die in the fashion so practised by the Morevian Queen, I shall die with a smile upon my face." Rafe winked, refusing the wine brought to him by one of Kergagi's servants. "But no, my dear lords, Tekira here is quite the rare Morevian emerald. To assassinate the First Queen of Morevi and live to tell the tale?" Rafe placed two fingers underneath Askana's chin, lifting her eyes to his own, his thumb caressing the soft skin just underneath her lips, "How could I refuse such a treasure?"

Askana felt herself smile in return, but she could also feel her control slipping as the privateer took full advantage of the situation. It was that intimate, familiar tone he took with her in the Palace Courtyard. A blatant disregard for her class and standing as queen. Then she looked deeper into Rafe's eyes. Was he speaking or were they just standing there in silence? She could see it clearly. This was not impertinence but merely the will to deceive. She felt the calm she knew just before a kill wash over her as he laughed softly.

He released Askana and returned his attention to The Merchants' Circle, taking the chair opposite of Kergagi, "I doubt very sincerely that you have all gathered here to discuss my recruiting tactics."

"Very well then, Rafton, what have you got for us?" Kergagi asked.

"Gentlemen, I bring you what could be my last run for some time against Morevi." Rafe sighed heavily as if ready to fend off protests. None arose. "I have a few crates of Morevian tea in my possession, barely worth the risks in plundering it, but still just as valuable and worth its weight. I am offering you this at half the normal price. Consider it a farewell token from me. Something to remember me by."

"HALF?!" A young member of the Circle stepped forward. He was tall, passably handsome. His youthful attractiveness made him unique amongst the fatter, softer merchant-lords surrounding him. Unlike Yonella who held respect in being the only female member of the Circle, this one's originality warranted looks of inattention and slight regard. This whelp was new to the order. "This is quite a token, pirate. Why are you making so generous an offer? Is the tea rotten? Poor quality?"

"Not in the least, Ganniman." Rafe gave a nonchalant shrug, leaning back in the chair to prop his feet upon the tabletop. "Allow me to refresh your memories. A month ago, you asked me to take arms against Morevi. I refused. You asked me for a reason and I gave you none, but with this last haul I shall finally tell you why.

"I received a similar offer for my services from a representative within the Morevian Court. I was uncertain what to make of it until I saw the cargo hold—or what little there was of it—of this last raid. Morevian courtiers approaching mercenaries? Cargo holds growing smaller and smaller, as if exports are now being handled by a different source? I am no politician, dear friends, but a soldier recognises overtures to civil war. Would you not agree?"

Askana watched the pirate with growing satisfaction. The explanation behind what few crates they had was a stroke of brilliance. She found herself appreciating the Captain's talents in "improvisation".

"And there is young Tekira here. Proof that Morevi is about to reach a state of anarchy. It seems that Askana Moldarin did not have as tight a hold on her people as once believed. That presumption will rest with her eternally.

"And this is where I must bid you all farewell. Civil war always raises the risks for piracy what with the protection of trade routes and possible blockades. I already tempt Fate enough with sacking her ships during times of peace. So until the dust settles in the Palace of a Thousand Suns, I will return to my own realm. The tea I can deliver to you upon your request, provided you are interested, my most noble lords. This offer I make to you is for your favour in whatever future unfolds between Eyrie and Morevi."

Kergagi held up his hand, silencing the room. "Well then, Captain Rafton, I believe we can come to an arrangement. We will take the tea off your hands in exchange for something I think you will find invaluable."

"And what is that?" he asked.

"Enlightenment," Kergagi smiled.

Hands emerged from the shadows, grabbing Nassir and Askana from behind, preventing them from drawing weapons. Rafe went for his rapier only to feel two bulky Eyriener guards lift him from his chair and throw him against the long table. The merchant-lords stepped back, creating a disturbing circle in the half-shadow, half-light, silently watching the three struggle against their captors.

Then, at the opposite end of the table, a pair of hands extended into the dim lighting of the chandelier. The figure was hidden in a dark cloak. Only slender, gloved hands reaching from the folds of fabric were visible, passing to Ganniman an ornate cup with a deep crimson liquid in it. Before returning to the room's darkness, Askana noted the fine craftsmanship of the gloves.

They had the style and markings of riding gloves. Morevian embroidery. Too expensive for common folk with their indulgent gold-work. Nobility.

As Ganniman brought the cup into the light, the shadowy figure quietly stood. The Eyrieners, even the guards, bowed in reverence as attendants ushered this cloaked figure to the door. At the doorway, the figure paused, looked back in Askana's direction for a brief moment, and then boarded an awaiting coach.

"Yes, Captain, enlightenment." Kergagi nodded as he slipped on a pair of worn, brown leather gloves, "You see, while we find your story most intriguing, our Morevian contact has told us a slightly different one. Her story is of a fair-haired stranger intervening in an assassination attempt on the Queen followed by her sudden disappearance. While we have little trust for these Morevian savages, we cannot blindly trust your word. I believe you should enlighten us on what is fact and what is folklore between your own story and that of our Morevian ally. Otherwise we, The Merchants' Circle of Eyrie, will enlighten you on a poison banned—or should I say, once banned—from use in Her Majesty's realm. The blood of the Kir'shia."

Kergagi carefully took the cup from Ganniman, lowering it to Rafe's eye-level, "We know what the poison does to men of this realm, but you are not of this realm, Captain Rafton. You come from across The Rift. I believe we should all indulge in a bit of enlightenment and discover exactly what this poison would do to you."

Rafe looked away from Kergagi and called out to his earlier advocate, "Yonella, do have a care. Now you know me well, far more intimately than these good gentlemen. Be a dear and vouch for my loyalty."

"Dear Rafe," sighed the merchant-woman, shaking her head with a transparent smile. "What we share is personal. This is strictly business."

So much for the Rafton charm, Rafe thought. He glanced at the tiny hourglass dangling by Askana's side. *A few more minutes.*

Keeping her eyes fixed on Rafe, Askana continued to work the fingers of the hand pinned to the small of her back, ignoring stabs of pain the guard now forced up her shoulders. Slowly, her fingertips loosened a dart from the gauntlet still concealed under the filthy sleeve of her shirt.

"My good Lord Kergagi," Rafe stated with the hint of a smile, only his eyes betraying tension. "Do you think I am that brave a man to challenge both the assassins of Morevi *and* The Merchants' Circle? Why would I betray my most profitable allies of this realm? And why would the same Queen who, if memory serves me correctly, publicly called for my carcass to be her latest Throne Room tapestry, employ me for services to Her Crown?"

"Why, indeed?" Kergagi loomed over him, a profile of mass layering with mass. Clearly by his smile and the sweat covering his podgy face, he was savouring this heady sensation of power.

Askana could feel the dart slip lower into her hand, almost free of its leather groove.

"He is stalling, Kergagi, merely postponing the inevitable." Ganniman shuffled nervously, still unaccustomed to the aggressive practices of his counterparts. "Discover what he knows and then be done with him!"

"Tut, tut, young Ganniman, the search for knowledge should never be rushed. And, Captain Rafton," Kergagi nodded, "I intend to take my time to find out everything you know."

Rafe laughed heartily, mocking his clear disadvantage to his captors. "My dear Kergagi and good lad Ganniman, what do you *think* I know? I am merely telling you what I have seen with my own eyes. Morevian cargo ships are yielding less and less, hardly worth facing those shirai-wielding wenches. I am being petitioned by both Eyrieners and Morevians to take arms against their Queen. As for young Tekira here, she sought refuge in my service following her crimes to the crown. It was luck that crossed her path with mine, and as you know, luck has always favoured me."

Askana took her eyes away from Rafe for a moment as she could hear a dry, hushed voice next to her. It was Nassir, whispering a string of insults, the sharp anger in his speech forming spittle around his bottom lip. The guard holding him gave a grunt and finally smacked the Moor with a steel gauntlet. His verbal assaults, now spoken in his own native Persian tongue, caught Kergagi's attention. The guard went to strike him a second time but the merchant-lord merely raised a finger, taking the cup away from Rafe's face.

"And does luck favour your crew as well? I understand you are very conscientious of them, Captain Rafton," Kergagi spoke as he moved toward them, stalking, pacing before them with the rhythm of a pendulum. A single nod to the guard and Nassir was hoisted to his feet, face-to-face with the fat merchant-lord. "Would you like to see him try the poison first? Such size, such strength." The giant Moor bared his teeth in a snarl. "A man like him, maddened by the Kir'shia blood and I would make a tidy profit at the game-pits."

He turned abruptly to Askana. She flinched as a hint of the blood slopped over the rim of the goblet to harmlessly wet his leather glove. He held out the cup as the guard shoved her forward, the sudden movement causing her to let out a quick, tiny moan. "A rather fine piece you have pillaged here, Rafton. Tell me, have you sampled her yet? A touch of Kir'shia against this lovely's skin, and she becomes as eager as a bitch in heat."

With a grotesque smile, Kergagi brought the Kir'shia-kissed fingertips closer to her face, as if to caress her cheek lovingly with the poison. Ice formed in the pit of her stomach at the blood's sharp tang.

"You cannot imagine the things an addict would do for more of this. She would be yours to do with as you please from sunrise to sunset, and perhaps longer," Kergagi said, breathing heavily in a twisted moment of ecstasy.

"NO!" Rafe snapped. "My crew have nothing to do with this."

Kergagi's hand stopped abruptly. Askana watched a single drop begin to follow the curve of his beefy finger, the blood hugging the leather and eventually slipping into his palm. In his face was a look of promise to see if this theory of the Kir'shia effects on her would prove true.

"Unfortunately, they do," Kergagi sighed as he returned his attention to Rafe. "You see, Captain Rafton, they follow your orders to the letter. No doubt they have seen things, perhaps even drawn their own conclusions. And then there is the matter of your latest addition to the *Defiant*. I'm sure Tekira is quite knowledgeable of who is being honest and who is trying to deceive. So unless you can, without a doubt, prove our contact wrong, I will simply have to recruit you and your crew for our own purposes." Kergagi dipped his gloved fingers into the Kir'shia once more, slowly rubbing the fingertips together with delight. "One way or another."

With a desperate twist of her wrist Askana felt the dart drop into her hand. The instant it was tight in her grasp, she turned, first into the guard's body then sharply away from him using his own imbalance to break his grasp. The guard howled in pain as Askana's dart sank deep into his thick wrist. He would not live to howl long. The poison it carried was not as vicious as the Kir'shia, but just as deadly. He stumbled back, staring at the dart in amazement, its toxin quickly taking hold. He then looked up languidly only to see Askana's heel strike his face in a graceful high side-kick. The hulking corpse went through the main window of the workshop, taking the curtains, shutters, and window itself away in a deafening shatter of glass and wood.

Taking his cue, Nassir took his own guard by surprise with a strong elbow to the stomach. He jerked the doubled-over guard's helm free and slammed it into the soldier's face, "That was for that crack on the head!" He followed this assault with a left cross to the jaw, "And THAT is merely for your being born!"

Two more darts in quick succession took down the guards holding Rafe. Another two smacked into a wooden pillar just above Kergagi's head as he ducked while covering the chalice of Kir'shia with his free hand.

Askana turned to the gaping hole where the window to the tinker's workshop once was to see the three guards from across the street running to aid The Merchants' Circle, crossbows still loaded and ready to loose.

"Privateer," Askana called as she drew from her gauntlet the tiny throwing dagger. It quickly found a new sheath in an approaching guard's neck. "Your plan for getting us out of here?"

"Working on one!" Rafe leapt for the iron chandelier, swinging out to kick a pair of guards in the face and then returning back to his vantage point on the tabletop.

The soldiers with crossbows shouldered found aiming at a clear target impossible. Panic had overtaken The Merchants' Circle who now outnumbered their protectors by nearly three-to-one! One crossbowman loosed at Rafe, a better target on the tabletop. The bolt, however, struck a merchant-lord running blindly towards any exit, throwing him heavily to the stone floor. The crazed minor nobility grabbed onto their leather armour and pleaded wildly for protection. One poor merchant-lord shook a soldier so passionately that his crossbow loosed accidentally, its bolt piercing his heart. The guards were compelled to use only hand-to-hand or short sword tactics, provided they could reach the privateers. A challenge in itself with merchant-lords and their attendants in the way.

Yonella found herself pushed backwards by one of the older, stockier merchants. She would have lost her balance completely had not someone seized her by the shoulders. The hands spun her around to face her rescuer. With a shrug and a playful wink to the Eyriener beauty, Rafe struck her soundly across the jaw.

"Nothing personal, love," Rafe smiled. "That was strictly business."

With guards coming in from the front of the workshop, The Merchants' Circle now made for a smaller service door near the back wall, Ganniman leading the charge. Askana grabbed from the tinker's wall of equipment a crescent-edged tool and hurled it at the rope suspending the candle-chandelier. It swung free of the ceiling and slammed against Ganniman, the cast iron arms driving through his and two other merchant-lords' backs.

Kergagi went for the side door as well, approaching from the other side of the grand table, but found his path blocked by Askana. Her eyes were blind with anger at his betrayal. She could hear another Eyriener guard running up from behind her. With her falcon-cry, Askana's foot kicked behind her, dropping the soldier before she twisted and kicked the chalice into Kergagi's face.

The chaos appeared to slow in a dream-like manner as Kergagi, covered in the Kir'shia, let out a blood-curdling shriek.

Rafe managed to fend off three guards from the tabletop, recovering his épée from an overanxious soldier who wielded the elegant weapon as he would a broadsword. A swift jump-kick to the guard's chest and the cherished Rafton sword soon returned to a familiar grasp. Rafe leapt to the floor, landing before a pair of guards armed with short swords. One lunged clumsily, trying to get in underneath the pirate's thin blade, but instead felt a sharp tingle across his neck and fell to the floor, dead. The second guard practised more caution as he tried to knock the blade from Rafe's hand with repeated hacking strokes. Rafe slipped to the left and the soldier's short sword swept past him, embedding itself into a nearby support beam. The pirate could only shake his head in commiseration before running his sword to the hilt into the man's belly.

He pulled his blade free of the dead soldier and turned to face Kergagi. With a single punch, Rafe was sent across the room. The merchant-lord, lost in the effects of the poison covering his face, searched the melee for one other. His fingers curled when he found Askana, and charged at her armed only with his bare hands and a wild scream. It seemed, with what he intended for her, he would need no weapon. The shot from Nassir's pistol ripped through the sounds of battle, and Kergagi fell hard to the cold floor.

"I am well," Rafe groaned as Askana and Nassir both lifted him to his feet. "He just took me by surprise!"

They recoiled suddenly, looking at Rafe in horror. The dark, bloody fist print against his cheek caught the light of room's candles. Before he could reach up to touch the blood, he felt a euphoric rush of excitement, his heart quickening its pace. The hair on his arms stood on end. He could hear muscles tensing in his arm as he gripped his rapier. The shadows of the workshop revealed their hidden details to him. He was a god. Invulnerable. Immortal. *No*, he thought with his last shred of discipline, *this is the Kir'shia.* He brought his weapon and duelling dagger up, dismissing any concern for the repercussions of Kergagi's assault. If handled right, Rafe knew this curse could play in his favour. For now.

Their backs hit the wall as the guards were quickly growing in numbers while the remaining merchants desperately shoved past reinforcements in order to put distance between them and this business gone bad.

"Privateer, that escape plan of yours?" Askana asked.

His eyes immediately went to the small sandglass attached to her side. The last few grains slipped free of the top chamber. With a new-found strength, Rafe overturned the grand table before them to create a small shield between themselves, the regiment of soldiers, and the wall opposite of the alleyway.

"With pleasure, Your Grace!" Rafe pulled Askana down to the musty stone floor of the workshop and shouted, "Down, Nassir!"

Ignited by the smouldering cigar, the trail of black powder had begun its slow burn. White fire and sparks crept along the floor, illuminating only a few inches around itself while burning its way to the larger powder kegs. Rafe had timed this course of events for no longer than thirty minutes.

Rafe's estimate had been extremely accurate.

Askana rarely screamed in pure terror. The sudden roar followed by a cocoon of heat and fire, their only shield from a horrific death the heavy table and a bare wall behind them, warranted such a response. The inferno and screams of the guards now crying in agony conjured images of Xorinok, the Morevian after-world where the dishonourable and the wicked reside, facing turmoil and torture throughout eternity. A second explosion followed soon after, causing Rafe to tighten his embrace on Askana as another wave of fire, smoke, and debris swept around them.

Long moments passed. The heat and flames began to rise, making each breath harder to take with each minute. Rafe remained still. Confident there would be enough time to get away before the next volley of explosions, he nodded to Nassir and released Askana. Only two walls of the workshop remained standing. Their table-shield was smouldering at its edges while around them lay corpse after corpse wrapped in fire. Rafe pulled the wide-eyed Queen up to her feet as she looked around her in shock at the sudden destruction.

"What in the name of Nadinath was that?" Askana shouted over the flames.

"Insurance, Your Majesty," Rafe said proudly while pulling her through the debris.

Across the street waited a cart, its two horses stamping their hooves nervously at the growing chaos around them. It had originally brought reinforcements for The Merchants' Circle but now its driver waited for survivors. He continued to pull back on the team's reins to keep them steady as townspeople ran from every direction to fight the growing fire. With his focus on the two horses, he never saw Nassir approaching. The reins were quickly in the Moor's grasp while his other fist came across the guard's jaw then back across his face. The driver fell to the ground with a dull thud of body mass and leather armour.

Rafe and Askana hopped into the back of the cart as Nassir gave the reins a quick snap. The horses kicked their front hooves into the air and were more than co-operative in getting the three of them away from the tinker's workshop, now engulfed in flames.

"A friend of mine in England fancies himself a tinker," Rafe said. "At his workshop, he has a variety of supplies in stock. One he has in abundance is black powder!" Another explosion ripped through the quarter of the city as Rafe looked back in pure delight, "While this world uses it for fireworks, we English from across The Rift have put it to a more conventional use!"

Nassir whipped the reins harder as two Eyriener sentries began pursuit of the only cart heading *away* from the raging fire. Askana loosed her last dart with deadly accuracy, landing it deep in the neck of one rider. The other guard urged his horse forward and with a surprising agility leapt from his steed to the cart speeding its way through Taighar.

Rafe turned toward the sound of something massive landing inside the cart and was dealt a strong punch to his jaw. He found himself pinned by the Eyriener over the wagon's side, his face inching toward a rapidly spinning wheel. In desperation, he opened his mouth and bit hard into the guard's hand, but his face only crept closer to the wheel, its spokes a mere blur as they turned, kicking up mud, dirt and small pebbles. Then came a surprisingly high-pitched scream as Askana's foot crushed the bridge of the soldier's nose. Released from his descent, Rafe rolled on his back and kicked the guard in his side, unbalancing him. As the man's hands flailed wildly, the Queen and Captain hit him square in the chest, sending him crashing through a shop's display window.

"Nassir!" Rafe shouted over the continuing explosions and screams of the townspeople. "Get to the Sanctuary from the Sea and collect Elunear. Her Majesty and I will draw some of this crossfire! You know where to meet us!"

"Yes, my Captain!" Nassir nodded.

"Draw their crossfire?" Askana, her hair flying across her face, turned her head toward the small militia of ten forming behind them, "And just how do you propose we do that?"

From his belt pouch, Rafe produced the small grappling hook and cable they had used before in Songkusai. He threw it in the air, connecting with a weather vane atop one of the more prominent street shops. "Simple." The pirate wrapped his arm around Askana's waist, "Let's go shopping!"

The rope tightened for a moment, pulling them free of the cart, across the street, and through the window of a perfumery's boutique. Surrounded by the heavy scents of colognes, powders, and perfumes, they pulled themselves up to their feet and quickly ascended the stairs. Behind them came the sounds of soldiers charging into the shop, but they had already reached the rooftop by the time the last guard dismounted.

The boutique was clearly a well-established business in Taighar as it did not have the conventional thatch but a solid rooftop. Rafe had shopped there many times for Yonella and was well aware of this merchant's success in the trade.

He also knew the perfume maker's neighbour as well. "This way, Your Majesty," Rafe whispered as he motioned to the high top of the angled roof.

They had reached the perfumery's summit as the guards inside could be heard lumbering their way to the rooftop.

"Now what, privateer?" Askana spat.

Rafe pointed to the building behind the boutique. The perfume maker's neighbour was, in fact, the public stables, complete with haystack between it and the shop.

They could hear the first guard call out to his comrades as they leapt. The soldiers were now thundering down the steps of the boutique, but Askana and Rafe had already grabbed one of their horses. Whipping the strong white steed around in place, they caught the attention of the remaining herd and led them through the city now covered in a shimmering white-gold light from the inferno consuming the lower quarter of Taighar.

"Privateer, where are you taking us?"

"Outside the city is a tor called North Pointe. We'll be meeting Nassir and Elunear at a smuggler's dock. We maritime entrepreneurs use it when merchants wish to be discreet about our cargo." He shouted over the rumble of the herd's hoof beats, "Imports like your fine Morevian wines come to mind."

It was a grand entrance they made at North Pointe — Captain, Queen, and a team of powerful war steeds. At the edge of the cliff, dimly illuminated by grey moonlight, stood a small shack with a pulley that extended to a makeshift dock in the heart of what was known in the realm as Lyssander's Bay. Nassir and Elunear were there anxiously awaiting them with packs upon their backs. From North Pointe, it appeared that half the city was now engulfed in flames. Not everyone's attention was bent on saving the port as a row of eight torches were quickly riding to their position.

"I told you, mistress," Rafe laughed to Elunear with a wild glee he was aware of but powerless to stop. "You would know the signal when I sent it!"

Askana looked off the tor and held her breath at the sight of the giant ship awaiting them in Lyssander's Bay. Its sails were rising upwards as the voices of its crew distantly echoed off the cliff's craggy walls. She could also see in the twin moonlight a black banner waving proudly from the highest mast, no doubt the moniker of the Sea Wolf. This was the sailing vessel *Defiant*, more impressive than Askana could have pictured it.

Rafe wrapped Askana's arms around his waist and took a strong hold of the hooks hanging from the ropes above his head. Nassir, with Elunear holding tightly to him, also took hold of a second set of hooks behind Rafe. The oncoming horses were just in earshot as they pushed themselves free of the cliff. They slid along the pulley's rope to reach the small platform with a dull thud. Crossbow bolts and arrows could be heard whizzing past them, one or two lucky shots striking the side of their dinghy. Another crossbow bolt struck inches from Nassir's hand as the four climbed into the tiny boat and started for the grand pirate ship. Rafe primed his pistol and fired into the air. Darkness yielded for an instant to a bright flash and a deafening thunder as the *Defiant*'s port cannons fired on North Pointe. Alongside the vessel hung heavy rope where Nassir secured the dinghy while Rafe, Askana, and Elunear pulled themselves up to the ship's main deck.

"Wonderful stuff that Kir'shia!" Rafe laughed as a second volley of cannons fired at the tor.

"Pirate, I do not know whether to be impressed or outraged." Askana shook her head, "Such recklessness and insanity."

"Two of my more commendable traits, I assure you, Your Grace," he quipped. Rafe could feel the strength slowly ebb from his body, but braced himself by the side of his ship with a strong arm as he continued, "Come. We should retire for the night."

Rafe offered a hand to Askana, only to have it slapped away by Elunear. She had not struck him hard, but in the sudden weakness from the Kir'shia, he was knocked off his feet. Rafe could hear one or two small daggers drawn free of their scabbards.

"Stand fast in the ranks!" he snapped, holding up a cautionary hand. Rafe reached for the thick rope of the ship's rigging and pulled himself back to his feet, his mind fighting for focus as the poison continued to run its course. "This woman is a queen and shall be respected as such. Any man showing less to either of these women will answer to me. Understood? Now back to your posts. We set a course for The Rift."

Nassir finally appeared over the deck, his bulk and muscle calling for three privateers to help him over the railing. He looked about to see his crew dispersing, grumbling discontentedly and giving cold stares to the Morevians, and his Captain leaning precariously against the *Defiant's* port railing. He caught hold of Rafe's arm and spoke softly as not to be heard by Askana and Elunear, "My Captain, Elunear was waiting for me at the Sanctuary. Jailene never appeared."

"Very well. Keep a close watch. We could have a stowaway to contend with unless Jailene is dead or returning to her masters." Rafe pulled himself free of Nassir's assistance, refusing to let the Kir'shia get the better of him as he summoned up enough strength to join Askana and her guard at the main mast of his ship. "Ladies, will you follow me?"

After days of being helpless in tending to her sovereign, Elunear was finally given leave to wash away two days' worth of filth from Askana's skin. While the young girl looked at the opportunity to bathe her Queen as a high honour, Askana looked at the bath as an honour in itself. Hot water scented with her perfume of sandalwood, jasmine, and lily. A welcome change from the stench of travel and combat. Elunear gently massaged her queen's shoulders, but the girl's efforts only eased physical tension. Askana's mind lingered on the gloves of the unseen patron of The Merchants' Circle. Only women of Morevian Court would wear gloves of such a fashion. To be so close to the instigator of this coup d'état and be unable to strike. This treachery was all the more reprehensible as it was under a guise of an alliance with Eyrie. An alliance with no foundation. This would be King Cedric's opportunity for the conquest of Morevi.

Elunear slipped Askana's evening robes across her now-clean skin, ushering her to the centre of Rafe's massive bed. It was comfortable even by royal standards, adorned with satin and silk sheets, and soft goose feather pillows at the head of the bed. The comfort of the Captain's bed and Elunear's insistent pampering had been the first time since leaving Morevi that Askana actually felt like a queen. She could feel her eyes close as she slipped into *yuk-re-mun*, the meditation Kubi-Sogi would always have her perform before their morning bouts. It had been so long since their flight from Morevi, and now she finally found a moment's peace.

Light perfumes were being applied on her neck and wrists when Rafe barged into his quarters, heading straight for the large table covered in a variety of maps. His entrance snapped Askana out of her meditation but it was the young Maiden who appeared to take offence.

"You were not given permission to enter!" snapped Elunear.

"Indeed, for these are my quarters and this is my ship," Rafe said sharply, advancing on them both so swiftly Elunear reached for her shirai. "Her Majesty may be Queen of Morevi, but on this ship I am Captain. Do not forget that."

Askana watched him carefully. His strength had returned for the time being, but his hands were trembling and his ears appeared slightly red as if the blood was flowing quickly in his veins. She heard him muttering random thoughts as he frantically searched for parchment to write down everything, regardless if it were important or trivial. It was the Fever of the Kir'shia giving him this slight edge that could easily get him killed.

"If he orders his men to show us respect, we must return the favour," Askana replied softly, her eyes never shifting from him. "Captain Rafton is master of this vessel, and his kindness is so noted for offering his quarters to the Crown. You may retire for the night."

"My Queen?" Elunear whispered, gripping her shirai.

"Captain Rafton has prepared sleeping quarters for you as well. Take advantage of them, for now may be the only time we get rest. You have my leave."

Elunear's eyes narrowed as she watched the Captain turn back and forth between navigational charts, referring back to a giant master chart, its edges frayed and colour faded with great age. She did not care for the thought of this pirate on the same vessel with her Queen, let alone in the same chambers. As Rafe's erratic attentions were shared between the maps and a large hammock opposite the Captain's bed, this appeared to be the arrangements made. Askana's eyes assured Elunear that she would be safe. With a final bow to her Queen, she left Askana alone with Rafe.

From outside the grand bay windows of the Captain's Quarters, however, deep emerald eyes dutifully kept watch over her Queen. She had stowed away on the ship when it had left The Barrier Reef after hearing rumours of its captain making a pact with a queen known as "The Black Widow". She knew that name well—a name given in the spirit of irony, for the woman was reputed to have worn armour for her mourning garb. She watched the Captain closely...

...was amused with their travels in the jungles...

...saw his crewmate die...

...followed the dark giant and her sister warrior to their night-time rendezvous...

...waiting for the right time to make her presence known. The ship was about to cross The Rift again. She peered from the darkness to try and see on the Captain's charts what course was being plotted.

Rafe's back was to Askana but she could see from the state of his shirt that he was sweating profusely. If he were not tended to, he would never sleep. He would work himself to a point of exhaustion and eventually die of it. Normally, her agility and talents for stealth would keep her silent, but she was unaccustomed to such sailing ships as the *Defiant*. The creak of a wood plank underneath her seemed to echo in the ship's quarters. Rafe, his eyes almost blind with excitement and confusion, turned to the sound so quickly it caused her to start.

Askana gently took his trembling hand into her own, "Perhaps you should rest as well, Captain."

"No rest for the wicked," Rafe laughed as he returned to the charts. "We have a perilous journey ahead of us."

"Across the Rift?"

Rafe pushed aside the other maps and Askana's eyes grew wide at the master chart revealed. It was a giant blue canvas of criss-crossing paths with co-ordinates running along them, circles overlapping circles displaying symbols commonly found on astrolabes and compasses, and a giant grid, all referring to a central point within the map. This was a navigation chart for The Rift, Captain Rafton's secret in navigating to her world.

"Aye, Your Majesty, home to England. We have an appointment to make with his majesty, King Henry the VIII."

Merely Players

Morning dawned pleasantly across Morevi, a warm golden-yellow with none of the scorching heat that would assail the streets and steam the jungles at midday. In the country estates, farming villages, mines, and various towns between cities, life went on as usual. Shops in Anderis opened their doors. Farmers and herbalists sold their goods in the marketplaces of Renai and Lahsa. There was, however, something very unique about this particular day. Across the realm, commoners' talk centred around one topic—the events occurring in the capital city of Songkusai. There, whispers abounded. Its people, so used to upheaval, were worried.

Whispers from the Palace of a Thousand Suns reached the townspeople in the form of rumour as rain would trickle down a mountainside to eventually create a lake. None of these rumours or speculations could be substantiated, of course. *"The Queen is dead"* was the word on the streets. No word had come from the Palace or the Council, either of confirmation or negation. No funeral arrangements or mourning time had been made. Knowing full well one could lose their tongue or their very life for perpetuating rumours of this fashion, people conversed in lowered voices and silent looks to the Palace looming in the horizon, not knowing that the Council of a Hundred Turi had already begun session.

A very heated session, at that.

"Point of Order!" Lady Shrimaan of House Tiar, Chosen Speaker of the Council, snapped as the din of the Council swelled to an almost deafening volume. "It is most certain that Her Majesty has taken it upon herself to discover what enemies we may have within our alliances. There is no need for such conjecture!"

"Then why fake her own death?" challenged the pale skinned Min-Lu. Her voice of dissent caused murmurs to rise among the assembled Ladies.

Min-Lu of House Annaki had always been a strong supporter of the Queen and, in the eyes of many in Council, Askana's selected pupil. In the War of the Fan and Slipper, they had literally fought side-by-side. She abandoned her pious beliefs in El'Baz to embrace Askana's Order of Nadinath. When a deciding vote fell to House Annaki, it would, without question, go to House Moldarin. In turn, House Annaki won many issues that went to the Queen for a final decision. Now, in the Queen's absence, the royal favourite spoke with a new-found passion and drive committed against her strongest advocate.

"Askana has acted without consulting the Council, seeking neither its approval nor support." She rose from her seat with all the confidence and assurance of a skilled gamester, knowing whatever the choice of sport would be, she would emerge victorious. "This Council was formed upon the good faith and understanding of Her Majesty that no one woman would rule alone. We were to be more than just advisers, fresh perspectives, or devil's advocates. We were to be the voice of the New Regime, heralding an age of Morevi where the voice of its subjects would be heard. Now we see the true colours of the Queen." She fell silent for a moment, her gaze going across the collected assembly as if assuring herself their attention was undivided. "Crimson. The bloodshed of a trusted innocent, of Noble Ladies of our own Council, the slaughter of honourable Servants to the Crown, and now reports of fatalities and destruction in the Eyriener ports of Taighar." Her eyes narrowed sharply, "These overtures to war were not sanctioned by the Council!"

"Nor was the deployment of the Morev'ar!" Kubi-Sogi spoke, a razor's edge in his tone. He stood by the vacant throne of the Queen, determined to fulfil his charge and serve as Askana's voice. He could only pray that she knew what she was doing without consulting him first.

"Your voice is mute here, old man! Your blind loyalty to the Queen is well known."

"My loyalty to the Queen is my choice, just as it was her choice to grant me her voice in this Council!" he stated, holding up the Royal Seal. Gasps from some Councilwomen mingled with murmurs of disbelief, confidence, and bitter scorn at the sight of Askana's crest. The Blademaster would not be denied now for he had the blessing of the First Queen. "Her Majesty has taken flight, yes, for she is not safe in the Palace of a Thousand Suns. How can you expect her to approach the Council for approval to go into hiding? She has fled in order to return, armed with the truth as to who in this Council plots against her!"

"The truth?" Min-Lu asked repeatedly over the clamour of voices surrounding them, eventually subsiding as Lady Shrimaan, again, called the Great Hall to order. "It is time, old man, that you see the truth! The Morev'ar were a necessity after the discovery of treason, not against the Crown, but against the very state."

A silence blanketed the chambers now as the word 'treason' hung heavily in the air.

"From whom?" Lady Shrimaan asked as she slowly rose to her feet.

"From the very saviour of Morevi." Min-Lu held the eyes of the Council members with her dark, cold gaze and spoke the name with disdain, "Askana Moldarin."

Cries of protest and support erupted from the collection of delegates. Lady Shrimaan snatched the staff of office and struck the floor hard, "Order from the Council! We must have order!" Min-Lu remained motionless across the table, her lips pulled back in a chilling smile as Shrimaan spoke, "This is quite a claim you bring before the Council. We have no proof that the disaster at the Taighar ports is her doing. It could have been a result of Eyriener plots to implicate the Queen and incite the people, or more likely, Eyriener carelessness. Allegations without proof are slander, and this applies to the claim you bring before us. I pray you have evidence to substantiate such claims. Otherwise, you yourself face execution for treason!"

"I do." Undaunted by the reprimand, Min-Lu motioned to a soldier of her house guard, who disappeared out of one of the many archways. "I wished not to alert the Council of my findings. Sources must always be protected."

Heads turned at the commotion coming down one of the corridors towards the Great Hall. Whoever the source was, she certainly did not look as if she had enjoyed protection of any kind. She was young, and seemed on the brink of fainting, all self-possession now tatters along with her sweat and blood-stained clothing. Her bruised body was as lifeless as that of a rag doll thrown in the middle of the Council Chambers. Her sobs were the only sounds that broke the stillness surrounding her.

"Guard, lift her." Min-Lu walked from behind the great table and stood before the girl, now being held upright by her long, mahogany hair. Min-Lu struck her hard against the jaw, the broken woman's sobs rising in volume for a moment, subsiding as the menacing Council member spoke, "Welcome, traitor, to the Great Hall of Dawn. A sight you know well. Now, for our records, state your name before us."

"I am Jailene of House Risa. Lieutenant of the Royal Guard. Personal guard to Askana Moldarin, First Queen of Morevi."

Lady Shrimaan, who had opened her mouth to voice protest at the girl's treatment and the fact that she had been tortured without trial or sentencing, remained still. Startled gasps escaped some of the ladies as others stared, surprise turning to resignation or anger. To see disloyalty from within the highest ranks of the military was unthinkable, but there it was, corporal proof that such deception was evident in Morevi. Her condition and her pathetic wails were reminders that as a Royal Guard she was also a Maiden of the Night. The thought was in many minds that, bar the Council or a Court of Three, only the Temple of Nadinath could have ordered that the girl be interrogated and broken this way. Min-Lu was indeed a member of that faith. Another damning finger pointed at the Queen if the Temple had thought the matter serious enough to break one of their Order.

"Speak, traitor," Min-Lu hissed. "Tell the Council what you told me."

"Her Majesty is not what she appears to be. She is not the voice of the New Order, but merely the old voice of tyranny under a new guise," Jailene sobbed. "She is secretly planning an alliance with the Eyriener merchants." With each word she caught her breath, struggling to remain loyal to her Queen but unable to fight against the pain of torture. "I heard her plan with the fair-haired stranger. She intends to incite war with Eyrie, against the will of the Council. Once she had...once...she..." Her voice began to trail off as she shook her head in a feeble protest against the secrets she was now forced to tell.

Min-Lu's hand was merely a blur in the air as she struck the former Guard, sending her to the floor. Jailene gasped and began speaking again as the diminutive Lady moved in threateningly. "Once she has taken Eyrie and combined military forces, the Queen intends to engage the Elves, determined to vanquish them and seize Arathelle."

"By the Goddess herself," came the appalled voice of one Councilwoman. "The Queen has become mad with power!"

Again a clamour exploded as Jailene collapsed into a lifeless heap at the feet of Min-Lu, who did not even bother to look down as she said, "Guard, remove this filth from the Council Chambers."

Shrimaan called for order as Kubi-Sogi raised his voice before the Ruling Ladies, "This is madness to be certain! The Queen who established relations with the Elves would be the last one to attack them. No one knows better than Askana Moldarin the extent of their power! If indeed the Queen is conspiring against her own people, why was her most trusted handmaid Tekira trying to assassinate her at the very time when two of her strongest supporters in the Council were killed?"

"Because her 'strongest supporters' were involved in the plot, and Tekira was a patriot who could no longer keep silent over this plot against her kingdom!" Min-Lu snapped, glaring at the old Blademaster. "She believed in the preservation of Morevi, and a war against the Mists of Arathelle would mean our extinction! We all know this! But the Queen has found her lips whetted with the wine of absolute power, and she is now drunk with that wine."

As both the Speaker and Kubi-Sogi saw with despair, the Noble Ladies were now seized by the new accusations, and leaning with Min-Lu as trees would during a storm. Their voices would not be heard, but feeling the Royal Seal tight in his grasp Kubi-Sogi would try for his Queen.

"I have trained many a mind, body, and spirit in my years. None so keen and disciplined as Her Majesty." He breathed deeply, attempting to keep his patience long enough to break through to the new ruling class, "I believe her sacrifices to the wishes of the Council have been evident. Her heart belongs to Morevi, not to whims of temptation or otherwise."

"Her sacrifices?" Min-Lu laughed mockingly. "Banishing a freakish pet whom she let loose to rampage among our families and loved ones and tempering her desires to rule Morevi with a vision only her own is nothing in comparison to sacrifices we all would make in lands, soldiers, and resources waging a war that is not winnable." Min-Lu composed herself, "We are without a leader. *Three* of our number have been murdered! Word spreads across Naruihm that Eyrieners grow bold and have their eye on Morevi. This is no time to have the Throne vacant!"

"I agree," a voice rang sharply, making every Council member look to the arched double doorway of the main entrance and then stand in reverence of the late arrival. "Forgive my tardiness, but I have been dealing with pressing affairs of my House."

"The Council recognises Sister Dirare and her Adviser, please join us." Shrimaan announced, her tone one of relief.

Dirare and Arnese moved to the section reserved for House Jarahd. In the great arcs of seats around the floor, other Noble Ladies and their silent personal retainers watched her slow ascent. Dirare gave no sign that the collected stares of the Council discomfited her in the least. Arnese pulled the seat back for her Lady and sank down onto a cushion at her side. She performed the ceremonial seating that recognised her House and acknowledged the Speaker, then stood up and made her way with alacrity down to the floor.

There was a formality always in her voice when she spoke, demanding respect from the collected Houses, "My Sister of the Council speaks true. It would appear that for reasons unknown—"

"Not for reasons unknown!" Min-Lu shouted to Dirare, resentful at having to give up control to the woman who gave the appearance of a tall, elegant flame in her red robes. "We have heard the testimony—"

"Of a frightened girl," Dirare purred, bringing an almost terrifying calm to the matter before the Council. "It is obvious that the girl had been maltreated. Whether that was at the command of the Priestesses of Nadinath or not I will be sure to check, but we all know that under 'persuasive measures', I believe you call them, Min-Lu, the girl would have told her interrogators anything they wanted to hear." Dirare paused significantly to let that sink in, then gave a small laugh, "She would have told us that the fires of Xorinok had been quenched and in its place there is an endless winter."

Polite laughter rose, breaking the tension and making them more amenable to guidance as she well knew. Min-Lu, bridled by the implication against her, stared at the Councilwoman coldly.

"Glaring is a child's tactic, my Sister." Dirare said, her eyes never turning to Min-Lu. "But perhaps, considering your disturbed state of mind, the mistake you made concerning your Queen is understandable. We understand that you love Askana Moldarin deeply and that her sudden disappearance must worry you very much. As such I do not think we will consider your outburst treason."

Min-Lu took a long, deep breath and slowly returned to her seat.

"So what are the thoughts of House Jarahd?" came the voice of Kirine of House Demandar. "Even if the Queen is not guilty of treason, there is no denying that she has left her country in stealth. Some would call that running away."

Dirare looked around the Council. "The question is, from what? I doubt very much that our murdered Sisters were involved in the plot that poor Guard claims to have discovered. We do not know for sure whether Askana Moldarin left to escape her assassins, whether she was taken by them, whether she is dead or alive. What is clear is that we are without a ruler."

Absolute silence reigned in the Great Hall.

"Now then, members of Council, I agree with Lady Min-Lu that we should raise new blood to the throne, but not in the manner of which she speaks. First and foremost comes the simple question, what are the wishes of Askana Moldarin? Not what we think her impulsive actions of these past few days are, but what was her vision when she brought the New Age to Morevi, from the very first day? For that is why we have come as far as we have."

Dirare smiled inwardly as she heard her peers discussing her question and why Askana's political rival was suddenly defending her.

"Remember, my Sisters," she said with great gravity, "do not be influenced by the chaos of the past few days. Remember that we stand for the New Age, itself a vision of our lost Queen, and that we must act wisely so as not to undo all that we have worked for. We must honour this vision and secure the throne for future bloodlines."

A delegate from one of the border estates, Lao-Chin of House Giedoshi, raised her hand in question, "Are you suggesting we proceed with the Raising in the absence of Her Majesty? Forgive me for saying so, Sister, but it is clear to us that you already have someone in mind."

As Arnese had predicted, faces turned hard at this. Each and every one of these women assumed Dirare had designs on the Throne herself. Supporters and detractors immediately masked themselves.

"I mean it for the Consort, Jermal Sandhuilean."

Before an outburst could resume, Dirare nodded with a raised hand, "A role tempered by the voices of the Council. I have taken it upon myself to serve as liaison between the Consort and the Council until such a time wherein a successor for the Throne is chosen, one whom the Consort will honour and cherish and who will rule supreme in this most glorious of ages for our Kingdom."

Already some of the more seasoned members of the Council had caught on to what this meant. Dirare indirectly in power, yet a pleasing temporary arrangement that would harm none. If the Queen came back there would be no opposition from the Regent or any blame to lay on the Council. If the Queen did not, then there would be time to jostle for position.

A mild applause came from supportive members of the Council, but Min-Lu was on her feet again, her eyes blind with fury. "Such beautiful and inspirational words, *Sister.*" Dirare raised an eyebrow, the true intent behind Min-Lu's address to her clear to everyone in Council. Min-Lu continued, unfaltering. "However, the evidence cannot be denied that Her Majesty Askana Moldarin is acting on her own accord without consulting the Council."

"Then I propose," Dirare spoke, cutting off Min-Lu's rebuttal, "we establish a High Council consisting of representatives of the Houses of Morevi who will advise an appointed High Regent to the Consort-King. If it is discovered that the Queen is dead or has no intention of returning, we will put it to a vote whether or not the Consort stays upon the Throne or if the Council shall take full control of the government until a new queen is named."

Voices of support seconded the bold move on Dirare's part. Kubi-Sogi caught Dirare's eye and received no response at all. For whatever reason she had seen fit to grant the Queen reprieve, but for what reason he did not know. What he did know for a fact was that Dirare had possession of the Consort, and it would be Dirare who ruled until Askana's return. He also knew she would not give up power that easily. He had already seen how easily the Noble Ladies were swayed if played right. Even if they knew the right, they would support the wrong if it suited their own ends.

And what of Jailene's claims? He had no doubt that they were false, but it was disconcerting how one of the Royal Guard Askana had taken with her had fallen into Min-Lu of Annaki's hands. As these questions repeated in his mind, Kubi-Sogi noticed his own dim reflection in the polished marble table before him, but he did not smile at the irony of the setting.

Being a man in a woman's world was not easy.

With the right application of mud, dirt, and tattered clothes, it was ridiculously easy to blend in with the Eyriener surroundings. Kalea made her way across the borders posing as a wandering peddler of charms and potions. She knew that the Council must have begun its session, and she was having misgivings about leaving Kubi-Sogi to it. She hoped he could stand his ground against the opposition.

The air was still misty with morning as she approached the port city of Taighar, nodding to the Eyriener soldiers who dismissed her immediately as they got close. She shook her head ruefully as they pressed forward along their patrols. Any of her Guard would have known enough to at least question a wanderer. She felt a proud smile at the thought but had to mask it as another patrol approached.

The number of soldiers abroad at this time of the morning was quite unusual. Even in her guise as a harmless gypsy, she could feel their scrutiny, an air of wariness about them. Kalea took notice of their direction—they were all heading for the mountainous border range. It was not as if invading armies could come through the Sleeping Dragons. The mountain passes were too narrow and too treacherous for such numbers. She also took notice at their demeanour. The closer she got to Taighar, the soldiers grew more gruff, their eyes trusting no one and suspecting everyone.

Then, as she cleared the rise overlooking the Eyriener ports, she understood why.

The sight was horrific yet impressive all at once. It managed to take away the seasoned Anjara's breath. The port town looked as if the Goddess' fingertip had touched it out of anger. Charred remains of shops and buildings refusing to fall reached upwards in vain, only a memory of what they once had been. The ruins were crawling with carpenters and city planners assessing the damage and estimating the costs of rebuilding. Kalea slowly walked through the damaged city, listening to merchants cursing and shouting over their losses, crying for retribution. A funeral procession passed before her in one of the town squares. The size of the processions indicated that the mourning was for people of wealth and stature. In some disbelief, Kalea recognised one of the charred bodies borne aloft as that of Kergagi, whom she had known as a contact for the Queen.

Boys were passing out parchments to passers-by. Kalea accepted one simply from a reflex action. She did not ask why the boy was doing this and to whom he paid homage. She was about to discard the thick paper until her eyes caught a name written across the bottom of it—The Sea Wolf.

The man could have passed for an Eyriener noble, but the artist had darkened the eyes of the sketch, making them appear harsh and heartless. A description pieced together from the reports of the survivors now gave the Sea Wolf a name—Rafe Rafton. An unusual name, neither Morevian, Arathellian, or Islander. Rumour had it that he was not of this world. She was impressed by the amount of the bounty that had been set, almost matching the one her Queen placed on him. Kalea's mind raced as she rolled up the parchment. She had come here seeking answers only to find the seaport in ruin and the man responsible an ally to the Eyriener Crown.

Her thoughts were interrupted by the flight of a drunk through the doors of a tavern, aided by an innkeeper and a truly monstrous town deputy.

"An' if you wish to drink i' my tavern, you should think to bring coin next time!" the innkeeper barked as the deputy dusted off his hands. "Wendell, make sure 'e and 'is like don' cross the threshol' o' my pub!" he said with a sharp nod and a saturnine grin before returning to his tavern.

The offending patron sat up and let out a grotesque belch. Even from a few feet away Kalea could smell the stench of alcohol on his breath. She looked up, clutching the hood of her ragged, muddy cloak to her, to see the inn's sign slowly swaying in the morning breeze.

"Sanctuary from the Sea," she whispered to herself, as she stared at the carvings of mermaids and sailing ships around the peeling gold letters.

She kept her hood close about her as she entered the Sanctuary. The smells were not so unpleasant, but it was clearly a pub for sailors and workingmen. She made her way past the barmaids, who ignored her after making sure that she was no competition. At the bar, she tossed a few odd brass pieces upon the counter to catch the innkeeper's attention.

"That will cos' you more, witch, if'n you wish to sit there," Drakkan said as he mopped down the counter. Laughter rose from the watching patrons of the Sanctuary. "An' you can forget about showing me your goods, as I am not one believin' in charms or love potions. Only your money."

"But surely, this is enough for a bit of ale?" Kalea counted the pieces again, subduing her insulted pride and keeping her guise intact.

"Aye, you can buy an ale wi' tha'. But to drink it *in that chair* will cos' you two gold crowns."

"Two gold crowns?!" Her breath momentarily taken away by the cheek of the demand, Kalea swore. "What in the name of Na—" She caught herself just in time. Kalea then asked in what she hoped was a humble tone, "Does it cost more to enjoy drink at your tavern?"

"No, jus' *that* particular seat belongs to Cap'n Rafton." Drakkan winked in pride. "An' after las' night's fireworks, it'll cost anyone two crowns to rest their backsides there. Been thinkin' of puttin' a sign out front abou' it. Probably draw curious travellers, it might."

A rousing cheer sounded, and a sailor lifted his mug in a toast to this wanted criminal of Morevi, and now Eyrie. "Here's to The Sea Wolf. The pirate who knows how to make an exit!"

Assuming the naivete of a stranger Kalea unrolled the paper. "You are raising your glasses to this man?" she asked incredulously.

The bartender merely shook his head, laughing heartily as he motioned to her, "Peddler, you mus've slept 'arder than the dead if'n you didn' hear the commotion two nights ago."

"You mean *one man* did all this to your city?"

"Aye," Drakkan smiled widely as he poured himself a cup of ale. "One Man. And fireworks."

"Fireworks?" Kalea asked as she slid into another seat. "How could fireworks cause such destruction?"

"The Festival of Onarg, God of the Sea, is in three days time. As part o' the celebrations there's always fireworks, and there's this tinker in town and always prepares a display. I mean, Barrows usually 'as black powder on hand anyways, what wi' his inventing and such. As he is charged with providin' the Festival's fireworks, he 'ad stocked up on it, promisin' a display not soon forgotten. Well, Tinker Barrows was right abou' tha'! In one night, Captain Rafton took out two taverns. Business couldn't be better!"

A laughter-filled roar came from the patrons as they raised their glasses again in tribute. Drakkan pointed to a small shelf behind the bar where rested a small glass snifter with an engraved "R" upon it.

"That be Captain Rafton's *scotch glass*," he said, emphasising the words "scotch glass" as if he spoke of a rare treasure from a far-off land. "You see, this spirit called *scotch* is his preferred drink. I keep a bottle 'ere jus' for 'im. Brings it from across The Rift, he does! I have other items of his for sale."

Kalea nodded slowly, her eyes resembling those of a wide-eyed innocent hanging on the tavernkeep's every word. It never ceased to amaze her that in disreputable dens like this, people knew more of the realm than the highest ministers of state. This bartender talked about The Rift as if it was as ordinary as a changing of seasons. This commoner even had a growing collection of artefacts from an unknown realm and was now offering them to the highest bidder!

He reached underneath the bar, a leering smile across his face as he spoke, "So, does this strike your fancy, peddler?"

Kalea's eyes grew wide as Drakkan produced a beautiful silk scarf bearing the emblem of Askana's house. She could see the Eyriener bartender did not recognise the Turi flower insignia upon the delicate material. Drakkan nodded slowly as he unfurled the scarf before her.

He gave a wink to one of his serving wenches who took his place behind the bar, "I'm cert'in we could find *something* for trade."

"Yes." Kalea's eyes motioned to the store room behind the bar, a dimly lit chamber with a heavy oak door separating barrels of ale, wine, and supplies from the tavern, "But I prefer to do business in private."

"Well spoken, woman." Drakkan stood back to let her come around the bar, trying in vain to make out her form under the cloak. The woman had a good voice and a nice mouth under that hood of hers. Sometimes a man liked surprises. A bawdy jest or two followed them as the door closed.

In a few moments the quick rhythmic pounding against the store-room door raised a hearty laugh from the patrons. Another sailor raised his glass in a mock cheer. "It looks like Drakkan has been taking lessons from Captain Rafton on how to make an exit!"

The patrons began the chorus of a bawdy drinking song as the pounding against the door grew quicker and wilder. The singing continued with zest and vigour as they drank toast after toast in honour of the defiant captain.

Min-Lu continued down the corridor to her guest chambers in the Palace. She spoke not a word as she entered with her guards in attendance, not even as she looked over the person on her knees in the centre of the room. The girl had been brought in through one of the many private passageways by House Annaki guards, unseen by any who was in attendance in the Great Hall that day.

Min-Lu dismissed both guards and servants. Left alone with the girl, she closed her eyes for a moment and regulated her breathing. This exercise and the incense that had been lit helped calm her nerves after the confrontation with the Council. It also helped settle the excitement that was growing in the pit of her stomach. She smiled, for here was proof that she was still a child in some ways, unable to wait for a promised reward. When she opened her eyes, the girl was still kneeling there. A smile crept across Min-Lu's young face as she removed her heavy formal robes to slip into a more casual, gauzy one.

She had found such loyalty before. In Tekira. The foolish girl's refusal to betray her Queen had suitably impressed Min-Lu. After Tekira had been broken, Min-Lu set about finding herself just such a loyal hound. She found it in this kneeling girl.

"I must commend your performance." The Lady produced from her vanity a tall, ebony decanter and poured out sweet Anderisian amber wine into two silver goblets. The kneeling girl lifted her head to reveal a satisfied grin that Min-Lu returned, "I thought I had struck you too hard before the Council."

"My beloved Mistress, I suffered the blows in the name of duty." Jailene gave a slight groan as she lifted herself from the cold floor, "It was actually the second blow that took me by surprise. You are very strong." The Guard held back the urge to say *"for your size"*.

Min-Lu set the goblets aside and gently took the woman's hands in her own. "You must forgive me, Jailene. That was for effect. I knew support for the Queen would be strong in the Council and an allegation of such magnitude as to shock them out of their fixed ways of thinking was what I needed. I needed you to be convincing enough. Remember the Council's motto—it is for the New Order!"

Jailene laughed. They both knew what Min-Lu meant by "New Order". "I was not sure if my claims swayed the Council much after Lady Dirare's appearance."

"That was most unfortunate. I did not anticipate her move. Be assured that we have planted the seed of doubt in many minds today." Min-Lu took up the goblets, offering one to Jailene, "Whether they follow Dirare's pointing finger like sheep or not is no indication of what they believe."

"It is so much less than we planned," she replied, accepting the wine.

"Always plan beyond your expectations. That way you will always win something." Min-Lu smiled warmly, "Without your testimonial, the Council would have never considered voting on whether Askana should remain on the Throne or not. In their narrow little minds they have always taken for granted that Askana has indisputable rights to the Throne simply because she led the revolution. If anything, Askana is a general. She does not possess a drop of *royal* blood in her House, so there is no reason why anyone else should not dispute her claim if they are more fit to fill the office."

"To the bright and glorious reign of the New Dawn." Jailene smiled proudly as she took a mouthful of wine.

"I am so very pleased with your loyalty to me, Jailene," said her Lady, tracing the rim of her goblet with a single fingertip as she spoke. "You have braved such risk, such danger for me."

"My Mistress honours me." Jailene made a strange picture, standing erectly and proudly in her stained rags.

"Jailene," Min-Lu walked slowly to the balcony of her apartments, watching the sun, now a deep blood red, sink below the horizon. "Your service will not go forgotten."

The sudden clanging of a goblet striking the floor gave her a moment's pause as she reflected on the words she had said before the Council. Treason, she knew some murmured now. Or had they been words of revolution? Might they come to be known later in history as words of reformation? Jailene's violent gagging did not move her in the least. She turned to look at the trembling woman whose face was twisted with shock and disbelief. The girl could not find a voice to cry for help as her windpipe was swollen shut, nor did she feel the floor as she struck it hard.

As Min-Lu set her goblet down on a table, two of her guards entered her chambers as they were told to do when Jailene was "attended to". She studied the body on the floor with some fascination, part of her understanding the attraction to the apothecary's craft. *It was so easy*, she thought with a hint of elation.

"Jerick," she spoke to the guard, motioning to the body on the floor, "it seems that I need the services of one of my maids."

The man bowed and motioned to his fellow soldier to fetch a servant. "My Lady," he said softly. "*He* is here, awaiting your presence in the West Chamber Passageway."

"Then Jerick, you are with me."

The guard joined Min-Lu as she slid back a disguised panel in the West Wall of her quarters. Shadows danced along the high walls of the passageway, illuminated by the torch Jerick held. Her steps ceased for a moment as she heard through small chinks in the wall the sounds of people reassessing the day's events. As narcissistic as it appeared, Min-Lu always loved to hear her name spoken by the members of the Council. Her name would be on many lips this night in Morevi.

Silhouetted by torchlight, he came towards her as he had in the beginning. Dressed in dark, flowing robes, a fine silk mask across his face, he was merely a shadow emerging from those trapped in the corridor walls. His ominous, powerful voice was sweet to her ears. "My beautiful one," the man's voice came whispering down the secret passageway. "I have been waiting to hear of your journey to Eyrie."

"My Lord Ruain, I have news for you," she said eagerly, wrapping her arms around his solid frame. "Before I crossed the borders, the King was already blaming the disaster at Taighar ports on the Queen and is eager for vengeance. Everything is proceeding as we have planned."

"So the little Guard is dead," the robed figure nodded slowly. "I have heard that a Raising will take place. When?"

"Soon, my love. Dirare has the Consort under a protective shield that even I dare not try and penetrate."

"Dirare?" He laughed softly, "She is simply playing the Great Game with the Council members as par-stern counters. We will allow the Consort to come to us. As for the Queen?"

From underneath his robes, polished gold buttons caught the dim torchlight of the corridor. In his waistcoat and breeches cut of the latest Eyriener fashion, he was known in the social circles of the Eyriener Embassy and in his own realm as the "Dark Merchant". She knew him by his name, a name she did not mind calling out when they were alone in her chambers. He was unlike any man she had ever known and the power he exuded was alone enough to make her love him.

"The Queen is no more," Min-Lu said, throwing her head back in a delighted laugh. "She now plays the part of an outcast in the company of some upstart sea captain. An Otherworlder."

She felt his posture stiffen in their embrace. His hands slid up along her arms, only to grab them firmly, "And this Otherworlder—tall, gold hair, and wore an ivory handled rapier by his side?"

Min-Lu winced, feeling his grip tighten on her arms. "Yes, my Lord."

He released her and stepped back into the shadow, his eyes studying the torchlight in the corridor. "Most unexpected. Something I must deal with personally."

"I think you take too much onto your shoulders," Min-Lu teased as she returned to his embrace under the cloak. Making a pout with her plump mouth, she complained, "Why must you concern yourself with this pirate? Isn't he merely a trifle, my Lord?"

She felt his fingers take her jaw and squeeze harder than necessary. "You know little of what you speak of," he said softly, menacingly. "This man is a very real threat. Knowing his tactics, he is no doubt the true cause of the destruction at Taighar. He pilfers from your trade ships and you cannot even stop him." The fingers shook her. "You should thank that Goddess of yours for saving your skin or you might have joined Kergagi and his friends in a fiery death!"

Min-Lu gave a quick moan as he pulled her closer, "They are all dead?"

"I received the news this morning at the embassy," he spat, releasing her with a shove. "This *trifle* eliminated The Merchants' Circle in one night."

She bowed her head, thinking his anger justified. He must have worried about her, that she could have died in the destruction that swept through Taighar that night. She had originally been there to finalise plans for her coup. Then came the news of the Otherworlder wanting to meet with the Merchants' Circle. She had thought it was Tekira at first glance. It made perfect sense. The girl had killed the Queen and understandably needed to run from everyone, including Min-Lu herself. Then upon her return to Songkusai, the doctors sent her word that the dead body they held was, in fact, Tekira. The Queen had allied herself with a new player in the Great Game, a player cunning enough to give her beloved pause.

"This captain from across the Rift," Lord Ruain said to her. "You know him as the Sea Wolf, but I know him by his true name."

"Rafe Rafton, miss! His name is Rafe Rafton!" Drakkan choked out as her fingers tightened around his throat.

His heels were knocking wildly against the oak door as they dangled a few inches above the ground. Kalea could only assume the innkeeper was hoping for one of the lads to come rescue him, but the patrons outside were singing some old sea-shanty to give their good friend Drakkan his privacy.

"Tell me more." She released her hold and let him drop to the ground, coughing and gasping for air.

"I don' know much more! All I remember is him turnin' up here wi' his First Mate and a couple of women. They looked Morevian, now I think about it. They 'ad that arrog—er, *confident* look, you see? The Cap'n said he 'ad business tha' night! Said he 'ad a feeling about the deal."

"What feeling? That the Morevians might turn him into a capon?" Kalea mocked, mentally apologising to Kubi-Sogi for the slur.

"A *good* feeling." Drakkan pushed himself up onto his knees, wincing. "A boy from the Messengers' Guild brought 'im word that th' Merchants' Circle were to meet 'im that night. I saw 'im leave with 'is Mate and one of the Morevian women."

"And?" Kalea prodded, pressing two fingers lightly against his throat.

Drakkan racked his brains, his eyes darting upward as if trying to find the answers in his storeroom's ceiling. "Wait! Another woman come before them, I remember now! A thing o' beauty she was, but she left wi' one of Rafton's men before the Captain 'imself arrived. They were looking for 'er."

The Anjara's fingers pressed a little harder. "Where have they gone?"

"I don' know!" he said, his words growing more uncomfortable as she pressed into his throat. "I think 'is Mate mentioned something about The Rift. That's all, I swear by the soul of Myrian!"

"I set no store by the name of a mere wife to a God." Kalea removed her fingers from him and smiled broadly to the bartender, "I hope you have enjoyed sampling my wares." And then she hit him square in the chin, knocking him out cold. She watched him slump into unconsciousness amidst the packs of flour, sugar, and other dry supplies.

There seemed to be no rhyme or reason to Askana's actions, but that was the least of her concerns. The Queen of Morevi was now in the keeping of the Sea Wolf.

CHAPTER SIX

Second Chance

To describe her bed as "comfortable" would have been a gross understatement. It was luxurious. The mattress was surely down, cradled in a four-posted frame of dark, lustrous wood built soundly into the wall. A mound of cushions surmounted the shimmering satin sheets and the coverlet was of swan's-down, silver edged with white fur. This was a bed proper for a Queen.

All the more strange that it belonged to a man.

She could not sleep. Her skin shone with a faint sheen of sweat that made the light robes stick to her. She was not used to sleeping in outer robes, but tonight she did not think it prudent to place comfort before safety. The harsh, rapid breathing from the other side of the cabin would not let her forget the man who now slept fitfully in a suspended hammock. Ordinarily she would not have cared to spare his "sensibilities", but she was not about to tease a man half-crazed by the blood of the Kir'shia.

Rafe spent two hours pounding the ceiling and walls, crying out that he could *feel* the ship drifting off course. She would never claim to understand or decipher the mathematical symbols and numbers jotted on the assorted pieces of parchment scattered across his great desk. Yet she knew enough of nautical matters to know that no ship could go seriously off course within two minutes of sailing. Still, at the top of his voice, he insisted on a course correction. It reached a point where Rafe was priming pistols, intending to shoot those in charge of the ship's whip staff. The Moor coaxed Rafe back into his cabin, but not before the Captain threatened him with an unsteady pistol, accusing the bewildered officer of mutiny. Askana had managed to make him drink some wine, trying to reason with him in his fever-induced state.

"Come, you must rest," she had said to him, watching him warily as the poison warred with the man.

"Do not lie to me," Rafe had laughed. *"I know my days are numbered now thanks to my ineptitude in not seeing Kergagi in time. I must do all I can before answering to St. Peter and the All-Mighty in Heaven."*

"These men can wait for one more night, privateer." She had managed to lead him back to the hammock, *"Lie down, just for a moment."*

Now, thankfully, he slept.

She lay staring up at the canopy, cursing the luck that had given Rafe a taste of the Kir'shia. Though she bitterly resented it, this had happened to him because he was in her employment and therefore, her responsibility. In this moment he was not so different from the Sisters who would charge with her into battle. Under her command and answering to her call, she cared for them all. Now the privateer had fallen under her care. It was not as if the plan could not continue without him, but he had served her well, and so far, loyally.

Askana was the Mistress of Poisons. No one was more skilled at this art than she. But this one poison was beyond her skill to counter. He had already suffered bouts of cold and raging fever. She sat by him during the evening, gently wiping his face with a wet cloth to ease his fits. First Queen of Morevi. High Priestess of Nadinath. Nursemaid for sick pirates! The sight would have made the Palace Guard, rival courtiers, and sworn enemies all laugh their heads off. Yet in some ways she was the ideal nurse. Her hands were strong yet tender as she combed back the thick blonde hair plastered to his forehead. She fed him wine with her own sleeping draught mixed into it.

Askana could not help but wonder if she was, in fact, mellowing with age.

Jermal had been her first sign of weakness. She knew she had been desperate, on the brink of some inner darkness, hollow and empty, when she had gone off to seek Lubria at The Barrier Reef. She had been alone, truly alone, despite all the young women she had taken under her wing. Despite her guards. Despite the young Min-Lu. In the ship's darkness she admitted to herself that she had used them all selfishly, searching for a Lubria in each and every one of them. She believed in the existence of soulmates for every person as did all the Daughters of the Goddess. Those who found theirs often took them as blood-sisters. She had not dared to perform the ceremony with Lubria for fear of censure, and not a day passed that she had regretted it.

She had, in a moment of weakness, thought that Jermal might have been another of her soulmates. Their meeting was too significant to have been the workings of chance. She was sorely mistaken. That mistake had seen her boxed into taking him as Consort instead of King. A situation she would not have chosen, but which did serve to warm lonely nights. As Kalea and a few Noble Ladies had clucked at her, "A woman needs a warm bed and a lover's arms sometimes." She had not the heart to tell them that she neither kept nor desired another lover in the true sense of the word, since Telmrant. She knew Jermal was utterly devoted to her, but it was nothing like the passion she had known once so briefly.

It was an example of life's irony that her only true lover had not been mortal, but Elven. He had shown her that love was not war under another name, but something glowing, joyful and precious. He gave her support and security without asking for anything in return. That was truly a rare gift. With him, she began to think that perhaps love was a fragment of the Divine. Then he perished at the hand of an Eyriener assassin. He who would have lived immortal through the ages had it not been for his association with her. No one would have dreamt of harming an elf, but for the fact that they knew him for her weak point.

She deserved the name of Black Widow better than anyone could imagine.

Askana had a choice with this privateer. She could save him, but not by herself. She would need *her* help and she knew the price would be heavy. Was he was worth such a price? He was not dear to her. *It was merely a matter of time before you faced the wrath of Nadinath*, Askana thought. Her imagination pictured him standing before the Goddess to pay for his deeds against the Sisterhood. No doubt there were many. He made no pretence that he enjoyed the company of women. She would be naïve to believe the luxurious bed was for his benefit alone. Askana could also see him standing before Nadinath with his chin lifted slightly and that defiant smile she found so irritating. *Would you show this man mercy, Goddess of the Night?*

He is a man, responded the voice of Nadinath in a chorus of three that thought as one in this waking dream. *Perhaps one of the more reprehensible of his kind. A man who would gladly enjoy the gifts of your flesh as Lord Norisht did at one time. Strike him down in the name of the Sisterhood to avenge those lives he took and restore the honour he robbed from so many.*

Her eyes drifted to the table of navigation charts. The twin moons of Naruihm cast their light through the windowpanes, creating a second grid of shadow across the large, aged chart covering the others. It would be so easy for her. Use the amulet to return to Morevi with the chart of The Rift. She could take her own ships to the world across it and demand an audience with King Henry the VIII by dint of royal blood. If he refused her, there might be many other lands, many other potential allies to be bought with silks, perfumes, and tea. Everything in her told her she should not leave Elunear behind, but she knew that the Guard herself would have insisted on it. The girl would lay down her life for Queen and Realm. The pirate would fall into a sleep that would eventually lead to death.

She slipped out of the bed and approached the hammock on stealthy feet. In sleep, he looked innocent, so trusting of her. She knew Elunear would look the same. It was a hard thing to live up to other people's expectations. She must be all-wise, all knowing, all powerful. Mistakes and privacy were not allowed.

She made her choice, and was surprised by the relief it brought her.

Askana fumbled around the dark cabin, moving as silently as the infernal rocking of the ship would allow. She discovered her gauntlet and placed it beside the shirai that lay across the bed. She quickly checked the small haversack. She had with her a sharpening stone for her shirai blade and an assortment of small bottles and pouches of herbs used for mixing either poisons or remedies. There was also a small leather wallet that kept the darts for her gauntlet. She opened it to find only two remaining. Elunear had more in her supplies. If she awakened her and faced questions, she would never leave the ship alone. She loaded the two darts into the gauntlet and hoped they would not be needed.

It then dawned on her that she had no proper clothes here. Biting her lip in frustration, she remembered all her clothes were also with Elunear. Then, by great luck, the moonlight struck a mirror that briefly illuminated a carved wardrobe in which she found shirts, coats, and breeches.

Of course, they were his clothes.

As I intend to save your life, privateer, you should not mind. She thought with a crooked smile, *Even if I do take the very shirt off your back.*

She had her own deerskin boots, better suited for their travel than the traditional slippers worn in court. His shirt reached down to her knees and his breeches, snug on him, hung loose and long on her. She wrapped one of his belts around her waist twice, cinching the shirt and breeches about her waist, then tucked the breeches' cuffs inside her own boots. Slipping the gauntlet over the folded-back shirt cuff and taking up the shirai, she closed her eyes and said a quick prayer to Nadinath.

When she opened her eyes, the moonlight caught her reflection. It was sight that would have made her laugh in any other situation. She was The Pirate-Queen of Morevi. What she found startling above all was how the Captain's ensemble actually suited her.

Askana paused by his hammock as she lightly touched the leather strip of the talisman. He was snoring lightly. He would have another day or two remaining and then nothing would awaken him. "You had better be worth it, privateer," she whispered.

She gripped the talisman, and the void opened, sucking her in. The dizziness and disorientation came again. She felt the sensation of crumbling away, sifted like sand between open fingers, and spread as a puff of dust in a breeze, meshing into a whirlwind of time and space that was the portal.

Askana stepped into a dark grove illuminated by an eerie, greenish light, a sign of the magic that thrived along with lush plant life and nightbird song in the Tangled Southern Wood. This area of forest and jungle south of Anderis had been declared "off limits" by the Fellowship of the Jewels, even though it was part of her kingdom. The faint smell of rotting leaf mould came to her, not overly unpleasant, but strange and faintly spicy, unlike the smells of the jungle west of Songkusai. The trees were huge in width, gnarled and twisted into strange shapes. Their huge roots intertwined along the ground. Clumps of Old-man's Beard draped the branches and swayed ghostlike in the wind. The glittering dust that existed only in the Southern Wood shimmered in the coloured light almost as if someone had thrown a sparkling powder in the air. There was an ethereal beauty here.

There was also danger, more danger than any jungle could devise for unwary feet.

She grasped her shirai in a loose fist, not clenching her fingers, but in a strong, flexible hold that would allow her to spin the staff and strike with deadly accuracy in a moment. Askana had never come here without her armour before. She felt exposed and unprotected in the loose shirt and breeches, and soft, supple leather boots encasing her legs. Since she was here, no use in worrying or waiting.

She set off at a steady pace, but the coils of the Southern Wood taxed her abilities. Small creatures and birds abounded in the sorcery-touched forest. Its trees tightly wound in their branches, roots, and stems around each other and any rock, stump, or growth from the earth in their path. She vaulted over gnarled roots piled waist high, sometimes only to splash into pools of standing water. Brambles scratched her and tore the fine linen shirt, snagging on the heavy coils of her hair twisted into a knot at the base of her neck. Gold specks clung to her sweat-dampened skin, the dust itself making it difficult to judge distance and perspective clearly.

She pushed through this deceptively serene forest for perhaps two or three miles before hearing the sounds of feet keeping pace with her. She slowed, coming to a stop at a leviathan of the Southern Wood, an enormous tree spanning centuries upon centuries of age, its roots creating a great wall behind her. The sound of her unseen companions also came to a halt, and then she saw them appear over the rise before her. Hulking, scaly-skinned creatures whose yellow eyes were the brightest quality about them. She knew these hideous beasts as the *Balesskis*, the eyes of a pack of twelve glowing in the dimness occasionally broken by the flash of fang and claw.

At least it was not one of the ravenous, blindly horrifying *Wyrms* this time.

She slid into a crouch, shirai spinning in her hand allowing it to fall neatly across both palms, its deadly edge turned outwards. The light reflected off the curved blade, and the pack snarled. Moments passed slowly as she watched them and they watched her, both Queen and beasts taking careful account of each other. Askana knew they were trying to circle her, but the huge tree at her back kept them from effectively doing so.

The first one sprang, jaws agape and forearms outstretched. The butt of the shirai slammed into its muzzle, and a flick of her wrist sent the blade up to cut deeply into the short, corded neck. Dark blood spurted as the creature gurgled, flailing uselessly, its throat slashed by the razor-fine edge. She twisted the blade, ending its cries abruptly. Planting her foot in its chest, Askana pushed the dead hulk off her blade and into the middle of the clearing.

It was all over in a matter of seconds.

There were no howls of rage from the others. Rather their movements grew more wary. The second one, a larger individual with a row of paler green spines down its muscled back charged in, avoiding a swipe of her blade. Clawed feet kicked up loose soil as it jumped backward then again at her. It came so close that she felt its fetid breath in her face. Its weight jarred her arms right up to the shoulders as she held it off with the shaft of the shirai. Askana quickly loosed her two darts into the beast's belly. The creature yelped quickly as the small projectiles buried themselves in flesh. Her leg came up, and she kicked the weakened creature away. As the second attacker stumbled back, the poison beginning to course through its blood, making its four legs unsteady. A third leapt for her. The Queen stepped aside and dropped to one knee, bringing the blade around in a great arc and viciously gutting the creature as it soared past her. The predator landed clumsily. Its limbs twitched and jerked as its entrails slipped past the cut she made along its stomach. She returned to her feet as the poisoned beast dropped where it stood.

Three down, and Askana could feel herself tire.

Movement in the undergrowth. Yellow eyes staring from mist. Three pairs like glowing moons. Her skin crawled as she gripped the shirai, blinking the gold dust and sweat free of her eyes. And then they attacked—three of them—springing out of the shadows with sudden roars that shattered the silence. She ducked a blow from a clawed paw and lashed out with a kick, feeling her foot slam into slabs of muscle while simultaneously cracking another across the face with the shirai shaft. They retreated a little, careful of the blade spinning in her hands.

Askana then stopped the weapon before her, the hard realisation striking her as hard as their attacks. These "beasts" were drawing it out, trying to wear her down. Her shirt clung damply to her back, her mind reeling in alarm. She had once watched a pack of these beast-hounds bait a cornered stag. They hemmed it in, dancing and snapping, even taking blows from its sharp hooves and horns, as others slunk silently through the bush behind, waiting to rush in and sink their teeth into their surprised quarry's throat.

In the corner of her eye, a large form disappeared into the upper branches of a great thorn nearby. Slowly the three advanced on her, long tongues licking their snouts, their legs moving slowly only to pause in mid-step as she would cut the air between them with her shirai.

The leaves above her rustled. Something was moving swiftly down to her, low enough to strike out with its claws.

Suddenly, the whole tree shook with the sounds of a scuffle and leaves rained down, startling the balesski. The thick branches shuddered with the struggles of her would-be attackers, then came the sound of a whip-crack soon followed by a yelp of pain and fear. The scent of singed flesh filled the air as the pack quickly sprinted back to the safety of the mists, their retreating howl echoing throughout the grove.

"And be off with thee, thou errant children of the Wood! Get thee back to thy own lairs and learn that those who walk to Grainne's doors are not for prey."

Askana turned to the direction of the voice, releasing a growl of her own as she struggled to keep her shirai steady. Her gasps for breath subsided as a girl swung down out of the tree, holding a willow switch in her hand. The Queen's heart rose in her throat. The child looked no older than five. She was tall and almost too thin for her height. Pale, silvery white hair fell about her triangular face as black eyes looked her over with a boldness few had ever been able to evince.

"Why art thou afraid, stranger? Dost thou not know that Grainne watches over those who come hither seeking her? We did know the very moment of thy arrival." The graceful words sounded very odd spoken in her high, childish treble, and she spoke with all the frankness that only curiosity and spirit could give as she turned to lead the way. "Come, I am to be thy guide from here."

Askana's voice sounded like the croak of a frog to herself. "What is your name? Who are you?"

"I am named Lissellone. Grainne cares for me." was her childish answer. "Set thy worries of Old Ugly and his family aside. I merely gave him a lash that will vex his simple thoughts for some time." The child gave an innocent giggle, "Judge not Old Ugly in haste. His children must needs eat, and humans be simple prey." Delivered in her silvery voice, the words and the mindset behind them were disturbing in their truth.

"I...I have not been to see Grainne in a long time."

"All the more reason why thou shouldst hasten thy steps! Come!"

The girl moved with the grace of a deer, easily sliding through the tangle of the Southern Wood. Strong as she was from the demands of her training, Askana found it hard to keep up.

From a distance, it looked like a simple hovel surrounded by trees and thicket, a warm light shining from its doorway and windows. A closer inspection revealed the house was built into a cave. Its front was actually woven willow walls daubed with clay and its thatched roof belied the actual size of the dwelling. Flowers bloomed in colourful profusion, not a tended garden but great beauty growing wild around this hut of rock and earth.

Grainne, the Caillech of the Southern Wood, was indeed waiting for them. Being a grouchy old woman, she did not like waiting. Stooped and wrinkled as she was, she was still clearly a strong-willed soul who preferred to be obeyed. Her dignity, which utterly refused to bow itself to any, was enough to make her chastisement of a queen seem appropriate.

"Askana, my girl, it has been almost five years and still you haven't learned how to be punctual! I have better things to do than wait on you." She drew her pipe out of her mouth, frowning prodigiously with bristling brows, and snapped, "Get inside, Queen of Morevi, before I take it into my head to spank you! Something someone should have done to you long ago."

Askana gave her a half-smile. "How is it every time I come here I fully set my mind on berating you for my travails in your forest, and yet the minute that we meet, I find myself the chastened child?"

The light words were a sham front. Though the Caillech was a friend of sorts, it was painful to look at her. She unearthed too many bad memories. Some thought Grainne a practitioner of Black Arts. In truth, she had exiled herself deep in the Southern Wood, appalled at what the Fellowship of the Jewels had become over time. She now had little patience for that "sect of necromancers suffering from delusions of godhood" as she described them. As far as Askana knew, the Caillech was the last of those with a true understanding of magic. Grainne had once explained to her, there was no such thing as "dark" or "light" magic. The source was neutral, and only the use which its practitioners put it to was questionable. Remembering the circumstances of that conversation, Askana's jaw tightened as she walked by the old woman. The Caillech noted this, sending a puff of bitter tobacco smoke from her pipe into the Queen's face as she passed.

As Askana entered the hovel, she heard Lissellone asking, "She is a queen?" followed by Grainne snorting, "Like so many other fool girls. Less sense than a chicken. Be off with you, child! You'd stand there prattling all day if I let you."

The steps of the little wooden house creaked as Grainne came up. The door snapped closed behind her. "Do you remember how we first met, Askana Moldarin? You begged me to bring the dead back to life."

Askana closed her eyes tight. The Caillech did not waste time with tact or decency. She wondered what her point was in reminding her of old wounds, as if the child outside was not a reminder enough. "She is beautiful, Grainne."

"Aye, like her parents," Grainne sighed heavily, her voice softening as she looked towards the door. She turned to Askana, staring at her for a moment, and then shook her head in disgust as she hobbled back to a tiny kitchen to set a humble tea tray. "She learns fast, and there is true magic in her. Magic I have not seen in some time. I have no doubt, if she were not in my care, she would have caught the attention of Arathelle long ago. Mark my words, she could bring about some much-needed change in the Fellowship."

"Who taught her the First Tongue?"

"Who do you think?" Grainne huffed as she removed the teapot from the hearth and poured a cup of sharp-scented tea, "I did, of course. It is part of her heritage, after all."

"I never hear you speak it." Askana said as she reached for the cup in Grainne's hand.

"It's like reading, girl." Grainne smiled as she took a seat, the hot tea she poured still in her own hands. She spoke mildly, her concentration divided between continuing her convoluted train of thought, taking the seat opposite of Askana, and calling the cup to her lips while keeping all its contents inside it. An effort at one time not so difficult, but now a grand display considering her years. "Everyone knows how to do it, but not all of us choose to do it." Grainne took a sip of her tea and motioned to the pot with her own cup, "There is enough tea for us both and your arm does not appear broken. Pour yourself some before it goes cold."

Askana took a deep breath, keeping her own tongue still. Grainne had always been contrary. She suspected the woman derived some kind of pleasure from it. She had to be careful not to think too much of it as Grainne could easily sift through her thoughts. She poured herself a cup of the strong tea and spoke sharply, "You let her wander alone in the Tangled Southern Wood, with all those beasts, the Bogs, and the traps out there?"

"My dear girl, I'd think you were beginning to care for the child." Grainne paused before taking another sip, "She is of no concern to you, remember?"

Her teacup and saucer returned to the table just as she had picked it up. It rattled so loudly that the Caillech laughed gruffly, her chuckle grinding in her throat. Had Askana let them strike the table any harder, the chipped cup and mended plate would have shattered.

"You don't trust the magic I teach, Askana? Well, you never had faith in it unless it served your purposes." The tea appeared to soften the grating quality of her speech. Her smile widened as she thought of the child, "We rule the Southern Wood, she and I, but not the way you rule your country. Lissellone could walk blindfolded safely through the Wood, whereas you would need an arsenal of weapons and ten eyes simply to relieve yourself during a lengthy session of Council." Grainne leaned forward, her tone suddenly mocking, "And as you heard, I have chosen an Elven name for the girl.

Now tell me, why did you come here? It was not to visit me, I know." The witch set her teacup and saucer next to the still brewing pot, the steam emitting from its spout curving into the air in a serpentine fashion only to disappear into the dark corners of the room. "And it certainly was not to check on Lissellone."

Askana was silent.

"What is it, girl? Speak up!" Grainne reached for Askana's saucer and cup, which were surrendered without effort. "You want my help, don't you?"

She bit her lip. "Yes."

Grainne shook her head, the ill-kept, thinning white hair waving slightly as she gave another gruff, grinding laugh from her throat. "Be careful. The day may come when what I ask from you will not be what you wish to give."

"I have no choice. He—"

"It's a man again?" Grainne slapped her knee and cackled like a hen that had just laid an egg. "For a Black Widow, you are a sorry sight. Who is he? Another elf? A poor soul desiring his death before his time? Tell me of this new love."

"I do not love him!" she flared, unable to ignore the very sharp thrust of Grainne's references. "You know my love lies in the grave that I dug with my own hands, and you know well enough of my last lesson. I seek no more brothers." She paused for a moment, gathering her self-control before continuing. "This is different. Very different. This man is my instrument in unearthing a conspiracy against the New Regime. With this man, I have dealt my own blow by eliminating a nest of Eyriener snakes. Through him, I may gain aid from beyond The Rift, and return with forces needed to keep the throne. Without him, this plan will come to nothing."

"From beyond The Rift, is he?" Grainne looked up at her with keen eyes. "Why seek such dangerous company? If it is allies you need, there are other nations within your reach. The people of Lydonnesse, perhaps, or even those of the Cynerian Isles."

"You know well enough that they will not be an accomplice in war if it comes to that. They fear the Fellowship and well they should since Andoulin is well within reach of their borders."

"So you say, girl, but make sure you don't make excuses to yourself. You know I don't take an interest in politics, particularly between countries. What does he need?"

"His life," she said grimly. "He was poisoned with Kir'shia blood."

Grainne went still. "I thought you outlawed Kir'shia."

"So did I."

Both were silent as the Caillech sat back in her chair as she lit her pipe's leaf. Was she running through her mind the different spells she had to counteract the poison? Was she considering the cost of such a remedy to the Queen? Askana waited, her hands in tight fists as she waited on Grainne's word.

"I cannot help you this time, Askana Moldarin," she said suddenly, taking a long drag from her pipe. "You will simply have to find other allies for this crusade of yours."

"Why?" The vehemence of the question startled even the Caillech. "I have seen you bring souls back from Death's door, heal mortal wounds, command the elements— why not this small thing? He was only touched by a little of it."

Grainne rose, the sounds of her bones rising with the creaks of the chair's bark and wood yielding its occupant. "You know as well as I do that the only difference the amount makes is in how long it takes him to die. I cannot help you."

She turned to go, but a hand caught her sleeve, fingers clenching in the folds of brown wool. The Caillech of the Southern Wood looked at the hand, then at the woman through her pale eyes.

"You know you can. I can't see why you won't. I've always returned the many favours you did me." There was desperation in the Queen's eyes as she spoke, her grasp on the Caillech's dirty sleeve tightening with each word. "I gave you my light to brighten your days so don't treat me as you would the petitioners you selfishly scorn though it is well within your power to help them! I need that man alive and I can't do it on my own, you know that!"

"What you need—" Grainne's voice never rose above a gentle tone, but clearly it would be Askana's only warning. "—is to remember your place. Now release me." Askana's trembling hand let go of the thick sleeve as she returned to her seat. Grainne looked hard at the Queen for a very long time without saying anything. Then she tipped back her head and said, "It's like that, is it? Well then, there may be a way to save this man of yours, but it will test your boundaries, Queen of Morevi. Pain is the least of it."

Her own fingers trembled as the last drops fell into the clay bottle and she sealed its neck with a cork. Although the young woman crumpled at her feet had long since subsided into whimpering, her screams still seemed to echo in the room. They both ached with tiredness, but at last the task was done.

Askana loathed tampering with magic. It bordered on the unholy, but she knew it was her only option in this matter.

During the ritual, through the chinks where moss and clay had been carefully scraped out of the willow matting, the child kept watch. Her dark eyes had watched the Caillech collect the blood and tears of the woman who was a queen. She had seen many come into the forest to ask for help from the Caillech. Usually they were turned away, but she had sensed instinctively that this one would receive Grainne's help. The Caillech, in the midst of her chanting, had given the windowpane a rap with her knotted cane as a reminder of the scolding she would give her young ward if her chores were not finished. What the young elf-girl did not know was that Grainne wanted to spare her the sight. The spell she was performing was not for Lissellone's eyes, and hopefully would never be. Elven magic was clean. Pure. It caused no pain, and Grainne wanted that for the little girl whom she had grown to cherish.

Feeling her age in light of both the mental and physical demands of the spell, the Caillech stooped and laid a hand on Askana's sweat-soaked shoulder. "Listen, child. The potion is ready. I have drained a great deal of your blood as it is essential for this remedy. He must drink every drop of this potion." The old woman held up a cautionary finger as she spoke, "The core of it is this—by drinking your blood, he shall be *linked* to you. You shall feel one another's pain. In battle, every blow against him shall count against you as well. The effect may last a few months, a few years, perhaps forever." Grainne could not help but give Askana a wry smile as she told her, "I cannot tell. This meddling with the Fates is very unpredictable. There is a benefit. You both will share immortality, of a sort. One of you cannot die without the other. In order to strike you down, your enemies must strike fatal blows against the both of you in the same place at the same time. And be forewarned—another touch of Kir'shia blood on either one of you, and you both suffer the same fate. Only then, no remedy will cure you."

"And so this the price you ask of me," Askana winced as she laboured into the privateer's shirt, the fabric sticking to her sweat-soaked skin, "To share a bond with the privateer? You must be experiencing a moment of kindness, Grainne, to ask so little."

With the vial firm in her grasp, Askana touched the amulet to open the void. She took a step to the portal, stopping for a moment and turning to Grainne as if she was going to thank her. She saw nothing in the crone's cold, grey eyes. Askana remained silent as she returned to the privateer's ship.

The Caillech took several puffs from the pipe as she watched the void wink out of existence. The girl's arrogance yearned for humbling. All this for a kingdom, a piece of earth occupied by trees, buildings, and mighty stone walls surrounding it all. There was more to life, and far more to her potential in this life than being a queen. She simply needed to choose. A choice had already been made for the poor man, whoever he was. Grainne knew that. The potion had already been employed before the cork was placed in the vial's mouth.

She snorted and looked for her jar of tobacco to replenish her pipe. Askana's final words to her were still ringing in her ears. Perhaps the humbling that Askana Moldarin needed was now at hand.

"Privateer, wake up."

Rafe felt a hand shaking his shoulder, pulling him out of fevered dreams of excitement that, oddly enough, he could not remember. He had been struggling to the surface of sleep. His instincts warned him of danger. He vaguely recalled eyes watching him. *Two* sets of eyes. One of them was the Queen's. There was something in the way she looked at him, as if evaluating his worth. It was the other pair of eyes that, even in his fever-dream, caused the hair on the back of his neck to stand upright. Brilliant green, like emeralds. He remembered a sound, a soft rumbling that had come with the unsettling stare. The eyes looked him over from head to foot and Rafe could have sworn he had felt something sharp touch his cheek.

Such bizarre dreams.

He now opened his eyes to the grey light of a morning not yet dawned, feeling the ache in his shoulders from a night in the hammock. His first sight of the new day was the First Queen of Morevi leaning over him as she had the night before, only this time looking pale and unsteady.

Stretching, the Pirate Captain yawned, "Why, it is not even dawn yet!" The yawn stopped midway. "Why are you wearing my clothes?"

"Explanations later." She held out a small, clay vial to him. "Drink this."

Without question, as he was still waking up from his nightmare-riddled slumber, Rafe placed the bottle to his lips and tipped his head back. His eyes went wide as the taste of what he drank suddenly slapped him awake. He was about to spit the medicine out when Askana's hand slapped over his mouth, her other hand braced against the back of his head.

"Swallow," she said evenly.

Rafe could not tell if it was a Royal Decree or a warning, but left with very little choice he followed the Queen's bidding. Across both realms, Rafe had sampled many types of drink. Scotch of the Northern Highlands. Wines of Portugal, Italy, and Morevi. And, of course, ale from all parts of England, the Germanies, Eyrie, and Lydonnesse.

Nothing he had ever sampled in his travels was as foul or vile as the elixir that burned its way down his throat, leaving a foul aftertaste on his tongue.

"Good God, Your Majesty, are you trying to kill me?!" Rafe snapped as he offered the vial back to Askana.

"The bad taste will not linger." Askana's eyes narrowed, "Finish it!"

"Indeed, Your Grace, you speak easily for one who does not drink this swill!" With a deep exhale, Rafe took the remaining dose of remedy, but not without a melodramatic groan as he forced it down. "There, I have taken my medicine, mum. Now may I go out and play with the other pirates?"

"Believe me, privateer, your 'sacrifice' in drinking the potion is less than it cost to make it," she replied curtly, the rigors in making the remedy beginning to creep over her. "I know what went into this potion and it is what you need for your fever."

"Bullocks!" Rafe forced himself out of the hammock, his body still weak from the Kir'shia as well as Askana's drugged wine that had helped him sleep. "The poison has no remedy. You yourself told me this. Now I awaken to find you in my clothes with a cure speedily to hand?" Rafe fought to keep himself steady as he snapped, "I will not tolerate witchcraft of any kind aboard my ship!"

Askana's already frayed temper slipped a notch. "You ungrateful bastard! The Ancient Art might very well be the only thing to save your life!" Her voice was beginning to rise in volume when she felt weakness steal through her. "The potion is…" Her voice faded, "The potion…"

The Queen's eyes seemed to glaze over for a moment and then roll back into her head. The travel across the void coupled with the battle in the Southern Wood and the spell itself had completely drained her, and now the effects took hold. Rafe was in no condition to support her, but he summoned enough strength to catch Askana in his arms before she could hit the floor. It was when he pulled his hands away from her, seeing them covered in blood, that he understood Askana's pallid look. He ripped open the back of the shirt she wore, and a curse caught deep in his throat at what he saw. The cuts were clean and precise, a row of chevrons cut all the way down her back.

He did the only thing he could do. *"Elunear!!!"* Rafe cried at the top of his lungs, *"The Queen is hurt!"*

The girl nearly kicked the door off its hinges, her shirai in hand as her eyes searched the room. It hit the floor with a dull thud when she saw Rafe struggling to lift Askana.

"My Queen!" Elunear cried, taking her into her arms and placing her in the centre of the luxurious bed, "Her skin is cold." Her hands pulled away from Askana, covered in blood. "What have you—"

"Elunear, please listen to me, I need your help." Rafe blinked his eyes tightly. Without warning, the Kir'shia fever had returned, only this time warring with the potion that the Caillech had composed for him. "Have Nassir fetch a tankard of boiling water, and then in the cabinets above my liquor store you will find a small collection of vials and jars. Bring them all to me. Hurry!"

Elunear bolted for the main deck, her voice calling out for Nassir.

Following Rafe's instructions, select herbs were combined with a mix of tea kept in the Captain's Quarters. Askana turned her face away from the sharp wood scent rising from the mug, but Elunear—quite forgetting her reverence for the Queen—took Askana's face into her free hand and pressed against her cheeks, forcing her mouth open. Nassir held Askana steady as she tried to fight against swallowing the bitter mix. Even in her weakened state, the Moor found it difficult to restrain her. Rafe watched carefully as she reluctantly swallowed a good portion of the tea. He knew that soon the tranquillising herbs would soothe her to sleep.

"She will rest now." Even Rafe was alarmed by how slurred his speech had become. Whatever mix Askana had given him was having a similar effect as his tea. "This is what she needs."

Elunear, her eyes never leaving her Queen, asked nervously, "What was that vile mix you had us force on her?"

"It's a 'black powder remedy'. A mix of Earl Grey, Sage, Chamomile, and Cinnamon. Along with rose petals and a few secret ingredients that I keep for my own. It's a cure-all for fatigue and severe blood loss, which Her Grace is suffering." He felt absurdly sleepy, considering he had just woke up. He noticed the fever he was under now seemed to be breaking. "I have no clue how this happened to her," he protested in a slur.

"My Captain, you need rest as well." Nassir spoke softly. "You rest. Mister Bayliss and I will keep the ship steady."

The First Mate walked his Captain over to the hammock, and in a gesture that Elunear found curiously graceful, pressed his hand over Rafe's heart. "My Captain, before you sleep you must know this. Supplies are disappearing. I think we have a wanderer in our midst."

"Elunear is capable..." Rafe gave Nassir's hand a gentle pat of assurance, "...but I trust your instincts, my friend. If you wish to post another watch, do so." Rafe opened his eyes, fighting the urge to sleep so that he could give one last order. "So take this ship across The Rift safely, Mister Nassir, or I shall have you hanging by the yardarm."

"Yes, my Captain." Nassir smiled.

The door closed behind them. Rafe's eyes turned drowsily to the bay windows of his quarters. The soft light of morning began to replace the dark of early dawn aboard the *Defiant*, streaks of blue creeping across the black canvas of night in the sky above. He knew when he awakened they would be close to home. Askana was deep in a relaxed sleep, something she had needed for quite a time. Rafe thought to himself that he had never seen the Queen look more radiant.

"Indeed, Your Grace," Rafe thought aloud as he slipped away, "we are the lucky ones."

CHAPTER SEVEN

Merely the Beginning

Askana stretched lazily within the comforts of the satins, forgetting for a moment her whereabouts. Then she awoke with a start. The sudden movement aggravated the wounds along her back, causing her to wince with a hiss. She recalled returning from the Southern Wood, arguing with the pirate, and then it was nothing more than the darkness of a deep sleep. *What is this horrific taste in my mouth?* she asked herself, slipping out of the enormous bed. Her eyes quickly went to the empty hammock that swayed gently with the rocking of the vessel. Grey moonlight and the bed's white linens revealed the blood from her wounds. She had been laid to rest in haste. Askana removed the now-ruined shirt from her skin, replacing it with one of her own silk garments that conveniently waited by the bed. Elunear's touch. Her travel robe was not enough to remove the biting chill of the Captain's Quarters. Slipping into a heavier sleeved doublet belonging, no doubt, to the Captain, Askana cast a glance outside the Quarter's bay window to see if any recognisable landmarks were in sight. Surrounded only by the dark surface of the open ocean and a canvas of pinpoint lights, Askana made her way to the main deck. She opened the door to find Elunear dutifully standing guard. The young warrior smiled. Her apparent worry allayed at the sight of her Queen. She immediately returned to Askana's side only to be relieved for the evening.

Above her were countless stars as she had seen in her realm on crisp, cool evenings when skies were clear of clouds. However she could not find the constellations of Nadinath, the Shirai, or Reya the Huntress, an easy constellation to find for the three stars that created her belt. She then noticed the Northern Star that was a constant in her sky was not where it was supposed to be. This was not her sky. She was across The Rift and, presumably, in Captain Rafton's realm.

The solitary moonlight gave the ship a dreamlike quality as it created shadows stretching across its entire length. Men walked along the decks, smoking pipes that sent puffs of sweet tobacco briefly into the night air. Laughter came from those playing cards and dice. Behind this light din of activity, Askana could hear the *Defiant* itself slicing through the black waters surrounding its hull. Over all this came the song from a tiny flute, a tune that played from the heart and soul. Full of wonder. A hint of sorrow. The song was as haunting as it was beautiful. Askana followed the tin whistle ballad to the ship's aftercastle, overlooking the main deck.

The musician was Rafe Rafton, performing the simple melody to an audience of stars. He appeared merely a cut-out against the night. She crept up behind him silently, listening to him play. The notes would rise then fall in a graceful cascade, mimicking the waves that caressed the *Defiant*. The song touched in her images of wide-eyed innocence and tales of adventures in far-off lands. Askana could feel her skin tingle lightly, not from the chill but in response to this long-forgotten sense of wonderment. *Behind these notes is the true story of Rafe Rafton*, she thought musingly.

"Well played, privateer," Askana said as Rafe concluded his song. "You did not strike me as a patron of the arts."

"There are many sides to me, Your Grace," Rafe smiled, still looking over the star-filled horizon, "that remain uncharted to you."

"Perhaps that is for the better, privateer. I do not believe in allowing allies or enemies to know all aspects of my soul." The Queen pulled the opening of the doublet tighter to fend off the chill. "There are some things best kept hidden."

Rafe nodded, "So in that, I suppose we share something in common. A man of my occupation must also choose his confidants carefully. And when we find ourselves absent of a confidant, we must revel in isolation." He sighed heavily, his breath forming faintly beyond his lips, "I find music provides a peaceful alternative to those lonely times."

Askana gave her head a slight tilt, letting her jet-black hair slip across the shoulder of his doublet. She found him to be a curious fascination. Her reports had painted him out to be nothing more than a common criminal, common in his actions anyway. His tactics, strategies, and uncanny talents to elude her assassins were respectable. Still, he was nothing more than a pirate from some unknown realm. But musician? No, that was something she did not expect. Perhaps indulging curiosity would not cost her greatly at this time, seeing as there was nowhere else to go on this vessel. "Have you been a pirate all your life?"

Rafe took in a deep breath of the sea air and turned to the Queen, looking almost ghostly in the pale moonlight. "In my heart, all my life. But I took to the oceans a few years ago. The title of 'Captain' and this ship were gifts of gratitude from His Majesty upon returning to England after visiting your realm. No easy feat, I assure you. The Hand of God, and perhaps a bit of luck, brought us to The Barrier Reef. And that same bit of luck provided us a nautical chart that would bring us safely across realms. It did not take long to build a reputation for the *Defiant*. And my own, I suppose. Rafe Rafton, the Sea Wolf." He shook his head in spite of himself. "Sometimes being a kasam-de-nim is not everything as one would hope. The stories cannot even begin to describe me properly! Eyes as blue as the sea. No, green as emeralds. Oh, no— dark as those of Death itself! Most difficult being a pirate with hazel eyes."

Askana could not help but surrender a soft laugh of her own. "But you have not always been a pirate?"

"No, Your Grace," Rafe smiled, "I spent most of my life in London alongside my sister Serena, and my mother."

"And your father?"

"I know very little of him, apart from that he was a visiting nobleman from the Spanish Court, hence my name Rafael. My mother was a courtesan."

His father of noble blood and his mother a courtesan? This explained much in his manners and profession, refined and of a higher class but still hard and rough around the edges as those of a commoner. Askana nodded, her tone losing a hint of its warmth. "I see."

"Yes, my mother was quite the vision, and her talents gave her a reputation with good King Henry's Court. That reputation was enough to grant Serena and I some privileges without the status." He watched the Queen's posture and expression change before him, returning to that original pomp and loftiness when they first met at The Barrier Reef. "There is nothing to gain in pretending my mother is something she is not nor in rejecting her for a choice. She did what she had to do in order to provide for us. She raised us and loved us, and this was all Serena and I needed. When she died, there was only Serena and myself. It was our mother's love that taught us the importance of family. And survival."

"Your sister—is she a courtesan as well?"

"No, she is not," he replied quickly, then his voice softened once more. "Serena and I realised that together we could accomplish anything. We used our God-given talents—beauty, intelligence, intellect, and cunning—to befriend ourselves with higher classes of society. We lived quite well off the generosity of others."

Askana's tone continued to sharpen as he opened up to her, "And does your sister continue to live this lifestyle of toying with the confidences of strangers?"

So much for kindness from the Crown, Rafe thought. He was silent for a time, carefully selecting his answer to the Queen's outward disdain toward him and his family. Finally, he answered with a voice dripping of civility. "Serena lives comfortably in a small town called Plymouth in the shire of Devon. She is managing quite well for herself as a minor noble lady. How she governs her own counsels is her own business. Not subject to my opinions. Or yours."

Vulnerability. He did not care for his class standing holding him under scrutiny. He liked it even less when his family stood judgement. Perhaps an advantage to exploit later. "London?" the Queen asked quickly in order to change subjects. "A city in this place called England?"

"Not merely a city, but *the* city. A truly beautiful place of culture, romance, and pageantry. My home. It was there I learned the art of the rapier. London being a centre of culture, I met ladies from all over the world." His voice grew distant as he revelled in the memories of his realm. "So many beautiful ladies."

Askana's eyebrow raised slightly at the pride in his promiscuity, "Did you love any of these beautiful ladies?"

"Oh, yes, Your Grace." Rafe smiled wickedly, "Repeatedly."

She watched him for a moment. His demeanour was now quite contrary to the song he had played on the tin whistle. "I pity you, privateer."

"Pity me, Your Grace?"

"To have never been in love," Askana stated.

For a few moments, the only sounds breaking the silence were the groans and creaks of the *Defiant.* Rafe stared upward, studying the familiar constellations guiding them home as Askana continued to stare at him. She could see the truth of it all. He was so alone, both in her realm and his own. And this solitude was his choice. *I do pity you, privateer,* Askana thought, *to not know love.*

"I wanted to thank you, Your Grace," Rafe spoke suddenly, "for risking your own life to save mine."

"What do you mean, privateer?"

"I saw the condition of my lucky shirt. It seems it came in good use for you as well."

"What I did," Askana looked away from Rafe as she stated factually, "I did for the greater good of Morevi. I have invested a great deal in you, privateer. I will not lose you so early in this venture."

Again came the silence.

"Morevi is so fortunate to have a monarch so dedicated to its welfare," nodded the Captain as he slipped the tin whistle into his belt. "I recommend you get more rest, Your Grace. We should be in London by tomorrow morning."

"Very good then," Askana responded, looking past Rafe to the dark horizon where the stars disappeared into the sea. "Tomorrow morning."

Rafe walked past Askana, leaving her to the privacy of the aftercastle. Her hand went to her chest as she suddenly became short of breath. It was a momentary feeling, as if her heart ceased for a moment in reaction to this chill. As she stared into the heavens, she said a quick prayer to Nadinath to watch over Kubi-Sogi. She knew he would seek out the Anjara and together they would stand for her.

The twinge in her chest came again, and she steadied herself against the side of the ship. Perhaps the pirate was correct. Rest was what she needed. She turned to leave and then froze. The boatswain's eyes were fixed on the destination ahead. The crew strolled about the decks stepping in and out of shadow. There was nothing amiss.

But Askana could feel the other set of eyes upon her. She knew this gaze. Somewhere on the *Defiant*, she was there. Watching, waiting.

Askana whispered into the darkness, "Lubria?"

The cold chilled her, the air sharp and clear. She could feel every nerve alive and tingling under the gaze of this unseen being. The question remained unanswered. A sea wind caressed her skin, lifting her hair. Her hand went automatically to her waist, but she was wearing his clothes. No weapon to be had. Then her eye caught movement in the shadows opposite of her, the sound of something skittering across the gangway above the lower decks, only a few men turning to the sound it made but quickly dismissing it as sounds of the ship's hull settling after their Rift-crossing. Askana kept her eyes fixed on the source of the sounds as she moved like a panther stalking in shadow. Now familiar with the movements of the *Defiant*, she slipped stealthily into the ship's cargo hold where the sounds led her. Here the darkness was thick, unrelieved by lanterns. She moved deeper into the shadows, boards creaking gently under her boots.

A sudden rush of movement. Something slammed into Askana, knocking her off-balance. She felt limbs and hands trying to close around her throat, a sharp pain in the back of her neck suddenly. Her attacker could not lock their hands into the chokehold as Askana brought her chin down and stiffened her neck muscles in defence.

The fingers relaxed for a moment, the moment Askana needed. She thrust stiff-fingered hands between her attacker's forearms, breaking the hold on her. She quickly encircled her hands, now tightened into fists, back to her side and thrust forward into her opponent's now-unprotected chest. Her attack merely grazed the shadow as it twisted aside and vanished. Then came a rush of air followed by the anticipated sweep of an arm towards her head. Askana caught the arm and, using the momentum of the swing, threw her opponent amongst the crates. There was no crash to tell her that a body had fallen, only soft thuds against the wooden surface of the *Defiant's* hold.

Askana was hardly surprised at her opponent's agility, for during the brief struggle she had felt its strange skin, warm and silken-soft. Silken-soft as the pelt of a tiger.

"The years of ease have not softened you," purred a familiar voice.

Askana smiled, "You still fight like a demon."

Footsteps resounded on boards above their heads. Shouting broke through their words as the crew converged on the ship's hold. Firelight washed over Askana causing her to blink at the abrupt change of illumination. Nassir stood at the head of a small crowd of men, some carrying torches and lanterns that cast their light across blades of daggers and barrels of pistols. They reached the hold only to recoil as a group at the sight of the creature standing only a few feet from the Morevian Queen.

The snarl began low and throbbing, and rose in cadence till it grated on the ears of everyone present. It had been some time since Askana had heard it. Its savagery reminded her of why Morevians feared it.

"Witchcraft!" came a cry from one pirate. "The Devil himself has put a monster on the ship!"

Nassir held his place within arm's reach of the Queen, his grasp tightening around the hilt of a sabre. "Stand fast, men!"

The creature crouched against crates appeared as a woman. Her skin was unmistakably the black-striped pelt of a tiger. Red-gold hair fell in a cascading mass about a face from which glared two brilliant emerald eyes with golden tongues of flame in their centres. The ferocity in those green eyes never curbed. Her snarl revealed sharp teeth. Wickedly hooked black claws were now fully distended from her fingers and toes, and a long, slender tail lashed from side to side, occasionally striking one of the wooden crates.

"The quality of company you keep, Your Majesty, has deteriorated. Declining to the common criminals? How fast and far you have fallen, First Queen of Morevi."

Another pirate quickly crossed himself as he stammered, "It speaks!"

"Not '*it*', man," the tiger-woman's eyes flashed lightly in the fire's light, her words spat out venomously. "I am no dumb beast."

Askana stepped closer. "Lubria, these men will not harm you if you do likewise."

"I do not trust the mercies of men." There was a faint crunching sound as she flexed her claws, gouging small grooves into the wood of the deck.

"Get away from the beast, Your Grace," Nassir said tautly. With his free hand, he reached quickly for Askana, taking hold of her wrist.

"How dare you lay hands upon the Queen!" she snarled.

Lubria's words were Nassir's only warning. He leapt back in reaction to the sudden blur of her swift attack, but not before black claws slashed across his arm. A pistol discharged, the gunfire sounding like a crack of lightning. Others blindly shot forward into the shadows where Lubria had been. Askana quickly crouched down upon on knee, pressing her back against the nearby crates. The acrid scent of black powder filled the air of the ship's hold as Lubria landed softly on top of cargo, her mocking laughter sending a chill across their skin.

"STOP!" Askana's shouted over random exclamations of the terrified crew.

"I do hope that is not pistol fire I hear in my ship's hold," came a shout from behind the crew. Rafe and Elunear pushed their way through the pirates as he continued his tirade. "For if my men are firing pistols in the same hold where we store black powder..."

His words stopped abruptly at the sight of the creature.

"Lubria!"

It sounded so much like a child's squeal that Rafe looked askance at Elunear as she pushed passed him and the other men to stand at the base of the crates.

"I remember you, little one." Lubria sprang down with ease, powerful muscles rippling under a magnificent striped hide enveloping her entire body. "You've grown since I saw you last."

Elunear embraced her, Lubria towering over her by at least a head. The young girl-warrior stepped back. "No scars," she gasped.

"The Earth between realms is truly blessed." Lubria smiled, her fangs still chilling to behold in such a tender moment. "The scars I earned in serving Her Majesty were mended as I slept in the Mother's body."

"Who is she?" Rafe whispered to Nassir, one hand rubbing his nape.

The Moor, his bleeding arm kept close to his chest, winced as he looked quickly at the wound and then to the creature. "Our hidden passenger from Eyrie?"

"Your Grace," Rafe hissed to Askana, "by the Mass, who is she?"

Askana pretended not to hear him. *Not now, privateer, I must focus on her. I must know if she still carries the pain of our parting.*

Lubria's eyes fell on Elunear's shirai, and with a delightful purr she took the weapon into her hands. The privateers took another step back and spent pistols that had fired earlier were being primed again as Lubria handled the weapon as a seasoned veteran.

"A fine weapon." Lubria caressed the polished shaft, "You are a warrior already, little one? I regret not keeping one of these elegant creations with me." The Fae-woman reminisced as she whirled the weapon about her body, spinning, stabbing, and slashing as she tested its worth.

Since their escape from Morevi, Rafe Rafton had destroyed half a port city, endured a vicious poison, and been fed a cure that tasted worse than Irish whiskey. He thought there would be little remaining in this venture that would surprise him. That was before Askana's cure began to show side effects. Moments before the sounds of pistol fire, he had suddenly been knocked off his feet by nothing, as if the planks of his ship had been yanked from underneath him. His next surprise took form in this spawn of darkness demonstrating basic shirai tactics. Now the woman that he knew possessed all the answers to his questions chose not to acknowledge him. To top this boiling kettle of frustration, his nape itched unbearably. Rafe slowly moved for Askana, believing Lubria was oblivious to him as she was reminiscing with Elunear.

"Of course, I was born with my own weapons, but I find the grace of this one enthralling," Lubria purred, launching suddenly into fluid movement with the weapon. Its blade stopped just under Rafe's chin. A judgement of distance and perception so accurate that the sharp edge merely rested against skin.

A host of *"clicks"* snapped through the cargo hold as every pistol now drew aim on Lubria. Rafe's gaze slowly met her own, her emerald eyes glistening in delight over this false stalemate. She had seen guns before. Even if the privateers shot, the Fae-woman could kill Rafe before any bullet reached her. She gave a gentle purr to the Captain, pressing the blade a fraction more as if daring to cut him.

I am growing far too familiar with Morevian blades against my skin, Rafe thought.

"Let him go, Lubria," spoke Askana as she slowly closed in behind Rafe. "He is the Captain of this ship and working for me."

"Your Majesty, I am no longer under your command. Do you not remember that day you had me break my vows of service before sending me to The Barrier Reef? You told me that I was a free woman, and I should listen to no voice but my own."

"Ah, The Reef," Rafe said suddenly, acknowledging their common bond. He had no way of knowing if she would actually slit his throat or not, and from the look on Askana's face, she was just as uncertain. Nothing to lose in this gamble. "I have been there a few times myself. Good wine, good food. Interesting people, but none as the like of you. Tell me, sweet lass, what do you do there?"

Her eyes narrowed at being called "sweet lass". Lubria looked him up and down in contempt. "I am a hunter for hire. Some of the meat served is what I put on the table."

"Really?" His mind raced for something else to say. "What do you hunt?"

Lubria's head leaned to one side, intrigued by Rafe's question, "Deer, boar, fowl, hare, *humans*." She said with a feral smile, "Don't flinch. I would not want to cut you before your time."

"Surely your talents are wasted at a simple pub." He was acutely aware of Askana standing close behind him. Why did she say nothing?

Lubria's eyes darkened for a moment as they glanced to Askana and then her head tipped forward, hair spilling over one shoulder forming the shape of flame. "I am content. Why the question?"

Rafe touched a nerve. That he could see clearly. "Because we need you," he said. "More to the point, your Queen needs you. Those sworn to protect her have betrayed the Throne. As we speak, unknown enemies grapple for her Realm. She has fled with a total stranger. A pirate whom she must blindly trust. She needs your help and protection. Perhaps even from me."

He could feel his heart leap into his throat when Askana touched his shoulder. Her body brushed against him as she placed a hand on the shirai, lowering the weapon away from his chin. "I am asking you to do this for your love of me whom you once called sister."

The blade moved away from Askana's touch with a threatening rush of air. Rafe remained where he stood, knowing full well he could be at the shirai's point in an instant.

"It was very hard to learn love," Lubria said slowly, painfully. "I do love you, my Queen, but what do you do here now? With *him*? What is he to you? You, who taught me never to put trust in a man?" The creature smiled confidently as she glanced to Rafe and his crew, "Should I aid you to what may be the path to your doom? Your resolve seems to be weakening, your hate diluted. Why should I not kill him here and end it?"

Rafe now heard knives being removed from belts but a quick look to Nassir was enough for his First Mate and crew to stand down. He felt Askana tense against him as his neck now began to burn. The Queen suddenly let out a soft, gentle laugh and with slow steps came around to face him, looking up into his face. Mocking, teasing. She draped herself over him, a hand going around his neck, the other pressing widespread fingers against his doublet as Askana looked over her shoulder to Lubria.

"You ask me what I *do* with him?" Her smile was something that he had never seen before, warmly inviting and almost wicked. "Why, look at him, Lubria." A finger traced his jawline. "A handsome man, a man such as I would never find in Morevi. He pleases me. A pleasant diversion. You say you do not know love. Well, I say you do not know *desire*. Desire can go hand-in-hand with hate. And for the time being, I desire this man. Do believe me, Lubria, he serves me well!"

Suddenly, she rose on her toes, pulling Rafe even closer.

"This is necessary!" she whispered fiercely before kissing him full on the mouth.

The crew erupted into catcalls and ribald jests. Hammers returned to a safe position as pistols lowered. Even Nassir shook his head slowly as he watched his Captain enjoy the lips of this foreign queen.

His hands rose to push her off, but she had locked her arms with his. He could not break their false intimacy. She held him fast, the kiss growing with intensity. Rafe heard her lewd moans of delight as she made their kiss linger. A memory awakened in the Privateer Captain and he pulled her closer, his rage returning the ferocity of this mock affection.

She broke the kiss. Both their eyes were maddened with anger. Askana could still taste the privateer in her mouth. She knew his sudden return of the kiss was nothing more than revenge. The moment between them felt like an eternity. Askana closed her eyes for a moment to soften them again and she turned to face Lubria, a delightful and contented smile crossing her face.

Lubria's eyes narrowed, but she nodded in acknowledgement. "You loved once, and I could not understand or approve of that love. Yet this desire is what men use, is it not? Prettily is it turned on this one. Then shall I as a Sister of Nadinath choose to follow you, my Queen."

Askana nodded, "Go with Elunear, then. The girl is eager to rediscover the warrior she worshipped in her youth." She felt her heartbeat relax and calm. *Thank you, Goddess,* Askana thought.

"Nassir, see to that wound of yours. I cannot afford to lose my First Mate." Rafe nodded curtly to Askana, motioning to the open night air of the main deck. "Your Grace, may we?"

The crew resumed their chorus of approval and praise, but a sharp look from their Captain silenced and dispersed them. Askana gently caressed his cheek as she passed and walked out across the deck. In a fury, he strode after her. Once reaching the privacy of the *Defiant's* forecastle, he stepped sharply in front of her. Askana's face in the span of time between the cargo hold and there had quickly changed from seductive to disgusted.

"What the Hell do you call that, Your Majesty?!" Rafe snapped.

"You will be silent, privateer, and thank Nadinath that you are alive!" she snapped. "I could never control Lubria, even when she was mine. Fate made her love me, and what she did for me she did out of love. If she had been uncertain of you, she would have cut your throat for love of me! I had to make you appear subservient."

"Please, Your Grace, leave the improvisation to me! If she had been loyal to you once, could she not be trusted to know about our business? Why, of all things of Heaven and Earth, did you choose such degradation for you and I?"

"Do not insult me, Captain." Askana spat, "From what you insinuate, you have enjoyed such exploits with those above you in class!"

"Do you not see the damage you have done?" Rafe shrugged helplessly as he spoke, "I am trying to maintain an amount of respect and decorum towards you and your Guard as an example to my men. In one swift act, you appeared before them exactly in the image I am trying to dispel!"

Rafe was correct but Askana would not admit it. She was also disgusted by her actions. She turned to leave him but the Captain quickly took hold of her arm and forced her to face him, well into his personal fury. "How do you feel now? Is the Crown of Morevi contented, Your Grace? Did you find pleasure in it?"

Askana held her breath for a moment. Rafe's tight grip on her took her back to another's cold, cruel embrace. In this moment, she returned to that time under his hold. His violation of her. The sting of his hand across her face. *That time is past, he is dead, and I am Queen,* Askana thought sharply.

With an unbridled growl Askana ripped free of his grasp and shoved him in the chest, sending him against the forecastle's railing. *"I found no pleasure in my actions, pirate!"* she screamed, her voice causing crew members in the topcastles to look down from their watch. Askana fought back her building blood rage, her deep breath sounding almost desperate as Rafe picked himself up from the deck. "There! Are you satisfied now, pirate, at the error of the Morevian crown? You think I have not heard such words used upon me? I too carry pain! Pain does not recognise nor pay reverence to royalty. How do I feel, privateer? I feel as I once did under the rule of Lord Norisht. Like some tavern-dancer, some whore performing for a master!"

"Lord Norisht?" Rafe asked. "Who is Lord Norisht?"

Askana was completely unaware she had spoken the name. This privateer did not need to know any more. "For what I am paying you on this endeavour, you will play this part of consort for Lubria's benefit. This audience is over, privateer."

She turned to leave the Captain with only the soft ambience of the ocean parting underneath the ship's hull for companionship. The abrupt movement whipped her hair back, and Rafe's eye caught sight of it in the moonlight. It was a dark blemish against her pale white skin. She felt his hand catch her arm, more gently this time, and turn her to face him again. Her instinct brought her hand up to deflect his touch in a swift motion. Rafe paused, waiting for Askana to see he was beyond his earlier anger. His hand continued to her neck before she realised what he was doing and could stop him again.

It came away smeared with blood.

Lubria's half-sheathed claw had given her a long scratch. If it had been fully distended it would have dealt a lethal cut. As he stared at his blood-stained fingers, he felt where his neck itched. The exact same spot.

And where he had held her fast by the arm, his own arm tingled lightly.

Askana avoided Rafe's gaze.

"Your Grace," Rafe said as evenly as he could. "I think we need to talk."

"I do not know whether she will help you," the Lady Armenia said. "She has taken a turn for the worse of late and her sickness eats at her like a canker."

Kubi-Sogi sighed heavily as he rose to his feet. "My Lady Armenia, you were much beloved by the Queen for your past kindness to her when she was but a girl. Now in this most desperate time, I must speak to her mother. Perhaps she can help me find the way her daughter has chosen."

Lady Armenia inclined her head. The small jade ornaments in her silvering hair softly caught the sunlight filtering into the arboretum. Something flickered in her eyes for a moment when she looked up to the Blademaster. "I am not one to deny a request from you, Kubi-Sogi."

The old man shook his head, "That is not why I ask this of you. I do it out of loyalty to my Queen."

"Still you refuse to see, Blademaster," smiled Armenia warmly. She glanced toward the sound of collected birdsong, "You may see her."

Kubi-Sogi bowed as the Lady rose. He followed her slight form down one of the many paths in the great garden of her country manor. Armenia, unlike the other women who had ascended to power following the War of the Fan and Slipper, had retired from life at Court and professed a wish to live out her days in peace, surrounded by beauty. She was past middle-age and still undeniably handsome. It was her elegance that the Blademaster found irresistible.

Armenia wore humble robes absent of the typical Court adornments and gardening slippers. Instead of a fan, a pair of clippers hung from her sash. She kept no bevy of maids or pages around her, only a modest collection of young women and men attending to the manor that bowed as they passed. Kubi-Sogi smiled. That was so like Armenia. All the rights and ceremonies entitled to one of her high nobility traded for household tools and simple pleasures. No nonsense at all, and still achieving an unparalleled elegance. Then the smile disappeared as they approached a small pavilion in the centre of a beautifully trimmed lawn.

The young guards bowed as they opened the teakwood doors for Mistress and Blademaster. The smell of flowers, rainwater, and excrement assailed Kubi-Sogi so hard that he turned his head slightly to take one last gasp of fresh, uncontaminated air behind him. Armenia did not flinch in the slightest as she had grown accustomed to the flowers attempting to mask the more offensive scents. She guided him through the halls adorned with birdcages. Row after row of them, all delicate and beautifully shaped, some gilded or studded with pieces of coloured glass and draped with expensive cloths. Songbirds chirped, whistled, and sang as the maids fed them.

But not all the birds were songbirds. Some were chickens. Others were more exotic such as flamingos and peacocks. Dominating over the eclectic mix of birds were ravens. They were kept in the most elaborate and bejewelled cages in the manor. The last cage was the largest in the collection with a perch large enough to seat a man. It was empty.

He was led to an indoor atrium. Sunlight streamed in, and brilliantly coloured flowers bloomed in profusion. Water flowed in an artificial waterfall down into an unsurpassed lily-pond. Small birds as colourful as the flowers flitted free in this little paradise, and in the centre of it all sat a strange figure at a rattan table. A maid dutifully fanned the old woman with a peacock-feather fan as she cooed to her birds and fed a small finch with seeds placed on her tongue. The attendant tried to put on a better face for Armenia and Kubi-Sogi, but was overwhelmed in sadness towards the poor wretch to whom she served.

The Dowager Queen-Mother was small, shrivelled up into herself. Her hair was a dishevelled mass of iron-grey streaked with white, done up in an Old Court-style that rapidly lost its intricate hold. Precious ornaments studded with small gems were stuck haphazardly into the whole, giving her head the semblance of a living pincushion. The old woman had applied a thick coat of paint to her face, and this was melting in the warmth of the sunlight. She looked lost in a magnificent overcoat of gold-shot red that clashed with the green and purple of her inner robes. The years after her husband's death had been cruel. The worry of wandering homeless and penniless slowly consumed her, eventually driving her to the desperate measure of arranging her daughter's marriage. Watching her beloved child reduced to a concubine under Lord Norisht's rule had been a mental torture. The sorrow and guilt claimed her mind before Askana's dizzying rise to power.

Yet he would try.

"A reverence I make to the Queen-Mother of the Thousand Suns." Kubi-Sogi made a deep obeisance. "A greeting on this fair morning."

The old woman cackled suddenly, frightening the finch off her hand. "A mother of the Suns you say? Are you mad? My insides would have been cooked to a crisp if I bore a ball of flame for a child. No, I lay eggs, but they keep taking them away."

"Eggs, madam?" he asked seriously.

"Yes, eggs. The most beautiful red things. I know they would hatch if only these people around me would not keep stealing them. Taking advantage of a poor old woman." She smiled vacantly at him. "Do you like my eggs?"

"Never seen more beautiful things in my life, madam," Kubi-Sogi said with a smile of commiseration.

"Good, good! Sit down, dear boy!" She shooed away the birds with sweeping motions of her arms, feathers flying in the air. As he approached, she gripped his arm with bony fingers and drew him into a chair across from her. She spoke with the pride and excitement of a small child, "I am a bird, you know. Sometimes I like to climb up to perch on a windowsill. I would fly, but the nurse says that if I flew away all my darlings would be so lonely. So I do not fly away. I stay to love my darlings."

"Your darlings, madam?"

"Yes, my babies!" She swept a hand to all the cages, nearly knocking the bag of seed off the table. "They are my children, you know."

"They're very beautiful, madam," Kubi-Sogi took a deep breath of the foul air and focused on the Dowager Queen's eyes for a hint of clarity and reason, "but did you not have a human daughter too?"

The old woman frowned. "Did I?" She turned to look at Armenia. "Did I ever bear such a great clumsy creature as that? And such an ugly thing? No colour. No soft feathers. No wings."

"Dear Sister, you have no wings yourself," Armenia said gently.

"Rubbish!" the Queen-Mother snorted. "I have wings, big beautiful wings the colour of the clouds above. And all my children come out of eggs." Her voice trailed off as her head nodded quickly, the words repeating again and again, "So pretty, my eggs..."

"I would like you to think very hard, madam. You had a daughter—Askana. And a son—Markuna." The old woman said nothing, peering at him with beady eyes that never blinked. Kubi-Sogi pressed on gently, "You had a husband once. A Lord of this land. Do you remember this land—Morevi? Your husband died of the red fever."

For a moment, no one spoke, only the sounds of birdsong interrupting their silence. Then a single word. Clear, full of reason. "No."

The old woman said it again. "No." She was no longer looking at Kubi-Sogi or Armenia. Her eyes still did not blink as they stared forward, her head shaking back and forth as she added, "He did not die! It was the changing of the season. He merely took flight to a brighter place." Then the Dowager Queen erupted into wild screams of "No! No! No! No!" She thrashed in the chair as her fantasy gradually surrendered to reality. "My husband, my husband! *All gone! All dead and gone!* My baby! My little Markuna gone and dead and buried under the earth and rotting." Agitated birds called and cawed as they flew and wheeled around in the atrium. She looked up to the birds darting high above her, nodding to their song as if they were talking directly to her. The old woman's chair rocked wildly as she began to caw like her ravens. The chair toppled. The Dowager Queen reached for the bag of seed as she fell, spilling it across the floor as her caws became long, pitiful wails. "My daughter, the whore of court! My baby! My baby! My Markuna gone, gone, gone, gone!"

Kubi-Sogi hung his head at this pathetic sight. He held his hand up to keep Armenia back as he stood. The birdseed crunched under his steps as he crossed to the mad woman sobbing at his feet. He placed a gentle hand on her back and went to speak.

Her head shot up quickly and the sound that came from her was not human.

The Queen-Mother's bony fingers grabbed Kubi-Sogi's robes and pushed him back against the table, knocking the table and its contents aside with a loud clamour, sending the birds into a wild frenzy. Armenia called for more attendants as the Queen-Mother growled to the Blademaster, "Where is my Maeve? Tell me! You hide her from me! Why!?" Then she stopped suddenly, her eyes looking Kubi-Sogi up and down. She whispered, "You killed her, didn't you? You killed her for she knew your true nature." Her voice grew as she shook him, "You murderess! You filthy, filthy whore! I'll scratch out your eyes I will! You hide in the Cursed Wood with that sorceress, but I will find you. I will find you and kill you!"

Attendants grabbed for the Dowager Queen, pulling her off the stunned Kubi-Sogi. She spat upon all of them, her eyes wide with hatred and clouded with madness. She screamed like a hawk upon the hunt as the handmaids struggled against her wrists and ankles. Some birds were daring to fly in close to help themselves to the spilt seed across the atrium floor, assaulting the maids and Blademaster by flapping their wings into hair and faces as they did so.

"The cage!" Armenia was calling as she fended off the greedy birds with a peacock-feather fan. "Open the cage!"

The Blademaster watched in sickened fascination as they opened the door of the large, empty cage and put the old woman upon its floor. Slamming the cage door shut, the Queen-Mother grasped the bars just above her head and shook them wildly, her cries mingling with horrific wails as if mourning the death of a loved one.

"Bird, bird. Shhh now. Sing, pretty bird, sing me to sleep." Armenia cooed as she went to the cage, whispering and whistling as she would to a songbird.

The old woman began to calm at the sound of Armenia's voice. Like some old frog she crouched on the floor of the cage, looking up at her as if waking from a daze. Then slowly she clambered up onto the perch. She swung back and forth slowly on it—a chilling *"creak-creak-creak"* sounding above all the other birdsong—and began humming some garbled tune to herself. Her head turned quickly back and forth like that of her "darlings" as she sang.

"Is she like this every time?" Kubi-Sogi asked in amazement.

Armenia smiled wanly, her weariness now showing her true age. "Talking of her past always does this to her. Mostly though, she is quiet, playing with her 'darlings'."

Kubi-Sogi reached out to gently stroke Armenia's hair. "You must be strong to have dealt and lived with her all these years."

She looked down, leaning into his tender gesture. "No stronger than most."

"Who is Maeve?"

She spread her hands helplessly. "We do not know. I have never been able to find out. The murderess she refers to, though, is Askana."

The birds were calmer now, save for the ravens that cawed relentlessly in seeing the other birds helping themselves to spilt seed. Kubi-Sogi could only feel his heart sink at this sad state. The mother blamed her daughter, the last remaining relative of her bloodline, for the death of her son. If the Queen-Mother could only know her daughter, "the murderess," punished herself for Markuna's death every day of her life.

But who was Maeve?

He had not realised that he spoke aloud till Armenia laughed sadly.

"In the Tangled Southern Wood. You will find the answers there."

"My Lord," the girl whispered in his ear as they lay together in the great bed, the carved screens closed around them.

On either side of the bed, cakes of incense burned in censers, tingeing the air with a sweet musk scent that she claimed would enhance their desire and sensuality. The odour made him slightly sick.

"My Lady," he smiled down at her, trailing a hand through her hair. She had auburn hair, wavy and thick, and she was proud of it for the colour was very rare in Morevi. He had seen women with manes more beautiful in Eyrie and he toyed with the idea of telling her that. She was young and vain, but she also had a sharp mind. He knew it would be difficult to find another with her skills in the Great Game. Such a pity she did not know it well enough to know when she was being manipulated. He could see in her eyes deep love and devotion. It made control over her so much easier.

Her fingers strayed upwards towards his face. He caught her wrist before she could touch the black mask across his nose and mouth.

Min-Lu smiled at him. "Why will you not let me see your face, Ruain? Is our love not strong enough?"

"Even if it were our bridal bed I would still hide my face." He sat up, disentangling himself from her arms and getting out of the bed. "I am not fool enough to confuse love with trust."

"But you trust me enough in this plot of ours," she snapped while gathering the sheets around her naked body.

Underneath the mask, he smiled at Min-Lu's attempt at chastity. He could still hear her moaning and whimpering while he pleasured her. How she loved to show her prowess and agility during their love-making, perhaps to vaunt skills unknown to Eyriener women. Now she tried to cover her body like an innocent virgin would if an intruder walked into her chambers.

"You are too deeply involved to back out now, but you would not want to do that now. Would you?" he mocked as he slipped into a high-collared, exquisitely cut coat that reached down to his shins. "This close to the life-vein of Askana Moldarin, you could not nor would not stop. You are too much of a power-hungry little witch."

In a fit of rage, Min-Lu abandoned the bed sheets and spoke sharply *"Hasha-tiak!"*

The Morevian curse was his only warning as her hands reached for him, fingers curled into claws. He easily stopped her attempt to scratch him by batting her hands away and wrapping a single hand around her delicate throat. He was not choking her, but he knew it would be effortless for him to snap her neck.

She took in a deep breath and fixed her gaze on his eyes, the only visible feature of his face. "You wear Eyriener clothes, the clothes of a merchant-lord, but you have brown eyes and dark hair like an Eastern man of Lahsa. It would not be so hard to find out who you are and turn you over to the Council, you devil!"

"A devil, am I?" He pushed her back on the bed, enjoying the sight of her nude and vulnerable atop the sheets. He braced his hand against her bare chest, keeping her down as he leaned over her in a sudden, menacing movement. "But isn't that what makes you love me?" His free hand caught her chin. "Is that not what makes me irresistible to you? This darkness about me? The very fact that I am not cowed like your Morevian men?" His breath passed through the fine, sheer material of his mask, brushing her cheek as he spoke. "And what of this power I have over you, proud member of the Council? You forget yourself, I am your Lord by your own words." He released her chin and gently caressed her face with his gloved hand, "When all is done you shall discover the man behind this mask. Until then, our kisses shall only be shared under cover of night."

Min-Lu's face softened at the feel of his leather glove touching her skin. Her leg slipped out from underneath him and moved across the sheets. She was ready for him once more. A little moan escaped her lips as he ran his fingers across her cheek.

The Dark Merchant could see the want in her face. He let out a soft laugh, watching the proud Council member part her legs and writhe lewdly. He gave her a light shove away and stepped back from the bed. His laugh grew in its cadence as he left her there. Her transformation from pious Sister of Nadinath to common paramour never ceased to entertain him.

Walking down the silent corridors, flanked by Min-Lu's guard, the Dark Merchant grinned in deep satisfaction under the folds of his black cloak and hood. He knew so well how to manage her. First the whip, then the reward. Striking just the right balance between the two. It was the right way to control one of her ilk. Min-Lu was no challenge for she made him the dark hero of her girlish fantasies. No, his challenge would finally come with the First Queen of Morevi. His revenge for all the wrongs she had dealt him began with the death of Telmrant. It would end with her beloved realm under *his* rule.

Right now though, she was in the company of Rafe Rafton, a pirate who bested him one time too many in the eyes of the Merchants' Circle. He could never prove that the Sea Wolf led unexpected raids against the Eyriener Merchant Navy. He, on the other hand, knew this to be true. Now the Merchants' Circle was dead and he was the last of their Order. Unlike his fallen brothers, he was well aware of the Sea Wolf's loyalties.

He knew where they would go, and Captain Rafton was not the only one who possessed means to navigate through The Rift.

When was the last time she shared tea with a man? The memory of the last time she had shared any semblance of company with a man escaped her as she took a long puff from her pipe. She still kept, for some odd reason, the etching of herself in her younger and wilder days. Perhaps her magic was not as powerful then as it was now. But in her youth, the magic was in her beauty that bewitched men with little effort. That time seemed so long past.

Now, after years of solitude and lacking the company of men, she had a caller. Bitter irony struck her when she thought of how useless he was in any type of carnal needs. As he emerged from the embrace of the mists with Lissellone as his guide, that thought remained at the forefront of her mind.

"Kubi-Sogi, is it not?" Grainne looked him over with cold, grey eyes. Before he could answer, she huffed, "Yes, you have that look of a follower. A subject."

His posture straightened slightly at the little insult. *So this is the infamous Caillech of the Tangled Southern Wood*, Kubi-Sogi thought. *Not what I expected from what legends tell.*

Grainne gave a rough, gravely laugh as she poured tea into an old, chipped cup, "And just what did you expect, Blademaster? Stone circles, boiling cauldrons, and skins of animals hanging everywhere about?"

Impressive, he thought. *But why read my mind?*

"Because I make it my office to know the needs of those who risk their lives to find me. You are in my realm now, Blademaster. A realm the Fellowship of the Jewels would care to make disappear from the face of Naruihm if they still possessed the ability to do so. The Fellowship and your Queen have no hold here. Therefore I do as I please," she spoke flatly as she set a cup of steaming tea aside for him. "Her Majesty believes herself mistress of her own fate. Bah! Askana Moldarin could not begin to grasp the events she has set in motion."

"These events." Kubi-Sogi asked, "They date back before the arrival of this pirate, do they not?"

"Perhaps, Blademaster," Grainne winked as she took her own cup of tea and a seat by a modest table and an empty chair. "Will you join me? It has been so long since I have enjoyed the company of a gentleman-caller."

Kubi-Sogi smiled pleasantly at the unexpected invitation. It would seem this sorceress of legend and myth was, at one time, a woman who enjoyed her courtiers. The old master took the seat across from the Caillech and dropped two small sugar cubes into her teacup. The kindly gesture gained a chuckle from her.

"I tend to read individuals as well," he said softly while stirring her tea. "Only without the magic on which you tend to rely."

"You would say your martial arts are not magic? Oh, but they are. The sorcery of combat. All magic comes from a spirit. With your art, the spirit is war. With my magic, it is the lifeforce within nature. And then there is love." Kubi-Sogi paused in the stirring of his own tea. Her face grew distant as she talked, "A powerful magic that no necromancer can command. If one dares try, it only brings misery to that poor wretch."

Kubi-Sogi forged ahead gently. "Mistress Armenia told me I would find the answer to an enigma here."

"You think your kingdom is so important, do you?" Grainne shook her head ruefully as she took a deep sip of her tea, "And tell me what has this great kingdom yielded? A mad mother who believes herself to be a songbird. A brother now providing a banquet for worms and beetles. A trail of blood that could encircle the world ten times over. Women bickering between one another over land titles as if they were colour schemes for quilts! A small fortune in light of the sacrifices *that you know of*, Blademaster. Your Majesty has not been forthcoming in her consequences to become Queen."

"Such as Maeve?"

Grainne stopped her teacup in mid-lift, her gaze fixed on mist slipping between the tangled trees. "A name uttered in a fit of insanity."

"But within the madness of Lady Kimali Chesia, there is clarity. I know of the death of Her Majesty's brother Markuna, but the Dowager Queen laments for this one called Maeve. She also curses her only living offspring and you, the Caillech of the Southern Wood."

"She curses me?" Grainne smiled, "It is so pleasing to be remembered in the minds of the demented."

Lissellone could not help to spy on the two elders through her chink in the hovel's willow matting. It was so exciting for her. Within a few days, Grainne had accepted *two* visitors, and one of them had been a queen. The child wondered if this old man were a great wizard or some elderly king in search of lost youth. She watched them sit in silence and fought a growing urge to giggle as she remained undiscovered.

Grainne suddenly leapt from her chair, striking the crack in the wall with her knotted cane. "To your chores, girl! Lest I give you a thrashing that will give you something to remember the next time you hear words that were not for your ears!" As the young feet scampered away, Grainne shook her head. "I must have been mad to think I could raise a child at my age." She slowly eased back into the cushions as she spoke. "Perhaps I should show you the way to your answer. It does not matter. Your Queen is lost."

Kubi-Sogi slumped in his seat, a hand going to his forehead as he lowered his face, "By the grace of Nadinath, Her Majesty is dead."

The Caillech let out hearty laugh as she rocked back and forth in her chair, "Oh no, the great Askana Moldarin still lives. Her fate, chosen by her, is far worse than that of death!" Grainne smiled as she nodded, "Far worse." She leaned forward in her chair, poking his arm with the smoking tip of her pipe, "Instead of teaching that girl how to play with knives, swords, and other baubles, you should teach her what you of all in her Court know better. How to listen. Particularly to her elders." She reclined back with a gentle laugh, her smile revealing a new-found contentment.

"Maeve." Kubi-Sogi said, his growing exasperation now warring with his patience. "Please tell me who the Dowager Queen laments for."

She knew he would not leave without an answer, but there was a sport in watching the desperate achieve enlightenment. She closed her eyes for a moment, recalling dark and turbulent memories. With a deep breath, Grainne began.

"Blademaster, there is a reason why this Dowager Queen is reduced to the broken soul her attendants see. A harsh jest that fate would play with her bloodline. It is this fate that has made Askana Moldarin who she is. Part of this fate is Maeve. Maeve is a part of the duality that Nadinath or the one this pirate simply calls 'God' creates to achieve a sense of harmony within the world."

Kubi-Sogi leaned forward, setting his teacup aside. "What do you mean by duality?"

"Have you not noticed it in your own travels, Blademaster? Surely you have! You of all people. But like most, you are blind to such obvious answers." She took a slow drag of the remaining tobacco and then tapped the pipe against her shoe as she spoke, "In battle, there is the victor and the vanquished, is there not? There is time for opening wounds followed by a time to heal. And when the Sword of War sleeps, there is Peace."

"This is the duality of which you speak?"

"Yes, it is everywhere, Blademaster. The blessed earth from whence you came breathed life at the same time the Southern Wood came to be. Light and dark are companions eternal. And even in the brief time we spend in this age, there is the duality of husband and wife. Parent and child."

"Sister and brother?"

"Aye, young Blademaster." Kubi-Sogi could not help but smile at being referred to as "young" but it did humble him slightly as he pondered in that instant this woman's age. She nodded in approval, "You are a quick study. There is also the duality of sanity and madness, something The Queen-Mother now knows on a more intimate level. Poor soul. How could she know now such secrets are best taken to her grave?" Grainne shook her head. "It was not the bearing of her family's responsibility nor the loss of Askana to Lord Norisht. It was the turmoil within that tore her apart."

"But Markuna was one of Askana's most powerful allies in the War. They were as close as family serves. Askana still carries the guilt of her bother's death."

"Markuna was the product of a minor noble's inability to resist a passing fancy with one of his servant-girls. Askana loved him as a true brother, but they were not true in their bond. This is not the duality of which I speak."

Kubi-Sogi's eyes seemed to illuminate for a moment as he spoke the words. "You speak of a twin! This one the Dowager Queen calls Maeve was a twin sister to Askana!"

"That she was." The Caillech shuddered lightly as if a chill passed through her old bones, "And there was no evil paralleled with Maeve."

"But Her Majesty never told me of—"

"Because she was exiled in secret. Imprisoned in a sealed keep in the barren wastelands far east of Morevi. She was a demon spawn, that Maeve. She was the coldest, most lethal of adversaries. When Askana began her ascent, Maeve grew more and more distant. Before you were enlisted into the Queen's service, Maeve had reduced herself to a forgotten name. She watched Askana from the shadows. She was enclosed in her own ambitions, living like a hermit in their own manor. She was never seen or called upon. Maeve disapproved of Askana's outward compliance to Lord Norisht, and that disapproval only festered into hatred as she watched her sister bed powerful men to reach the throne. In her isolation and twisted perspective, Maeve indulged in the Ancient Arts. Her only desire was to watch Askana suffer as their beloved mother had. Maeve even went so far as to have her own banner created. A raven with wings spread wide and talons stretched out in attack. Maeve's own arrow took her bastard brother's life when she allied herself with the opposition. Had the strike itself not proven fatal, the arrow's tip was anointed. Maeve left nothing to chance."

Kubi-Sogi stared at her incredulously, "You said Askana banished her?"

Grainne nodded slowly. "The banishment of Lubria, you recall, was over the Fae-woman's blood rage unleashed against those remaining men plotting against Askana. She discovered, following Lubria's banishment, that Maeve allied herself with these men, *leading* their movement against her. She found her twin sister filling their mother's head with nonsense of Askana's contempt for her and how it was Askana that brought about the deaths of those she loved. Askana nearly killed Maeve before her mother's eyes. It was Telmrant who stopped Askana, and it was Telmrant who took Maeve to the far-off uncharted wastelands. Under cover of darkness, the Elf locked her in a keep with food to last only a few months. He had hoped she would perish with time. The Elf underestimated the Arts she practised in secret and how fate would intervene.

"The death of Telmrant dealt a severe blow to Askana, but not as severe as the knowledge of who killed her love. The assassin left his battle-axe embedded within Telmrant's chest. The blow was to the heart. Engraved upon the axe was the symbol of a raven killing its prey."

Kubi-Sogi's mind returned to that day. Telmrant's body was brought before Askana. The weapon was lodged so deep in his chest that no one could remove it. He had never heard the Queen wail in such a fashion. Kubi-Sogi was convinced the Palace walls would have fallen from the force of her cries. Then, in a strange moment, she went silent. He looked to her, and Askana's eyes were simply staring at the insignia on the axe. Her face was vacant.

"Askana alone set out for the deserts of the Uncharted Lands. I believe she told you it was a pilgrimage in honour of her love, Telmrant. Sometimes the greatest deceptions are concealed in hints of truth," she laughed, giving the Blademaster a wink. "When Askana arrived to the keep, she found the seal to the doors broken. Maeve's 'prison' was adorned with fine silks and decorations from Morevi with the raven crest in full view. She even had two Court hounds tethered to her own private throne. It was her way of flaunting her influences within Morevi, even in banishment. Askana ran her through with a shirai and left her there to rot. She spent the rest of her 'pilgrimage' wandering the wastelands, endlessly grieving. Pathetic, she was then."

"And this is what weighs so heavily upon the Dowager Queen?" Kubi-Sogi felt a numbness come from all this new-found knowledge of his Queen. He noticed his hands were trembling.

"Shhh, 'tis well, Blademaster." The Caillech, in a rare moment of tenderness, reached for his hands and took them into hers. There was a slight chill in her skin at first, but within moments it became a comforting warmth. "And now you have found the answer you have sought."

"I have?!" Kubi-Sogi said sharply, releasing himself from the old woman's grasp. "You give me nothing more than secrets and lies! I have discovered nothing save that my Queen has concealed the murder of her true sister! Nothing more! This has nothing to do with current threat to the Throne or the disappearance of the Queen!"

"Tut-tut, my young Blademaster," she smiled, still remaining serene in the face of Kubi-Sogi's anger. "You must look closer."

"What do you mean, witch?!" he shouted, his patience now abandoned and maddened by what the Caillech revealed to him. "Tell me, crone!"

Grainne took a hold of his hand once more. A sudden calm washed over Kubi-Sogi as she continued. "Look at the echoes of this tragedy. They will not only provide the answer you seek, but also shed light upon events in motion." She smiled as she lifted herself to her feet, "Think on this while I fetch Lissellone. She will see you safely through the Southern Wood, back to that precious kingdom of yours."

Left alone on the porch of her tiny hut, Kubi-Sogi meditated on the shadows of the great trees and the sounds of life within the enchanted forest. The feelings of betrayal and deception tore at his resolve. He felt closer to the Queen than anyone in her service. The fact she entrusted him with the Royal Seal was evidence that she felt the same in this. Why then could she have not entrusted him with this? What other secrets did she keep? Perhaps that was one of the few privileges of a queen that she allowed herself—family secrets.

He continued a slow, deep breathing while he waited for his guide to join him. The last words of the Caillech repeated in his head. *"Look at the echoes of this tragedy. They will not only provide the answer you seek, but also shed light upon events in motion."*

The echoes of this tragedy, Kubi-Sogi thought. *What did the old witch mean by that?*

Then he reflected on the story of the sealed keep. Banishment, never to be seen by eyes again. The death of Telmrant dealt from a weapon bearing the crest of Maeve. The lavish, pampering possessions of the Queen's sister, coming from the marketplace of Morevi.

Maeve had an ally, one who had influences in Morevi, be it merchants or traders from other lands. Other lands close to Morevi's borders. And Eyrie's. This ally even risked their own life in a war that was not theirs, to seek vengeance in Maeve's name.

This was not just a sworn ally to Maeve, he thought as he opened his eyes to look upon the curious stare of Lissellone, *but a lover.*

Homecoming

A fortress of stone called "The Tower" welcomed them into a hive of people, activity, and magnificence. Large buildings reached into the morning sky of crystal blue. Children rushed from cart to cart while traders and merchants proudly displayed their wares in the open marketplaces. Sweet music filled the air, occasionally drowned out by the call of a town crier or bawd from an open window of a house of ill repute. Quickly Rafe pulled the Morevians away from underneath windows where housemaids would dump piss-pots free of their foul contents. The women ranged in all ranks of class. Askana noted one or two wide-eyed and familiar looks shared between the ladies and Captain Rafton. From the appealing to the abhorrent, a concert of sounds and sights filled the air. Askana, Elunear, and the cloak-concealed Lubria kept outwardly stoic expressions, but could not completely bury their wonderment at this new world. They could not deny the hypnotic spell woven by this place that Rafe Rafton called home.

London.

Askana wanted so much to ask Rafe question after question on her new surroundings. However, her words reserved themselves to only what was necessary. Rafe had barely spoken to her since their talk in his cabin. He stood there motionless before her as she told him of the cure's origins and the price it carried.

Linked. Perhaps for only a fleeting moment. Perhaps forever. Even she could not say for sure which.

Being an explorer, Rafe knew sights and sounds fascinating and incredible to the eye, especially with his own travels across The Rift. He had grown accustomed to the presence of magic, never wholly accepting of it. Sorcery was a bending of God's Will in his eyes. It was tampering with nature in such a fashion that he could only see as an invitation for some Divine Retribution. It was still a part of her realm, something he understood with an apprehensive acceptance. He was the grand exception to the rule of his world. No effort would be made to understand, and carrying this secret only compounded Rafe's challenges. Lubria would have to remain out of curious courtiers' sight as the subjects of King Henry VIII would deem the Child of the Mists as a product of witchcraft. If his own bond with Askana were to be discovered, it would lead to public burnings, beheadings, or some other horrific torture.

Looking at Askana, he truly wished he had surrendered to the Spanish and never crossed The Rift.

Listening to Rafe was merely a formality to approach that fragile ego of his. Askana did not question or regret her act. It was a necessity, and her right as First Queen would not exclude Otherworlders. He would be ruled by her so long as he accepted payment from her. Still, a hint of guilt touched her. His words sounded very much like her own. Askana knew the price of magic first hand. In this distrust of sorcery, she was on common ground with this privateer. The guilt was quickly dismissed. He was merely a subject to her rule. Even less than that. A criminal against her throne, and to be treated as such once their agreement came to an honourable close.

The escort from the palace gates was a wide-eyed boy, eager to please as were many in his office. He was to serve as their liaison to Court before their meeting with His Majesty, King Henry the VIII.

"And how is Her Majesty, Queen Anne?" Rafe asked, his voice echoing in the palace corridors, "Still being welcomed to her new home by her people?"

The young boy turned to Rafe excitedly, "Master Rafton, have you not heard the good tidings for our King? I suppose being out to sea, word did not reach your vessel. His Majesty has remarried!"

"You mean, Anne of Cleves has fallen out of favour with His Majesty?"

His smile grew wide in bearing what he thought was joyous news. "On the contrary, Captain, the King's Sister is quite content and still loved by her people."

"The King's *Sister?*" Rafe asked incredulously.

"That is what good King Henry calls her now. Her official title of Court." The page gave a quick look around in the massive corridor and chuckled in a hushed voice. "Better than when he called her a Flanders Mare, eh, Captain?" Askana's eyes darkened at the disrespect of this servant as he continued, "No, His Majesty was not fond of his marriage to Queen Anne. But all's well that ends well. His marriage with Queen Kathryn Howard has proven to be a blessing from God Himself."

"Kathryn *Howard?*" Rafe swallowed hard, his skin turning slightly pale. "Kathryn *Howard* now sits upon the throne?"

"Indeed, Master Rafton. She is the Tudor rose without a thorn. What a difference she has made as queen. I've been told His Majesty has not appeared this jovial since his days married to Queen Jane, may God rest her soul." The page was a fount of knowledge and gossip on the topic of King Henry's marriages. He continued to prattle on, brazenly offering his own opinions on the King's dissolving of the Catholic Church in order to divorce Catherine of Aragon and how the beheading his second wife, Anne Boleyn, was just as she had "bewitched" the King into marrying her. "Following this ill-marriage of six months to the Flanders Mare, good King Henry is entitled to a wife as sweet and pure as Kathryn," he beamed.

Askana's mind was reeling.

"But not all has been revels and celebrations. We are still discovering those who will betray the Crown, and these traitors are being found far too close to the King for my liking. Had it not been for the gracious Duke of Norfolk's diligence, the traitorous Cromwell would still be in power as he had once been."

Rafe's stopped in his tracks. "Thomas Cromwell? The Lord of the King's Privy Council was denounced as a traitor to the crown?"

"And who is this Duke of Norfolk that makes him the King's Right Hand?" asked Askana suddenly, unable to remain silent in the wake of this alarming insight to the English Court.

"Thomas Howard." Rafe flinched, "The Third Duke of Norfolk, and Kathryn's uncle. I have endured the man's company. On any given day, the good duke is far too busy to deal with a simple privateer, but catch the attention of the King as I have and you have his patronage to be sure." The page quickly hushed him as serving maids crossed before them, curtsied in respect, and then hurried off to their duties. Rafe continued, "He is a true believer in the ways of status and the power that comes with it. I would not doubt for a moment he is basking in his new appointments thanks to his niece."

"Please, Master Rafton!" The page whispered, now breaking into a fear-induced sweat, "Lord Norfolk is loyal to a fault and as humble as we lowly subjects to King Henry!"

Rafe scoffed, "It will take more than the favour of a king and a new position for a tiger to change its stripes."

A chilly whisper from Lubria sounded in his ears, "Watch thy tongue, human."

The servant stopped before a huge open door revealing specious chambers offering modest luxuries. They were far from the grand, bright marble of The Palace of a Thousand Suns, but Askana cared little about her lodgings. All that truly mattered was her objective—obtaining allies.

Rafe nodded in approval, "This will do Her Grace well. Now what of me?"

"Captain?" The young page blushed, "These are your lodgings as well. Lord Norfolk, well aware of your fondness for the fairer sex, did think you would wish to share quarters with the ladies."

"Well, I do not wish it." Rafe leaned into the servant's face, "The quarters across the hall. Are they taken?"

"No, Master Rafton," he stammered.

"Good." Rafe pulled him closer by the collar of his tunic, "While I have the assurance of the Lord Chancellor, make certain that our audience is assured with the King. I would not wish to be an unexpected surprise to the King this day. Perhaps when you come to fetch us, I will have forgotten this blatant disrespect. Now go. Leave us."

The page was released with a hard shove. His feet never stopped moving as he stumbled back, turned, and flew down the corridor, the pirate's warning still ringing in his ears.

Askana looked at Rafe with an emotionless stare, "You wish to have your own quarters this evening?"

"I wish to have some privacy," Rafe spoke curtly, "not to mention some sleep before our audience with His Majesty. I received none yesternight with all the excitement on the ship." Lubria gave a soft growl from underneath the cowl of her cloak. "Which reminds me, Lubria, it may be best if you stay within chambers during this meeting. The cloak conceals you, but all we need is a brief glance from a handmaid, a royal command, and then it's off to The Tower with the lot of us."

"I serve my Queen, not the wishes of you, human!" Lubria hissed.

"Stay in chambers this night, Lubria," the Queen said gently. "We must be subtle with your presence in this superstitious realm."

"I will tend to you later." Rafe turned to his own chambers, "You know where I am if you need me."

Lubria growled, "Human, you forget yourself. The Queen has not dismissed you yet."

"No, sweet lass," spoke Rafe over his shoulder, "she has not."

With that, the door slammed shut with a deafening echo in the corridor.

"I know not if I trust this human, Your Grace." Lubria peered at the heavy door that had so rudely shut before them. "His actions appear noble, but—"

"Lubria," Askana's sharp tone surprised both her companions. "I desire your services, not your counsel."

Both Lubria and Elunear looked to one another with concern to their Queen. They were strangers in a strange world with a pirate as their guide. By the sound in her voice, their Queen was agitated and needed rest. The three remained silent as they entered the spacious, stone chambers.

While their escape from Morevi was in haste, it was not without some forethought. In the haversack originally carried by Jailene, Askana had packed clothes and accessories suited for a royal audience. The radiant Court robes were an impressive display of emerald green and pearl white, the seal of House Moldarin proudly displayed in gold across the back. She wore the breathtaking ensemble proudly over her more practical white silk robes. The make-up design native to her Court was a chalk white with a deep crimson colour accenting her lips. The final touch rested on top of her head—a delicate tiara of gold from which fine emeralds hung and rested against her forehead. An audience with King Henry had become a contingency plan for Askana since Rafe's casual offer back at The Barrier Reef. It would only benefit her to leave the Palace prepared for royal audiences such as this.

She was a vision appearing unearthly, fragile. Yet the crown, make-up, and Court gown gave her a demeanour that would not be dismissed due to her gender, culture, or race. She was a queen unmistakably. Elunear, dressed in the nondescript silks of a handmaid, had ceremoniously decorated her shirai with beads and feathers she had packed in her own haversack. They were both pristine and proud representatives of their realm, ready for a meeting with their host monarch.

It appeared from the assortment of castle servants that had knocked upon their door all asking for Captain Rafton that all, save for the ladies of Morevi, knew nothing of his own chambers across the hall. Reluctantly, Elunear summoned Captain Rafton to the corridor outside their chambers. When he appeared, he was no longer the portrait of a pirate but dressed in a fine sleeved doublet and breeches of brown and forest greens, trace accents of gold, silver, and chocolate brown leather. The ensemble bestowed upon its wearer an almost noble aura, even finer than how he had appeared in Eyrie. The elegance and refinement of his clothes gave strong contrast to the weapons he wore. Askana's dark eyebrow arched slightly. It seemed that she was not alone in being prepared for anything.

The silence they shared earlier that day remained between them as a page escorted them to the Great Hall.

Trumpets sounded with pomp and circumstance, heralding royalty, their attendants, and guests to the palace. Towering over all in his company was the great King Henry the VIII. His heavy, obese face was framed by a beard of brilliant red, threads of grey and white intertwined within it. His eyes were sharp, cold, accenting the hard features of a king who led a nation. It was apparent in his limp and his girth that time was beginning to wear on this grand monarch Askana had heard talk of at The Barrier Reef. She still could not deny the nobility King Henry conveyed. She would have never pictured humans reaching such a height as he did. For all his shortcomings, both in his physical ailments and questionable morals, this monarch was nothing less than impressive.

The ageing King did nurture a sparkle in his eyes, and it came from the child-bride walking alongside him. He was man reaching fifty while his new Queen was merely in her late teens, an appropriate age for the Rights of Ascension if she were in the Order. Askana could tell, however, this child was nothing like the strong Maidens of Nadinath. Kathryn Howard basked in the wonder and ceremony in being a queen. To her, it was a delightful game of play-pretend. She was a ruler free of any responsibility or duty to her office. This façade of a queen was King Henry's personal salvation. If she did possess any power, it was to push back time for the ageing monarch, returning him to the days of youth when he would indulge in wine, sport, and delights of all manner and still have the drive and the strength to rule a nation. It was as if this child-queen were an unexpected summer on the eve of this King's winter.

The voice resembled thunder in its volume and a cannon in its power, "Who be the first that will have an audience with Us?"

"Your Majesty," Stepping forward was a man dressed entirely in fine robes of blue, red, and gold accented by a fur pelt. He wore his chains of office proudly. The King, Queen, and nobility looked upon him in reverence while visiting lords and ladies bowed deeply. Askana glanced to Rafe, his own bow polite, but not respectful. She deduced this must be the one known as Lord Thomas Howard, the Third Duke of Norfolk, the King's self-appointed Right Hand, and uncle to the young queen. "Captain Rafe Rafton, a simple privateer in Your Majesty's service requests Your—"

"Ah, Captain Rafton, We are most pleased to see thee again." The King smiled warmly as he stroked his red-grey beard, "Your exploits are well known to Us, indeed! We are most pleased with your gifts to the Crown. Such bounty that pleases King and Court well."

"Aye, i'faith!" The English Queen chimed in sweetly, "We are most pleased indeed with your imports and tales of adventures across the Atlantic. Mayhaps you would grant Us an audience in the future to hear of your exploits abroad."

At that invitation, Rafe made eye contact with the young Queen. Both he and Askana could not have foreseen what came from the Throne of England.

Queen Kathryn Howard *winked* at the Privateer Captain.

Askana joined Rafe in the centre of the Great Hall, trying desperately to remember formal etiquette as practised during the Old Regime. She had shed many of these traditions in her own Court as she always held a low tolerance for the use of the royal "We" and "Us". She found it utterly pompous and nothing less than obscene. Equally offensive was the tradition of Court to speak in First Tongue. Only Elves could speak it properly. Now she needed these grandiloquent traditions to establish equal footing with this monarch now studying her from his grand throne.

"You bless me with your praise." Rafe said, his voice tinged with wariness in wake of Kathryn's wink. He turned a hand towards Askana, "Allow me, Your Majesty, to introduce to the Court— "

"In particular," the King continued, "it would please Us greatly if you did acquire more of that lovely tea from—what is the name of that country? That far-off land of savages you did tell Us of—*Morevi*, We did think you called it."

Rafe's eyes went from English King to Morevian Queen, the light sweat on his brow now becoming a sweat creeping up his back.

"Granted," Queen Kathryn grinned, quite pleased with herself, "since We discovered the benefits of honey and chamomile, We find its taste more pleasing to Our *civilised* palette."

Askana's eyes narrowed further as she took Rafe's hand, pulling her sleeve back far enough to reveal the array of poison darts. The anger in her gaze promised Rafe that these insults against her homeland would not go unanswered.

He subtly pulled her sleeve over the gauntlet as they approached the throne. "Just follow my lead, Your Grace." Rafe whispered to her as they neared the King, "Remember, your kingdom relies on this alliance." He took a deep breath and announced to the court, "Allow me to introduce Queen Askana Moldarin. Of Morevi."

A foreboding quiet fell over Court as Henry's face darkened, twisting into a scowl. Kathryn remained proud and overconfident in her throne of power as she looked down on the foreign queen, completely unaware of why the King was growing angry. Henry slowly rose from his throne, his subjects bowing together in reverence.

Askana remained motionless, standing strong as those around her remained upon one knee.

"Askana," Rafe whispered sharply as Henry's footsteps grew near. "For the love of God, bow!"

"No," she answered, never taking her eyes from the approaching King. "He is challenging me. I will not stand down."

Henry Tudor stopped before her, resting one hand firmly on his great hip. The top of Askana's crown barely reached to his stomach. Askana kept her gaze with Henry's, showing nothing in her expression. All she returned was a blank stare to her equal.

Elunear, following her sovereign's lead, stood proudly behind Askana. The young warrior was trying her best to appear fearless and lethal, but she could not help to stare wide-eyed at the sight of this behemoth towering over them both.

His voice was not as booming as it was before, but the undeniable power still resonated strong. "Rafton, what be this deception to Our Royal Person? We were not told of a monarch visiting Our Realm."

"I do crave Your Majesty's pardon, but we are travelling under cover of shadow." Rafe spoke carefully, "Her Majesty, Askana Moldarin, comes from lands in the Far East. The *extremely* Far East. There is a conspiracy within her realm and we have come to beg a boon of your most Royal Majesty."

"Is this true, Your Grace?" King Henry asked of her.

"Your Majesty, We are here on behalf of the people of Morevi. Treachery is growing within Our Council, and We are a nation healing from civil war. Our new government is young and We crave peace for Our New Regime. To obtain this dream, We need allies—powerful allies such as Your valiant subjects—to come to our aid."

"Truly?" sounded the voice of Queen Kathryn from her throne. "And this be the reason You hath placed Your own safety into the keeping of a privateer? If Your judgement in state is as sound as the company You keep, it doth come as no surprise You need help of Us!" A polite laughter rose from the Court, but neither King, pirate, nor visiting Queen found Kathryn's comments amusing. "So tell Us, Queen of Savages, what can You give Us in trade that We do not already take?"

Askana's eyes narrowed upon Queen Kathryn. The child spoke with a voice of headstrong youth, the spoils of privileges, and ignorance of the world. Only four guards flanked her. *An easy target*, Askana thought in passing.

"Your Majesty, We in Morevi have certain techniques in combat that We could teach your soldiers. Advanced training in hand-to-hand combat. Ways of the sword unknown to you. Talents in espionage and intrigue that would benefit Your network of spies."

"Indeed?" King Henry's face softened, "And where will be the soldier that will show his strength before Our Royal Person?"

"*She* stands before Your Majesty," Askana answered. A collected, horrified gasp came from the ladies, disbelieving chuckles from the gentlemen. Askana stepped back, "Elunear, remove Our coat."

The formal garments easily slipped free of her and she now appeared before Henry in simple robes similar to Elunear's. The modest silks liberated the movement of her arms and legs. The brilliant white in her robes matched the white of her Court make-up. It gave her the haunting semblance of a wraith, but still she carried herself as a queen.

"Your Majesty, send five guards to Us," Askana said confidently. "Our martial skills will protect Us and disable Your most skilled warriors."

Intrigued by this boastful yet confident challenge, King Henry nodded to a courtier. The subject bowed in reverence and turned to the archway behind him. He called sharply, "*Landsknechts, einsinstretten!*"

The men that answered this call were lumbering, beefy men dressed in heavy armour and clothing of various fabrics and colours. They also brandished heavy weapons of bulky, wide blades, and huge pistols. The courtier, apparently their commander, spoke to them in a language guttural and harsh, motioning to Askana. They looked at Askana and shook their heads, laughing incredulously while surrounding the painted maiden. One brave Landsknecht approached her as if to embrace her in some silly bear-hug. She leapt high into the air, delivering a harsh kick to the unsuspecting soldier's face. His nose shattered in the instant. He tipped back, landing hard against one of his comrades, and then unconscious against the floor.

A moment's hesitation and then two soldiers charged for her. Askana stepped to one side and attached herself to the back of one soldier, covering his eyes. The burly man spun about in a blind panic, causing Askana's legs to swing out and wrap around the second's neck. While she closed her legs on the second soldier, she tightened her grasp around the first. Both guards struggled for air. Slowly, they began to melt before the onlookers of Court and eventually fell with the sounds of their armour ringing dully against the floor.

Aksana stood over the unconscious guards, her court make-up still appearing flawless and fresh. For the first time since her arrival in London, her lips peeled back to form a smile as her eyes came to rest on the last two guards. The remaining Landsknechts drew heavy short swords no bigger than a man's forearm. Three of their brothers had fallen to this savage and they refused to let their honour be slandered any longer.

They both shouted at the top of their lungs, "*Noch Weiter!*"

One guard found his extended sword arm caught in an odd hand-lock from Askana who pushed the weapon aside. She delivered a hard strike against his elbow that forced the arm to bend unnaturally inward. The bone crunch was accompanied by a howl of pain. A quick side-kick to his kidneys knocked him to one side. The last soldier swung at her but Askana quickly slid up and swept her leg in a crescent-kick against his wrist, blocking the weapon and knocking it out of his hand. She leapt forward with another side-kick to finish this challenge, but the Landsknecht evaded better than she anticipated. He grabbed Askana from behind and held her still. His laugh was extremely indulgent. She struggled against his girth, the smell of sausage and beer offending her senses.

"Oh, this savage is so delightful!" Queen Kathryn clapped gleefully, "She speaks as sweetly as a poet and fights as bravely as a soldier. What other tricks can she do, Captain Rafton?"

Askana had reached her limit with this child's insolence. She kicked swiftly behind her, dealing a hard strike to the soldier's knee. The heavy soldier dropped and her elbow connected hard with his temple, knocking him out cold. In the scuffle, her appearance had been dramatically altered. Her Court make-up, particularly around her lips and eyelashes, was smeared. Her hair, once styled in a Courtly fashion, released huge strands that hung across her face. With the look in her eyes, she did appear wild, savage. In a blur of movement and rush of silk, Askana launched in Queen Kathryn's direction two of her anointed darts. They cut through the air, their sound melding with the scream of the horrified Kathryn Howard.

The darts buried themselves into the Queen's French hood, half an inch above the top of her head. The headdress was now secured into the high back of her throne that she looked at with a pale, horrified look.

"Protect the Queen!" shrieked Kathryn, her hands coming up in tight fists as if she were trying to hide behind the folds of her wide sleeves.

Landsknechts seemed to appear out of every archway. Halberds stretched out over the gathered audience as shrieks and calls to arms filled the Hall. Noblemen either drew daggers in a feeble gesture to protect their beloved Queen or caught ladies that were swooning from all the excitement. In the middle of this pandemonium, surrounded by vanquished guards, was Askana Moldarin. Her eyes were now blind with rage as she began to size up her potential opponents. Elunear stood back-to-back with her Queen, shirai poised and ready to impale any that dared threaten her Sovereign.

Somehow, a hand reached through this chaos and took a gentle hold of her wrist. She could not explain how, but Rafe's words brought a calm to her. "You have made your point, my Queen."

"My Queen." Respect and reverence from the last person she expected to find it. The dark eyes softened as Rafe unconsciously stroked her hand. Her breath slowed. Elunear shoved him away before returning Askana back into the more formal Royal coat. There was a pounding in her head. The Queen closed her eyes for a moment to try and ease was she thought was her heartbeat. Her composure returned but the pounding continued.

The pounding was the boisterous laughter of King Henry the VIII. "Most excellently done, Your Grace!" bellowed the King as he looked to his terrified wife, amused beyond description at the trembling Kathryn. "You have shown Us that You are strong in stature as well as proud of Your God-given nobility. Mayhaps an alliance can be forged betwixt Us. We must needs think on't. For Your lands are far from Our own."

"You have no idea, Your Majesty," Rafe whispered to himself.

"We will unfold Our mind to You anon. Please, do stay here as Our guest in Our most fair city of London and Our Realm of England. Captain Rafton shall serve as ambassador to You as he is so familiar with the ways of Your people." Henry's eyes turned to Rafe with a very contented grin, "We thank you, Captain Rafton, for thy pains. Here is for thy coffer." A page appeared with a small, fist-sized bag of gold coins that the King tossed to Rafe, "You have Our leave."

The assembled parted quickly, giving the Queen, her guard, and the pirate a wide berth. This was not the way in which Rafe would have conducted matters between Askana and King Henry. Nonetheless, the Morevian Queen's prowess had surprisingly opened a dialogue between Morevi and England. Rafe glanced over his shoulder, catching sight of the King and Lord Norfolk exchanging whispers apart from the Court.

He had watched Lord Norfolk betray complete strangers, close friends, and family all in the name of recognition and blessings from the Crown. Watching this man so close to the King did not set his heart at ease.

Rafe excused their page as they continued down the corridor in private. Elunear handed Askana a cloth into which she spat and began removing the formal Court make-up ruined by combat. The smudges and smears made her look ridiculous. By her ferocity in wiping the make-up away, she was still hearing in her mind the taunts and jeers of the English Queen.

"Well, Your Grace," Rafe spoke, breaking the tension in the air. "If this is how fortune smiles on you in politics, I would hate to play you in cards or a game of Hazzard."

"I will have silence from you, privateer!" Askana snapped, spitting once again into the cloth, "Never have I known such disrespect and insolence from members of nobility."

"I see," Rafe nodded. "So is this how you arrange an alliance with an unknown power? By assassinating the Queen of the reigning monarch?"

"If I wanted her dead, I would have taken my aim two inches lower. But with a skull as thick as hers, I would be surprised if my darts could do any damage!" She shook her head in disgust. "What a bloated bombast, your King! So pleased with the entertainment provided by the savage? No doubt his subjects follow his lead."

"No doubt," Rafe nodded, keeping his calm.

"Such arrogance," continued the Queen. "He believes the sun rises and sets at his bidding! Perhaps he and his subjects could use a lesson or two in humility."

Lubria had made certain the hallway was clear before greeting them by their chambers. She displayed a very contented smile as her tail twitched gently from side-to-side, "I could hear the battle from here, Your Grace. It doth appear you made an unforgettable impression upon these humans."

"Despicable people, these English!" Askana called back into the direction of the Great Hall, "If I had my wish right now, I would have them all drawn and quartered in my public square! And that detestable creature of a queen, her head would be spitted upon the tip of my shirai, surrounded by the rotting corpses of her beloved subjects!"

Before Elunear or Lubria could leap to her defence, Rafe took hold of the Queen's arm and braced her against the corridor wall. His technique was so swift it even caught Askana by surprise. Only the flickering of corridor torches interrupted the stillness of the moment, a moment appeared frozen for an eternity.

Then Rafe spoke his mind. "Every subject's duty is to the King and Country. But no King, Queen, or Country holds counsel over a subject's soul." Rafe released her with a shove, "Namely, *this* subject's soul."

"Of course not, privateer," Askana rubbed her arm where Rafe dared to hold her fast. "You sell yours to the highest bidder."

"Think on this, Your Grace, my loyalty to you does carry a heavy price, but what you have subjected me to with your dark magic goes well beyond my fee! Be certain to thank that faceted deity of yours I did not throw you and your companions to the sharks after discovering your witchcraft."

"Your Grace, give me word to rip his heart out," Lubria growled. "This human tests your most royal person."

"There would be no gain in such a word, Lubria," the Queen spoke softly. "How can you rip out his heart when he has none?"

Rafe stepped closer, his body almost touching hers. "Bitch."

Lubria's lips peeled back into a menacing hiss, but Askana raised her hand, the gesture enough to hold the Fae-woman at bay. Regardless of the Caillech's spell, she wanted to lash out at him. There were so many options before her, seeing as to how close he was. A simple blow to the throat, or a well-delivered strike to the nose. He would not be able to defend himself and it would only cost her a momentary discomfort. Why could she not strike him down? The Queen stared into his eyes. Unlike his King's, Captain Rafton's were not challenging. Nor were they defiant. It was regret she found in his eyes, contrary to his stance and demeanour.

"I will retire for the night," Rafe spat. "By your leave?"

"You have it," Askana said flatly. "Use it."

Rafe shut the door to his quarters and rested his forehead against the thick oak, giving his head a few light taps against the wood. *Well done, Rafton,* he thought to himself, *you let your heart speak instead of your head.*

He could see the Baroness now, far too vividly for his liking. Rafe's heart carried her image with him on the most desolate of nights at sea. How Askana was so much like her in spirit and demeanour. This is what bothered him most about the entire venture. He needed to remember that the Baroness was in the past, never to be seen or heard from again, and that Her Majesty was nothing more than an employer. His heart had no business in being moved or influenced, nor to speak out of turn as it had just then. Again, he thought upon the Baroness and reminded himself of what a great lie were those three words she had once uttered to him...

"Good evening, master," her silky voice caressed his ears.

No, Rafe thought to himself flippantly, *those were not the three words she had said to me.*

He turned to face the exquisite creature stretched out across his bed. She wore a bejewelled top accented by transparent veils that attempted to cover her toned legs. He followed the sensual curves of her breasts and stomach as she sat up on her knees, the shadows only adding definition to her body. From her head flowed a blanket of hair that matched the darkness in her eyes and the hazelnut colour of her skin.

"I am A'idah, and I am for you."

"Truly?" Rafe smiled wickedly, raising an eyebrow. He unbuttoned his doublet as he approached the bed. With each step, she became more and more enticing, "And pray, what have I done to be gifted with such a jewel from the Nile?"

"I was deemed appropriate." Rafe reached out to her to stroke her cheek that had a lovely, delicate smoothness to it. She leaned into his caress, her lips softly kissing his own fingertips. "I was told that your actions warranted my bounty to you."

With those words, she removed her top slowly to reveal her dark breasts. She breathed deeply as the back of Rafe's fingers traced the curve of her exquisite figure. A gentle moan escaped her lips as she tipped her head back. She reached up to him, her hands running along the outside of his shirt. Rafe could not help but think to himself as her lips gently touched his, *This is exactly what I need tonight.*

Askana's eyes remained shut, occasionally closing tighter as Elunear rubbed the soreness away from her muscles. Lubria had fallen asleep at the foot of the bed, her tail twitching slightly as she dreamed. The Queen reached down to gently scratch between the Fae-woman's shoulder blades. She heard a soft rumble come from her. A smile formed on Lubria's lips. Askana had missed her "sister" more than she realised. The Queen had masqueraded the loss of Lubria as setting her free so she could find her own voice. Everyone she loved she lost for the Crown, for the sake of her birthright. This birthright now led her here to a strange land, far from home to seek an alliance with a king uncertain in his mind, and the only ally she could trust and rely on was this—

"Cursed pirate." Elunear seethed as she worked on her Queen's tense back muscles, "How dare he insult the Crown."

"Sister Elunear," Askana groaned. "His verbal insults pale in comparison to your assault upon my shoulder."

"I am sorry, my Gracious Sovereign."

"No apologies necessary, Elunear. Just vent your temper through your voice, not your touch."

"I do not understand why you let him live," Elunear pulled the thin muslin away from Askana's body to where it exposed her back fully. "He swears no allegiance and grants no respect to any. His words betray even his own King."

"But his words are honest. There has been no deception on his part and yet that is his business, the art of deception, is it not? He knows I could have him killed with little or no hesitation, but it is his honesty—whether I care to hear it or not—that keeps him alive."

And then there was the spell of Grainne's. She could not tell Elunear. Not now. Perhaps on the journey's end...

"Forgive me, my Queen, for being so bold," Elunear's hands trembled a bit as she took a deep breath, "but I think Your Majesty misjudges the loyalty of this privateer. He would sell your soul if the price was so offered."

"I said the man was honest, not loyal." Askana glanced at Lubria, still deep in slumber. "There is a difference."

Elunear paused for a moment, "My Queen?"

"Elunear, you are of the Royal Guard, sworn to protect my life and die for the greater good of Morevi if so called upon." Askana looked over her shoulder and stared deeply into her Guard's eyes, "But tell me, do you think I warranted the insult from Captain Rafton?"

"No, my most blessed Queen!" Elunear was horrified at the mere notion of siding with the brash pirate. "I would not dare speak such an insult."

"But would you think it?"

The young girl hesitated for a moment and then found her voice, but the words choked in her throat. The hesitation had betrayed her true thoughts. She could not help to ask why her Queen's anger, though justified, was directed to the one who had risked his own life two times over? True, this pirate was brash, but enigmatic for a mercenary. Fighting alongside her against the Morev'ar. Their escape from Eyrie. His respect to her in King Henry's Great Hall. These were not the actions of a simple hired blade.

"And this is what separates you from the Captain," Askana laid back upon the bed, casually stroking the lovely red hair of Lubria. "You think your heart whereas Captain Rafton speaks his."

Askana felt a sudden tightness in her throat as she looked to the door of her chambers. His insult was honest and perhaps that is what made it hurt all the more. She had been called far worse in her time, but it was out of passion, politics, or blind hatred. Never out of honesty. True honesty grew harder to find the closer she came to the Throne. She noted regret in his eyes, the first time she had seen regret in this bravado Captain. She remembered the sad little tune Rafe played upon the deck of his ship. *"There are many sides to me, Your Grace,"* he had said to her upon the deck of his grand vessel, *"that remain uncharted to you."*

Perhaps, she thought as the tightness swelled again in her throat, *there are some realms best left uncharted.*

"Elunear, open a window." Askana sighed as she tried to block out the memory of Rafe's honesty, "I find the air too still in here."

A'idah threw her head back, her gasp evolving into a delighted moan of ecstasy. Her leg muscles tensed around his waist as she gave another erotic cry that echoed in his chambers, her nipples tight in excitement of feeling him so close. She looked down to him and tried to find the words, but his own gasps said exactly what she felt.

Rafe struggled for air as the bejewelled top that she had casually removed now tightened around his neck. His gasps became rougher and harder, his intake of air far less than before. He remembered the feel of her lips against his own as she removed his shirt. He remembered her legs wrapping around his waist while she played with his blonde hair. He vaguely remembered the feeling of her thin, flimsy garment being gently draped around his neck. He just managed to slip his fingers in between his neck and her top before she pulled against it. He did not count on the woman's strength pressing his fingers against his windpipe, his only leverage against her attack now slowly turning against him.

"They told me you would be an exquisite kill," she gasped. "I had no idea you would be this magnificent!" She plunged her tongue deep into his mouth, making breathing for him close to impossible.

The door over her shoulder grew blurry in his sight. The colours of his chambers began to run together and he could feel his eyes roll back into his head. A'idah's legs tightened around his waist as his strength ebbed away.

Then he reached for a moment, one single moment of clarity, and he found a solution. He had to hit it just right.

Rafe pulled his hands free of the halter, feeling the rough fabric, jewels, and gold against his bare neck. He grabbed A'idah in an embrace that brought her to a frenzy of delight.

"Yes, my dearest!" She gave the garment around his neck a long, slow tug, "Embrace me, the mistress of your death! Oh, yes!"

With his last remaining strength, Rafe charged at the closest stone wall of his chambers, striking it with A'idah's shoulder. Her shriek in pain was satisfying, but Rafe delighted more in the quick crack her shoulder made when it dislocated. The shock of the blow loosened her grip enough for Rafe to push free of her. He fell to one knee, gasping for air, coughing harshly. The flash of his own dagger brought him back to his feet. A'idah had landed by his weapons and freed his duelling dagger from its sheath. She now appeared less graceful as her left arm swayed helplessly by her side. She lunged for Rafe, but he quickly locked his hands around her forearm and tossed her towards a large window. Her body shattered the intricate stained glass design. A'idah's screams echoed as she fell, abruptly stopping on her body striking the courtyard.

The pirate rubbed his neck as he peered through the hole where his window once was. He watched her twitch a few times before going still on the stone path underneath her. The calls to arms sounded as guards rushed to find the assassin's body, see where it fell from, and disperse to protect their King, Queen, and guests.

Askana.

Rafe freed his rapier from its scabbard and rushed across the hall, kicking the door open. Lubria leapt from her state of sleep and growled sharply. Elunear dropped the tray of tea and produced two small throwing blades from her hairpiece. Askana produced a shirai from the shadows of her bed. With the exception of Lubria, weapons lowered as they noticed it was Rafe.

Shirtless.

Rafe seemed too preoccupied to notice Askana was wearing only a small loincloth about her waist. "Elunear," Askana said sharply. "A robe."

Rafe's eyes darted from corner to corner of the guest chambers, his rapier slowly lowering. Lubria's eyes seemed to flash with an emerald glow as she watched the pirate closely, waiting and hoping for a reason to pounce. Askana secured the robe about her and tossed the shirai to Elunear as she approached the disoriented pirate.

"Well, privateer, I cannot begin to imagine why you would burst into my chambers unannounced. And half-dressed?"

"Your Grace," Rafe said, completely disregarding her words, "you are alone?"

"No," she said incredulously. "Lubria and Elunear have been in my company all the while. Is this the imperative question you have come to ask of me in this waning hour?"

"I had a caller." Rafe finally stepped into the brighter torchlight, revealing to Askana the abrasions on his neck, "A delightful mistress with a most engaging personality."

"Your neck! Elunear, fetch me the basin!" Askana guided the Captain to the edge of her bed, starring at the redness in his neck. "I assure you there is no one here other than who you see."

Rafe looked to Lubria, "No callers while we were away?"

Lubria stared at the doorway.

Askana immersed a linen into a basin of cool water as she spoke, "Lubria, were there any callers during our audience with King Henry?"

"No, my Queen," she replied.

"Well then, this complicates things," Rafe winced as Askana softly touched the cold cloth to his neck. "My assassin was waiting for me in my chambers. No one knew I was there apart from our Court Page. Then again, with the way that young whip gossips, he could have probably told all of England, Ireland, Scotland, and Wales by now. Someone in Court is not happy with me serving as your ambassador. Someone in the palace wants me dead and Your Grace unguarded." Elunear straightened up slightly, the shirai staff tapping against the stone floor, "No offence intended, young one. We must be cautious, even in Royal company."

"Should we not leave, Your Majesty?" Elunear asked.

"I would advise against it," Rafe answered quickly. "King Henry would not ally himself with a guest who would leave unannounced. You must wait for the King to announce his decision. Therefore, if you don't mind, I will stay here this evening. We must stay close."

The women looked at the privateer coldly.

"Not that close," Rafe assured them. "I intend to sleep on the floor within arm's reach of rapier and pistol."

"Lubria, stand watch," Askana motioned for the shirai she handed to Elunear. She placed it along the length of the bed, well within her reach if she were awakened unexpectedly. "We stay for the evening."

Rafe wondered if he would catch any sleep tonight. He had returned home hoping for a royal audience. He was now a moving target. What of Askana? Was she a target as well? His thoughts were broken on noticing Elunear staring him down.

Rafe finally broke the tense silence as he rested his weapon casually upon his shoulder. "Do you object, my lady?"

"I do, privateer," Elunear sneered.

"Good," He smiled, moving towards the door. "I was afraid you were suddenly developing a sense of respect for me." He returned to Askana's chambers a moment later with his belongings, dropping them where he stood. "I assure you my intentions are and will remain strictly honourable." The pirate reclined against the side of Askana's bed, resting his head against the mattress with his formal doublet serving as a pillow. "I suggest you try and sleep, Your Grace. We can only hope King Henry does not dally in his decision."

Lubria crept to the shadows of the chambers, her eyes never leaving the privateer who slipped off to sleep with his rapier draped across his lap. Elunear gave her own shirai a twirl in her hand, her eyes also watching Rafe closely. Askana read in her Guard's eyes a strange mix of mistrust and envy. Pulling the folds of her thin robe closer to her body, Askana reclined back into the comforts of the bed. Random thoughts of Kubi-Sogi, the delicate balance of her kingdom, and Morevi kept mingling with King Henry's laugh and the insults of Kathryn Howard. This myriad of priorities and distractions eventually lulled her to a deep sleep she desperately needed.

The warmth of sunlight awakened Askana. Her first sight was truly reassuring. Lubria was still dutifully keeping her post by the door, gingerly stroking the brilliant golden waves of the young guard asleep in her lap. There was a peaceful smile upon Elunear's face, perhaps a subconscious reaction to the Fae-woman's gentle touch. It delighted Askana to see them together once more, recalling their bond of friendship.

A sharp cry from the balcony caused her to turn her head with a snap. It was Rafe. He appeared to be practising a martial art similar to one from Kubi-Sogi's vast knowledge of styles. Rafe's technique, although needing improvement in stances and one or two of the more difficult kicks, was nothing short of impressive. A low block across the body, then slowly moving into a knife-hand block. His morning workout caused his body to glisten in the morning sunlight as he came about with a lethal blow followed by a sharp cry. Taking in his features in more detail than she had at the lake, Rafe's torso was not overly muscular. It was smooth and defined with an even amount of hair across his pectoral muscles. She lingered on the sight of him, perhaps since she was still waking from her rest. Then he came to a halt in his exercise with a deep intake of air.

Askana gave a light laugh, "Where did you learn the ancient arts of *TanTeKassa*? I see the way your people move. The King's Guard, in particular, lumber in such a manner that make Eyrieners appear graceful."

The Captain smiled as he took a cloth soaking in rose water, still chilled from the morning air. "Indeed, we English are not the most elegant of fighters. My sister and I spent a glorious year in Italy where I learned this art. My master knew it by another name."

"Italy?" Askana pondered on the name. *England. Italy. Such strange names for countries and kingdoms.*

"Yes, part of the Gateway to the East." Rafe smiled as he padded his face with the cloth, "A cultural treasure. I found a master there who agreed to teach me this ancient form of combat. I must say, it has made me the better swordsman."

"You have potential, Captain," Askana nodded in approval.

Rafe gave a bow to her, "And after seeing you fight, I am certain you would make an excellent teacher, Your Grace."

Askana could hear in his words the same reverence he bestowed to her yesterday in the Grand Hall. It would appear the events in the corridor were behind them. "I am honoured."

As Rafe continued his quick rubdown, Askana turned to Lubria, still keeping watch. "No callers or curious servants last night?"

"Neither, my sovereign," Lubria nodded as Elunear wrinkled her nose, a reflex to the fur in Lubria's paw tickling her. "I gave Elunear leave to rest."

"She needed it." Askana smiled, "Thank you, Lubria. I have missed you."

"In your own way, perhaps." There was an unsettling chill in her tone. "So tell me, my Queen, how skilled is the man in combat?"

Before Askana could answer, Elunear stirred. "My Queen?" she said, her voice still heavy with sleep, "Forgive me in falling asleep. I did—"

"Nothing that you did not earn, Elunear." Askana nodded, "Be assured you have served your Queen well and did not falter in your duties."

Rafe, now dressed and adorning his weapons, extended a hand to Askana. The Queen was uncertain about this gesture at first. Perhaps it was the evening's rest they finally had taken or his personal reflection during his exercise, but Rafe's demeanour was much softer than before. The privateer was humbled, more reverent to the Queen than he has ever shown since their adventure's start.

"Your Grace, once you are dressed, would you indulge me this afternoon?" He smiled warmly, "I have a diversion in mind for us. As the King has appointed me your ambassador, I wish to introduce you to my home of London."

"Do you really think it wise in light of last night's attempt on you?" Askana asked, taken aback by Rafe's sudden wild abandon of reason.

"On the contrary, I find surrounding ourselves with people in the light of day the wisest course of action. Assassins tend to be shy and prefer to work covertly, preferably at night. We simply must take caution as we stay in plain sight of the good people of England, and in plain sight of each other." He extended his hand once more, "Trust me, Your Grace."

As Askana hesitantly took his hand, Rafe spoke to Lubria and Elunear. "I suggest that Elunear, taking into account last night's excitement, pays a call on the *Defiant* this morning. Tell Nassir if he does not hear from us in two days time to sail for Devon and await orders there. As for you, sweet lass," Rafe turned to Lubria, "remain here. We will return from the afternoon to gather our remaining items, hear the mind of my King, and then we will return to Morevi, hopefully with the allies we need."

Lubria remained silent, her eyes showing no acknowledgement of the Captain's words.

"Lubria," Askana spoke softly, "remain here. You will return to Morevi with us and, we hope, the allies needed in our endeavours."

"As you wish, my Queen." Lubria purred.

The streets of London were as they had been on their arrival, overflowing with activity, sounds, and life that never abated. Askana, absent of Court make-up and formal robes, could not hide her status. Even wearing the crown that appeared as an exotic headdress and simple travel robes of white silk, she commanded respect and reverence. Rafe seemed completely unaffected by the attention the two of them attracted as they continued through the streets. Oddly enough, it seemed that Rafe welcomed it.

With the Queen to his right, Rafe proudly pointed out landmarks that made England renowned. These landmarks were obviously leading to the final destination he intended for them—an open marketplace of musicians, artisans, and carefree revels. A celebration. Here, peasants and lesser nobility caroused together in dance, games, and commerce. Rafe referred to it as a "Festival Day".

He told her that before and after the harvest, his people would revel and feast in hopes that God would smile upon them and grant them bountiful crops. Askana shook her head in the contradiction of this realm. They feared sorcery and magic, yet they believed their celebration would yield plentiful crops. *Such folly*, Askana thought.

These English were a very different breed compared to Morevians but commonality would reach across The Rift to link their two worlds in this Festival of the Harvest. Chickens fluttered wildly as they were stuffed into bags while only a few steps away a wrestling match commenced between two husky men. An elaborately dressed street performer would exhale a cone of fire skyward for the amusement and patronage of onlookers. Rafe would throw a few shillings towards the musicians upon the street corners, showing a generosity at the music of "bagpipes". He was not from this land called "Scotland", but he admired their people's spirit and resolve.

The appearance of this instrument called bagpipes unsettled Askana, though not nearly as much as the shrill sounds that erupted from the series of pipes that seemed to hang free from itself. The "music" resembled that of a hawk or a falcon in distress or perhaps a *Shamaraj* being skinned alive. Or both.

The market teemed over with activity and life, a celebration of a successful planting season. Rafe's eyes seemed to illuminate with rapture as they walked through the city streets. It was obvious that he was happy to return home—brief as his stay would be—but to return during the Harvest Celebration was something special to him. Askana could not help but be reminded of the same activity that she would find in her own streets of Songkusai.

Rafe led Askana to a small clearing where a vendor of games, puzzles, and other challenges had set up two small archery targets. Before the master of games, a pair of bows and a dozen arrows awaited the skill of a hunter or warrior.

"If memory serves me right, Askana Moldarin, First Queen of Morevi," Rafe chuckled in a jovial manner as if introducing her to the surrounding masses, "is known to be quite the archer. Would you care to live up to your reputation?"

Askana, her senses growing accustomed to the festivities around her, never cracked a grin as she approached the archery challenge. There was purpose to this diversion and it still remained unknown to her. A moment's peace, perhaps? Recreation to ease the soul for just a moment? Not this one. There was a reason he was known in the Trade Circles of her realm as "The Sea Wolf". She watched him more carefully than ever. It would be in this time that men of his nature would dare to make overtures towards her. Perhaps this challenge would serve to humble the overconfident Rafe Rafton.

"Merchant," Askana spoke evenly with little elation, "move the target back another one hundred paces."

"But my Lady," the vendor guffawed, "the target is a hundred paces back already. Such a challenge would be a wasted effort."

Askana gripped the bow, her fingers moving the bowstring back and forth slowly. It was not the quality of bow she was accustomed to but it would do. "Move the target back."

Her tone now struck the vendor less as a request and more as a warning. The game master's eyes turned to Rafe who, behind Askana's back, made with his fingers the image of a crown over his head while motioning to Askana. The vendor bowed, his skin growing pale in realising his slur towards nobility, "Yes, Your Majesty, do forgive my insolence."

The target seemed to grow smaller as the peasant moved it an additional one hundred paces into the open field. A few passers-by paused for a moment to see this oddly adorned woman handle a bow and arrow as a skilled archer would on the battlefield. Askana was presented with six arrows. The game master's body language betrayed his scepticism at her skill. Queen, huntsman, or seasoned soldier would find this challenge near impossible. With no further words as to insult visiting royalty, he stood to one side as onlookers gathered.

Askana's dark eyes narrowed upon the target. She would have preferred it to be another fifty paces distant, but that would be boastful. This distance would suffice. The bowstring never wavered as she pulled back. The arrow sailed through the air. Its journey was silent and swift as it impacted with the target.

Bullseye.

The next one followed instantly. Her technique and dexterity in nocking her second arrow appeared unnatural and inhuman. This was from her archery training with the Elves. Their methods were not easy for humans to learn, but with discipline and focus it was possible. Under the Elves' tutorage, an archer's ability could double in efficiency and speed. This was why she did not take a moment to aim her second arrow. She did not need to. She had a feel for this simple bow and adapted with the conditions of her surroundings.

A second bullseye.

Rafe's eyebrows lifted, his head nodding in acknowledgement of Askana's skill. The onlookers gasped as she landed yet a third arrow in between the two already residing in the centre of the target. Whispers echoing "savage" and "most improper" filtered through the din of wonder Askana's skill warranted. It was clear that these dim English could not accept the fact that a woman, particularly one foreign to their realm, could be far superior in the ways of combat. *Very well, then,* Askana thought with a trace smile. *The pirate has been dealt his warning. Now it was time for the English to receive one of their own.*

The fourth arrow pulled slowly back along the top of her hand. Her eyes narrowed slightly as she focused on her target. The Elven technique washed through her body, every muscle relaxed and yet every muscle steady and taut. The more distant observers wondered if she was a statue as she appeared so still in her poise.

Then her fingers released the bowstring. The arrowhead spilt her first arrow's shaft in two. The spectators went silent.

"She must know Robin of the Hood!" a young girl exclaimed.

Before Askana could respond, the mother snatched up her child and disappeared from sight. Perhaps it was the way she looked or the unmistakable fact that she was nobility. She felt it from all of them. Askana caught fear in their eyes. Her awareness of just how different she was from them heightened. She turned her eyes to Rafe. It was time to shift attention elsewhere.

"Now, privateer," Askana said as she set the bow before him. "Impress the Crown of Morevi and your people with your skill."

Rafe was caught completely off guard. He blinked, hoping he had not heard Askana correctly. "I beg your pardon, Your Grace?"

"You issued the challenge. Now let Us see how truly capable you English are." Askana looked to the still-growing crowd and then turned back to Rafe, "We desire it. Deny not Our wishes lest We complain to your King."

All eyes now rested on Captain Rafael Stringfellow Rafton.

He picked up the bow and let out a heavy sigh, shaking his head lightly. He stared at the clean target one hundred paces away from him. The vendor offered to move it back another one hundred, but a quick look from Rafe told him this was not an option. If anything, Rafe wanted it closer. Say, within arm's reach.

Two arrows. The pride of his realm rested in his skill with two arrows. With a deep breath, he pulled the first arrow back with his two fingers and released.

The arrow sailed past the target, never brushing its coloured canvas.

A few giggles and snickers could be heard as the wooden shaft skimmed the grass and rocks behind the target. Rafe was trying to focus on keeping his hands steady. Instead, he found himself fumbling with the final arrow as he brought his bow back up. He swallowed hard and pulled back on the bowstring. He could see in the corner of his eye the Queen of Morevi struggling to subdue her own laughter. Rafe quietly muttered a prayer to God and released the arrow. The crowd watched as it sailed through the air, landing squarely into the target.

Three feet to the left of the bullseye.

Groans of disappointment rose from the onlookers. Before the vendor could comment jovially on Rafe's defeat, a pistol appeared. A small capsule of powder had been dumped into its pan and its hammer was pulled back into a firing position.

The gunshot ripped through the sounds of the celebration, and the crowd cowered back in surprise. For a moment, the surrounding revels ceased and every head turned to the sudden sound of pistol fire. When the smoke cleared, Rafe's target was reduced a collection of splinters, straw, and bits of canvas. The crowd erupted into laughter as Rafe firmly placed a small sack of gold coins into the vendor's palm. Askana even let a good laugh escape as the pirate returned his pistol to its resting place in his belt.

"Captain, you are a brilliant tactician as a privateer and extremely gifted with a blade." Askana shook her head in total amazement, nearly doubling over with laughter as she spoke, "But your skills in archery are quite lacking. I think the children of Morevi shoot better than yourself."

"Now you see why I use a pistol, Your Grace," Rafe scoffed. "Never did care for archery."

Her jibes reminded him of growing up with his sister, Serena, whenever she would best him in a playful rapier fight. A sweet innocence seasoned with satisfaction at his shortcomings. There was little vindictiveness in her words. The sight of the destroyed target now struck Rafe as a rather ridiculous sight. He returned the laughter, savouring this fleeting image of the Morevian Queen.

Askana thought she should have felt guilt for enjoying herself, but instead she only felt a release. A glorious release followed by a light euphoria. *When was the last time I laughed like this*, she thought distantly.

Rafe finally spoke, his words a bit awkward as if he wanted to assure what he uttered was composed perfectly. "Your Grace, I wish to convey my regret for what was said yesternight. I have never developed a faith or trust in magic. There is too much in your world for my taste, nor do I care for it practised upon me without consent. But you did save my life and I would not wish you to think I did not appreciate such a gesture."

"Pirate," Askana could feel herself taking his words to heart. Sincerity matching his honesty. She cleared her mind quickly. "There is no need for your thanks or gratitude. I did what I did for the greater—"

"— good of Morevi. Yes, I know. So you love to tell me again and again. I also know that pirates are not rare in your world or mine. You could have easily let me die and offered the price to another."

Askana desperately searched for words to countermand his. As she did, she silently cursed his logic that she found even more infuriating than his honesty.

"Your Grace, my words last night were rash. Ill-timed in your present situation, so far from home. I simply wanted you to know that I am grateful."

"I see there is simply no end to your indignities to the Crown, privateer," Askana smirked playfully. "Very well then. Apology accepted and you are welcome, privateer."

"Please, Your Grace, call me Rafe."

The smile suddenly melted away. "It would not be proper, pirate. You are a servant of Morevi. And when our transaction concludes, you will still be regarded as an enemy of the state. This treaty between you and Morevi is only binding while in my service."

Rafe offered his hand to Askana as a formal escort and nodded, his words less elated than before, "You are quite correct, Your Grace. Forgive me for not knowing my place."

They had not taken two steps further before they noticed the crowd ahead parting quickly. An order of the King's Guard made their way down the street with the Duke of Norfolk walking between them. Thomas Howard, dressed now in black robes and wearing ornate gold chains of office, lightly tapped his cane twice against the stone walk. The large guards surrounding him assumed a parade rest as he approached Rafe and Askana, his black robes billowing with each step. One soldier had a bandage across his nose while another displayed a black eye and slight limp. They both gave the visiting Queen cold stares, still feeling the sting of humiliation from the day before in the Great Hall.

As Lord Norfolk approached, Askana could feel the light hair on the back of her neck stand, a cold sweat forming at the base of her spine. Something in Thomas Howard's eyes, a void of blind ambition and absent ethics, made every instinct in her sink to a defensive crouch.

"Good Captain Rafton," Lord Norfolk smiled as he extended a hand to Rafe. "I trust you have entertained Her Majesty well this afternoon? London does have so much to offer this visitor from far-off lands."

"That it does, my most gracious Duke, but we are tired and were about to retire for the day." Rafe nodded, his hand casually resting against the pommel of his rapier. "I was just about to escort Her Grace back to Her chambers."

"I have been sent as emissary from the King to bring you before His Majesty to discuss plans for supplying allies to Morevi."

Askana's heart soared. Rafe beamed brightly, perhaps mirroring her elation. "Excellent. I shall attend to His Majesty once Queen Askan—"

"Captain, if you would not mind, my guards will escort you to His Majesty who waits upon you. It would honour me if I could partake in the pleasure of the Queen's company. I shall personally serve as her escort back to the palace."

She felt her blood run cold at the thought. As if by instinct, Askana's hand tightened slightly around Rafe's. The privateer smiled cordially as he gave Lord Norfolk a slight bow. "Well, my gracious Duke, I am certain the Queen will be delighted. May I share a moment with Her Majesty in private before you are on your way?"

A hint of impatience crossed Lord Norfolk's face as Rafe took Askana aside for a brief audience.

She remained static and formal, but her instincts were telling her not to let Rafe out of sight. "Privateer, I do not trust this Thomas Howard."

"Neither do I, Your Grace," Rafe cast a quick glance over her shoulder to the Duke. "Give me an occasional nod as if you are accepting counsel. When you speak to me now, make it appear as if you are giving me orders."

"Why pretend? I am giving you a Royal Order—do not turn me over to the Duke of Norfolk. There is something unsettling about him."

"I would not argue that for all the world, Your Grace, but we must play this hand out. I do not wish to take chances with King Henry. His mind is as constant as the colour of a sunset. If he has truly agreed to allies, then we need to act quickly. Lord Norfolk is not the most trustworthy of gentlemen, but he is still a servant to the King. If any harm befalls on you while in his company, it will be his head joining his dear Boleyn relative. Do not worry, Your Grace. I am not as concerned of him taking action against you so much as you taking action against him. I will not be there to stop you." Rafe leaned in closer to her with a smile, "And if I were, I probably would not."

His flippancy was comforting for a change. Returning to the tiny procession of Lord Norfolk's, Rafe took Askana's hand and passed it from himself to Howard, the most civil of smiles shared between the two men as the Captain bowed in respect. She took in a deep breath as the privateer under the King's Guard disappeared into the crowded streets of London.

The sun was setting quickly and Thomas Howard's appeal did not improve with the growing shadows of nightfall. "Your Majesty, this is indeed an honour for me," smiled the Duke as they began to walk in the direction of the palace. "You made quite an impression upon the King, and he wished me to serve as ambassador to you during your stay."

"Rafe Rafton fills that office very capably," Askana said curtly.

"Aye, Your Majesty, as far as privateers go. Captain Rafton is a bit more 'refined' as far as his kind are, but he is quite ignorant of what we are accustomed to in Court."

Her eyebrow arched slightly at his presumption. "And just what are we accustomed to in Court?"

"Revels of chance." Howard said smugly as they took a sharp turn away from the main footpath.

The growing darkness engulfed them. Askana noted the narrowing of streets as she followed Howard's lead. She thought rather comically how this was a direct antithesis to the Southern Wood. Instead of open mists and concealed threats, these spaces were confined and claustrophobic, the shadows attempting in vain to cover their dangerous omens. It was at this moment Askana realised she and Lord Norfolk were unescorted by guards or attendants. They were alone in the darker back streets of London.

Part of her wondered if she would not be safer now in the Tangled Southern Wood.

"My Lord, my Lady," the poor wretch hidden under the layers of his cloak moaned. "Spare a penny for a leper."

Lord Norfolk continued along as if he did not notice. Askana caught a hint of movement from the opposite side of the narrow street. Clumsy and primitive as it was, they had stepped into a thieves' trap. She moved for her wrist darts but the flash of silver seemed to lash out like a dragon's tongue. The blade sunk deeply into the gut of the advancing attacker and Howard gave his weapon a few ghoulish twists, scrambling the insides of the assailant. Pushing the dying man off the sword, he then turned to the leper and removed his hood and mask to reveal a terrified peasant suffering only of hunger and desperation. The Duke's blade slipped across his neck before he could beg again. For mercy.

Askana removed her hand from the wrist gauntlet as Lord Norfolk sheathed the sword back into the concealment of his cane.

"Is this what you do in the English Court for entertainment?" Askana asked as she watched the life ebb away from their attackers.

"Forgive the King's subjects." The Duke shrugged as Askana apprehensively took his hand. "No, the entertainment I truly enjoy is sport of a different nature." Lord Norfolk stopped at a single level building, its windows covered with a thick fog from the heat of the people gathered inside. The muffled cheers rose for a prolonged moment of frenzy and then subsided to a murmur, the sound of coins quickly exchanging hands. Howard rapped upon the door with his cane twice, paused, and then rapped twice again. An attendant opened the door. His face was covered in sweat and his look was that of one who would not be bothered trivially. Catching sight of the Duke of Norfolk, the man's expression melted and he bowed in reverence as the door opened wide. "And it is just ahead of us in here. Follow me, Your Majesty."

Lord Norfolk led Askana through a collection of men and women. The privileged and the peasants were all gathered here. The atmosphere was not like the carefree innocence of Rafe's Festival. Royal advisers, merchants, wenches, gentlemen and ladies of Court were pressed next to one another, all sharing one common thirst in that moment. A thirst crossing class boundaries. A thirst their cries begged for satisfaction.

A thirst for blood.

They were all peering down into a submerged, circular pit, reminiscent to the gaming pits of Eyrie. Askana had seen them when she and a handful of soldiers infiltrated the city walls of Iambourgh to discover more of their foe to the west. But unlike the gaming pits of Eyrie, a massive post was embedded in the ground close to one edge of the circle, and fixed to the post was a chain attached to the back ankle of a massive bear. Howard and Askana took proper seats, apparently reserved for the Duke. It appeared from the preferential treatment bestowed on him that the Lord Norfolk was a regular at these barbaric revels. Two dogs, snarling and foaming at the mouth, were thrown into the pit just out of the bear's reach. The cheers became wild as the two canines nipped at the beast, joining the hall with her own cries. A massive paw sent one of the canines against the wall. The yelp as the dog hit the wall would be its last sound. It landed with a dull, dead thud against the ground. The ones who had bet on the bear howled in delight. The jingling of coins exchanging hands filled the air as the bear gave a pathetic grunt, tugging in vain at the manacle around its one ankle.

Askana could not mask her revulsion at this display. *These English dare to call me a savage*, she thought bitterly. "What is this atrocity you have brought me to witness?"

"We call this bear baiting," The Duke said proudly, signalling to the game masters to begin another round. "If we feel particularly bold, we will sometimes throw in a man. This particular pit was inspired by the gaming pits of your world."

Askana turned to face him, now oblivious to the barbarism commencing in the pit, "You know of Naruihm and The Rift?"

"There are many issues a loyal servant to the Crown must make himself aware of. The King is made aware of them if they have a direct effect upon the Throne." Howard savoured the continuing combat of bear versus canines as he continued to speak with the Queen, "Other trivialities, however, I take a personal interest in, such as The Barrier Reef. A quaint little tavern in the heart of The Rift—how intriguing! The current political standing in Morevi, I find most stimulating. There are also the growing tensions between your realm and Eyrie."

"And your King knows none of this?"

"It would not hold his limited interest. His Majesty cares little about our own 'New World' outside of how it can better his own kingdom! He only knows you come from a far-off land and your political tensions have you in need of allies, but that is not his concern so much as his attentions upon you."

Askana sat back in her chair, the cheers of the maddening crowd causing her own blood to course quickly as she recognised an old pattern beginning to form, "But your King is married, is he not?"

"Aye, Your Majesty, to my niece. My sweet, little strumpet of a niece." Howard spat. "I wish I could say all is well with Court. Sadly, it is not." Lord Norfolk sat back as the two canines took full advantage of the bear, now drained from the night of combat. The dogs sank their teeth into the bear's neck, the calls of elation and disappointment driving the animals all the more in their killing frenzy. "I thought my niece would bring the name of Howard back to greatness and she has, but the little slut is threatening everything. It has come to my attention that she is enjoying relations with some of the younger gentlemen of Court, in particular a young rogue by the name of Culpeper. I know word has reached the King and he is refuting what he believes to be nothing more than jealous Court gossip. But his confidence is beginning to falter. I cannot afford that." Askana could see in the corner of her eye the wranglers dragging out the bear's lifeless body while Howard continued, "His Majesty was most impressed with your abilities in the Great Hall. The fact you are pleasing to the eye is a blessing of God's that should be taken to its full advantage."

Askana could feel the beginnings of a blood rage as Howard smiled smugly. "Exactly what do you want me to do?"

"Your Majesty, my niece is but a young and tender child, and therefore easily swayed. She constantly wants what she cannot or should not have. However, Kathryn does so enjoy being the Northern Star of Court, always bright and the centre of the Heavens. Therefore, I want you to show an interest in His Majesty. Serve him well as a mistress should. It is nothing new to His Majesty. He has enjoyed his fair share of mistresses in the past. If you win His Majesty's attention, my niece will endeavour to win him back and keep him." A sudden sparkle came to Howard's eye, "And if your union provides offspring, I would not be surprised at all if the son you bore would have a strength far superior to that poor whelp Edward." He stared distantly into the gaming pit, the attendants removing the chain from the post, leaving it completely bare. "How we legitimise the bastard child will be a challenge, though."

"And what if I were to refuse your proposal to serve as the King's mistress?" Askana hissed. "This would mean King Henry loses interest in aiding my people?"

"Only if you are most fortunate." A warning. A clear, confident warning. "I will have your word that you will give your attentions and affections to our King. Once my little whore of a niece abandons her dalliances and resumes her rightful duty, you may leave with the allies you need." Howard then slowly turned to Askana, his expression now foreboding enough to give her pause. "I will do what I must in order to keep the power I wield. I have fallen once from the grace of the Throne. Never again."

"And you believe bringing me to this 'bear baiting' will entice me into agreeing to your proposal?"

"No, Your Majesty, I believe the night's entertainment is just beginning."

An unearthly growl filled the hall. Askana's eyes averted away from Lord Norfolk to the screaming patrons who caught sight of the heavy sack that concealed a wild beast demanding to be released. Its claws tore through the sack that imprisoned it. The wranglers threw it into the pit before its binds could be removed completely. The sack opened and Lubria shook her hair from her face and released a deafening roar that horrified the crowd. Some women fainted at the sight of her while some of the drunken patrons threw bits of food at her. The crowd watched her with a strange combination of terror, delight, and anticipation.

Then the betting began. There was no care of effrontery to laws of God and Man. There was no talk of witchcraft or Satan's doing. All that mattered were the bets placed before the combat began. Their screams of fear exploded into a crazed elation as *four* canines were released into the pit.

Lubria was a skilled assassin, her abilities unmatched by any mortal. Her victims, however, were men. Awkward creatures that lacked the grace and form she possessed and controlled so well. She underestimated the agility of the canines as one sank its fangs deep into her leg. Lubria's scream chilled Askana, awakening abominable memories of her talents in battle. The Fae-woman braced her hands around the attacking dog's snout and face. Its neck quickly snapped with a twist. Already another dog leapt for her but Lubria merely shot out her hand. Her claws effortlessly sank into the dog's belly, protruding through the other side. She hurtled the corpse to the remaining two dogs and released a roar. The canines recoiled for a moment, then crouched low in preparation of a strike. Before her wide-eyed queen, Lubria eliminated the remaining two with an incredible ferocity and swiftness that answered to the cries of the cheering horde. The blood of the dogs as well as Lubria's own wounds stained her thick striped coat. The scent of the dead beasts excited her and the roar of the onlookers, unexpectedly, gave her an indescribable pleasure. Lubria looked about her in a mad frenzy, the growl staying in a constant rhythm in her throat.

Howard leaned forward studying the frenzied creature in the pit, "An amazing beast. We became aware of it in your chambers when you arrived. She hid herself well, but did not remain so. It would have been wise for Captain Rafton to check for spyholes, particularly in the ceiling."

Askana could not take her eyes from Lubria, their eyes suddenly locking on one another. The Fae-woman's growl grew at sight of her Queen. This was the part of Lubria that Askana had tried to starve away. She wanted Lubria to find her true self, the unique and extraordinary creation she was born to be, not a creature twisted by cruelty and scorn. Now she was forced to watch Lubria succumb to more primal instincts, to that part of her comprised of violence and hate. Where Lubria was in her mind, there was no reason. Only the joy of the kill mattered.

Askana turned to Lord Norfolk, her hand slipping towards the poison dart array about her wrist.

"Dogs are a but child's play to this beast," Lord Norfolk pouted. "Perhaps we should increase the stakes."

He gave a nod to the game master. The four wranglers struggled against the fighter's protest, but he had no choice as he was lifted above the crowd and landed at the feet of Lubria. The impact knocked the wind out of him, losing him in a moment of disorientation. She backed away at first, taken aback by such large prey following the dogs. Her eyes took in the new opponent and a delightful smile bore her blood-stained fangs to her new opponent.

"Rafe," Askana whispered.

Lord Norfolk leaned forward with delight as he said to Askana, "Now begins the *Royal* entertainment."

Rafe was armed only with his abilities and his wits, and he had never felt so outgunned in his life. He slowly pressed himself against the wall of the game pit, his eyes focusing on the elated Lubria. He shot a quick glance to Askana and found little comfort in her helpless, overwhelmed expression. Lubria moved with the agility of the Fae. She was nothing more than a blur. No matter what direction Rafe turned, Lubria blocked his path. He lunged desperately to Lubria's right, hoping to clear her reach. Her claws cut the surrounding air, ripping into Rafe's right arm. The blow spun him about and he hit the ground hard.

Askana flinched slightly as she felt an intense stinging sensation in her own right arm.

His blood appeared black against the white-and-tan sand floor of the game pit. Rafe looked up to Lubria who licked his blood away from her long talons. Its taste sent a slight tremble through her body. He could see she had missed the thrill of this kind of combat. The claws retracted slightly as he pulled himself up again, his right arm cradled close to his chest. He looked to Askana once more, shaking his head as if to tell her he had no choice. His fingers detached from around his waist a chain-link belt from where hung a silver leaf ornament. The ornament hanging free of the belt split in two, revealing a fine razor's edge. Rafe began a rapid circling motion with the belt, its sound cutting the air above his head. Lubria found this trinket amusing, giving a slight laugh as she crouched low to attack. Rafe whipped the chain around Lubria's calf. The small blade sliced into her skin. Upon her scream, Rafe pulled hard against the belt, knocking Lubria off balance and tearing the weapon free of her. With no hesitation he whirled the belt-weapon over his head and struck again. This time it wrapped around her forearm, the blade's edge digging into her striped pelt. Rafe pulled against the belt and threw her against the far wall. The crowd cheered wildly as he did this again and again in hopes of knocking her unconscious.

Her counter-tactic was unexpected, terrifying in Rafe's eyes. She wrapped her wrist around the chain-belt and tugged. Its blade sank deeper into her muscles and sinews, but she had gained control. She pulled hard on the belt. Rafe came flying at her. With her free arm Lubria delivered a strong punch to his already injured arm, knocking him clear across the pit. He slammed hard against the thick wooden post. The crowd's delight drowned out Rafe's agonising cries as he fought to stay conscious.

Askana felt another sting in her arm and a sudden cramp in her back. It was a valiant, if not desperate, act of defence. His efforts had only made Lubria descend deeper into a blood rage, completely beyond reason or control.

"Well, it would appear this beast of yours is having far better luck than the emissary I sent yesternight." Lord Norfolk nodded in approval.

"You tried to kill Rafe?" Askana asked, turning her eyes away from the combat for only a moment.

"As King Henry had voiced an interest in you, I had to remove any possible distractions. Captain Rafton's reputation is well known." He smiled as Lubria struck him again with a solid punch to the face, "Especially by my niece. I intended to leave nothing to chance. Whereas my first attempt did fail, this one could very well succeed." Lord Norfolk leaned over to her, touching a fold of her white robes, "That is, if you continue to dally. So how stands your mind on my offer?"

Askana tasted the coppery flavour of her own blood on her lips where her teeth cut through soft flesh. She had already paid a price for the privateer's life. Now the contract before her carried the sentence of two. The terms did not seem so high, but everything in Askana screamed against it. The proposition was reprehensible. It meant that not only her body, but any result of this agreement would belong to a King and Court void of honour or devotion. It was shades of her own realm's past under the rule of men, corrupt and soulless men that cared little beyond their own individual gain.

Down in the pit, Lubria kicked Rafe. Black claws tore bloody rents in the breeches of one leg, and the sound of his pain cut thinly through the obscene excitement of the crowd. The fire burning up her thigh caused Askana to cry out lightly as beads of sweat formed under the emerald suspended across her forehead by a fine chain.

"Do not torture yourself so. You are a stranger here." Howard actually sounded sympathetic, pitying. "How could you have known my true nature?"

Askana's fingers gripped the wooden railing, her knuckles turning white. She had no other choice. Her head dropped on her long neck like a bruised lily, the delicate winged headdress fluttering like a bird about to take flight from the blue-black masses of her hair. She silently wished she had Court paint on her face. It could have concealed the agony now displayed on her face for all to see.

"Look at him, Your Majesty," Howard whispered into her ear. It was the delight in his tone that caused her to turn quickly, facing him with dark eyes. If he were not so close to the King, this whisper would mingle with his last breath. "He is looking here. Oh, I think he has seen you! He must believe in your abilities very much, because I do think hope appears in his eyes."

"Stop!" Askana hissed through gritted teeth. The pain, an agony of wounds that were not hers, burned in her body as Rafe stumbled. Lubria slowly circled around his body, prolonging the crowd's demands for a fatal end to this carnage. "Stop it! I agree. I accept your offer!"

"Good," Howard said promptly.

Her voice creaked from the strain. "I will do as you wish, now stop this!"

"Actually, Your Grace," Lord Norfolk sighed remorsefully, "I cannot."

The roar of the crowd drowned out Askana's cry. "What?"

"I know nothing in controlling that creature of yours." With a little chuckle, he sat forward in his chair, the theatre of gore reaching its apex.

In the blink of an eye Askana descended on him, the pain of Rafe's and her own anger now filling her with an inhuman strength. Her fingers wrapped around Howard's neck in a choke-hold, forcing him against the back of the chair. Behind her, Lubria spun around on one leg, her other foot striking Rafe with a hard hook-kick that dropped Rafe to his knees. Askana's head swam from the force of the blow, but she merely tightened her grasp. One simple thrust away from crushing his windpipe.

"Think twice, Your Majesty, before killing me." Lord Norfolk wheezed, his breath giving life to carefully chosen words. "I am the only man here with the power to keep your beast there your secret. I can arrange to have the spawn delivered to the Archbishop Cranmer. I assure you, the Church of England will not be so accepting as the masses here."

Her fingers squeezed a fraction more, bringing his brows together and his hands up to his throat in a futile attempt to break her grasp. "Gracious Lord Duke of Norfolk," It was a serpent's hiss that gave even this vile man in her grasp a moment's terror. "Enjoy tonight's revels for you will regret the day you crossed me."

In a swirl of silk and linen, she was gone.

Askana turned to the edge of the pit just in time to see Lubria hurl Rafe against the opposite wall. She winced and fought to remain standing. Lubria, savouring the smell of his blood and heat of the kill, was directly under her.

"One of you cannot die without the other. In order to strike you down, your enemies must strike fatal blows against the both of you in the same place at the same time."

The Caillech's words rang in her mind. Rafe would not die, but if she delayed any longer he might wish he could. Askana also understood Lubria's present intent. Lubria had made her loathing of the privateer evident. Now was her opportunity to toy with Rafe, enjoy the sweet ecstasy of his kill and gain praise through the adoration of his countrymen. It was poetic, and Lubria's love of the arts let her see that. It was an elegant kill on so many fronts. Lubria intended to enjoy this to the fullest.

Askana's hand flicked up, triggering one of the poisoned darts housed in her gauntlet. Noiselessly, it embedded itself into Lubria's shoulder. The Fae-Woman roared in rage and surprise, clawing wildly at the dart. The crowd did not see it, but they took in the display of added ferocity with glee. Askana leapt down into the pit from an impossible height, appearing fairy-like as the robes she wore billowed flowing and graceful. She landed in a crouch between the combatants, the soft boots and leggings she wore silencing her movement.

Lubria finally dropped, senseless and motionless, to the ground. Askana bent over her, extracting a small vial from its place alongside the darts. She quickly poured the contents of the vial down Lubria's throat. She did not know whether death was possible for her sister, but she refused to leave anything to chance. The Fae-woman's breathing was rapid as if she had just finished a hunt spanning several groves, but her chest gradually slowed.

The crowd saw there would be no kill, and their heightened thirst for blood now turned to boos, curses, and cries of disapproval. From his chair, Lord Norfolk stood, his hand lightly massaging life back into his now tender throat. Impressions of Askana's grasp still burned in his skin. Now that the Queen had agreed to his proposition, he had to keep those in her party alive as leverage. If the situation warranted, they could still be threatened if Askana were to waver in their agreement.

"Empty the house!" he commanded.

Rafe was trying desperately not to surrender to this strange delirium of exhaustion and pain. The sight of Askana's pale face hovering over him brought a weak smile to his face. It became his focus, keeping him conscious. "So now I know. Angels come not from Heaven, but from Morevi."

"Silence, privateer. This is no time for your flattery."

"I remember seeing you disappear with Lord Norfolk. We had rounded a corner when the King's Guard turned on me." Rafe winced, "It never ceases to amaze me what those Landsknecht bastards will do for a few gold crowns!"

She silenced him by gently pressing her finger against his lips, the strange gesture now habitual to her. When she touched the open, bleeding gashes in his right arm, she flinched, reminding him with a jolt of the bond and the pain that they shared. His jaw was swelling purple on one side. The gashes along his thigh were just as frightful. He looked terrible, but he would heal under her care and return to his brash bravado with only scars underneath his doublet to show for the night's excitement.

"Captain Rafton," Askana sighed, "sometimes I think you should never have accepted my offer."

Defiantly, Rafe tried to sit up. A sharp pain shot up their backs that made him wince and her lips tighten. "Your Grace, this is all merely part of the grand adventure," he jested as she gently guided him inch by inch to comfortably rest his head in her lap, his blood staining the brilliant white of her robes. He was silent for a moment. "I truly thought Lubria would kill me, and that you would let her."

"No," Askana broke in, her fingers gently stroking sweat and blood-stained hair away from his face. "You cannot die unless I die with you, felled by the same wound." Her voice reduced to a whisper as she continued, "There is good to the Caillech's spell, as you see. You have, Captain Rafton, a form of immortality."

"Well then," Rafe winced. "Fortune smiles upon me indeed, does it not?"

The doors of the pit flung open and two rows of armoured soldiers marched in quickly. Rafe's lips drew back from his teeth when he saw Lord Norfolk approach them.

"Worry not, Captain Rafton," smiled the Duke. "Her Majesty has ensured your well-being by paying the piper's price." He turned to the men, "Escort the Queen back to her chambers. She is to be treated with the utmost respect and her safety guaranteed. Any reports of unsatisfactory behaviour will be dealt with severely."

Rafe's mind, still too groggy from his fight to stay awake and aware, tried to comprehend what he was hearing. "Why were you here, Your Grace?" he asked Askana. "Why Lubria? What price?" Too late he realised that the trap had been for Askana as well. But why? "Askana?" Rafe asked.

"Captain Rafton, do not to take such liberties with Her Majesty!" snapped Lord Norfolk. "Keep your distance, your behaviour proper, humble, and respectful, and remember your place! If you do so, you may be allowed to continue serving as ambassador. Our great and august King looks upon Queen Askana with favourable eyes, and Queen Askana of Morevi returns His admiration. I am here to assure you do not compromise this budding relationship between our realms."

Rafe could say nothing. His eyes turned to Askana and closed. His last conscious feeling was her fingertips gently running through his hair.

The Consort Who Would Be King

"What means this?" the tall man asked, his grey eyes never straying from the Anjara's.

Since returning from Eyrie, Kalea and Kubi-Sogi had been preparing both their regiments for political upheaval. He was silent, a rarity for the warrior-adviser, when she had told him of their Queen being in the company of the Sea Wolf. She would take the image of Blademaster's stare of wonder to her grave. This would have been cause for alarm had the Sea Wolf not been held responsible for the destruction of the Taighar ports. Both knew in light of this information that Askana would return, perhaps in the company of a privateer under her employment. The military would have to be ready.

"I will find who in the Palace Guard are true to me," Kubi-Sogi had told her, *"My Guard may not be entirely happy with the New Regime but they are loyal to me and will follow my orders. I will meet you in four days time in Arathelle with my men. The Council and assembled Noble Houses will be in session for the Royal Commencement, no doubt given by the Consort who will be raised by that time."*

Four days. This was the time Kalea had remaining to gather her own Royal Guard and stand for her High Priestess and Queen. She was also facing the challenge of discovering who in her own Guard was truly loyal. After hearing Kubi-Sogi recount the testimony before Council, she could not afford another Jailene.

Kalea could not help but notice that other embassies of Songkusai were pulling out of Morevi. Irshian. Coromvar. Lydonnesse. Embassies were quickly abandoning their posts, all save one. This came as no surprise or coincidence to her. She stood before the ambassador in a sleeveless tunic of red linen and brown hide that barely covered her knees. Her rank was signified with gilded guards and heavy cuffs of worked gold encompassing her shins and upper arms. The brightly polished helmet she wore swept up her grey hair, a long trail of it spilling out the back as if it were a horsehair plume. Her thick hair mingled with the helm's ornaments of the green, red, and blue iridescence of Murgi bird's feathers. A step behind her stood two other women, one still in her youth and the other closer to Kalea's age. Their shin guards were unadorned and their wrist gauntlets a simple polished bronze. This and the sweeping white feathers of the Achingo decorating their helms signified a lieutenant's rank.

"Why do you remain in Morevi, Ambassador Peregrin, when others have fled?" Kalea asked.

Of late, Ambassador Olaf Peregrin had felt every minute of his age, his brown hair thinning and wrinkles deepening around his light-coloured eyes. He knew this appointment would be a never-ending challenge. Nothing could have prepared him for the past two weeks of growing unrest. His position as Eyriener Ambassador to Morevi was growing exceedingly difficult. Still, he would not abandon his post.

He studied the women standing behind their Anjara. Their heads were arrogantly held high and faces menacing through the open visor of their helms. He tried to compare these women to any of his three daughters. Tried and failed. The differences were just too mind-boggling.

Peregrin never knew if it would be bluntness or subtlety with the Anjara. Oftentimes, it was both. "I received no order telling me to leave, from either side," The ambassador replied stiffly.

Since Askana Moldarin's disappearance, all foreign tradesmen and nationals had fled for the safety of home. He, however, defiantly stood his ground, bound by his duty to be the voice of his people in this realm. Peregrin saw a potential in this nation. Being land-locked, Morevi had done well enough to earn itself the title of The Silken Box of Naruihm. Turi essence, chocha, sandalwood, tea, and silk—it was a gold mine of natural resources. The price of such riches was in the soil, depleted of many nutrients for prime crops. The Old Regime had chosen isolationism and starvation instead of opening trade relations with other countries. Askana surprised her people and neighbouring kingdoms by promoting commerce outside her realm's borders, their greatest coup being an alliance with Arathelle, the Elven Kingdom. This was their "strongest" relation. Other kingdoms kept tenuous agreements with Morevi as its New Regime was still in its infancy and so radically different from any other monarchy in Naruihm.

Peregrin felt that his country needed Morevi as badly as Morevi needed them. Eyrie could offer their resources of agriculture and industry in exchange for this realm's exotic riches. King Cedric, however, saw this regime's recovery from civil war as an opportunity to claim the Silken Box for Eyrie alone. This had become his goal, a lofty dream the ambassador himself scoffed at. King Cedric was charismatic though, and could convince his people to charge on Andoulin if he desired it. Peregrin hoped this embassy would send a contrary message to both regimes. For Morevi, it would be an optimistic vision of a future together. For his own realm, it would present an alternative to conquest.

Since his arrival, tensions between nations had only grown worse. Now the infamous Royal Guard were at his door. He thought briefly of his beloved wife at home with his three daughters and two sons. They were having a family portrait done for his fiftieth birthday, and he remembered his oldest daughter, Alise, told him she was wearing a white dress with pink ribbons on the bodice and rose-slashed skirts. She looked so precious and sweet in that ensemble.

Precious and sweet. Two words he would not use to describe the armed woman standing in front of him.

"You are a brave man, Ambassador," said the Anjara as she removed her helmet. "But surely you would find it safer in the ports of Arathelle? Or across the Sleeping Dragons in the comfort and security of your own lands?"

"Comfort and security, indeed!" Peregrin replied with a wry twist of his mouth. "A week ago, the port city of Taighar was nearly destroyed by a series of explosions. Half the town market decimated by fire, many hurt. Merchant-lords also died in the calamity. The High Lord Kergagi was amongst them. King Cedric is understandably furious as those responsible have yet to be apprehended. He has already implicated Morevi in his addresses to the people. And the military."

Eyriener news arrived to him through a variety of sources. It was carrier pigeons that provided the latest news from home. News so incredulous, he had to wait for a confirmation message this morning to believe what had been reported to him several days earlier. A Morevian servant wanted for an assassination attempt on her Queen was reported in the company of a fair-haired Otherworlder. These were the facts he managed to decipher from absolute conjecture. Something of a conspiracy against the throne of Morevi itself. King Cedric in league with The Merchants' Circle and hiring mercenaries to take arms with Eyrieners in a full-scale invasion. He prayed that the last was nothing more than just an outlandish rumour.

"I know of this destruction, Ambassador, but your loss pales in comparison to ours. Our Queen is missing, dead, or held captive. We do not know for certain. The rumours we hear say that Eyriener soldiers will march on us. There is also talk of dark sorcery at work, stealing our Queen from her throne and leading your forces to our city gates."

"Magic? Think, woman! No member of the Fellowship of the Jewels has been here in decades. They would not stand for such outward indifference to their laws and decrees." He stifled a sigh, his tolerance disintegrating with this brash woman. "Do you honestly believe King Cedric would dare risk breaking the Sacred Laws of the Fellowship?"

"I believe young King Cedric is weighing his considerable ambition against that long absence. No one of the Fellowship has left Andoulin in decades. Who or what would prevent him from calling upon the Dark Arts to achieve his goals? And if the sorcery he called upon were powerful enough, why would his ambition end with taking Morevi?" The Anjara let her words trail off, her face making no effort to mask her accusations.

He laughed. A harsh sound to the Morevians. "Are you suggesting that Eyrie will wage war against the Elves? Our King may be ambitious, but he is not mad! It is most fortunate for us all the Elves possess no desire for power or conquest. Even if Eyrie did move against Morevi, our forces would have no other choice but to move through Arathelle. While they prefer neutrality, no one truly knows the Elves' allegiance other than the Elves. For all we could know, the Elves would defend Morevi, in light of the Queen's affair with—"

One flash of the Anjara's eyes quelled him. "Be careful. By law, none can speak of that."

"But if she were to speak of it openly, it might give King Cedric pause."

"The story of a lost love would convince your King to remain on the other side of the Sleeping Dragons? This, an intimate bond shared with an elf, would accomplish? You give far too much credence to your King."

The ambassador threw his hands up in disgust, "I tire of this talk. If you have come to arrest me, do your office and be done with it!"

"That was not my reason for coming. You may stay, Ambassador." The feathers rasped against the smooth surface of her helmet as she set it on a small table. Kalea casually perused an array of carefully tended bonsai as she spoke to him. "Although Her Majesty knows of Eyrie's growing ambition to rule over her realm, she does hold a respect for any brave enough to represent his lands in the heart of his enemy's. I would suggest that you do not stray far from the embassy, and keep your Eyriener guard close. I cannot control all my people. There are many who do not hold Eyrieners in high regard right now."

He watched Kalea carefully as she leaned in for a closer inspection of his garden.

"Did you know," she said while gently caressing the yellow blooms of one miniature plant, "in the recent meeting of the Council, the Queen was accused of treachery against her own Kingdom?"

Peregrin could not stop himself from starting, discovering truth to one of the rumours he had earlier deemed outlandish. "Impossible! Askana Moldarin is known for her ferocious love of her kingdom and its people."

"The Lady Min-Lu of House Annaki brought forward proof. According to an unsubstantiated account, our Queen means to wrest control of Eyrie and Arathelle, then continue further conquest by breaching Andoulin."

"Why do you tell me this?" he asked abruptly. "You know that I am an ambassador for Eyrie. A rival nation. I could easily divulge this information to my Lord and King as my duty dictates. Why would I care what happens to this realm?"

"Because Her Majesty knows you are not of the same mind as your King. She knows of your desire to unite Morevi and Eyrie as fast allies. She finds the notion repugnant. Yet, she admires the passion for a dream. Winning the admiration of our Queen should not be taken lightly. So yes, you should have great care for what happens here. You know the best way to keep peace is to maintain a balance of power. An attack from Eyrie would upset that balance, and King Cedric may find himself in a war he cannot win."

The Anjara was cut off by the sound of horns sending a hollow chorus into the sky. Two soldiers bearing the sigil of the Turi beside the symbol of the Kingdom, approached, flanking the diminutive man in short-skirted clothes of a herald. His voice boomed, ricocheting off the high walls of the courtyard. "A Royal Summons! An assembly of the Council of the Hundred Turi, High Power of the Kingdom of Morevi, has passed a motion brought forward by High Lady Dirare of House Jarahd, acting Regent in the absence of Her Majesty Askana Moldarin. For the good of the Realm and continuation of the rule of House Moldarin, High Lady Dirare has appointed a ruler according to the wishes of the Queen. The Ceremony of a Thousand Suns has taken place, and the people of Morevi shall bow in reverence to their King, Jermal Sandhuilean. Long live His Majesty. May the thousand rays of His Rule shine!"

Ambassador Peregrin went silent with shock. The lieutenants went so far as to break their attention stance to stare in amazement. Only the Anjara nodded as if knowing this was about to happen. She glanced at the beaded calendar in view of Peregrin's study as she donned her helm. Four days. She now had four days to build her forces while accepting the cold consequence of Dirare's move.

A *king* ruled once more in Morevi.

The immense Hall of Dawn was packed to full capacity with men and women in Court dress. The tension was palpable. Already the unstable base of politics was moving, and all eyes watched one another as if to discover a hint to who was allying with whom. Those fiercely loyal to the Order of Nadinath and Askana Moldarin silently seethed as the reality of this ceremony struck them as morning's first rays on a new day. The Morevian dynasty under the rule of women now turned to the men for guidance.

In the Great Hall of the Palace of a Thousand Suns, the pecking order of Morevian families illustrated itself with all the grandeur and majesty of a proud nation rich in history. Crossing the newly laid mosaic pattern of the Turi flower underneath the grand rotunda, the most powerful houses took their places around the ring of the dais. Their ruling heads led in front, the heirs next, and to the rear were the young, old, and few remaining men of the House. Although this regime was new, this impressive display served as a reminder of Morevi's heritage. This splendour was matched only by the spectacle of the Great Hall itself. Magnificent pillars of red-veined stone soared upward to a vaulted ceiling of plasterwork so dainty it appeared like a distant sea of lace. Wood carvings hid corners and spread along the walls. Light from the torches and coals in the incense-sprinkled paper lanterns glimmered, reflecting against the black marble floor. Standing diligently over these proceedings, receiving uneasy looks from some of the Houses, were the Morev'ar. Their skin glistened from oil and a dusting of gold glitter. Underneath crossed arms, they wielded the discus-shaped atriah. Tattoos adorning their bodies gave their skin the countenance of marble, making them appear all the more statuesque in the presence of the Families of the Blood.

It should have been a breathtaking spectacle for the Raising of a Consort, but the tension could not so easily be dismissed. Speculation. Distrust. Raw anger. Askana Moldarin had fought so hard for this new dynasty. Now she was gone, abandoning her beloved home or taken against her will for reasons unknown. The tension only intensified the silence.

All fell quiet as Jermal, dressed in formal Court robes, took his rightful place before the dais. The words of a new King echoed for what felt like a brief eternity in the Hall of Dawn.

"I do not pretend to be royal. I do not pretend to know you better than you know yourselves. I am a man, an ordinary man. I do promise you I will rule justly in accordance to the wishes of your beloved matriarch, Askana Moldarin. I will ensure that none are oppressed, taken for granted, or misjudged. The hungry shall be fed. The weak, protected.

"I am a man, not of Morevian blood. While viewed as an inadequacy in the eyes of some, I say it is not. My resolve and character was forged in faraway lands, realms where both men and women live in harmony. Realms most of you can only see in dreams."

There was some murmuring among the Ladies, but Jermal did not falter. His posture still radiated confidence and purpose. He knew Dirare was smiling behind the fan. How pleasing it must have been to hear her own words spoken by her rival's trusted Consort. He caught sight of her in the corner of his eye. Dressed in her ornate red and gold brocade, she looked every inch the Regent, a position that everyone knew would fall upon her.

"But do not mistake, I am only one man. The burden of the Crown is far too great for one pair of shoulders. Before you, the Collected Houses of Morevi, I choose my advisers. You, who have sworn your allegiance to me this day. From this day to the last twilight cast across the lands of Naruihm, these select few shall be revered as the High Council."

The shimmering veil Jermal wore "to shield his brilliance from the eyes of his subjects" kept getting in the way. It would catch in between his lips as he would take in a breath. He could not tell if his voice was as confident as his stance. He could not show weakness or uncertainty. Dirare's liquid black eyes drove him on.

"To the position of Chancellor of the Kingdom," Jermal began, the slight treble of anxiety noticeable for the first time in his voice. "I raise the High Lady Miarad of House Harlin."

Murmurs and scattered applause rose as the tall, hard-edged woman approached the dais and made obeisance. The Mistress of Ceremonies laid the heavy strand of gold across the King's hands, and slowly he slipped it over her head. The links of the chain, shaped like miniature stars, clinked lightly as they came to rest against High Lady Miarad. With a motion of his hand, Jermal directed her to the five cushions on the dais before him.

"As the Minister of Trade and Commerce, I raise the High Lady Pira of House Charmar." More applause followed the slight, slender-looking High Lady Pira. She could not contain a smug smile on receiving the heavy chain of crescent moons. She sank into a cushion beside Miarad, her fellow High Council member obstinately refusing to acknowledge her.

"As the Keeper of the City and Lands of a Thousand Suns, I raise the High Lady Pura of House Charmar." The murmurs were louder this time as Pura rose from her place to accept the office, darting a swift look to her sister Pira as she neared the dais. Jermal thought with dry amusement that in a single moment, weeks of plotting and manoeuvring were shattered.

He then noticed Dirare's fan stop abruptly.

This was not part of the script they had rehearsed. She had been so careful to orchestrate everything from the appointments he made to words emphasised in his address. Jermal could not help but smile at catching her by surprise. Many of the Collected Houses, in particular the esteemed Lady Dirare, would be unhappy that both sisters of House Charmar controlled county, city, and trade ports in Arathelle. Jermal knew better than anyone present of Askana's intentions to form a High Council. It was something Dirare did not know they shared in common. As for the appointment of the sisters, Askana would have wanted this. No one could disregard the enmity between them, especially in the looks exchanged as Pura took her place beside her sister. It was not hate, but intense sibling rivalry. They would stand together against a common enemy, the bond of family uniting them to make them unbreakable. Their own petty squabbling would in turn keep each other's power in check.

"As the Minister of Internal Affairs, I raise the High Lady Radna of House Nishien."

The pleasant-faced, grey-haired woman ascended the dais, her modest robes of dove-grey silk possessing a certain simplicity pleasing to the eye in the midst of all the ostentation of court.

Dirare's fan resumed moving, but at a slower rate.

"And as the Regent of the Kingdom, the Right Hand of a Thousand Suns, I raise the High Lady Dirare of House Jarahd."

When the applause came, it was considerable. Power struggles or no, the Council and nobles recognised the strength of House Jarahd. While the regime had changed dramatically in recent years, the influence and power of Dirare's House remained constant. She was the most vocal against Askana Moldarin, sometimes single-handedly challenging the Queen before Council. Dirare could not enjoy the power she now held without Askana. Without Dirare's influence, Askana could not remain queen. It was a delicate balance. They needed each other, but refused to become allies.

Some of the applause was also for the strategy of the Consort-King, regardless of Dirare's influence on him. In one stroke, Jermal eliminated the five most powerful contenders for the throne by tying them to him and opening the field for play against each other. Jermal could see this in the faces of nobles closest to him and he could not help but to stand taller. He thought for a moment of the pride and approval Askana would have bestowed on him for his first appearance before the Families of the Blood.

As he watched Dirare approach, Jermal's confidence wavered.

Graceful and fully aware of her power, Dirare ascended the dais and paid homage. Before she did so, her eyes looked into his for a long moment. He slipped into a queer, bizarre state of unconsciousness, fully aware yet detached from his actions, as if he watched himself from outside his body. He placed the heavy chain of gold sunbursts around Dirare's neck. Dirare's head bowed slightly as he bestowed a Royal Blessing with a simple gesture of his hand. He watched himself do this as a king would do for the most loyal of his subjects.

Through it all, Dirare's eyes never left him.

The brush of brocade and unfamiliar scent of her light perfume snapped him out of this strange dream-like state. He was now suddenly in an antithesis. A heightened awareness of the hundreds of eyes fixed upon him struck him hard. The Houses of Morevi all awaited words from their new King. Their collected gaze tore away at his skin and flesh. The delight that came in reaching the end of appointments left him just as quickly.

After Dirare assumed her place, he held his stand for a long moment. Under the heavy Court robes, he had broken into a sweat. The moment stretched into minutes. Dirare's fan was moving again, faster than ever. An excruciating pain, the grating of muscle against muscle, ripped through Jermal's throat as he swallowed hard. The dryness persisted, but it was time for him to speak. It was time to tell his High Regent that he was not her puppet.

"Ladies of the Blood, nobles and rulers in your own right, as you well know my coronation was not a matter of my choice, nor yours either. My own Raising was a matter of circumstance and need." Jermal could not help but be impressed by his own stamina, amazed that he had not lost consciousness between struggling with the veil and the wild pace his heart kept. "Many of you feel that I will not be a competent ruler. Some fear that as a stranger to your realm, not born of Morevian blood, I will change the structure of your lives. This is not my intention for I do love this land as deeply as does its Queen. And my love for Morevi is only matched by that love I feel for her.

"I do not believe that she is dead. Your King decrees she will return to again take the throne and lead her beloved Morevi into the New Dawn. In her absence, I will rule according to Her Laws and My Judgements. I will speak as Her Voice. For the unfounded rumours of her betrayal to Her Beloved Realm, your King proclaims that they are false. Nothing more than allegations of envy and jealousy and hereby decreed punishable by death. So speaks your King."

The murmurs were not murmurs anymore and Dirare's eyes were a furnace. He understood. He could have undermined himself with those words, but he made his stand clear. Her retribution could wait till later.

The sails billowed firmly from the force of the winds, the yards creaking under the strain as the sleek-sided ship sliced through the waves. Normally, the rowers were thankful for such strong wind as it exempted them from labour, but the madman onboard wanted speed. They did not dare to voice displeasure of any kind. They were free rowers who worked for the Captain of the ship, paid well for their services.

They called their sponsor "madman" only in private. He always wore black, the cut of his clothes definitely of Eyriener fashion and a mask of black silk across his face. The mask concealed everything save a pair of lifeless black eyes, not the telltale grey eyes of an Eyriener. He inspired fear. His every word was to be obeyed as a command. He also carried the Royal Seal of King Cedric, a recognition even the now-extinct Merchants' Circle could not obtain. It was the manner in how the Assassins' Guild answered to him that terrified them above all this.

The Assassins' Guild deferred to no one, neither ruler nor noble. Now their Order was under the absolute command of the madman. They arrived several days after a carrier pigeon delivered news that visibly angered the Dark Merchant. It had angered him enough to override their Captain's authority and turn the ship back toward what was left standing of Taighar's ports. The next day, members of the Assassins' Guild boarded their vessel.

The crew was convinced the madman commanded dark forces. Messenger birds arrived out of thin air. They were in the open sea, the coastal ports of Naruihm far off. No land for miles around. Where were these birds coming from? Then there were the strange events of yesterday. Without reason, the crew was suddenly ordered below into the ship's cargo hold, secured in the darkness for over two hours. They could hear the shouts of their Captain and the Dark Merchant who silenced him with threats that sounded more like promises. The madman spoke in some bizarre gibberish made up of all languages of Naruihm, turning the waters wild as if he himself called upon some unearthly storm. When the seas calmed, the crew emerged to find their Captain pale and ashen-faced, and their ship sailing across a grey ocean with the help of a hard, cold wind.

A benefit of the additional rowing was that it kept them reasonably warm in this biting chill.

The Dark Merchant glanced up from the news he had just received via his trained birds. He caught the words "bewitched pigeon" from a rower. He paused by the man. Behind his mask, a smile crossed his face as the rower kept his eyes forward, not daring to look up. Continuing his walk along the length of the ship, the High Lord Coumiran returned his attentions to the small parchment in his hand. This news was far better than that of several days prior when the English nobleman granted the full protection of his monarch and kingdom over Askana Moldarin. The bitch was close to obtaining allies, and that was something he had not foreseen. For a moment his mind entertained the gratifying idea of having the man gutted, but Howard did have one last task to fulfill that would save his life.

His little Morevian had informed him of The Raising, the Queen's Consort now King. *Fine*, he thought. *Let the Lady Dirare crown her Puppet-King and rule as High Regent.* Min-Lu informed him she was gathering allies and planning her own little military coup. So long as she waited on his word, the plan would proceed.

As for the little problem of Askana Moldarin and her bewitching of a king, he would be in London soon. *Perhaps this little intrigue of mine will benefit both realms across The Rift*, he thought as the coastline of England began to appear over the horizon. The Duke was no fool, his loyalty not completely blind. The Dark Merchant saw much of himself in this servant to King Henry the VIII, precisely why he would never trust him completely but take full advantage of his frailties. He smiled under his mask as the letter ignited in his hand, seemingly of its own accord. In a matter of moments it was ash that eddied away on the breeze.

And when I have finished with Askana Moldarin, she would be little more than that. Coumiran tipped his head back in a memory. *I had forgotten how delightful the intrigue of Court could be,* he thought with delight.

"What delusion of grandeur were you suffering from in the Hall of Dawn?!"

Jermal expected this. He knew this confrontation was inevitable. He also knew that the repercussions from Dirare would be swift and harsh. What he had not prepared himself for was the immense satisfaction in watching Dirare pace. Pride. Jermal had almost forgotten its taste. It had been so long since he had allowed himself this indulgence. It tasted as sweet, as rich, and as potent as dark chocha. He thought to himself that at the rate she was going, she would wear out the marble underneath her feet. Jermal was unaware that his thoughts were beginning to show on his face. A cynical smile was forming on his lip.

"This was not what we had discussed nor rehearsed. In future you will follow the counsel I give you to the very letter, do you understand?"

Dirare turned to face him, intending to continue her tirade when she noticed his grin. With no word of warning she marched over to him hotly and connected her hand with his cheek. The blow snapped his head to the side and the smile vanished.

"Do not presume that your current status gives you any power with me, thief!" Dirare screamed.

The echo of her own voice and tingling of her hand gave her pause. She watched Jermal turn his head back slowly to face her. His grey eyes registered a hint of shock. They were also calculating this significant loss in control. She took a deep breath as she slowly backed away from him. He was still in his ceremonial robes from the Raising in the Hall of Dawn. It was a reminder that a change in approach was required.

"When you collect yourself, Your Majesty, join me." Her voice rang sharply, "Servants! The King desires nourishment and music."

On her command, Palace Servants appeared from concealed corridors. They hesitated for an instant at the scene. Dirare's face was tense with a hint of blush, a shade similar to the handprint on Jermal's face. Something was clearly wrong. The attendants kept their eyes averted from the growing redness in his cheek as they removed his robes and gingerly escorted him to sit opposite of his High Regent.

Soon the dulcet tones of three stringed instruments rang in Dirare's chambers. She tilted her head back proudly, and stepped up onto the raised area in the centre of the room where rugs and embroidered cushions invited guests to sit around a low, lacquered table.

Jermal still had not developed a taste for Morevian arts. He still had a long way to go before he could appreciate the music.

Dirare casually reclined among the comforts of the pillows and silks as she enjoyed a sze-rine bun. "Jermal, you must forgive my outburst but I am somewhat cross with you." She spoke to him as if he was a child. "You cannot say you were undeserving of my displeasure. You diverted from the plan we agreed on for the Ceremony. You have shown good sense to realise that you need my help and protection. The unexpected appointments are a cause for some concern." She motioned with her fingertips and a servant produced for her a small, steaming cloth perfumed with rose, citrus, and cinnamon. "My dear Jermal, I do not care for surprises."

"Nor do I care to be led by a leash and commanded to perform trained pet tricks for Court!" The thief, now crowned King, snapped at his Regent.

Dirare paused in the rubbing of her hands and smiled politely at his posturing. It struck her as precious that Askana's little consort now wanted to play "King". She resumed wiping her lips and cheeks with the scented water. She could not help but be curious as to what Jermal had prepared to say next.

"I agreed to your protection and to your counsel in Askana's absence, but do not for one moment take me for one of these sad, beaten-down men of your realm. I was not completely oblivious of her talk concerning Morevian politics. I paid attention, you know."

"So you would have me believe that all that time we thought you were focusing your love-struck eyes on Askana you were actually planning your own political platform?" Her laugh cut through the music, causing the musicians to pause. She noticed the sudden silence. With a simple look from her, the music played once more. "Tell me, Jermal, do you truly believe Askana will grant you a place in the High Council upon her return? Or perhaps regard you as anything other than Consort? Consider it fortunate that you were named King at all. The Court is already in a state of shock. Your Raising rather chafes against the old precept of consorts never being given the power to rule. The only thing keeping you alive is Askana's lingering memory and my allegiance."

"I will not allow you to work me from the shadows so easily, Dirare," Jermal warned. "I meant every word I uttered in the Hall of Dawn. I do love Askana Moldarin and believe she is not this treacherous creature that she is accused of being."

"Nor do I."

Jermal went silent. The red colour faded a little from his face, making her handprint more pronounced on his cheek. His grey eyes were now tinged with confusion.

Dirare opened her fan with a gentle snap, slowly fanning a scent of rose and cinnamon into the air. She knew the motion and scent could be soothing. Her eyes revealed nothing. Neither did her tone as she spoke, "Dear Jermal, do you truly believe I would support unsubstantiated claims of Min-Lu over the reputation of the Queen? Askana Moldarin is no traitor to her own Crown, nor is she some mad tyrant longing for war. Believe me, I know Askana well enough. What Min-Lu claims is ridiculous to say the least. I am encouraging ties with the young noblewoman in order to keep her close. I do not wish to oppose her at present for she has influences within the Council. We can put her influences to better use if she does not oppose us openly. I find it intriguing that Askana's 'little sister' should suddenly show such hatred for her."

"And so you intend to offer Min-Lu this alliance so you may find out what?"

"Her true intentions, of course." Dirare extended a slender hand and a nearby servant placed a steaming cup of chocha in it. The aroma was pleasing to her in its complexity. "Now then Jermal, as your High Regent, I give you my first bit of advice. Take advantage of your power and our offer of friendship to House Annaki. Discover why Min-Lu is so swift to implicate the Queen." She took a sip of the steaming beverage, then added, "I have often thought the young woman a little too fond of the fruits of power."

Jermal knew in his heart of hearts that if Askana returned to find Dirare too deeply entrenched, it would be his fault. Through him Dirare held Morevi in the palm of her hand, much like the cup of choca she now savoured. The governors of the four major cities had already paid their respects to her. To *her*, not to him. He knew tributes would be arriving from the towns and villages. It was all a splendid sham. A moment of uncertainty took hold. How would Askana react if she found him on the throne in her stead? His Raising now went far beyond the boundaries of their relationship and into the political arena. He would have to fight to keep himself alive, remain useful to Dirare, and somehow hold the throne for Askana.

He was King, though. He had the raw materials at his disposal. The uncertainty began to disappear. Yes, he was now King. He could feel himself smile again as he looked at Dirare. Jermal was determined to become as good at the Great Game as any woman of Court. Even his High Regent.

He sank into a more casual posture across from Dirare, extended his hand, and a fresh cup of choca was gently placed in his waiting palm. She raised an eyebrow at this regal gesture from a man not two hours King. As in the Great Hall, Jermal knew he had scored a hit. "As you see, the subjects are duty bound. Regardless of your feelings or level of respect, I am King. You have made me so."

Regardless of his heart pounding wildly, Jermal kept an exterior of stillness. The woman who sat across from him was terrifying. Not outwardly so, for she was no tyrant. It was what she did not show—her ability to plan and plot against those closest to her—that scared him. He took a sip of the hot chocha and replaced it on the saucer. The cup vibrated lightly as Jermal set it upon the small table before him. He wondered if the sound came from his trying to keep the fragile cup balanced or if his nerves were showing. But had he not done this before as a thief? Outwitted nobility? There was no difference here. Merely the games would be played in the open. He knew he could do this. His heart slowed. He was in control.

"No, I am not drunk with power nor do I intend to rule with reckless abandon until Askana returns to take her rightful place." Jermal reclined as she did on the cushions. "I will, however, be the voice of Askana in her absence."

"Your faith in the Black Widow is inspiring," Dirare stated flatly. "You truly believe she will return."

"She loves Morevi more than you could ever know. She has lost too many loved ones and sacrificed too much to simply abandon it. This love will bring her home. I believe whatever she is doing is for the greater good of Morevi."

Dirare laughed softly as she shook her head, "And you think I am manipulating you?" Her eyes darkened as she spoke, "Tell me something, *Your Majesty*, the words you just uttered—were they your own or Askana's? I thought for a moment I heard her voice."

"Not her words," Jermal returned. "But her influences. Dirare, I made you High Regent because of your earlier kindness and protection, calculated as it was. Now we must work together, trust one another until Askana returns. We are on the brink of civil war. I, for one, do not desire to deal with her *when* she returns to find her kingdom in disarray." It was a lightly veiled threat, a reminder of what Askana might do.

Dirare nodded. She took another sip of the rich drink in her hands. The Consort was growing a backbone. She was *very* clear when she said she did not care for surprises.

"I know if I were to truly rule in her absence, I need to acquire an understanding of Morevian politics and legislation. I have much to learn." Jermal raised himself to his feet, servants appearing as if from thin air to help him back into ceremonial robes. "That will be your office. To guide me as I rule until Her Majesty's return."

Dirare watched him quietly, her manner as placid as a lake in the early morning. "I will endeavour to serve you and keep the people of Morevi faithful, My Sovereign."

"Good," Jermal stated. "For we need one another. You need to keep your office. I need a voice in the New Regime. And we both must keep the realm intact. I will be in my chambers. I must formally address the Families of the Blood before they return home." His head tipped back as hers would habitually do when giving him direction. "Write something appropriate. We shall review it together. I am certain we will find a voice that suits us both."

"I will wait upon you, My Sovereign." Dirare gave a slight bow with her head as Jermal adjusted his robes.

"I do not doubt it, High Regent." He turned to the door. Jermal's regal robes billowed around him as he spoke over his shoulder to her, "I will call on you when I am ready."

As the door closed with a gentle click of a latch, the delightful, gentle music continued. It came to an abrupt halt as Dirare's eyes slowly came to rest upon the musicians. They could not have left her chambers any faster. Attendants disappeared with equal alacrity as her gaze fell on them. With a final soft, dull thud of the servant's access door, she was enveloped in silence.

Jermal.

Askana's name was constantly on his lips, and she knew however foolish it sounded, he was deadly serious. Control would be much more difficult than she had anticipated, but not impossible. She finished her cup of cold chocha resolute in her first duty as High Regent—to teach the King how powerless he truly was.

Tudor by Torchlight

Something was wrong with his eyes. The room listed hazily as colours ran into each other like pools of liquid paint. Eventually, the colours ended their coupling. Sharpness gave form to the formless. His vision blurred and wavered once or twice for a moment. Then all was still again.

He was lying in a deep, soft bed. A grand bed fit for a king, or perhaps a guest of a king. The chambers he awoke in were not rocking with the soothing motions of the *Defiant*. He stared up at the canopy suspended above him, the earlier blurred image now coming into focus. It depicted a hunting scene. His current dizziness seemed to give the hunters and the game their own motion.

Rafe tried to turn his head and sit up, but stabs of pain shooting through his shoulder kept him still. The muscles of his back and neck throbbed. Stifling a gasp, he sank back against the pillows. At least the sharp pain brought him to a full state of awareness. *Where the Hell am I?* His head swam in random images and thoughts. *The last thing I remember is Lord Norfolk. Some pit. Askana…*

There was a rustle of movement beside the bed. Instinctively, disregarding the blinding pain sweeping over his body, his hand went for his rapier. He then realised he was not wearing his belt. In fact, he was not wearing anything at all.

Elunear's head popped up from the left of the raised bed. Rafe scrambled to draw the sheets over himself. The instinct cost him in another sensation of agony as if his skin were slowly being torn in two. Rafe could not remember being in such pain, even after facing the worst squall at sea.

"Oh, you have awakened," said the young Maiden. Her honey-coloured hair was tousled, making her appear much younger than he remembered. "Try not to move. You will only tear your stitches open."

Rafe's mind reeled. *Tear my stitches?* He was about to open his mouth to ask what had happened when another head rose up on a level with his, moving with an impossibly rapid, serpentine grace. The green eyes glittered as her lips peeled back into a sensual, horrifying hiss. He then recalled Lubria snarling at him. Her fangs were mere inches from his face. He was bleeding copiously from where she had clawed him. Then the world was a blur as she flung him backwards. He went flying through the air until hitting a stone wall.

With this memory came another. A recent memory. Another time, another place. All urgency lost and clouded. The sun was shining brightly outside, and he remembered ordering from the barkeep a scotch. A beautiful woman sat beside him in the strangest of clothes. He knew her. They were talking of battle plans, silenced thoughts, and personal regret.

Then in an instant Rafe returned to the pair of emerald eyes and white fangs.

"Careful!" Elunear's hand pushed firmly against his chest, keeping Rafe restrained with a strength her youthful exterior concealed. "You will tear them, I said." She gave Lubria a scornful look, but could not help to smirk at the Fae-woman's taunting of Rafe.

He followed Elunear's eyes to his shoulder and his own went wide. Four parallel lines raked down the smooth skin and muscle. The wound was kept sealed by stitches so minute that they would have been quite unnoticeable had the thread not been black. A lift of the blankets and a glance at his leg told him that the case was much the same there.

"Pretty marks, are they not?" Lubria purred at him, her voice incongruously velvety and caressing, "Wear them with pride. You are the only mortal to draw my blood in combat and still draw breath to tell the tale."

Rafe noted Lubria's right forearm and calf were wrapped in a clean dressing that covered the wounds from his belt-weapon and scoffed, "Something tells me you fared better than I did."

The Fae-woman laughed, "Do not take my actions to heart. I was, after all, not quite myself at the time." Her smile turned feral as she gasped in pleasure. "Your blood has a good taste."

"Well then the next time you try to tear me to pieces, sweet lass, I will remember to ask if you are yourself first."

The smile melted away. "Call me 'sweet lass' once more and I will finish what I started."

"Please, do not make such idle threats. They do not suit you," Rafe then leaned in to her with a wry smile, "sweet lass."

"Stop this snapping," Elunear warned. She dabbed ointment firmly on the stitches in Rafe's arm causing him to wince. "Now that you are awake, you had better turn your resolve to aiding the Queen."

"Yes," hissed Lubria, backing away from him. "Tell me, human, why is your kind so inept in controlling your primal urges? A king who rules his country by the ache in his loins is hardly fit to be a royal footman, yet this wretch remains King. And his subjects are hardly redeeming."

Rafe stared at her with shrewd surprise in receiving a lecture from Lubria on "controlling primal urges".

"That creature Howard has hinted the King will refuse Her Majesty allies if she does not share the King's bed," said Lubria. "You have brought us here, human. Now get us out."

Rafe knew he should feel a sense of shock or surprise in Lubria's words, but somehow he already knew of this sacrifice that she intended to make. *"And why not?"* Askana said to him once before. *"It is not such a bad trade. Myself for a kingdom. I have sold my body for less."* A vivid memory, fresh in his mind.

"That will not happen, not in my lifetime," he said aloud as if responding to the Queen's words. *I had said that to her,* Rafe thought. *But when and where did we share this exchange?* He then noticed Elunear and Lubria both looking at him quizzically. *What in the name of Beelzebub is happening to me?* Rafe tipped his head back deeper into the pillows, trying to clear his mind. The sleep, the pain, and now strange memories of conversations never shared were all too overwhelming.

Lubria suddenly moved in close to Rafe once more, knowing it unnerved him when she did. Her eyes sparkled as she spoke, "Whilst you slept, Elunear has been trying to convince me of your loyalty to Queen Askana. A most loyal advocate you have gained in her, human. She seems quite taken with you."

Elunear set down the cloth and moved away, blushing lightly as Rafe looked at her. Askana said that she had two years of celibacy to go. He wondered with a grin if those two years now appeared as two thousand.

"I do not trust you," Lubria stated quite plainly. "But so long as the Queen wishes it, I will work with you if only for the good of the Queen and the realm she treasures. Human folly that it is."

"Does that mean you shall avoid gutting me today?" Rafe asked painfully as he kept the sheets close and manoeuvred into a sitting position.

She purred with the sharp-toothed grin. "There is always tomorrow, human." Watching Rafe struggle to keep himself covered brought Lubria's grin to a full smile. "You do not need to be so modest around us, human. Elunear has already seen all that there is to be seen."

The girl's skin tone now deepened to scarlet. Elunear then firmly grasped Lubria's bandaged forearm. The shot of pain caused her to break her stare with Rafe. Her hiss ended abruptly at the sight of Elunear's own death stare. "I should keep an eye on this bandage," she snapped. "Make certain it is secure."

"So how long have I been asleep? Who sewed me up?"

"You have kept us all awake with your repugnant snoring for four days by my count," Lubria said as she rubbed her forearm, her eyes still fixed on Elunear. "Her Majesty and Elunear tended to your wounds. They are both trained in the Healing Arts. I have no understanding or interest in such skills. I do not inflict wounds merely to repair them," she said blandly.

"Where is Her Grace?" Rafe asked, looking about their chambers.

"Your King summoned her," said Elunear, the blush finally subsiding from her skin. "So, you had best turn your mind to thinking up a plan to get us out of here. Preferably with allies."

With that decree clearly being the final word from either woman, they settled down to resume playing Cat's Cradle.

Rafe stifled a groan. Stand against his King, rescue Askana, and depart from England with allies, all without the Duke of Norfolk's knowledge.

He stared at a small goblet of water by his bed, wondering if it would be any easier to turn it into a fine wine.

The sweet tones of the singing girl soared with the melody of the dulcimer and harp, then fell to velvety, dark tones reverberating with feeling. The song was a remorseful ballad of a young man's unrequited love and desire over a woman, a woman he would never know and a love forever lost.

The richly-attired nobles listened, the servants listened, the imposing man on the dais and the woman in russet on his right listened, but Askana Moldarin's attention was far from the Great Hall where the music played. She forced a smile for the homage paid to her in this song. The tune, as it was made painfully evident again and again in its repetitive chorus, was called "Greensleeves", penned by the very King who now looked at her adoringly from his throne.

Silently, she prayed for Nadinath to touch her robes and change their colours from white and green to yellow and pale blue.

This was the fourth day of court life, and Askana found it nothing beyond an extreme exercise of purest boredom. True, she was gaining a feel for the politics of the land. The performers and artisans entertaining the court were exceedingly talented. The games were also simple enough to master, making it easier to "lose gracefully" to her opponent which, in most cases, was King Henry himself.

But doing the same thing for days upon days on end?

After the second day she had given up on her make-up. It was a formality of her Court, but the English found her outward appearance intimidating. Adding to this was her gauntlets and throwing-knives, which she wore only on the first day. All she carried now was the large silk fan that hung on a tasseled cord from her girdle. She needed to win their trust and admiration, especially of their King.

She wore the faintest rouge to accent her cheeks and lips. Keeping with her own realm's fashion and traditions, her hair was piled up in elaborate braids and ornamented with emerald pins, offset by the crown of Her Realm. Even without the Court paint and weapons, she still remained outstanding with her hard, muscular features sharply contrasting the rounded, plump features of the English females who looked as if they had never handled a weapon or fought for a cause in their life of privilege.

Queen Kathryn conveyed a contrived civility in Askana's presence. Not surprising in the least, especially in light of King Henry's behaviour if he too was present. The child had hardly forgotten the incident in the Great Hall, but she appeared to be the only lady of Court still refusing to forgo Askana's impressionable introduction.

The English women all shared in common a voracious eagerness to talk. Their talk, however, was far from stimulating. Avid questions about Askana's "strange" manners and lack of "modesty" as well as the lesser facets of Morevian life. A few of the more pious tried to convert Askana to Christianity. Some implored her of how to appear more alluring and exotic to their husbands. It was either open talk of what their religion promised or whispers of what their religion forbade. Other than that, it was fashion, embroidery, and gossip.

Only the men had anything useful to say by way of trade, politics, or war. The real work of the country was not for her eyes though and done behind closed doors. Yet even they preferred dedicating hours to games and gambling. Like over-indulged children, they played at cards, dice, and elementary games called "croquet" and "bowls"! The hunting and jousting, on the other hand, Askana found more to her liking.

As for the "object of her desire", King Henry was rather self-indulgent, revelling in past prowess at sports his age and health now made either difficult or impossible. He was fond of praise and flattery, though he was shrewd enough to recognise it for what it was. A trait Askana could admire but a single trait easily outnumbered by a multitude of shortcomings. The religion that he ruled as "Supreme Head" merely served to justify his rulings. He also showed little tolerance for any ideas, opinions, or concepts opposing his own. Then there were his sexual urges and desires that had not dwindled with age as his behaviour insinuated with both Kathryn and herself.

And with each passing day, King Henry was becoming more informal as was evident from this morning's events, still fresh and lingering in her mind...

Stifled by the inactivity and constant feasting, she had chosen to practice *Yelan-Chi* in the small stretch of gardens visible from her chambers. She was assured of privacy as the greens were partially enclosed by a low wall. Yelan-Chi was one of the many styles of martial arts that she trained in, but it was by far her favourite, being not only an art of self-defence but also an excellent program of stretching and swift movement. One form would consist of slow, fluid movements covertly working every muscle in her body while another form would require swift attacks, precise control, and abrupt bursts of speed and strength. This art also gave Askana a sense of peace, a sweet solitude in its discipline and philosophy, ascending her mind to a higher state of clarity.

Askana had asked Elunear to spar with her. The girl was eager to comply. Her pride was still stinging from the humiliation of being found tied up like a turkey behind the bed. It was after her return from the *Defiant* that Lord Norfolk made his bold move in abducting Lubria, costing him two of his men and dealing a serious blow to her self-confidence. The young girl wanted to remind herself that she was of the Queen's Royal Guard, the highest and most elite of the Maidens.

Elunear's hunger for redemption was refreshing following the company of bland, latent English women. The young warrior fell into a crouch and tried to sweep out Askana's feet from under her, following up immediately with a series of vicious hook-and turn-kicks. Her unbound ferocity caused Askana to retreat quickly with several backward somersaults and a back-flip onto the low wall.

"Te-shi, *Elunear!*" she said from her crouch, her body glistening with sweat despite the morning chill. Elunear stopped in her counter-attack, still waiting to pounce, her breathing deep and controlled. Askana swept her long black mane away from her face with a gentle laugh, *"Keep channelling your anger into the exercise, and your Queen will need another Royal Guard to protect her from her Royal Guard."*

"An unfortunate predicament We would have you avoid," said a booming voice from behind her.

Askana quickly turned, her eyes wide at the sight of King Henry with noblemen and attendants surrounding him. Under the guise of privacy, she had shed her white robes and wore only a simple red and tan loincloth so that she could move completely uninhibited. His small eyes insolently looked her up and down as a lewd smile formed on his face. Only Nadinath knew how long they had been there, watching her, eyeing her like a simple wanton displaying her wares for the highest bidder. All those charming words and Courtly manners, merely the surface of a pool where underneath the slime and mud settles. No substance. No sincerity. This is what they had wanted from her since her arrival. The exotic savage, unleashed and alluring unlike their own female cattle.

Elunear had already slipped the white silks over Askana's shoulders when she finally spoke. *"We were told this footpath was seldom used, Your Majesty,"* she said curtly. *"We did not expect to be disturbed."*

"We came to pay You a morning visit, Queen Askana. If We had known this would be the display before Us, methinks We would have made a habit of coming this way every *morning."* He then laughed heartily, his courtiers quickly following his lead. *"Finer than an English sunrise, by Jove!"*

As she had been this morning, Askana was the centre of his attention. Kathryn seethed from her throne, making no attempt to hide her disliking of the "savage queen". Askana cared little if she won the respect of the child-queen for she had no say in King Henry's decisions over the realm or its subjects.

The scorn Kathryn dealt allayed when Thomas Culpeper entered the Great Hall. He was attractive by the shallow standards of these English Court ladies. "A fine, turned leg" they would whisper with adolescent giggles. He was, on outward appearances, of good breeding. The young man also carried with him a reputation of being a mighty opponent in battle. Kathryn enjoyed the attentions of men, but clearly her favourite was this Culpeper. This was evident in her initial reaction. Askana remembered that look. It had been a distant lifetime ago when one's presence would cause her face to radiate so brightly.

Kathryn spared a moment's elation when Culpeper appeared, then quickly returned to the demeanour proper for a queen. Then her eyes met Askana's. For a long moment, they held a stare. Kathryn knew with Askana's look that her secret was now shared with the "savage". Her skin grew pale, but in the warm light of the burning tallow no one took notice.

Except for one. Askana broke her stare with one Howard only to lock eyes with another. Thomas Howard had been unctuously polite all evening but kept a constant watch over her. From underneath the sleeves of his robes Lord Norfolk produced a small locket of Lubria's fiery red hair. Only Askana could see it from where she sat. A convenient reminder of the hold he had on her.

She knew Kathryn's secret, but could share it with no one.

As the tedious chorus began once more, she closed her eyes to turn her thoughts to the man she left slumbering in her chambers. A few moments ago she had felt a twinge in her shoulder, then her thigh. In a day the stitches would come out, though he would have to be careful not to tear the wounds. *Finally, the sleeper has returned from his Dreamwalk*, Askana smiled. *I hope he found the journey a pleasant one.*

She was unaware she was smiling until opening her eyes to find King Henry returning the smile. Could she protect the privateer from his own King? Then the memory came to her, sudden and vivid. *There is, of course, another option*, he said with new-found resolve in his voice. But when did this conversation take place? *I will not fail you, Your Grace*, Rafe had said.

The surreal recollection caused her smile to fade away as the girl sang the closing refrain. The courtiers applauded, but the King's attentions were on Askana. "Something ails you, Queen Askana? Was the song not pleasing?"

"We are not accustomed to such music, Your Majesty," she said tactfully. "In Our Land it is most different," she smiled as her memory recalled the exquisite enchantment of Elven-Song. "But yes, it was perchance a little melancholy."

"What means this? The Queen is bored?" asked Henry in good humour. "'Tis true. We have lulled our senses with sweet music, but perhaps Our guest would care for something more rousing?" Askana merely smiled politely, feigning a modest embarrassment to the King's unending attentions. He gave a hearty laugh and clapped his hands loudly. "Minstrels!"

The sound of conversation elevated and animated laughter filled the chamber hall as ladies rose eagerly to their feet, followed by their lords. Servants scurried to remove chairs and tables as musicians took their places at one end of the hall. The older gentlemen took themselves to the walls and alcoves where they could talk. Some in jest, some in earnest scheming. The younger came forward as the ancient game of courtship that had already begun earlier in the evening was about to reach a pivotal stage.

The torchlight flickered on the walls as King Henry stood, towering above all on the raised dais. The cut of the doublet made his broad shoulders even broader, and jewels flashed on his fingers and winked on his dalmatica as his Court waited for his signal to begin. Kathryn smiled brightly at the sight of her King, her back arching slightly upward to give her an illusion of extra height. She looked nothing less than the sweet treasure of the Tudor Crown that could not be denied.

Instead, King Henry turned to Askana, "Will the Queen favour us with a dance?"

No one could overlook the impact of this gesture. Facing the Morevian Queen, Henry had turned his back completely on his own. Kathryn's hands twisted a lace handkerchief. Her face fell and boldly she looked to Culpeper for strength.

Askana could see in the young noble's eyes a painful want to take Kathryn into his strong arms and carry her off to some far-away paradise. Instead, he forced himself to look away. She then glanced at Kathryn's uncle, Thomas Howard, grinning with overwhelming contentment at the progress of his plans to secure his own high standing in Court. The child-queen was now totally and utterly alone.

Askana's reply surprised everyone, including Askana herself. "Many thanks, King Henry, but We fear We are not familiar with this dance. Perchance You might ask Your Queen and wife to accompany You."

The drop of a pin would have sounded like a thunder-clap.

Lord Norfolk's grin faded into a slight scowl.

The King's laugh broke this absolute silence, but it was no longer so good-humoured as he turned to face his own wife. "So says the wise ruler of Morevi. But We think Our Queen appears as pale as moonlight. We think the Queen should retire to Her chambers for the night."

There was no way she could refuse. Kathryn was determined to end the evening with her dignity intact. "As Our King wishes," she answered, sinking into a curtsy as her ladies gathered round her. The awkward silence continued as Askana rose and bowed to her. Kathryn paused for a moment, and then continued on her way, refusing to return the homage. Whispers of shock and disdain continued to follow her as she proceeded through the corridors of the palace.

"Well, that is that," Henry said, completely overlooking Kathryn's defiance. At his sweeping gesture, the musicians began playing. Henry bowed low to the Queen of Morevi before turning to his Court.

The initial crash in the Great Hall sounded like the roar of a wild beast. Shards of glass fell as raindrops against stone. Through the shattering of high windows, three black-clad figures hit the floor in a roll, immediately returning to their feet. Screams rose into the air as the cries of alarm and for the King's Guard echoed in the chambers.

Askana remained still, biting down a curse as she recognised them for what they were. Members of the Assassins' Guild from across The Rift. *In England?*

She caught a glimpse of the red collar and sash on one before his hand pulled back and slashed forward. The room whirled as her hands found the back of the King's heavy wooden throne and she somersaulted over it. The throwing knife embedding itself into its back, tore the edge of her hem as she slipped behind it. Two more knives bit into the back of the throne with meaty thuds, their points just poking through the thick wood.

By Nadinath! A Shokara, thought Askana wildly. *A master-assassin.*

With a roar, two Landsknechts charged another assassin with their halberds forward. A noble effort, but not a wise one. Another black-wrapped man sprang up in the air, his arms outstretched and legs tucked up to his chest. He then lashed out with both feet to either side. His sash was blue. A *Minawa*, specialised in stealth. The armoured men dropped like stones.

The third assassin snatched something from a fold of his garments and threw with unerring aim. In quick succession three charging gentlemen fell, the serrated edges of the throwing discs biting deep into their throats between the points of their collars. He also wore a sash of blue.

At least there was no yellow. The *Yusana* were killing machines, trained to kill their targets and anyone in the vicinity, armed or unarmed.

Several of the women had fainted. The hall resounded with the ring of swords, but the noblemen's complacency now haunted them as they faced demons dressed in black. The elder gentlemen protected the women while the younger nobles charged forward.

Askana experienced a fluttering of panic. These were men of her realm and would kill them all in an instant. She knew. She had contracted with them.

The Shokara made his move. Without a sound he took a run, climbing up along the wall and pushing himself into the open air. His feet knocked aside Earl William FitzWilliam and Sir Thomas Audley, who had placed themselves before their King. As if they shared one mind, the Minawa moved to flank their brother, moving through the Hall as deadly shadows that closed on King Henry.

The assassins had sadly forgotten one thing—their *primary* target.

There was the rushing swish of fabric. The torches fluttered fitfully. She appeared as an avenging angel of white and green silk, a single malevolent green eye of fire glaring at the Shokara above two pools of dark anger. A booted foot drove deep into his belly, throwing him clear of King Henry whom she landed in front of, causing the advancing Minawa to recoil. The Shokara twisted effortlessly to a full-standing position and slipped back into a defensive back stance.

She slowly ran the tip of her tongue across her top lip, a dark smile across her face accompanying a soft, cat-like hiss. She then darted forward, feigning a high kick, then dropping suddenly to the ground to sweep the Shokara's feet out from under him. He back-flipped, but as swift as a striking panther she followed. Her foot slammed into the side of his head, and then she twisted and kicked him in the ribs repeatedly. Her attack crunched into his ribs, and with a sweep of silk she leapt into the air. The scene seemed to freeze as her arms rose like a butterfly's wings, her knees folded under her with a deadly grace till her right leg unfolded, foot catching the man under the chin.

His head snapped back audibly.

She landed silently only to turn and stop the advancing Minawa with a powerful side-kick to the knee. She curled her fingers into claws and struck him across the face, her nails taking the assassin's skin as well as his black mask, revealing his face. Her other hand slid a small, slender blade out of its concealment inside her fan as she whirled around him. Askana locked her hand underneath his chin, forcing his head back against her shoulder. A single flick of her wrist and the tiny fan-dagger rested against his neck.

The remaining Minawa moved for the King with dagger unsheathed. Now that she held his brother, the secondary target could be taken without interference. He was about to reach the mammoth King until something stopped his advance abruptly. His eyes looked quickly to Askana. She still grasped his comrade. Then he looked down to see the halberd's ornate blade buried deep into his chest.

He had taken Askana into account. He had not done so for the Landsknecht reinforcements.

She turned her eyes back to the Minawa in her hold. He was younger than expected, straight-nosed and actually handsome. Blood flowed down from her nail-marks as he fixed his coldest stare with hers.

"You embraced death, boy, when you came here," spat Askana.

He smiled, despite the insult. "I am glad you tore away the bindings of silence. Now I can tell you with my own words that you will die. Be it here or on your own soil, you will die by my master's hand."

The fan-dagger disappeared only to have her hand close around his throat like a vice. "Who is your master?"

"Only before you draw your last breath will you know that." With no warning, seizing her face suddenly with both hands, he kissed her full on the mouth. It lasted only seconds, and then he fell to the floor as she released him. "A good fight. An excellent way to die. I have sampled the Black Widow and found her lips sweet."

His eyes glittered lightly. Sweat burst from every pore of his skin. He tossed fitfully before an eerie calm came across his limbs and his eyes closed gently.

Askana stood there for a long moment looking at the dead Minawa. Her lip rouge had mixed into it a swift poison that paralysed first and then gave a painless death. Prepared with an infusion of her own saliva, it had no affect on her. It was her preferred method of killing when she wished to be merciful, or when the kill had to be made in bed. This man knew of it. Her trademark was his escape so that he would not be questioned.

Askana stood amidst the death in the Great Hall. The silence was absolute.

"Queen Askana." The King's voice caused everyone to start. Her blade vanished inside her fan before he took her hand in his. "We know not the meaning behind this attack upon the Throne, but are deeply indebted to You." He stood close to her, his large hand all but engulfing hers and his breathing still fast from the shock of the attack. "You have saved England's King, thus You have saved England." He turned to those remaining in the Hall. "We owe Our life to Queen Askana, and forthwith We deem Her worthy of any boon She seeks within Our power to grant."

"Sovereign of England," Askana bowed, her heart pounding against her ribs as she spoke, "of Your generosity We will partake. You have offered Us a boon. This will We ask of You and Your Country. We desire a fleet of ships and an army of men, for Our Realm is shadowed by a threat, a threat greater than what We have seen tonight." She took a deep breath and stared imploringly into the King's eyes, "Time is against Us, and We must move against those who oppose Us. Please, Your Majesty, grant Your Sister and Her Realm this boon."

The great hand around hers tightened, then released it as he smiled warmly.

"Sire!" Lord Norfolk could not contain himself any longer. "As a subject most loyal to you, this is too much to ask! Forgive my boldness, but are we certain this attack was not orchestrated by her? They fight as she does and are undoubtedly from her lands. Her Majesty's presence in England has brought this danger to us all!" He straightened his robes and smiled dryly, his eyes never leaving Askana's. "Give me leave, Your Majesty, to investigate this matter further. I do suspect the Queen harbours secrets against Your Majesty's well-being."

Askana felt a chill run through her as Howard casually toyed with the braid of Lubria's hair, this time openly before the King and Court.

King Henry's eyebrow arched slightly as the words of Lord Norfolk echoed in his ears. He then looked at the faces of the assassins. The noblemen had torn away their masks as if demanding to know who they were. Did it matter though? They had no identity in this world. The Duke was right. These men were from *her* realm. A brutal, deadly realm from their expressions suspended in death.

He now contemplated this foreign Queen standing before him, awaiting the answer to her request for allies. He noticed her eyes were now cast downward under his hard gaze. A habit of His Court she had never practised before until now. She appeared so fragile and delicate in the soft light of the Great Hall. A look could shatter this fine treasure before Him. He knew now, however, this was not her true nature.

Even in its gentle tone, his voice commanded reverence. "Leave Us."

The chambers began to clear, attendants and nobles bowing in respect and departing quietly, the night's horror continuing to play in their minds. Askana's eyes never rose to meet the King's. Howard, it seemed, had given the monarch pause. She had moved only a few steps away from the King when his voice again shattered the unnerving quiet of the room.

"Yet for Our Royal Cousin, Askana Moldarin, We desire Her to remain here with Us," The King uttered. "We wish to share confidence with Her."

Lord Norfolk's demeanour changed abruptly, his shoulders dropping slightly as the locket of hair disappeared from view. It was time for Askana to "earn" her allies and consummate the King's affections. Soon, his little niece would hear of this night and fight to win back her "beloved husband and King". As for granting allies in exchange for her affections, Howard merely grinned. He would make certain no ship would leave English ports to serve this savage. With his own agenda close to completion, he bowed and left the room.

Askana froze. Her eyes now fixed on a series of glass shards that shimmered in the reflection of the torchlight. She watched the shadows of Henry's subjects pass by her, one by one, as they departed on their King's command. She heard the doors close. Askana remained motionless. They were alone. She could feel his eyes staring at her, watching her. Her fingernails dug into her palms, her hands in taut fists that grew paler as she tightened them. *What are you waiting for?* Askana screamed the challenge in her mind, *Either take me or kill me, and be done with it!*

"Your Grace," King Henry moved to Askana, his massive hand reaching underneath her chin and gently raising her eyes to his own, "We are a rare breed in this world of commonalties. Above all others in Our Right. Monarchs born to rule. Embodiments of Our lands, its subjects, and its heritage. Rarely are we allowed the luxury to bear Our souls honestly and openly." The King took in a deep breath and moved to the shattered window, the remains of the stained glass grinding underneath his steps, "Tonight, however, I desire a confidant. Someone I can speak with honestly and openly."

"I", Askana thought with surprise. *Not "We".* She could feel her body soften in its posture, but her guard remained. *Is this a ploy to charm me into his bed?* Years under the hand of man made her so very cautious in settings such as these, but there was something in Henry's words Askana had not heard since arriving to Court. Her intuition kept her quiet.

"England is my home by birth, but England is also my responsibility by God. A heavy responsibility, indeed. I have asked for this audience to speak my soul." His gaze returned to the dancing firelight in the far-off streets of London that stretched across the horizon before him. "I wish to speak to you not as a king, but as a man. I was thunderstruck by your spirit, your strength, and your beauty. I was once more brought back to the time I met my Kathryn. My rose without a thorn. She is..." Henry searched for a word appropriate. Perhaps not accurate, but appropriate. "...vivacious."

Askana held her breath in amazement. He knew it was true. He knew everything about Kathryn and her secret affairs was true.

"In my eyes, Askana Moldarin, you are quite extraordinary. I know that my overtures have been hinting to something more intimate between us, but I know not what I would fear more. Living in the shadow you would unknowingly cast over me, or subduing that fire that burns so brightly in your soul. Or perhaps what I truly fear is how I appear before my subjects. They want their king young, powerful, and stalwart." Henry laughed bitterly, "In my efforts to return to my youth, I appear as an even larger doddering old fool!"

The King finally turned away from the panoramic view of his beloved realm to face Askana. "You will have your fleet, Queen Askana, and our debt will be paid. Where shall I send them?"

Her smile could not be contained, and the sight of it brought a gentle laugh from King Henry. She crossed to a small table with parchment and quill upon it. Her hand seemed to move upon its own accord as she quickly jotted a series of numbers, angles, and a rough outline of what looked like a coastline. She recognised it as that of a place called "Wales" and another outline she knew was "Ireland". These were "co-ordinates" and "headings" that helped sailors across the oceans, and these would aid a fleet across The Rift and bring them safely to Arathelle.

"Tell your fleet to follow these course headings to the letter." Askana handed King Henry the parchment, its fresh ink almost appearing to shine in the torchlight. "The first set will take them to a place called The Graveyard of Lost Ships. If they maintain this course *to the letter*, they will reach a port called Arathelle where we will meet them. Once there, we will proceed to Morevi on foot." She removed from her hand a tiny signet ring of her House Crest and placed it in his hand, "Tell your Captain he sails into Arathelle with the blessings of Morevi's Sovereign."

The King smiled widely, "A lady of strategy as well. You possess many talents, Your Grace. But where did you come by these co-ordinates? You did tell me Morevi is land-locked. How could you know of such things as maritime bearings?"

Again, a memory of what never happened came to her. She watched the Pirate Captain jot down numbers, plot courses, and his eyes flashed with optimism. *"We will meet in the safe ports of Arathelle and then onward to Morevi, and return you to your rightful place!"* Such conviction in Rafe's voice that she felt a moment's euphoria pass over her as she looked up to King Henry. "You could say," Askana stared at her own handwriting in some bit of wonderment, "they came to me in a dream."

He took a deep breath and nodded as he placed the parchment in his belt, "It shall be done." Henry returned to the window overlooking London, "It has been so long since I have borne my heart this way. Only one other held the key to my soul as you do now, Askana." His face fell slightly as he spoke his name, "Dear Thomas. In these hours I do miss him so."

"The Duke of Norfolk?" asked Askana incredulously.

"By the Mass, not Howard! I humour the man. He is one I keep close in order to know where his loyalties lie on that particular day. No, this gentleman was very much like you—an individual of integrity, undaunted courage, and an honest soul. He commanded from me nothing but a friendship and trust unmatched in my Court. Sir Thomas More. In more personal moments, he would dare to call me 'Hal'. God's Peace, in these most intimate of hours do I now understand why he was known as 'a man for all seasons'. There are times..."

The King's voice trailed off as his head bowed slowly in shame. Askana recognised his pain. She had seen it before when she looked into her own mirror. "And what became of Sir Thomas More?"

His eyes were closed and his voice betrayed a vulnerability. "I had him executed." The words seem to catch in his throat. "He would not sign the oath accepting me as Supreme Head of the Church of England. A simple signature. That was all I needed. For my kingdom, my people. I did it all for England. I did, Askana."

"I, too, have paid heavy prices for my Crown." Askana felt her heart come full circle on this King. He was much like her in his determination and resolve, and in his regret. A man of power and might in a desperate search of justification for his past. In the most quiet of hours when regalia and revels were at an end and only the sounds of night provided company within the Royal Chambers, she had also been in his turmoil. "If it is absolution you seek from me, I cannot grant it. You must find that within yourself." A friendly smile came across her face, "Hal."

Henry's laugh came as a gentle rumble that shook his entire body. "So much like Thomas, you are." He returned his eyes to the comforting sight of his realm, the lights of London winking back at him. "Sometimes I do wonder—this sacrifice for a country— is it truly worth it? Does this band of gold, velvet, and jewels that I wear across my brow truly merit the sacrifice? As King, I believed the world would be mine for the taking, and yet I find myself denied of the simplest things that would make me..." He searched for a moment and then sighed heavily, his breath creating a light fog in the cool night air around him, "...complete."

A chill had now overtaken the warmth of the dying fire that burned in the Great Hall's hearth. Askana could feel her skin tingle from its sensation. Her light shiver was Henry's cue that the night's revels had come to an end. He straightened his back to assume a most regal posture and extended his hand to her.

"Allow Us to escort You to Your chambers," Henry bellowed in his full voice.

Askana took his hand gently, "Know always, King Henry the VIII of England, that you will have a confidant in the Sovereign of Morevi."

"We would desire a kiss to seal this new alliance betwixt Us, but We have seen the effect Your kiss hath on men." Henry grinned with a playful wink, "Mayhaps We shall practice more modesty."

He granted her hand the lightest of kisses, managing a smile from her.

The door closed behind her with a soft *"click"*, and Askana let out a sigh of relief as the King's promise returned to her.

She had done it.

Then came the sound of the door's latch locking from the outside, reminding her of the diplomacy practised by Lord Norfolk.

The sound of clasps fastening satchels caught her attention. Lubria and Elunear were at the four-poster bed packing their last few belongings and placing their haversacks on one another's backs. Both had secured their shirai through a series of ties and loops across the satchels. It was evident that Lubria had prepared Askana's bag and now bore it upon her own back for the Queen. Elunear double-checked the securing of her own shirai, then turned to Askana, giving her reverence followed by her wrist gauntlet.

"My Queen," Elunear said, "we are ready."

Askana looked around the room as she replaced the gauntlet to her wrist. "Where is—"

Before Askana could finish her thought, she felt an intense shock in her leg. Her eyes immediately went to the door of an adjoining chamber. Rafe emerged from a changing room, fully dressed and fully armed. Stitches in his leg caused him to limp slightly. Askana could literally feel the pain in his every step as he crossed to the bed and placed his own haversack upon his back.

"Time to leave, Your Grace," he uttered dryly.

His forehead was already breaking into a sweat. As she also felt the tearing pain with his steps, Askana could not understand how he could be walking with only the slight limp. Then she noticed a slight tingling in her chest, bringing her slender hand to his own. His eyes lowered in a dream-like state as Askana's head snapped up, her dark gaze staring at him in shock. His heart was racing frantically, but his skin was cold. His breath was still even and controlled. His eyes appeared as gemstones, glassy and brilliant in the torch's light.

"Elunear!" One look to her Guard and Askana knew Elunear had gone into her supplies and created a remedy of some kind for Captain Rafton's pain. This was a skill that Elunear was still a novice at, and a skill she had not practised for some time.

"My Sovereign, he insisted. The Captain would not heed my warnings."

"There will be no need for you to lie with King Henry." Rafe took a deep breath, a smile crossing his face. "I have an alternative, Your Grace."

"An alternative." Why were these words so familiar to her?

"That will not be necessary, privateer." Askana nodded, placing a hand upon his shoulder, "We have our army and King Henry has his co-ordinates to bring his fleet across The Rift."

Elunear and Lubria looked at their Queen in shock. Eventually their gazes turned to Rafe whose face now turned a shade paler than before. In his eyes resided a conflicting medley of emotions and Askana could feel her blood rushing a bit faster. *Was this anger? Rage? No,* she thought to herself, *there is something else here.*

"Captain, I do not—"

"Your Grace, please." His words were sharp and curt. The pirate secured his pack and moved to the window. It would be a long trip down the side of the castle, but the Morevian cure in his blood should last him long enough. "Now that the Duke of Norfolk has what he wants, we have become a hindrance. Any moment now, his men will come for us." He finally looked at her, unable to find any words appropriate for what he felt. "Follow me," he spoke, his voice barely audible.

Askana could not help but flinch slightly as Rafe pulled himself over the balcony, followed by Elunear and Lubria. She could read it in all their faces. Had he not cut her off in mid-sentence, Askana would have explained to them all that no carnal transaction had occurred, the allies a token of appreciation in saving the King from an assassination attempt. An assassination attempt meant for her. As she slipped out of her outer robes, wearing only the plain white robes of a handmaid, she wondered if she would find a moment to restore her honour with Lubria and Elunear.

The full moon bathed the four in a haunting pale grey light, their shadows reflecting their soundless descent to the ground below. Occasionally, their climb halted as guards below walked heavily underneath them. Their armour sounding against the stone walkway preceded their approach, and pleasant words were exchanged between the dutiful night regiment. The evening conversation echoed in the night, ending with a slight nod to one another and then disappearing into their uneventful watch. Had the sentries merely cast their eyes upward, the monotony of their duty would have ended in an instant.

Rafe slowly moved his arm downward and the Morevians continued to follow their guide along the wall.

They crept from shadow to shadow, making their way along the perimeter of the castle. Their journey seemed to lengthen with each step. She crept past Lubria and Elunear and slipped to Rafe's side. She watched his eyes carefully as they peered forward to a soft glow that dispelled the cover of night that concealed them. Rafe's smile found its way to his sweat-drenched face as a steed's boastful voice broke the gentle air around them.

"Your Grace," Rafe whispered, motioning to the stables, "your steed awaits you."

Their eyes adjusted for a moment to the yellow light of the few lamps that remained lit for the evening. A magnificent black stallion turned its head in the direction of Lubria who locked eyes with it. She quietly approached the horse and uttered something in a language Rafe had never heard before. Askana knew this as a talent of the Fae. Another horse of a dark chestnut colour approached them and looked to its fellow mare. The stallion let out a soft whinny and nodded. The deep brown eyes returned to Askana and it nuzzled her gently.

"We have friends here," Lubria purred happily. "They know of our plight and are willing to help us."

"Your Grace, do you have your wrist gauntlet?" Rafe asked, pulling himself up to the black steed's back.

"Yes, fully loaded."

"Excellent." Rafe extended a hand to Elunear who looked to her Queen uncertainly at first before taking his hand. He pulled her up to sit behind her. Askana winced as pain shot down along her side. "The main gate is still open as many of the King's guests are leaving tonight for some strange reason. You will need to take out the gate sentries if we have any problems in our exit."

Askana mounted the second horse and then gave a check to the darts. By the blue-coloured feathering of the tiny darts, four were loaded that were not lethal. Lubria joined her and they set off down the loose gravel path from the stables that led to the main path.

There were several carriages making their way from the entrance of the King's Palace to the open gates. Rafe and Askana casually rode up to the final coach and joined the modest collection of attendants, also riding on horseback. Askana was only a few paces behind Rafe, concealed in shadow as Lubria was in plain sight. The guards politely waved them through as they neared the giant iron gates. Rafe then gave a gentle nod to the Queen as they passed the final sentries. With a snap of reins, they rode ahead of their adopted train of carriages, disappearing into the shadows of London.

From the balcony of his own chambers, King Henry watched his numerous guests hastening their way home. *At least it will be said that at King Henry's manor, a dull moment is rarely had*, he thought with a tiny smile. He also watched Rafe and Askana easily slip amongst the train of carriages and then slip away into the night. His eyes turned to the parchment of co-ordinates in his hand. There would be opposition to this action, of risking valiant English lives for a realm of savages. Perhaps, but he was still King. His word was the will of God. Beyond that, he would not fail his confidant. His heart said a quick prayer for this ally from the far-off land of Morevi. He wondered if he would ever see her again.

"Godspeed, Askana Moldarin," Henry uttered softly.

The *Defiant* had set sail during the King's Evening Feast welcoming the Savage Queen to England, bound for an unknown rendezvous point. A regiment of the King's Guard under the command of the Third Duke of Norfolk were provided several ports to patrol, ports that Rafe Rafton frequented. It was important to try and catch the *Defiant* before it set sail for the open sea. These were their orders, issued by the Duke himself who was outraged at the complete failure of the English soldiers keeping watch over the Palace Gates. It should not have been difficult to notice a pirate, two savages, and a creature of witchcraft. He then issued the orders for the capture of Captain Rafe Rafton, the heathen queen, and those in their company. Whether they were returned to London dead or alive depended on how much they resisted.

Lord Norfolk's parting words to them were clear as crystal. *"Ride forth to find them. If you fail to do so, do not bother to return."*

Four soldiers had just finished their rounds in the port of Plymouth and found no sign of Captain Rafton. However, the *Defiant* was spotted dropping anchor there, so this port had to be their rendezvous point. They were on their return to London to inform the Duke and gather reinforcements when they came across a carriage en route to the shores of Devon. To Plymouth. As their orders mandated, this carriage like any other coach, be it of minor or highest nobility, was subject to a search.

"Halt, in the name of Thomas Howard, the Duke of Norfolk." Bundled in a series of bulky cloaks to ward off the chill, a diminutive driver pulled back on the reins, bringing the carriage to a halt. The Captain and his second dismounted while the others, remaining on their horses, loaded crossbows. "In the name of the Duke, tell us the nature of your business in this county." The cab remained silent, save for the muffled sound of rapid chattering coming from inside it. The leader of the four approached the carriage closer, "I am an officer of the Duke of Nor—"

He managed to finish the word "Norfolk," but the latter half of it sounded more like an obscenity and less of a title as the carriage door suddenly swung open, slamming him in his face. Its owner was apparently in the middle of a fascinating story to her guest, and both were unaware of being stopped by soldiers. The Captain, rubbing his tender nose, turned to silence the talking lady and paused at the sight her. Hair as black as a raven with eyes to match. Impressive high cheek bones and a voice that had a playful, sultry edge to it. Both she and her companion displayed stunning bodies in their extravagant outfits. Perhaps they were fashions from Europe as they were most provocative in their exposure of the neck and chest. It was difficult to make out the second woman's features as she remained concealed behind a fan, her black eyes remaining attentive to her friend's story. The men on horseback lowered their crossbows, appreciating both women's lack of modesty as they displayed ample bosoms from their expensive, exotic fashions.

The Captain and his yeoman could not manage to get in a word as the first woman continued in her prattle. "And so there I was, completely naked as upon the day of my birth, and all Lord Thomas Seymour could say was 'Praised be God I shall finally live up to my family name.' If he did *see* any *more* he would have to enlist into the medical profession!"

Both women guffawed and cackled loudly, completely oblivious to the guards in front of them.

"Excuse me, my Lady," the officer said, his faculties finally returning to him.

"That does remind me of *another* story..." she chortled as her companion merely nodded with wide, vacant eyes.

"Viscountess?"

"Yes, we had this darling young man come in to take charge of the local parish. I was making up the most fantastic stories just to have a reason to 'make confession' to this lovely looking man..."

He tried another tactic, "Your Ladyship?"

The woman continued on, heaving her bosoms upward, "Bless me, Father, for I wish to sin..."

"YOUR LADYSHIP!" bellowed the officer.

She stopped abruptly. Both women turned to the Captain in unison, their dark eyebrows arching upward giving their gazes an obtuse quality. The soldier could now get a better look at these women. Obviously neither one of them were the privateer in some elaborate disguise for both of these women were unmistakable in their gender. The first lady was quite lovely but as dim as many of their class.

"My Lady, I have orders from the Duke of Norfolk—"

"Who?" shrugged the Viscountess.

"Thomas Howard, my Lady, the Third Duke of Norfolk and uncle to Her Majesty, Queen Kathryn Howard." He began to feel a sinking regret in following his orders to the letter and stopping this particular coach. "We are charged to search your carriage for criminals wanted for treason against the Crown."

"Oh, how exciting!" The noble lady smiled, her dark eyes widening as she slid closer to the guard, "Such responsibility. The Duke must trust you implicitly to send you on such a mission of importance to the country."

As the dark lady traced the Captain's jawline with her fan, the second beauty slowly approached the two guards on horseback. Her tilted dark eyes seemed to enjoy the sight of them.

The larger soldier leaned in his saddle towards the other, "I like this one, Colin," he said gruffly. "She's quiet."

"We are blessed with trusted agents of Lord Norfolk," purred the Viscountess. She moved away from the Captain and now gently took in her hand the yeoman's chin, turning his eyes away from the empty, luxurious cab. "And what is your name, noble agent to the Duke?"

The younger guard smiled awkwardly. This woman could be old enough to be his mother. Time, however, had not stolen her beauty nor would it do so in the near future. He felt a shudder as she looked him up and down with her dark gaze. "My name is Geoffrey." The young guard blushed as he heard his voice crack slightly.

"Geoffrey," the woman sang as she rested her hand against his chest. "Men in positions such as yours must be entrusted with heavy duties of keeping our King and Country safe."

"Aye," smiled Geoffrey proudly, puffing his chest out as he spoke. "We are responsible for the security of England and its most gracious sovereign. *God save the King!*" His accolade went unanswered as the crossbowmen remained silent, staring at the woman concealed behind her fan.

The Viscountess returned to the Captain. "Then you gentlemen can keep a secret?" she smiled as she dragged her fan across his neck.

"It is our office to be trusted with secrets, My Lady."

The Viscountess leaned into him, her ruby red lips turning into a smile as she whispered into his ear, "The Savage Queen you seek is standing right over there."

The woman's ornate, beautifully painted fan shut with a piercing snap. Her fan flinched sharply in her wrist and on its opening two threads of silk extended from their spines and sank deep into the crossbowmen's necks.

Geoffrey went for his sword but he suddenly went rigid. A small dart carrying the same paralysing agent landed in the nape of his neck. It had been fired from the wrist gauntlet the female driver wore.

Before the Captain could draw his sword, a dagger's blade rested against his neck, halting his actions.

"Now, noble agent of Lord Norfolk," mocked the dark Viscountess, pressing the cool blade closer to his skin. "We are but defenceless women. Thanks be to God that you have come to our rescue." Askana removed the broadsword from his grasp and passed it to Elunear, holding tight the reins of the carriage's team. The lady lowered her dagger and caressed his cheek, "A kiss for my hero."

It was a gentle, lingering kiss accompanied with a sweet, erotic moan as she ran her fingers through his thick, chestnut hair. The Captain was about to pull away in protest but then he felt a chill in his fingertips. The chill crept throughout his arms. Up along his back. Worked down his legs. He could not tell if he was falling or not. He knew he was being gently laid down in the rolling green grass of Devon. It would be his best night's sleep in years.

"Oh, Your Majesty, I *must* have more of this lip rouge," the Viscountess smiled with glee.

"It has been mixed for you, specifically," the Queen said, turning her attention to the cab. "Consider it a token of gratitude in helping us escape."

Both ladies returned to the carriage. Askana lifted the seat cushion and Lubria stretched flexibility back into her fine muscles. Serena removed the other cushion, her expression quickly turning to one of concern. Wrapped in a heavy wool blanket, Rafe shivered as if caught in a biting chill. During their journey to Devon, Askana could feel tingling and sharp pain throughout her body. They had to get to the *Defiant* so she could properly tend to him.

"Brother," Serena cooed. Whenever she spoke that word, a softness and intimacy would overtake her tones. The woman bestowed to the privateer a warm, brilliant smile as she ran fingers across his sweaty brow, "We are just outside of Plymouth. Be strong."

"How I wish you would come with me, Serena," Rafe whispered through chattering teeth. "You missed your calling. You would have made a formidable pirate."

Askana gave Lubria's long red hair a gentle caress, "Conceal yourself for only a few moments longer. We are almost there."

With a huff, the Fae-woman curled back up into the tiny compartment under the seat. Askana replaced the cushion and then returned to Rafe. She spoke as softly as his sister had, "Privateer, try to remain still. You have torn your stitches. I will tend to you once we are in your quarters."

Rafe grinned wearily as his grip tightened on Serena's hand, "Dear sister, do you hear? I am to fall under the care of a queen."

Askana could see in Serena Rafton a growing fear at seeing her brother this way. There was no world outside of them. Closer than lovers. Stronger than the longest of friendships. With no hesitation, they would lay down their lives for one another. Both shared the bond of family making them unstoppable, the world around them an endless bounty of good fortune.

She had seen this touching portrait once before. A part of her died when Markuna fell.

"Rafe," she smiled, rolling the "r" in his name across the tip of her tongue as she lowered the seat. "Remain still. We will have you aboard the *Defiant* soon." Serena called to Elunear through the window, "Follow the main road. We are looking for a pub called The Boar and The Bull."

The carriage resumed its journey once more, leaving behind Howard's four guards asleep on the side of the road. Through the coach's window, Askana took in a final look of the English landscape. A beautiful country cloaked in a deep green still vibrant even in the dying light of day. A part of her silently, selfishly wished she could return to this country simply to travel across its rolling hills.

"Thank you, Lady Serena, for aiding us in our escape," Askana said, her voice breaking the silence she had become acutely aware of in the cab.

"You can thank me, Your Grace, by taking care of my brother." The sight of seeing Rafe's condition no better than their escape from London had given Serena's voice its curt, sharp edge. Even the sight of Lubria had not sent her into a frightened frenzy as did the condition of her brother. Her voice softened even as she lowered her eyes, "Forgive me, Your Grace. I do forget myself."

"No, Serena, you do not," Askana spoke gently. "I had a brother. We shared a bond much like what you share with the privateer. I cannot explain to you why, but he will not die."

"You sound so certain of this, Your Majesty," Serena stated as she glanced nervously out the window. Over the horizon she could make out the top of the *Defiant's* masts. Not much longer. First it would be meeting Nassir at The Boar and The Bull and then weeks of worrying until a messenger would deliver Rafe's latest correspondence of his adventures between realms. "I wish I shared your confidence."

"I assure you," Askana nodded. "Your brother is an ally I cannot afford to lose. He is not of the same nature as the men I have known. Granted, he is an outlaw. He is also a scoundrel. But his heart is noble. Above all this he is a good man, and that is rare."

"You are a good man, Captain Rafton. And that is rare. So very rare." Another distant, vivid memory of words never uttered. *I have said this before to Captain Rafton. But when?*

"We are here," Serena nodded as she knocked lightly on the top of the cab.

Elunear brought the carriage to a halt before a modest looking pub with a newly carved wooden sign swinging in the evening wind that read "The Boar and The Bull". Nassir enveloped Serena Rafton in a friendly embrace on their arrival. He looked as if he had not slept in days. He was relieved to see his Captain but when he noted Rafe was unable to stand without help from Askana and Elunear, the urgency to return to the *Defiant* became clear.

Serena watched the cart ride toward the pirate vessel moored in the docks of Plymouth, wringing her hands anxiously as Askana and Elunear crouched over Rafe. Lubria, concealed by the cloaks Elunear had worn as the carriage driver, sat motionless next to the First Mate. *Only my little brother would find such strange companions*, she thought quickly. It was never easy being the older sister to a brother like Rafe. His colourful correspondences thrilled her but also kept her awake at night. She was proud of him. She was worried to death about him. It could not be helped.

In the eyes of the English court, he was Captain Rafe Rafton. In the realms of Naruihm, he was the Sea Wolf.

Yet in the eyes of Serena Rafton, he would always be her "dear little brother".

He could feel the Captain's sweat upon his own ebony skin, "He is cold to the touch, Miss."

Askana placed the back of her hand against Rafe's brow. Ice. His skin was that of a corpse and continuing to pale. "Elunear, what did you give him?"

"This is his bidding!" Elunear insisted, her voice not of a warrior but of a child caught in some misbehaviour. "When I was tending to him, he asked me if I knew the Healing Art as you did. He wanted me give him something for the pain, something that would make our escape possible!"

"What did you give him?" Askana demanded again.

"Genshi root," Elunear replied. Askana's eyes widened, but this was merely the first ingredient in Elunear's medicine. "Mixed with Jad-Henna. I added Gnysnig to give him strength."

Askana stared at her guard for a moment, beyond words for what she thought, until, "In the Goddess' Name, you could have killed him!" She turned to Lubria, "Fetch my medicines and herbs. They are in my pack." The Fae-woman remained still. Askana suddenly erupted, *"Do not question me, Lubria. Just do so!"*

Lubria could feel the fur of her coat stand slightly along her back. With only a gentle snarl of disdain as her reply, she rummaged through clothes and weaponry to find several leather pouches. Askana quickly rubbed her hands together as Lubria laid out on a small, low shelf next to them several different dried herbs, fresh weed, and roots both pulverised and in whole chunks. As she arranged the small bottles and pouches of herbs, Elunear took a step forward to aid her Queen as was her duty. Askana shot a look to her, stopping her in her tracks.

"Stand watch, Elunear," she spoke, her anger and displeasure evident. "We will discuss your taking the position of apothecary at a later time."

If she were to question the words of her Queen in Morevi, it would have been a blessing to simply be expelled from the Royal Guard after severe penance. However, Elunear had grown tired of her Queen showing concern for this man who had done nothing to prevent her Sovereign from surrendering to his King. The cost of a simple pirate in escaping an existence of servitude was acceptable.

"I was only thinking of Your Majesty and Your well-being! Unlike this infidel who could not prevent Your Majesty from giving herself—"

"I can take care of my own person. The only exchange between myself and King Henry was an oath. Nothing more." She would have preferred to tell them both under better circumstances, but Elunear would not back down. Now she knew as did Lubria. Both paused in surprise. "Leave me," Askana seethed.

Genshi root was an unpredictable ingredient, reserved only for Sisters possessing skills parallel to hers. The root, if prepared properly, created a physic that would take the body into a deep sleep in order to heal. The Jad-Henna served as the healing agent, but the blend between them had to be precise. The addition of Gnysnig, however, was something Askana had never dared to try. With the increase of strength, the body could alter the original compound, cancel out the Jad-Henna, and push the body into a deep coma. If Nadinath blessed them, the girl's skill was better than Askana gave credit.

Nassir watched her toil over his Captain, his eyes never leaving her or Lubria. Various powders, herbs, and oils were meticulously applied. It was this way for hours. The Moor turned the hourglass over a fourth time. Even with Askana's repeated assurances and Lubria's threats, he refused to leave his Captain in this time of need. Still, he could hear Rafe's words in his mind as if berating him from his unconscious state for not assuming command. *First priority, Nassir, is the crew. Have a care for them and they will have a care for you.*

"I must see to the ship, Your Majesty." Nassir spoke as Askana finished new stitches for Rafe's shoulder wound. He cast a worried glance over the Queen's shoulder as she worked, "His sleep is a bit heavier than I have ever seen."

"It is a healing sleep." Askana bit at the stitch to sever it. She had done all she could for Rafe. "He will sleep until his wounds heal."

"Yes, he will need to as he's been in a bit of a tumble. Good thing your stitches are keeping him whole." Nassir turned for the door, then hesitated. "Your Majesty should know, we follow Captain Rafton because he pays us well. We also follow him because he is a fine captain who takes care of his crew. If the Captain does not come back to us, the crew will want to find someone to blame, be it soldier or queen."

Lubria slipped away from Askana's side into the shadows of the room. A rush of air swept through the cabin. She then stood between Nassir and the door, "Is that a threat, pirate?"

"No, Miss," Nassir said. "A promise."

"Lubria," Askana spoke softly, "stand down."

It was no surprise to Askana. She knew the crew merely needed or, more to the point, *wanted* a reason to act against them. Their superstition had been tested enough with the presence of Lubria, and it was Captain Rafton who kept them back. Now their Captain was in his quarters under her care. If he did cross the threshold into a "living death", Askana and Elunear would answer for it, provided the privateers could overpower Lubria.

The Fae-woman curled up against the foot of Rafe's bed and slipped into sleep. Askana continued to watch over him, her eyes growing heavier as the firelight of the oil lamps dwindled. She purposefully thought to refresh them for more light, but her body refused to move. She placed a hand on Rafe's chest as the lamp's flame snuffed itself out and only the light of the full moon illuminated the room. The bay window created a criss-cross pattern in the quarters and across the slumbering Rafe Rafton. His face appeared almost dreamlike, the grey light giving him a colourless look. She could make out the empty hammock swaying in the darkness, but her body pleaded for her to stay where she was. Askana continued to gently brush his hair with her fingertips. They had come so far in their travels and yet the future still remained as uncertain as in the beginning.

The heaviness in her mind contributed to the heaviness in her eyelids. She felt her body soften as the strokes against Rafe's hair slowed.

Eventually, Askana surrendered herself to her own voyage deep within a dreamscape.

It was The Barrier Reef. The place where this adventure had began, but something was very different about it. Askana's eyes looked about the dingy, wooden tavern, its patrons the odd assortment of different races and realms, all finding their way across The Rift to this oasis. She looked down to see she was wearing her battle armour. Her mind searched as to when she had been dressed in it, as well as how she got it when it had been left behind in Morevi. It announced her presence with each step, but no one in the tavern seemed to take notice. The majority of patrons this day were women, females of all types ranging from the mild and meek to the strong and powerful. They all had different looks and demeanours but they moved about the tavern in a slow, languid manner.

She had finally reached the bar, her body compensating for movement in her battle dress. "Barkeep, you have a bottle of Morevian wine there," Askana spoke confidently. "Serve it to me."

Osgood paid no mind to her, but continued to clean the pint glass in his hand.

"Barkeep!" Askana said again, "Morevian wine."

Still, his silent routine continued as if he were a clockwork figure.

"Why not sample this fine claret from your realm?" A voice from behind her asked.

The table was tucked away in the back corner shadows of The Barrier Reef, and its lone occupant appeared dishevelled and unkempt. A bottle of Morevian wine and an empty glass sat across from his own snifter and bottle of scotch. The contents of his bottle were slowly dwindling, and the privateer consuming it looked as if he were trying to kill himself by drinking.

"Captain Rafton, you are a mess," Askana said, turning her nose upward.

"Am I?" Rafe snapped defiantly. "A thousand pardons, Your Worship, but forgive me if I have lost my ability to care." He raised his glass and laughed, "A toast, Your Grace. To the witchcraft you have subjected me to that has linked us in body and soul." He downed the contents of the snifter and Askana watched in horror as Rafe grew even more pallid.

She then looked about herself again, noting the movements of the patrons and then her own armour, and her head lowered, "Damn you, Caillech!" She looked to Rafe and slapped the half-full snifter of scotch away from his hand. He watched with a long face as the glass shattered against the knotted wood floor. Askana grabbed his wrist as it reached for the scotch bottle, "Have you caught yourself repeating words you have never spoken? Recalled conversations between us that have never occurred?"

"And if I have, Your Grace, what of it?"

"This is a dream, privateer. This is why we are haunted by such images of one another and familiar words shared. A dream-link."

"Fancy that," Rafe sneered as he released himself from Askana's grasp.

As it had been before, the half-full snifter rested in his palm. Askana looked to the floor where she had knocked the glass to only as moment ago. The floor was dry. Not a chard of glass or drop of scotch spilt there.

With a delighted snicker, Rafe set the glass down and looked to Askana, "I think I am getting to like this dream realm. But if you are to share this with me, you will not be dressed like that."

Askana's skin tingled as the armour moulded itself into another form. The intimidating battle-dress soon turned itself into the flowing, low-cut morning robes similar to the ones she wore during Kubi-Sogi training sessions, only more intimate. Rafe smiled warmly as he leaned forward, savouring how the robes accentuated her figure.

"There we are. Much more to my liking."

Askana's hand came across his face hard. Rafe continued to grin smugly, even though in this dream-realm the pain he felt was quite real. The burning of his cheek seemed to relent a bit as he took a deep sip of the scotch.

"Well, that has been building up for some time, has it?" quipped Rafe.

"Do not push any strange fantasy upon me in this realm, pirate. I have dream-linked before and know how to take control of this realm."

"I see. A past love teach you that? You two sharing a bit of sorcery that would push the bounds of pleasure beyond comprehension of this simple God-fearing Christian?"

She could feel her face struggling against painful memories of Telmrant. "Do not speak of what you do not know, privateer."

"Are you insinuating that I do not know of Telmrant? A prince he was, heir to the Elven throne of Arathelle. He won your heart. Your only love, stolen from you in battle." There was a bitterness in his tone. Not directed toward her. "There is so much one can learn in a dream link, would you not agree?"

He was challenging her. He wanted her to cut him down. She could see it in his eyes—Rafe was trying to kill himself within this dream-realm. How much had he learned about her in other dreamwalks? Did he truly understand what he was tempting? If Rafe were to die in a dream, be it this one or another, he would fall deeper into sleep. Normally, a dreamer's body would gradually die, but the Caillech's spell would keep Rafe alive. An eternal living death.

Askana would have to serve as a guide for him. Through this walk, then back home.

She poured herself a glass of the Morevian wine and took a deep sip, the oak flavour mixing with the bitterness of fermented, dark reccaberries creating a pleasant taste. In fact, she drew a hint of resolve from her homeland's vintage. "Captain, we cannot stay in this realm. It is important that you return with me."

"Oh, I am afraid that is quite impossible." Rafe shook his head as he motioned behind Askana. "I am afraid *she* may have something to say against that."

The woman was a stunning slender creature of beauty, long brown hair and demanding blue eyes. She was dressed in the same fashion of Rafe's England, but there were subtle differences in her clothes that led her to believe she was not of the English Court. Her gaze was cruel and mocking, and the sharp laugh she gave him only amplified the chill she evoked from Askana. The Queen was reminded of several members in her Council that possessed this same look, but Rafe's dream-mistress outshone them all.

"Who is she, Rafton?" Askana asked, her eyes never turning away from the mysterious woman.

"That is a lady of the Holy Roman Empire named Karoline Baronesse vom Greifenfels." Rafe refused to look at her, but Askana could see that her laugh touched him deeply. "We were lovers at one time. I loved her, perhaps it should be said. She meant a great deal to me. And then, the fairy tale ended. She returned to her homeland and I remained in London."

The woman rose from her table and walked over to where they sat. Askana could feel the hair on the nape of her neck stand upright as this spectre closed in on them. She did not walk so much as glide across the tavern floor. She knew this was merely a dream of Rafe Rafton's but something was very unsettling about her.

"Well met, Your Grace." Her voice was lifeless, a cold harmony of breath and thought lacking warmth or passion. She spoke with a slight accent reminiscent of the Landsknechts she had grappled with in King Henry's Court.

Askana knew this ghost was an overpowering image that would reign in his dreamscape. She had once dealt with a creature such as this. It had taken the form of Telmrant. She had lost months in dreams where she could, once more, feel his arms around her, savour the touch of his lips, and listen to the music of his laugh.

He was as she. A dream. An illusion.

"Do not mind this clever rogue. He is pretty and well worth his price." The Baroness cooed as she played with Rafe's hair, "But alas, this poor romantic falls in love so easily."

Askana swallowed hard, watching her touch draw more life from Rafe who refused to look at either one of them. "What do you mean by that, Baroness?"

"Why look at him, Your Grace." One of her pale, slender fingers traced his jawline, "A handsome man, a man such as I would never find in Court. He pleases me. A pleasant diversion."

The Queen's eyes grew wide in hearing her own words. The Baroness had at one time used those very words upon Rafe. His outburst on the ship that night became so very clear to her.

"I failed you, Your Grace." Tears welled in his eyes as he spoke. He brought the snifter closer to him. "You gave yourself to my King for reinforcements. This was not why I brought you to London. This was not the bargain I agreed to here at The Reef."

"Captain Rafton," Askana straightened in her seat while the Baroness moved away from Rafe, still laughing at him mockingly, "we are not done in this endeavour. You will receive your payment in full once we reach—"

"You truly believe I am in this for payment, Your Grace?" Rafe snapped. It was all in his voice. An outpouring of emotions that he could never tell Askana in the waking world, not even if they found themselves alone. "Do you really think the risks I have taken are justified by fifteen thousand gold crowns? Perhaps in the beginning, but now fifteen thousand crowns would not even begin to cover the risks I have taken on this enterprise. What I have done on this venture I have done because..." Rafe looked over Askana's shoulder to the Baroness, her laugh ringing in his ears, "...you matter."

So many words had passed between them in their travels across The Rift. In this instance, Askana could not respond to the privateer. There were no words appropriate.

A hand fell upon her shoulder. She knew it was the Baroness. She grew weary of this harpy's presence, especially since the creature chose to stand behind her. She turned to face this ghost of Rafe's past and stepped back in a cold terror at the sight before her.

The Baroness' face had changed and now it was a doppelganger of Askana Moldarin laughing at Rafe.

This was nothing more than a dream, but if Rafe lost hope to live he would exist merely in the physical presence. Nothing more. Askana tried to shut out the taunting of the Baroness, now a dark reflection of herself, as she knelt by him. With a gentle touch of her fingertips, she turned his face towards her own.

"Captain, I did not lie with your King. We were attacked by the Assassins' Guild. I saved your King and won his allegiance." She gave him a gentle smile, lightly touching his cheek with the back of her fingertips. "You have not failed me, privateer. We are en route to Morevi. Do not give up on this venture for I cannot do this without you."

"Are you certain of that, Askana?"

He called her "Askana". Most improper, and yet she was flattered by it.

She gently bit her lip and opened her heart to the possibility of what lay ahead of them, "I have made it this far under your care, Rafe. I intend for you to be present when I return to my throne." Askana pushed the snifter and scotch away and smiled at him warmly, "Try the wine. You will find it an excellent vintage."

The reflection of her had disappeared, perhaps slipping back amongst the phantoms of this tavern. Before Askana stepped out of The Barrier Reef, she looked back to see Rafe still sitting at the table. He now sampled the Morevian claret she left behind. A bit of colour returned to his face, and he was smiling at its taste. She could not decide if the image of herself in place of the Baroness was an insult to her or a warning to him. What of the words he had shared with her here in this dream?

"What I have done on this venture I have done because you matter." It had been some time since anyone uttered words like that to her.

As she passed through the doorway to a calm silence, Askana wondered if Rafe Rafton would remember any of this shared dream on his return to the waking world.

CHAPTER ELEVEN
The Voices of Nadinath

The cool of the evening sapped away much of the jungle's heavy heat. The brilliant flowers of morning closed, for now was the time of the shy, fragrant blooms of night. A nightingale lifted its flute-like voice somewhere in the thick foliage, its song punctuated by the *"kapok! kapok!"* cry of the Achingo bird. Yet even in the tranquil silence of the blue-grey evening, life moved in the jungle's depths. Creatures stalked, hunted, died. There was no real serenity, no real stillness.

So it was with the structure, massive and dark, that rose up in the midst of the White Falls. Weather-stained and bedecked with creepers, its glorious and sometimes grotesque stone carvings covered every inch of its surface. It stood on a bed of solid rock. The waters of the wide, low falls frothed and roiled around it, disappearing into the dark pool that swirled around its rocky base. Two weathered stone bridges, strongly arched and also covered with fantastic carvings and statuary, led across the pool to the building itself. Torches flickered along the bridges and on the many levels of the building, casting ominous, dancing shadows of the monsters that stood sentinel at the gates. The creatures were, in fact, guardians sworn to protect their sanctuary. They possessed uncanny strength, their identity concealed by elaborate masks. Huge, gaping-mouthed heads from which sprouted manes of feathers and bristles. This was the Temple of Nadinath.

Within, the sound of cymbals, thin, rapid notes of the stringed *mehrus*, and the harmonious sound of many female voices echoed through the halls. Their soft chorus lifted through chambers and alcoves, finally reverberating in gathering places ornately decorated with walls and floors of mosaic, huge marble pillars, and bronze incense braziers. Rooms were separated by walls of cream stone, often exquisitely carved with friezes of birds and beasts, scenes of feminine life and fertility. Beaded curtains, falls of silk and gauze formed doors. Corridors and chambers were illuminated by the gleam of gold and polished copper. Colours ran riot in peacock plumes, mosaics, and gems, all gathering in a display of costly offerings in the chambers of worship. Everywhere was the image of the faceted Nadinath. Lover, Mother, Destroyer.

In the cavernous hall that was the heart of the temple, hundreds of women were gathered before the three great statues of Nadinath to offer evening prayer. There was the white marble of Nadinath the Maid, slender and dancing, the free spirit. Next to Her was the redstone of Nadinath the Mother, round-bellied and heavy-breasted, the giver of life to all. These representations of the Goddess were embodied in the Priestesses and their Maidens, either dressed in white for the Maid or in red for the Mother. While the facets of Nadinath were very different, they all answered to the Goddess as one. They were unique, yet a single voice of the Sisterhood. It was not rare to find the Maids offering gifts and prayer to the Mother, as well as the Mother devotees giving thanks before the white marbled Maid. It was this common thread of their femininity that united the Sisterhood.

So it was tonight, but tonight the prayers went to one facet of the Goddess. Not of the innocent Maid nor to the giving Mother, but to the third facet. Tonight, the prayers swelled to Nadinath the Destroyer.

She was cut from obsidian, sleek and ferocious, weapons of war in Her many hands. In Her face was a strange coupling of tranquillity and unleashed rage, its shadows bringing this semblance of the Destroyer to life. The women had been gathering from all corners of Morevi, some openly, some in secret, since the day the High Priestess was lost. Many, many more had come recently, after a man was again proclaimed as ruler of Morevi.

The sweet hymns rose once more through floors and levels of the Temple. Their voices faintly reached its pinnacle, giving the Anjara reason to turn towards the distant harmony. The Spirit of the Goddess herself was awakening. She turned back to the Priestesses, the reason why she was here. Before her were the voices of Nadinath, these three women second only to Askana, the Queen and High Priestess of the Temple. Kalea now only had a day remaining before joining Kubi-Sogi in Arathelle. Her own Royal Guard were ready, but she had come here to discover the mind of the Temple.

Light and incense played and mingled in the beautiful chamber where more than fifty women were informally gathered. Amidst the flowing white of the Maid and the red robes of the Mother were women adorned in black leather and cloth, weapons at hand even though armour had been laid aside. Yet, different as they were, they sat together on the polished steps, reclined upon divans and rested against the high backs of carved chairs together, some braiding each other's hair. They were anything but idle, though, as they listened to Kalea with quiet gravity.

"I know the Temple has always remained detached from the politics of Council. No doubt a wise choice. Yet I must remind you, my Sisters, that the High Priestess is also our Queen. The War of the Fan and Slipper won us our freedom, and we now live a dream that our mothers never lived to see made flesh. Under Askana Moldarin's rule we have become a symbol of hope, salvation, and power. Women flock to the Temple, some coming from distant lands to escape oppression."

Kalea paused, her eyes meeting with the Priestesses' for a moment. Then she continued, "Now we see that dream, our vision, threatened. Sisters have died. The Queen has disappeared. A king has been crowned again, an Otherworlder! Now news has come that the Eyrieners take up arms, holding Morevi and Her Queen responsible for the tragedy at Taighar." She prayed to Nadinath to forgive her for the white lie. "They are a nation of men, my Sisters. We know what they are capable of unleashing. We know what hatred they hold for us. The Royal Guard loyal to the Queen are in need of aid. The Temple has the power to aid us! If you have influence even in other nations, covert or not, then surely you can help to protect the realm and its people!"

"A bleak picture you paint, my Sister," Priestess Maghda nodded, "but you must remember that the new King is firmly in the hands of the High Lady Dirare. All his ruling ministers are strong women. You may not care for House Jarahd holding the reins of power, but that should not be your concern." Maghda stroked the panther-kitten curled in her white-covered lap, her voice the calm of one devoted to study and meditation. "Your concern should be for continuation of female rule. Dirare is a strong woman, even if she is not of our Order."

"We know something of the Eyrieners' movements," Priestess Illora said, shifting in her divan with a clink of metal and a whispered rasp of leather on leather.

"The Elves have spoken with us as we cross their borders for our herbs." Priestess Messara added as she tied off the end of the plait she had made of Illora's hair. She adjusted her red robes as she turned her full attention to the Anjara. "They are always warmer, if not faintly amused, with us Healers. Perhaps because of our role as Nurturers.

Elves value their children and are willing to protect them at all cost. They tell us that the Eyrieners have met with the Elven Queen and King. Arathelle has agreed to allow Eyriener ships into its waters."

A muscle twitched in Kalea's jaw. "And you do not find that strange? The Elves have never been fond of Eyrieners. Though trade does occur between them, no Eyriener craft has been allowed to enter Arathelle's waters for centuries! Only Morevian craft enjoy that privilege. Eyrie could dock a fleet at Arathelle and lay siege to Songkusai! The Elves' agreement is almost tantamount to a betrayal."

"Not so." Maghda shook her head. "The Elves of Arathelle have always been separated from Naruihm in ways we do not understand. They posses great magic that was outlawed ages ago. They now turn to their own disciplines to temper their darkness and remain at peace. They will not oppose Eyrie so long as the threat is not directly turned on them."

"They protect their way of life through their neutrality," said Messara the moment Maghda's thought finished. Priestesses always did that. Part of their study. They always preferred giving the impression that they were a collective of one voice and one mind. "The opening of their ports to Eyrie is not out of malice. Queen Esharana is a good woman. Strong of heart and true of word."

Kalea closed her eyes briefly as she thought of the Elven Queen. Askana had politely refused to see Eharon, the Elven King. It had been but a year after the War and the purges were still ongoing. Males, even of another race, had not been welcome at this delicate time. Askana's motives, though, were more personal. Eharon was Telmrant's younger brother. It was forever etched in Askana's mind that he occupied a throne that was not his.

Kalea had openly cursed the Queen's ill-timed action. As a result, she was given the Royal Decree to meet with the Elven Queen and King. Still a young woman, green to the ways of governance, her heart thudded against her ribs as she walked up the rise to the waiting delegation. Elven warriors in glittering armour. Nobles in silks and beautiful fabrics that had no name. Willowy maidens wearing snowy robes parted the curtains of the litter that drifted in mid-air. She shivered as she looked up at the white banners bearing the stylised gold sun of Arathelle. They rippled in a breeze that was not there. She felt unseen eyes study her.

The Elven Queen had slipped out from the litter with a grace no human woman could match. Esharana was taller by at least head and shoulders than any of the Morevians. Skin pale as pearl, shimmering in her gown of diaphanous white. Her ornaments were of iridescent *ashurbal* brought from the Elven mines of Naruihm. The working of this enchanted metal was only known to them. Within the litter Kalea caught the green-eyed gaze of the King before its curtain dropped.

In this distant memory, Kalea could still hear the Elven Queen's clear, pure voice. Her own Elven tongue echoed like a breeze passing through treetops as she spoke...

"Peace to thy Queen, peace to thee. Peace upon thy Kingdom for the offer of goodwill from thee and thine. Thou hast asked for peace, thou shalt have peace. Thy Queen offers trade, so shall the Road of the Moon be open to her people, her tradesmen, so long as they stray not into our woods. Food they shall have, places of rest they shall have. Thy Kingdom's ships may find welcome in our ports for thy gifts of silk and perfume, and thy courtesy. In times of strife they shall have our protection. This, Esharana pir Coulad pey Eirelle and my lord Eharon pir Hathar pey Casura, do promise."

The Elven Word was as binding as a contract. Kalea remembered searching for appropriate words to thank the Queen, and perhaps to apologise for Askana's slur against the Elven King. Esharana, ancient and ageless, beautiful and solemn, smiled. She knew Kalea's mind as she spoke once more.

"Thy Queen is young, too young even for human wisdom. Eharon and I take no offence from the child. She is beloved of Telmrant, and therefore our sister." Esharana had paused, and the sorrow that entered her deep blue eyes had touched Kalea then, and still did in her memory. *"Yet I would not like this exclusion of all that is male to continue. Life is two halves. Male and female. One cannot do without the other nor rise above the other. Thou hast righted a wrong with thy war, but take care thy feet lead thee not down that same path. Wouldst thou take on the tyrant's mantle and be to the men what they were to thee? The philosophy of segregation is not what the Great Mother intended. Perceive — take the bulls away from the cows, and there will be no calves, the stallions from the mares and there will be no foals. I fear that in trying to cure one ill, thou shalt truly never heal."* The Elven Queen's face brightened and Kalea had felt an elation pass though her she had never experienced since that meeting. *"True joy, child, is birthed from understanding and love."*

The memory was so vivid that she wanted to remain there. The sound of sharp prayer and chanting, no doubt given to the Destroyer in the Temple underneath them, brought Kalea back before the Priestesses.

"So, you will not fight for Morevi? You will let Dirare rule the Puppet-King? How long the Consort will serve a puppet is the question. Lords may see this as their chance to reclaim Morevi. They may already see the fall of the New Regime in the accusations of Lady Min-Lu."

"We did not say we will not fight," Illora said, her voice showing a slight offence to Kalea's claim. She was a Priestess of the Destroyer, opting never to lay aside the shirai. "We will fight to the death if needs be, but only for the Temple and our High Priestess. Not for political manoeuvring, not even for Morevi. If the Eyrieners come, we will be ready, but we will not strike first."

"The Lady Min-Lu is one of our Order," Maghda said, continuing that same disorienting manner of two voices sharing one thought. "We have taken steps to ensure she does not malign the High Priestess again. We will not meddle directly with House Jarahd as she is not of the Sisterhood."

"Steadily the women have been coming. Some from the farthest reaches of the Goddess' voice," said Messara in a soft, maternal voice as her eyes went across the room to other Maidens and Priestesses with features that marked them as of a race or descent outside of Morevi. "Many that have arrived represent the Houses assembled at the Palace even now. Some are Sisters or Daughters of the Blood. All are committed to the protection of the Temple and the High Priestess."

"Since the discovery of Tekira's betrayal, we have purged the ranks of the Maidens before the fire and the altar," Illora said, her shirai blade catching the flicker of torchlight. "We found no betrayers."

"We are calling upon our influences outside Morevi," Maghda spoke. "But we cannot make them risk everything with overt action. Those caught in Eyrie are executed without question, cast aside by their own fathers, brothers, and husbands. Can you ask them to give more?"

The silence from the Priestesses was Kalea's indication that the audience was over. She donned her own helm and took up her shirai. The coolness of the helmet felt good against her burning skin. It was borderline pomposity on the part of the Temple. They would not move without the command of the High Priestess unless they were directly threatened. How could their High Priestess give the word if she were missing? Provided Askana did reappear, it would be too late once the attack came. She would have to rely on the remaining forces of the Royal Guard.

Perhaps Kubi-Sogi would provide better news on the loyalties of his own Palace Guard when they met in Arathelle.

The Lady Min-Lu's knees were quaking. She might not want to admit it, but they were.

The woman who sat across from her wore black wrappings and gleaming black armour. Black leather. Much in the style of the Black Widow herself, which was more than Min-Lu cared to be reminded of at the moment. The Destroyer's lap was covered by a large cat that purred loudly as she scratched between its shoulders. Min-Lu watched the feline uneasily. One of the few things she had not liked at all about the worship of Nadinath was the cats. Not just normal cats. Shamaraj were hunters of the jungle. Tan coloured and muscular with large, five-taloned paws. She did not like their eyes, their stares. It was not uncommon for these cats to sometimes accompany Priestesses.

At least this Priestess had not domesticated one of the tigers that sometimes strolled in.

"Of course, with all the political turmoil of late, we have kept a constant watch. The Raising, so soon after accusations against the High Priestess..." The Priestess let her voice trail off, playing with the tufted ears of the shamaraj that leaned into her touch.

Why on earth had they sent a Priestess of the Destroyer to her? They could not possibly know of her plans. Was this a threat? If this was a threat, should she be afraid? Of course! She should be very afraid. A Death Priestess. She fought to keep her breathing even.

"You see, young Sister, there are some things we cannot have our devotees doing at this time. One of which is raising certain issues, if you understand me," smiled the Priestess.

Min-Lu kept her glance directed demurely to the polished tabletop. "I thought that the Temple was not politically inclined, Priestess. As a member of the Council, it is my honour-bound duty to take action for the good of the realm. To expose that which may lead to its downfall. The Temple should at least empathise with me. Even in the Order of Nadinath, anyone with sufficient proof may name a betrayer. I clearly had such proof." She could feel under her layers of silk a sweat begin to form at the small of her back.

The Priestess laughed softly, companionably. "True, young Sister, but recollect. To accuse at the Temple, one must ensure that the accused and the accuser are both present so that a fair trial before the Goddess can take place. Here, the accused is missing, and there was no time for anyone to examine the proof. It is most unfortunate that Sister Jailene died," continued the Priestess as her fingers scratched behind the cat's ears, the shamaraj staring at Min-Lu with unblinking yellow eyes. "We very much wanted to conduct our own trial in the Temple as well. After all, your accusations do concern the High Priestess, and are of a serious nature. It is easy, Child, to blacken a name. Stir up hate. It is so very easy to do, even unwittingly, when only the tale of one side is heard. Your intentions, young Sister, are good, but I must remind you that method counts as well." She shifted easily on the cushions, sipping hot tea from the small porcelain cup. A silence fell, a tense silence during which the only sound was that of the cat purring.

Min-Lu bowed her head respectfully, gritting her teeth. *Trial of Nadinath*, she thought, hiding a shudder. *A trial before Nadinath would not have shown me, Jailene, nor Tekira, any mercy.*

"We have missed you at the Temple gatherings, Sister. Many come to give their support and prayers for our absent High Priestess. Others are frantic after the raising of a king."

At last, common ground. "I was against the Raising of Jermal from the beginning, Priestess. The newly appointed Regent, High Lady Dirare, intimidated the rest of Council to bend to her wishes, as is her way. Being not of the Order, she does not see as far as we do. She does not see all the consequences of her action."

Min-Lu's weak smile faded as she watched the cat yawn and stretch, revealing all its hooked claws and sharp teeth. The interior of its mouth was pinkly wet.

"Dirare is a capable ruler for the time being. She keeps the man safely in her control." The Priestess noted Min-Lu's discomfort. "The creature's presence disturbs you, young Sister? Some share the same nervousness with the greater cats as well. They find it difficult to accept that a wild thing, once hunger sated, can be as calm and quiet as a small house cat. Others find it disconcerting to feel the wet nose of a curious panther as they are at prayer." The Priestess shifted some of the cat's weight off her affectionately. "Do you know why, though, we invite cats into our Temple halls?"

Min-Lu wearily opened her mouth to recite the words of Nadinath as they had been taught to her. Just because she had outgrown the doctrines did not mean she still could not recite them word-for-word. Their meaning had been lost to her for so long now.

The Priestess forestalled her as she stood up, the shamaraj bounding off her lap to look at Min-Lu for a moment then return to the heels of the Priestess. "They have the Eyes of Truth." Simple, clean, cryptic. "A good day to you, young Sister."

Min-Lu's muscles relaxed as the screen door slid shut, but her face contorted with a mixture of frustration, extreme irritation, and fear. It had been a long time since she felt true fear, and she did not like it.

She rose from the table in a swirl of silken robes, tearing impatiently at the artful curls and coils of her hair until it fell fine and wavy down her back. She closed her eyes tight as her fingers quickly massaged and scratched her scalp. High Lord Ruain had not replied. A reply should not have taken so long. Where was he? What was he doing? What was the delay? Should she move or not?

In a strange, bizarre gesture, she dropped to her knees. Her stare went out of her window into the horizon. She could see the Road of the Moon that led to Arathelle.

"My Lord Ruain," she called to him in a dry, whispered prayer. "Sometimes you unduly try my patience, but love keeps me strong. You must hurry. When we are wed I will gladly renounce my beliefs and embrace the Dark Arts you will teach me. I am still a cog in the Temple system and I truly do fear them. Their wrath can be terrible. You must be swift. The world can be ours, it only remains to reach out and grasp it!" Her clasped hands tightened on one another as she pressed them to her forehead, "Make haste, my love. Make haste."

She returned to her feet, a small part of her appeased in her appeal to a lover that could not hear her. The agitation began to grow once more. She paused as her eyes fell on the small, beautifully made altar to the Goddess. As a girl she had loved the worship, loved the abandon, and loved the strength Nadinath gave her. Now it was just too small for her. She would not simply have power only to place it in the hands of a deity that no longer gave her satisfaction. When she became mistress of Ruain's Dark Arts, she would show the Temple that they no longer held sway over her. She would be Queen! A true monarch would finally lead! In her hands would the power lie, and nothing would be able to make her feel debilitating fear again. Not in the arms of her love.

With a snarl of hate she struck out at the statue of Nadinath, knocking the porcelain bowls of offerings and flowers. The scented water splattered over the tile, mosaic, and gilding. Curls of incense were broken and glowing embers showered to the floor, snuffed out with a tiny hiss when touched by the water running from the desecrated altar.

Call of the Cannon

"My Sovereign?"

It was Elunear's voice. Askana could not recall when she fell asleep, nor could she recall how long it had been since she slept so soundly. It was a feeling of security, one she had not felt in a long while. She knew she was safe in the belly of the *Defiant*.

Then she became aware of where she was. Sometime during the night, she had gone from a sitting position to bundled in bedclothes. Her robes were still on her person, but she could not remember how or when she had reclined back fully to enjoy a good night's rest. Askana remembered watching over Rafe as he slept, playing with his hair in an odd fascination.

She also remembered the dream at The Barrier Reef.

"How long have I slept, Elunear?" Askana asked, her voice still groggy.

"It is nearly mid-day by the pirate's clock today. Our third day at sea. When he awoke earlier this morning, he insisted on letting you sleep." Elunear was producing for Askana a variety of clothes on loan from the Captain, a change from the robes she had worn since their adventure's start. She also set by the end table Askana's perfume oil after adding a few drops of the scent into a small bath prepared for her. "His wounds are nearly healed. I removed the stitches just yesterday. He is resuming his office, but I have suggested he proceed gently."

Askana laughed as she slipped into the bath, a quick moment's escape before their return to her realm. "I doubt sincerely if he knows the meaning of the word."

She knew Elunear continued to keep her eyes averted as her prior actions still had not been discussed. It was a fool-hearty action to put Captain Rafton at such risk. She could also tell the young girl was anxious to return to her home, familiar ground with familiar faces. This journey had pushed the Guard beyond her limits and perhaps matured into her own womanhood before she was fully prepared. Askana could not help but grin as she watched Elunear inspect her shirai. Evidently, the Maiden felt a premonition of battle in the air. She could not help but be proud of her and her growth.

The ensemble she wore was similar to the one she had created before in the dark of the Captain's Quarters. She tucked the leggings into her boots and cinched the shirt at her waist. The fabric of the shirt's wide sleeves were rolled up high into makeshift cuffs. As she stepped out of the Captain's Quarters onto the main deck, the breeze warmed her skin. There was a certain scent in the air that told her she was across The Rift. With Elunear and Lubria at her side, Askana made her way to the upper deck where Nassir and Rafe plotted their course to the ports of Arathelle. The Captain looked up from his charts and smiled brightly as the strong sea breeze toyed with his hair. There was a very different look in his eyes as he approached her. Elunear and Lubria watched intently as he kissed the Queen's hand with a gentleman's bow and that confident grin Askana had now grown to appreciate.

"Your Grace," he smiled as he motioned behind her. "Welcome home."

Askana turned around to see the coast of Naruihm stretching across the horizon. From the distance, she could see the colourless profile of the Sleeping Dragons. Even from here, her heart leapt at the anticipation of returning home. The days had run together, overlapping as hues and shadows upon a canvas that created a panoramic landscape. Only now did she realise how much she missed her beloved Morevi.

"I am still uneasy about this return, my Queen," Lubria said as she walked to the foremost railing of the top deck.

"As we all are, Lubria," Rafe chimed in to her surprise, causing her head to whip around to face him. "I do not expect the gates of Morevi to swing open and welcome us with open arms, but this is providing we reach Arathelle in one piece. In light of our recent visit to Taighar, we are in extremely unfriendly waters at present."

As if taking a cue from Rafe's concern, the watch cried, "Ship ahoy!"

Immediately, the crew joined their Captain along the starboard side of the *Defiant*. Distant ships, merely specks against the massive dark backdrop of land, slowly followed the coastline. "Mister Conner," Rafe called, extending a hand, "spyglass." He moved the telescope back and forth along the line of ships, counting to himself. "Thirty-eight...thirty-nine...forty. Quite the navy you have built there, Cedric." Rafe turned to Askana, offering her the telescope. "Care for a look, Your Grace?"

Askana looked at the device quizzically. Rafe gently positioned her hands upon the brass cylinder and gave her a gentle nod of assurance. He stepped behind her, his arms carefully encompassing her, and whispered to her lessons in finding bearings between land, sea, and target objects. Askana smiled in fascination as his words helped her bring the group of slow moving sea vessels into the centre of the spyglass' view.

She could feel his body pressed to her own. She cast a glance to Elunear and Lubria who watched his forwardness with concern. Askana merely grinned. Any man who would dare attempt to get this close would embrace a quick death from one of her concealed blades. There was a part of her that enjoyed how this privateer tempted her, tempted death. He had done it before with her. She sensed that he enjoyed doing so.

She counted forty ships moving in a basic formation along the coast, using the landmass as a guide for their destination. A considerable distance in the lead was a single ship. No doubt, the flagship.

Askana lowered the telescope slowly, "Do you think it is some kind of blockade?"

"That would mean the Captain of the flagship would know of our return to Morevi. The ships travel too close together." Rafe gave a heavy sigh, shaking his head slowly, "I doubt they are an Eyriener welcoming committee."

"An invasion fleet," Askana whispered. "They would not dare take arms against the Elves! It would be suicide."

"Or, an agreement. A truce between Arathelle and Eyrie, allowing the Eyriener navy in their ports?"

"Neutrality?" Askana huffed, "Would Arathelle truly think they could survive as a neutral power, reaching bargains with these Eyriener barbarians?"

"Believe me, Your Grace, profitable commonwealths are founded on deals such as this. We call them 'The Swiss' in my world." Rafe turned to his First Mate, "Assemble the crew."

Nassir passed the call and soon the main deck and gangway of the *Defiant* filled with privateers. They were neither the cleanest nor the friendliest-looking lot. A mix of men, women, and races, all united in their service to King Henry the VIII and their exploits on the open seas. His crew numbered eighty. They did not stand in formation nor did they appear to be in any sort of order. When Rafe stepped forward, they did not snap to attention as her soldiers would with pride and an attitude of invincibility. Nevertheless, this crew was duty and honour bound much like her Royal Guard. It was in their eyes.

"Well, here we are, lads." A light laughter passed over the crew as their Captain referred to both man and woman as "lad". Rafe placed his foot upon the rail overlooking the main deck and leaned on his knee as he continued, "I am certain none of you thought our most prized bounty within these waters would be our benefactor, nor would any of you foresee our mission to be that of Royal Protectors of the Crown. Yet, here we are, lads. We return to Morevi with the Black Widow herself, and it is my intent to return her to the throne. We all know the price this venture carries. The windfall may settle debts for some of you, allow others to retire somewhere to try their hand at farming." Rafe shot a playful look at Nassir that, again, gave the crew a bit of levity. "But to restore Her Grace to the throne we must board the flagship of the Eyriener fleet and discover what they intend for Her Majesty's realm. That flagship is followed by an impressive Eyriener Navy with their course set for the ports of Arathelle."

Askana's eyes grew wide. She cast a glance to Lubria and Elunear behind her, both looking to their Queen in horror. Rafe intended to take on the flagship alone, without the reinforcements promised by King Henry.

"I know what risk this carries. This would mean some of us will not return to our beloved England or wherever we do call home. One ship against forty. Most bleak, indeed. But if we do pull off this raid, there shall be plenty of talk in the pubs about us!" He flashed the crew a smile and their voices raised in an almost carefree laughter. Only the women of Morevi looked over the crew and the Captain, unable to comprehend what they heard. "So here is my offer. Whoever wishes not to join me in this attack on the Eyriener flagship, step forward now. Coins shall be given to that person and I will load the dinghies with supplies that will allow you to reach the safety of the Eyriener ports. There will be no judgement or shame passed upon you by this crew. I would rather have a crew of one whose heart is in the trim, than a crew of a thousand who could not stand by me in the fray with full confidence. What I am asking is something I swore never to ask of you again—a leap of faith." He cast another glance at the oncoming fleet and then back to his eclectic crew, "Shall we?"

Askana could see that Rafe was holding his breath and she felt her own heart keeping pace with his. It was a lapse of reason to think they would survive a direct assault against the Eyriener Navy. Then slowly, a part of her began to see the method within his madness. The *Defiant* was faster than any ship in these waters. Their objective was not to sink the flagship but get what information they needed and then escape. She could see the crew following this thought process as well. Something in a plan so ludicrous and inconceivable held a probability of success *because* it was so ludicrous and inconceivable. Were they justifying a desperate act? Or were they beginning to think like their Captain? Crewmembers looked to one another. There were whispers being shared between them, nothing intelligible to Rafe and Askana who stood upon the top deck awaiting word.

One of the pirates, Mister Stewart, spoke suddenly in his rough, Scottish accent, "Fo'ty ships. A'tee pirates. Two men fa' ev'rie ship! Tha's odds a Scottsm'n liv's fa!"

The crew erupted in laughter as another crewman named Gower made his voice heard, "I cannot think of a better way to die than taking arms alongside Captain Rafton!"

"If the Captain promises me a farewell kiss," remarked Sarah Reiley, a shapely female pirate whose long red hair cascaded along her shoulders, "I will follow him to the doorstep of Beelzebub himself!"

Rafe turned to Nassir with a grin, "I will breathe easier, my friend, if you were to fight alongside me."

The Moor laughed heartily as he shook his head, "It may be a fool's death I invite, My Captain. But better to die with the sweet smell of cannon fire than the smell of pig shit with that farm I dream of!"

"God save the Queen!" cried one of the pirates, his sword waving above his head.

The crew drew their weapons in a salute to Askana Moldarin. *"God save the Queen!"*

It was an odd sight. Swords-for-hire, brigands, and cutthroats pledging their loyalty to a land where they carried death sentences for their crimes. Still, their loyalty was binding. She knew it was for their Captain. It was that same kind of loyalty from Captain Rafton she could not fully understand.

"What I have done on this venture I have done because you matter."

Could not, she thought to herself, *or would not.*

"Brave words, human," Lubria hissed. "But I wonder if they will truly possess the courage you think they have when we engage in battle."

"I suppose you will have to trust me then, Lubria," Rafe smiled with a devilish wink. She let out a soft *"whuff"* in response. He rapped the Moor against his broad chest. "Nassir, plot an intercept course for the fleet. Hoist our banner. Let us give these Eyrieners a proper English welcoming!"

"No," Askana said quickly, taking a hold of Rafe's arm as she spoke, "Captain, I have an idea you may find to your liking."

Rafe looked over his shoulder to his First Mate, "I do think, Nassir, our Morevian Queen may become a pirate after all." With a hearty laugh, Rafe gave Askana a nod, "What do you propose, Your Grace?"

"Have the ship's cook supply me with a few chickens."

He tipped his head to one side, "Chickens, Your Grace?"

"Yes." Askana turned to Elunear with a very wicked gleam in her eye, "Elunear, it is time to make amends for your error in London. We shall work together on this, so watch and learn, my Sister."

The banner of Eyrie whipped high above the crew's heads as their vessel moved alongside the coast. Captain Urlich Fenn looked over his shoulder to see the impressive fleet of ships trailing behind them, but it did nothing to ease his nerves contemplating this aggressive move against Morevi. Since assuming the throne, his King enjoyed taking chances. King Cedric believed this land, a land where civil unrest yielded a warrior-queen upon its throne, easily won. When patrols began to disappear, Morevi was considered unobtainable for the moment. It became an obsession with the Eyriener King. Now Fenn was the second-in-command to the beginning of a war against a land of savages.

He looked behind the *Archangel* once again to see the ships trailing in a typical, military V-formation. The winds were particularly strong this day, but only the flagship insisted on utilising the rowing crew to keep pace ahead of the fleet. He wondered if it was a tactical strategy to scout ahead for the benefit of the navy or if this was merely a sign of arrogance that his ship would lead Eyrie to victory over Morevi.

"My dear Captain Fenn," High Lord Coumiran purred as he joined him on the top deck overlooking the crew, "I do believe that is the third time in the past twenty minutes you have cast a glance over your shoulder. I assure you, where we go, the fleet will follow."

"High Lord, you must forgive me, but this is the first time I have served as Captain of an invasion fleet," Fenn swallowed hard, hoping his speech would not be taken as insolence. "This was not part of our bargain. I was instructed to take you across The Rift—"

"Which you did with all speed, but that was merely the beginning of your task. You should remember that King Cedric gave me full control of this vessel. That means you will follow my wishes without question. Those wishes include leading an invasion fleet. Is that clear?"

Captain Fenn did not care for the tone of this "Dark Merchant" as he heard one of the sailors call him. He knew the payment standards King Cedric set for successful Rift-crossings. They were profitable to say the least. He was completely unaware that in the case of this particular crossing, his King had literally sold him and his ship to this masked beast.

"Boatswain, maintain course and speed," Fenn sighed, a captain only in title for the time being.

"Ship to port side," called the watch from high above the deck. "Ship to port!"

"Can you make out a banner?"

The quartermaster produced a telescope from his side and peered across the horizon of open sea. The ship flew no banner. No movement could be spotted upon its decks. "It appears to be dead, sir." Fenn scratched his salt-and-pepper beard as he saw the ship, sails full, close upon them. It was a big ship, but not like those of Eyrie or Arathelle. His quartermaster joined him on the top deck, handing him the spyglass. "Perhaps it came across The Rift?" he asked. "All hands lost?"

Coumiran narrowed his eyes slightly, "Captain, I must voice a concern about this supposed ghost ship. I can see from here it is definitely from across The Rift. I would not be at all surprised if—"

"Wait!" Fenn moved to a stationary telescope, more powerful than his quartermaster's. He anxiously swung it about to get a closer look. "I see something on the top deck. A sailor. He is in the mizzen's topcastle. Definitely an Otherworlder from the looks of his clothes. He appears dead. Boatswain, prepare a boarding party."

"I think not, Captain!" snapped Coumiran. "I have command of this vessel."

"We have to board it!" This time, the Captain would not yield. "This is maritime law! We have no idea what is on that ship, and if its course is true then it will collide with the fleet. We must gain control of that vessel, therefore we are boarding it!"

Coumiran glanced at the oncoming vessel, clenching his fists at this distraction. "Very well."

"Pray it is a ship hauling powder kegs," Fenn huffed. "We will need every last bit of it to take Morevi in King Cedric's name."

The High Lord watched the ship with narrowing eyes. A dead ship adrift on an intercept course with the Eyriener fleet. This was all too coincidental. He would not be caught off guard, not this day. Too much planning for this day. No surprise would spoil this day of reckoning.

The Boatswain pulled himself over the side of the ship and froze at the sight of carnage before him. Bodies splattered with blood surrounded him. Men and women were locked in a struggle, their faces frozen in death. The deck was littered with weapons soaked in a brilliant crimson gore. He spun upon his heels at a sudden rush of sound, but it was merely a comrade's foot slipping in a small puddle of blood. They were a boarding party of five. If this ship were dead, they would be enough to change its course. If there were survivors, they would be able to handle trouble well enough. There was still an uneasiness in standing amidst so much death.

"Come on, men." Boatswain Heinrik found it difficult not to feel ill but he kept his midday meal in his stomach as he led his men through the collection of bodies. "Top deck."

They found a dark-skinned pirate slumped over the Captain's Pedestal. A blood soaked length of chain was wrapped around his neck. At his feet appeared to be a gentleman, perhaps the captain himself. Beside him, a female pirate lay next to him, her slender hands reaching for a blood-stained cudgel only a few inches away from her fingertips. Heinrik bent down beside the dead gentleman and moved his face upward to see it in full. Half of the corpse's face was covered in a deep scarlet, obviously from a head wound dealt by the woman. He leaned in closer. Slowly he recalled the dead man's face from placards he had seen at Taighar.

"Rafe Rafton," gasped Heinrik. "His own crew mutinied against him."

"Is he dead?" one of the sailors whispered, his sword raising upward in a defensive fashion.

Heinrik pressed his palm against the chest of the Captain. The pirate did not flinch. The body felt cold to the touch. Sunlight caught the mirror briefly as he produced it from his pouch. The mirror remained clear. No fog. No breath. "The Sea Wolf is dead, mates. I suppose this means we have a new vessel to add to the fleet." He held the tiny mirror towards the direction of the fleet, its reflective surface catching the brilliant midday sun, "Once we secure the whip staff, we can start getting rid of the dead. All save for Captain Rafton here. His carcass is worth a few coins back home."

Fenn breathed a bit easier as he saw the three flashes from the Boatswain's mirror, a pause, and then three flashes. The ship was secured. Soon, they would be expecting a small crew to man her. It was much closer now and seemed to grow larger with each passing moment. The vessel would make an impressive show when they reached the Arathellian ports.

"No surprises, Captain?" the Dark Merchant hissed as he noted the Captain's relaxed smile.

"We have an armada of forty-one, it would seem." The Captain turned to Coumiran with a new resolve. "My Lord, you have command over this ship, but never question the laws of the open seas. In these matters, I am the word of Onarg. Judge, jury, and executioner. Never doubt that."

High Lord Coumiran gave Captain Fenn a respectful bow as he returned to his charts. Perhaps the time had arrived for this Eyriener to step down from command. He did not care for having his word challenged or answering to doctrines that were not his own. Maritime laws, indeed.

His dark eyes studied the markings of the ship. Something about this felt familiar. The High Lord motioned to his footman, a wide-eyed boy whom he bought one afternoon at the Eyriener markets.

"Fetch my sidearms," he spoke evenly.

It felt all too familiar.

The creaking of the ship caused the hair on his arms to stand. This was Eryk's first voyage with the Eyriener navy and the images his mind conjured of marching triumphantly through the gates of Morevi was enough to convince him of volunteering for this invasion. He knew of the mystical beauty of Morevian women, matched only by their ferociousness. He thought to himself how glorious this ascension to manhood would be. Conquest of a city. Conquest of a Morevian native. The prospect of hearing a savage wench screaming for mercy as he defiled her, his right ordained by victory in battle, excited him all the more.

"Quiet, Eryk!" Vasyr whispered sharply. "You're breathing heavy."

They were sent to secure the vessel's whip staff, tucked away in the hold underneath the top deck. It was midday at sea but there were still parts of the ship immersed in darkness. Where the whip staff was located was such a place. There was still no movement either on the top deck, main deck, or here. That is what made it all the more unsettling. Vasyr had already tripped over two bodies. It grew increasingly difficult to see the corpses as the rear of the ship was secured tight. Very little light pierced through the shadows.

"Stop!" Eryk whispered, "Did you see that?"

Vasyr turned his face upward to Eryk who stood a few paces behind him. Why he was constantly getting paired up with the young recruits remained a mystery to him. "See what?"

"I thought I saw something move," he answered nervously, motioning to the thick shadows with his dagger.

"Then I wish I had your eyes," Vasyr shrugged, "because all I see is darkness!"

The sound of a door creaking caused them both to crouch and then give a loud exhale as they saw a shaft of white light. It came from a small open hatch, a shaft of light illuminating dust that hung in the air of the corridor.

"Finally, some light," Vasyr stepped into the darkness. He disappeared from Eryk's eyes for a moment, and then reappeared as a disembodied head floating in space. His eyes glanced into the empty chamber before him, "Eryk, you whelp, will you come on?"

Vasyr entered the dingy chamber of the ship, the shaft of light moving up and down as the vessel rode the waves of the ocean. He could make out in the shadows the large shaft that controlled the ship's rudder. As soon as that green recruit joined him, they would finally take full control of this fine ship and add it to the Eyriener navy. There was a light stench in the air. Perhaps they ate in here. He had heard stories that sometimes Otherworlders would sleep in the same chambers with a ship's whip staff. There was another rumour some of these vessels from across The Rift were so small, the sailors did both! *How could men live like this,* Vasyr thought to himself.

It would be the last thought he would have.

"Vasyr?"

Eryk finally crept into the darkness of the compartment where he last saw his shipmate. Vasyr had suddenly gone quiet. Vasyr was not usually so quiet.

The dagger was still trembling in his hand as his eyes darted about the small aft chamber. The ray of light still shone in the middle of the darkness. He could hear the soft, long creaks of the ship's hull from the wood settling in Naruihm waters. He tried to find comfort that this ship was of sturdy build. If it could survive a Rift crossing with all hands lost, it could really take a pounding. Another long, slow groan that he actually felt underneath his feet caused him to pause. Nothing. Only the light, and his heartbeat. So where was Vasyr?

He wanted the dagger to stop shaking. This was not the constitution of a true Eyriener warrior. How would Morevian women cower at the sight of him as he approached to steal their sweet innocence if he could not keep a simple dagger ready? He thought of the glory, of spitting upon the chained and shackled Whore-Queen of Morevi as she passed by him. The dagger began to steady. Once Morevi fell to the rule of King Cedric, it would only be a matter of time before the Elves would recognise the true power of Eyrie. Then would the proud and mighty Elves surrender Arathelle to him, *Captain* Eryk Soroyan, the Black Hand of the Eyriener Navy. He would be known far and wide for his ruthlessness, the dead floating in the wake of his grand sailing vessel!

The sunlight caught the shine of the blade, still as the air within the quarters.

He smiled as the light cast reflections around the chambers. It was no longer a simple dagger but a charmed sword that he would wield triumphant in battle. He was about to step forward when his blood went cold. The glint from the dagger caught a pair of emerald eyes that watched him from the darkness. It was only for an instant but they were, beyond a doubt, the prettiest eyes he had ever seen.

His death was as quick as his shipmate's.

Auric and Geylan leaned over the body of the infamous Captain Rafton. In Eyrie, he was considered a "living legend". He sacked junks bearing the seal of Morevi, and lived to tell about it. Then came the night of the Great Dock Fire, when he was seen in the company of a young Morevian woman. Rumours claimed it was The Black Widow herself. Now *two* nations wanted him dead. It was truly a surprise that his own crew would undo the "legend".

"Lads, staring at his body will not move it any faster." Heinrik barked. "The man's dead and we need to move him below. Otherwise, he'll get in the way of the relief crew. So get him moved! And mind the head wound. From the amount of blood, it's a wide berth."

Auric turned Rafton's head to one side and followed the blood to his blonde hair, now sticky and stained. The golden strands that mixed with the deep brown now clumped together in a sickening red mass. The blow must have been severe. He moved in closer to Rafe's scalp, his own head tilting to one side quizzically. Where was the fatal wound?

The sting across his neck caused Auric's eyes to go wide in terror. His last sight was Geylan with a woman's hand around his throat.

The Boatswain cast a casual glance over his shoulder to the dull cracking sound. He had no time to draw his dagger as Nassir's strong hands clasped his head firmly. Heinrik's neck also snapped as cleanly as Geylan's.

The dead crew, one by one, were now returning to life. Askana gave Elunear a very proud smile as their mixture had timed out precisely. The simulated death passed and now the *Defiant* made ready for battle. The crew remained low, priming rifles and pistols. Nassir quickly began undressing the Boatswain, passing the Eyriener's clothes to Rafe.

"These are not my best colours," Rafe huffed as he slipped into the ill-fitting garments.

"So long as they suit the eyes of the Eyriener Navy," Askana whispered as she peered over the aftercastle railing.

"Stay down, Your Grace," Rafe hissed sharply. "Leave nothing to chance."

He took his usual place at the Captain's Podium, only now wearing the clothes of an Eyriener Boatswain. Askana could not help but give a small laugh at how ridiculous Rafe appeared in clothes far too big for him.

"Ah, I see. This is your revenge for dressing you like a pirate so long ago," Rafe nodded. "This is my thanks in endeavouring to bring you home. Very well then."

His voice shattered the *Defiant*'s silence as he called to the whip staff crew. The ship now began to move closer to the Eyriener flagship, his crew remaining low and out-of-sight. With a simple nod, the Captain ordered half of his crew across the main deck to descend into the lower compartments of the ship. A few moments later, sounds of heavy weights could be heard moving inside the *Defiant*'s hull.

Sounds of the wind striking sails and oars cutting through the water were the only sounds in his ears. No one spoke to him, not even the captain who from the top deck casually smoked his pipe as they continued their voyage to Arathelle. The fleet still kept their distance behind them, locked in formation. Coumiran knew the notion of any attack without reinforcements was nothing short of madness.

Yet this "latest addition" to their fleet appeared to be *gaining* upon them.

He did not like feeling uneasy. Control was his discipline. Control was his power. From one as low as his slave who primed a second pistol for him to one as high as Min-Lu, the art of control would fulfil his promise to his lost love.

He could still see her body lying before him, a grotesque sight. He could hear his screams of fury reverberating within the lonely keep. She was so beautiful, both of body and of mind. He still kept on his person her scarf, stained with her blood from that fateful day. Time had turned the stain from a deep red to a dull rust colour. The dryness of the blood gave coarseness to the elegant smoothness of the material. *It was so much like her,* he thought.

The ship was still closing, not to join the fleet but to intercept them. Coumiran returned to the top deck where Captain Fenn enjoyed another healthy puff of his pipe.

"Why are they not falling into formation?" Coumiran asked as he watched the vessel close in on them. "I thought your orders were clear."

"They were," the captain nodded, enjoying the sight of this Dark Merchant actually answering to him. "As you can see from here, Heinrik has control of the ship. Perhaps there was something found in its hold that needs my immediate attention."

"I see." Coumiran suddenly turned Captain Fenn to face him, locking the look of the Captain's surprise with his own cold gaze, his grip tight on the man's waistcoat. "As I am somewhat lacking in these 'laws of the sea', tell me what would be in that ship's hold that would demand your immediate attention?"

Their heads turned as they heard something strike hard against the inside of the approaching vessel's hull. Hatches from the lower deck flipped up and cast iron barrels slowly extended forward. On the deck above them, another battalion of black metal moved into firing position. The Dark Merchant released the old captain whose pipe carelessly fell from his gaping mouth.

"Rafton," Coumiran uttered.

"Open fire!" Rafe shouted.

The *Archangel* lurched suddenly as its port side felt a thunder delivered from the *Defiant*. The cannon fire tore through the flagship's upper deck, but very little damage was dealt to the lower hull. The cannons retreated back into the hold for reloading while a line of ten riflemen appeared from the side of the ship.

Coumiran, however, had taken precautions of his own. "Cannons fire!"

A volley of cannonballs responded to the *Defiant*'s original assault, knocking two riflemen clear of their posts. Nassir gave word and the air filled with the sharp cracks of rifle fire. Rifles and pistols also fired from the forecastle. Eyrieners had finally reloaded their own cannons but never fired a shot as the *Defiant* upper cannons released another lethal volley. Amidst this melee, a young boy bolted across the *Defiant*'s main deck. He pulled with all his might and heart upon a series of ropes, hoisting high above the clouds of smoke a large black banner with the Ace of Spades above a sword and a black rose—the banner of Rafe Rafton. The Pirate Captain gave a playful salute as the lower line of the *Defiant*'s guns fired, tearing away at the flagship's hull. The oars alongside the *Archangel* came to a halt at their sudden breach.

Nassir spun about to see the approaching fleet of Eyrie, their oars slowly beginning to reach from the sides of their ships, as if they were sprouting wooden legs and intended to walk across the water. "We are running out of time, My Captain!" Nassir shouted over rifle fire, both ships now firing at will.

"Then let us not dally!" Rafe shouted to his crew. "First boarding party—*now!*"

They flew through the air from thick ropes secured on the various yards of the *Defiant*. Askana led the first team. Her feet landed against the flagship's main deck with her shirai spinning up to a ready position. In one lethal move, the staff slammed against the jaw of an unsuspecting crew member while her blade thrust back into the belly of a gunner. Two more soldiers attempted to flank her, but her shirai seemed to move with a life of its own as the blade sliced across one man's neck while its shaft shattered the knee of the other. His scream of pain was quickly silenced by her next attack.

The second team boarded, Rafe leading this assault. He had two pistols primed and ready, but they were merely that, at the ready when needed. His ivory handled rapier cut through the air, moving elegantly from blade to blade of soldiers who tried to find an opening. The first one felt his blade across his sword arm while another felt his throat neatly cut. He turned towards the Captain's Quarters when three crewmen leapt from the aftercastle to the gangway, making a human shield between Rafe and his objective. Their own rapiers were drawn, and they waited for him.

From his boot, Rafe produced his duelling knife. "Lads, you seem new to this," he smirked, shaking his head before leaping into an attack. As he would parry a blade with his rapier, the dagger would cut low to block the other two. He then spoke evenly and informatively as would a wise teacher, "On this day, allow me to bestow you the three basic lessons of swordplay. Lesson One: Always keep your balance."

Rafe quickly ducked underneath an approaching blade and swept his leg across the gangway, catching his first attacker behind his ankle and sending him to the hard wood of the main deck. Rafe spun to his feet and quickly blocked the oncoming blades.

"Lesson Two: Always be aware of your environment."

He pushed the blades clear and turned into the closest Eyriener. He gave his opponent's mouth a sharp rap with his elbow. The disoriented soldier stumbled back, unaware of how close he was to the *Archangel's* main mast. His head bounced hard against it, rendering him unconscious.

The last Eyriener charged at Rafe, bringing his own rapier blade down for the Captain's head. He blocked the incoming strike with both rapier and dagger over him. "And Lesson Three: When in doubt, cheat!"

Rafe kicked hard into the young man's genitals, lifting the poor soldier off the gangway. The sailor let out a high pitched yelp and gasped desperately for air. He landed on his knees and Rafe quickly relieved him of any misery by kicking him square in the face.

"Here endeth the lesson," Rafe nodded, continuing down the gangway.

Lubria's claws etched lethal patterns across Eyriener faces and throats. She could taste their blood on her lips. She showed no signs of fatigue or wear, merely sweeping gracefully in and around her opponents with the agility of the Fae. Lubria herded the Eyrieners like cattle towards Elunear who would finish the men with her shirai. There was a chilling efficiency in how they fought. She could not help but savour a long-missed elation fighting alongside her beloved Sister Elunear.

Suddenly, the shirai was halted by a lucky position of a sailor's quarterstaff. Elunear felt the thick oak slam against her face, knocking her down along Lubria's feet. Lubria turned on her heels quickly, but the dagger was already descending towards her. Then came a loud snap and the Eyriener lurched back. A patch of blood appeared square in his chest as he fell before them. Lubria turned back over her shoulder, following the scent of gunpowder.

The smoke was still slipping away from the barrel of his pistol. Rafe returned the discharged weapon into the back of his belt and gave a nod to Lubria. His smile said it all.

Rafe made a run for the door leading to the Captain's Quarters. Through the smoke of cannon and pistol fire on the aftercastle, Askana emerged. Her face was stained with soot, her shirai with Eyriener blood. She threw herself against the outside of the Captain's Quarters, opposite of Rafe.

"This is a quick visit!" Rafe said over the battle. "Remember that."

They burst through the door to find a grand table similar to the one in his own quarters. The maps were different, more of a military nature in the detail of topography surrounding and leading to Morevi. Rafe quickly rolled up the map and tucked it in his belt. He was nearly out the door when his eyes fell upon an open crate. His eyes widened as he saw its contents. A collection of firearms. Rifles and single-shot pistols. From his business with the Merchants' Circle, Rafe knew Eyrieners were just reaching the ability to construct proper cannons. It seemed that the Dark Merchant had made connections of his own across The Rift. These weapons were of English craftsmanship. Unmistakably.

Three volleys of cannon fire cut through the air, and the whistle of cannonballs sounded loudly. Most of them landed in the sea, but a few managed to strike Rafe's ship.

"Time to leave, Captain."

Flames rose before them as the privateers had set fire to parts of the *Archangel* during their retreat. Askana and Rafe charged into the thick black smoke, emerging through it to find the wide plank that created a makeshift bridge between the two vessels. The pirates quickly returned to the safety of the *Defiant* as Eyrieners left alive from the surprise attack were either bailing water from the hold or squelching the fires raging across the *Archangel*'s main deck.

Rafe gave the order for Nassir to pull free as he reached the *Defiant*'s main deck. Askana placed a foot upon the wood plank to begin her own cross to safety.

The bullet reached her first.

The lead ball struck her in the shoulder, causing her to spin off balance. From underneath his mask, Coumiran gave a smile at the sight of the proud Black Widow of Morevi scrambling for her shirai, a rush of bright scarlet slowly ebbing its way along her arm.

"The Queen is down!" Elunear screamed.

She lurched forward to join her Queen's side, but Rafe—fighting the stinging sensation in his own shoulder—pulled Elunear back and shoved the chart he had stolen from the flagship into her hands.

"Get this map to Nassir. English armies or no, tell him to take the crew to Songkusai and make ready to defend the city. We will catch up to you. Go!"

Before his crew could grab a hold of him, Rafe leapt from the *Defiant* back to the *Archangel*. "Go!" Rafe shouted to Nassir as another volley of cannon fire struck his vessel.

He turned around to stare down the barrel of a pistol. The hammer pulled back with a quick *"click-click"*. The index finger was encased in the finest black leather of Eyriener craftsmanship and it rested gently against the trigger. The flagship's captain strode hotly around Rafe, his face red with anger at being outwitted by this Otherworlder upstart. Askana winced at a sharp sting against the back of her head as Fenn slapped the Pirate Captain hard. Rafe cast a glance to her at his feet, giving a gentle nod. As he returned his eyes back to the High Lord, he could see the outline of a smile forming underneath the silk mask.

"By order of His Majesty, King Cedric of Eyrie," Coumiran could not help but say this with a hint of gloating, "and the just wishes of the Merchants' Circle, I hereby arrest you, Rafe Rafton, for crimes of property destruction, piracy, and murder against The Crown."

Rafe laughed as the barrel held its target, "By God, my friend, good to see you! Who would have thought it would come to this, eh? Well, I was never one for lengthy farewells. Let us end this relationship."

"By all means," the adversary hissed as he straightened the arm holding the pistol. Askana jumped as the pistol discharged above her.

"Captain Fenn believed himself to be master of this boat," Coumiran said as Fenn's body tipped over the side of the ship. "He was sadly mistaken." The Dark Merchant lowered the pistol and shook his head slowly. "I have waited a long time for this, Rafton. It would be a pity to waste a bullet on you."

By now, the Eyrieners had formed a circle around them. Fires were dying of their own accord. The fleet had eventually caught up with their crippled flagship, and crewmen from the *Archangel* and other ships were quickly diving into the water to check the hull breaches. The priority here was not pursuit of the *Defiant*, but the repair of their most powerful warship.

"Well, as my conquest of Morevi is to be detained momentarily, perhaps I should retire for the time being. Men, strip them of their clothes, clean them up, and take them below to my study." The High Lord leaned in even closer to Rafe. "I will enjoy this more than you will ever know, Rafton."

"A request—" Rafe continued to wear a grin, even as he watched the *Defiant* disappear into the horizon, "—from bastard to bastard? The Queen wears about her neck my signet ring. A token from myself, commemorating our adventure together. If we are to die, let her wear it upon her finger."

"A simple request," he nodded. "Consider it your last."

With a wave of his hand, Rafe and Askana were dragged off to the lower decks of the *Archangel*. Coumiran produced a portion of his love's scarf and took in its scent, a hint of her perfume mixing with the staleness of an aged bloodstain.

"And so, my love, it begins."

They were bound by rope restraints to a pair of grand tables, face down with their arms outstretched to either side of them. They had been cleaned free of the blood, smoke, and soot from battle and left only in their breeches, but as they were face down

Rafe was still deprived of that provocative view as he had been back in The Barrier Reef. The bullet was removed from Askana's shoulder and the wound finally had stopped bleeding.

Her first bullet wound. It glittered in the dim light of the cast iron chandelier and throbbed a bit when Askana looked at it.

Rafe felt it as well.

It seemed that the High Lord did have a sense of honour. Upon Askana's finger was the signet ring of Rafe Rafton, his crest of the Ace of Spades, the rose, and the sword. He smiled warmly as he looked at the ring. At least he could still look upon her as they were facing one another.

"It is how I won the charts providing me safe passage across The Rift," he said, suddenly breaking the silence around them.

Askana looked up at him. "What, privateer?"

"The signet. You wanted to know the story behind it. I thought now would be a good time as we are in no rush." Askana rolled her eyes in disbelief as Rafe continued, "The rose crossing the rapier is my family axiom, 'Love by the Rose, Live by the Sword'. The Ace of Spades, my key to conquering The Rift."

"The Ace of Spades?"

"I was simply another privateer in the King's service, until Fate and Mistress Luck would make me captain of my vessel. Once safely across The Rift, we were stranded. Our first attempt home delivered me and my crew to the Oasis within The Rift, and consequently, The Barrier Reef. We happened upon a game of One-and-Thirty. After many dealings and good fortune, it was down to myself, another sea-captain, and one final hand. I was dealing. The ante was my ship against his charts granting navigation across The Rift. He had a fine hand, and I needed only one card to top his."

Askana nodded, her eyes looking about the room for options on how to escape, "And naturally, the Goddess smiled upon you and dealt you the Ace of Spades."

"Actually, no." Rafe grinned, "I did have a Ten, a King, and a Queen. As the dealer, I knew the next card I drew was a tres of hearts. The hand would have cost me my ship."

Askana stopped, her attention piqued with curiosity at the pirate's tale, "So how did you win?"

"When I gamble for such high stakes, I always keep a few select cards up my sleeve. As he perused the deed to my old ship, I switched the tres card with the Ace of Spades."

She stared at him for a moment, completely stunned by his lack of honour. He possessed such potential, yet it would seem he preferred a more common, base life. "So typical of your sex, privateer. So typical. You cheated."

"Cheated?" The tone in Rafe's voice caught Askana's eye. He had a mocking look of offence, touched with a hint of humour. "My dear Queen, you insult me so in associating me with such an ugly word. I prefer to think of myself as one who controls his own fate." Rafe then motioned with his head to the ring on her finger. "Turn my signet ring inward to face your palm." Rafe watched with a grin as she did. "Excellent. Now with your thumb, press against my crest."

A tiny *"click"* sounded. Askana turned her head to look at the ring. Along the outer edge of the signet, a small blade appeared. She gently caressed its edge with her thumb. The blade was tiny, yet as sharp as her own shirai.

"Well, Your Grace," Rafe winked. "Start cutting."

Askana returned his wicked smile with one of her own. Indeed, this privateer made his own luck when necessary. Her fingers moved back and forth tediously, an eagerness in her heart swelling at the slow progress of the blade. Still, she could feel it begin to cut through the thick rope that bound her wrist.

She finally spoke over the faint sound of the tiny blade working its way into the restraints. "Please talk to me, privateer, so we do not drive ourselves mad with anticipation. What do you intend to do with your payment?"

Rafe lifted his head slowly. He found himself taken aback by her sudden optimism. The confidence Askana found in his efforts, even in this bleak dilemma, was refreshing. There was also the sudden interest in where he would be bound after concluding business with her. He could not help but take it as a compliment.

"Well, I would naturally pay a share to Nassir. He has been by my side since the beginning and taken considerably more risk and responsibility than any of the crew. With this payment he could retire back to his native Persian homelands, or perhaps acquire his own ship. He is ready for his own command, I am most certain of that. Another share would go to the crew to be split amongst them evenly. They have truly earned it upon this little adventure."

"And your share?" Askana's wrist bent as far as it could. It was awkward but the sound of the rope fraying made it all worthwhile.

"The Sea Wolf would return to his den and disappear."

Askana stopped for a moment and looked him incredulously, "Captain?"

"My share, no doubt, is the largest. A tidy sum of ten thousand crowns. With ten thousand, I—our time is fleeting, Your Grace, cut!" As he watched Askana resume working against the ropes, Rafe continued, "With ten thousand, I could find a small manor of my own, purchase myself a proper crest, and enjoy the status of a gentleman."

"So Rafe Rafton would finally be lord of his own manor?" Askana smiled, not thinking her next words so carefully, "Do you think this change in status will win back your Baroness?"

He looked at her blankly, recalling the shared dream and uncertain as to how to react to words he carried in his heart. Askana's agreement with the King voided. The image of the Baroness. It was a dream, but she had been there.

She paused for a moment, chiding herself silently for her sudden abandon of tact. Askana stumbled over her words as she spoke, "I am so sorry, Rafe."

"Pay no mind to it, Your Grace. I suppose I knew but was just not certain of it." He shook his head, bewildered, " So we shared a dream?"

"Indeed, Captain," Askana blushed slightly as she continued on the ropes. "The Elves call it *Ill'ethstréa*. Dreamwalking. It would seem we are bonded in the dreamscape as well as the waking one."

Another dull snap of fibre sounded. For a few moments no words were exchanged between them.

"You remind me a bit of her," Rafe spoke up suddenly, "but believe me when I say you are nothing like her. I met her while engaged in a scandalous affair with one of her in-laws. When we were formally introduced, I had thought the world itself came to a stop. At first, our affair began as nothing more than a dalliance. I assumed I was merely a brief fascination. She led me to believe otherwise. I found myself wanting time with her, not the profits of her family's estate. I gave her my heart. And she gave me hers.

"Then, as winter began to fall, she called for me. I was greeted by her entourage who rewarded me with a small chest of gold. For *services rendered*. After bestowing to her lackeys a few lessons in swordplay, I finally reached her chambers. Apparently, the Baroness had received word that she was to return to her homeland to assume her rightful place in Court and wed some lad she had known all her life. I asked why I could not marry her. It was the best I could do at a wedding proposal on such short notice, Your Grace," Rafe said with a slight grin. "That was when she laughed at me, referring to me as an improper gentleman. Baroness Karoline then spoke plainly so that my 'dull peasant wit' would understand, as she put it. I was merely a pleasant diversion from the many boring men of Court. She again extended the payment to me. I took the money."

Askana's eyes widened, "Why would you—"

"Basic instinct, Your Grace." Rafe shook his head slowly, "I rode to Plymouth for one last plea to her. She caught sight of me as I reached the docks. Then she turned her eyes away to the horizon. I watched the ship sail to Europe, her standing on the deck in the arms of some other gentlemen. A *proper* gentleman. She never looked back." Rafe's voice was distant. It amazed him at how vivid the memory remained, "She never looked back."

"She did not know you, Captain," Askana spoke softly, "to think you were nothing more than a simple peasant."

"But she did know me, Your Grace. She knew me all too well, and turned my weaknesses against me. There is no pain more cruel than that."

Askana paused in her cutting and locked a sorrowful gaze on the privateer, "I would disagree. There are other kinds of pain far worse. My love knew my heart and opened parts of my soul that I thought were dead."

"A most fortunate man," Rafe smiled warmly.

"He was not human." Askana stated, "He was an Elf."

It was simply fact to her. Rafe's mind, however, conjured images of the Morevian Queen frolicking in endless fields of heather with a slight creature sporting pointed ears and a green hat akin to Celtic folk tales.

"Ah," he said quickly.

"His name was Telmrant, a being of pure light. I rediscovered so much of life's wonders with him. I found the Song of the Goddess once more and rejoiced in its beloved melodies." Askana found it difficult to see Rafe for a moment. Her memory was also vivid, regardless of the time now past. "I mourned his passing for a year. I still mourn his passing."

"A most rare individual then," Rafe smiled. "To be let in to your life as such. I do envy him."

Askana could feel the bind around her hand and wrist give way. Suddenly, the door latch lifted up. Her hand continued back and forth, now in minute gestures as the Dark Merchant entered the room with a soldier by his side. He looked them both over as his attendant set a covered tray close beside them. Rafe could tell in the High Lord's posture that this was, perhaps, the happiest day in his life.

"You Majesty, welcome to my study." For a moment, Askana was reminded of one of Lubria's soft purrs. She could hear the same delight in his voice. "It is here I come to relax. Broaden my mind, as it were. With you and the Sea Wolf as my subjects, I am quite anxious to see what I can learn from you both."

"I am simply the hired help, my friend," said Rafe.

"Do not underestimate yourself, Captain Rafton. I make it a habit to watch the world around me. I watch the world very carefully—" Coumiran laughed in a chilling manner as he approached Askana, " —as I watched the two of you sack my flagship."

He angrily grabbed Askana's shoulder and buried his thumb into the bullet wound, twisting it as he did so. She fought back a howl, clenching her teeth as she tried to breathe through the intense pain. She forced her head upward to look into the Dark Merchant's eyes. He continued to dig into her shoulder, but his eyes were not watching her.

Rafe's jaw was taut and his face tense, his eyes shut tightly from the sharp pain in his shoulder. He fought against it as Coumiran drove his thumb into sinews of muscle and nerves. He suddenly yanked his thumb free of the wound. Both Askana and Rafe released a loud gasp as their bodies slumped in unison against their respective tables. His shoulder throbbed lightly as Askana breathed through continuous ripples of pain from the aggravated wound.

"It seems someone has paid a visit to the Caillech." Coumiran nodded as he revealed the contents of the tray next to them, "This should prove most enlightening."

A variety of blades, all of the finest sharpness and quality, were unveiled before them. Pots of strange-smelling unguents were opened. Askana recognised the scents of sulphur and raw salt.

"Shall we begin?" he asked in a delightful manner.

"And just what do you intend to gain by all this, my friend?" Rafe panted, still feeling a tingle within his shoulder.

Coumiran grabbed Rafe's hair and yanked his head back to speak directly into his face, "Personal satisfaction, Rafton, for having you as a thorn in my side. You have no idea how difficult it is to compete for the favours of the Merchants' Circle when you are outdone by an Otherworlder."

"Outdone?" Rafe quipped defiantly, "You sure you don't mean 'outwitted', my friend?"

He slapped Rafe against the back of his head and huffed, his black mask quickly moving back and forth with his breath, "Personal satisfaction, Rafton. Knowing I will hear you plea for your life, or kill you as you try to mask your pain with that annoying English arrogance of yours."

"I suppose, my friend. At least with my death, you can finally remove that mask of yours. Must be awful being so embarrassed of living in my shadow."

"Worry not, *my friend*," he hissed. "My face, unmasked, will be the image you take to your grave." He then slowly turned to Askana while reaching into his robes. A small ebony box encrusted with jade was gently placed in front of her face, "But as for you, Your Majesty, I wanted you to know who it was that brought you down from your grand splendour."

When the lid was removed from the box, Askana and Rafe both turned their heads away in revulsion. A strong, pungent odour of rotting flesh mixed with a variety of incenses and ointments assaulted them. Then, as if a sudden fit took over, Askana's eyes welled with tears. A series of short gasps and moans of the darkest agony escaped from her lips. The tears that ran down her cheeks were beyond her control. She found it difficult to breathe. In her eyes formed a dizzying madness of anger, sorrow, and lament. She wanted to reach out from her restraints to try and claw at him, but she merely sobbed helplessly.

Rafe's eyes finally turned to the grotesque contents of the small keepsake box. Resting upon a small bed of crushed red velvet were a pair of fingers, apparently the primary bow fingers of an archer. Rafe could not tell if it was decay with time or their natural pigment, but the skin colour was that of fine ivory. They were far longer and more slender than a normal man's fingers. Still upon the bony, withered finger was a signet ring. The crest was the Dragon, Tiger, and Phoenix surrounding the Turi flower, the House Crest of Askana Moldarin.

It had taken her hours to dig his grave. Arms trembling, aching with every shovelful of dirt, digging till she fell, tasting the bitter earth and the salt of her own tears. She fell again, and again, and again. She had not stopped, not until the white-shrouded body was lying under the moist earth, until the acorn had been planted on the fresh grave, a symbol of strength for a corpse laid incomplete to rest.

"Where is it?" A snarl, a rolling growl that could not have come from a woman's throat, emitted from her. "Where is the heart?"

The High Lord slid the fingers closer to her, just enough for her to be unable to avert her eyes away from the gory sight of Telmrant's bow-fingers. He let out a delighted sigh, as if her misery was a chorus of angelic voices. He looked at them both and took up the first instrument, a long, thin blade, in his grasp. With a slight gesture of the scalpel, the attending guard left the study. He watched the door close tightly before returning his attention to Askana.

"I will kill you!" she wailed through her sobs.

"You can do better than that, Askana." Assured of privacy, he spoke openly. "I am, after all, family."

Her expression remained incensed with rage, completely constant in light of his claim.

"You disappoint me, Askana. I expected the Black Widow to know who the Dark Merchant of Eyrie was. So many spies in your service and still they could not find my true identity or allegiance?" He leaned in close to her, his breath passing through the silk of his mask to touch her face, to mingle with the scents of the ebony box. "Allow me, my dear Queen, to enlighten you. I want you to know who I am. I want my face to be burnt into your memory in the long hours before your death."

His gloved hands removed the cowl covering his head. Folds of fabric whispered down, revealing a snarl of triumph on his fully visible face. There was a vicious light in his jet-black eyes. Faintly golden skin, black hair. This High Lord of Eyrie was Morevian, at least half-Morevian. His build and skin tone suggested another race tingeing his bloodline. With the silks now away from his face, the reason behind the mask was revealed. Scar tissue from a severe burn, slightly faded with time but etched in his skin, ran down the left side of his face. Morevian characters spelling out the word "outcast".

For a moment, no one moved. The only audible sounds were that of water lapping against the sides of the *Archangel.*

"How dramatic," Rafe stated flatly.

Yet he tensed when his rival closed in on Askana, and he knew that across the room Askana did likewise. She felt the rope slacken as a few more strands severed.

"You truly do not remember me, do you? You were just a girl then. I saw you once, but it was enough to last. You stole from me my birthright. You cast my father out of Morevi."

"So, you were the son of one of those Lords driven out during the Purging. It means nothing to me. There were so many of you I cannot tell one from the other," she said coldly. "Like so many ants in a line."

His hand slammed down in front of her, his voice sharp as the scalpel underneath the flat hand. "Oh no, I am more to you than that, Askana Moldarin. Do you not remember your cousin, Coumiran of House Ke-Rashu? My father was to inherit the Moldarin estates as was his right. Until you, a mere girl of fourteen, brought about his downfall. You witch, liar, serpent! You who wriggled your way into Norisht's bed. You who would not be content with the dazzling life he gave you at Court." The breath hissed between his teeth as his face contorted from recalling the pain of his family. "What was the wrong my father committed upon you? Was his crime marrying an Eyriener? You did not know either one of them. You had never set eyes on my family as we were living in Eyrie at the time of your father's demise. For a decade, my father longed to return to Morevi. Then, with the death of your father, the stars finally smiled on him. He spoke of relatives with whom we would reunite—you, Maeve, and your mother. He gladly would have given you a place on the estate, regarding you and your family as his own."

"I remember the first time I saw you." His fingers clenched around the handle of the scalpel. "We had just begun to settle into our rightful estate when we were evicted without warning. Our servants, slaughtered before our eyes. Our possessions, reduced to cinders and ash. They dragged us out like thieves from a home that, by the laws of my father's beloved Morevi, was our own. My father shouting, my mother screaming, and I recklessly trying to stop Norisht's men. That is how I came by this unfortunate trait," Coumiran spat, motioning to the scars on his face. "I saw you. You were sitting in your litter, and I saw you. I saw you as the breeze nudged aside the filmy curtains. Dressed in white silk, pearls strung on fine gold chains through your loose hair, the veil half-over your face, your eyes cast down so meekly. I saw you. Norisht took your hand and kissed it. 'Is this what you wish?' he asked you."

The table shuddered as his hands slammed down again. "Is this what you wish?!" His eyes glittered with rage and hate. "I saw you," he whispered repeatedly, waving the scalpel as a cautionary finger.

"Norisht struck my father down! My mother fainted. He kicked her, called her an Eyriener bitch. Her hair, I remember, her hair came loose and matted in a puddle of muddy water. And you, with the finest silks against your skin and little pearls glistening in your shiny black hair! You watched from behind that accursed veil with no expression whatsoever! I saw you.

"We did return to Eyrie, eventually, but not without cost. My father was knifed trying to get us off a rickety ferryboat. My mother and I made it back to her father's house where I was condemned to a life of concealment. My mother died months later of a broken heart."

Askana closed her eyes. She remembered, faintly, that night. A passing mention to her Lord Norisht of wanting her father's lands returned to the rightful name of Moldarin. He was in one of his more caring moods that day, caring as far as his own gains permitted. She remembered watching him unleash his cruelty on this family of strangers. Helpless, powerless to stop him in his tirade. Unable to watch, wincing at the screams and wails that tormented her in dark dreams, even after her ascension. She knew Norisht had always delighted in causing more pain than was necessary. She had not been spared it herself.

212

"I had not vowed to break you yet at that time. I came into my own when my grandfather died. By then you had killed Norisht and usurped his lands like the bloodsucker you are. I took arms as a mercenary, a means in adding to my influence in The Merchants' Circle and with the Eyriener Crown. I was scouting the Uncharted Wastelands when I came across a solitary keep. It had been built by the Elves, unquestionably. It was there I met Maeve."

His voice cracked. Moments passed before he spoke again, personal demons and horrific memories passing before his eyes as he spoke. "I nearly killed her, believing that she was you. Maeve was your shadow. She had her pain, her own darkness, and remained overshadowed by you, the glorious elder sister! She was wilting, dying, when I found her. My Maeve." Coumiran leaned in even closer, almost as if he would kiss Askana on her cheek. "Where is the bastard Elf's heart? I fed it to her dogs."

Her rise of pity vanished like a candle's flame in a thunderstorm. The table rattled as her back arched, muscles contracting with the strain as she struggled to break free. Heels kicked the table surface as she pulled against the rope that still firmly bound her.

Coumiran eyed the scalpel for a moment, "No, I do not think I shall start with this." He carefully returned the scalpel to the tray of tools and removed from a wall displaying a collection of blades a long dagger. It was marked with the raven crest of Maeve's estate. "Yes, this is much more appropriate," he nodded approvingly, lips drawn back in a snarl.

The surviving son of House Ke-Rashu leaned over her, his blade caressing her cheek and cutting across it leaving a thin red line in its trail. She pulled once more with all her strength, and the weakened rope snapped, freeing her right hand. She snatched the dagger in a blinding, blurring movement that caught Coumiran completely unaware. Before he could speak, she slammed the pommel of the dagger against the bridge of his nose.

He stumbled back, cursing as blood ran down his mouth and chin. One slash freed her other arm and another her feet. Her arm snapped like a whip, sending the dagger at the rope holding Rafe's left wrist. The blade's sharpness and the force with which she threw it easily severed the coil.

"Bless you, Your Majesty," Rafe whispered as he grabbed the dagger to free himself, "for remembering that I am left-handed."

"Guards!" bellowed Coumiran, blood spraying from his nose as he backed quickly to the door of the cabin.

Coumiran's attendant opened the door in time to see the dagger thrown at him. It landed square in his chest, cutting through the thin leather armour he wore. The door swung back revealing Coumiran, now setting his own nose back in place with a high-pitched howl. Rafe rolled across his table to where the instruments were laid out and snatched up two scalpels. They caught the light as they whirled, slicing through the air towards Coumiran.

"*Rahiv'al tar!*" Coumiran said with a single hand outstretched, fingers spread wide. The blades froze in mid-air for an instant before clattering to the ground.

"Damn it all," Rafe swore. "I hate magic!"

More crewmen rushed through the doorway of Coumiran's study. Coumiran himself pushed his way through the handful of soldiers, disappearing from sight.

Askana immediately leapt for the nearest Eyriener, driving the ridge of her hand into his ribs with all the force of her weight, bones crunching from her strike. The heel of her other hand snapped his chin up, and then drove two stiff fingers into his throat. The man gasped his last breath, gurgling with a crushed windpipe before stumbling across the room and crashing to the ground. His broadsword was now in the Queen's grasp.

She could hear Coumiran's footsteps pounding against the wood of the steps leading to the *Archangel*'s main deck. Coming from the pent-up fury of everything—the High Lord's identity, Telmrant, his personal vendetta against her—Askana released a guttural roar, like that of a lioness losing track of prey after a drought. The foremost soldiers stepped back at the sight of this half-crazed, half-dressed woman, her own blood streaming down one side of her face and a broadsword in her tight grip. This moment's hesitation was their last.

The broadsword came around, its blade glinting quickly before taking the head of another Eyriener soldier and severing the arm of the comrade standing next to him. Askana placed her boot on the one-armed soldier's belly and pushed him free of her blade. The remaining two soldier fumbled for their weapons, their eyes never leaving Askana's wild gaze.

Then came the sound of the other broadsword, cutting through the air as he approached. Rafe had taken this blade from the wall of Coumiran's study. It was not as light and flexible as his rapier, but he knew this weapon well enough. Unlike the rapier, this sword could cut through bone. A death-blow did not necessarily require a thrust as an unsuspecting Eyriener found out.

"We have to get out of here!" Rafe shouted to her, his heavy blade blocking the remaining Eyriener soldier's attack with a loud clang. The blades locked in a bind. Rafe brought the swords around, and slammed his elbow into the man's cheek. The Eyriener stumbled back to land with a thud in the doorway.

Above their heads came the sounds of sailors and soldiers all running to the doorway leading to *Archangel*'s main deck. A skinny, grey-eyed Eyriener officer met Rafe in the stairwell, a club raised high in the air. Turning the flat of the broadsword to him, Rafe struck the sailor hard across the face. The man's eyes rolled back in his head and the club slipped from his fingers. Before he fell down the remainder of the staircase, the privateer caught him by the collar, removing the coat from the unconscious body.

"Let me thank you in advance for the fine doublet, my good man." Rafe handed Askana the garment, a twinkle in his eyes. "You might be needing this. Modesty is a virtue amongst the Royal."

He smiled widely, finally enjoying that provocative view he had been so long denied.

"If you have taken your fill of gawking at me, pirate," Askana spat as she slipped into the waistcoat, "may I remind you we are still trapped on this vessel! The *Defiant* has sailed off into Arathellian waters and King Henry's fleet should be arriving soon!"

"And I do hate being tardy for important social engagements," quipped Rafe as the stairwell was now blocked by three oncoming sailors. "I suppose we will just have to take over this vessel," he said with a shrug.

A massive blade cut above Rafe's head, dealing more damage to the surrounding stairwell than to its intended target. He pinned the Eyriener's blade against the wall, giving Askana the target she needed. Her own sword sheathed itself in the man's stomach. The remaining sailors charged, screaming wildly with their small cudgels high in the air. On an unspoken cue, Askana and Rafe grabbed the Eyrieners by their shirt-collars and cracked their skulls together, sending them to the pile of bodies collecting at the bottom of the staircase.

Askana kicked open the door leading to the main deck, her broadsword at the ready. She then felt a strong grasp on her good shoulder, then a push to one side just as a sharp 'crack' ripped the air. The bullet left a smoking hole in the door where her forehead would have been.

Askana looked to Rafe in shock. "Someone has supplied the Eyrieners with pistols!"

"Yes, I failed to mention that I discovered a tiny arsenal in our earlier raid. I believe that your distant relative is enjoying a friendship with our dear friend of the English Court. The crate of pistols and rifles bore the family crest of none other than the Duke of Norfolk." He caught her wrist and pulled her behind a pile of barrels as gunfire riddled the hatch. "This is turning out to be a very educative day," he groaned.

Looking up, he saw just what he needed. He charged at the mizzen mast's rigging and with a single slash brought the heavy wood pole down on the novice marksmen, knocking them clear of the main deck and into the ocean.

Springing from deck to bulwark and from step to deck again, Askana dashed with frightening speed to the ship's stern, felling anything that moved in her path. By the time she had reached the *Archangel's* upper deck, there was a trail of dead and wounded in her wake. She had paid a price, however, at the scarlet signs of a dozen different injuries. The Boatswain took one look at the enraged, blood-soaked she-demon bearing down on him and abandoned the Captain's Podium, leaping into the ocean below. He had seen too many men, his Captain one of them, die today. He thought it was high time for a transfer to another ship.

She did not hear the trap-door open, or the whisk of fabric. She did not see the sword rise behind her, but someone else did.

"Askana!" Rafe called from behind her.

Hearing Rafe call to her by her given name sent her to the deck instantly just as the sword descended. It bit into wood next to her. She scrambled away desperately as the High Lord Coumiran hacked into the deck, bearing down on her.

A blur of muscle, flesh, and bone slammed into the High Lord, sending him flying only to roll over and move into a crouch again, blade held ready. Breathing hard, Rafe also raised his broadsword, giving his long-time adversary from The Merchants' Circle a nod. Their blades met with such force that each man's arms felt the shock. Rafe fought with all his skill, but knew something was wrong. He could feel his blows weakening. His shoulders and arms were beginning to ache while Coumiran was still fresh. Slowly the Captain's advance turned to retreat. The blow came for his head, but he blocked the blade, bound it away, then ducked under Coumiran's sword with a defiant kick to the High Lord's backsides.

"To think you cannot beat me when I am worn from battle," Rafe bragged, attempting to bait Coumiran into a clumsy attack. "You could never match me on the oceans. You cannot match me with the blade either."

The deck of the ship whirled around him as he fought to keep Coumiran's broadsword from touching him. Back. Back. Then he met with the railing of the aftercastle. Nowhere to go but into the sea.

Coumiran rose his sword with a growl. In a last desperate act, Rafe flipped back over the railing, catching Coumiran's chin with a kick and landing with a dull thud in one of the rowboats lashed to the side of the ship.

The Dark Merchant stumbled back from the surprise kick, then turned suddenly on his heels to parry what would have been a lethal strike to his side. Askana pushed him away with an unexpected strength and stepped between him and the aftercastle's rail, her teeth bared in a snarl. Coumiran raised the sword high over his head, taunting her with a gloved hand, inviting her to attack. She gladly accepted.

Rafe had just pulled himself to his feet when he heard Askana's cry followed by two heavy blades striking one another. He was reaching for the ladder built into the hull of the *Archangel* when he caught a rush of black fabric above him. Coumiran's blade severed the rope in a single blow. The boat now rocked unsteadily as it began to drift free of the flagship. He was still within reach of the ladder, until something unseen hit him hard across the face and his head reeled as he stumbled back into the dinghy

On the upper deck, Coumiran had just back-handed Askana across the face. She was tiring. Her attacker could see it. Triumph rose in his chest as she stumbled, the parry of his stroke nearly knocking her off balance. The bullet wound was hindering her attacks and her numerous wounds now caught up with her. He knocked aside her next cut and struck her again with his gloved fist, watching with delight as her head snapped around. With a final summoning of her remaining strength, she bound his blade upward and kicked her opponent under the ribs. From the reflex of her strike, his sword came around again, knocking Askana's out of her grip. Seizing her chance, she leapt away, over a pile of barrels and net, hooking her arm around the mizzen mast. She landed heavily on her feet, the upper deck beginning to blur in her vision. She had to get off this ship.

She felt the length of silk pass around her throat and she was pulled back against the mast, her head cracking painfully against wood as the scarf snapped tight.

In the tiny boat below, Rafe felt a tingling around his neck. Everything around him grew soft, hazy. He could not find the oars, but he knew the currents were dragging him further away from the *Archangel*. "Askana!" He could breathe, but it hurt to do so. He felt her dizziness, her choking. He continued calling to her, knowing she could not hear his pleas. "Askana!"

Coumiran wrapped the ends of the silk tighter around his fingers. Askana Moldarin would die at his hands this day, and he would gain strength with her death. His revenge, at last. Morevi would fall, burning and subdued under the Eyriener armies. Min-Lu would take care of the pathetic High Council her way. After that, he would take care of her, *his* way. He would sit on the Throne of a Thousand Suns, the banner of the Turi torn down, burnt, and the standard of the Raven risen in its place.

Maeve! His mind wailed, *Maeve!*

Her blood on the scarf. Her lying on the ground with wide, unseeing eyes. Askana choking, thrashing, tearing at the scarf. *Maeve. Askana. Maeve. Askana.* The same face in the throes of death. In the agonised peace of death...

The tingling suddenly stopped. Rafe's vision was now returning. The waves of the *Archangel* and two relief vessels created even stronger currents that sent him adrift. The Eyriener Navy was growing farther and farther off while the shores of Naruihm were now closer. He was powerless to do anything but be borne away. He threw back his head and screamed, a single howl to the sky. A cursing of God, Nadinath, or perhaps both. A damnation to the powers that moved Askana and himself as pieces on a chessboard.

He picked up the oars and began rowing in the direction of Arathelle. *No, Askana,* Rafe thought, *it will not end this way. Not this way.*

Captain Galdric paced the floor of the stateroom, plucking fiercely at his yellow beard. His eyes, furious. "We should knife her and be done with it!"

The cloaked, hooded figure straightened slightly from his bent posture over the bed. Next to him, a thin, wiry little man with sharp grey eyes tended over the woman who lay asleep. A typical sickbed scene, save for iron cuffs around the patient's wrists and ankles, chaining her to the bed.

"You are letting anger cloud your logic, my good Captain. To King Cedric, she is worth much more alive than dead. The Morevians might just surrender without too much of a fight." He placed a gentle hand on the healer's shoulder as he said, "Small stitches now."

Intent on sewing up the livid gash in the woman's cheek and appeasing the Dark Merchant, the healer did not dare to look up.

"The Black Widow of Morevi," Galdric said with utter loathing. "She lives up to her reputation. What is left on the *Archangel* is nothing more than a skeleton crew." A scarf of sorts was draped about the sleeping woman's neck, presumably to catch the blood. A fine silk scarf, already bloodstained. "I must leave, with your permission, High Lord, before my hands decide to break her neck."

"Leave then, Captain." Galdric turned to leave, but stopped as Coumiran spoke. "I understand your ship collected my Boatswain."

"Yes, High Lord."

"He abandoned his post during the melee with the Queen and the pirate. If in the next thirty minutes I do not see him hanging from the *Sea-Eagle*'s main mast as your new banner, I will have the both of you served as the main course of my dinner table. Am I clear?"

Galdric was silent.

"Very well then. You have my leave. Husar, if you have finished you may go, too. Leave me be."

The door shut softly behind them.

Coumiran eased himself into a chair by the bed. He had nearly killed her before it became clear to him, like a flash of lightning. *Maeve and Askana. Askana and Maeve.* His love was well-educated in the Dark Arts. She had once collected spell books. Much of their teachings were the simpler spells cast merely by will, incantation, or gesture. After her death, he found some of her documents and lessons, but the more powerful spell books remained hidden. Forever lost in a maze of catacombs underneath the Palace of a Thousand Suns. She told him in a night's embrace of a powerful and terrible spell, one she wanted him to use if they were ever separated by Death. With it, souls of the damned could be raised. With it, the dead would live again, provided a body could be found to house the soul.

He found the perfect body here.

The only obstacle would be Min-Lu. The devious little bitch. She would not hesitate in killing Askana once she grew wise to his agenda. He could not let that happen. Smiling, he produced an unopened note she had sent him earlier. He knew its contents before breaking the seal. Words of love. Visions of a new queen with her faithful love by her side. A pledge of devotion to Lord Ruain. A love that, much like Lord Ruain, did not exist.

A few whispered syllables, and the letter were but ashes in his palm. *My response, sweet little Min-Lu,* he thought dispassionately.

Leaning over, he caressed the sleeper's cheek tenderly. He had no intention of delivering Askana Moldarin to Eyrie. She must be unharmed. She must be kept perfect.

CHAPTER THIRTEEN

In the Company of Elves

Lord Bartholemew Marlow fanned himself with his hat as he nervously paced the confines of his quarters. It was a beautiful vista from his window. A wind rippled the surface of a clear blue sea. Under a cloudless sky, the modest fleet of ten ships rode the waves gallantly like horses of the sea. There was, unfortunately, a heavy humidity in the air. It coaxed the sweat from his skin and made his eyelids feel heavy. A hot summer's day in England had never rivalled this even by half. He opened another window in a futile attempt for more ventilation. Marlow returned to the map once more, unlacing his doublet and loosening the ruff around his neck. *So this,* he thought to himself as he checked the co-ordinates once more, *was the land beyond that strangeness men called the Graveyard of Lost Ships.*

This whole venture smacked of madness. First, there was the call to King Henry's Palace in the dead of night. Only the Lord Chancellor and Keeper of the Privy Seal were in attendance with the King. He and his fellow captains were sworn to secrecy and then charged with this gesture of thanks to the Savage Queen for saving His life. As Marlow was the only Lordship among the captains, it was he who would lead this tiny fleet of ships to this far-off realm. It was his first command over a fleet, and it was barely that as there were only ten ships in his company. To add insult to injury, he could not tell a soul.

Lord Marlow was one of the few who knew, however, that the King's motives were not all of a sentimental or romantic nature. During her stay, the Queen spoke of emeralds, tea, silks, and perfumes in exchange for allies. King Henry needed money to continue building up the English Navy, and it was this promise of what Morevi offered that kept the attentions of the Earl of Southampton and Sir Thomas Audley. With sufficient funds, England could, in time, become a great maritime power. Perhaps strong enough to hold its own against France and Spain.

He could understand the interest of FitzWilliam and Audley, but the King's insistence in aiding this savage escaped him. She was merely a woman with not an inkling of proper manners and modesty. Clearly, she was a heathen. He was convinced that this Rift was her work, in league with the Devil Himself. Did His Majesty truly know what God-forsaken place her co-ordinates would take his subjects to? Did he even know, or care to know, what they would face there? As a gesture of thanks, Marlow would have understood the King granting no more than two ships for this venture. This was fleet of ten, including two of the navy's best! It came as a surprise to Marlow that the King did not offer up the *Mary Rose* to the Savage Queen's service. He did not care for this adventure in the slightest, yet he realised what gain this might mean for England. The reports were that Spain was already making a fortune from the New World.

Suddenly, a grinding crunch. The floor tilted, books slid off their shelves, and charts fell to the floor as the *Winged Victory* slowly righted herself again. They were now dead in the water.

"There was no mention of rocks or reefs!" Marlow replaced his hat and strapped on his rapier. Already a frantic hammering was shaking his door, along with the cries of his name stretching, it seemed, from fore to aft of his vessel.

He flung open the door, bellowing over the terrified voices of his crew. "What is it?"

Steel rang as it was drawn with a sound unearthly sweet like nothing he had ever heard. A cold edge came to rest just under his chin. His jaw would have dropped if not for the blade beneath it. "God's Teeth!" was all that he could say as he stared in amazement.

The cries of his crew were growing silent as they were being herded to the centre of the main deck, imprisoned in what looked like a dome of shimmering glass. A few remaining sailors were pushed through the barrier by armoured forms. He watched them as they beat and yelled soundlessly against the barrier, their feeble strikes merely causing the dome to ripple as the water's surface would when broken by a stone. The lookout boy came floating down from the fore topcastle straight into the hands of another of their unearthly captors.

He then turned his eyes away from one wonderment to view another one far grander. A sleek white ship suddenly appeared beside his, pure white from sails to hull, shining in the sunlight. It was twice the size of the *Winged Victory* but bore no armament. He noted the vessel dwarfing his own did not disturb the water around its hull. If he was not certain of his senses—and he was not certain of anything at this moment except for the steel holding him at bay—Marlow swore the ship was actually *part* of the ocean. He finally followed the blade to the face of the one who wielded it. In this single moment, his faith and understanding of the world was challenged, and then abandoned.

The being wore snowy armour of a metal resembling polished silver, yet its sheen was far more brilliant. The visible plates were made of light chain mail, fitted closely to his body and ornamented with intricate, swirling designs akin to the endless knots of Celtic origin. His helmet clove to the head, curving like shells. Long, silver-white hair flowed out behind to rasp on metal. Fine white skin stretched over the bones of a face that was too delicate and too strange to be human. There was something feline about the being's solemn, yet fierce features.

It was the eyes though, that held Marlow speechless. They were of the deepest gold, different shades from the lightest hint of gauzy sun to the dark richness of Cat's Eye, gleaming like fractured diamonds. There was sorrow in them, faint but palpable. There was also joy, music, and laughter in his melancholy gaze.

The sight of long peaked ears set close to his head reminded Marlow of childhood tales. Small creatures with red caps raced through his mind, followed by the more ominous myths of the Sidhe, the Fair-Folk who can be cruel as well as kind. When Marlow broke eye contact, he could feel a tear run down his cheek. His hand rose tremblingly to make the sign of the Cross.

Then Marlow felt his heart in his throat at the sound of a voice. A voice that was severe, but light just the same. It was as though an undercurrent of joy ran through it. "What dost thou do?" the Elf-knight asked. The words flowed like music struck from a deep-toned bell while underneath it echoed a whisper of the same words spoken in a different tongue.

"I—" He was thrilled to have found his own voice. Then his mind struggled to remember what he was doing to provoke the question. "I was making the sign of the Cross."

"A spell?" The being asked him with almost childlike curiosity, "Art thou a human mage?"

"Mage?" Marlow made a sound like a surprised bark. "Witchcraft is not practised in King Henry's armies!"

"Armies." The voice chilled perceptibly. "We know not of thy King Henry."

The sudden tension was broken by the sight of movement at the starboard railing. Two hands took hold of the railing not far from them and another sleek, armoured body pulled itself effortlessly over the side of the ship. Graceful, silent, and awesome in appearance, Marlow quickly began to understand how the *Winged Victory* was boarded. Not a drop of water marred the deck.

The one who held Captain Marlow merely turned his head. "Messilura, what word from Borimvar?"

"He wishes that the leaders among these intruders be brought to him, and the nature of their intrusion made known." Messilura doffed her helm. Pale silver hair, dry, spilled out over her armour as she walked right up to Marlow. "He be the one, Jasilan?"

"Yea," spoke the one still holding Marlow at sword's point.

She was eye to eye with him, a tall creature of beauty but still hard and stern in her own armour. There was in her eyes that same look of unfettered joy below solemnity. In this lady's gaze, however, resided a deeper, darker thread of some past injury running so deep that Marlow wondered whether she herself was even aware of it. Her voice, also with the haunting echo-whisper of a foreign tongue, sounded so sweet to him. "Who are thou, mortal?"

He was beginning to believe he was in the company of angels, until the condescending tone of the word "mortal" cut him to the quick. Some riled defiance bubbled to the surface as he drew himself up and glared at her. "I am Barthloemew Marlow, Lord of Ettingsborough, Captain in service to its Sovereign, His Majesty King Henry the VIII of England." He felt his chest puff out. Regardless if these beings' speech was honey-sweet, it would not diminish his responsibility to his crew or the Crown. "I command this fleet. As emissaries of His Majesty, I demand to know who holds my fleet and person."

She looked at the proud man with the slightest smile of amusement crossing her face. His words and titles meant nothing, but his sudden pride was refreshing. Clearly, he was not of this realm. "I am Messilura, a Captain of the Forces of Arathelle, and he who holds thy ship is Borimvar, Guardian of the Coast and Ports at the command of King Eharon and Queen Esharana. He," she gestured to the male who slowly withdrew his sword from Marlow's throat, "is Jasilan, also a Captain of the Forces."

Marlow felt the hairs prickle on the back of his neck as the question formed in his mind. He could see in her eyes that she knew the question before he asked it. Still he wanted to hear his own voice, if only to be certain he was not deep in a dream. *"What are you?"*

Her stern look softened in light of the man's innocent question and her smile grew wider. "We are the First Race. The Walkers of the Dream and the Children of Celeron. Thou mortals call us Elven-folk."

"Elves!" chortled a voice from behind Marlow. This voice was not of the melodic, haunting tones of the Elves. It was definitely English. "We knew it even before we left Wales, Lord Marlow. The Savage Queen is a witch and this is a land of enchantment."

The defiant, brash English gentleman was being escorted by two other Elves, one sword at his neck and another's tip close to his back. His doublet was slashed, evidence that some sort of minor struggle had taken place, but otherwise he was impeccably dressed right down to the triple plumes of his hat. "Greetings, Elven Mistress, I am Sir Thomas Eshton, at your service. I would bestow upon you a bow, though I would fear your lad's fine Elven steel would cut my fine English throat."

No one cracked a smile. Eshton still kept the grin across his face.

"I do not believe this!" spluttered Marlow. "Elves are the stuff of fairy-tales and childhood imaginings!"

"In fairy-tales, yes." Eshton laughed brightly, looking with new and avid eyes around him. "Obviously, my Lord, this is no fairy-tale."

Marlow opened his mouth to silence the rantings of his second-in-command, but then Eshton's logic struck him. For all those old legends in their realm, perhaps some of these creatures passed through that Rift before. Perhaps hundreds and hundreds of years ago. Perhaps the Irish were not so crazy after all.

His dizzying conclusion from Eshton's flippancy was quickly forgotten as the brilliant white blades around them returned to their scabbards. "Whether thou believe or nay," said Jasilan with a steely gaze, "thy fleet hast intruded in Arathellian waters. Thy reasons must needs be good."

"They are!" Silently praising God for familiar ground, Marlow fumbled through a small pouch hanging from his belt. He produced a small silver ring with the insignia of House Moldarin as he spoke the words as taught to him by his King. "We sail into Arathelle with the blessings of Morevi's Sovereign, Queen Askana Moldarin."

Brows snapped up, and the Elves quickly looked to one another. "Her Majesty, Queen Askana? She hath been missing by nearly a moon."

"Yet this is without question her sigil on the ring." Messilura touched it with one long, slender finger. "Our Queen knows. There will be bloodshed here ere long."

"A mortal squabble that we have naught to do with," said Jasilan coldly.

"Arathelle doth lies between the two foes."

"If it comes to that, the Elders shall seal off everything save the Road of the Moon. It hath been done in times past. Come!" Jasilan strode away to where rope ladders led down to silver rowboats.

Messilura paused, looking at Eshton, "As you are Lord Marlow's second, thou must come with us."

"Excellent!" He swept her a perfect bow with his triple-plumed hat. "I shall follow wherever you lead, my Lady."

Marlow remained where he stood, still staring at the place where the Elves once stood. He jumped with a start and a small yelp as Eshton slapped him on his shoulder.

"Elves, witchcraft, and a battle on the horizon." Sir Thomas sighed with a mischievous gleam in his eye, "This, my Lord, has all the makings of a grand adventure!"

With a hearty laugh, he eagerly followed Jasilan and Messilura to the awaiting rowboats.

Music rippled and flowed, washing over all in a shimmering wave of notes. Perfume seemed to emanate from the white sails. The bells on the tassels of the instruments tinged with the harmonies their players brought from them. Lord Marlow and Master Eshton stood on the enormous deck of the Elven ship. It was the largest craft they had ever seen. It housed them and the captains of King Henry's fleet in a luxury the finest palaces of England, France, and Spain could never begin to touch. This ship was an embodiment of their Heaven. Still, Marlow frowned in uneasiness at the nature of the Elves and the loss his fleet now suffered.

Three captains were dead. One had refused to obey orders to come peaceably and was killed as he and several crewmen charged the Elven warriors. He had watched in fascination and horror as the arrows made no sound when drawn, loosed, or striking the advancing English. The second captain died of shock when he felt invisible bonds lifting him. The third screamed gibberish about agents of Satan, witchcraft, and God delivering him from evil before leaping overboard. He hoped the count among the sailors during the initial boarding of this fine vessel was not too high.

Now, after a day in the Elves' company, many of them did not want to leave. They were fed well on strange foods, milk, and honey that lifted their spirits and tasted unlike any delicacy of their kingdom. Both captain and crewmate were treated with equal respect and reverence. They were not prisoners of the Elves, but their guests.

They had been brought before Borimvar the night before. It was a grand feast of meats, succulent fruits, and wine that could truly take away sorrow for a period of time, along with most other sensations, save euphoria. Borimvar, the English captains were to discover, was a Lord of his people and served as a supreme commander over the Elven fleet. He was also the ruling lord over the port city they now knew was called Iomer. Borimvar stood out from the others not only in his distinctions, but also in his appearance. He was taller than his kind, black-haired, and spoke with the voice of a seasoned warrior. Lord Marlow perceived that he was older than the other Elves, yet time and age had not touched him. They touched none of the "Children of Celeron" as the Elves called themselves. Marlow could see knowledge and wisdom in Borimvar's face. The sorrow that only hinted in the eyes of the others marked him clearly, making his fine face cold.

Marlow explained the charge handed down by his King, upon the requests of the Morevian Queen. He caught himself tripping over his words as Borimvar's eyes seemed to read his very heart before he spoke. He was convinced the Elven Lord knew of the displeasure and uneasiness about this mission that he kept buried inside him. Still, he would not fail good King Henry as he presented his royal decree.

The Elven commander, remaining stoic and silent, rose from his chair at the grand table to retire for the evening. As if on cue, the other Elven warriors also rose and escorted the English back to their own chambers.

Now Lord Marlow stood against the deck-rail, arms folded across his chest as he silently watched the shining towers and buildings of the Elven ports come into view. The port city of Iomer, the gateway to the realm known as Arathelle, seemed to stand out as a collection of pearl, ivory, and white marble surrounded by a lush jungle. Seeing the brilliance of the city nestled in rolling green, he could not help but be reminded of the stories of King Arthur and the descriptions of Camelot. With all that he had seen in his short stay in this bewitched realm, it would not surprise him to trip over Excalibur itself, perhaps lying idly by a footpath.

Something was in the morning air. They were encouraged to bathe and dress in the best clothes their cabins could offer. In due course, they were led up to the main deck. *Wide and deep enough to accept a proper Royal Procession*, Lord Marlow thought absently. Still no response from Borimvar on what was to be done with King Henry's fleet, although he could see the shores closing. At last, the Elves began gathering.

Today the Elven men wore billowing cloaks of many colours over their mail and armour, fastened at the left shoulder with a stylised sun made of both a light, brilliant silver he heard them call "ashurbal" and resplendent moonstones. The women had undergone a total change. Their armour was replaced by clouds of fine fabric. He recognised only silks, both plain and embroidered. The others remained nameless, some rich and heavy and shot with gold thread. Light, gauzy, and moving with every breath of the breeze so that one saw the pearly paleness of a rounded arm under vapory wrapping. The sun insignia shone at their left shoulders, as well. They appeared as naiads rising out of the water in trailing robes, slender shapes now visible through veils of mist.

Thomas Eshton bowed low as Messilura took a place beside him, her silver braids swept up off her pale blue drapery. "The dawn of morning never held such beauty as do you on this fair day, my lady."

Messilura arched a silver brow, her deep blue eyes startling against all her paleness. "Thy verse, Sir Thomas, lacks some polish."

The blunt, coarse response came as no surprise to him. The apparent equality between the genders was something the English could not grasp, and therefore approached the women as they would in their own realm. The Elven maids seemed faintly amused, if not slightly annoyed, at the antics of a few of the younger men. Sir Thomas could not help but to continue in his courting undaunted. He was taken by the numerous women soldiers. Pallid, beautiful Valkyries in silver armour. However, the Elven directness that bordered on tactless proved sobering for many of the English.

Not to Sir Thomas Eshton. "But what we mortals lack in polish we make up for in ardour," he grinned. "What means this gathering today, and why the change of attire?"

"Thou shalt see soon enough, Sir Thomas."

Overhead, the gulls suddenly took wing, scattering with piercing cries. A great sigh rose from the gathered Elves.

"They come," whispered Messilura. "Lord Marlow, Sir Eshton, attend."

They followed Messilura to the main deck where Borimvar stood silent. Their eyes never left the sight of what now extended from the shores of Arathelle to the ship. A ribbon of glistening light reached towards them through the air, far above the surface of the ocean. It stretched longer and longer, sweeping out over the sea until it was close enough for mortal eyes to make out.

"A bridge!" whispered Marlow in amazement.

The light eventually touched the deck of their vessel. The musicians onboard had long fallen silent, yet still they heard the sweet strains of music with the ethereal sound of voices singing in that hauntingly fluid Elven tongue, carried forward by the wind. Banners waved and snapped as they came. Fifty knights marched in perfect precision, their swords at their sides, white surcoats and grey-green cloaks draping over chain-mail of the brightest ashurbal. Contrasting the armour and weapons were wreaths of flowers that adorned their armour in colourful bursts of sweetness and softness. Orderly and swiftly, this procession made two long rows on either side of Borimvar who waited at the aft portion of the deck.

Then came the sound of thunder, soft and rolling in their ears. Sir Thomas could not help but give an innocent laugh at the splendour unfolding before him. Two magnificent horses, one dapple-grey and the other jet black, rode along the light-bridge. They were the size of Shires, beautifully proportioned with strong, powerful muscles under smooth, glossy coats. Unlike the work horses of their realm, these creatured moved with all the light grace and elegance of Arabians. They held their heads high, a mighty call coming from them as their long manes tossed in the breeze. Their majesty and pride befitted them as Elven steeds, particularly as they carried the rulers of Arathelle.

Like a wave rolling in the tide, all knelt, Elves and men alike. There was no hesitance for there was no doubt that these were two worthy of reverence. Marlow was likewise kneeling, his brain wanting to deny the reality of everything happening here yet he could feel the stomp of the Elven mare on the deck vibrate underneath him and the faint brush of the honour guard's robes that billowed in the breeze. He cast a glance over to Sir Thomas.

Eshton was absolutely enraptured by it all, relishing every minute of it.

"Borimvar, blessed be," spoke the voice of the Elven King.

Marlow's heart ceased beating at the sound of the monarch's voice. It was as if he had heard a clarion call of charge across a bloody battlefield when victory was certain. He trembled to think of the man to match the voice.

"Blessed be, my Sovereign," murmured the voice of Borimvar. "Thy presence graces us at last."

"Thou hast been Our loyal servant and highest champion. Why should We doubt thy word?" asked the voice of the King gently.

"We have given welcome to the Morevians, three days past," added the voice of the Queen.

The hairs raised on the back of Marlow's neck, his head still bowed. While trying to picture the King behind such a voice, the female voice thrilled him to the bone. It was the soothing caress of a moonlit river, the whisper of forest trees, and the purple of shadowed night. It sang more than spoke, drawing his heart to her eternal service. "The Morevians now know Our intent."

"Not the new King, my Queen?" questioned Borimvar.

"Nay. Those who know the mind of My King and Mine Own are allies sworn true to Queen Askana. Rest easy, My Borimvar." The voice broke in a note as soft as any wood bird's. "Ah, but We forget our manners! Where are the mortal Lords who have come hither on the Morevian Queen's behest, whom We should have greeted beforehand as courtesy dictates?"

"There, my Queen."

Lord Marlow watched the feet of Borimvar step to one side. He now felt something akin to sunlight, but it was not warm. It was peaceful, tranquil. He knew the Elven King and Queen now waited on him. He could not feel his legs, or his hands. He was unsure if he still drew breath. *I may have proven to be made of jelly till now,* thought Marlow, *but enough is enough!* He could feel his resolve growing like a tiny fire inside him. *Even a dog will snap when cornered. I am an Englishman! I will not shame my England or good King Henry Tudor by trembling on my knees. I will not!*

He stood proudly, sweeping his hat and making an elegant bow. "Lord Bartholomew Marlow, Royal Emissary of the Court of His Royal Highness King Henry the VIII of England, Your Most Esteemed Majesties. How may I serve?"

He forced his gaze up to meet theirs, and dropped his hat.

The Elven Queen smiled, and it was like no smile he had received from any woman. "A fine man and a fitting commander of this fleet thou art. Thy King should be proud of thee, for thy courtesy."

Her words continued to echo in their minds, touching their hearts as well as their ears. Eshton could no longer contain himself as he rose to his feet, picking up Lord Marlow's hat as he did. Returning it to him in a subtle manner, he boldly faced the King and Queen of Arathelle.

"Sir Thomas Eshton of the Court of King Henry the VIII," he spoke boldly waving his triple-plumed hat, "at your service, most reverent and gracious Sovereigns."

The remaining captains kept their heads bowed, shameful of their cowardice before these awesome beings of pure light and joy. As if feeling their anguish, a voice touched them in their minds. *Rise, noble men of thy King,* spoke the voice of the Elven Queen, *and be known to Us.* This silent absolution brought the other men to their feet and their names called out proudly across the deck of the Elven vessel. Sir Wallace Borrows. Sir Julian Sommers. Master Jonathan Perceival. Some referred to themselves as "Sir" while others "Master," equal titles interchangeable in their kingdom. The names continued until the last man stepped forward boldly.

"Lord Miles Agecroft," he spoke, then with a deep breath for courage, added, "God bless the King and Queen of Arathelle."

"You are all welcome to Arathelle, so say King Eharon and Queen Esharana." The Queen motioned to the Royal Guards closest to her, "Bring those sworn to Our Sister, Askana, hither to Us."

"Most Revered Majesty," Lord Marlow asked, bowing his head as he addressed the Elven Queen. "Might I humbly inquire who are those sworn to Her Majesty, Queen Askana?"

The King and Queen glanced at one another, before Esharana answered. "Those who serve Queen Askana Moldarin, whom thou must work with to carry out Her Command."

"But, my Queen, we have received no commands. Therein lies our problem."

A trill of laughter came from Her. "Thinkest thou so? Thou wilt see soon enough."

"What?" murmured Sir Thomas.

"Shhh—silence awhile, mortal," whispered Messilura. "Curb thy bold curiosity for but a moment."

This time, the approach was heralded by the tramp of many feet.

The women who jogged down the ramp were a fantastic sight in their own right, marvellously savage yet exotic, vibrant, and obviously human among the Elves. Lord Marlow was shaken slightly in how forcibly they reminded him of Queen Askana. Most shared her strange, golden-skin colouring. One or two could have passed for English, if not for their dark eyes and fierce air. Some were young, some were older. A small amount were pretty, a few strikingly beautiful. All had the look only seen before on hardened soldiers. To his surprise, judging from what he had heard and seen of Queen Askana, there were men too, men who wore heavy battle armour, unlike the women.

Their lines parted and a middle-aged woman stepped forward with a white-bearded old man also dressed in heavy armour as were the men. Two long blades of a type that Marlow had never seen were strapped to his back while the woman gripped a weapon similar to that of Askana's attendant. These two boldly stepped up to the Elven rulers, hardly dazzled or even impressed by their splendour.

The woman stood for a moment, looking first at the Queen, then at the King. Then slowly, she bowed from the waist, fist to heart, and sank down on one knee. "Blessed be, Sovereign King and Queen of fair Arathelle."

He saw Queen Esharana smile again as all the newcomers followed their leader's example.

"Stand, Mine guests," said King Eharon. "Stand, all. We would not have thee kneel all day."

"You are most kind, Sovereign Lord," puffed the old man as he returned to his feet. "The run does not agree with men my age."

"We should have allowed thee thy steed. It was Our oversight, Royal Master of the Blades," the Queen sighed. "Kalea, Anjara of Morevi, Captain of the Queen's Guard. We welcome thee, friend. Time has changed thee much."

"As time does to those not gifted with immortality," the woman answered with a smile on her hard face. Her tilted, dark eyes then fell on Marlow, Eshton, and the other English captains. "I see strangers amongst us, Sovereign Queen. Was I mistaken to think only we and the Eyrieners could pass into these waters?"

Silence. Sir Thomas fought back a laugh. It seemed that the Morevians shared with the Elves that gift of blunt honesty.

"It is a strange and important scene played here today," Esharana spoke as if recalling a dream. "Three nations shall meet to decide the fate of two, and the fourth shall wait for the morrow's eve. We cannot and will not play the games of mortals. That is Our Creed. We are far from the Snows and the Singing Winds of Home. For the sake of Our people We take the Middle Way." The silvery voice deepened, "Yet, thou art a friend, Anjara. Thou hast given Us peace and kept thy promises even for thy short mortal span. We believe thy realm and the Queen shall continue likewise. Thou acknowledged my Lord and our King out of thy courtesy. Thy Queen is Our Sister."

"We tell thee," said King Eharon. "Only the Road of the Moon shall be open on the day of war. Thou knowest where it begins, thou knowest where it ends. We will give no aid to them, but neither can thou expect warlike aid from Us."

Madness, thought Lord Marlow. *Madness. What could the King have been thinking? To bring His subjects into a war that is not our own?*

The Anjara's proud bearing sagged a little, her voice heavier than earlier. "The thanks of my people, Sovereign King, but we are at a loss. Our people stand divided, our Council in argument. Our King is new and raw. To speak truth, our women will not follow a king who does not hold the approval of our Queen, only the approval of the High Regent." She cast a cold glance to the Palace Guard. "We had little time to prepare for this war."

"Wait awhile," spoke the Elven King. "We have tidings to give thee yet. These strangers are thy Queen's gift to thee. She has been found, yet lost again."

Palpable shock ran through them. The Anjara's head snapped around, plumes flying, as Kubi-Sogi barked, "Lost again?!"

Eharon lifted a hand and nodded gently, "Thine own people shall tell thee the tale. A Royal Guard and Maiden of Nadinath. The young maid did arrive here aboard a ship also from the other side of The Rift." His face suddenly darkened, "A young maid and another companion of this realm. Therein remains another matter."

"Attending the Guard was a Creature of the Mists," said the Queen quietly. "At the sight of Elven folk, she did turn to fury and anger whereupon we did restrain her."

The Anjara's eyes widened. "Lubria!"

"Thou knowest our law. We knew of this Creature of the Mists in Our Sister's company, many mortal years ago. Now she has come into Arathellian waters. By Our Law, We pass her back into the Mists, to the Lost Ones."

The sound of armoured footsteps stole their attention to the bridge. Three figures emerged from the light. The foremost was a young girl with long, golden hair, dressed much like the Morevian women. The other two were instantly recognised by the English as Nassir, the hulking, brown-skinned giant who served as Captain Rafton's First Mate, and the fiery-red haired Sarah Riley, his *Mistress* Gunner as Rafe liked to call her.

The girl took one look at the Morevians and dashed to fall before the Anjara's feet. "I lost the Queen, Anjara," she cried, her bronzed shoulders shuddering as she spoke to her commander. "I lost the Queen! I beg leave to go to the Temple! I must perform penance!"

The Elven Queen and King looked at her with nothing but compassion.

The two pirates were suitably round-eyed at the spectacle before them, until their eyes fell on the English captains standing among the Elves.

"Now I am *certain* that we have not ascended into the Kingdom of Allah," Nassir quipped sharply as he pointed to the English. "He would not stand for these Christian heathens to befoul His sacred temple!"

Sarah placed her hands on her hips, looking over Sir Thomas. "Knowing some of these 'gentleman's' likes, I can assure you they won't be anywhere near those holy grounds of Allah's."

Lord Marlow groaned, burying his face in his hands as Nassir bared his teeth in a friendly smile. He was not fond of pirates, Rafton's crew in particular. While they all answered to His Majesty, privateers and gentlemen rarely could socialise in the pubs without it leading to some raucousness. It was to be Rafton's privateers and an army of savages he would lead into battle. He thought back throughout the years, trying to remember any incident where he might have incurred King Henry's displeasure.

Sir Thomas merely gave Sarah a devious wink, her eyes still roaming up and down him as a lewd smile crossed her face.

A thunderous roar shook the deck, followed by ear-splitting screeches. Blood drained from most of the English faces as the terrible sounds came from the bridge and drew near. Elven faces lost their softness, and more than one hand opened to birth a ball of blue flame before clenching into a fist over it again. With the Morevians, an assortment of expressions crossed their faces, uppermost of which was recognition. The sounds melted into articulate, melodic words, though uttered in the coldest tones of damnation. It was another language, close to the tongue of the Elven whisper. If not used to curse, it would have outshone the Elven speech in its grace and beauty.

Sir Thomas caught Messilura flinching with a slight hiss. "What is it?" he asked.

"It uses the High Speech, the language of the Mists." This, of course, meant nothing whatsoever to Eshton, but his politeness and curiosity kept him on her every word. "It is the language of long ago, when the Firstborn were the only articulate race in the world. Now we have but the fragments of it, enough to understand but not to speak it well. Only the Lost Ones know it now. The Creature knows the Laws, and therefore curses the race of Elves. It curses even the memory of one it tolerated and protected for the Queen's sake. It does not desire to return to back into the Mists."

" 'It' can speak? What is —"

Thomas' unformed question found its answer when the two Elven captains emerged from the bridge. Suspended between them was a clear globe of the same make as had been used on the English. What was within it made the bold young Englishman pause and swallow. Lubria saw the Morevians, gave the sphere one last defiant kick, and then settled down in its centre to wait with narrowed eyes. She looked keenly at

Elunear, at Kalea, at those she knew to be Maidens. There were some faces that showed only fear. Her salvation would lay in the Sisterhood as they ironically saw her as a symbol of their Goddess.

Kalea stared for a long moment at Lubria, then raised her chin slightly as she spoke, summoning true courage in her plea. "Lubria is one of the blessed of Nadinath, Sovereign Queen. I pray you to let us take her back to the Temple. She had done good service to Your Sister, Askana Moldarin."

A clever tactic, but Esharana shook her head. "She cannot leave with thee. So it is writ in Ancient Law that what comes from the Mists must be returned, else shall the Children of Celeron suffer the price."

"We close Arathelle at sunset on the morrow before the Eyrieners land," said King Eharon. "It will take them two days to lead an army to thy kingdom."

"Then can the Sovereign Queen keep Lubria safe, till Queen Askana returns?"

"We cannot keep so many," Esharana sighed, motioning to the English. "It taxes our resources as well."

"Your Majesty," All eyes fell on Marlow who now spoke. This was the opportunity to make their presence known. "We are the subjects of King Henry, honour bound to serve the realm of Queen Askana. Allow us to return to the sea for there we shall aid her most valiantly. We can also supply arms and infantry for the Morevian army assembled here."

The Anjara drove the butt of her shirai into the deck of the Elven ship, arching her eyebrow sharply. "Just what do you believe you can do, *man*, on the open waters of Naruihm so far from Morevi?"

Lord Marlow now felt his English courage swell up in his breast as he approached her. Even watching her grip tighten against the weapon's staff did not intimidate him. After all he had seen, this savage was less than a trifle. "The enemy is coming here to Iomer, meaning they travel on the ocean. This Englishman has arrived with ten warships at his command. How many do you command, my *Lady*, in your land-locked nation?"

Kalea was silent. Kubi-Sogi could not hide his grin at the man's effrontery.

"So I thought," scoffed Marlow with a self-satisfied grin. "What could provide a better surprise for the Queen's enemy than a land-locked nation's *navy*?"

Even the Elven King and Queen could not hide their approval at Marlow's new-found resolve. He continued, bowing on one knee before them. "Therefore, with the blessings of the King and Queen of Arathelle, shall I do so for the people of Morevi and the good people—" He then paused awkwardly, looking at Esharana raise her eyebrow as the Anjara had. "—*Elves* of Arathelle."

Kubi-Sogi looked at the Englishman silently, his grin now a satisfied smile. Marlow locked eyes with him. He was uncertain why he was compelled to do so, perhaps out of assurance to the Morevians that they would fight alongside them as allies. He took out the signet ring and lifted it up to the Blademaster. The old man's face cleared as he reached into the wide sash across his stomach and produced a silver pendant that matched the signet.

With a gentle nod, Kubi-Sogi whispered to Kalea. After a moment, she asked, "Sovereign Queen, upon this charge shall we accept our allies. We will take some with us, while the others return to fight at sea. Would you then keep Lubria until Askana returns, Gracious Queen?"

Apparently, this would not be an issue easily resolved.

Eharon shook his head. "Creatures of the Mists are unique, immortal, unpredictable. They come from The Mists. Return there they must, for fear of what they could do in this world. We hear that this one has already done as much in thy land, yet Askana loves her. This once, shall We waive custom. We shall keep her safe, Anjara, whence thy Queen returns."

Elven faces hardly changed expression, but the mortals sensed the disturbance they felt at their King's promise to the Anjara. The uneasiness subsided very little as their attentions turned to one another. Privateers. English gentlemen. Morevian warriors divided clearly by gender and ideology.

In their uneasy alliance rested the fate of a nation.

Elven patrols were extended further due to the arrival of the Otherworlders and the impending threat of war. This was a war between mortals. While it did not concern them, their hearts were heavy just the same. It was war that scattered their race. Envy turned the race of Man against Elven-folk. The armies of Man swarmed through the forests and overran the mountains. The great cities of the Elves fell, the Four Tribes driven away from their rich homelands to the wastes and jungles of the east. Heartsick, one tribe took their ships and sailed away from the lands of Naruihm, never to return. Now, war drew close to them, unearthing memories and desires long suppressed.

Benhaar and Setreia, riding in the surf that lapped around their horses' hooves, were the descendants of that tribe. Despite their youth, they too felt that the shadow of war had touched them once more. They did long for the outside world. In this time of doubt when Man squabbled and the Elves remained hidden in Arathelle, there rose the faint wish that they would fight as they had been trained to do.

"Not that I wish war," Benhaar said. "Yet 'tis true as Friya says that we must remain upon the Middle Way. It is very well for the Elders to say that peace is all they desire, but thinkest thou it was the desire for peace that led to our weakness? The Elders did not wish to fight with Man, therefore we were driven away from the Snows and the Singing Winds."

"Dost thou desire to quest, then, Benhaar?" Setreia reined in her grey mare. "Nay, speak not yet. I too feel in my blood the call for something more. It pains me sorely that we should give way to everyone who challenges us."

"Why, think thou, that Roadan, Jarenissa, and the others agreed to go to Borimvar on Io? 'Tis because even joining the Fellowship of the Jewels is better than to stay here forever, without ever seeing other lands or trying our swords." Benhaar was almost sick with impatience, and his eyes flashed with something near anger. "The Fellowship demands a measure of our young. The world outside encroaches on us. The Rift has opened for reasons we do not know into the Lands of Old. It is as though all the world is afire with change save us. We are prisoners of our own divine stagnation!"

"Have a care, Benhaar." A mist passed over Setreia's pale green eyes. "Thy words carry some meaning that I fear." Her voice lowered, "I have dreamed."

"Of what did thou dream?" Benhaar backed his horse out of the surf and they continued more carefully, eyes scanning the horizon.

She turned her face away towards the sea and when she spoke, her voice was soft with sadness. "I dreamt of the snows of the mountains, of a streaming wind over a green-grey sea. I dreamt of the lonely harper on Aimeor's Rock. I dreamed of death."

When he took her hand, it was wet and chilled from the sea-foam. "'Tis only a mood, my love. What harm can there be coming for us, when we are soon to wed?" It was something they did not speak of often. He had but three hundred years behind him, and Setreia only two hundred and eighty four. Very young by the standards of their people.

"Others have dreamt it too," she murmured, riding over a dune and finding only a family of rabbits feeding on runners. "Mayhaps 'tis true what the Elders have seen in their Ill'ethstréa. What sickness of the blood causes us to revel in the ring of sword on sword and in the storms that lash the shores and howl on moonless nights? Our race is fading, or worse, I fear we may soon have the change that thou seekest."

He would have comforted her, but they had rounded a cliff-side and went silent at their find. In the light of the setting sun they saw the dark shape of a boat grounded half-in, half-out of the surf. It was from the ship of Man, and their quick eyes saw immediately that there were no footprints or other signs of life around it. Silently, as only Elves can, they dismounted and swiftly approached the craft, swords at the ready.

There was a mortal in the boat. He wore tattered breeches of an Eyriener, but he was an Otherworlder. His exposed torso was a bright red, his skin hot. The lightest of touches left a flash of white before it returned to the sunburned hue of scarlet. They could also see wounds on his forehead, arms, and chest, sealed with dried blood. His breeches were bloodied as well, as if he had been in a fight.

He stirred when their shadows fell over him. His lips were burnt and chapped. There were blisters on his hands, apparently from his rowing to shore. His voice was dry and hollow, but still he managed a smile as he murmured, "I made it to Heaven. Excellent well."

Then he subsided into unconsciousness.

Overtures

Askana's dark eyes cautiously moved from corner to corner of the pub. Usually crowded and bustling at any time of day, now only her own footfalls were heard. She felt a chill across her skin. She was not in her battle armour but in white morning robes. The planks underneath her feet creaked lightly as she continued towards the bar. No shadows moved. No barkeep welcomed patrons. No serving maids balanced trays as they moved between tables. She was completely alone in this familiar place, or so she thought.

"Well met, Your Grace."

It was his voice beyond doubt. Still arrogant, still brash. There he sat. The snifter before him, and a closed book on the table next to a solitary candle which cast its light in his face. This was how they had first met. He had been watching her as she entered The Barrier Reef, and hailed her when she passed by him with those very same words. He was a stranger to her then. Somehow she had come full circle and returned to the beginning of her journey.

This was not possible. There was a battle at sea. They had been taken captive and were in the Dark Merchant's "study". Rafe disappeared over the side of the ship. The look of victory in her cousin Coumiran's eyes as the silk tightened around her throat. She was on his ship and had slipped into darkness. Into dreams.

Wearily, she remembered the Caillech's spell. Grainne had outdone herself this time.

So this was a look inside the head of Rafe Rafton. The snifter of scotch, the relaxed seat, the outward bravado. The book, a sign of a learned gentleman. "I commend you, privateer, in mastering the skill of Ill'ethstréa in so short a span. You should be proud," she said with a touch of sarcasm. "Besides myself, only Elves and a precious few Magi have ever experienced it."

He merely raised an eyebrow at her needling. "I am afraid such witchcraft is punishable by death according to King Henry's law." He leaned back in his chair.

She wondered if this pirate always had to strut. Everything about him, from the foppish elegance to the putting on airs seemed a façade. But a façade over what? Sometimes she sensed the performance was solely for her benefit, but like the peacock he had no qualms about displaying for others. At least this whole scene meant that she was not dead, merely unconscious. She would still live to kill her dear cousin.

"Sit down, Askana." Rafe sipped from the snifter. "Have a scotch with me."

"I do not care for the taste of the drink, privateer." She kept her stance in the middle of the tavern. Being in her morning robes discomfited her. She knew they hid little, but had never worried about that before. Here, though, knowing they were sharing a dream, she felt too unprotected, too revealed, for her liking. Remembering what pieces she had gathered about Ill'ethstréa, she focused her mind on changing her clothes. Nothing happened. Perhaps Rafe had become more skilled at manipulating the Dreamscape than he had earlier indicated.

"Well then, have some Morevian wine," he winked. "The establishment is ours for the time being. The bar is always well stocked."

"Pirate, why have you brought me here?" Askana placed her hands on her hips, feeling more secure in a stronger, challenging stance. "It is a diversion I do not need."

"Oh, so our dreams are a diversion now, are they?" Rafe smirked as he leisurely swirled the scotch in its snifter. "Well, with everything we have endured, a moment's diversion should not be the end of Morevi's New Regime."

His contemptuous tone was a slap to her pride. She did not expect him to understand her motives or what drove her to protect the legacy she built for the generations to follow her. Still, he was deriding something she loved.

"Is this such a detestable place to be, Your Grace?" Rafe asked, spreading his arms wide as he motioned to their surroundings. "We are in The Barrier Reef once again. No Morevian guards. No cutthroats. No mad relatives to the Crown. There is only us." A corner of his mouth lifted sardonically. "Or is it that you, Askana, are afraid of sharing a moment alone with me?"

It was not only a challenge. He was also insinuating that she was afraid she would find him attractive. His egotism would have been laughable had there not been a grain of truth in it. Rafe *was* a handsome man.

"I do not fear you, pirate. I do not fear this dream. It is the power you hold in this dream that displeases me. It reminds me too much of my youth with Lord Norisht. Thanks to the education he gave me while I was his mistress, I developed a distaste for being under a man's control. I am not a precious doll for display."

"That was in public." Rafe smirked, "What were you to him when darkness settled over your estates and the servants were commanded away?"

"Lord Norisht considered himself something of a master-trainer. Of his animals, of his soldiers, of his women. I was to respond to his word with no question or contradiction. His command would be my action."

Askana suddenly realised what she was saying. She felt a heat rise in her as she looked at the privateer. *How dare you take advantage of our link!*

He did not pounce on the sordid confession. He just watched her with that infuriating smile still playing around his mouth. He rocked back and forth on the back legs of his chair. "Is that what you think is happening here, Askana? You put too much faith in my abilities. If what you believe is true, I could have you dancing for me right now, strictly for my pleasure."

"Do not forget your place, privateer!" She had never danced for any man's pleasure and she was not about to start now, not even in this common man's perverted dreamworld. "It is not as if you are ignorant to the ways of respect. You display that very well before your bloated King Henry. Perhaps you refuse to respect the Queen of Morevi?"

"Respect, Your Majesty, is earned. It is not a birthright."

Askana did not care for his tone or his words. "I suppose the glorified thief of the oceans thinks it his due to lecture others higher than he on the earning of respect. Maybe you refer to my noble lineage? We were left impoverished. I earned our bread and keep the only way I could with Lord Norisht. It was a world of men where women could not inherit land or conduct business. My only option was to become what I am now. If you cannot respect that, so be it. My hatred shaped me. I broke free of my shackles and gave hope to the women of my kingdom and of other realms. In that respect I am a self-made woman and if you still cannot respect me, no matter. You will either show proper reverence during our working relationship or I will demand it from you at blade-point."

She spoke from the heart. It was a summation of herself, of how she had come to be where she was, and it was not often that she explained this to anyone.

The brief silence following her words was shattered by the ridicule of his slow applause. "All that resentment, Askana, and all it taught you was the hatred of men? Let me tell you what I see, shall I?" He pressed a finger to his lips as would a learned scholar or philosopher preparing to answer the truly daunting questions of life. When he answered, his tone was elevated, condescending. "I see a woman created by the men in her life. Mourning the death of her father, who gave her freedom. Taken advantage of by Norisht, who gave her anger. Anger that could be channelled through the Art of War bestowed on her from Kubi-Sogi. Torn with guilt over the sacrifice of her bastard-brother, Markuna, who embodied her strength. And now she is a Queen, steely, hard, and ruthless, but carrying still in her soft core the ashes of a dead love, the dearly departed Telmrant."

Her fingers trembled for an instant, itching to reach for an imaginary sword. To mock her brother was sheer insolence, but he had gone too far with his last slur. "If you dare speak his name again, I will rip your tongue out with my bare hands." The timbre of her voice was civil, even polite, when she spoke. "Telmrant stands so far above you, pirate, that nothing you say touches him, or conceals your envy."

"Envious I may be." He continued, undaunted. "You, however, are blind with vengeance. It almost proved to be the death of you." He laughed callously, "All this for a lover buried under sod and soil with an acorn serving as his gravestone."

He had touched all the hidden hurts in her and mocked them. He mocked her pain. He mocked the loneliness she fought after Telmrant died. She lowered herself enough to try and make him understand who she was. He used it to attack her. It was a betrayal of trust.

This dream was over.

In a few strides she crossed the room and slapped him hard across the face, knocking him free of his chair. Still on the floor, he turned to face her. The blood trickling from the corner of his mouth was not enough. "You will never speak like that to me again! You will not befoul the name of Telmrant pir Hathar pey Casura with your breath!" She raised her hand to strike him again. It did not seem odd to her that she was suddenly clutching one of her daggers. "If you cannot treat me as a Queen then I shall have to make you do it, whether in your Dreamwalk or not."

Rafe's smile melted away as he slowly came to his feet, "Askana, what makes you think this is my dream?"

She could hear her heart pounding in her ears as she stared at Rafe. The conclusion she repeatedly reached was not to her liking. She eventually found her voice, "What in Nadinath's name are you talking about?"

"You say you lack control in this realm when I have been merely a servant to your will." Rafe wiped away the blood from his mouth with a slight laugh, "Think for a moment, Askana. How did I know about the loss of your father and the freedom he granted you when you were a child? How did I know about Markuna, your half-brother and his untimely death? And how did I know of Telmrant's grave? I am but a product of your desire, passions, and will. This is your dream, Askana Moldarin, and yours alone. I am here due to your bidding. I am here because *you* want me here."

"No." Askana shook her head slowly, taking a step back as Rafe closed the distance between them. "You lie, privateer. It is you who have brought me here."

"I am afraid not, Askana. Captain Rafton is not here. I am part of your Dreamscape. This is your dream, Askana Moldarin, and yours alone."

The image of Rafe slowly wove in between the empty tables towards her. Her hand came up quickly, her palm on his chest to make him keep his distance. His flesh felt warm, real. She could feel his chest rising and falling with his breath.

"Stop." Askana shook her head, trying to clear it, to think properly. The dagger was still in her grasp, yet she could not strike. Her mind screamed, *What is happening to me?*

"You know what is happening, Askana," answered Rafe. "I am the voice of your heart. Answer it." He took a step forward, but Askana's hand kept him at a distance. He lifted his chin slightly, grinning at her in the way she knew so well, "Askana, if you do not wish me here, command me away. This is your creation and you alone control it. This is your dream, Askana Moldarin, and yours alone."

"Stop saying that!" Askana could hear her voice beginning to falter. The images of her mind grew cloudy. Distant. Indistinct. She found the strength in her arm weakening, but Rafe did not advance. "This is merely a dream."

"And tell me, Askana, what is a dream? A shadow. Is not a shadow simply an extension of yourself? Even in the dead of night, your shadow is always with you." Rafe moved closer to Askana, her arm giving way to his advance. His hand reached up to her own, still resting against his chest. His grasp was gentle. Comforting. "If you do not want me here, take the dagger in your hand and strike me down with it." She felt her arm begin to go numb. The dagger fell from her grasp, striking with a light ring against the floor. She knew this was a dream, but his touch felt so real. "Let them go. Your father, your mother. Markuna. Telmrant. Even her whom you had to kill." His voice was gentle in her ear. "You must let them go and live, Askana."

Tears were slowly falling down her cheeks. She felt his fingers wipe them away as she wondered why she was crying.

She was then blinded by sunlight spilling into the Captain's Quarters. She wanted to cover her eyes, but something kept her from shielding the white light. She blinked her eyes several times and then turned away towards the opposite wall. There were simple items within view, a number of them being bottles of healing ointments, sutures for the closing of wounds, and a few blood-stained needles.

She was awake. She was alive.

Askana went to rise and found her movement hindered by the shackles on her wrists and ankles.

"You are awake," Coumiran purred. "You were moving in your sleep. A dream?" He laughed softly as his removed his gloves and casually stroked her bare side. "What were you dreaming? Of a lover, perhaps?"

She could not get away from him, from his touch. She schooled herself to lie still. The stroking was to unnerve her, she knew, and she was not going to give him the satisfaction of seeing her try to recoil. He was as close to her as Rafe had been in her dream. His touch was sobering, focusing her thoughts on the immediate present.

"So instead of torture from your scalpels and blades, I am to be tortured by your affections?" Askana tried to ignore the tingling burn in her cheek where the healing tissue tugged against the stitching. "You will regret not killing me."

"Will I, my beloved?" His voice lightened as he stroked the hair free from her face. She refused to react. She was very familiar with this stratagem. Men such as Coumiran were gentle before they struck. "They want to present you alive to King Cedric as part of the spoils of war, but I think otherwise. I have plans for you, my sweet." His head tilted to one side as he gently turned her face to look at the stitches along her jaw and cheek, "Such a pity about the scar." Coumiran took from his belt a small, ornamented knife and gently drew its edge over the stitches. She could not help wincing as the stitches gave way, followed by a slightly nauseating sensation of her skin parting slightly. "The doctor worked so hard to make the stitches small, but even mortal medicine has its limitations." Coumiran gently placed his fingers on the wound and smiled at her with his large black eyes as he spoke, *"Sa' kevit' mahn."*

The cold clutched her. Every muscle in Askana's body seized up, arching her back violently. Her lungs burned as she stopped breathing. Every muscle in her body tingled in the bitter chill. To her horror, she could see what little breath she had escape from her mouth and form into a small, grey puff of mist in the warm air of the cabin.

Then it was over.

Askana collapsed back onto the bed, gasping wildly for air as Coumiran watched with a small twist of satisfaction. While there was risk in attracting the Fellowship with such indulgent magic, it was essential for the body to be perfect. It would be the vessel for Maeve, and he wanted to provide an excellent temple for his goddess.

Askana became acutely aware of her body. She could no longer feel the tingle of a scar along her cheek nor could she feel the other injuries from her battle aboard the *Archangel*. They had all disappeared. She was certain scars from past battles were also erased. The chill still lingered underneath her skin, countered only by the burning rage inside her heart. She was growing to understand Rafe's distaste for sorcery. Coumiran's gloating was hard to bear.

She looked again at him. *No,* she thought, *not gloating—doting.* She could see tenderness in his eyes replacing the wild, obsessive revenge that had been there earlier. Fear began to form inside her.

"And what plans do you have for me?" Askana asked, her voice almost a whisper.

As Coumiran gently traced on her cheek where the scar once was, tears glimmered in his eyes. "I have been so alone in this realm since you left me, but the Fates have brought you back. Askana Moldarin took you from me but Askana Moldarin will also bring you back."

The Caillech had once told a young Askana about magic. All spells have a cost. The penance for the Dark Arts would usually mean one's soul, but for some it would be their sanity and reason. This was one of many reasons for the Fellowship of the Jewels and their strict edicts. Askana could see the toll of the Dark Arts, along with years of bitterness, wrought on Coumiran. The longing in his voice was real enough. She fought a surge of understanding, a sympathetic commiseration. In a strange way the story of his life paralleled hers. They knew the same loss, the same loneliness that always remained hidden so none would know their weakness.

She swallowed hard as she leaned her cheek into his gentle touch, "Tell me, my love," Askana's voice grew softer, a loving tone she had taken advantage of many times in her youth, "how will Askana Moldarin bring me back to you?"

"The Spell of Souls," Coumiran nodded. "I will perform it in the Palace of a Thousand Suns itself, and then you will come back to me."

As he gently laid his head on her chest, she remained perfectly still, not wanting to tip the delicate balance of his perception. It was a loving gesture on his part, meant not for her but for one long dead.

He closed his eyes, relishing the sound of her heart. "It will be all I've longed for, to have you by my side. My Maeve."

Her eyes looked out of the windows of the Eyriener vessel as a wall of sailing ships continued undaunted towards the ports of Arathelle. She could hear her own heartbeat quicken slightly, no doubt pleasing Coumiran. She, however, was cursing herself. All this time she had thought the greatest threat to be the conspiracy brewing against her in Morevi, and perhaps the threat of an Eyriener invasion.

Now the stakes had been raised.

"You failed me once before," Lady Min-Lu said as she surveyed the white magnolia blossom in her hand. "What assurance can you give me that you will not repeat that failure?"

"You will have to take my word for its worth, High Lady."

A bee buzzed happily deep in the breast of a yellow blossom just above her head. A flicker of movement through the fancy holes in the latticework where the blooming vine's tendrils twined assured her he was there, but was he listening to her? The Morev'ar were supposed to be the most lethal and effective faction of the Morevian military but she had not been impressed with their efforts to date.

"Fail me and you will face the consequences. Serve me well and the rewards will be beyond the scope of your dreams."

A soft laugh. "You will not be able to lay a finger on me either way, Lady Min-Lu. My kind make and break nobility. Kings and queens are of small interest to us. All that matters is the future of the realm, and we see a bright future with you upon its throne. Of course, I make it no secret that I covet the *Astarkhan's* place. Something you should consider in your ascent—my loyalty in contrast to his. The old fool is at present attempting to elevate the Morev'ar by supplanting the Royal Guard's position around the King."

She calmly crushed the magnolia in her palm, letting its sweet scent rise into the air. "Do not toy with me, Gidaron. Your task is simple enough. During the battle, our dear King and the High Regent must die while I marshal troops to defend my beloved kingdom. If members of the High Council happen to perish as well, why then all the better. When all is done I will rule Morevi. The Morev'ar will share my power and will have leave to stamp down the Temple."

"I thought you were a Daughter of the Temple, Lady."

He was sarcastic, biting. She would have to remember to remedy that later.

"No Gods or Goddesses determine my fate. No one does that but me." Min-Lu paused for a moment, here eyes studying the silhouette visible through the lattice. "No Kir'shia blood this time. I want their minds clear and the deed done cleanly. No trace must be found leading back to me."

"Those loyal to me shall do it, fear not. The Astarkhan shall fall valiantly protecting the King." A rustle of flowers and foliage followed his final words to her, and then only the sounds of birds and insects remained.

She let the magnolia fall from her hand. Her serving maid followed submissively with the parasol held aloft, protecting her mistress from the sun as they walked leisurely through the gardens. The girl was deaf, a perfect servant in that respect. It had grown tedious, disposing servants that knew too much. She did not believe in the ridiculous principle of treasuring one's own House's retainers beyond what was deemed as their actual worth. Yet having to constantly remove good maids was irritating. It always happened just as they were good enough to please her exacting tastes.

She looked over the clear, open spaces above the Sleeping Dragons. Still no word from Lord Ruain. She knew that he would put into the Arathellian ports soon. This meant time would be narrowing to make all ready. Soon, the Annaki Dynasty would rise.

Askana Moldarin had kept such a narrow view of the world. Her temperament would be her undoing. She answered to a mute Goddess lacking true strength. Above all this, she came from such a common background. Only a true royal should rule the "Silken Box" and Min-Lu had royalty in her blood. Though she enjoyed the freedom that the shift in power had wrought and the potential Morevi now possessed, she also knew that minor nobility should not lead the kingdom into its New Age.

Her eyes closed as she basked in the warmth of sunlight. A smile crept across her face in the vivid memory of her Lord Ruain. Together, they were the future of Eyrie and the destiny of Morevi. In two days time the King would formally address the Council of the Hundred Turi. It would be the last time he would ever do so. No one would know until it was too late. The trap was already set.

In three days time, she—Lady Min-Lu of House Annaki—would be Queen.

His lips were like dry parchment. He knew the feeling all too well from ill-starred ventures at sea. Dehydration, lips cracking from the salt air and sun, skin tingling from the burn. His memories were a muddled swirl of salt and silt, but he remembered rowing with the current in efforts to reach Arathelle before the Eyrieners. *Row*, he thought to himself, *row*. He felt the pain of her wounds becoming one with his own muscles straining against exhaustion.

He remembered eyes, brilliant eyes of joy, concern, and melancholy, looking down on him. The man gave him water that tasted as ambrosia itself. He heard music. A haunting melody stealing over him like weariness, lulling him to sleep.

The light blinded him as his eyes slowly opened. It was a brilliant, clean room. He could smell a hot meal of baked meats, sweet spices, and what he hoped was good wine. The feel of the bed, the size of the chambers, and the absence of windows was enough to tell him this was a prison. He knew he was not in Heaven. The pain in his body reminded him of his mortality. He closed his eyes and focused for a moment on the stinging of his muscles. He needed water. His eyes followed the scent of the meal awaiting him. He smiled pleasantly as he watched a second goblet appear, seemingly from thin air. He knew it contained water.

"I suppose," an icy voice came from as yet an unseen corner of the cell, "you will expect me to fetch it for you, human."

"No," he uttered in a hoarse voice. It was clear some sort of care had been given to him during his sleep. His skin was cool. No blisters on his hands or lips. Still, he was famished and suffered a harsh dryness in his throat. He did manage to summon some wry confidence to his voice, "I am quite capable of helping myself, Lady Lubria."

His knees quickly gave out from underneath him as he tried to stand, but Rafe managed to keep upright by bracing himself against the bed. Lubria merely hissed a laugh as she watched him slowly make his way to the table.

"Where is your arrogance now?" Lubria's tail thrashed from side to side, clearly showing her agitation at having Rafe with her in such close quarters. "I care not for being caged, but to be caged with you, human, is a cruel punishment."

Rafe downed the water loudly, the slurps and gulps magnified in their cell. Lubria twisted her face, repulsed by his grabbing of bread and mutton and stuffing his mouth like a glutton. She thought it ironic humans had called her "beast" when this creature walked freely among them.

He took several deep gulps of Elven wine and savoured the nourishment for a moment, "Our captors are very generous, although I fail to understand why they imprison me. When they found me I was near death."

"Had the Elves not a respect for all life, even for Otherworlders such as your kind, you would be dead upon the shore providing a banquet for vultures."

Rafe merely shook his head as he spoke through a mouthful of food, "I think my tenacity would surprise you." He swallowed the food quickly and grabbed a nearby fig as he finally turned to face his reluctant cellmate. "So I can assume by your presence the *Defiant* made it safely here. Had King Henry's men arrived as well?"

"The Arathellian ports reeked with the stench of Otherworlders. They only preserve you to keep their peace. I heard tell of plans for battles at land and on the sea. Perhaps when the forces of Morevi return, provided they do, we shall be released into the custody of the Queen."

He moved to the door of the cell, the only exit. He studied the strong silver bars as he spoke, "So King Henry's forces have arrived and a party from Morevi has met them. Very good. If the King's Navy proves valiant, we may still have several days lead before the Eyriener forces arrive at Arathelle."

"*They* have a day's lead, human." Lubria huffed, "*We* are imprisoned here."

"Not for long." Rafe reached through the bars of the cell door and felt the lock of the hatch. His fingertips felt the keyhole and gently tapped against the smooth metal casing of the door's lock. The quality of the lock was impressive, its metal a smooth, silvery substance the equal of which he had never seen. A single keyhole normally meant a single latch. The sturdiness of the hatch, however, meant within its casing were mechanics trigging several other latches. *This one would be a challenge*, he thought with a grin, *but not impossible*.

The privateer reached for the pouch normally hanging from his belt. The tools he needed were back on the *Defiant*. He was still wearing only the tattered breeches of the Eyriener sailor. Completely defenceless in this cursed land.

Then his eyes fell on Lubria.

"Why do you look at me that way, human?" Lubria's tail twitched nervously. She could feel a growl rising slowly deep in her chest as Rafe stared at her, a smile starting to form on his face.

"Lubria, we can get out of here. To do so, we have to work together." He held out his hand, but she merely stared at coldly, quietly. "Do not debate the matter any longer. Either kill me," Rafe extended his hand further, "or trust me. Whatever your instincts tell you, listen to them now."

What did her instincts tell her? *It would be so quick, perhaps not as satisfying as the slow death I wish to inflict upon him, but no one—not even the Black Widow—could save him from my grasp*. If she followed instincts alone she would have gutted him by now.

She had another tool humans often believed she lacked—reason. Reason told her Askana had seen fit to put her trust in this man. Perhaps trusting this creature was better than being returned to the Mists.

"I warn you," Lubria hissed as she took Rafe's hand. "Betray me as humans are prone to do and I assure you a painful death."

He gave her a pleasant nod. "And here I thought you would find it difficult to work with me. How silly to underestimate you."

Rafe looked at one of her fur-coated hands, stroking it gently as he studied it. He remembered Artemis, a kitten he and his sister Serena had nursed back to health. Their cat loved to paw and swipe at anything that moved. Balls of wool, lace hems, even the sheath of Rafe's rapier as he walked past. Lubria had all the abilities of a cat and more. *Perhaps she shares some of their anatomy as well,* Rafe thought as he gently pressed down on her knuckle.

The claw emerged slowly from her fingertip. His eyes widened at the length and sharpness of it, the ebony colour seeming to absorb the glare of their cell. Rafe gently felt the smoothness of it. The claw outwardly appeared fragile, but it was as sturdy as a dagger's blade. It would take a great amount of force to break this weapon.

Lubria smiled proudly, "Impressive, is it not? You are one of few mortals to study it so intimately and live."

"I do live a charmed life." Rafe winked as he gently guided her hand through the bars, slipping the tip of the claw into the keyhole.

Lubria found herself in a position she would had never dreamt nor desired. She was pinned between the door to freedom and this odious person of Man. She did not care to be this close to the human, and the growl in her chest swelled as his form pressed even closer to her own. She bucked against him in protest, throwing him a step back. For a moment the tips of the other claws showed themselves.

"Lubria," he smiled pleasantly, stifling the impulse to shove her back. "My intentions are strictly honourable."

"I do not like the liberty you take under these circumstances." Lubria's tail slapped against Rafe's side as she took a deep breath to relax.

"It is not a liberty I take with you," he quipped as he took her hand again. "It is a necessity."

Feeling his skin rubbing against her pelt, she seethed. "Your presence displeases me."

"Have a little faith in me, Lubria," Rafe smiled as he wiggled her hand quickly. "I may prove my worth yet. It takes an exceptional thief such as myself to know any treasure merely awaits an opportunity, any problem merely awaits a solution—"

Lubria's hand suddenly slipped and raised sharply. Rafe let out a small sigh of satisfaction as they heard latches slide away. The hatch swung open.

" —and that every lock merely awaits a key," Rafe bowed gracefully, his hand extending towards freedom. "After you, Mistress Lubria."

The claw tingled inside her hand as she stood apprehensively, massaging the odd sensation. His scent clung to her. She itched to purge it from her fur. Lubria never had much use for mortals, save for Askana and the females loyal to her, particularly at the Temple where she enjoyed the chance to study her lower "kindred" at leisure. It was only Askana who ever treated her with love. It was never a problem to look upon her as "sister". It did not matter to her that the others feared her.

Now she stood indebted to this fool—*twice*—for more than the Queen's life. She did not like owing a mortal.

"We have far to travel, human," Lubria moved by Rafe quickly, her nose in the air as if she was attempting to catch the scent of any Elven soldiers, "if we are to meet the Morevian forces. Come."

He struggled to keep up with her. He could not tell where he was. All the passageways looked the same. Bright white marble and pearl. Smooth surfaces showing no decay or age. Fleeting moments passed running through linking corridors before they emerged into a field where the Morevian troops had stood with their English counterparts. The tracks told Lubria all she needed to know and she slipped away like a shadow. Rafe almost lost her in the growing dusk as they made their escape.

Strange, fantastic buildings and spires loomed above them, silvered by faint starlight. Rafe could not help but turn about as he followed Lubria, his head cast back as a smile crossed his face. He so dearly would have loved to explore this place. The buildings themselves seemed to retain the dying sunlight and reflect the dim light of emerging stars and lit torches along the streets. A faint glow hung over everything.

"This is far too easy, Lubria," Rafe whispered as he caught up with her.

"I agree, human. There are no soldiers on patrol." Lubria stopped for a moment as she took another sniff of the air. "No one stirs in the city this eve." Lubria's head turned and she grinned, showing white, sharp teeth, "But I have the scent of the Morevian forces. They march for the capital city by the Road of the Moon."

"Road of the Moon?" Rafe asked, wishing he had his rapier at his side. "This leads to Morevi?"

"Aye. It doth."

Rafe grabbed a nearby torch and took a deep breath as he tried to see through the jungles ahead. "I follow your lead, Mistress Lubria."

"Even now, perchance they are already gone. Not that I doubt thee, my husband, but thou art sure this was the right action to be taken?"

"I do, though my heart weighs heavy at having to break Ancient Laws in allowing the Creature of the Mists to escape thence. Yet of a surety, if my Ill'ethstréa be not at fault, the path of these two lie together. She shall yet lead him to Morevi where his battle lies."

"Yet Dreams do not lie, my husband. We may not be able any longer to Walk the Dream to reach beyond the winds of Naruihm, but the Dreams that we may have do guide us true." Queen Esharana slipped her arm through his and lightly kissed her husband's shoulder. "Fret not, my King. The Mists shall ever wash towards the cities of Elven-kind like the sea upon the shore. Thou knowest as I do that ours is a stricken race. When the day comes that the Mists call to thee know that I shall be by thy side."

Eharon's brows furrowed for a moment. "Do the Elders question my judgement?"

"Thy reasons were sound. The Elders know as we do that to keep Arathelle safe, we must play the demands of one neighbouring nation against the other." Queen Esharana's tone deepened to the sorrow always beneath her surface. They had long passed their first few centuries when joy and light-heartiness of youth overcame even Elven longing for their homelands. "In my heart, I feel that right is on the side of Queen Askana. Victory must go to Morevi, or Cedric may grow overconfident and seek to extend his reach."

"Is it Thy belief that he wouldst aspire to so much? Yea, perhaps young wolves reach too high. How'ere, warring Eyrieners will be naught to worry us. It is the meddling of the Fellowship we cannot have. It is enough that We send some of Our young to them to learn their ways."

"We have moved rightly, my husband." Esharana leaned against the graceful curve of the balcony railings, gazing inland and already missing the fair city of Tir'Ghazal, hidden in the deep forests. "Mayhaps it will help Morevi, and Askana, on the way to healing."

They had remained anchored at sea for repairs. Finally, after two days, the *Archangel* was ready to resume course. The destroyed cannons were replaced by others in the fleet, and now the afternoon wind favoured their advancement towards Arathelle. The current, however, worked against them. The High Lord Coumiran ordered that oars be put to water. Once more with the *Archangel* leading the fleet, the Eyriener navy was an impressive sight.

The wind tried to snatch at his mask as he nodded in approval. "Boatswain, maintain course and speed." He walked across the top deck to look over charts, plotting their landing in Arathelle and march to Morevi. "Send word to Captain Galdric we will be putting to port before sunset. If the fleet cannot keep pace, give him and the other Fleet Captains orders to join the rowers."

"On your word, High Lord." Boatswain Gennar said nervously as he quickly took leave of him. Already two Boatswains had perished on this ship. He was not about to deny the Dark Merchant's wishes and make it a third.

"High Lord," First Officer Denir spoke. Denir prided himself as being smarter than the late Captain Fenn. He followed the Dark Merchant's orders without question or hesitation, but present cargo warranted his concern. "Please forgive this imprudence, My Lord, but the Morevian may prove an unnecessary hindrance once we set out for Morevi."

Coumiran did not like being questioned. Still, he sympathised with Denir's apprehension at having to travel through the jungles of Morevi with Askana in their midst. The body count was already high without them encountering proper Morevian warriors, but she was worth the risk. Askana was a skilled warrior, sturdy, and in excellent health. A perfect vessel. Maeve would certainly have no complaints.

"A valid question, First Officer." He waited for Denir's shoulders to relax, then continued, his voice never raising in its tenor. "I will explain things to you, but I demand absolute obedience and above all, loyalty. Captain Galdric may be the commander of this fleet now, but I am the leader of this invasion. What I decide is final and unquestionable. Am I clear?"

Denir remembered very well how The Dark Merchant meted out his punishment. He had already altered the Ship's Log to explain the death of Captain Fenn. He remembered his pledge to Eyrie and to the Crown. Safeguard and protect the waters of his homeland. It was an easier time for him back then, before this High Lord. There were either fellow Eyriener countrymen or enemies to the Crown. Darkness and light. Right and wrong. The higher he rose in the ranks of the King's Navy, the more blurred the lines had become.

Denir swallowed hard. "Your word is law on these waters, High Lord Coumiran."

"Excellent. We shall march through Arathelle with Askana Moldarin as our prisoner. She will be bound upon a litter and under heavy guard. Only I will care to her. If any so much as cast an ill eye upon her, they will have to deal with me. Once we enter the Gates of Morevi, we must secure the Palace of a Thousand Suns. When we have done so, I plan to conduct a little ritual—"

"A ritual, my Lord?"

"Yes," His tone told Denir clearly enough that he would tolerate no further questioning. "I will need men to hold the Palace while we are inside."

"Very good. Shall we inform—"

Coumiran's eyes snapped open and stepped closer to Denir, "No one. Only our regiment is to know of this. Am I making myself clear?"

Denir could not move away. There was something about this man that smacked of more than madness. That in itself made his hold on life tenuous. If he told a superior, he might as well be dead already. If he did not, he could still be killed to make sure the secret was never made known.

"Ship ahoy!" cried the *Archangel*'s watch. "Ships ahead!"

Coumiran moved to the edge of the top deck, his eyes scanning the horizon. There appeared to be three ships, grand in scale with sails full and the current rushing them along at a swift pace. Denir passed him a telescope and stood back nervously as Coumiran tried to make out the ships' banners. There was very little he could see at this distance apart from the ships' swiftness across the oceans.

His gloved hands tightened around the telescope but his tone did not change. "A message to Galdric," he spoke as Denir motioned for a quill and small parchment. "Tell him due to the damage we have suffered, we need to slow for further repairs. Allow the fleet to pass, then bring this vessel hard to port. I want a better look at those ships!"

The heavy oars ceased and the *Archangel* dropped back to the rear of the fleet, still approaching the large ships that made no attempts to change their path. With a nod from Coumiran, the order was given and *Archangel* veered away at a sharp angle, breaking off from the fleet's formation and protection. He could not dismiss the oddity about the three advancing ships. Elves usually sailed white ships. Morevi flew green and white colours and were mere junks. These ships were far more foreboding. He could hear calls from the closest vessels. Their pleas as to why the Eyriener flagship now broke free of them remained unanswered as his eyes remained fixed on the ships ahead.

Coumiran then caught the faint outline of another ship—three ships in fact—behind the lead ships. His eye strained through the refracting glass of the telescope to make out yet another three ships. There were now at least nine ships advancing upon them. He had heard of this tactic from the Duke of Norfolk. These were English ships on an intercept course! It meant they carried not only the fearsome cannons on their vessels, but something far more valuable than the arms the Duke of Norfolk had provided to him. Experience. Experience the Eyrieners severely lacked.

"Boatswain, set a course for the Iomer ports from these bearings. Send word to the *Nighthawk* and *Cedric's Pride*. Tell them to break formation." One regiment could take the Palace, but he would need at least three for a chance to reach it. He did not need to hold Songkusai or even the Palace for that matter. All he needed was time. Time to perform the ritual. "Tell them to follow us to Arathelle at all speed."

Pigeons took to the sky, flying for their respective vessels, before Coumiran could finish his orders to the *Archangel*. "Stay clear of those ships and have the rowers double their efforts. Under no circumstances will we deviate from this course."

"But High Lord," Denir spoke. "Three regiments are not enough to stand against the Morevian army. They will not surrender to merely—"

He struck the First Officer in the face with a gloved hand, his eyes quickly turning hard with fury. Denir could taste the coppery tang of his own blood at the corner of his mouth. At one time, he thought the Dark Merchant was mad. Now he was certain.

Sir Thomas Eshton could not help but feel a little disappointed. He was delighted to find the Morevians were a handsome race, and a pleasing number of the women were quite beautiful. They were, however, fierce as wolves! This was particularly true of the ones closest to the female commander called Kalea. He approached a delectable-looking pair who trailed white feathers from their headgear, armed only with compliments and sweet words. Discouragingly enough they debated between themselves whether to simply thrash him soundly or whether he merited a duel. Luckily, they had decided to only laugh full in his face.

Hoping to soften hearts, he approached Kalea, a sternly handsome older woman. Eshton did not mind older women, continuously referring to the Anjara as a "seasoned beauty". He approached her with a delicate flower he had plucked from some bush he saw alongside this "Road of the Moon". He bent to one knee and presented it to her as if it was a Tudor rose.

The shirai came very close to taking off his fingertips. The flower fell apart under his horrified gaze.

"The flower secretes a nectar that, following prolonged exposure, can give one brain fever," she explained before amused Morevians, both male and female. She then followed this humiliation with well-intentioned advice, "Focus on the task at hand, Englishman, the liberation of Morevi. No one needs distractions in battle."

His ears rang with the calls of cicadas, birds, and other unseen animals. Sometimes he could clearly make out the sounds of a fight for supremacy in the greenery, only for the unidentified quarrellers to disappear.

There were a few soft claps of thunder in the distance. Usually this meant an approaching storm. Eshton smiled widely as he looked up to the cloudless sky, a seamless blend from blue to orange to red. The thunder was rolling, rhythmic. To the English, the thunder was a familiar sound.

"Marlow has his hands full," Eshton replaced the pipe back between his lips and took a long puff as another sound of rolling "thunder" sounded over the jungle. "I think the battle has been raging for quite a spell. He may even fight well into the evening. What time and victory he grants us will be as cherished as a gift from Mount Olympus."

"Mount Olympus?" asked Kubi-Sogi as he lowered his own carved pipe. "Is this the palace of your King Henry?"

Eshton and the assembled nobles answered Kubi-Sogi's comment with a hearty guffaw that broke the tension of their sudden alliance. They liked the old Blademaster who had become a liaison between them and the uneasy female Guard. In their short time together, he was regarded by the English as their "grandfather". The term was more than an endearment, but out of respect in watching him handle his men and confer with the Anjara as the seasoned and cunning old commander that he was.

"It is just a bit of myth and legend," Sir Wallace laughed as he clapped Kubi-Sogi on the shoulder kindly.

Eshton took another drag from his pipe and called him, "Blademaster!" They all did so as they could not pronounce his name. "I have sampled many blends of tobacco, but this is lovely."

"Aye, that it is." Lord Agecroft nodded. The Morevian tobacco was not a leaf, but a thick, dark paste that neatly filled his pipe. "There is a delicate, smooth texture to this leaf. I have never enjoyed such a smoke as this."

"Indeed. I believe King Henry would enjoy having this delicacy in Court," added Sir Julian to a chorus of "Aye," and "God's Truth."

Eshton stared at the contents of his pipe, the leaf-paste's sweet scent tickling his nose as he spoke, "Interesting that it tastes so similar and even smokes the same as our import from the *other* New World." A few laughs lifted into the air. "We smoke the leaf itself but it looks as if this sweet tobacco was pulverised."

Kubi-Sogi smiled proudly, "Its preparation and our secret ingredient is what gives the tobacco such a distinct flavour. The leaf grown in our realm is very bitter taken alone so it is cultivated carefully in greenhouses and we must be discerning about the blend."

Agecroft leaned forward to ask curiously, "Pray, what is this secret ingredient?"

"An ingredient found only in Morevi," Kubi-Sogi proclaimed. "We grind the chopped leaf with the night-soil of the *Bek'ria*, a type of small omnivore of the jungle, resembling a cat, which we now breed—"

The gentlemen froze with eyes wide, some in mid-puff of this momentary diversion. Eventually, their gazes returned to Kubi-Sogi who was still describing the Bek'ria in detail.

"Night-soil?" Agecroft finally asked, interrupting Kubi-Sogi's dissertation. "You mean this paste is the dung of a wild cat?"

"We use it as fertiliser as well," Kubi-Sogi peered at Lord Agecroft with a look that made it clear he found the interruption rude. "When the leaves are ground with the night-soil, the end result is what we enjoy now. I am certain we can arrange shipment of the Bek'ria's deposits, provided we can think of a proper way to transport it from..."

As if following choreographed moves in a dance, the English gentlemen set aside their fine pipes. The sweet smell of the tobacco surrounded their cosy fire, its scent now turning some of the gentlemen as green as the surrounding jungles.

All except for Eshton who shrugged and took another deep puff from his pipe, "A fine smoke unparalleled, Blademaster." He scrubbed a hand through his hair as a shrill series of ascending trills and one descending note repeated itself once more. "God's Wounds, when will that blasted bird stop singing?"

"The lookout," Kubi-Sogi said evenly. "Warning the watch of her approach."

Darkness was quickly closing in on their temporary base and the light of campfires danced through the gloom of dusk. They were two days away from Morevi. If the English warships bought them time, there would be three days at the most to prepare for an attack. Both English and Morevian soldiers kept watch along the camp's perimeter as Kubi-Sogi and the Englishmen joined Kalea there.

"The warning came from the watch-leader," she stated, her eyes staring off into the dense jungles before them.

Elunear appeared from out of the growing darkness. Her form was striped with paint of dark green, brown, and black, making her seem invisible as she suddenly emerged out of the foliage. Eshton still had to accustom himself to the fact that in this realm women were the dominant sex. It was hard to accept that this child was the "watch-leader" but if her skill at this age was as fine as Kubi-Sogi and Kalea said it was, she would prove to be a formidable opponent in combat. This was hardly the terrified servant they met in Arathelle, suffering the blow to her honour and her conscience in losing the Queen.

"There is movement coming towards camp. We estimate two or three at the most who followed our tracks off the Road of the Moon."

"Elunear, you serve us well," the Anjara nodded.

The child's desperation was still fresh in her mind. She had been cleared of any suspicion towards the Crown following documented accounts from the Sea Wolf's crew. To allay misplaced guilt, the Anjara subjected her to several drills, a penance in itself. She needed her confidence restored before the impending battle and therefore was assigned as "watch-leader".

"Spies?" Agecroft asked with some concern.

"Spies of Eyrie work alone. If they are in pairs, it is less for surveillance and more for sabotage." Kalea motioned with her head to have Elunear stand alongside her.

"My Captain, there is more." The jungle sounds began to subside, eventually leaving only Elunear's voice against the eerie silence. "They did not move as the Eyrieners do. It was as if they had tracking dogs with them."

The sound of a branch rustling caused their heads to snap forward. There was only darkness. Something in the jungle had hushed the surrounding nightlife. Kubi-Sogi, Kalea, and Elunear grasped their shirai while Agecroft and Sir Julian produced rapiers and daggers. The idle talk around nearby fires died away, the camp's attention turning to the shadows of the jungle.

Then came the sound of a crow. It cawed three times. The bird sounded ill.

"Just a moment," Eshton smiled, removing from a nearby English soldier his rifle. "I think we can stand down. I believe we have a friend in our midst."

Eshton pulled back the hammer of the rifle and aimed high for the branches of the trees before them. The rifle fire cracked sharply in the dusk air, sending a flock of bats into the air with a series of high-pitched squeals. Bark and wood ripped away from the distant tree as a heavy branch fell.

"Damn you, Eshton!!!" a voice shouted from the darkness. "You bastard!"

Eshton gave a hearty laugh as his comrades' blades lowered, "As I suspected. It's Captain Rafton!"

Stepping into the light of many guards and soldiers were two figures, one an Englishmen and the other causing the Maidens to rise to their feet and the younger Englishmen to take to their heels into the shadows of the camp. Lubria's eyes glowed in the firelight as she and Rafe approached.

"Rafton!" Eshton called broadly over the rising exclamations of his peers, "Do you have those ten shillings I won from you at betting?"

"Eshton, you are of a higher station than I but do not forget that I am the better card player," Rafe huffed. "It will be a cold day in Hell before I pay you. You are a horrible cheat!"

"Not as horrible as that bird call." He slapped the privateer's shoulder lightly, "What was that? A crow striken by the plague?"

"You must forgive me for my ill-prepared call, but I have endured a rather horrid few days—"

Shirai blades seemed to reach from the darkness to surround the soldier and privateer. One step in any direction and Rafe's throat would be cut. An awkward silence fell over the English subjects as Kubi-Sogi and the Anjara stepped forward.

"So this is the pirate Rafe Rafton?" Kalea asked with an arched eyebrow, her eyes surveying him head to toe. So many ships had fallen to this man that the Queen herself had sworn to have his head presented to the Council. It was hard to believe this was the same man Askana had hired. "You have much to explain to Kubi-Sogi and I."

"The Queen lives, if that is what you want to know." Rafe's eyes nervously skipped from shirai to shirai.

"How can you speak so certainly?" Kalea seethed, her own shirai rising to rest at the base of Rafe's throat.

What is it about shirai blades and my throat? Rafe thought bitterly. "Believe me, I know." With so many Englishmen present, he dared not challenge their beliefs any more. He could only imagine with a grin their audience with the Elves of Arathelle. A shame to miss such a spectacle. He then turned his eyes to Kubi-Sogi. "She is prisoner on the flagship of the Eyriener navy—and oh, the stories I have to tell."

The shirai lowered and pulled away as Kubi-Sogi stepped forward, "Well, you have come full circle, boy. I thought your incautious tongue and your arrogance might have brought about your demise, either at the hands of Eyrieners or the Queen herself."

"Believe me, Blademaster," purred Lubria, "I do think he tries Her Majesty, but he has served her—" Lubria forced the next words from her lips, hints of surprise and frustration mixed in her almost inaudible tone, "—most valiantly."

"Has he?" The Anjara looked him over again, "This known enemy of Morevian sea trade is now Protector of the Crown?"

"The Queen lives because of him," Lubria nodded. "He hath delivered me from the captivity in Arathelle for he knows you do desire me to fight with you." Her eyes returned to Rafe, "The human speaks true. We have many tales to tell of this journey."

"My Captain!" boomed the voice of the Moor. Rafe found himself picked up in a friendly embrace by his loyal First Officer while his crew called out jests and cheers. The hard slap of hands on his shoulders and back rang in the air as Nassir beamed, "My Captain, you truly sail with the blessings of Muhammad! When we left you—"

"Aye, my friend," Rafe nodded, a touch overwhelmed by the reception of his crew. "But the good Lord was not ready for me in Heaven and Satan himself was afraid I would lead his minions in mutiny!" The laughter rose heartily as he made his way through his crew to Kubi-Sogi and Kalea, "We have a task before us. Someone fetch me proper clothes. I think these breeches could walk to Morevi without my aid."

As the privateers and Maidens dispersed, Rafe's hand caught Elunear's arm as she meant to return to her post. "Not yet, sweet lass." She shook free of his grasp. Before she could snap back with a retort, Rafe stopped her words with a smile, "Well done, Elunear. The Queen would be proud, but I need you here. You're part of this plan, too."

He needed sleep but he could not rest yet. Kubi-Sogi had brought to light a truth—he had almost come full circle in his adventure with Askana. He knew she lived. He knew Coumiran kept her alive for a reason, and it involved Morevi. Time to lead another leap of faith. "We have little time ahead of us. If we are to face the Eyriener forces, we have to devise a plan that will take advantage of this lead we possess."

"What do you propose, Rafton?" Eshton asked.

"We allow the Eyriener forces to march into Morevi. We give them no resistance. Allow them to enter the city without a shot being fired."

"We will not lay down our weapons so easily!" Kalea snapped loudly. "How can you ask us to surrender—"

"Not surrender, Anjara," Rafe said without letting her words deflate him. "I believe I am beginning to think like Queen Askana. She once told me that she was a weaver of traps. And I think Songkusai would be the perfect place to set a trap of *divide et impera*." The Morevians looked at Rafe blankly. "Divide and conquer. We must learn the city. Know every corner, alley, and crosspath. We must make the Palace their main objective, trap them inside the city, then break their ranks."

"Easier said than done, privateer," Kalea huffed. "Our numbers are small. While we could ask for aid from the Morev'ar, they are a faction of the military we cannot trust implicitly."

"I did not say this would be a perfect plan," Rafe shrugged. "This is a risk, as any strategy is, but with the proper execution, this will work. So—are we agreed?"

The camp fires flickered in the night. The heavens revealed endless pinpoints of light, creating a menagerie of infinity. Against the stars passed patches of clouds that would punch holes of darkness in night's canvas. Joining in the din of the campfires were insects, nightbirds, and other forms of jungle life.

The distant cannon fire had ceased. The Sea Wolf awaited an answer.

Nightmares and Negotiations

The first to see them were the border farmers.

They were simple folk, carving a living out of the jungles by cutting swathes from its green expanse with axe, hoe, and torch. They planted fields of green shoots that would grow into tapioca and corn plants and cultivated rice in paddies flooded with water from the rivers. They had been there since before the luxury crops of Turi and chocha came in demand, before the spices, sandalwood, and tea. Even though food production could never fill the demand, they were the central core of Morevi's agriculture.

Rumours flew fast in Morevi, and the farmers were anxious. Crops of war only yielded destruction, privation, and death. Sometimes total cessation of their way of life. In the days before the War, skirmishes between nobles were common. Nothing more then a few trampled fields, a few dead farmers, enough damage to a village that would serve as an annoyance. The poor and the lowly were never paid compensation. When it was all over, they would come out of hiding to attempt to build a new life out of the fragments of the old one, and pay taxes that were always due too soon. The system had not changed much nor had the time to change properly since the beginning of the New Regime, but the past few years had been fruitful ones. At least there were no more wars between nobles. To the people it seemed that the stars shone only for Queen Askana Moldarin.

Everything changed in the month. War was now imminent by the sounds preceding those on the Road of the Moon. Sounds of armour against armour, of running feet and galloping hooves. The rasp of hair against metal and the voices of men, women, and horses.

The borders of Morevi were marked on one side by the contour of the Sleeping Dragons, and extended to the last yard of explored jungle to the South and East, but North they shared a border with Arathelle. Here, lines were defined by markers of carved smoke quartz and scorched earth. Legend had it that the first Elves created a magical barrier as impenetrable as the side of the mountain. Anything that touched it turned to ash. The only way in and out was through carefully guarded doorways. Now only the lines and the tall markers remained. The Road of the Moon ended at one such line burnt into the ground, connecting to the wide road that led to Songkusai.

Late yesterday the shields of Arathelle were raised. Huge domes of misty blue that shone faintly in the sun and locked in all of the Elven nation, forest and jungle in a wall of magic. The only areas left clear were half a mile on either side of the ports, creating a path leading to the Road of the Moon. The sight was beautiful, awe-inspiring, and terrifying because it heralded a threat of greater proportions. Arathelle was no longer a buffer against Eyire.

Now, down the wide, dirt road, came the only line of defence against what was to come.

They had not brought horses with them. At first it had been the subject of a minor debate among the Morevians whether they would walk or, for the more fit, run. Eventually, the conclusion was that none of the Otherworlders were in the physical condition for such activity. As a result, all the Royal Guard and soldiers gave up their mounts, save Kubi-Sogi and Kalea. Even so, that provided only twenty horses. The English troops and pirates had to fend as best as they could on foot, with a lot of chivvying from their Morevian guides. It became a competition of sorts first between natives and Otherworlders, eventually turning into a battle of genders. The physical challenges were only the beginning. When they paused, weary and footsore, the English were drilled mercilessly by the Morevians on the layout of the capital city, which would serve to educate them until their arrival to the city itself.

Rafe urged his horse forward to draw abreast of the Anjara. "How much longer till we reach Songkusai?"

She glanced at him as one might glance at an annoying fly. "We shall be there before nightfall." Immediately her gaze settled elsewhere, and she spurred her brown charger forward.

He frowned, exasperated as he caught other gazes of the Royal Guard watching their leader. Watching him. It was a look that both Palace and Royal Guard shared when he was close. 'Chillingly civil' was the best description he could give for the Morevian attitude towards him so far.

"Not giving you the time of day, is she?" Eshton mournfully commented, "The lady spurns my attentions as well. Sometimes I think I may be losing my incomparable charm."

In spite of himself the privateer laughed. "By God, Eshton! And I thought my unending appreciation of the fairer sex was incorrigible! No, the Anjara, much like the rest of Her Grace's subjects are simply extending that endearing Morevian welcome that cuts me to the quick as would their shirai. After serving their Queen, I fail to understand it."

"I would believe the reason for it is obvious, if you pardon my interruption," said the Blademaster approaching from behind them.

"Why?" Rafe shrugged. "Because I am a man? But so are all the others!"

The old man clicked his tongue and chuckled, "Just a man, are you? You, the Sea Wolf of Naruihm?"

"The Sea Wolf?" Eshton asked with amusement.

Rafe had not made his alias common knowledge in his world for good reasons. Sir Thomas Eshton was one of them. "Not another word from you, Thomas."

Kubi-Sogi continued with a chiding grin, "You Otherworlders. Always so hasty. Contrary to what you may believe, the women of Morevi do not strive to murder every man they meet. In the first few months after the War, perhaps. Even then a good many sisters and wives, particularly among the common people, hid their menfolk so they would survive the Great Purging."

Eshton swallowed. "Somehow, that does not reassure me, and does not answer the Captain's question."

"Patience, youngling, is a virtue. Captain Rafton here believes himself to be just a man like any other man. In the eyes of a good many Morevians before his 'grand adventure' with our Queen, there was no trouble. Then suddenly we discover the Queen missing and in the company of a common privateer. Royal squabbles ensue among the members of the Council, splitting it down the middle. The Raising occurs, placing a king upon a throne reserved only for a queen. A stumble backwards for the Council and Ruling Ladies, even if the Consort is merely a puppet. Then Eyriener ports are decimated, provoking King Cedric to wage war. So, obviously, Captain Rafton is seen as an extraordinary man—the sole cause of the strife in Morevi." He then leaned over towards Eshton. "And if I were you, youngling, I would not annoy Kalea any further. Women tend to become snappish and bad-tempered at her time in life until true age catches up with them."

With that, the Blademaster moved ahead with a final glare at Rafe Rafton. *Just a man, indeed,* he scoffed silently.

"Canny old boy, is he not?" Eshton shook his head in light wonder. "She looks so much younger."

"You always did enjoy the favours of older women," Rafe said. "Heed the Blademaster's warning, my friend. Leave the Captain of the Royal Guard alone."

"I always enjoy a challenge," Eshton then gave Rafe a wry smile, "Master *Sea Wolf.*"

The only warning they received was the slight rustle of the undergrowth very close to them. Eshton's horse shied a little with a worried neigh.

"I wouldst suggest that you spur your mounts instead of prattling away like old women," Lubria hissed with her usual amiability. "Even on horseback thou art slower than the runners."

She was gone again, melting in to the green rows of corn alongside the road.

"Now *that,*" said Eshton dreamily at the last flash of the tiger-striped pelt, "is a challenge."

"I have only one piece of advice to give you concerning the Lady Lubria. Life is more pleasant when you have eyes to see it through."

Rafe had been to Songkusai before, always in secret. His crew thought he was insane in daring a closer look at the city. Now, in the dimming light of dusk, he approached it in the open. No disguise. No deception. This was his opportunity to explore. Two days to memorise every nook, every cranny. As its walls began to loom overhead, Rafe silently wished for another day, perhaps two by the grace of God and Lord Marlow's skill at warfare on the ocean. Their task began to take on a new, daunting quality as the massive city gates opened before them.

The trampling of feet announced the unit of soldiers marching through its entrance. Their procession came to a halt as these soldiers in red and gold enamelled armour took a defensive formation, digging their feet into the ground. Archers stood ready. Men gripped swords and maces. The English noticed the mark of the Turi was absent from their breast armour. These men were of the Old Guard who defended Morevi in the Old Regime. By the looks of the Royal Guard, and even Kubi-Sogi and his Palace Guard, there was an uncertainty if the Old Guard would give their loyalty to the new Queen. They remained loyal in their service to the realm. As it was with the Morev'ar, there was no proclamation from their commander in pledging their lives to Askana. Winning their service was one of Kubi-Sogi's goals.

The Old Guard's Captain stepped forward to issue his challenge, eyes running swiftly over the strange garb of the Englishmen. "Halt in the name of the King!"

"The word sits too easily on the man's tongue," the Anjara whispered angrily to the Blademaster. "I thought these men were loyal to you. How quickly they change in your absence."

"The way you snap, Kalea, I would have thought he pinched your rump," muttered Kubi-Sogi in a rare moment of irritation. "The King has been raised to his new position. Either they use his name or they are hanged for treason by the Regent's orders." As he edged his horse forward to the soldier, he raised his voice. "It is I, Kubi-Sogi Karoshiwa, Blademaster to the Queen and General of the Kingdom's Armies. Stand down and let us pass."

The officer relaxed visibly, hand leaving the hilt of his ru-yilei across his back, the beginnings of a smile dawning on his face. "It is good to have you back, General." His eye flickered over the company again. "You bring allies?"

"Yes, Her Majesty Queen Askana Moldarin has sent us allies from a far-off land called England."

"The Queen is alive?!"

Kubi-Sogi spoke deliberately and with conviction. "Yes. She comes home."

The captain turned to the Old Guard behind him and shouted *"Kashiro ti-wanshi! Re ghina ish Askana ha Molarin me kana! Te oshi ye-hasha!!!"* He raised his a fist into the air. The soldiers suddenly erupted into cheers, clapping their gauntlets against breastplates with a clatter that made the English raise their brows. He then turned back to Kubi-Sogi, "The Dawn smiles on us! We shall win this war and drive back the invaders. The Queen returns to Morevi!"

Rafe breathed a sigh of relief in his saddle. The odds were turning in their favour.

"The war has already begun at sea." The Blademaster's face turned grim. "We must make haste and prepare the city. Spread word to expect runners. Many runners, perhaps three hours later."

The officer bowed in traditional Morevian fashion, fist to heart. "Your pardon, General, but the Regent has issued a command directing every soldier to tell the Anjara and your honoured self to seek audience immediately upon your return."

Kubi-Sogi cast a glance to the Anjara and then to the Palace rising high in the distance. The Palace of a Thousand Suns was, in its own manner, a nation in itself. The Council and the Collected Houses were preparing for an address from their King. The Guard could still move in secret, provided the word passed between the troops was done in the Old Ways. "Use the network and call the Old Guard to order. We cannot announce our arrival to Court or Council. We must maintain our stealth in this conspiracy to the Crown and this war upon our horizon."

The commander repeated the salute, "On your word, General. May the Gods herald the return of our blessed sovereign, Askana Moldarin!"

"The love of the soldiers for their Queen seems great, but even greater is their faith in her," commented Eshton.

Rafe remained silent as he urged his horse forward into Morevi's capital city of Songkusai. He knew from the talk in the streets the War of the Fan and Slipper was still fresh in the men's minds. Hearing about this "Great Purging" could only make him wonder how deep the animosity could be against the First Queen. Still, one thing the men could not deny was Her Majesty's strength. Rafe knew from Morevi's history that Askana's prowess on the battlefield and from behind a planning table was nothing less than impressive. It helped that the last three kings were weak, spineless. Useless in war. Rafe felt a surprising pang for her suddenly. She sacrificed so much and worked so hard for her people to regard her only as a lioness to defend them from the wolves. Did they truly love her as she loved them? He regretted their inability to see the Queen he fought alongside. Their loyalty would never be questioned again.

Eshton suddenly spoke, breaking Rafe's solemn thought. "I am surprised that her armies are predominantly male. I expected—"

"The women warriors are in the Royal Guard, a faction large enough to form a sixth of the army," interjected Kalea. "An enormous achievement in the time since the days of the Great Ascension. Most of the Sisters, though, are with the Temple."

"What temple?" Eshton asked as the Anjara moved ahead to take lead.

The privateer hid a small smile at the stories he could tell the incorrigible woman-chaser beside him. "It makes for a long story, Sir Thomas, of epic proportions. Remind me to explain it to you another time."

His grin soon faded as they progressed further into the city. It was a beautiful place, concealed within the savagery of the jungle. Buildings of a cream-coloured hard stone, roofed with colourfully glazed tiles. Some buildings were constructed of pearl-white marble with scant traces of deep green, grey, and black. There were other domiciles with fanciful latticework and carved walls, doors, and window frames in the ornamental Morevian style. The streets were wide and clean unlike those of London, with a highly sophisticated drainage system that his country would do well to imitate. In matters of cleanliness and city-planning, the Morevians were high above the English.

Pleasant though it was, the ride raised the hairs on his nape.

There was a tense, thick feel to the air. The feeling of a city waiting for war. The streets were curiously empty of people. Where throngs should have moved, only a scant few conducted trade and went about their daily business. More than half the shops were closed, and there was a conspicuous absence of foreigners. The people stared at the English as they passed with unreadable dark eyes. They could feel gazes from behind doors and shutters. It was not disdain they sensed, not overt hostility. Just wariness. Suspicion. Anxiety. Rolling over them all like a fog. Apart from their own horses and the march of the armies, only the gurgling coos of pigeons could be heard in the streets.

"As still as a tomb, My Captain," came the thick Persian voice of Nassir.

Rafe gave a simple nod in reply as he continued to study the city. Generations built outward until the buildings bled into each other like a growing mass of coral, particularly in the older sections. A network of streets linked by narrow, dark alleys and made into a maze by later additions. An invading army could die there, under the swords of Morevi.

He looked at the city surrounding him once more, and felt a flame of hate for her. She was Morevi, a worn old dame made up with powder and paint and smothered in costly fabrics, crowned with riches over which her scheming nobility squabbled and sickened with corrupt politics, tradition, and dark-shadowed plots. *My country, for which I paid with blood and spirit and heart*, rang her words in his mind. Even though it was a dream, she held a ferocious love in her eyes as she said it. How could he explain to her that she loved an ageing whore? How could he explain to himself why he felt such jealousy?

Still far from the Palace of a Thousand Suns that rose high above the city, the forces came to a halt by a large building. A modest place for its people to meet. Here, the plans and strategies would be finalised.

"Time," Kalea said to Rafe in a sharp tone of annoyance. "We are running short of time."

He glanced up, "Remember, we must make their goal their trap. We will barricade alleyways and footpaths, leaving only a select few open. We will lead them to the Palace. There, we will make our stand and then drive back into the city, back to where we want them. Then, we will close in and systematically remove the threat to Morevi."

All around him, the men and women captains clutched shirai, atriah, and ru-yilei, outraged. The Anjara fixed him with a hard dark eye. "You ask much, pirate, particularly with the last. It will not be easy, but it shall be done." With a moment's glare at the privateer, she was gone.

"Is the whole war to take place in the city?" asked Eshton in astonishment.

"According to the plans from the *Archangel*, once Songkusai fell, it was to be their keep as they launched offensives against Renai, then Anderis. Lahsa and the surrounding villages would be last as Eyriener re-enforcements would arrive." Rafe stood over a giant map with Kubi-Sogi, Eshton, Agecroft, and Morevian lieutenants of both sexes around him. His fingers pointed to a barren spot of the map where he tapped it lightly, "Depending on what forces survive Marlow's front, we can greet any unwelcome guests here."

"The Kinessa Plains," Kubi-Sogi nodded approvingly. "A good place for a final stand. Yet we will not know the numbers to expect. Therein lies one of many flaws in your plan, boy."

"That is why this is called 'a leap of faith', Blademaster. Much of the success of this plan rides in the nautical capabilities of good Lord Marlow."

"Your faith is inspiring but you must know that moving in secret limits our numbers," Kubi-Sogi sighed heavily. The Morevians looked to one another, hanging their heads low. "Our collected infantry between the Old Guard, the Palace Guard, and the Royal Guard amounts to only six full garrisons."

"Six?" scoffed Rafe. "One ship in the Eyriener fleet holds a full garrison! Marlow is capable, but the Eyriener fleet numbered forty. Even if, by the Grace of God, the Eyrieners are reduced to six ships we will still be evenly matched."

"We can call upon House Soldiers from the Collected Nobility. If they make haste we can increase the numbers on the Kinessa Plains to a thousand, provided we can count on their numbers and their loyalty."

"We overlook one detail. The High Lord Coumiran. Knowing old Handsome as I do, I can assure you he will lead the invasion on Songkusai. He will be focused on one thing and one thing only—taking the Palace. We can use his ambition to our advantage by focusing our forces here," Rafe pointed at the city gates. "And, of course, at the Palace. The English will make a stand with your military while re-enforcements under the command of my crew will take positions throughout the city."

"Re-enforcements?" Kubi-Sogi asked. "Where will our re-enforcements come from?"

"The citizens of Morevi," Rafe said with a nod. "Every man, woman, and child. An army of the common people who have everything to lose if we do. With the people behind us, we can spare a garrison to lead the House Soldiers."

It was a plan unlike any conceived in the history of Morevi. It would either be their finest hour or the most horrific bloodbath of Naruihm. Rafe thought for a moment to the commoners he caught glimpses of in the streets. These terrified wretches would now turn the odds of this 'leap'. *Dear God*, Rafe prayed silently, *fight alongside us from Your Hallowed Kingdom!* "Rally the people of the city. Have them assemble here. Tell them they must fight to liberate she who travels now as prisoner of the enemy."

"Who?" Eshton asked, the pirate's tone stealing his attention from the map.

"The Queen," Rafe stated.

Kubi-Sogi's eyes narrowed under white brows, "How would you know such a thing, boy?"

"A hunch, General," Rafe said, his wrists tingling slightly as if the circulation were being cut off. "I follow my instincts."

"Exceptional. This is truly exceptional."

Jermal was beaming. He read the address to the Council for a third time, trying the words out in his mind. This was Dirare's writing, but she had carefully and cleverly tinged it with Askana's tone. The speech in his hands was his proof that the High Regent was wary enough to obey him in some things at least.

Her muscles ached from the smile she had chiselled into her face. The speech was a sop to his blind loyalty to Askana, but she could feel her tolerance ebbing away. She gave a slight bow to acknowledge his praise. "You honour me, Your Majesty," Dirare said evenly. Never had it pained her so much to speak those two words.

"Truly this is lovely, Dirare." Jermal set the address before him and refilled his chalice, "Join me for a drink to celebrate."

"A celebration?" Dirare relaxed her smile for a moment.

"To celebrate the New Age of Morevi." Jermal raised his glass, holding the dark wine to the light, "The Throne of Morevi is now complete with a King to sit alongside its Sovereign Queen. I think it's cause enough for celebration."

Dirare's smile had faded completely by the time the goblet reached his lips. She turned and climbed the two steps up to the cushions, knowing that he had more to say. Lately, his head had swollen to fit his crown and he would prattle incessantly as if his words held some sort of merit with her and the High Council.

"The War of the Fan and Slipper was a revolt, but it was also about revenge. The same stands for the Great Purging. Families were broken, men slaughtered and driven out of the kingdom. Women treated their menfolk harshly for fear of being accused of not supporting the reformation." Jermal shook his head as he reflected on Morevi's bloody history of recent years. Askana had brought her people so far since that time, perhaps bringing them from a dangerous brink of self-extinction, from their own sloth and corruption. Still, the kingdom was very vulnerable. Together, upon her return, Askana and he would change that. He spoke with the strength of conviction as he said, "I believe the arrival of a King to complement the Queen delivers a powerful message to the people. One of unity, and I dare hope, a measure of equality."

"It is quite a blessing to have a King with vision," Dirare said flatly. Again, her smile returned. Cordial. Dutiful. "We dared not hope that an Otherworlder would love so passionately a land that was not his."

Jermal stared at the intricate gold designs at the rim of his goblet, his grin the only response to the faint touch of sarcasm he heard. It was true. Somehow he had come to love this realm, regardless of its cruelty to his gender. "Sometimes I think there is sorcery in the air." He joined her on the cushions and said truthfully, "I cannot imagine a life outside of Morevi now. My old memories seem very distant."

Of course, Dirare thought. *The life of a king would make the life of a thief seem distant.* "Forgive my curiosity that questions Your Majesty, but do you think the High Council shares your vision?" There was some challenge to her voice. "You have my guidance and support, but I cannot speak for all."

"Dirare, your words reflect Askana's views and mine." He looked at her for a moment, picturing Dirare penning the speech with teeth clenched so hard they were probably cracked in several places. "The people know that I'm not ruling according to my own impulses. We are only progressing with the plan Askana laid out long ago. I want her to return to find her homeland further along the path towards peace, harmony, and prosperity."

"Your Majesty," Dirare intertwined her fingers together, touching her two index fingers lightly to her lips as she spoke carefully. "Have you given a moment's thought to the fate of Morevi if the Queen is dead?"

"No, for she is not, Dirare. I will have no one in my service or my company who wishes so."

Dirare's eyes quickly darted to Jermal. She was an accomplished politician. Jermal, barely a novice. She immediately heard the edge to his voice. "Your optimism is inspirational, but unrealistic, if I may be so bold—"

"You may not," Jermal stated sharply. He gave a deep sigh, shaking his head, "I thought this matter already closed."

"You made your wishes clear, Your Majesty, but as your Royal Adviser I would not be performing my duty if I did not bring to your attention every possible situation which might arise." She paused for emphasis then continued, "If the Queen is dead, we may face civil war."

Jermal tried not to think about the possibility. He knew in his heart that she was not dead. Regardless, the question remained—how long would it be before the people of Morevi lost hope and decided she was dead? The eventual proclamation that the dead body found in Askana's chambers was that of a handmaid barely beat back the rumours of her death. A monarch cannot leave her country for too long, even in capable hands. He knew that he was protected only by the lingering hope of the Queen's return.

He was well aware of the feelings in Council and Court. The women who thought they could rule Morevi better than Askana would enjoy seeing him fall so soon after The Raising. There were a few women, precious few, who enjoyed life under the Old Regime and were encouraged by his coronation. The people, still adjusting from male-rule to female-rule, swung like a pendulum.

His life hung by a thread.

Dirare watched his face and smiled to herself. He was but a few steps from being forced to the Centre of the Winds. It was time to position her Samsagi and Temples.

"Therefore, Your Grace, I think you should read *this* before the Collected Houses of Morevi." From the folds of her robes, Dirare produced a second parchment and handed it to Jermal, removing her original speech from his now faltering grasp. "The tone is *different* from what you requested, but I wholeheartedly believe this will be equally effective, if not more so, than the other."

As Jermal read the speech, a cold sweat broke out on his back. This new address remained notably free of any influences from the First Queen. The more he read, the less it sounded like a commencement to the Collected Houses. It was a eulogy. This address would all but formally pronounce the death of Askana Moldarin and remove the balance on which he stood so precariously.

"No." Even to himself Jermal's voice sounded dry. "This, Dirare, goes very far from protecting myself or Askana. I am surprised you had the brass to give this to me."

Dirare raised an eyebrow at his crass remark. It so proved her point about Jermal. Dress the man up in finery and gold, call him King, and still it does nothing but decorate a common, base nature.

"I know no other way," Dirare nodded slowly in satisfaction. "You choose the wrong tactic. You must put this uncertainty over the Queen to rest. Then only can you truly consolidate your position as King, integrate yourself with the different power factions. We must regain order."

"Not this way! Only under the guidance of Askana Molda—"

"Askana Moldarin is not present and you are but a figurehead representing her interests. Nothing more!" Dirare's eyes slit like the eyes of a predator as she addressed him with no reverence or respect. "The only reason you continue to represent her is because of my very real presence here. If you like, I can always step down as Regent and allow you to rule on your own merit. If you do well, I am sure the Morev'ar will lay down their lives to protect you."

"The Royal Guard will protect me." Jermal's fingers clenched on the parchment. In a fleeting moment, he wished it were the papers for Dirare's execution.

The final defence. His Sword was valiantly trying to protect him. This was a tactic she expected. Always the last, desperate act before forcing the Queen to surrender in the Centre of the Winds. "I am told that the Anjara and the Blademaster left with a good number of their captains and lieutenants a few days ago. Tactical training, so they said. It does make one curious as to what tactics they are training, in seclusion." She rose from her place opposite of Jermal. She gave no obeisance to him as she spoke, "I shall take my leave now, Your Majesty. I have already taken too much of your time."

Jermal watched her walk to the door. If she left his chambers with those words being the last shared between them, he would be completely and utterly alone. His rage turned to ashes in his mouth as he made himself say, "Wait, Dirare!" She paused three steps from the door, but did not turn back. "Please." He could not rule alone. He knew it. "I need you."

"Yes." Dirare remained with her back to him, turning her head ever so slightly in order to speak to him over her shoulder. Her voice never raised beyond a calm, polite tone. Control. Total. Absolute. "You need me, Jermal. Never forget that. For if the Morev'ar under the influences of the regime do not turn upon you, the women of Morevi will."

Jermal could not bring himself to speak. He silently stared at the new speech, the parchment crumpled where his hand had clenched on it. He had to believe that Askana would return. She could not be dead. Hearing the doors of his chambers close with a soft click, he felt a swift wave of hatred pass through him. For Askana in leaving him without a single word. For Dirare in the forcing of his hand. For Morevi and the women who rule it. *Survival*, Jermal thought to himself. That was all that mattered.

Outside the Royal Apartments, Dirare let the door close behind her. She had never looked more radiant.

The jungle was cool, for it was dusk. The time of twilight when the real and the unreal blended together into beauty. She could see the greys and greens so vividly, feel the brush of the cool leaves on her skin, smell the crushed vegetation under her feet and the heavy, intoxicating bloom of night flowers. A cathedral of lush wilderness, as magnificent as Morevi itself.

She wore the red linens and tan hide of the Royal Guard, a naked shirai in her hand, but her hair was loose, falling silken down her shoulders and braided with flowers, crowned with jasmine and magnolia. Beaten silver cuffs tight on her upper arms. She kept on walking, listening to the sounds of night. Everything was as familiar to her as home. In a way, it was home. A stand of venerable shodara trees came into view, old, immense in diameter, aerial roots hanging down like curtains.

Enter, the Voice called.

A cloud of small white butterflies rose in a spiralling column as she disturbed them, so that for a moment she did not see the statue in the clearing within the ring of trees. It was of grey stone, beautiful yet so simply carved. A figure split into three, facing in three directions. Three faces, three pairs of arms, three torsos in a pose of immeasurable grace captured in stone by the artist. The Maiden. The Mother. The Destroyer.

She knelt in the soft grass, and knew peace as she closed her eyes. "My Mother, the Mother of all women, the Goddess of the Eternal Garden."

The three faces were looking at her, the arms lowering, the eyes full of supreme life. The mouths did not open, yet the voices that spoke were of one mind, one heart. *Who art thou, My daughter?*

"I am Askana, Great Mother. A supplicant." There were no titles before Nadinath. She was no longer a queen, or even a High Priestess.

What dost thou wish of Me?

"I beg Your aid, Great Mother. Aid me to win this battle for the sake of all women, for the sake of Your Worship. Aid me in my fight for Morevi, the home of Your daughters. Aid me in my task to protect the Temple, or we shall be crushed again below the heels of men!"

The eyes blinked slowly, the heads swayed. *Temples mean naught to Me, My child, for I livest in the hearts of My children and truly so am I Eternal for I shall never die in memory. Thy kingdom means naught to Me, but for the love of thou and a fraction of My children bear for it. My true kingdom is not kept within mortal boundaries. My daughters live scattered across all the earth. I ask thee what is thy wish and thou hast not answered, daughter. Thou hast voiced the prayer for all My daughters, which I hear already, even in this hour. I ask thee, what dost thou wish of Me for thyself?*

"I am confused, O Goddess. What is Your meaning?"

Thou dost not know Me true, and thou dost not know thyself. Come to Me, daughter, ask of Me My Name.

As if lifted by unseen hands, she rose slowly to her feet. It was a mystery how she knew what must be done, but she approached the living statue, under the gaze of all eyes.

She asked the face on the left, "Who are you?"

The graceful lines of the arms flowed as if in dance. The hands held a flute and a book, the carved stone hair loose and rippling. *I am the Spring, the Beginning. I am Youth and that which is pure. I am Knowledge and Art. I am part of thee.*

"Who are you?" she asked the one in the centre.

The face was the same, yet wiser, placid. The hair was in a crown of braids, her breasts were not covered by her robes. Her hands held a vial and a flame. *I am the Fount of all Life. I am She who cares for all young and all wild things. I am the Healer and the Creator. I am part of thee.*

"Who are you?" she asked the one on the right.

In this face, there was no sweetness, no warmth. The brow was furrowed slightly, making her expression foreboding. The shirai and the ru-yilei drew back for her, and the face bent towards her.

I am Darkness, embarked on the course of world annihilation. I am Time, the Devourer of everything. I am She who prepares the way for the New Dawn. I am part of thee.

She stepped back. Again, the Goddess spoke. *Thou art incomplete, unhappy, discontent, for thou overlookst one side of Me and thyself.*

Askana stretched out her arms, beseeching. "What have I overlooked? Show me in Your mercy!"

Look behind Me, child. Ask Me who I am.

Mystified, she moved slowly around the pedestal as the three watched her. A bird twittered sweetly in the silence.

A fourth face smiled at her radiantly, *Here, my daughter.*

This one was embedded in the back of the central figure. Only part of her was visible. Half-finished, she was still beautifully carved and waiting for the artist to return and finish her work. Unlike the others, her features were alight with laughter and unabashed joy. Unlike the others, she was not clothed save for carved flowers, her perfect curvature lush and inviting. Her hands, reaching out from her indistinct body, held a blossom and a basin full of clear, still water. *My beloved child. Ask Me My Name.*

Her voice trembled in its whisper, "Who are you?"

A sigh like a thousand whispered words. *I am Womanhood and Fulfilment. I am Desire and Want. I am Sensuality. I am Love. Thou hast shut Me out of thee.*

She shuddered. Her heart pounded. All she wanted to do was run. Instead, she stepped forward, drawn by a force that seemed to come from the statue itself. Stone fingers wrapped around her wrists like the maw of a monster, holding her fast even as she pulled back in panic. She could not move, no matter how hard she struggled against the stone grip that gave a delicate warmth in its touch. Then, before her horrified eyes, the lines of the stone face began to change and move. The features of the Goddess melted away to her own face smiling back in smooth stone.

Terrified, she tugged backwards with all her weight. There was a deafening groan and the Fourth was split apart from Her Sisters. The fingers released her. The hands now cradled the basin. The living statue extended the bowl to her as the water in it began to shadow and colour as shapes floated into being.

Look upon the water. See the face of the one who has wakened Me in thee.

She jerked away, raising her arm to shield her face. Her heel hooked on a root and she fell backwards on the sward with a cry. A blinding light filled her vision, obscuring everything.

Do not ignore nor starve one side of thyself, for it is part of you. Neglect it and thou shalt remain incomplete and forever wandering. Now thou hast seen the fourth face of thyself, and thou art healed. Thou art whole and no force can withstand thee. List to your heart and thou shalt be the strongest force there be on this earth, as eternal as I am. The seas shall roll over but the rocks shall remain, My child.

The blinding light spread over her, and she was jolted awake.

She could not tell if she merely thought these words or was speaking aloud. *Where am I, Great Mother? What is happening to me?* She smelled the scent of the night flowers and the jungle. She heard the cicada-song. Yet all she saw was white, stark and sharp. She was not lying in the grass as she longed to be.

A horse whinnied, and everything came flooding back.

"We stop here for the night!" barked an Eyriener's thick voice. "Move the litter under the trees. We want it out of sight."

She felt the litter lurch into movement as the men led the horses deeper into the jungle clearing. The soldiers would be encamped closer to the road, to fend off opposition. An unlikely possibility. The road had been empty all the way.

As she had done hundreds of times already, she pulled at the leather bonds. They did not give one inch. The soft leather tightened uncomfortably as it had done before and cut the circulation briefly to her wrists and hands, giving them a slight tingle.

They had been travelling for two days and two nights. Soon, they would reach Songkusai. She closed her eyes after the futile efforts with the straps. The voyage home had become a nightmare...

Even though she could feel the sudden change in course, the roar of giant guns rolled over the sea like thunder, a sound to wake the dead as the Eyriener ships were engaged by the English navy. Her allies were outnumbered and outgunned but these rifles and pistols were new weapons to the Eyrieners. They were severely lacking in experience. Many of the Eyriener ships were not armed with cannons as they did not expect opposition on the sea. The English were more than willing to give them a costly lesson in nautical combat.

Some of the cannons fired heavy iron balls while many of the guns on the English vessels fired a series of small iron slabs. These chunks would inflict a wider area of hull damage than the single cannonball. The Eyrieners were also unaware of a tactic that the English unleashed on them that would not only rip into the ship but also catch decks, sails, and masts on fire. Their cannonballs were heated to an incredible temperature and then fired. She remembered Rafe mentioning it in passing as something called "hot shot".

Thinking this was just an elementary tactic to employ, the *Archangel* attempted to fire heated shot from their cannons when challenged by an English vessel. Those who did not succumb to the extreme heat and fumes released from the iron artillery were killed by the cannon itself, exploding before fired. From what she could hear in the chaos on the decks above her head, seven ships sank from the damage they inflicted upon themselves.

Askana was locked in the cabin alone, and somehow that had been more terrifying than being left alone with Coumiran. Restrained to her bed, she was forced to hear all this with only her imagination conjuring up horrific images of gruesome deaths. When *Archangel* was hit, the ship rocked like a toy in the hand of a giant. Books fell from their shelves and slid across the tilted floor. King Henry had most assuredly given His best to serve her. Now she wished they were not half so good. By a miracle of Nadinath, *Archangel* and two other vessels slipped past the English navy. Under Coumiran's direction, their vessels broke free of the fleet while the remaining ships battled against this unexpected ally of hers.

A hawk sent news to them today. The Eyrieners manage to sink three of the Otherworlder vessels. However, of the thirty-seven, only fifteen survived the English Navy. All hands were lost.

God save King Henry, she thought amusingly.

Since their journey from Arathelle, her dreams had been murky, restless. This most recent one remained etched in her mind. It was as disturbing as the others, yet she felt rested, even relieved and at peace until the reality of her captivity settled in once more. *What did it mean?*

The curtains fluttered, and maddeningly she smelled roses. His bestowing of a token to the vessel of his beloved. The delicate blooms could not stand the jungle heat and damp rot. Only the Elves grew them in their enchanted realm. While Coumiran meant for them as a gesture of ardour, the roses conjured the image of another. *Love by the Rose, Live by the Sword*. Askana closed her eyes, drawing a picture of the Privateer Captain in her mind. She felt a small twinge of hope when she saw the *Defiant* in the docks of Arathelle. She caught the disappointment in Coumiran's eyes when he noted the Elves extended their shields around it. *Where are you, privateer?* She silently wondered, *Are you with your comrades or adrift in the ocean?* If it were the latter, her fate was sealed. He was the only one who could tell them where to find her, if they managed to find her in time before she became someone else entirely.

"Good morning. I trust the journey went well?" Black-gloved hands laid the pale roses on the pillows beside her head even as she turned her face away. "Why so cold?" Coumiran continued pleasantly, "After all, you are home, my sweet, and in a day we both shall be." She felt him lean in to feel the leather straps. "Too tight. Have you been pulling again? You really should cease this rebellion, my dear. You will only hurt yourself in the end, and we simply cannot have that." She felt his fingers adjusting the bonds so they did not bite into her flesh.

"To go directly into the Palace itself?" She finally turned around to face him. "It is a madman's plan. If the Palace and Royal Guard do not cut you down, the Morev'ar most certainly will."

"I think you underestimate my abilities," he laughed softly. "What stands in my way, I ask you? You? Your Royal Guard? The Temple? Your Priestesses hide in their hallowed halls waiting for others to take the sting out of the foe. I suppose they expect to emerge like jackals to take the scraps of the lion's feast. Your Ladies plot against a Consort who fancies himself a king. As for the Servants of the Kingdom, no one commands the Morev'ar but the Morev'ar. You know that. As it was when Maeve was in her banishment, I have eyes and ears even in the very bosom of your Court. You have allowed yourself the illusion that you were the only one capable of holding Morevi. Your ingenious plan to unravel a conspiracy against you only hastened the fall of your precious regime. The slate shall be wiped clean for Maeve and I, clean for us, and then shall we begin anew."

It made the hair rise on her nape to hear him speak. One moment he saw her. The next he saw nothing but a vessel for the soul of a dead woman.

"Or could it be that you keep your faith with the Elves? You yourself saw the shields. Did you really think that those inhuman creatures would come to your rescue? They will die out, you know. They were never meant to inhabit the same world as we do. Like your former love, dear Telmrant."

She turned coldly to look at him. "Let me up. I have personal needs that require attention."

He touched her lightly on the neck. She kept her gaze locked with his, but in her weakened state, she flinched at the feel of his fingertips. "Of course. Stay close, my dearest. I do so hate to see you ill."

Her legs were weak from lying down so long, and she had to chafe her ankles to get the blood flowing properly again. Askana refused to stagger when she rose up out of the litter. She would not give him that satisfaction. Back straight, she made her way into the nearby underbrush.

Just out of view of Coumiran, she felt a light dizziness. This would be far enough then. She lowered herself awkwardly to the ground, finding a small amount of privacy in the surrounding foliage. She did not need his warning. The first time they stopped she had immediately knocked down three soldiers in a mad attempt to run, but she had not taken more than three steps before the muscles of her legs cramped and she fell to the ground, violently sick, head reeling. She had tried again, three times to be exact. Each time, the same result. The spell Coumiran apparently cast over her while she slept was his security in keeping her close.

Askana could feel herself grow weaker as they neared Morevi. She soon discovered along the Road to the Moon that his incantation worked on two levels. He told her that by the time they arrived in Songkusai, she would be "most agreeable" in making their way through the Palace.

He was proud of his work and confided in Askana the expectation of, once more, practising alongside of Maeve.

She had been so certain that victory was theirs from the moment King Henry granted her his fleet. The accursed Eyrieners had not expected to find an experienced navy awaiting them. Now, it seemed that Coumiran would win, all because of a single bullet to the shoulder.

"What did you mean, O Mother," she said bitterly, "when you said that no force could withstand me?"

CHAPTER SIXTEEN
Siege on Songkusai

The corridors of the Palace of a Thousand Suns were deserted, save for the immense Hall of Dawn. Servants moved about at their work like cautious wraiths. Every small sound echoed slightly under the pillared ceiling. While the streets of Songkusai mirrored the stillness of the Palace corridors, there was pageantry and splendour under the Hall's great dome. This commencement was a ceremonial affair, words of inspiration and hope for the future, yet this ceremony had a very different look from The Raising. There was a notable absence of both Royal and Palace Guard. The Morev'ar, however, were showing in full force and standing for the Consort-King. In light of their presence, the Collected Houses were on edge. They were now realising for the first time how fragile their New Regime was without their Queen. The threat of war was in the air, but would it be a war with another nation or would it be a war *within* a nation?

Throughout Songkusai, in their appointed areas, soldiers and guards rested fitfully. No more drills were conducted. The Kinessa Plains, silent and empty awaiting the bloodbath that the next day would bring. While the Eyrieners issued no formal declaration of war, proof of the inevitable presented itself when the shields of Arathelle were seen from the watchtowers. With invasion looming like a shadow above them all, the mood was grim. Morevi's armies were still far from unified. Generals Trokan, Idir, and Kabir managed to retain their positions as there were no women to replace them. The fact that these men were in charge of the male-dominated armies left many questioning their loyalty. Even more galling was that these men were the only option remaining. The female Royal Guard, efficient as they were, numbered so few. Ruling Ladies within the ranks now reconsidered a proposal championed by Miarad, Pira, and Kimali for more aggressive recruiting tactics. The New Regime would never feel completely safe until a majority of the military was female.

But at the Palace, cradled in their own isolation, the commencement had begun with the other religions of Morevi paying homage to the Priestesses of Nadinath. Two Maidens, Two Mothers, and Two Destroyers flanked the Throne of a Thousand Suns as the Procession of Faith was led by the chants of the yellow-robed priests of El-Baz, half-droning, half-chanting blessings upon the Council as their swinging censers filled the air with sweet smoke. Two devotees of Coma, the Goddess of the Seasons, cast flower petals along the marble floor while in the galleries their sisters raised ethereal voices. The pleasant smiles of the Order of Nadinath faded away on the approach of the priests of Haralth, stern and cold in their brown cassocks. Haralth had been the principal faith of Morevi before the War. He was the God of the Old Regime. Now His priests were lean and sour. His temples, the few that remained standing following the Great Purging, vacant.

"Utter foolishness!" Lady Arshana whispered furiously to Lady Jamila behind her fan, "My daughter is our Family's new ruling Head, and she abandons her responsibility to disappear in the jungles carrying armour and weapons as some bizarre penance for her beloved Order! She cannot even heft a sword!"

"This is the way of things now. It is the same with our Lina as well!" Jamila nodded. "What I cannot accept is Lina's *willingness* to fight. So she has recently been appointed to the Royal Guard's higher ranks. What of it? The Anjara calls and she believes it is her duty to answer. Ruling Ladies do not have to fight on the battlefield if they so choose, I said to her. She just shook her head at me and left without a word. These girls are becoming more headstrong every day!" She shook her head slowly, disappointed. "Too wild and too full of themselves to listen to their mothers. Next she will be wanting to train with the Anjara!"

"It is necessary," the man spoke softly. Lady Jamila started in surprise at the sound of Lord Khameel's voice coming from over his wife's shoulder. "If it is their right to rule in the place of men, so it is also their duty to rule completely in all matters, including war if they are so called." Jamila snapped her fan open and waved it slowly, eyeing Khameel. Undeterred, he continued, "It gives fighting men heart to have their Lady riding at their head. Those who rule have a duty to protect their people and lead their soldiers. It is only right that she embraces all the responsibilities her new role in society demands."

Lady Jamila smiled, a tolerant, amused smile one might indulgently use with a child. "So a man might say, Khameel, but it is a mother's task to raise a daughter. We should not have to dirty our hands on a battlefield."

"So is it your view, Jamila, that our Generals, loyal despite the hostility of the Council they serve, should fight this war on their own? Is it right that power should rest in the hands of women, but that men should fight and die to preserve it?" Lord Khameel did not blink, his voice gaining a new-found resolve. "In the days of a King, men not only governed but fought. Now you say we should remain the protectors and give our lives for a society where our voice is mute? With power comes responsibility." One or two High Ladies turned their heads towards them in hearing his voice, his tone now well above a whisper. "Queen Askana, whatever some may say of her, understood that. General Idir once told me that he remained in his office because of her respect for them. At least she bestowed that to the men who protect our kingdom. Respect they truly deserve. You refuse to do that in the threat of war? Then, I fear, your hold on power will not last very long."

"Husband, I feel we should discuss this at home," Lady Arshana said with slight embarrassment. "Not in formal company."

Jamila sniffed. Then the horns sounded, turning her mood in an instant to one hauntingly pleasant. "Your husband is so fond of a jest, Arshana. What is a slip of tongue between old friends?" She ran a cold eye over the tall, gaunt old man before glancing behind them and raising from her seat. "I see that High Lady Min-Lu has just entered. I think I shall go and greet her to see what news she has to tell."

With a polite, civil bow, the dowager moved off.

Arshana turned to her husband, whispering sharply. Not out of anger or embarrassment, but out of fear. "Khameel, you should be more careful of what you say! Every time you behave like this, the reputation of House Ghesselan is threatened! We cannot afford to jeopardise our standing, for Remini's sake." She sighed heavily, "Fortunately it was only Jamila, this time."

"Yes. Jamila. I remember we were old friends, you, Jamila, and I. She never treated me with such contempt before this New Regime." Lord Khameel swallowed his next words, then continued with a distance in his voice. "Did we men really mistreat you so?"

The horns blared again, and the clamour rose all around them. The members of the High Council were entering.

"You know that Jamila was widowed after Shuban fell from his horse," Arshana said in a low voice. "You know how she suffered when the Old Regime took her estate. She learned to be bitter in those years. It changed her, all that suffering." She took his hand with a feeble smile, "Not all men were like you and Shuban, Khameel. To lose such a loving marriage as that, and you remember what she married simply to retain her lands. Bidran was her stepson, and you saw how he treated her and her daughters after inheriting the estate. There is pain behind the hate."

"Did we not pay for the pain after the War? Did I not beg forgiveness for every sin I committed when I knelt and gave you my sword, hilt first, before the family altar? How many had blades pushed into their breasts? And how many, how many families were shattered on that day? What crime so awful could have been committed that sons fled their homes to live as fugitives in other lands, learning to hate the sisters who took their places and despise the parents who could not aid them?"

Arshana's eyes filled with tears as cheers, loud whether false or true, rose at the King's Entrance and the Singers of Coma loosed silvered streams of song as welcome.

Khameel paused for a moment, his face frowning at the mockery of a king that slowly walked to his throne. As he watched the King's entrance, he continued, "The Queen cannot expect the men of her land to simply accept this change and be done with it. No one can or should. Can you truly imagine the futility I felt as I woke this morning to see Remini dressing herself in her brother's armour with his ru-yilei *at her side*. I swore to protect you the day I wed you, Arshana, and Remini the day she was born. The day she paid consort-price to a Family of the Blood for their son, I sorrowed. When she disregards my advice on war to seek that of other inexperienced, naïve young Ruling Ladies, it hurts more than my words could ever say." His bony old hand gripped hers fast as her tears spilled over. "As Jamila would say—this is the way of things now."

"Do you think he truly despises us?" she beseeched.

He could not speak his name either. Their son had told them that morning in a heated exchange that the family name was now an insult to him. "I do not know, Arshana. There is always hope as long as he lives, that we can make atonement, someday."

As the cheers, cymbals, and singing crested and died, they sat in their seats, two old people embracing each other in the heart of a relentless, cruel swirl of forces they were powerless to control.

Once again, Jermal was standing before the Collected Houses of Morevi. The faces staring back at him looked very different. Many of the Ladies of the Blood present were not the Ruling Ladies of their House, but merely representatives. The thinned ranks of the Palace Guard were supplemented by House soldiers. He was told by some prattling servants the Ruling Ladies were already encamped on the Kinessa Plains with their regiments, or had disappeared shortly after The Raising to seeking guidance from the Temple. A very different audience this time. It sent a powerful message to him.

With Dirare's words in his mind, he was about to do the same. "My people." His voice carried, confident and strong, amazing him how regal it sounded in the moment. It was fortunate they did not know the truth. "I know how you are uncertain, worried, afraid. I am, after all, an Otherworlder. Yet even as an Otherworlder, I have come to love the Kingdom of Morevi, and in this time of turmoil nothing comes so clear to me as the need to protect. I am no longer one man alone, and there is no place for anything else in my heart, not even for love. With the invaluable aid given me by my trusted High Council, I have taken time to make peace with fate, destiny, and loss."

Murmurs rose. The King was beginning his commencement with mention of loss. One and all, they felt the approach of yet another tremor to shake the delicate balance of the New Regime. The Priestesses stood like statues of stone on either side of the throne. On the first tier, the High Council watched the room with hard, glass-bright eyes. Dirare showed no reaction, merely remained attentive as the Consort-King spoke her words. Jermal stood in his shimmering robes of gold and white, the brilliant sunlight flooding through the magnificent dome above, filtering through coloured-glass panels of blue, green, and gold. The brightest rays centred on Askana's vacant throne, truly making it appear to blaze with the light of a thousand suns.

"An epoch in my life and in the history of the Kingdom has passed. I am now a nation. I am Morevi. I am here to rule, and rule I shall with the aid of my High Council and under the direction of the High Regent, the High Lady Dirare. They will serve as my light in this time of darkness."

Subtle currents ran through those assembled, including those crowded into the standing audience galleries, separated from the room by wooden slatted screens. Jermal, in that moment, was more than willing to forgo the flowery speech and hand the reins of power over to the High Regent.

A company of House servants dressed in Morevian light armour of nondescript colour, their crests and faces obscured by dust from the road, progressed slowly towards the gates of Songkusai. They had carts packed with what looked like furniture and luggage. The curtains of the litter blew gently in the breeze and the number of attendants told the guards she was a Lady of some status.

"Halt where you stand!" called the watch. On the wall, arrows were nocked to bows. "Who approaches?"

"Lady Shinare of the House Shadao, cousin to High Lady Min-Lu of House Annaki. We go to House Shadao's apartments," returned the black-cloaked rider.

Proof was demanded, made evident by the sounds of bowstrings being pulled back from the watchtower. The rider answered with a series of clicks and whistles. House Shadao's password. He then unwrapped and held up the house staff, carved elegantly with symbols from House Annaki and Shado crests and winking with polished gems. With a nod from the watch, the guards withdrew and bowmen stood at ease. Moments later the city gates swung open.

The caravan rumbled through as the guards waited patiently, their attentions kept on the Road of the Moon and the jungles in the distance. One guard said jokingly to a soldier straggling near the rear, "Your Mistress must possess strong resolve if she moves her household so late. Those in the country should not feel themselves so safe."

"Ah, but those in the capital city should not think themselves safe either," returned the soldier in a strange, thick accent. The guard's eyes opened wide, but no scream came from him as blood bubbled out of his mouth from the dagger sheathed suddenly in his neck.

The Lady's attendants pulled back the covers of her carts to reveal fully armed Eyriener soldiers, loosing their crossbow bolts with a deafening *"whoosh"*, striking the guards on the battlements. The black rider held high the blood-stained scarf and waved it over his head.

Then came the cries of the soldiers, emerging from the jungle shadows and charging for the open gates of Songkusai.

"Even the luxury of remembrance is no longer mine. I admit here, now, that I am strong enough to face the truth present before us for some time." Jermal paused for a moment. They were simple words he spoke that had the power to change a nation. "My Queen is not coming back to us."

He was told to expect the cries and jeers from the Collected Houses. He continued over their voices, his own finally silencing the protest. "I must accept that Queen Askana Moldarin, my predecessor and my love, is not here to rule and will never return again to rule. Now, I must take the throne truly, and I will. We have come into a new age, a new rule. Change is what will occur under my direction and that of the High Council."

Some shouted approval, others heaped condemnation. The supporters of Dirare and, ironically, Min-Lu's faction, cheered the new announcement. Those who remembered, loved, or feared the Black Widow, argued and shouted. Those who feared change and civil war threw their hands upward, agitated with this throne unable to keep a ruler. Insults flew as fast as glances. No longer impassive, the Priestesses exchanged looks before quietly leaving the Great Hall, followed shortly by the servants of the other deities.

None, save for one High Lady, knew of the true power struggle currently unfolding in the streets of Songkusai.

Armed attackers flooded into the streets, spilling into the emptied marketplaces with cries shattering the silence like a hammer's blow. Taken by surprise, the few Palace and Royal Guard on patrol were forced back into the entrances of shops and warehouses. Each entrance was formed of stone arches leading into enclosed foyers. They served as small death traps.

The young Royal Guard deflected the sword of her Eyriener opponent, turned on her heels, and sliced open the man's belly. Already her arms were bathed to the elbows in blood as soldiers continued their charge through the street, all going in one direction—the Palace. They had arrived a day earlier than anticipated, but everything was still going according to the Otherworlder's plan.

When she began this patrol, they were a small combined team numbering five. Her Sisters and the Palace Guard were all dead. She now stood alone as the Eyrieners closed on her. She gave a shrill cry, wielding her shirai with a strength born of desperation, then felt a tugging sensation that jerked her off her feet. A wet, sticky warmth flooded over her fingers as the Eyrieners left her to die, returning to their push to the Palace. Soon she would return to the loving embrace of the Goddess. She had pleased the Maid and the Mother. Only one duty remained to gain the blessing of the Destroyer. The Royal Guard's fingers were steady as she drew the strange, short weapon from her belt. She could still remember in her slipping awareness where to deposit a small portion of black powder. The "flashpan" the Otherworlders had called it. Her finger slipped within the metal curve on the sleek weapon's underside, and raised it to the sky.

The gunshot exploded into the air like a crack of lightning.

The interior of the shop-house was dark, save for the odd candles that illuminated the room. All the shutters fastened and barred. The shopkeeper and her family were settling down to their afternoon meal when the pistol sounded, making them start. The youngest child knocked over the teapot. It crashed to the floor, shattering into pieces.

"Do not fear," the Otherworlder reassured the shopkeeper and her husband as they rose from the table. "Keep silent and barricade the doors the moment we leave."

From the shadows, a playing card flipped onto a sideboard. It landed face up. The Ace of Spades. "Time to 'Live by the Sword' in truth." They could hear the charge of the Eyrieners pass by their hiding place, a wave of trampling feet and battle cries. Rafe gave his own pistols, a pair of double wheel-locks, another glance before turning to the now-assembled group of commanders and soldiers. "Gentlemen, ladies, let us welcome our delegates from Eyrie."

Coumiran spurred his charger forward, the storefronts and buildings on either side of him merely a blur as he led the charge. He could hear close behind him the clatter of the litter, bouncing dangerously over the stone street. Its fastened curtains billowed like sails as its horses dashed madly forward, screaming, eyes rolling to show their whites in fear.

Three times they were challenged by Morevian units and drawn into pitched fighting. Three times they cut their way through, carving out a path with sword, mace, and axe. From these stinging attacks, Coumiran knew their siege was not a complete surprise. Still, he would not be denied. He ground his teeth as he pressed forward with his regiment. Nothing mattered more than gaining the Palace. With it taken, the war would be over before it even began. Thundering down the street, Coumiran's heart leapt as it came into view.

He did not notice the faint shimmer atop the Palace entrance until he reached the courtyard gates. The High Lord pulled back hard on the reins of his ivory-white steed, allowing some Eyrieners, lost in the heat of the charge, to continue past him.

They appeared at the top of the Palace steps, rising from a crouch. In unison, they dipped their arrowheads into the line of flame extending across the top step. They slowly raised the bows, pulling back smoothly and evenly.

"Archers," called the yeoman, "loose!"

The arrows appeared as mere gold and white rushes of flame, landing short of the charging infantry. The Palace suddenly disappeared in a blinding brilliance as the flaming arrows ignited oil mixed with a generous amount of black powder. Hidden underneath a thin blanket of dust and dirt, the Eyrieners never caught a hint of this trap. A wall of flame rose high above them, instantly devouring the men leading the push. The roar and heat of the explosion caused the soldiers alongside Coumiran to stumble and slide back.

"Min-Lu, you have failed me!" Coumiran spat, heeling his horse forward, resuming his charge. The remaining Eyrieners followed his lead. "It is a trap! It is a cursed trap!"

He wanted to save his strength for the Spell of Souls, but his present goal was the Palace. Coumiran would have to challenge his limits. His hand extended forward as he shouted over the cries of his armies, *"Mak'iltumris flamis ja telans!"* Before the horrified Morevians and English archers, the fire-barrier parted for Coumiran, a number of Eyriener soldiers, and a litter. Then with not even a glance behind him, he brought his hand down. The passage closed, consuming the stragglers in his wake. He was uncertain how many remained on the other side of the fire. Perhaps fifty perished. An acceptable loss. He had enough men with him. All that mattered was the Palace.

Fire rained down from the Palace entrance as the second line loosed, striking the first wave of Eyrieners that reached the marble steps. The first line stood again, bows ready to fire. The dark rider, along with the men under his lead, stopped just out of range. They did not know who this rider was but the great cry that rose from his white horse sent a chill into their hearts. Only the sound of the dwindling firewall behind him interrupted the silence before he spoke.

"Open the gates," Coumiran shouted.

In quick reply, three green-fletched arrows fell quivering before his charger's hooves.

Coumiran handled the shying horse easily with one hand while the other balled into a fist at his side. His whole frame tensed, the muscles in his arm contracting until the whole limb shook. The Eyrieners could hear him whispering a string of unintelligible words. Their sound was harsh, grating, and full of menace. His voice was growing louder with the sound of metal grinding against metal. The grinding became a groaning that caused the line of archers to turn around to see what was making it.

Coumiran's hand shot out, the whole arm and shoulder thrusting forward and upward, fingers splaying open as he now shouted this strange tongue. The explosion of the doors sent archers flying from their posts. Many of them were killed instantly by the shock of the blow while others snapped their necks on landing hard against stone paths. Those who managed to survive the destruction of the palace doors soon felt axes and daggers bury themselves into their stomachs and backs.

"In the name of King Cedric!" The roar went up as his white horse bounded forward up the Palace steps. "For fair Eyrie!" he shouted.

The Palace Guard and a handful of Morev'ar charged at the invaders now crossing the foyer. Coumiran snarled as he pulled up on the reins. His war-horse reared up, steel-shod hooves flailing, striking a pair of Morev'ar. Coumiran's sword released from its scabbard across the horse's flank and cleanly severed the arm of a Palace Guard, decorating the charger's steaming white coat and the litter's delicate silk curtains with tiny drops of deep red.

The voices of debate in the Great Hall drowned out everything, including the horns' warning. House members were now on their feet, their shouts echoing under the dome. Members of the High Council were attempting to silence the protest as the King remained in the centre of the Hall, bewildered. As the debate raged, Jermal finally stepped back from the edge of the dais and slumped in his own throne. He could do nothing but stare at the larger throne next to his, once the place of his beloved. It was a mockery of a Royal Commencement.

No one noticed the High Lady of House Annaki who, after a servant whispered quickly into her ear, quietly stood and slipped away.

In the corridors, Min-Lu's heart soared as the sound of the horns was loud and clear. She found herself just in time to stop the Palace Guard moving to evacuate the Council.

"My Lady, we are under attack!" The lead guard ran up to her side, the swords of his companions glinting from sunlight striking their edges as they bowed quickly before her. "We must empty the Hall of Dawn and usher the Collected Houses to safety!"

The High Lady Min-Lu tilted her head. "Why should we?"

"High Lady—?"

She stepped back before the knife hurtled through the air and buried itself between the man's shoulder blades. Five Morev'ar stepped out of the shadows of pillars. The remaining guards fell quickly as atriah lifted them off their feet, poisoned blades killing them instantly.

Min-Lu turned to the one wearing a gold circlet on his brow, "Gidaron, fasten the doors! Make sure these braying asses are kept in the Great Hall. Have your men bar those in the audience galleries as well."

He stepped up to her suddenly, smiling a bit when she flinched at his touch. It was merely to move her back to avoid the pool of blood spreading from the dead bodies of the Palace Guard. "It will be done. Now your ally must keep his end of the bargain. No Morev'ar must fall for he will not know my followers from the others. We will provide our own 'casualties'. Already those in my command are preparing to take care of the Astarkhan."

"Then I should address you as the new Astarkhan." She drew back regally, chin rising. "Take your positions in the catacombs. They will try to take the King out that way. Kill him there. If we are fortunate, Dirare will leave with him." She turned to leave, apparently towards the Royal Apartments. "In any event, both of them must die."

"Your Grace," Gidaron called. Min-Lu could not help but have her breath taken when she heard herself called by that formal address. "Will it not appear strange when they find you absent?" he asked.

She turned, and her smile was real. "By that time, it will not matter any longer."

Two hundred men. That was the number remaining after the Dark Merchant led the charge. It had begun with *six* hundred. Now those on the other side of the fire barrier were granted the rewards of their bravery—abandonment in a hostile, foreign city.

They were left with no choice. It was not a retreat, they assured themselves. It was merely dropping back to reassess the threat. There was the temptation to make a final stand with these impressive weapons of war, but an unfortunate problem with these "pistols" and "rifles" were that they could only be used once. Unlike a crossbow, they took a short eternity to reload! The fact they could not see their enemy—or people of any kind, for that matter—only reaffirmed their collected instinct to fall back.

Then it reached their ears. Not all at once, but they all eventually stopped and looked around them. It was the sound of something being moved slowly across sand and dirt. Whatever was being dragged was massive.

"No!" shouted a young recruit as his eyes looked behind him. "Myrian deliver us!"

The gates of Songkusai were closing. The outside world was quickly disappearing from view. The soldiers thought nothing of victory for Eyrie, the lost payment for not fulfilling their duties, or even the wrath of the Dark Merchant. Watching the huge gates close united them in one single thought—they had to leave *now!*

Once more they charged, but not for the glory of King and country. This time, their run was for survival. A few escaped the city with little effort, but as the exit passage between Songkusai's gates narrowed, soldiers tried to force themselves through, only to be caught between the massive doors by their armour. In their panic to escape, others began climbing over those trapped. Eventually they all were crushed by the doors now locking shut.

Before the Eyrieners trapped inside could regroup their numbers, they appeared in the battlements. A line of Morevian men and women, and beings not of Morevi—Otherworlders. Some standing amongst the soldiers looked like shopkeepers and simple merchants. They must have positioned themselves in the overlook battlements *after* their initial charge into the city. There was a still moment as the Eyrieners froze. They could see a rear line of archers that hastily nocked crossbows and long bows while this strange collection of warriors, peasants, and gentlemen lifted their own weapons. They did not know who spoke the words. For some, it would be the last words they would hear.

"First gunners, fire!"

It was a serving maid with an empty pitcher who discovered that the doors leading from the Great Hall to the servants' corridors were barred. The news was passed from servants to attendants. Attendants passed the news to the House guards. The guards informed their Noble Ladies. The protest raging for well over half an hour died down in a matter of moments. As the sounds of debate died, other sounds became audible. Sounds resembling fireworks. Horns. Shouts and cries of combat, filtering in from the outside.

The voices that once demanded a unified Morevi and the preservation of the realm now became pleas of self-preservation and panicked cries for escape.

There was a minor crush as nobility and attendants alike rushed the doors. Dignified Ladies of the Blood now clambered over seats and out of royal boxes, their court robes, head-dresses, and fans hardly hindering their desperate runs for any door or archway. Some shrieked. Some fainted. Those at the main doors were shouting for their guards to force them open, but they themselves were packed too close to the doors for anyone to do anything. Up above, in the audience galleries, an identical scene occurred. Then came the screams from the various archways. They could also hear the sounds of atriah flying through the air. The High Lady Shira of House Duma'ki was alone, running out from an archway she had disappeared into earlier, when the atriah struck her in the back. Because of the bright red lip rouge of her court makeup, no one noticed the blood coming from her mouth until she collapsed at the foot of another dignitary.

Dirare rose from her cushion and was about to descend into the crowd when Arnese caught her elbow, "That way is certain death, my Mistress!"

She paused, barely able to hear above the din. She was not a woman of action. Her place was in the Council and in the Court where she played the Great Game with skill. Yet she saw her guards, six of them, with Arnese, and the four Morev'ar responsible for the King behind them, all looking to her for guidance. Up above her she saw the King, glowing in his ceremonial robes.

"We have to get to the catacombs! Guards, Servants, surround us. Use your armour and bulk to shoulder our way through so we are not dragged down. Little mother, you must trust my judgement!"

Arnese lifted the hems of her robes as she took a place in the middle of Jarahd guards and Morev'ar. "I will follow, but we must go now!"

"El'Baz curse me for a fool!" Dirare darted up the platform. Jermal looked wildly at her as she seized his sleeve, "Come! We have not a moment to lose!"

The terrified servants screamed at the sight of a dark rider on a white horse, appearing as the spectre of Death. He was followed by four Eyrieners who carried a litter on their shoulders. Coumiran dismounted, watching the palace attendants flee. He did not bother with them. There was no need. With the number of men he brought with him and the Morev'ar allied with Min-Lu, it was done. They were far from securing the Palace, but they now held an invaluable advantage.

Using the map provided by Min-Lu, he led the litter to the grand staircase that led to the Royal Apartments. "Put it down."

Before it came to rest, Coumiran tore open the curtains, ripping the fine cloth. "You will have to do a bit of walking, cousin." Askana glared up at him, his spell now at its full potency as she fought to stay conscious. His dagger cut the leather cords that bound her. "Help her up," he ordered to his attendants.

She staggered as she was led up the stairs, shrugging off the guard angrily as the blood rushed painfully back into her legs. An Eyriener seized her shoulder roughly. Summoning her remaining strength, Askana turned and sank her teeth into his hand until she hit bone. With a growl of agony, the soldier struck her across the face. She stumbled back and rolled down the steps, landing hard against the floor. She could not even make an attempt to rise. The fall and Coumiran's spell kept her on the floor, retching as the soldier's blood, mixed with her own, dripped from her mouth.

With a hiss, Coumiran darted down the steps, sword flickering out like a lizard's tongue to drive deep into the soldier's breast. He watched the man's eyes go wide, perhaps searching in final thoughts for what offence he had committed. Coumiran pushed the body free of the blade, wiping his sword clean with the edge of his cloak.

"Pick her up and carry her!" he shouted to the remaining Eyeriners. He stared at her for a moment, the madness creeping upon him, but only for a moment. He had to remember why he brought her, why she must remain unspoiled. "We have no time for distractions such as this, my sweet." Coumiran then turned conversational in his tone to Askana as they progressed through the empty corridors of the Palace. "It was clever of you, really. No one would have ever imagined you kept her possessions there of all places. After the ritual, it will be convenient for you too, my love. I remember how you always liked your study to be close to your bedchamber."

"Your ally in Morevi must be very close to me to have provided a map to the Palace and its catacombs," Askana rasped, recovering painfully from the effects of the spell.

"Oh, she was! You have no idea." He turned suddenly and took her chin in his hand, holding it firm in his grasp. "Do not worry, Your Majesty. I will not keep you in suspense for long. You shall meet your adversary very soon."

He kicked opened the set of doors with loud growl. Elegant rays of sunlight filtered through the windows, illuminating the splendour of Askana's chambers. Faint and elusive, the scent of her perfume still lingered in the air. Her rooms were in the same condition as she had left them. The same furnishings, small articles of hers still on the tables, books on the shelves, and her harp in its corner. Had Askana not been a prisoner, she would have been elated to find herself in this inner sanctum, far from the eyes of the people and sequestered from the bickering and plotting of the Council.

Then, as she was carried in, she saw objects that did not belong there. A suit of armour, an impressive work of white and gold studded with gems, hung on an ornate display rack. It was a suit fit for a king, a king who had replaced her. And the boots on the hearth, the morning robe discarded on the floor. They were obviously for a man.

They went relentlessly through room after room until Coumiran flung open the doors of her bedchamber. A surge of distaste, strong enough to overpower her lingering nausea and the pain in her limbs, rose in her at this man defiling her most private sanctuaries. Then her nose caught another scent. A perfume with a distant, vague memory about it. It came from the slight girl in lavish, pale blue robes that sat at her vanity, calmly brushing her auburn hair with Askana's own brush. She rose from the stool and turned to her with a pleasant smile.

"Welcome back, Askana." Min-Lu said as she crossed the room to Coumiran's side. "Things are not quite the same as when you left, are they?"

"You?" Askana whispered, "You are the traitor."

"The word 'traitor' is so subjective," she smiled. "To you, maybe I am. But when I become Queen I will not have betrayed Morevi. I will be revered as its saviour. You see, High Lord Ruain and I have an arrangement concerning the Eyrieners."

"Lord Ruain?" asked Askana distantly. Was this another Eyriener conspirator she had not met yet? Then she followed Min-Lu's eyes to Coumiran. It was his alias. Min-Lu had no idea of his true identity or agenda. Before she could share her thoughts, her tongue swelled, causing her to gag sharply. It seemed that Coumiran's spell kept her from betraying him even with words. Askana hung her head low, giving a soft laugh at Min-Lu's naivete. "You would trust him? Do you believe even for a moment that he would let you rule?"

"Oh, but I will. Why would I stand between Morevi and a more proper ruler for its borders?" Coumiran took Min-Lu into his arms. "You see, Askana, she loves me."

She wanted to shout, to scream out to Min-Lu that it was a lie. The man she loved by a false name was still obsessed with a dead woman. This was the girl whom she had begun personally training, whom she had once viewed with affection. Min-Lu had once shown such promise, so much promise that Askana had been willing to overlook the little signs of boredom and disregard for ethics evident. In her fascination for poisons and aptitude for learning, Askana saw an image of herself. The girl's seemingly natural, charming affection—a bond she lost with Lubria's banishment—was a deception. She lacked control, whole-heartedly throwing herself into actions with no thought for implications.

Now she had thrown her whole being into a love for this man. Askana's stomach cramped horribly and she retched again, dryly, choking as she fell. Her vision hazed but she could still see Coumiran. She knew he was smiling under that mask of silk, smiling at her inability to warn Min-Lu of this mockery of love.

"My Lord." Min-Lu reached up and caressed his black mask tenderly.

A soldier lifted Askana back to her feet and now served as a human crutch. The Queen's tilted eyes, even in the sickness of Coumiran's spell, lost none of their edge as Min-Lu slipped out of her lover's arms and approached her.

"It was all too easy," she whispered to Askana. "When you destroyed the Taighar ports, King Cedric was furious! It took little urging to have him send an army here with Lord Ruain at its head." Min-Lu lovingly stroked Askana's hair, "King Cedric shall never set foot in Morevi, that much I can promise you. Take that solace with you as you travel to the Gates of Tián'ba."

She giggled, eyes sparkling as she turned back to her lover, "The entire Council and Collected Houses are locked in the Great Hall, including Lady Dirare, her 'High Council', and the Consort-King." She looked at Askana, "Oh, yes Your Majesty— your charming Consort was made King by Dirare. I must commend you. Your control over him was so absolute it lasted even in your absence. You should have been here to hear him speak. Such an apt student of yours! A shame he will not live out the rest of his days, either as a king, consort, or thief."

"Like all the others. Markuna. Telmrant. And poor Captain Rafton, adrift in the oceans of Naruihm." Coumiran mocked, "You should stop caring for men. It proves detrimental to their health."

Askana did not have to speak. The hatred in her eyes was evident.

"Come, my Lady," Coumiran held out his arms to Min-Lu. "We have work to do. Your map, my sweet?"

She handed him from the folds of her court robes a parchment, carrying the stamp of Kubi-Sogi's office. Min-Lu walked past Coumiran, and with her oblivious to them in the moment, he looked to Askana. His expression was chilling.

It was true what Min-Lu had said. Askana could control men. So too could Maeve. From beyond the grave. The High Lady of House Annaki would shortly experience the worst betrayal of her life. For that, Askana could almost pity her.

They headed to the huge wardrobe at the end of the room where her full suit of battle armour stood on a model figure. Beside it, also on a similar figure, the costume of the High Priestess. The soldiers flung the closet doors open, revealing royal garments tailor-made for both Jermal and herself.

Min-Lu glanced over her shoulder at Coumiran before walking into Askana's closet, feeling inside its moulding. Finding a tiny knob tucked inside the wardrobe's doorway, she pushed it. The armour model's pedestal slowly slid to one side, taking part of the wall with it. There was a rush of cool, stale air as they stood before the opening of a passageway leading into darkness.

"It is true then." Coumiran's glance was almost hungry, raw with anticipation, as he looked at Askana. He whispered, *"Me'djea!"*

The torch that hung inside the entrance to this labyrinth has not been lit in many years, but exploded with light on Coumiran's word. He removed it from its sconce and led the party into the maze underneath the Palace.

Before descending into the catacombs, Askana could see from her window dark clouds beginning to gather in the sky.

"Simarda rea, andrain erda …" Soft, low, and haunting sounded the hymn that every woman sang whether gentle and whispering or clear and pure. A hymn of death and the peaceful journey beyond the corporal world. It was the way of the worshippers of Nadinath. To sing for those who would die in the coming battle. This time though, the song had special meaning.

Amber light washed over the great statues of Nadinath, painting everything red and gold. Flames sent shimmering colours running up and down the ceremonial hangings. Devotees sat on cushions or mats on the floor. The Temple was full this day. Some were there for sanctuary. Many were waiting for a word, and as the messenger soared in from the outside, it appeared the wait was finally over. The falcon sailed in silently to one of the perches before the giant statues and landed with the soft, fluttering sound of beating wings.

A red-robed Priestess stood and ascended the steps to the stands. The bird let her take the rolled message from its leg without protest. She unrolled the tiny slip and read it slowly, carefully. Then, she descended from the falcon's perch to the other Priestesses, one in white robes and the other in black armour. They conferred for a few moments before taking their rightful places before the statue of Nadinath, each before the facet they represented.

Illora glanced at the Maiden playing the harp, and the music stopped. "The war has begun." She spoke solemnly, "Songkusai has been attacked."

Silence.

"The King has declared the High Priestess dead, and the High Lady Dirare has been formally given the power to rule."

Soft sighs overtook the vast quiet of the Temple like waves slipping over the sands of a shore.

Silently, Maghda and Messara walked over to the two immense silver bells on one side of the statues. They lifted large mallets and rang them so their tones shivered through the whole Temple. Three times in unison, the bells tolled softly.

Within moments more women entered the spacious hall. Many wore the garb of Priestesses, many more were Maidens. Some old, some young. Some devotees were mothers who had left their sleeping children to answer the call of the bells, and others were daughters leaving their bedside vigils over their aged guardians. They were from all standings of class. They were not all of Morevi. Their numbers were vast. Silent in reverence to Nadinath, they entered and stood along the walls as the women who had been there from the start made room for newcomers. When all had gathered, filling the cavernous place that kept the giant statue of the Goddess, they appeared as a sea of women.

Illora spoke again, her voice reaching every ear. "Since the audience with the Anjara, we have been waiting for proof, and it is here. Sister Kalea told us that the Eyrieners would strike at the city, and they have. If the men take Morevi, we shall not live out our lives, and the worship of the Mother shall cease to exist. So it comes to this." The sound of her shirai-butt striking the floor echoed through the Temple. "As the Priestess of the Destroyer, in the absence of the High Priestess of Nadinath, I declare the Temple at war."

Silence once more. Illora was joined by Maghda and Messara, all three of them wielding shirai. They ascended the steps to the base of Nadinath and, with a quick twirl of their shirai, inserted the blades into three slits in the stone floor. They turned to descend as the sounds of stone sliding against stone could be heard filling the Temple. With a hollow groan, the golden sunburst mosaic in the centre of the great chamber split apart, each half slowly moving as the women moved aside. A gaping hole fifteen feet in diameter was revealed and from it raised a great bronze basin. It slowly rose from the darkness of this pit until its base fitted level with the floor. Red priestesses approached with pails of perfumed oil which they poured into the basin as the word tolled as the bells did earlier in the Temple.

"War," Maghda's and Messara's voices echoed in unison.

"War," echoed the young Maidens.

"War," sighed the devotees.

"War," spoke Illora as she lowered a lit torch into the basin.

The flames leapt high into the air, throwing frenzied shadows over everyone, the voice of the flame the only sound in the Temple for this moment.

Illora was now joined by others dressed in the menacing dark armour of the Destroyer. They formed a large ring around the basin, shirai held horizontally at waist-height with the blades pointing in as they circled the leaping fire. "Vengeance on those who affront the Mother. We go to the battlefields to protect in the name of the Destroyer." The Maidens echoed, punctuating the end of each sentence with a rap of their shirai on the ground.

Through a break in the circle Red priestesses entered and formed a ring within the Black, each holding a ru-yilei. Again, the weapons were held with the point inwards as they spoke. "Vengeance on those who come against the Mother and her daughters. We stay with the Temple to heal and protect, and to give sanctuary, in the name of the Mother."

Again, the break, and the White formed the innermost circle. The sweet ring of steel echoed a thousandfold as they struck the side of the basin with the circular atriah, holding them high above their heads, sending rings into the ceiling as firelight caught the curve of their blades. "Vengeance on those who attack and spill blood on the Mother's ground. We go to the Palace, to protect and to retrieve, in the name of the Maiden."

"The flame shall burn undying till the war is ended in the name of Nadinath," Illora intoned.

As if given a signal, all began to move out of the Temple.

The soldiers were hot, tired, and quite lost, separated from their brothers. There were ten of them altogether, and they were Eyrieners lost in this maze of the Morevian capital.

Following the massacre at the gates, the remaining soldiers returned to the main street leading back to the Palace. They were trying desperately to find an alleyway or some side street for escape. It seemed that every avenue was blocked, but eventually one opened and they took it eagerly. Their numbers became smaller and smaller as the roads they took shrank into winding alleys that crossed and bisected each other. After a few minutes of running, the streets all looked the same, hemmed in by walls and tall buildings, narrow and dark. Over-development of the capital city had caused some of the balconies to overhang the streets and roofs to stack above or underneath one another.

Taloss had been leading his men for the better part of an hour. He was hoping to find the main street that led back to the gates. He was now feeling less foolish and more alarmed. "Curse these Morevians! How could anyone *not* get lost in the city?!" He leaned against a wall, removing his leather helm as he combed back with his fingers the brown hair wetly plastered to his forehead. Taloss then noticed one of the younger soldiers looking up and down the street, as if trying to confirm or allay a fear. "Lennis, boy, come into the shade! This Morevian sun will roast you—"

"Did anybody notice something about this place?" he asked suddenly.

"What? That we are trapped in some forsaken shithole in Naruihm?" Rendiann snapped. "We have seen nothing but shuttered windows and barred doors."

"No, these barricades." Lennis looked across the intersected streets, his voice growing more anxious. "They're not just random junk tossed in the alleys. There's a pattern." He then looked at the windows surrounding them, each a potential spot for anyone armed with a crossbow. "As if they *wanted* us to come down here."

The men leapt back to their feet with weapons drawn.

"We should have stayed on the ship." Lennis groaned.

"We should have stayed in bed," quipped Rendiann.

"Would you argue with the Dark Merchant? Or King Cedric for that matter?" snapped Taloss, grabbing Rendiann by his armour. "Nobles and Merchant-Lords need no excuses for their actions. This is a blood-price issued for the destruction of our seaport."

"That display alone should have served as a message!" Rendiann shouted back, giving Taloss a hard shove to the chest. "Leave Morevi be!"

As other soldiers, the heat and confusion wearing thin on their tempers as well, pulled Rendiann and Taloss away from one another, eyes watched them from the shadows. Smiles crept across their faces as the Eyrieners began to turn on each other, just as they had hoped.

"The point of the present is we are still here, wherever that may be." Lennis said sharply. He pointed to a visible tower reaching upward to a sky filling with dark storm clouds, "I say we return to the Palace. As far as we know, the High Lord still holds that part of the city. If we reach it, we can make a stand."

"And just who put you in command, boy?" Taloss asked menacingly, motioning to his armour's insignia rank. He was not an officer, but still higher than Lennis. "We will continue down this street until we find another platoon, then plan a—"

"No!" Rendiann barked defiantly. "I have reached my fill of closed doors, empty streets, and these parlour games of bait-and-switch!" Moving back, he took a run at a small door, turning his armoured shoulder against it. "There are people in there, I wager. A city this big has to have people!" Again, his shoulder slammed against the door, causing it to shudder on its hinges.

"Who is it?" the pleasant voice sang.

Everyone froze.

"This is a bad dream," Lennis uttered, "A very bad dream."

Rendiann gave the door a hard rap with his gauntlet, shouting wildly, "Open this door, you savage! We are taking this city in the name of Eyrie."

The door's latches slid back. The Eyrieners poised their weapons as the wooden hatch opened with a long, hard creak.

The woman stepped into the sunlight just reaching the doorway. She was a full foot taller than most women of Morevi or Eyrie. Hair as red as a sunset sky. The shirt she wore was cut low revealing a most pleasing chest and cinched just above her stomach. Tight, form-fitting breeches encompassed her legs along with fine dark boots reaching halfway up her fine-toned calves. She was a stunning creature of beauty. She was the sole occupant of the dwelling.

She was not Morevian.

"Who are you?" were the only words Rendiann could find appropriate.

"The hired help, lad," the woman spoke as she raised the pistol up to Renidann's face.

His head snapped back and he remained standing for a moment before falling to the ground with a dead thud, the bullet lodged in the centre of his brow. The others fell as quickly when archers and riflemen opened fire from the rooftops surrounding them.

Rafe smiled brightly as he fended off the Eyriener captain. The man he challenged out of the group of eight turned out to be a ranking officer who knew his swordplay.

"Thank you, kind sir," Rafe said with delight as he cut at the man's head, slicing through the air, "I was afraid to spend this day's battle amidst unprimed cubs, not meeting a suitable opponent!"

His opponent merely replied with a growl and a vicious series of thrusts to Rafe's belly, all of which he danced around with a series of binds and parries.

"Rafton, I must honestly say I have not enjoyed myself so much all my life!" shouted Eshton as he punched an Eyriener with the butt of his shirai. "If this is the life you privateers live, I might give some thought in joining your crew!"

"You, take orders from me? God forbid!" He ducked as the sword whistled over his head. "You would prove the death of us all. You are a rogue, a risk-taker, and a braggart!"

"As are you. I think you are losing your sense of humour these days," Eshton quipped as he drove the butt of his shirai into his opponent's stomach. "Sorry, lad," he said as he brought the shirai staff up across the soldier's face.

"Will the both of you stop," Sir Julian gritted his teeth as the Eyriener forced him back against the wall, blade to blade, "and lend a hand? I would like very much to live to the autumn of my life, preferably on a country estate somewhere in Essex!"

Eshton's former quarterstaff training made the shirai a true delight to wield. He twirled it gracefully in his grasp, then hurled it at Sir Julian's opponent, driving the shirai blade into the man's back. Its tip just barely broke through the Eyriener's chest, giving Julian a slight poke in his doublet.

"I must have one of these shirai for Court!" Eshton smiled.

"Your arrogance, Otherworlder, is intolerable!" the old Eyriener growled as he cornered Rafe. "Your skill is lacking to back your boasts."

"But what I lack in skill I make up with in ingenuity!" Rafe pushed his opponent back and hacked at a clay pipe coming down the wall. Waste and stagnant water sprayed out onto the officer, blinding him long enough for Rafe to cut across the old man's neck.

"Poor sot," Rafe said to his cohorts, "he now reeks of more than Death!"

"Privateer!" the voice called from behind him.

The Royal Guard dragged her right leg as the broken-off shaft of an arrow protruded from her calf. Rafe caught her as she fell, her lips uttering words that sent a chill through him, "The Queen!"

Instantly, his bravado disappeared. "Where?" he demanded, pushing back the girl's long black hair gently.

"The black rider," she gasped, her mind attempting to stay focused with the pain of her wound calling for attention. "The Queen is with him! Inside the Palace..."

"Rafton!" shouted Eshton. *"Rafton!"*

Rafe was already gone.

The caverns threw back every small sound. The torches held by the guards sputtered and smoked slightly in the occasional drafts that came from the myriad of doorways that yawned like black mouths.

"Where are we?" Jermal's voice echoed in the tunnels, bouncing off the stone walls.

"The catacombs," Arnese shuddered. "The regime that built the Palace had this series of secret passages built just above the sewers. These paths have not been used in more than three hundred years."

"Except by those who put them to use," snapped Dirare. "The Blademaster gave me a map. Many of us in Council have such maps, a plan of escape in case of invasions such as this. This will lead us out of the Palace, and if what the map says is true, we will emerge on the very street where my townhouse is. We shall be safe there."

The sudden rustling of clothing behind her made Dirare turn to Jermal. He now tore the veil from his face with disgust and lifted the headdress off his head, casting it aside much to the horror of the Morevian guards and to Arnese's amusement. She glared coldly at him as he removed his outer robe, "If you intend to disrobe, Your Majesty, kindly keep in mind that we are not serving maids."

"Forgive me if I forgo the respect and reverence, Dirare," bit Jermal, his words dripping with sarcasm. "The way I see things here is that we are on equal ground for the moment as we are both on the run! As we are on the run, I would prefer to do so in my day robes. In this ridiculous outfit I might as well have a bull's-eye painted on my back." He tossed the rest down to the cavern floor, keeping only the ornate ru-yilei.

Dirare raised a brow. "I did not think you could fight."

"It is an easy weapon to use," he shrugged. "Point the sharp end at your man, and run at him. Pretty simple."

Sudden, sharp battle cries echoed through the tunnels, making the attackers sound greater in numbers than what they truly were. The guards drew their swords but were already falling to bare-chested men with oiled skin, their white loincloths luminescent in the dark.

"Servants of the Kingdom, this is your King you attack!" the attending Morev'ar shouted to his brother.

He was answered with the blade of an atriah across his throat.

"My Lady!" Arnese's shrill screech caused Dirare to turn. The old lady pushed Dirare aside. The flat of a sword struck her hard, knocking her against the stone wall of the catacombs.

Dirare felt the air move over her head with the passage of the heavy, long-bladed knife. One of her guards saw this and swung. The Morev'ar's blood spattered her, the warm fluid seeping into her red robes.

"High Regent, back!" shouted one of the King's guards as he twisted to avoid the thrusting knife of a Morev'ar. "They mean to kill us!"

She was numb with horror. With trembling fingers, Dirare reached up to her headdress, which was askew. Her fingers came away soaked with blood. With a small scream she clawed it off her head, scattering pins, yanking her fingers away from where blood soaked her hair as if its touch burned her.

In the shadows of the catacombs, torches lying on the ground and casting light haphazardly around this melee, there was no way to know who fought against whom. Dirare only knew if something moved towards her, it was a foe. She could make out a form that was pushed off the stair's edge, his screams echoing and fading as he plummeted into the darkness of the chasm. Dirare watched intently as the sounds of blades cutting through skin and muscles became fewer and fewer, and then eventually ceased. She could hear only one other breathing, one shadow remaining. The torch lying on the steps cast no light on who it could be.

She extended a hand to the form.

The shadow raised a weapon into the air.

The ru-yilei thrust through his chest with such force that the tip protruded through his back. Lifting a foot, Jermal pushed the still-warm body off his blade.

Dirare stared at him in shock. He caught her arm and thrust the bloody weapon into her hand, a fallen torch in the other. "There are more coming!" Jermal picked up the unconscious Arnese, carrying her in his arms as if she were a wounded child. "Stay close to me. I saw a small tunnel a ways back."

He moved so fast that Dirare almost tripped over her hems in her haste to keep up with him. Footfalls sounded above them. Jermal counted three forms approaching just before slipping in to the alcove.

The tunnel was short, and small. A dead end in the rock. He laid Arnese down at the far end. "Stay with her. She is not dead, but we don't know how bad that crack on her head is."

Dirare gently laid her adviser's head on her lap. "Arnese?" A tear fell onto the old woman's face.

Jermal touched her shoulder comfortingly, "She'll be all right. Stay here with her!"

The tunnel was narrow, allowing only one man in at a time. He could see the Servant's long, menacing scymitar leading the way. He caught the shadows of two more at the mouth of the corridor, probably awaiting the end of the kill or ready to charge if he proved lucky.

Jermal stood before him, his feet planted wide apart, his blade already stained with the blood of a Morev'ar. A soft, menacing laugh ebbed through the tunnel. An intimidation tactic. The King raised his head proudly as he slipped into a defensive stance. His eyes were bright, his head high.

Gidaron smiled as he surveyed the results of the fight between his men, the loyal Morev'ar, and Lady Dirare's guard. The High Lady Min-Lu had given him a very good copy of the map to the catacombs, not that it was needed. He knew how to stalk in the darkness without losing his way in these forgotten, unexplored tunnels. He leisurely stepped over the corpses of the High Regent's guard. Armed only with a ceremonial sword against three of his men, the Consort-King and Regent were as good as dead.

The sound that reached his ears was indistinct at first, or his mind rejected it because it was so absurd to hear it in these surroundings. Then it came again, and this time his mind placed it. Laughter. Feminine laughter.

His hand slowly unsheathed his long, heavy knife as it came again. Clearer, closer this time, rippling madly. It lasted longer too, a hair-raising, almost insane laughter with a curl to the sound that he could not quite place.

"Come out, whoever you are. Woman! Ghost! Monster! Come out in the open where I can see you."

The pause lasted so long he fully did not expect the voice that answered. When it did, Gidaron wished the voice had remained silent. "Your guesses are all wrong."

There was nothing more than the distant firelight coming from where the guards fell, casting titanic shadows that filled the cavernous abyss surrounding him. He cursed himself for not taking a torch with him. His hand felt along the wall desperately until stopping at a sconce that, as were many of the torches in the catacombs, had remained unlit for centuries. He removed the ancient light from its brace and dragged it across his chest, using the ceremonial oils as a fuel. He then frantically struck the metal of his atriah and dagger together to nurse a spark. The voice found this amusing. The laugh was unsettling but he continued his efforts. The spark caught. The torch came to life. Gidaron held the flame high above his head and extended his dagger forward.

There was nothing to return his challenge but silence. He was alone.

Then, he turned around.

He was bolting across the courtyard, the shirai in his hands mowing down any opponent that challenged him. In the circles he travelled, this was known as a "dead run". The last act of a desperate man or someone completely lost in the heat of battle. The eyes watching him charge towards the Palace of a Thousand Suns knew him as reckless and perhaps touched by madness. That did not prevent them from joining him. In this short time, the Sisters of Nadinath had come to believe in the man's loyalty to the Queen. The English had come to believe in his cause. Perhaps his madness was having an influence over them all.

Gunfire from the Eyrieners that held the entrance to the Palace caused Rafe, Eshton, and a small number of Royal Guard to dive behind an overturned wagon of fruit crates and grain, now serving as cover for Kalea, Nassir, and Kubi-Sogi. Crossbow bolts whistled past this makeshift outpost, sinking deep into the Morevian earth. Nassir huffed as he primed a rifle and quickly appeared over the wagon. Amidst the shouts and sounds of battle, the Moor's gunfire ripped through the air. The scream of an Eyriener soon followed. Eshton set aside his own shirai and prepared pistols while two Royal Guard stood to draw back on their bows. A volley of shots sounded but not before the young warriors sent their arrows on their way. One bullet struck the taller of the two. The pellet still burned in her shoulder as she wailed in pain. Her Sister tried to hold her down so she would not injure herself further. Kalea fired her own bow in retaliation but only one soldier fell as another rank of Eyrieners, all armed with rifles and crossbows, took position behind the first line.

"Most of the Eyriener horde is lost within the city," Kalea spoke to Rafe as she laid out arrows beside her. From a belt pouch, she produced a small vial and anointed their tips with her poison. "These are the true exception of Eyriener nature. They were intelligent enough to return to the Palace and make a stand!"

"They are fortifying their position!" Rafe shouted over the rifle fire, "Does anyone have a clue how many we number here?"

"Before we took shelter, I saw at least one unit divided amongst the houses and streets here. All we await is an opportunity." Eshton leapt up and fired both pistols.

"We have a problem." Rafe gnashed his teeth as enemy gunners fired, bits of the wagon tossed into the air around them. "I did not anticipate the Eyrieners taking so well to firearms. We need to take out that line of gunners or they will just exhaust our supplies!"

"You need an opening, My Captain?" Nassir snatched up a small barrel of black powder, "Then an opening you shall have!" The Moor extended a muscular arm and pulled Rafe close, "The Queen is a good queen, but she is a better woman than any we have seen in our travels." He flashed a brilliant smile and gave him a rap against his chest, "Do not disappoint me, my friend!"

Nassir shoved Rafe into Eshton and Kalea, and ran free of the wagon. He could hear the plea of his captain distant in his ears, but he refused to stop in his lone charge. The first crossbow bolt entered his shoulder, giving him a shock and knocking him to one knee. He continued undaunted in his climb up the steps past fallen soldiers. Another bolt entered his thigh, but he only gave a deep moan as he neared the soldiers with rifles pointing at him. The first volley resonated in his ears, a mix of hammers simply clicking in the sounds of a misfire while others ignited the power within the pan. He felt two bullets enter him, but he knew at least four hit him. He felt blood spatter against his cheek when the bullet made contact with his shoulder and he could feel himself drop again to his knee. He was close enough. Nassir ripped open the small barrel and pulled back the hammer of his own pistol.

He said something that was neither Morevian, Eyriener, or English. *"Allah barikh Askana Moldarin."*

"God save Askana Moldarin," he had said in his homeland's tongue.

Then he pulled the trigger.

The powder keg's explosion ignited small powder pouches attached to the Eyriener soldiers, nearby kegs intended for the keeping of the Palace, and clothes stained and soiled with powder residue. It was a chain reaction of fire, blinding flashes of white light, and thick smoke accompanied by the screams of Eyrieners, now human torches wildly searching for anything that could extinguish the flame gorging on their flesh.

The Palace entrance, decorated with smouldering debris and corpses that burned like Christmastide logs, was open and awaiting the Morevian-English allies. They charged up the steps, a melody of battle cries filling the air as they ran through the horrific stench of burned flesh and black powder.

Rafe hesitated for a moment as he found, covered in powder burns and blood, his fallen First Mate. He wished to give his friend a proper farewell, but Nassir had made an oath for him to keep. He passed through the doors, ripped apart by an unnatural force, with a sinking feeling. By the look of the entrance and foyer, Coumiran was close.

This feeling of dread only worsened at the sight of the dead Palace Guard. They had died with a look of surprise on their faces. His own footfalls seemed to echo in the nearly deserted corridor as their numbers fanned out upon entering. A pair of More'var guards were running towards him. Rafe did not take a challenger's stance, but kept a grip on his shirai, keeping in mind his past experiences with the Morev'ar.

"So who are we, lads?" he asked as they closed on him. "Friends or foes?"

A curved weapon flying towards him was the reply.

Rafe felt someone tackle him, followed a moment later by the rush of air from the weapon's wake as it passed alarmingly close to his neck and embedded itself into the thick marble wall behind him.

"Foes," the Blademaster scoffed, still holding Rafe in his grasp.

The Morev'ar released a guttural howl as they charged. Rafe brought the shirai around as Kubi-Sogi unsheathed his own ru-yilei. He faced an opponent wielding an atriah as a buckler against Rafe, knocking his shirai's blade aside as the privateer twisted and twirled it in his hands. The disc-weapon had several hooked openings, similar to Spanish and Italian rapiers he fought against in his world, and worked the same way when in skilled hands. The atriah caught the shirai shaft, and with a bind-twist removed it from the privateer's grasp. The More'var gripped the atriah and howled as he leapt forward, bringing it across his opponent's chest.

Another weapon appeared between them. A flash of red hair, and then the Morev'ar felt a curious stinging sensation run up along his left side. He fell wide-eyed in shock at his defeat to this Otherworlder. He also caught the final moments of his brother Servant dying under the old Blademaster's ru-yilei, but a last glance to the privateer's saviour granted him a hint of satisfaction.

"Sarah, bless you, lass!" Rafe smiled widely, "You have never looked so lovely."

"Even in my torn chemise?" Sarah grinned, motioning to the wound she sported from saving her Captain, "And this was my finest wear."

"Well then, when we return to our own world, perhaps we shall sack an Italian barkentine and find you the finest—"

Before Rafe could finish his thought, his fellow privateer dropped to one knee. It appeared as if her muscles stopped working. He took the woman into his embrace as her body fought against the poison from the Morev'ar's weapon. Her breathing came in quick, short gasps while fear filled her eyes. She tightened her grip on his shirt and doublet as her body jerked against his. Her breath began to slow. Rafe had never seen his Mistress Gunner so terrified in her life.

Sarah chose her words carefully, still holding Rafe as she spoke. "Captain, I must insist on our agreed payment."

Rafe tipped her head back and pressed his lips to her own. She could taste the salt of his sweat, the sweetness of his tobacco indulgence, and the vitality of his own life that ebbed away from her. Sarah pulled him closer as a cold eased upward from her feet to her legs. She could not feel her limbs but she knew he was close and she would not let go. Then her lips released his own and her head fell limp in his arm.

Sarah was gone. Paid in full.

"Sweet dreams, lass," Rafe whispered. "Give Nassir my regards." He stood, anger driving back his fatigue as he checked his own pistols while he spoke. "Kalea, rally our forces. We must bring this battle to a close."

His eyes stared down the long corridors of the Palace, the storm clouds blocking out the sun and casting a strange blue-grey colour over the stark white and brilliant gold. Somewhere in the vast number of corridors and hallways were Askana Moldarin, High Lord Coumiran, and the traitor to the throne.

Nassir's and Sarah's deaths would not go unanswered.

Jermal never cared for the sword as a weapon, but within these close quarters, it served him well. The Morev'ar was big and the scymitar limited his movement in the narrow passageway. The hulking Servant swung at him clumsily. Returning to his old tricks as a thief, he easily slipped around the lumbering attacks to drive his sword into the slave's belly. He knew it was not his skill that won him the fight. It was luck. Sheer, unabated luck. Now he moved slowly for the archway where the other two waited. His blade was steady though his heart raced as he emerged into the dim lighting of the labyrinth. His eyes went from corner to corner, searching.

Only the flickering from dropped torches broke the tomb-like silence. A thin trail of blood on the ground was the solitary sign that someone had been there. Jermal turned back to the tunnel. He opened his mouth to call to them, but stopped as the torch he picked up from the stone floor caught a tiny glint. He lowered it closer to the shape. It was a pattern created in blood. A footprint. A footprint that did not appear human.

"Dirare!" His whisper echoed through the stone corridors, a multitude of calls each one syllable slower than the other. "We have got to go! They are gone."

"What do you mean 'gone'? It cannot be so! The Morev'ar simply do not leave." Her voice wavered in fear. Jermal could hear her gather up the unconscious Arnese in her arms. "There were three that pursued us and only one—"

"I assure you, we are alone." He extended the torch back towards their original path as Dirare now joined him. "We have to go before more of them arrive. I don't think we should try for your estate."

"Indeed?" Dirare could still hear the hysterical edge to her voice, but having Jermal issue commands to her was sobering. "Please do let me know, my King, why you think that is such an ill-planned idea?"

"How about the More'var who ambushed us in this passage? They came from ahead of us. I think your estate, High Lady, is a bit too obvious a choice."

"So where shall we go?" Dirare asked, pulling Arnese closer to her.

"We double back. Perhaps there is another escape route we can take. A servant's quarters or even the kitchens." The High Regent looked at Jermal blankly, her eyes hard and cool as she tried to regain her control. "Dirare, I think you need to trust me on this." Still no response. He could see shock beginning to set in. Jermal prodded further, admittedly with a twinge of satisfaction, "Otherwise you are on your own. I think now *you* need *me* in order to survive."

Those words won him a dark glare.

They began their climb upward. Sounds of the occasional gunshot filtered down through the vents of the caverns. They shared no words as they continued through the twisting darkness of this underground maze, one corridor connecting with another, then another. Eventually, the faint echoes of battle silenced as they entered a juncture. Their torch sputtered suddenly as they struggled to decipher keystones above the stone archways surrounding them.

"The map," Jermal whispered, sheathing the torch into a sconce.

Dirare gently laid her trusted adviser on the juncture floor, resting the old woman's head back in her lap. She then produced her map of the catacombs. Dirare's eyes puckered in frustration as she studied it in the dimness of the single torch. "This junction is the first we encountered shortly after escaping the Great Hall." She peered at the first keystone, "This tunnel will return us there."

"Then we know which way not to go," Jermal smirked.

Dirare shot him a look as Arnese stirred. With a sharp sigh to stamp down her frustration, she continued. "The tunnel to the right will take us to the main street directly under the Grand Arch of Songkusai—"

"— and right into the middle of the battle. No thank you," he stated calmly, now turning to a passage to his left. "What about this tunnel?"

Jermal was lifting the torch to its keystone when a gloved hand reached from out of the darkness and clasped around his throat. The shock of the grasp sent his ru-yilei clattering to the floor as he was suddenly raised into the air. Jermal's desperate gasps for air joined Dirare's screams as the giant figure stepped into their juncture.

"This passage" murmured the new voice, "leads to the crypt vaults of Morevi which also connect to the Royal Chambers."

He was dressed in Eyriener clothes of black and gold. There was something in his eyes though. They were not proper for that realm. Choking for breath, Jermal thrashed wildly. His fingers snagged the silk mask, pulling it free. There was a momentary flash of his face before Jermal was tossed aside. The man scrambled to cover his features, but the glimpse was long enough for Dirare and the semi-conscious Arnese to see what he tried to conceal. Not his branding. His heritage.

"You are of Morevi, child." Arnese uttered in a moment of awareness.

Dirare's head turned sharply from her fallen mentor to the black-cloaked stranger. She knew his face. It was faintly, naggingly familiar. The frightening figure had under his arm a heavy book with mouldering leather covers, the crest of Morevi's First Dynasty singed on its spine. The sign marked it as one of the forbidden books from the Libraries of Ancient Texts that most remembered only from myth. *How had he found it, this book?* Dirare thought quickly. *Who led him to the vaults?*

As if in answer to the silent questions, Min-Lu's smiling face moved into the light. Dirare's heart sank as she saw the young noble lovingly slip her arm around his. She watched this surreal scene unfold further as an Eyriener soldier in blood-stained armour forced Askana Moldarin out of the shadows. An almost unrecognisable Askana Moldarin, pale and ill in stained white robes, a woman who would have fallen to the floor without support.

"Well spotted," Coumiran said softly to Arnese, making Dirare's head jerk up. Swiftly, before Dirare could draw back he lunged forward and took Arnese's chin in his hand. "That done, what more have you to do on this earth, old mother?"

Dirare felt the crack of Arnese's neck deep in her lap. She looked down in stupefied horror at Arnese's head turned sharply the wrong way in her arms. She was trembling uncontrollably, completely unaware of Jermal's tight grip as he drew her from underneath Arnese's corpse, away from Coumiran. The man had killed Arnese in her arms. In her own arms.

When Dirare finally tore her eyes away from Arnese to Coumiran, he simply placed his gloved finger to his masked mouth and said gently, slowly, "Shhh..." He did not do this to console her. He did this to warn her.

"Your face holds back anger well, thief," Min-Lu laughed at Jermal, "but your eyes betray you. You think you see the fall of Morevi? You are actually witnessing its rebirth. From the ashes of war and bloodshed, it will emerge as a nation unchallenged in this world."

Coumiran returned his attentions to the book in his hands. Its dry, dusty pages between cracked leather were as valuable as gold to him. He realised now that nothing else mattered save what he held before him. Not the people around him, not the ground beneath his feet, not the kingdom above. It was a good feeling, to be holding all his purpose in his hands.

"Come, my love," he said. "It is time."

As they stepped into the darkness of the tunnel, Dirare could not help but reflect on the words of this stranger. She could see Min-Lu brighten as he spoke the words *"Come, my love..."* but it was obvious that his words were not meant for her.

Eyes watched them in the darkness. Green eyes ringed with gold.

Silently she loosed her hold on the stone pillar and dropped to the ground, silent and invisible in the darkness that was her friend. She sensed the terrible power in the black-cloaked man. She knew she did not have the means to bring him down now, formidable though she was.

Lubria loved the glory of battle. Her predatory instincts woke to the scent of blood. Like the greater cats of the jungles, she could kill for no other reason save sport. Yet on the streets above she had caught Askana's scent. That had been enough to lure her away from the fighting. In the catacombs, the hunt began.

The trail led her through the madness of the Palace into the catacombs. She would have watched Coumiran and Min-Lu without distraction had it not been for the sound of familiar voices and fighting in the corridors. Her hatred towards Dirare ran deep. She would not save the woman who banished her from the only true home she had ever known. She was faintly impressed by the courage of the man protecting Dirare and Arnese. She smelt his fear, but he stood his ground. Such bravery deserved a reward, and so came the deaths of the two Morev'ar. After amusing herself with the Morev'ar leader, she disappeared again into the shadows.

Now she thought about what she had seen. She was proud of her sister, fighting a spell as well-woven as any from the Elves. She cared little for Morevi, but her loyalty to Askana was unquestionable. As such, she knew she needed help in her rescue. The only help she trusted was the human. The privateer whose scent curdled in her nostrils.

As she loped away into the darkness Lubria savoured the pain she saw in Dirare's eyes as Arnese's lifeless body fell to the floor. Blood for exile. A fair enough exchange.

CHAPTER SEVENTEEN
The Spell of Souls

One of the huge windows in the Great Hall had been smashed. Glass shards twinkling softly in the light of flickering torches lay scattered on the mosaic covering the floor. The wind tore at his robes just as it tore through angry black clouds in the sky. Looking out over the Sleeping Dragons, Coumiran could not help but marvel at the beauty of the lush green jungle slipping under shades of grey, an occasional ray of sunlight breaking through the thick cloud cover. He used to wonder, long ago, whether there was still hidden magic in this land, though it had been bred out of the people long ago. The mystique of Morevi. The way the very name symbolised wealth and instigated awe was inexplicable, particularly given its isolation. His father once loved this kingdom to the point of obsession. Now, as he watched the storm block out sunlight and wash twilight shadows over the land, he finally felt he understood the attraction of this realm. It would be a magnificent gift. His wedding gift to the woman he loved.

"You shall have your vengeance, Father." Coumiran caressed the book in his arms as he spoke, "Mother, embrace him with care and look upon your son with pride, for he shall rule in his father's name."

No one else heard his quiet words. He turned slowly to savour the sight of the Hall of Dawn. Council members under the watch of his Eyrieners openly grieved over the loss of Lady Arnese. Many of these strong Morevians struggled to keep their pride intact as they stared at their captors defiantly, their jaws tight and eyes cold as they tried not to think about the lifeless servants, guards, and Ladies of the Blood. Women hard-edged in politics were now struck dumb by true violence. Husbands, once warriors in their own right, tended to those injured in the earlier rush for the barred doors. Powerless against these familiar and foreign weapons.

The Collected Houses could only watch in horror as a struggling Askana Moldarin, her absence now explained, was secured with leather bonds to a waist-high marble slab. Normally a place for ceremonial chalices, gifts from tributaries, and objects for ritual, it now became a sacrificial altar as she lay there, her sluggishness and feeble efforts at resistance a sign of defeat to her uncomprehending subjects. That and the burnt sign stamped on the book Coumiran placed on a lectern above Askana's head cast a sense of foreboding over the Hall, both for the Morevians and the Eyrieners.

"Council of a Hundred Turi, dear nobility of the Collected Houses, and you men who have so graciously surrendered your masculinity, I bring you greetings from King Cedric of Eyrie." His soft laugh could be heard over the light din of anguish and protest. Coumiran offered a hand to Min-Lu as he continued his address. "I do understand the difficulties in addressing the Collected Houses and the representatives of Council all at once. Therefore, I have called upon the services of Lady Min-Lu of House Annaki to usher in the New Age of Morevi."

The eyes of ladies who opposed the ambitious Min-Lu narrowed as she slipped closer to Coumiran. Their fists clenched at the sight of this traitor's slightly elevated chin and subtle smile upon her face.

"Those of you who have allied yourselves with me in the past shall remain my allies in this new chapter of the history and the future of Morevi," Min-Lu stated proudly, placing her hand into Coumiran's warm grasp. "With my beloved High Lord Ruain at my side, we shall bring Morevi into the Light of Prosperity, beginning with a glorious new alliance with Eyrie, bonded forever by our monarchy and the heirs we provide..."

Her words faded. Min-Lu paused, bringing her hand to her chest. She could not catch her breath. She could feel a slow, swelling sensation in her throat. There was a strange taste in her mouth. Sharp and bitter. She brought her fingertips up to her lips, and her eyes went wide at the sight of fresh blood covering them. Min-Lu quickly looked to Coumiran, opening her mouth to ask for his help. Only a gurgle came from her lips. She looked down to see a long streak of the deepest red trailing along the brilliant pale blue silk of her court dress. She could not understand what was happening to her.

Min-Lu then realised Coumiran's grip on her hand was tighter, and he was whispering something. He was not whispering *to her* so much as he was whispering *at her*. His eyes were completely void of emotion or compassion as his voice rose in volume.

"*Alysi te-kur-durmas*, Min-Lu *re* Annaki. *Malateri mortis sam inflamis te richarsha,*" he repeated over and over again while clutching her hand tightly.

She could feel a single tear fall down her cheek as she finally made a sound. A low, pathetic wail. Min-Lu then felt another wave of agony pass through her and she released another sickening gurgle. Then her air stopped. With her free hand, she reached for the silk mask and tore it free of his face.

She could see it in the features of his dark eyes and skin. He was not of pure Eyriener descent. He was half-Morevian, horribly disfigured from some kind of branding. The burn marks appeared to be some sort of Morevian writing. Min-Lu tried to make out the words, but she could not see them clearly. There was something in her eyes. Something thick and stinging.

The Hall filled with screams as it did earlier. The Council and Nobles watched, terrified, as Min-Lu fell at the feet of Coumiran. His face was free of the black silk mask and now his true heritage was made known to both Eyrieners and Morevians.

"My *beloved*," he purred, gently caressing the smooth auburn hair of the dead lady. Blood still ran from her eyes, ears, and mouth as her body twitched lightly. Faint glimmers of a life he took quite easily. "You brought me through the city gates, guided me through the catacombs, delivered to me the Collected Houses, and provided in idle hours pleasant entertainment. You have served your purpose."

Coumiran worked his foot underneath Min-Lu's body and callously rolled it down the steps of the dais. He returned his attentions to the book, gently caressing the pages as he glanced at spell after spell. He waited for the commotion to subside before addressing them in a chilling, calm tone. "There is no need to worry. You will not share the same fate as my sweet Min-Lu, even those of you who shared her vision for this realm's future. My Maeve had a vision of her own—" A small gasp broke his sentence as, underneath his fingertips, he saw the Spell of Souls. The ink was fading but still visible on the aged parchment. Its page shivered under his fingertips as he looked at the restrained Askana. "Now the vision shall become a reality."

One hand reached upward to the giant dome above the Hall of Dawn while the other traced the arcane symbols as he began, his voice barely audible. A sharp chill rustled through the rotunda. A light dust of gold and yellow light swirled around his body and Askana's for an instant, then faded away. Underneath everyone's feet, a tremor was growing. The tiny hairs along everyone's arms prickled. They could feel its presence, its hostility, its malice. *Something* was gathering in the vast, enclosed space beneath the dome. The Morevians clutched to one another with an indescribable fear in hearing a dialect not spoken in centuries—the Old Language of forbidden magic.

The Eyrieners just stood their ground, earlier doubt becoming certainty. They dared not move against their leader of Morevian descent. Their comtempt for these people was quelled by their fear of this half-breed, this fear only growing as they watched him command what was forbade by the Fellowship. He truly was a devil, but what he called forth they instinctively knew was far more evil.

Coumiran's voice settled into a ritualistic rhythm, rising and falling from a whisper to loudness and back again. Askana's body twitched, convulsed, each word driving into her like a blade. Instead of the nausea that rendered her unable to speak or fight, there were now waves of pain rolling through her, making her heart race erratically and cold sweat bead on her skin. She wanted to call out to her people to stand up and fight, to pull Coumiran down while his attention was focused on the spell. Askana could only keep her eyes shut tight, struggling against a chill clamped around her throat. In the darkness of her closed eyelids, grey shadows were forming, twisting, and dispersing, but always coming closer, reaching for her. The presence of *another* grew stronger.

Then another shock of pain came, pain that she had never felt even in the throes of battle. It rolled up like fire from her legs to her body. It forced her eyes open and tore a scream from her throat.

What Askana saw above her made her wish they had remained shut.

"Second line, fire!"

The volley of rifle fire ripped through the air, raising flocks of jungle birds screaming their alarm to the ominous sky above them. The darkness had rolled in like a tide from the sea, frightening both attackers and defenders. It also made aiming a challenge. Thankfully, many of the invaders dropped.

This was the second part of Captain Rafton's plan, led by Lord Miles Agecroft. Open the city gates and push the Eyrieners back into the surrounding jungles. He was not certain how hard the enemy had been hit, but they were far less than what had appeared in the morning's attack. Before the third line of riflemen composed of Morevians and Englishmen could step forward, Eyrieners and Morev'ar were in full retreat from Songkusai.

Agecroft frowned as cheers of men and women filled the air around him. The last of the Eyrieners made a mad dash for the jungles, using bloodied swords to cut through brush and foliage. He knew this was a victory for them. It was obvious in the enemy's retreat, but he could not find a reason to celebrate.

"Send the runner! Inform the forces at Kinessa we have the city!" cried the Maiden standing beside Lord Agecroft. "Blessed be Nadinath for this victory!"

He turned to catch the sharp-edged satisfaction sparkling harshly in dark eyes, eyes that he would have found otherwise pretty. "Dear lass, far be it from me to question your Goddess," he sighed heavily, "but perhaps you celebrate in haste."

The young woman had been charged by the Anjara herself to work alongside this Otherworlder. She found his clothes flamboyant, his manners distasteful, and his arrogance nothing less than nauseating, yet she refused to fail in her duty. She would endure the man's short-comings and serve Morevi well. Still, she could not stand being referred to as "lass".

"Is this how you Otherworlders embrace victory?" huffed the Maiden.

"A retreat means victory? My dear lass..." His eyes caught her body stiffening lightly. He gave a gentle nod and smiled, "What is your name?"

She lifted her chin and spoke, "Majin, third dan of the shirai and First Daughter of the House of—"

"Good lady Majin, spare the titles and listen." Agecroft returned his gaze to the wall of trees and plant life trembling from Eyriener and Morev'ar blades cutting a path through them, "It is a victory, lass, but not *the* victory."

Her eyes flashed, hot with the remaining wildness of battle. "Have you no faith in the Anjara and the Blademaster?"

"I have every faith in their abilities, as well as Captain Rafton's. But these men do not scatter in terror. They are heading in the same direction. They go to meet their comrades en route, so that we shall all meet again," he spoke as he slowly shook his head. "On the Kinessa Plains."

Majin blew her ram's horn repeatedly as Agecroft sent a single gunshot into the air. It was a call for the allies to meet at the city gates. Majin's eyes turned skyward to the grey clouds turning black as night.

The Eyrieners and More'var guarding the doors to the Great Hall heard their cry from down the corridor. A handful of men and women following an Otherworlder dressed in black. The privateer was yelling at the top of his lungs, gripping a shirai tight in his hands. His cry was answered by the raised voices of those who charged with him into what would be a slaughter of a last stand. The Eyrieners and Morev'ar were certain that this was a desperate tactic. Either that, or they were all stark-raving mad.

Then came the cries from the rear.

Kalea and her Royal Guard filled the corridor, soldier after soldier. The enemy was now trapped between the Anjara's battalion and the pirate's. Eyrieners against Maidens, Morev'ar against Otherworlders, Morev'ar against Morevians. Bodies covered one another in pools of blood. They all fought valiantly, but fatigue was slowing swords and straining muscles. The enemy still outnumbered them. A Palace Guard protecting Rafe's right flank shrieked his death as a heavy blade smashed through his armour.

The growl, when it came, cut through the sounds of fighting. The Morev'ar froze at the sound of it, praying it was merely thunder from the growing storm outside. They were the first to look up to the rafters where a nightmare in stripes smiled her razor-toothed smile at them before dropping down into the centre of this struggle. Her talons ripped effortlessly through armour as if tearing through cheesecloth. A great shout went up from the Morevians and Englishmen as they pushed forward again while the Anjara advanced from the rear and Lubria worked from the inside, clawing her way out.

The last man standing was a Morev'ar.

"We refuse the false Queen who will lead Morevi into an age of darkness!" he spat, "We will fight till every last traitor is brought down! We will not die for we, the True Spirit of Morevi, are eternal!"

The Morev'ar charged for Rafe, his heavy, long knife raised high above his head. No one moved, however, as Rafe calmly lifted his pistol and fired into the slave. The Servant staggered back and joined his fellow Morev'ar on the floor.

"Well, it appears the 'Spirit of Morevi' is not bullet-proof," Rafe shrugged.

"I know where they hold the Queen, human," hissed Lubria, her face fearsomely spattered with blood. "It is in the Great Hall. The one called Coumiran is with her." Her deep green eyes turned to Kubi-Sogi and Kalea, "Coumiran had a book with him. I did recognise it as one of the crypt books."

Rafe watched Kubi-Sogi and Kalea turn pale at Lubria's words. The massive carven doors of the Great Hall towered before him, and a strange quiet fell over them all in the corridor. He sensed that something was very, very wrong.

Eshton pulled back the hammers of his pistols, "Best to be prepared for anything. Ready, Rafton?"

Rafe backed away from the doors, his own shirai poised. "Gentlemen, ladies." He did not speak with a battle cry. He was controlled, focused. He simply met their gaze, all waiting on his word. He smiled and spoke evenly, "For Askana Moldarin."

They did not have to shout this pledge. The conviction was there. "For Askana Moldarin," came a wave of voices. Clear. Devoted.

Flanked by English and Maidens, Rafe gave a nod. They made to charge for the doors, only to have them burst open from the force of a howling gale that knocked everyone off their feet. Several of the slighter Maidens were blown back to crash into pillars and walls. Those on the floor fought to keep from being swept away as the wind screamed at them.

Even as he fought to keep his eyes open in the gale, Rafe heard her scream. It was a scream of torment such as no one should ever hear. It was the first scream that felt as if it cut him in two.

"Askana!" Rafe called over the howling cold.

They could see the ranks of seats lining the vast chamber, empty now as the Council members and Nobles were picking themselves up from the ground where they had thrown themselves. The splendour of the Great Hall was shattered. Windows destroyed by the onslaught of wind, great tapestries torn down, ornamental weapons thrown into the centre of the room and remaining there. No one moved to gather them up to fight against the Eyrieners.

Then, one by one, English and Morevian eyes turned upward to the rotunda.

"By the Goddess," Kalea whispered, her voice dry.

The great dome was now obscured by a darkness even deeper than that outside. This darkness, however, was nothing seen by human eyes in several millennia. It should have been nothingness, a mere void, but this darkness moved as if it were alive, swirling and stretching like a pulsing, sickly surface. Voices, some whispers and others wild shrieks, were coming from it. Something pushed against its surface from the other side, eventually breaking through the dark barrier. Something wispy, something with an undeniable form. Something reaching for Askana as she lay screaming on the pedestal. The unnatural voices were intelligible now. They were calling a name, as if imploring it to return.

"Maeve," uttered Kubi-Sogi with the unearthly chorus.

Rafe was frozen, reminded of every single reason why he hated magic. He could feel a strain on his heart, the blood rushing to every tip of his being in fear and agony. He helplessly watched this hellish scene unfold, his weapon slowly lowering with those around him.

The ghost opened her mouth, and the Great Hall filled with an unholy screech. A chill swept across them all. They were assailed by a nauseating, dead stench as the scream rung in their ears.

It was Lubria that led the charge, fearlessly leaping in to disable the disorientated Eyriener soldiers who cowered in as much fear as their prisoners. What she had seen in her past to inure her to this, no one wanted to know, but her movement restored resolve.

"Gunners, fire!" snapped Eshton.

Their rifles shouldered as if it was a reflex action to his words. The first volley sounded over the wails and shrieks from the dome. As the first offensive line dropped to reload, the second line stepped forward, but paused in shouldering their weapons. The bullets meant for Coumiran suddenly stopped, caught by an invisible shield, then dropped harmlessly to the mosaic floor. The second line turned their weapons upward and fired courageously at the horror above them. Unearthly voices shrieked in anger. This time the pellets rebounded, striking down riflemen and archers.

"This is witchcraft!" cried one of the gunners. "The Devil's work!"

"No, this is ancient sorcery! Banned generations ago." The Blademaster's trembling hand grabbed Rafe's arm and spun him about, "Coumiran intends to bring Maeve back by replacing Askana's soul with hers!"

The Anjara held her shirai above her head, releasing a shrill battle cry before she and three soldiers charged across the Great Hall with weapons poised to cut down Coumiran. With no warning, they were swept aside by an unseen hand. The Maidens flew across the hall, their bodies slamming hard against the bare walls. Kalea and her second let out slight gasps of pain as their shirai slid across the marble floor. The other two wrapped around the large marble columns of the Great Hall. Their necks snapped on impact.

"Archers, loose!" cried Kubi-Sogi.

With an almost deafening howl, arrows flew through the air across the Hall to their target. As with the bullets, they only stopped in their flight. An odd arrow glanced off the slab and lectern.

Something about this caught Rafe. *If I were to be certain of anything in my life*, Rafe prayed silently, *please let this be the time*. Snatching a bow from a nearby yeoman, he fought to keep the arrow in his grasp from trembling as he immersed its tip into a nearby lamp's oil basin. He could feel her fear and her pain because they *were* his. His eyes narrowed on his target as he pulled the flaming arrow back steadily. The thing that was Maeve had almost freed herself from the barrier, her ghostly form stretched painfully thin. It was touching Askana's cheek, and he felt sick as he saw the outline of a woman's face in that stretched darkness.

Kubi-Sogi's eyes widened as he looked at Rafe and his target, "You are aiming for the Queen!"

"No!" Heads snapped around at Elunear's scream. "You cannot kill the Queen!"

Royal Guard, Maidens and Lubria bore down on him. Rafe felt the instant Elunear's fingertips touch his shoulder, the instant Lubria's fur pelt brushed up his side, and the instant his fingertips released the drawn bowstring.

Coumiran could hear Askana's screams now turning into sharp gasps and whimpers of agony as a translucent grey hand reached deep into her chest and clutched her heart. He would not let this sight overwhelm him, yet his anticipation ripped a gasp from him. His Maeve was so close to being. He shouted into the maelstrom above, arms raised to the blurry forms of the envious spirits on the opposite side of the barrier, keeping them back as Maeve reached again into the mortal plane.

Then in the corner of his eye, he caught sight of the blazing arrow soaring towards Askana. He continued undaunted. He had prepared for any desperate attempt to save her, even if it meant killing her. The protection spell he uttered before beginning the ritual covered both him and Askana. The arrow would stop as the bullets that tried to strike him down.

What he did not anticipate on was the archer's skill as it struck *three feet to the left of its target*.

The arrow sank deep into the book. The dry, brittle pages were consumed in a quick, sharp roar of heat and flame. Coumiran stepped back, his eyes blinded for an instant by the burst that singed his face and caught his robes, breaking the incantation as he screamed with pain, beating at the fire. The moment's distraction released a powerful surge against its weaver, and threw Coumiran clear of the altar. The book smouldered before him, its words gone forever, yet he could see the Spell in his mind. The final stanza was there. He knew it. Merely on the tip of his tongue.

Then came the shriek from above.

She had taken a near-solid form, travelling so far from its Darkness to touch her sister's heart. To feel the sensations of a corporal existence. To feel the energy of life. The moment his spell stopped calling her, protecting her from the agents that kept her in the Darkness, she was lost. Maeve's head arched back, her shriek desperate this time as she made a last, futile lunge for Askana. Then black, inky claws sank into her still incorporeal form. Fingers and hands reached for her as her fellow spirits quickly gathered to pull her back. Coumiran watched as the phantom of his true love was torn into disconnected puffs of light and smoke. The unintelligible cries for help reverberated against marble walls and echoed in his ears as he forced himself back up to his feet, stumbling as he reached for her, not heeding the demonic hands ripping through the air. He reached for her transparent hand, his cries of sorrow joining with her own frantic pleas for help. For him. His grasp passed through the collection of fog, light, and dust. Then came a deafening roar, a rush of wind, and Maeve's screams giving one final call to him. Her imploring was drowned out by the growls of the Darkness' guardians as they dragged this lost soul back to its proper place.

Silence.

Askana, still bound to the ceremonial slab, gasped deeply for air to fill her lungs. She was still aware. She—Askana, not Maeve—was alive.

The ancient text was reduced to a collection of burning embers between covers of scorched leather, smouldering parchment falling at his feet like dead leaves in autumn. The Darkness and its agents were gone. Coumiran looked about him vacantly, confused. English soldiers, privateers, and Morevian warriors barred his escape through the main corridor. They shouldered rifles and held pistols forward. Shirai were held at the ready, waiting for him to move. He did not seem to care. Nothing mattered in the man's eyes. Nothing mattered until his eyes fell on the Otherworlder returning to his feet. The bow was still in his hand. He was a blur of black and silver to Coumiran's smoke-reddened eyes, but he was more than recognizable to the hate that now rose like a wave in his heart. A visceral wanting, a malice more than any human being had ever wished on another swelled inside him.

No more, Coumiran thought. *It ends now.*

The unseen force gripped Rafe and cast him effortlessly against one of the marble pillars. The attack could have killed him, but it was only meant to deal pain. Lingering pain. Before the privateer could pick himself up, he was thrown against the opposite wall by another wave of intense power. Only a last-minute twist of his body saved Rafe from a cracked skull.

A privateer aimed a rifle at Coumiran only to feel something grab his head. With a single, sharp sweep of his arm and a quick utterance, he broke the gunner's neck.

"*Kel'an Sia!*" hissed Coumiran again at Rafe, his eyes red with anger.

A third attack sent Rafe flying across the Great Hall, his body landing like dead weight in the middle of the floor. The assault was harder now, but he refused to fall completely. He felt as if every bone in his body was broken. Every breath hurt him. He held himself up on his hands and knees, coughing up blood that swelled in his mouth and throat. His eyes shut tight as he thought of what this was doing to Askana.

Rafe's thoughts of concern were broken abruptly when Coumiran grabbed him by the hair. He tried to pull free of the gloved grasp, but could do nothing as he was dragged up to the dais. Rafe was tossed next to the ceremonial slab next to Askana, also suffering in the throws of Coumiran's hate-driven assault. His scalp was still tingling after Coumiran released him.

Rafe looked up at him defiantly, "I liked you better with the mask."

"No, Rafton, not this time!" Coumiran bellowed, his voice amplified by the rotunda of the Great Hall. "You have daunted me for the last time! I intend to make you pay for every bit of anguish you have caused me, both professionally..." He choked back tears as his eyes looked high into the ornate decorations of the overhead dome, "...and personally." With each hand, Coumiran grabbed Rafe and Askana by their jaws, forcing their mouths open. "I learned a great deal in my study, Rafton. I think I understand this spell well enough. *Alysi te-kur-durmas*, Rafe Rafton. *Malateri mortis sam inflamis te richarsha. Alysi te-kur-durmas*, Askana *re* Moldarin. *Malateri mortis sam inflamis te richarsha...*"

Both Rafe and Askana lurched sharply as a fire swept through them both. It felt as if their insides were boiling in their own blood. With each of Coumiran's words, their pain stung harder. Rafe could taste blood in his mouth on the third mention of his name.

"So if you feel one another's pain," Coumiran's whisper came to him, "then with this simultaneous blow, there is nothing left. Except death. Death for you and for Askana Moldarin. *Alysi te-kur-durmas*, Rafe Rafton..."

Rafe closed his eyes at the building torture inside his body. Faces then flashed through his mind. O'Donnell. Reiley. Nassir. Fellow Englishmen lying dead in the streets outside. Maidens cut down in the bloom of youth. So much waste and death caused by the bitter ambitions and blind vengeance of this man. Rafe's eyes opened wide. Coumiran's grip was firm on both of them, his eyes completely blinded by a need for retribution. Eyes so blinded that they failed to notice Askana's dagger still sheathed in Rafe's wrist gauntlet.

Coumiran's spell stopped abruptly. His grip remained on them both, softening only a little. His eyes went wide. He could not understand why suddenly he could not speak nor breathe. Coumiran blinked at this sudden distraction. He slowly shook his head, as if to clear his mind, and that was when he noticed the dagger in his throat, run up to its tiny hilt. He could feel his lips mouthing the curse, but there was no sound. Rafe pulled the dagger free of his throat, pushing Coumiran back. His unsteady feet tripped on the steps of the dais and he fell, his head cracking hard against the marble floor. He continued to roll down the steps, his progress eventually stopped by Min-Lu's corpse.

Eyrieners standing guard over the Hall of Dawn did not react soon enough as the Royal Guard drove them down to one knee and English gunners pulled their rifle hammers back. They could have put up a resistance, but there seemed to be little point. Their entire campaign had been a lie, a complete and utter lie. Driven by an obsession over a dead Morevian woman. For years, they had answered to him. For years, they had feared him. For years, they had taken orders and cowered to a man of Morevian blood. The will to fight was no more. Barely a thought.

Rafe pulled himself up to the pedestal, every movement of his body screaming out to him, begging him to remain still. He ignored the pain as he cut Askana free. On the last bond snapping in two, he found himself caught in Askana's embrace. She was trembling. Was that a sob he heard? Then, in the midst of his own personal agony, it dawned on him what she had endured. He wrapped his own arms around her, gently stroking her long, dark hair as she sobbed softly. He closed his eyes gently at the feel of her head nuzzled in his shoulder as she fought to catch her breath. She clutched tightly to his doublet. He could feel it in her grasp. She would not let go.

Then he opened his eyes. "Your Grace," he whispered. "We are not alone."

Askana turned to look out into the Great Hall. Jermal, High Lady Dirare, and the Collected Houses and Council of Morevi all stared at her and the privateer. Many eyes, Jermal's in particular, stared at her with growing questions on their minds. Allies of her House were gazing at her in wonder. Would nothing, not even the darkest magic, strike her down? Others sworn to oppose her harboured a hint of fear and apprehension in their eyes. They, too, wondered if she truly was invincible. All eyes of her trusted Royal Guard and loyal Palace Guard looked to their Gracious Sovereign for a word, a command. They, along with their English allies, struggled to remain standing. They were all battle-weary. Then there was her sister Lubria who stood proudly, her striped skin decorated with the blood of the enemy.

She returned her eyes back to Rafe. They had come so far in their travels. It came to her in a flood of memories and emotions. The journey to Eyrie. The trials of the English Court. The gambit against the Eyriener fleet. *It was all for the greater good of Morevi*, she had told herself. This was why she took a risk in hiring this privateer, to uncover the treachery against the Morevian Crown. Askana gently traced his cheek with the back of her fingers and smiled as she once did for him in London.

Rafe toyed for a moment in pointing out her playing the quintessential role of the maiden sacrifice to be rescued by a dashing hero, and she had played it before her Court when she needed her reputation and the respect it brought to win back her throne. There was no place here for jibes, wit, or slight regard. As always, she was Queen, first and foremost.

He lowered himself to one knee, "Your Majesty, my charge has been fulfilled."

All eyes turned to Askana, now flanked by Kubi-Sogi and Kalea who assisted her off the altar. Her dark eyes passed slowly over the terrified prisoners. She could see them all pale and sick with fear, perhaps recollecting the reports of their border patrols.

This invasion of her realm and deaths of her kinsmen demanded action. Retaliation. Revenge. She paused, her eyes turning to Rafe for a moment, then back to her own people.

Askana's decree took everyone by surprise. "We will grant these prisoners safe passage to Arathelle and then home to Eyrie, along with their dead. This shall be our message to King Cedric. Enough blood has been spilt for one day."

"This will be a most long, grim night ahead of us," Kubi-Sogi stated sombrely. He turned to Elunear, "Send word to the forces holding the city walls and on the Kinessa Plains. The Palace is ours. We must gather the dead and separate Eyriener from Morevian, soldier from officer."

Askana gave a gentle nod to Kalea, "Make certain, Anjara, the prisoners are well kept. They shall be sent on their way at sunrise."

They could hear an occasional crack from the direction of Songkusai. The unfamiliar crack of gunfire. On the Kinessa Plains prayers were being said to the gods and goddesses through the rasp of weapons being sharpened. They prayed that the capital would hold, that the Otherworlders' plan would work. During the preparations for this battle, the English told them of a battle in their world where they had been outnumbered yet emerged victorious. They called it the Battle of Agincourt.

They did not care about past battles of the Otherworlds. This was here. This was Morevi, faced by enemies that outnumbered her forces, no matter the endeavours of the Otherworlder ships.

In a tent a young woman sat, her ru-yilei across her knees. She had been made commander only a day after the English allies arrived. Her armour did not fit her properly. Her mother protested with tears against her decision to lead their House soldiers on the field. Her father had remained silent as she strapped on armour intended for her brother. Fear was much like failure in this decision not only to fight but lead the Morevian women against the barbaric Eyrieners—not an option. Yet she knew her commission was not for her abilities with the ru-yilei. It was for her family's history. She now prayed the blood of her father and her grandfather would be enough to lead her House soldiers to victory.

The tent flaps parted with an address the girl was still unaccustomed to hearing. "Commander Remini."

The woman who entered was Leanna Kai, a seasoned warrior in service to Askana Moldarin. She was a commander of the famed House Moldarin soldiers, trained on the Moldarin estate and second only to the Anjara herself. "We are to meet in General Trokan's tent to discuss battle plans for the break of day."

Remini replaced the elegant sword in its scabbard then secured it across her back as Leanna had shown her earlier that night, "Any word from the capital city?"

"None," she said as they began their walk across the encampment, "We should receive word sometime in the evening of their fate. If we hear nothing before daybreak, we fight for the memory of our beloved home."

The collection of fires in the distance suspended themselves in the growing darkness of night. As they walked in silence, Remini could not help but enjoy the simple beauty of this sight. A proud people. Men and women. All under the glow of campfires, together for their Queen. Perhaps there was a divide between them, yet they were bonded in this night.

"Commander Leanna," Remini's voice cracked slightly as she summoned the courage to speak, "you are not optimistic. I know little of the ways of war, but I do know when people use their faces as masks."

"Do you, Commander?" Leanna raised an eyebrow. She might have reprimanded another, even an equal, for this slight remark. She knew all too well the fear this untrained girl was fighting. In her heart, Leanna agreed with the male commanders under the Generals. There was only the Royal Guard. A far cry from a true female army. Putting these girls in command of their House soldiers, at the head of the lines, was nothing but a farce that would cost lives.

"My mother and father practice the art very well, in particular when Council members call upon us in social situations."

"I see." Leanna smiled with a gentle laugh, "Perhaps this perceptive talent will aid you in leading your regiment into battle. It will reveal to you who will fight and who will defend."

Remini cast a nervous glance to her, knowing her next words tempted insubordination. "I also see you disapprove of my commission, a rank that does not suit my experience. The male regiments disapprove as well, and with good reason."

Leanna was impressed by the girl's perception. "I cannot question the appointments made by General Kubi-Sogi and the Anjara for it is not my place. We need experience and skill in the city. We need numbers on the field." She stopped, placing a strong hand on the young girl's shoulder, "You have a noble family history. Fight for the glory of your family's name. This will serve as an example to your company. Win their hearts, and their bodies will follow."

"All I am is a name," Remini whispered.

"Sometimes, that is enough."

The tent, hazy with tobacco smoke, was crowded with both male and female commanders. The men, leaders of both Palace and Old Guard regiments, stood apart. The women commanding their House Soldiers were tight-lipped, from fear, scorn, or both. Remini quietly entered and assumed a proper neutral stance, a stance the few-trained female commanders were also taking.

"Welcome," said General Trokan gruffly. His was a face that might have been handsome had it not aged overnight. With him sat Idir and Kabir, who barely gave civil nods.

"So, we gather for the greater good of Morevi," Trokan said, tapping the great map stretched out and tacked to the table. Small markers indicated the reported numbers seen making their way towards the Kinessa Plains. The opponents' markers overwhelmed their own, not including the markers resting on the rendering of Songkusai. "We fight in the name of our mothers, our fathers, our families, and for the subjects of the true Queen of Morevi, Askana Moldarin, and the King Jermal Sandhuilean."

"For Morevi," softly rose the collected voices in unison.

Trokan stifled an inner sigh at what he faced on the morning. The young noble-women commanded a large portion of the collected infantry. They were inexperienced, and terrified. The seasoned, skilled Royal Guard present numbered too few to keep them under strict direction. Looming over all this was the tension between the men and women, Morevi's reminder of the past and promise for the future. He knew better than to give into the worry about their numbers and the divisions among them. They did not even know for certain if the Queen still lived. There was so much room for doubt. He searched for words to comfort one group and inspire the other.

The female voice cut through the uneasy silence of the tent. "We of the Temple of Nadinath bring you blessings in this time of strife, beloved Daughters of Morevi."

The voice came from behind Leanna. As men started from their chairs, women entered. The speaker wore white and silver. The other wore the dark wrappings and ebony metal of death. Both women removed their helms as all the women dropped to one knee in reverence.

The men did not.

Trokan fought an urge to embrace the Priestesses. These women followed Askana Moldarin, trained with her, and fought with her ferocity. From their ranks came women like the Anjara. They followed the discipline of their Temple. In them he could find field captains and commanders to keep control of the Nobles.

"Welcome, Priestesses of Nadinath." He was out of his chair in a moment and grasping the hand of the one in black.

"The Palace sends children to fight for the Mother's ground," Illora said sharply with a look around the tent. She then turned her eyes to Trokan. "General, we accept your welcome. We have come to fight by your side. Women *and* men, this time." There was reluctance in her voice, but she said it.

"We follow a strategy unfamiliar to us." Leanna spoke bravely, still kneeling on the ground. She wished to sound like a true High Commander, but her voice resembled more of an apology than a report. "We have allies from a far-off realm. They fight alongside our Sisters."

"Allies?" Maghda questioned, bringing Leanna to her feet. "Who are these allies?"

"They come from an Otherworld called England. They fight for Songkusai alongside the Royal and Palace Guard. Their leader is a captain of the seas named Rafe Rafton." Leanna led them both to the battle map, General Trokan following. "He proposed a very inventive plan of defence."

General Idir tapped the map as he spoke, "Lure the enemy in and break their numbers in the alleyways of the city. He calls this strategy 'divide-and-conquer'."

All heads turned sharply as a young messenger bolted into the tent. She halted, wide-eyed at the sight of the Priestesses, then quickly knelt before them as she held up a scroll.

"This runner, Priestess, brings us news of the battle within the city." Trokan broke the wax seal, unfurling the parchment. He seemed to read it two times over before turning his attention to the map. There were light gasps of amazement as he began to remove marker after marker from the capital city. Sounds of joy grew as the Eyriener markers grew less in number, but Trokan held up his hand. "Hold your celebration. This is the report from Commander Majin who defends the city alongside an Otherworlder named Agecroft. They have the city—" His hand pointed to a small number of markers resting upon the Palace, "—but as for the Palace and the Queen, we do not know. The Eyrieners flee towards our position. They will return with reinforcements. Now comes the call of Morevi. We must fight."

"A moment." Illora studied the map, noting the markers within the capital city, "To have taken the city with the numbers he had, this privateer must have been blessed by the Goddess." She began to smile as the thought came clear to her. "General, I have a suggestion concerning the morning's battle plans."

From the Road of the Moon, just outside the city, they came. The morning's rays caught the gleam of their metal. From the Kinessa Plains came the tall, grey-eyed Eyriener men armed with swords that hung from their belts and shoulder baldrics, bouncing lightly with each step they took. At their front ranks the bronze-skinned, bare-chested Morev'ar loyal to Gidaron. A strange alliance, but one that served King Cedric for the time being. Their ranks lined up along the edge of the jungle. It would not be a charge this day. Simply a march on Songkusai. Their numbers, combined with those who managed to retreat successfully from the city, reached just over three thousand.

Their ranks were eight thousand when they had left Eyrie.

Many of their fleet fell to the Otherworlder navy. Some Eyriener ships were fortunate to escape the battle and dock at Arathelle. The Dark Merchant had left explicit orders for them to meet the Morevian armies on the Kinessa Plains, where he would join them once the Palace fell. From what the survivors of the charge told them, it was uncertain what to expect. They also heard about the strange battle tactics of the Otherworlders. Grim-faced and determined to avenge their losses, they marched at speed, only to find a readied field and the colourful tents of the Morevians abandoned. No word from the High Lord or the Palace.

A dark, transparent veil hung over the city. Not a morning mist but an indication of fires that burned during the previous day. There were some pillars of smoke still reaching into the morning sky. They could see no activity nor any Morevians walking patrols outside or along the city walls, and no sign of the runaway Morevian army. Every man felt scorn at the cowardly escape. Now they felt the beginnings of cold triumph. Perhaps this would not be a day of combat but a hero's welcome as they would find their High Lord in control of the Palace of a Thousand Suns. From the capital city, Eyrie could begin its conquest over The Silken Box of Naruihm.

The advancing infantry came to a halt when they saw the train of carts exit the gates of Songkusai. From where they stood, they could see that the carts carried men. Soldiers. Men who wore Eyriener surcoats and armour, bound at the wrists and ankles. Flanking the carts were Morevians, Royal Guard and Palace Guard. Both men and women wore the stains of battle, but they walked free with weapons held ready. Then at the rear of the train came eight carts piled high with Eyriener dead, also with an armed escort.

The Eyrieners began sharp, grating war-chants, beating their now-drawn swords against chest armour. At the sound of the shouted curses, the grim procession came to a halt. Then two figures leading the train, one being a Morevian woman and the other appearing to be an Otherworlder, continued forward to the Eyriener ranks. Gritting their teeth but still observant of the rules of engagement, the commanders rode forward to meet them. Their soldiers continued to holler and scream wildly to intimidate the few guards of the procession. The Morevian escort did not bother to raise their shirai or ru-yilei in response to their challenges.

The commander held his hand high, silencing the distant bellowing from the Eyriener invaders. The Morevian and Otherworlder wore clothes torn and bloodied, their faces stained with ash and dust. They did not recoil before the blowing, stamping horses that drew before them. Neither did their gazes falter as the three riders eyed them with contempt. The commander dismounted from his steed. His two officers remained on horseback, pulling from their saddles two nocked crossbows.

"The Whore-Queen of Morevi and the traitorous Sea Wolf," Commander Iom Geshalt barked. "This is indeed a pleasure."

"Commander," Rafe sighed as he dusted off his now-ruined doublet and meticulously removed his damaged leather gloves. "We have endured a most trying night sorting out the ranks of the dead, grieving for family, and bidding adieu to friends. I myself have hardly any energy left for banter, if you'll excuse me."

"I see." Geshalt's mouth smiled but it did little to soften his grey eyes. "I take it you want to negotiate the terms of surrender?"

"I am sorry, Commander, but you address to the wrong person. I present Askana Moldarin, First Queen of Morevi."

His lip curled in distaste. "There is no need for me to speak to the woman."

"Then I shall speak while you listen, Commander." Askana's black eyes were steady. Her voice was dry from the shed tears for so many the night before, but still she remained strong. "I am covered in the blood of my Sisters, my people, and my comrades of the shirai. A good amount of blood on me, however, comes from Eyrie. There is to be no surrender. We come to deliver your men, many whom you will wish to carry home to those who shall mourn them. You will find your High Lord Coumiran in the final cart. With him, a woman who loved him by the name of Min-Lu. Bury them together. I deem that a fitting punishment for them both."

Geshalt and his fellows could not help but laugh at her audacity. "Madam, are you suggesting we retrieve our dead and return home with nothing but rotting corpses to show for our efforts?"

"No," Askana's voice never lost its power as she spoke. "I am *commanding* you to retrieve your dead and return home."

His smile faded, "Tell me what my fate will be if I do not heed your Royal Decree?"

"Then will you pay for your arrogance with Eyriener blood," she stated. There was no need to give her words any hint of warning or malice. She spoke her heart.

"With your army decamping before swords were even drawn, your words are worth less than a wild boast," he huffed.

This news sank like a stone in deep waters, leaving not a single ripple. Perhaps somewhere in the back of her mind, she considered it a mystery, but there was no time to think on it now. There was no more time to think or to plan. She needed all her strength for what was to come.

"Madam, it will be a slaughter." Geshalt mounted his horse quickly. It danced sideways, the whites of its eyes rolling as he reined it in. "You can barely stand as you are now."

"I am sure your High Lord thought the same when setting your forty ships against Captain Marlow and his ten. I am sure he thought as much when he attempted to take Songkusai. Now he is embracing the Devil himself, welcomed into Hell's company."

"Do not spurn us as you would a wild dog," he hissed, his patience nearing its end. "We shall enter your city and claim it for our beloved King Cedric and fair Eyrie."

She did not need to look over her shoulder to know Rafe was close. She could feel the heat rising from his body. She knew that he would support her until the end. Die with her if need be, for a cause that was not his own. She felt a precious moment of peace, the blankness that comes in the face of death.

Thou art whole and no force can withstand thee.

A falcon's cry pierced the morning silence. Rafe glanced upward and saw only a breathtaking, crystal blue above him, ushering in a lovely day. "A perfect day to be upon the water," Rafe said with a heavy sigh. "Then again, on one as beautiful as this, no better day to die."

Askana smiled widely, a new life seeming to spring in her dark gaze, "No, privateer. Not today."

Her own falcon-cry lifted towards the sky. It caught the commanders and Rafe by surprise. Then it echoed in the morning air. A blast from a ram's horn, not from Morevi but from the distance. Another blast answered. Then another, and another after it. From the wall outposts of Songkusai, weary soldiers pulled back hammers on rifles and pistols, preparing for a final stand. Townspeople also climbed up to the battlements to watch what was happening. The Anjara and Kubi-Sogi stepped out into the open air, just outside Songkusai's entrance.

They came from over the rolling hills of the Kinessa Plains, sunlight glittering across a forest of blades. They appeared over the ridges and west of Songkusai. Black armour gleamed darkly. Their numbers massed on the ridges, interspersed with the well-ordered ranks of the Morevian army. Pennants and flags of Houses flapped brilliantly in the breeze. From all sides they surrounded the invaders and Songkusai, their voices rising and falling in a rhythmic chant that was more ominous than the rattle of sword on shield.

"Welcome, Commander, to the Realm of the First Queen, Askana Moldarin." Her voice could not have sounded so utterly terrifying as it did in that instant. A near-whisper that carried a chill of death with it. "Welcome to Morevi."

One of Geshalt's commanders shouldered his crossbow, but a tiny disc soared from the thicket of trees and embedded itself deep within the soldier's neck, knocking him off his horse.

Women in blinding silver armour now emerged from the jungles behind the Eyriener ranks. Their numbers were equally vast. They continued to appear from every possible cover. Shadow. Thicket. Foliage. The Eyriener soldiers looked about themselves wildly. One man raised his battle axe only to feel a white arrow sink deep into his chest. The weapons of the invading army lowered, but never left their grasp. Their eyes continued to look in awe as the endless barrier of men and women seemed to close in around them.

"Take your men and your dead home to Eyrie," Askana spoke evenly, a hint of victory in her words. "You are assured safe passage to Arathelle. Provided you leave now."

Geshalt's own words echoed in his mind. Yes, it would be a slaughter. Their own. "Send the cart to us," he spoke finally, all confidence lost in his speech.

Rafe waved to the carts and they rumbled forward once more. He then noticed in the train an Eyriener he did not recognise from battle. Too well-dressed for a soldier. He walked free, flanked by two Royal Guards. They did not keep him prisoner. This was a small honour bestowed to him. A proper escort.

"Ambassador Peregrin," Askana spoke to the man, "You are welcome to stay in Morevi if you wish. You have the guarantee of my protection, and your property will remain your own."

"You honour me with this, Your Majesty, but take no insult when I tell you it shall be some time before I return to Morevi." Peregrin seemed to appear as if a burden had been lifted free of him. "I have some time to spend with my wife and children."

"A safe journey before you, Ambassador." Askana gave a gentle nod as he passed.

The carts continued their slow procession to the hands of the Eyrieners, but Rafe's eyes could only look around him at the seemingly endless presence of warriors surrounding them.

"You are nervous, privateer?" Askana purred, "These are the Priestesses and Maidens from the Temple of Nadinath, protector of Queen, Palace, and Lands of Morevi."

"I am most thankful to be on your side, Your Grace," Rafe nodded.

"So you should be." She enjoyed watching him in this uneasiness. "One visit with the Maidens of the Temple would humble that outward bravado of yours."

"Really?" He nodded, raising an eyebrow while resting his hands on his hips, "Well then, perhaps I should learn to keep my temper in check knowing you have such a card up *your* sleeve as this Temple."

"Come, privateer." Askana's head tipped back in a proud fashion suiting a queen, "The Maidens from the Temple will wish to pay tribute to those fallen in battle. Then, on sunset, we shall honour those in our service and celebrate our victory."

A decree from the Queen of Morevi to celebrate. Rafe thought with a delightful smile, *A royal charge I will fulfil above and beyond its call.*

CHAPTER EIGHTEEN
The Cost of a Crown

By nightfall, Songkusai glittered with the glow of a thousand fires. They burned in bronze braziers along the streets, in paper lanterns decorated with Morevian calligraphy of characters for "Peace", "Prosperity", and "Victory", and on torches held aloft over the heads of joyous merrymakers. The smell of incense ate away at the lingering scent of gunpowder and blood.

In the two days since the retreat of the Eyriener forces, rumours and legends already began to filter through the streets and other cities of the realm. Those who had fled to the jungle returned to their Queen restored to the Throne and the most fantastic stories recounting the battle for Songkusai. The Queen had risen from the dead to cut the Eyriener horde down armed only with a shirai, some said. Others said that Eyrieners had called for a Master-Demon from Xorinok whom she swallowed alive, as Nadinath once did. Some stories claimed magic long forbidden by the Fellowship of the Jewels reached over land and sea, and delivered strangers that valiantly defended the Palace. These tales, wandering bards hastily composed into epic ballads. Only one thing was certain—it had been a glorious battle.

Some also said the Queen herself assumed the role of Goddess—*The Destroyer*. There were other whispers of a more personal and more deviant nature. There were those who claimed she allied herself with a devil. A demon from the ocean answering her call with a laugh of thunder and a flash of yellow-gold eyes. His name was a name merchants spat out with hate, Maidens swore against, and mothers used to frighten naughty children even so far from the sea. Could it be that the Destroyer kept a male counterpart, albeit a less powerful, subservient one?

So, when the ram's horns blared throughout the capital and messenger birds sent word to the other cities and villages of the realm declaring the days of celebration, the citizens of Morevi flocked to Songkusai. They came to see for themselves these men and women of legend, and to learn the truth.

The Priests of El'Baz walked through the streets with their censers, intoning words of blessing and cleansing side-by-side with the Priestesses of Nadinath, performing their duty as the two foremost religious bodies in Morevi. Great feasts were prepared. Street performers, tricksters, and dancers would be tonight's ruling class. Before the revels commenced, the Palace would recognise the heroes and honour the spirits of the dead. There could be no merrymaking until all debts were paid.

The powerful, ethereal voices of the Singers of Coma floated over the crowds gathered in the main courtyard before the Palace of a Thousand Suns, allaying them. The Collected Houses kept silently to their places, heads bowed as if in deep reflection. The entire Court in all their splendour were arrayed around and below the palanquin at the top of the Palace steps, the conveyance bearing a figure in green, white, and gold, seated gracefully and silently. To her left, on a lower seat, was the man who had once been King, also dressed in splendid white and gold. They did not attract the most glances, though, for at the base of the steps stood ranks of men in rich but strange clothing. Some were leaders, and others obviously subordinates. In front of them stood a man in burgundy and black. His eyes never strayed far from the Queen of the Morevi.

Melodies of the *nami*, cymbals, and mehrus rose as the Blademaster and General of the Armies made obeisance before his Queen in proper fashion, on hands and knees, touching his forehead to the patterned rugs on the floor. Two Red Priestesses sprinkled him with scented oil and perfume from golden bowls, and another held the tray before the Queen. With fitting ceremony she rose and beckoned him to stand as a Priestess laid the heavy strand over her hands, golden suns studded with jewels, intricately interlinked with stylised Turi flowers, the symbol of Royal Favour and the prize of a hero.

The Queen draped the strand over his shoulders, but the pride in his eyes was as though he were the giver and she the receiver.

"I am proud of you, Askana," Kubi-Sogi smiled, choking back tears as those of a father upon his daughter's wedding day. "You have come so far under my eyes."

"You have been my father and my teacher, Kubi-Sogi. You will have my gratitude as long as you live. You will have my respect even longer than that." She took the deep blue folds of the embroidered cape from the tray, shaking it out in a swirl of gleaming material, the mark of the Turi shining in silver on its back.

The female herald's voice rang out, amplified within the six-foot long carved horn used for such purposes, "Kubi-Sogi Karoshiwa, Blademaster of the Order, General of the Armies of the Kingdom of the Sun, henceforth High Lord and Adviser to the Queen. Servant of the Kingdom, his name shall be written in the Golden Books for all generations to revere and remember, on account of his services to the Kingdom."

The cheers were thunderous, rising over the music for a moment as the dignified old man began the long descent down the steps, his back straight, the magnificent cape of office flowing out behind him.

The Anjara came next. Her eyes held a certain cynicism and amusement as she rose on her knees, even as her Queen laid the heavy strand across her shoulders, and swept a cape of the same blue over her tunic. "My thanks, my Queen. It seems Kubi-Sogi and I are fated to go into the next life arguing together."

"If he were not Blademaster," Askana arched her eyebrow sharply with her playful warning, "I would have you both wed. Thank your stars, good friend."

If any wondered why the second Royal Adviser looked torn between laughter and distaste as she came down, they did not ask.

Elunear's knees looked unsteady as she sank to the ground and made her obeisance, but when she rose, her eyes were too full of pride to be uncertain. Askana smiled on her as she laid the heavy strand on her shoulders. Attendants armoured her with a white-feathered, gilded helm, and decorated shin and forearm guards studded with moonstones and opals, marked with the Turi and the Sun. Elunear could not refrain a gasp as a ceremonial fan of yellow and silver was laid in her hands.

"Elunear Machalan, raised to the Ranks of the Blood by Royal Decree, now Lady Elunear of House Machalan, granted estates to the North of the Kingdom. Raised to the rank of Lieutenant of the Royal Guard. Servant of the Kingdom, her name shall be written..."

"Do well, young Elunear. I see great things in your future," the Queen whispered softly.

Then, a ripple of surprise as one of the strange, pale-skinned Otherworlders detached himself from the group and ascended the stairs. He did not make proper obeisance when he reached the top. Instead, he swept off his odd hat and bowed with a flourish to the Queen, who smiled as the Priestesses sprinkled this stranger with oils.

With a little hesitance on the part of the herald, "Barthloemew Marlow, Lord of Ettingsborough, Captain in service to its Sovereign, His Majesty King Henry VIII of England, thrice-blessed for his service to our nation. Servant of the Kingdom, his name shall be written in the Golden Books for all generations to revere and remember, in his service to the Queen. He and all his descendants are henceforth always made welcome in the Kingdom of the Sun."

Eshton sighed a little as Marlow descended. He looked back to the distant open gates of Songkusai. His mind travelled beyond the city walls, along the Road of the Moon, back to Arathelle. The Singers of Coma were impressive, but their voices grew distant as his ears longed for the sound of Elvensong. Word was received from the Elven kingdom that tonight the shields would be lowered. He was surprised to feel tears gather in his eyes. Would his being a hero of Morevi gain him entrance into a world that haunted his dreams, whose voices whispered in his mind?

On it went, name after name, one after another. This was a night that would stand out in the history of Morevi forever, as until now there were only a few hundred names in the Golden Books. None of them Otherworlders. Even from their seats, in their silence, courtiers schemed and plotted, trying to find how these honours extended to those not of Morevi could play for or against the Queen. In between the names and bestowing of reverence, Askana looked about her to see the Great Game progressing. Even in this time of celebration, it never ceased.

Silence passed across the onlookers, those of The Blood, and Council as he stepped forward. Silence as he climbed the steps. Silence as he stopped before the Queen. The Sea Wolf. For a long moment he stood before her. Even the Priestesses wondered if he intended to receive his honours at all. The gasps from onlookers was audible as the privateer dropped to his knees and made obeisance before the Queen in proper fashion—on hands and knees, touching his forehead to the patterned rugs before her feet.

Kubi-Sogi taught him another gesture to add into the tribute for lasting impression. Rafe slowly brought his hands to his forehead, then to his heart, and then he crossed his arms against his chest with fists clenched. *To you, my Queen, I pledge my mind, my heart, and my strength for Morevi.*

The Queen was radiant.

Oil was sprinkled on him, the heavy chain draped over his shoulders and the ornamented ru-yilei placed in his grasp. The great ruby eyes of the wolf's head that was its hilt winked in the light. Murmurs from the spectators had the countenance of thunder as the Queen stepped forward, her eyes flickering with those of the wolf-hilt. As he rose, she gave him her hand.

"Rafael Stringfellow Rafton, Captain of the *Defiant*, in service to his Sovereign, King Henry VIII. His name shall be written in the Golden Books for all generations to revere and remember in his service to the Queen. For his valour and his unquestioned loyalty to Her Majesty Queen Askana Moldarin, Light of a Thousand Suns and Throne of Morevi, he has the favour of the Throne and eternal welcome in the Kingdom of the Sun."

On his throne, Jermal smiled a small, tight smile.

The privateers were next, honours in addition to the payment they would each receive, but the names seemed too few. Three heavy strands of gold and gemstones remained on the tray, to be fastened over the shoulders of the bodies in the embalming chambers, made sweet and preserved with all the art that Morevi could give, so they would be buried at sea. As the dead were called out to be listed into the Golden Books, no one saw the Queen watch their leader, seeing his jaw tighten when the name "Nassir Jalhammad" echoed over the crowd.

My poor privateer, Askana lamented silently, *you lost your First Mate and your friend. His actions will be remembered in Morevi, always.*

Gongs and cymbals crashed and the trumpets sounded as the ceremony concluded. A roar of approval went up from the people as the Queen rose to her feet, opening her arms as if to embrace them all.

"My people. My flesh and blood. My children, all. We have won our lives and our freedom. I will continue this fight, to lead you till the name of Morevi is a name to make others tremble in fear or wonder with awe at its mere mention. For now, I have grown tired of warfare. Tired of bloodshed among ourselves. Tired of the stench and smoke of battle. I do pledge to raise Morevi into the state she enjoyed in the time of our earliest forefathers. It shall be more than a New Regime, but a Golden Age. This is my oath to the Goddess and to you, my people.

"The beginning of this Golden Age shall be remembered as a celebration, and my first decree to you shall be this—feast, drink, and rejoice! Life is but a brief time that must be savoured. Our allies from across The Rift know the people of Morevi understand the meaning of war, victory, and honour. Now let us show them that the people of Morevi understand the meaning of merriment!"

On these words, a quick display of fireworks exploded into the night sky as gigantic drums sounded and cymbals crashed in rhythm. Still, the display high above and sweet sounds of musicians were lost in the cheer of the collected masses. Throughout the squares and marketplaces, merchants kept their establishments open to peddle their wares to citizens and visitors while entertainers performed their talents of juggling, illusions, and theatre on makeshift stages.

The Nobles stirred in their seats as Palace servants set long tables laden with food and drink. Before them, the main stage was lit for the Royal Players to enact their own adaptations of the battle for Morevi, even as jesters and bards strolled though the courtyard recounting the same battles in song.

"Rafton!" called Sir Wallace over the roar of celebration. "Come crush a cup of wine with us! This promises to be an evening not soon forgotten!"

The privateer seemed preoccupied. He gave a shake of his head as he passed, without so much as a word in return.

"What ails him?" Lord Agecroft asked. "He usually needs restraint when it comes to wine and wenching."

Eshton's eyes narrowed as he watched the privateer begin the climb up the steps. "It would seem, my Lord, the good Captain has other revels in mind this eve."

Rafe heard none of them, nor could he be bothered. She was at the top of the Palace steps. She was smiling at him.

"Do you note," he said wryly, refilling his chalice with wine, "that we are the subject of many curious glances? Well, some more than curious. Others, simply poisonous." Rafe looked pointedly at Jermal, who on catching Rafe's eye quickly returned to his talk with Eshton and Kubi-Sogi.

"Are you uncomfortable at being by my side this eve?" Askana broke a pomegranate open.

He grinned. "It seems he is." The grin faded away just as quickly. "Do you intend to keep him as your Consort?"

"It was never my intention. I expected better things from him than such an office." A servant poured wine into her cup, and both were silent for a moment. "Truth be told, I do not know what to do with Jermal now. The kindest thing would be to return him to his world, perhaps..." Her voice trailed off in sorrow. She had expected far more from Jermal. By now, the reports from various sources had told her of his brief reign as king and his complete surrender to Dirare. She did not doubt he would have tried to stand his ground, but he refused to risk his own death for her ideals. A chilling realisation as to the type of man he was. A creature of survival. It did not make him any better or worse of a man. It simply brought to light his true nature.

"Do you desire him?" asked Rafe bluntly.

"Captain Rafael Stringfellow Rafton, you have no right to ask me such a question." She fixed her eyes with his, "You have my favour, but even that has its boundaries. As you have shown in the past, you forget your place far too easily."

"Ah, that is one of my many talents, Your Grace. Besides, on this night, I think you should answer all questions I put before you." She gave a soft laugh, shaking her head at his audacity, and then went silent. He was not jesting with her. The light in his eyes was deadly serious. "It is a boon I ask of the Crown of Morevi."

"Very well, Captain," Askana smiled, popping another pomegranate seed in her mouth, enjoying its bitter-sweetness. "The Queen grants you this boon."

"Very well." The moments seemed to pass slowly as he suddenly found himself at a loss of what to ask. *Speak your heart, Rafton,* he assured himself. "Your Majesty, I—"

"Good eve, Your Majesty." The woman in grey who rose from her obeisance before them was plump and cheerful looking, but her eyes were fastened on Askana like a hawk's. "I trust I am not interrupting?"

"Good eve, High Lady Radna," smiled the Queen pleasantly, rinsing her fingers in the petal-strewn water provided. "Nadinath's Grace upon you. Quite a celebration, would you not agree?"

"Indeed, Your Majesty," Radna bowed her head. "I must speak to you, Your Grace, of a matter of import—"

Askana's words were as smooth as cream. "Are you not going to greet Captain Rafton, High Lady Radna?"

The woman froze. Her eyes turned to Rafe, as if noticing him there for the first time. She continued to look quickly from her Queen to the privateer and back again. "Of course, Your Majesty." She bowed slightly to a smiling Rafe, murmured a quick, cursory greeting, and then returned to her Queen. "Your Majesty, I must speak to you in private."

"Here will do, High Lady Radna. I have decreed that this night is for rest and merriment," Askana smiled, "and any matter that is weighty enough to merit a private audience is too weighty for discussion now."

For a moment, Rafe thought that Lady Radna was going to burst under her placidity, but the woman gathered herself with effort. He could catch in Radna's look a strong desire to wish him elsewhere. Perhaps back in England, if she had such power.

"Your Majesty, in your unfortunate absence the King formed a change within the government. The matter of the High Council and—"

Lisa Lee & Tee Morris

"I have heard of it, High Lady." Askana lifted a hand. An attendant stepped forward with a peacock feather fan to waft a cooling breeze over them. She let a silence fall. She cast a glance to Rafe to make certain he too was benefiting from the fan. Unseen to High Lady Radna, she gave him a playful wink.

Very good, Rafe thought with some admiration. *If High Lady Radna's composure had been shaken earlier, it had to be toppling by now.*

The woman's eyes were downcast. They had already betrayed her need for haste. Now she was sweating in the excruciating silence as her Sovereign picked a few seeds from the pomegranate and slipped them between her lips leisurely.

"As you know, High Lady, all decrees made by the King are now void, as is the position of King itself."

Lady Radna's headdress quivered as she kept her eyes down. "I never presumed to disagree, my Queen. The purpose of my coming of Your Majesty was to ask what we should make of it as the High Reg—" Askana's eyebrows rising slightly with her inquisitive expression caught Radna in mid-speech. As was just stated, the King's decrees were void. This included newly-appointed titles. "I do mean, High Lady Dirare. She has not yet come forward."

Rafe's lips twitched as he fought back a guffaw. He disguised this desire to laugh by taking a sip of the wine, an action that no doubt upped him a few notches in the embarrassed Radna's bad books. He could see her reading his eyes and actions as he was with her. She was insinuating that the High Council was entirely Dirare's doing, implying that she had not willingly gone along with it.

"I will decide what is to be done later," Askana replied with a sweet smile. "Tonight, enjoy the festivities. Thank you, High Lady Radna."

Radna rose to her feet, but even after the dismissal was visibly unwilling to leave. "Your Majesty, if—"

"Thank you, High Lady Radna."

The woman had no choice but to leave.

"You leave her hanging on the rope, not knowing which way to turn or which side to take." Rafe chuckled deep in his chest as he considered her. "Sometimes I wonder if I am wise to linger in your company. You are ruthless. Quite the devious player of politics. I think you would not hesitate to order my execution tonight if it furthered your standing in the eyes of Council and Nobility."

"If that were the case, privateer, you would already be headless." She smiled, her eyes dancing in the torchlight. "I was expecting one of them to come forward, actually."

"Why?" Rafe shook his head ruefully. "It is a bit easier to understand the life of the ocean. A ship approaches and nothing happens—friend. A ship approaches and fires on you—foe." The privateer shrugged, "I was never made for politics, Your Grace."

"Why do you think I linger here when I would rather be elsewhere?" Askana said in a playful, flirtatious manner. "I tell you, over the course of the next half-hour, one by one all the members of the High Council will come to me, each with their own version of what happened and what the others thought or did. Each hoping beyond hope that I will let them keep their new positions and demote the others. Since Dirare is absent, they will all implicate her."

"And where is this High Lady Dirare of whom I have heard so much?"

"She mourns for Arnese, her Adviser. I watched Coumiran kill her in cold-blood." Askana paused and reflected, "Dirare has served me admirably, though no doubt for her own causes. Yet—" She sighed, "Perhaps I favour the wrong people, and those who could truly serve me I dislike because they are too much like me for comfort."

"What are you going to do about the High Council, really?"

"Why, let them remain, of course. It was an excellent idea. One I had considered myself, just never implemented. Those appointed are all capable women."

Rafe laughed, shaking his head in amazement. "You are beyond belief, Your Grace!" He cocked his head to one side and smiled, "Considering my earlier boon, might I ask where do you wish you were now, seeing that you enjoy playing with your poor courtiers so much?"

"Someplace where we can talk." The dark eyes looked at him intently, her smile light. "Perhaps, in private."

"Well, Your Grace, do hold that thought, for I see a pair of high-born sisters at the bottom of the steps."

"Pira and Pura." Her face slowly grew featureless like a kabuki mask. Her demeanour, soft and approachable. "It begins again."

The women were getting closer. Rafe's voice was no more than a whisper, only audible to Askana, "But did you not say to High Lady Radna that this night is for merriment, and any matter to merit a private audience is too weighty for discussion?"

Askana arched her dark eyebrow as she did when Rafe grew impertinent. "It is *because* this is a night for merriment that I wish to be someplace where we can talk *in private*."

"Good eve, Your Majesty," spoke both women, bowing deeply.

With a quick glance to her sister, High Lady Pira spoke. "We trust we are not interrupting?"

"Good eve, High Lady Pira, High Lady Pura," Askana smiled pleasantly, rinsing her fingers in the petal-strewn water provided. Exactly as with High Lady Radna. "Nadinath's Grace upon you. Quite a celebration, would you not agree?"

As the High Ladies spoke the words he had heard mere moments ago only with High Lady Radna, Rafe felt something passed into his hands from under the table. It was the other half of the pomegranate, its seeds winking red like the rubies of his ru-yilei.

"And what will your Court think, disappearing unannounced with a known outlaw of the seas?" Rafe huffed breathlessly as they burst through an archway of a private garden. "Tut-tut, Your Grace! You have no modesty!"

"Modesty has many definitions. Yours is an English one," she laughed as she spun around in a swirl of silk and brocade, her veils floating around her face. "I cannot explain it but I have not felt this way since girlhood."

And like a girl void of all decorum, she danced lightly over the grass, keeping time with the far-off music of Palace minstrels and English sailors. Marlow's crews had brought from their ships a different kind of Otherworlder arsenal for the celebration— bagpipes, bodhrans, and fiddles. Along with a few tin whistles, they shared with the people of Morevi their own carefree songs of dance. Two cultures merging through joyous music. The sounds of music, laughter, and mirth reached them in this courtyard attached to the Palace. Yet it seemed shut out in this haven of cool darkness, out of place with the fragrance of greenery and night-blooms. He watched her dance in the light of the twin moons, completely surrendering to the song of two worlds.

Askana had reached a far corner of the garden and froze in her stance. Her arms slowly came to her sides as she stared into the shadows.

He ran across the smooth, green grass to stop beside this frozen image of a queen, her gaiety now replaced by a more quiet, sombre expression. "What is it, Your Grace?"

She was looking fixedly at the ebony statue in the corner of this garden, rising on its pedestal in a pool of clear water, surrounded by lacy ferns. It was a statue of Nadinath, bathed in the light of paper lanterns.

"Dear Lord!" Rafe exclaimed, his hand going to his chest, "Please don't tell me I have to endure the 'Little Death' again!" His jibe earned no reaction. Her eyes never left the statue. "Ah, the worship of a true devotee!"

He walked around the statue, perusing it with a mock air of scholarly pomposity. A fine statue, crafted of the darkest obsidian. The curves and folds of the fingers. The crease at the Maiden's neck as she tilted her head. The flowing hair caught forever in stone. He could see where a belt sank slightly with its weight into the flesh of a hip so that it folded a tiny bit over its edge. The third facet of the warrior, particularly with the shadows cast by moonlight and lanterns, caused Rafe to step back nervously. In the lanterns' soft glow, Rafe could swear the statue moved of its own accord. It breathed. It watched him study Her facets. As he rounded to the back of the statue, he stopped and peered closer, giving a slight gasp of awe.

"Now this is exquisite work!" Rafe smiled in sincerity, looking at the back of the statue from different viewpoints. "I know of artists that create illusions within their work to give it a mark of distinction. Whoever made this must be such an artist. From the back it is as if there is a fourth form here, obscure but hinted at in the stone. A fourth woman."

He could not see the Queen start slightly, her eyes widening. He also could not see her step back from the statue. Askana wanted to call out to him, to warn him the statue would come to life and take hold of him.

"A trick of the light and shadows, no doubt. I always wondered why the Goddess only faced in three directions." He winked at Nadinath with his usual irreverence. "She must have been quite a woman."

"You would not have liked Her." Askana's voice was quiet, subdued now. "What do you know of the worship of the Goddess?"

"Only that her Priestesses hate men, that it is a woman's religion."

She continued to watch the statue as he returned to her side. "Nadinath was the Creator of the World, the life-force that gave it birth. Some call Her the Great Mother, and see Her as a manifestation of the feminine power of the Earth itself. She is the one who gives Birth, the one who Nurtures, and the one who Kills." Askana paused, a catch in her voice suddenly. "She created the world out of Night and Nothingness. She spread life over it. She created the animals, the plants, the men, and the Gods who serve Her. All are under Her, Her children. The Creation of Man was not enough as there were no living images of Her. So for one year, She took a husband every night, and devoured him whole in the morning. At the end of that year, She gave birth to Woman. The Goddess placed her beside the men as a gift to them for their sacrifice. There are many stories and legends in Her Worship, but this is the basis of them all."

"Your Nadinath sounds like a bloodthirsty Goddess." He looked at her. "I hope you do not practice such things now, or ever did." The ghost of a smile crossed his face. "Poor Jermal would not stand a fighting chance."

"Bloodthirsty?" Askana snapped, her head rising slightly at his innocent insult. "No more than your Christian God. In the name of religion you English went on Crusades against peoples who were of another religion, is it not so? You went there to force your edicts in the name of a powerful God and his Son who wanted only to love others. Those who opposed these beliefs would be slaughtered. Your people tried and failed." Askana's smile was spiteful. "As you see Captain, I learned a great deal in King Henry's Court about your world's God. Acts of sacrifice. Decimation of whole cities. Genocide by flood or 'Angels of Death' by your *benevolent* God!" she stated sharply. "There are no beliefs in your world, or mine, that have no blood to their name."

"Does that make bloodshed right?" implored Rafe as he reached for Askana. His touch on her shoulder made her shiver suddenly. "My words were ill-chosen, Askana. I admit knowing little about Nadinath. I do know of the darkness in her towards men, in particular. That is not your true self. At least not in the Askana Moldarin I have come to know."

"Do you think there are not sides of me that remain uncharted to you, Captain? Without Nadinath as our strength and teacher, we are kept submissive. It is the way of men—the need to dominate. Take your own world for instance. Would your society accept a Queen as its true monarch? I feel the most pity for the one, Elizabeth. The youngest of Henry's daughters. By her own father's decree, she will never rule your England."

In the distance, the musicians ended with cheers and applause from the revellers. Askana looked to the sounds of celebration for a moment, pausing in her thoughts. She then remembered what brought her here, with him. He was silent, humbled. Askana could see in his face the loss of all mirth. Struck down, regardless of his good intentions.

"I presume too much, I suppose," Rafe finally spoke. "I have just seen a woman very different from what the stories do tell. You see how well we have done together, yes? We restored a kingdom. Together. Perhaps I hoped to convince you to end this cycle of persecution, otherwise your permission allows the viciousness to come out—"

"Please, Rafe," she said, stepping closer, resting her cheek against his chest. "Let us not speak of such things tonight. I have a lifetime to speak of duty. Tonight I am Askana. A woman like any other woman." She stared at Nadinath. It looked back at her, silent and mute. No life in it. It was a statue, a *three*-faceted statue. Nothing more.

Ask Me My name.

The sensation of her weight against him, the strange feel of her arms around his waist, made his breath catch in his throat and his heart knock against his ribs. *A woman like any other?* Rafe smiled, enjoying the scent of her perfume. *No. Never. Not you, my Queen.* Her veils fluttered against his hand as he touched her hair lightly. Soft, silken.

Again came the voices of the Goddess. *Pull Me out of stone, My child.* A shiver passed down her spine at his touch. The scent of him. She placed her palm on his chest, felt his heart beating. Then her fingers curled into claws, grasping at his doublet. A decision made in a fleeting moment.

"Come with me," Askana smiled, her eyes turning to the path leading to the near-empty Palace of a Thousand Suns.

He smiled, somewhat devious, but nonetheless suspicious, as she took his hands in her own. "And just where you are taking me, First Queen of Morevi?"

Her own smile was slow and wide, her eyes smouldering with light and fire as the moonlight touched her. "There will be fireworks this eve. The Grand Balcony bears a better view."

Her voice touched something within him, something he had kept well hidden. She went to lead him, but Rafe pulled her back into a tight embrace. His smile mirrored hers.

"Lead the way," Rafe released her but kept a hold of her hands as an idea came to him. "And as this is a night of revels, let us make this a game. If I catch you, my prize is a kiss. Agreed?"

Yes, said her Heart. *It has been so long, and you have forgotten what joy there is in it.* "If you catch me?"

"If I catch you," he nodded.

Her tiny laugh was sweeter than any music he had heard that night. "Agreed. A kiss for the brash, arrogant, and overconfident Sea Wolf—"

Her leg suddenly swept under him, catching him by the back of his ankle and knocking him down to the soft, dew-covered grass of the courtyard.

"—if you catch me."

She was gone. Her playful laughter intertwining with the sounds of music and celebration. With a laugh of his own, Rafe picked himself up and followed the flutter of white robes running to the Palace of a Thousand Suns.

Chandeliers were lit, a soft amber glow reflecting off crystals and mirrors. Hallways stretched out before her to every side. She heard Rafe stop for a moment in the corridor, assuredly uncertain as to where he was. She watched him in the reflection of a hallway mirror searching for a hint of her. A glimpse of white silk. The sounds of footfalls. She remained still. The only noise apart from the nearby torch were the festivities out in the city streets.

"Privateer," Askana whispered sharply, allowing her voice to be caught in a haunting echo that maddened Rafe as he looked around wildly.

Then he saw her shadow extending around the corner and the faint reflection in brightly polished marble. With a swish of skirts and a laugh she was gone again, leading him through the Palace.

She could not recall when such a spirit was within her. So different from her carriage as a queen. Something new in its place. An impish soul. Carefree. Happy.

Rafe caught another flash of white silk and charged, their laughter becoming one voice echoing through the corridors. "I am upon your heels, Askana Moldarin," he called to her in delight. "Take care if you wish not to be caught!"

Her pulse was racing. Her heart pounded in her chest from efforts to smother the laughter and excitement of this childish game. Turning into the first of five interlinked rooms, she stopped just inside the door and gave a piercing whistle. She then slipped behind a large tapestry in the chamber, and waited in the tiny alcove of a hidden doorway that would return her to the corridor. She watched the brilliant gold door handle turn downward slowly. As Rafe entered, she continued through the concealed exit. Then, gathering her skirts, Askana bounded for the stairs leading to her apartments.

The privateer considered himself an exceptional navigator, blessed with a skill that could successfully bring him back and forth across The Rift. In the Palace of a Thousand Suns, however, he showed no more skill in finding his way than a wide-eyed cabin boy. He was back in the first of the five rooms. Still no sign of Askana. It was a delightful idea, but now he was wondering how intelligent it was to challenge a queen so familiar with the Palace in a game of hide-and-seek. He slumped into a luxurious divan, absolutely frustrated with himself. This would not have been the first time his mouth had granted him a night alone. *A rare opportunity with a queen, lost to a moment of bravado,* he thought to himself bitterly.

Then he noticed a tapestry billow lightly. It billowed, but all the windows of the chamber were closed.

He pulled the arras back. In her haste to elude him, Askana had failed to close the hidden door fully.

She is a crafty one, he thought as he found himself back in the corridor. He could hear the quick pads of footsteps ascending to the chambers above him. Rafe smiled as he asked himself, *Was that a giggle?* The reputation of The Black Widow of Morevi said nothing about her giggling! He knew she was almost to her Royal Apartments. She could easily barricade herself in there and he would lose the wager he put to her.

On that thought, his eyes fell on an open window at the opposite end of an adjoining corridor. From that huge arch, the Grand Balcony was in full view.

Rafe shrugged as he reached for the tiny rope and grappling hook in his belt pouch. "If you are going to make this leap," he said aloud, "then jump in, feet first."

He used this clever agent in his trade many times to scale walls and board ships. He even used it in their escape from Songkusai. This was the first time he ever used it in a game of hide-and-seek. Its talons reached for the fine marble and stone and fastened itself to the balcony. Rafe leapt into the darkness and silently rested against the exterior walls, the soft roar of Markuna Falls far below him once again. His own laughter made the climb more difficult than it would normally be. He had to laugh though at the lengths and risks he was taking for this woman. The cable could snap. The hook could slip free. He could loose his grip and fall to his death, his body found weeks later against the cold hard rocks. This was utter madness.

He loved every minute of it!

He never felt more alive as he pulled himself over the Grand Balcony's railing. Rafe crept through Askana Moldarin's dimly lit chambers, his eyes peering at the grand doors before him. The shadows of her feet broke the light slipping in from the hallway.

Askana nearly tripped over her court gown's hem as she reached her chambers. She quietly unlatched the doors and waited. Her plan would be one to share with Ladies of the Blood in social gatherings, to break tensions and enjoy a shared amusement. She would slip into her chambers and go out onto the balcony. By the time he found her, he would be flustered and hot, and she would be as composed as ever with ample time to rest.

Askana took a light breath and held it to let only the distant revels and the torches fill her ears.

The hall was empty.

"More the fool you, Rafe Rafton!" she said exultantly, flushed and laughing, as she entered her dimly-lit chambers. She paused a while to smooth her skirts and brush a hand over her hopelessly disordered hair before stepping out into the cool night air. Askana leaned against the railing and looked up to the full twin moons. It was truly a night of abandon she had never known. The divan waited in the centre of the Grand Balcony, inviting her to rest. She smiled wickedly as she moved towards it. *I have won this one*, she thought as she reclined back to view the multitude of pinpoint lights far above her.

The privateer watched her from the darkness of her own chambers. He could not help but to relish her self-satisfaction in losing him in the chase. *It would be a shame to burst such a proud bubble*, he thought sadly, *but maybe the Queen needs a bit of humility.*

The sharp clearing of his throat caused her to leap free of the divan. Like a hart, her first instinct was to bolt.

"The places where ours paths do cross." Rafe clicked his tongue, shaking his head. "People shall talk of this, Askana Moldarin." She was so certain she had evaded this pirate. Her eyes narrowed at the sight of his figure emerging from the shadows, his smile growing with each step closer to her. "You are right, Your Grace, the view from here is quite lovely."

His eyes, however, were not enjoying the panoramic view behind her.

The Queen's eyes looked past him. The door was close. An easy escape. "A sailor should take a hunter's advice. Never consider cornered prey caught." With a sudden, fluid motion she made for her escape.

His hands seemed to move in the style of his ship's banner in the wind as he grabbed a hold of Askana and pulled her close once again, "I believe the game belongs to me."

She knew no harm would come to her in his grasp. His touch was warm against her arm. His heat passed through her robes, caressing her skin. It was so intense that for a moment she thought flames would consume her. He was firm, not rough, but assuring her that he had won. They were so close.

My child, the voice whispered to her.

Lost to it, she wound her arms up around his neck, "Then, take your due."

Rafe tried to slow his heart, but it raced faster now than when he chased her through the Palace corridors. *I have to be dreaming*, Rafe thought silently as she tipped her head back, her lips parting slightly. If indeed he was in a dream, he resolved to enjoy it to the fullest.

His lips touched hers gently at first. Then, he felt her arms pull him closer. Their kiss became another, then another, deeper and growing in a zeal that brought them to this point. *Her lips are sweet*, he thought. *Her mouth, so warm and soft.* Their tongues caressed one another in an intense, full embrace that brought their breathing into a loud pitch that filtered into the Royal Chambers.

No, Rafe thought as he pulled away from her slowly, *this was definitely not a dream.*

The kiss turned her blood to honeyed fire that raced through her veins. It was unreserved, unbridled. She had not felt this in so long. She knew where she would have it end. His arms were still tight around her, his fingers splayed across her lower back. She knew what she wanted. What she needed. What she desired.

She looked at him with command in her dark eyes, all the force of her will behind what she spoke. "Share my bed this night, Rafe. The Queen of Morevi commands it."

His mind raced. It was no longer a moment of passion but a decree from the Queen. A duty to be fulfilled. "You *command* it?" he asked, his voice losing confidence. His eyes went cold as he reached behind him and broke the hold she kept. Rafe backed away from her as if she were some hellish creature spawned from a nightmare, "The Queen *commands* me to take to her bed? Have I been raised to the role of Consort now?"

The sharp explosion startled them both as the first of the night's fireworks exploded in the sky. A shower of sparks that washed their scene with red and lurid white. She felt the desire being torn from her as Rafe looked at her with a chilling gaze. He was *angry*.

Askana stepped forward, her tone confused and lost within the conflicting emotions exchanged, "Is it not what you want? Do you find the concept so repugnant?" She felt a flush of embarrassment, sudden uncertainty. She could feel herself tremble as a virgin upon her first night as she ran through her mind what it was that she had done to turn him against her. She asked herself desperately *Am I not attractive enough?* She had not felt this way since...

Norisht.

His name flashing in her mind sparked a fury, and her eyes hardened as did her resolve. *I will not be made so vulnerable again,* she thought bitterly.

The noise of the fireworks and the cheers nearly overwhelmed everything. Nearly. Rafe's anger could be heard as clear as a thunderclap. *"What I want?"* He pointed sharply at her, his words raising in intensity, "How dare you toy with me as you would with one of your old maid councilwomen! I can assure you it is not simply your favours I want. I could retrieve the same pleasures from any common whore in London!"

Askana had been called that before, but this time the word struck her heart, "Whore? Do I remind you of a whore?!" Her eyes flamed. "Do you think I do not know what you felt when your arms tightened around me mere moments ago? Does the fact that your kiss touched me to the quick make me a whore? And dare you deny that you wanted me? I have granted you this desire by Royal Decree. Call it what you want— lust, desire, need—but I dare face it and you dare not Rafe Rafton! So much for manhood."

Askana turned her back upon him as if in disgust, inwardly trembling at the horrid harshness of their words, flinching at the crashes of the fireworks in the sky. She made to leave. His hands grabbed her shoulders and pushed her back hard against the wall. There was an edge, an intensity, in his touch. A mix of passion, rage, frustration, and something running underneath it all that Askana could not understand.

His voice was deep and sharp as he spoke to her, his anger giving way to pain. He was going to be heard whether she wished to listen to him or not. "Tell me what *you* want. Not what the Queen commands, but what you, *Askana*, want."

"What I want?" Askana scoffed, "I have said what I want, but you are not man enough to take what you want!" She spat her final insult, with all the hurt and malice she could muster. "In return for this insult, in return for your inabilities, perhaps Jermal shall take to my bed tonight."

The very thought sickened her.

Rafe lowered his eyes away from hers. She did not understand. His anger was now being driven by a growing frustration. Regardless of where this night would end, he would make her understand. "If I do lie with you, I do not intend to fulfil an obligation a consort cannot. I do not want to bed a queen. I wish to lie with Askana Moldarin. What do you desire, Askana?" Rafe pushed harder against her, his hand striking the wall by her head, *"SAY IT!"*

She looked stubbornly back at him, furious, forced to bow lower and be rejected, "Damn you, Rafe! Is it so hard to see? I want you. If that makes me no better than a whore in your eyes, then so be it. Now *RELEASE ME* before I hurt you as I long to do!"

She felt herself free of his grasp but now his hands were uncertain of what to do. She could tell he wanted to hold her close. He was afraid to touch her. His hands trembled as he fell to his knees before her. Askana could not comprehend this pain. Men were not supposed to be such creatures of emotion. Her hand apprehensively stroked the head of blonde hair as he clutched her fine robes. He was shaking. *By Nadinath, what did this Baroness do to you?* Askana empathised as he pulled himself back to his feet, *Such pain.*

"No. It does not make you a whore," Rafe said, his voice cracking. He could not bring himself to look at her. "It makes what you want real to me. Not a duty for your realm."

He went to apologise, to ask for a thousand pardons. She saw it in his eyes. There it was again, that curious gesture of placing a single finger against his lips as to not let him spoil their silence. He slowly took a hold of her hand and opened it to kiss her palm. She heard herself gasp at the sensation this sent to every part of her being. His lips pressed against hers again, a furious and desperate kiss. He wanted to take her back to their first kiss, before their words. Rafe's hand reached for the robe's neck opening and pulled hard against the delicate silk fabric as his kiss deepened. The pressure of his mouth and the rip of fabric made her gasp louder than the popping of the fireworks overhead. The air rushed over her skin for one sweet moment, before she felt the warmth of his hands, and the world dissolved into nothing but the two of them and the fire they shared. She returned the force of his kiss, her arms winding around him, clutching at his shoulders in desperation.

There is far too much between our flesh, Rafe thought as he pulled at the robes surrounding her body. Her skin could not have felt more delightful to his lips as her robes freed themselves from her torso. His lips worked down her neck, across her chest and he could feel her nipples tighten under his fingertips. Rafe followed the curve of her breast with his lips. Her nipple was sweet to the taste and he pulled her even closer. The warmth of her skin and the feel of her fingers running through his hair maddened his senses.

Liquid fire raced along her spine, jerking through every nerve in her body as she clasped his head closer, arching her back. She suddenly pushed him away, her fingers still clenching his coat as she pulled him back into the chambers. Their steps were quick and awkward as they continued to feel one another's bodies in the dark, his fingers never leaving the feel of her skin. She paused for a moment as her hip bumped a pedestal displaying an exquisite vase. The hesitation was Rafe's moment to return his lips to her own, his kiss desperate, for the moments between their touch were too long for his liking. Askana reached behind her, bracing herself against the white pedestal. The vase toppled. A treasure from an earlier Morevian dynasty, reduced to powder and shards, all in one moment of fleeting ecstasy.

The privateer tore his lips from hers for a brief moment, "Was that valuable?" His breath was heavy, his voice harsh with passion but brushed with a hint of mirth.

Her own laughter reverberated deep in her throat, her eyes dark with a thousand meanings. "Not worth one of you," she said quickly before kissing him again swiftly, heatedly. Her fingers caught the fabric of his clothes. *So complicated*, she thought in silent frustration. "If you value this fine doublet, you should remove it before I tear it free of you."

Rafe shrugged, "I will purchase another."

"No, I will purchase it for you, so that I will charge the tailor to make the removing of it easier in the future."

Reaching up, she brought his head down, her lips aggressively seeking his again. They stumbled through the doorway into another room, not caring if they fell against shelves or bumped into tables. She felt, at last, the ornate carvings of her bedchamber doors against her back. With her heel she kicked them open. Here there was a low, soft light from lamps the maids lit.

The enormous bed of ornate decoration and silks opened before him as Askana backed away slowly. Her eyes seemed to glaze over in a blind desire as she extended Rafe's arms to their full reach. He felt a hint of intimidation at the sight of the bed. A large, perfect oval, its magnificent frame and canopy was modeled in the likeness of a peacock. The bird's spread-fan of tail feathers was the headboard, and its neck arched up, its golden beak holding the bed curtains of pale green and gold gauze. The curtains had been drawn back for the day, and already the night-robe had been laid out neatly on silken sheets. The doors to the balcony had been left open, and the breeze fluttered the curtains and the drapery of the bed itself. Flames of the scattered candles flickered, causing a wave of movement to roll over the mosaic floor and the patterns of cloth and plaster, then everything shivered and was still again.

"I don't know whether to make love to you in this bed or admire it!" quipped Rafe.

"Why choose when you can have both?" Askana smiled wickedly.

Her eyes playfully dared him to follow her as she moved slowly around the bed, releasing the layers of drapery from the posts where they were tethered with silken tassels. The great eyes of the peacock seemed to look down benevolently on both of them, its ebony gaze as dark and liquid as her own. Stopping in front of the bed, she lifted her hands to her head and removed the great fan of white feathers that was her headdress, letting her hair fall free around her like a waterfall. She dragged her fingers through it, scattering emerald-decorated pins in every direction. The blanket of dark hair cast seductive lines and shades across her face as she stood at the foot of the grand bed, watching Rafe as a panther would watch its prey.

Her fingers went to the belt this time, but she did not smile. Rafe bent to kiss her, but in a graceful attack fashion she gave him a push full in the chest sending the unsuspecting privateer back through the bed curtains. His arms spread wide as he landed against the mattresses with a playful laugh. He watched her face full of determination turn to triumph as she pulled the belt free of him. Rafe struggled with his own shirt as Askana pulled the breeches free of his body. In a swift motion, Rafe's own hand slipped inside her arms and loosened the sash about her waist. Her robes had not finished their descent to the floor before he grabbed her by the hips and pulled her into bed with him.

Candlelight filtering in through the bed curtains washed over them both as they clung desperately to each other. Their affections, their touch far from gentle. It was set free and now claiming every moment as its own, as though they fought each other in the cradle of the peacock bed, their figures dimly seen through the curtains. They discovered something bittersweet and fleeting about the fragility of this night. Neither of them wanted to waste it.

Rafe caught hold of Askana's shoulders and rolled her upon her back, pinning her so she could not move. He felt her legs part slowly, her breathing wild and erratic. His own trembling was contrasted by the calm smile on Aksana's face, her thigh and calf gently bending, caressing his own leg, beckoning him closer. He had no problem slipping inside of her, but neither of them anticipated the pleasure that enveloped them both. Perhaps it came from the building emotion between them. Perhaps it was something as primal as raw desire. They both wondered if this was the witchcraft of the Caillech. His penetration. Her acceptance. Together. They shared one another's pleasure as they experienced their own. Sensations riding and cresting as curling waves that would crash against the shore as he moved with her, sweetly and savagely. They both knew this act, but no experience could not or would not parallel tonight due to the link they shared. This was a return to innocence.

The emotion flowering in her burst into full bloom, and her breath caught in her throat from the sheer sensation of him inside her. She arched up against him, burying her face in the flesh of his neck, perhaps to hide. Her fingers dug into the skin of his shoulder as she closed her eyes tightly, her breath coming fast and harsh, gritting her teeth as she felt herself open. Body, heart, and mind. Askana would not deny what she felt. It was new. It was fiercely demanding. The spell of the Caillech only enhanced the sensation, both the physical and emotional.

She frightened him, but he would not give into his fears. Neither would she. Ghosts of the past, both his and hers, could be answered later. As his anxiety grew, his thrusts intensified. Nothing mattered save the rhythm and instinct, the imperceptible rocking of the bed, the swaying of the hangings. A sharp sting tickled her lips. In a moment's zeal, she had bit his lip. It brought a smile to his face. Even the lightest pain she inflected brought him pleasure.

"Rafe," she called, strained and desperate. She bit his shoulder in the grip of an ecstasy that he continued to give her.

Then his body slowed, fighting the urge to let himself go completely in her embrace. He could feel her wanting to release, but his movements diminished. Slower. Slower.

"Askana," Rafe whispered gently. "Look at me. Please."

Like a wraith stealing through a mist, his voice reached her. Turning her head, tasting the tang of his blood on her tongue, she opened her eyes. His expression melted her heart as she raised a hand to his face, "You do not have to humble yourself to me, Rafe. Not now, not ever."

He smiled, leaning into her touch, "I just want to see your eyes." He wanted to reveal so much to her in this one night. He already had given so much to her and still she drew from him unconsciously. "You matter so much to me. What you feel matters to me. I want to watch you—"

Before Rafe could finish words she once heard him speak in a dream, Askana turned him over to his back, their bodies never losing connection as she sat up. Her head tipped back in delight as her hair cascaded down her back, gently touching Rafe's legs.

"Then look at me, Rafe," Askana smiled, her eyes looking into his own, "and know what pleasure you bring me."

It was Askana who now took control of their coupling. She leaned forward once more, forearms resting on his chest as her pleasure-filled eyes fixed on his. Never taking her eyes off him, she began to move. She knew how to prolong this pleasure.

The tenderness of her control eventually yielded to movement sharp and fast as their laboured breathing carried them both closer. Every muscle in his body went taught as he released a groan of pleasure and yielding. He could see in the dim light of the chambers her eyes widening at his complete acquiescence to her. She continued to feed off the pleasures of his body as he shuddered beneath her. She took his face into her hands, her own voice crying out at she felt herself surrender. Askana could feel tears well in her eyes, now understanding why Rafe wanted so much to look upon her in this moment. In this most vulnerable and intimate moment, she could not conceal anything nor could he. *I will not, Rafe,* she told him with her gaze. They were the same body. One soul. One life.

Thou art whole and no force can withstand thee. List to your heart and thou shalt be the strongest force there be on this earth.

They shared no words for the moment. Askana had made a pact never to surrender herself so completely to any man. The oppression of Lord Norisht. The void in her family with the death of Markuna. The loss of Telmrant. She refused to subject herself to this vulnerability again. Askana had done so for so long and now she was Queen of her home. With him, for the first time in her life, she felt complete. Hurt was somewhere outside of her, unable to touch her as they lay together in the aftermath like tigers resting in the grass. Dangerous creatures, lonely by nature, brought together by necessity.

Rafe found his voice, a hint of playfulness attempting to mask the apprehension in his words, "So as you did say, Queen Askana Moldarin, that our business agreement was not a pardon for past crimes, I must ask—what shall you do with me? At the moment, I am at the Crown's mercy."

"That you are, Captain Rafton, " she replied with drowsy amusement. "And I, the Black Widow of Morevi, do have a reputation to maintain." Teasingly she flicked her tongue over his collarbone and was rewarded by a rumble of laughter. "Perhaps I should lessen your death sentence, privateer. Instead of decorating my Great Hall with your carcass, I shall keep you prisoner." Askana purred as she ran her palms along the inside of Rafe's outstretched arms. Her fingernail would occasionally graze his skin, causing him to shudder in delight. "But no, not in the dungeons. A man of your make is far too fine to be kept in such dank settings. No, I shall keep you here within my bedchambers." Again the privateer laughed as Askana pulled the fine sheets of her bed closer to Rafe, placing him in a makeshift cocoon, "I will encase you within my finest silks, and tend to you upon my own whims."

Rafe caught her fingers within his own and locked them into a tight grasp. Askana tried to pull free but he would not release her. The smile on his own face was equally playful, "And what if I were to live up to my reputation of eluding the Black Widow? What if the Sea Wolf was to take the Queen of Morevi once more and hold her for ransom? The Council pays well, but in a roar of cannon fire and under the concealment of smoke, the Sea Wolf disappears with their Queen." Her eyebrow arched sharply as Rafe's smile widened, "And I make you my cabin wench. Keep my quarters neat and tidy. Cook my meals when I am hungry." Askana let out a small gasp of shock and revulsion as Rafe continued, "If I decide to have you occupy my bed for the night, you will see to my every bidding. Keep your Captain happy. What say you?"

"A man can dream," Askana laughed, striking him with one of her down-filled pillows.

Their words were playful, even affectionate, but as their words grew quieter there was a certain awkwardness they both could feel. With a final, light kiss on his lips, she turned on her side, fitting neatly against him as he slipped an arm around her. They both drifted off uncertainly into sleep. The uneasiness could also have been the simple fact of this unexpected night. Perhaps a foreshadowing of loss, but she did not care about it now. She could still remember him lighting his cigar with the tiny statue of Nadinath. She wanted his hide, there and then. The memory brought a smile to her. As if by instinct, she nuzzled closer against him. Even with her guards never faltering in their service to her, she had never felt so safe.

I do like this feeling, she thought dreamily, *for it is right.*

That was her last conscious thought before falling asleep in Rafe's embrace.

As the grand peacock that was her bed frame seemed to watch over them, others also kept vigil from behind the grand mirrors of Askana's chambers.

It was a strange relief to see Rafe by the bed, slipping a leather belt securely about his waist. He made great efforts to be quiet only making more noise in the process, but it was his absence beside her that caused her to stir from deep sleep. She could see in his face he had matters needing attention, namely his ship and crew. Their country silently beckoned them to return with stories of heroism and valour. His services were also, no doubt, in need from King Henry. Rafe had to leave for home soon, but she could see it was not his desire.

His eyes happened to fall upon her own gaze, still wrestling against the grogginess most common with morning. "I must tend to duties on the *Defiant.* I would have..." His voice trailed off and Rafe blushed a bit as he began lacing his boots.

Askana tilted her head to one side, "You would have what, Rafe?"

He smiled as his face reddened more, "I would have kissed you goodbye, but you were asleep and I did not wish to disturb you."

The Queen pushed the few strands of hair away from her face, tucking them back behind her ear as he finished dressing. She could only smile at his words, so innocent and refreshing to her ears. He gave her a final awkward smile and headed for the window of her chambers.

"Rafe, where are you going?"

"Out," he shrugged. "I told you. My ship, docked at Arathelle? You know—Elven city, lovely music, a rather odd-looking lot with pointed ears live there. A day's hard ride from here along the Road to the Moon?"

"No," Askana shook her head in frustration. "Why are you leaving through the window?"

Rafe removed the rope from his belt, "Discretion is the better part of valour, is it not? I would rather not have your name tainted with my highly visible exit from your royal bedchambers."

Askana glanced to the doors leading into the hallway and her smile widened, "Leave by the door."

"My dear Askana," Rafe smiled, his hand resting against his belt. "We should treat this delicately. We just restored peace to your land. Must we mar it with something as scandalous as me exiting the Royal Chambers with a look of divine satisfaction?"

"You do forget where you are, Captain. This is Morevi." She slipped out of the grand bed, keeping the long satin sheet about her body. "Your leaving by my doors would be cause for speculation, nothing more. Court gossip, which, it is well known, is not tolerated in my presence. And if it is scandal they want," Askana let the sheet fall, her naked body now displayed in full light of the morning sun, "should we not give them something worthwhile?"

Rafe pulled her close with a devilish laugh that she matched. Her arms slipped about his neck as he took from her a deep kiss that reminded them both of their night together. She was exquisite to behold and her kiss would not be so easily forgotten.

He took in a deep breath and looked into her playful eyes, "You must be the genie I have released from Aladdin's lamp. What have I awakened in you?"

"The sooner you return to me, the sooner you shall discover," Askana smiled. "So come back to me in haste, Captain."

"I am needed in Arathelle for four days. Plotting courses, stocking up supplies, and things of that nature." He took a quick look at her and nodded, "I will return in two, Your Grace." With a final quick kiss and a soft laugh, Rafe slipped to the door, "Now for God's sake, you are a queen. Do get dressed!"

Being around him was like being caught up in a whirlwind. There was no time and no calm in which to organise her thoughts, yet as Askana sat before her mirror combing her hair she found that she did not wish to do so. She did not want to think coherently at all. This feeling was something she wanted to hold selfishly. Askana found it curious. The emotion was not exactly pleasant or easy as it had once been. With the privateer, boundaries were crossed. Theirs was hard to define. Difficult to pinpoint. Difficult to control. It made her worry, it made her angry, and it made her afraid. At other times, at the most unexpected moments, the memory of his face or his touch would bring a joy to her so pure in its intensity that it took her breath away. There was no logic to her feelings for this swashbuckler. It was a wondrous exercise in reckless abandon. It was this thought that caused Askana to smile as radiant as her crown, for she knew that she would have it no other way.

The day gave way to another clear night, ushering a delightful coolness in lieu of the warmth felt by the people in the street and the peasants in the field. Askana could hear revels commencing once again. The music of the English with its hard, percussive, driving tempos now made her heart soar. She could feel the drive of the Celtic notes begging her to dance.

No, Askana thought as she closed off the sound and turned to her harp, *I need to call to him with my own song.*

Her fingertips rested for a moment against the taut strings of the instrument and then notes leapt from them as her hands played a light and haunting melody. Her eyes closed slowly as she played this tune with no name. It poured from her heart, this simple collection of notes that Rafe had once played on the *Defiant*. In her mind, she heard a tin whistle play a counter-melody. It was a delightful union within her mind, but she could feel a burning emptiness grow.

No mind to it, Askana thought with a smile as she built upon her theme, *for he shall return on the morrow.*

The door opened behind her without warning, and her smiled widened. "You are back early. Should I call for an evening meal? Or would you care for me to arrange a morning repast?"

"I have already eaten. Thank you, Your Majesty," the cold voice spoke. "I have no intention in staying long this eve."

Her music ceased abruptly. She whipped around on her stool, every muscle tensing. High Lady Dirare stood at the door, splendidly arrayed in formal robes, her lacquered fan open in her hand as she fanned herself slowly.

"How dare you!" Askana began with a touch of heat in her voice.

Dirare forestalled her by matching the Queen's tone, "How dare you, *Askana!"*

She could feel her back arch. Askana reclaimed her composure and stood from her harp, still maintaining the growing displeasure in her voice, "I did not give you permission to speak so informally," she said cuttingly. "I am well aware of your appointment to Regent in my absence, but with such a lack of decorum I wonder if you are growing too accustomed to power."

"I would agree in other circumstances, for such a practice does not show proper respect to a ruler," Dirare did not bow in reverence as she approached Askana. She walked past the Queen, tapping her fan within her open palm, "but in this case I am not sure whether the ruler warrants such honour."

Her voice was ice, yet there was a triumphant edge to it that Askana's instincts quickened to immediately. Askana did not like it.

Dirare opened the doors of Askana's chambers that connected to an adjoining room, now tidy and clean from any evidence of the previous evening's activities. She stopped for a moment at an empty pedestal. "Pity," Dirare sighed, "I was quite fond of that artefact. It was from the Shu-Loan Dynasty, if memory serves me correctly. Most rare. And for what? Simply to indulge in the pleasure of a common man."

Askana did not like it at all.

Slowly Askana followed Dirare into the adjoining room and walked to the vanity. Her fingers gently pressed the depression hidden amidst the forest of vines that adorned the wooden edge. The small blade could easily find itself within her grasp if this Game continued. "I am most certain you can explain this indiscretion to the Crown of Morevi, and for your sake I do hope it satisfies me for such arrogance will not go unanswered."

"Well, I am not positive I will satisfy you as well as the pirate did within your bedchambers."

She reached the end of this and the knife concealed within the vanity slipped into her hand, "The Queen of Morevi will not stand for this insolence. And the Council will see this no better than the very treason instrumented by Min-Lu."

Dirare finally looked upon the knife-wielding queen, her look void of all reverence or respect, "Treason? I am sure the Council will think otherwise. In fact, some of them may even be contemplating on doing the same thing I am doing right now. Even your Priestesses are not happy about this little development between you and this supposed saviour of Morevi. At present, Your Majesty, it is merely—how did you so eloquently put it this morning—speculation. But I can assure you that can change as the direction of a summer's breeze."

Anger made a solid lump in her gullet. Dirare knew the words she shared in private with Rafe. Askana did not have to glance at the mirrors within her chambers. She knew of their "hidden advantages". She also knew it was forbidden for anyone other than her to gain access to the passages linked to her chambers. Whatever Dirare planned, she felt confident enough to risk her own reputation, and her life.

"Whatever rights my Councils may have, the selection of my lovers is not one of them." Askana lowered the knife to the vanity, "If you value your position in Court, Dirare, you will leave now. I shall look upon this as your grief over Arnese overwhelming your sense of sanity."

She folded her arms and arched one black-painted brow. "It does not matter. If I am silenced and blinded for my spying upon you, I will become a martyr. I was, after all, acting for the safety and preservation of the realm. The injustice to my family's house will not go unanswered!"

"What do you mean?" Askana's voice lowered in menace.

Dirare found a seat against one of the open windows. The sounds of celebration reached high into the night sky as she spoke, "Your display of power in quelling this attack has given some cause to be wary of how you intend to rule in this Golden Age, as you now call it. You have never been too co-operative with the Council, Askana, and now they wonder whether you will become a tyrant since you brought support of a powerful kingdom. From beyond The Rift, no less." Dirare turned her eyes towards the revels, a casual smile crossing her face, perhaps in fascination of the pleasures of simple people. "While you did win allies, you did so without the consent of the Council, and that gives us pause, if not fear, of what else you intend to do without proper approval. People who are afraid often have stronger convictions and are more dangerous than people who play the Game for profit." The woman turned her smile to Askana, as if she had just executed a final move to win a winner-take-all game of par-stern.

"And you?" Askana hissed, "You play the Game for the sheer joy of it." She could see the dagger resting on the vanity, but she did not need it. A simple decree from her and Dirare would be dead.

"Kill me if you wish, but I will tell you beforehand that it will only hasten your inevitable fate if you continue upon this path!"

She took out a roll of parchment from within the folds of her robe and presented it decorously to Askana. The motion, with bent head and both hands raised in utmost courtesy, was a mockery in itself.

One slash of the knife severed the traditional red thread binding the document, and Askana scanned it swiftly, keeping one eye on Dirare. The knife wavered in her hand as she found herself more and more drawn to the words and signatures. Her eyes read passages she had already seen, her mind praying they would have been misinterpreted or change into something different before her eyes.

Askana's voice was a dry whisper, "What is the meaning of this?"

"A document signed by all the members of the High Council. It is a document that states our belief that the Light of the Thousand Suns, Her Majesty the Queen of Morevi, may be fostering relationships with forces from across The Rift without the blessings of the Council of a Hundred Turi. These relationships are of an undoubtedly political nature, but their purpose is as yet unknown." Dirare's eyes glittered with an ecstatic satisfaction. "You know this law as well as I, Askana. You made it!"

A cold hand clutched at her throat, stopping any voice she would have in the moment. She did indeed know her laws by heart. For a monarch to make political overtures to another kingdom without the Council's knowledge was deemed treasonous. Such actions from the Crown was on a level with forming laws at will without the Council's consent. It would prelude the actions of a tyrant. She could be deposed. In one blinding flash, Dirare's meaning became clear to her.

Askana forced herself to speak very calmly. "You know as well as I do that I made that agreement with King Henry of England during a time of crisis. As Queen of Morevi I am permitted to do so."

Dirare rose from her chair and returned to the bedroom as she spoke, "Upon that point I must agree with you, but it is not that issue of which we speak. Since the crisis is over, the Otherworlders must be sent back promptly. Not only do you show no sign of doing so, it is apparent you are forging relations with the most infamous of them." Her fan dragged casually against the surface of the bed sheets as she continued towards the balcony.

"Dirare," Askana's voice wore dangerously thin. "You have not given the Crown acknowledgement since setting foot in here. Dispense with formality and make your intent clear."

"Fine," Dirare cooed and turned to Askana with eyes upon the same level as hers, but still managing to look down upon the Queen. "You have shared your bed with Captain Rafton. If this were some passing fascination as Jermal apparently has proven to be, it would be no matter. With Captain Rafton, the matter is far more dangerous. Not only is the man a known enemy of the Crown, he is allied with men far more powerful than King Cedric. The English navy made that quite clear. As of yet, no preparations have been made to supply the English ships for their return journey. They speak of establishing trade here. Such trade conducted across The Rift cannot be established without the approval of the Fellowship of the Jewels. If Morevi fails, either in commerce with the English or on a more personal nature between you and Captain Rafton, we will not only have Eyrie and the Fellowship to contend with, but this King Henry of England as well."

Askana could practically feel the blood receding from her face, replaced with white-hot anger. "You invent evidence! You have no proof to back these threats."

"I have proof. With my own eyes, High Lady Radna, and the assistance of two scribes of the Order of Nadinath, we observed your actions. Your own sacred courtyard where you and Rafe shared theological opinion. Your charming game of hide-and-seek in the Palace." Dirare turned away from Askana and continued to walk out onto the balcony of the royal bedchambers, "And, of course, the actions within these chambers, leading well into this morning. For a queen who so proudly proclaims her loyalty to Morevi and its people, I fail to understand your choice of lovers. Had you conveniently forgotten while you were in the throes of ecstasy how many ships of Morevi he raided? What lives he took upon the open waters? Those who starved in the streets when his actions cut off supplies? Had it not been for winning the favour of that grotesque beast-woman, I am most certain Kalea would have fulfilled her Royal Decree and buried a shirai in his chest."

Askana knew Dirare had to leave her chambers alive. She did not want to admit the truth, but Dirare was right. There were crossed boundaries she herself considered. They would assuredly be brought to light. She joined her on the Grand Balcony. "What do you want, Dirare? The crown?"

"Oh, my dear Askana," Dirare laughed incredulously. "You do jest. I could never replace you as Sovereign. I do this for your sake, Askana. Why do I have need for a crown when I have you upon a proper path now, better suited for a prosperous future." The brittle laugh ceased and Dirare smiled, "Send the English away and keep to your own kind. Send the privateer away, Askana, and all shall be well. If you do not, I will not answer for what happens." And with a nod of self-satisfaction, Dirare left Askana there, not bothering to request leave nor bow in a regained reverence.

The door closed with a loud 'click' behind the sweep of her red robes.

Trembling with rage, she sat upon the edge of her bed, her mind now lost even more so than it was in the chaos Rafe stirred within her. Dirare had immunity. She knew that. The High Regent pulled off a triumphant coup. If she followed her heart and killed Dirare, the documents with their incriminating claims would reach the Council and the people. It would mark the end of her reign and a beheading by her own guards.

Some might support her, but how many? Enough to keep a hold upon the throne and peace within Morevi? The changes within her regime after all were still too new. There were many High Ladies who still adhered somewhat to the Old Ways. Her private life had already been considered scandalous with a mixing of her blood with that of the Elves. She knew of the prejudice against the Elves and how some felt her actions invited the wrath of the Mists. What would they think now? After Min-Lu's demonstration on how love, lust, or infatuation could lead to disaster, would it not be convenient for them to jump to conclusions?

Could she take a chance and flee from Morevi forever? She could wander the seas of a different world with him, just another simple cutthroat on a ship with no worries save how to avoid capture and stave off poverty. She would be safe in the company of the Sea Wolf, the only outlaw who eluded Morevi. The idea was extremely seductive. To cast off the chains of her existence forever. To be free to soar as any bird of the sea winds. To be with him, forever by his side.

If she did so, others would die, those too loyal to her to be trusted. Kubi-Sogi. Kalea. Elunear. And what of the Temple, what would they do? Would the Order of Nadinath fall? Or would her own Maidens pledge a solemn oath to never stop until she was delivered before the Goddess to face death in abandoning the Temple?

Since his departure, she longed for his return. Now she prayed that Rafe would open the sails of his grand vessel and disappear from Morevi, her name dropped in bawdy conversations between sailors in the pubs and taverns he frequented. He would return to his many trysts and forget her.

She knew better. Fate would not be so kind to release her from his return.

CHAPTER NINETEEN
Question of Honour

The double doors opened simultaneously as Rafe's bright smile attempted to illuminate the room. He had done many impetuous and impulsive acts in his day. Entering into a Queen's chambers unannounced was still quite humbling. So were his thoughts and emotions running rampant. He had made haste and delegated his work amongst the crew so he could return to her, the woman he had not stopped thinking about since leaving Songkusai two days ago.

For now, in the presence of servants, decorum would be paramount. The smile faded. The doors slowly closed behind him as if leading to a church hall. The privateer straightened his doublet and bowed before Askana, his reflection in her vanity mirror looking at her, "Good morning, Your Grace."

The Queen of Morevi looked up from where she knelt on the cushions. Three maidservants flitted around her, attending to her hair, massaging her bare shoulders with fragrant oils. She did little to acknowledge his entry, save tighten the sash that held the white linen shift across her chest. "Good morning, Captain."

For the first time since she was a little girl, Askana was truly afraid. Not of Dirare's threat, but of truths the woman made open for her unwilling eyes to see. This was not something ordinary. He was as unique as the bond they shared, both in Grainne's sorcery and in her bedchambers. It was beyond her control as he was.

Rafe was trying not to fidget but it was difficult to talk to her openly in the company of others. Elunear's gaze did not provide much comfort either. He could not fathom why she had suddenly gone cold towards him. Perhaps it was the return to her homeland and to her ways. It was a very unsettling silence, needing to be broken. "Your Grace, I do realise that I may be imposing upon the Throne but could you...?" Rafe's voice faded as he cast a few quick glances to the surrounding servants.

"Of course. Kichala, Morein, Peiria." She rose gracefully as the maids slipped the gauzy silk sleeves of her morning robes up over her shoulders, leaving her hair hanging down her back, "The preparations may continue later." She smiled at the girls as they obeyed her. A nod to the guards relieved them of their posts, all except Elunear who remained stubbornly. Askana wondered if her loyal guard felt the danger of his hold on her. She could not help but ask why Morevi denied her what she wanted, what she needed. She spoke softly, "Elunear."

With a frown, the girl bowed low, grasped her shirai and stalked out.

"What has suddenly taken Elunear?" Rafe asked, shaking his head, "At least Lubria now calls me 'Captain' instead of 'human'. An accomplishment, I have no doubt. Now I suffer an onslaught of daggers from Elunear's gaze."

She was in the middle of applying full court paint. The stark white on her face and the deep red lines around her eyes would have made her appear intimidating to outsiders. Rafe could only see the face of the previous evening, free of such formal traditions, a vibrant smile. *Slow and easy,* he coached himself silently, *slow and easy, but do not deny what you feel. Speak your heart, Rafton. There is no need to fear it.*

"People change." She rose and went a few steps towards him. As if by reflex, she reached up to him and placed a hand on his cheek. She would remember him this way and look on him with tenderness for these last few moments. *Rafe, forgive me.*

Simply beautiful, he thought with a smile, yet those words could not do her justice. "Askana, your goldsmiths are quite talented and efficient. I commissioned this before the celebrations began. I gave him a few extra coins for haste. I believe the old boy is a descendent of Mercury himself. Brilliant work, would you not agree?"

The ring was a combination of white and yellow gold. A modest signet ring, but the signet in its simplicity could not help but prove a curiosity to those who would see it. The continuous knot formed the head of a wolf over an intertwined rose and Turi flower. The entire design was in the middle of a playing card — the Ace of Spades. Askana noticed its size was perfect for her own slender fingers.

Then she noticed an identical ring around his own finger. "Our adventure together has inspired this. My new banner."

Beautifully crafted, Askana thought, *and what love must have inspired its design.* "It is lovely, Rafe. So beautiful." In her moment's hesitation, Rafe slipped the ring upon her finger, her hand trembling a little, and with a smile he closed his fingers gently around hers. Askana studied their hands, one large, paler than hers even as his skin was sun-browned, the other slender and golden. The rings glowed with a quiet sheen on their fingers.

"What are you thinking about?" His breath tickled her ear as he slipped a hand about her waist. "Do I have to pay you a penny again?"

"A what?" she said distractedly. She felt the material of his doublet against her skin, smelled the warmth of the sun on him.

"A penny. As I did in the Sleeping Dragons. A saying from my realm. A penny for your thoughts."

She looked up at him, into his face, a final silent desperate plea. *Go, Rafe. Cast me aside. Please...*

She felt his hands at her waist. He lifted her off her feet gently so she was looking down at him instead of up, her hands on his shoulders. "My light, little Queen." He looked at her a moment longer as if to commit her face to memory, and put her gently down again.

"Rafe, please." Askana gingerly removed his arms from around her as she returned to the vanity. Her eyes closed gently as she tried to silence her heart, now screaming for her attention.

You must do this. It was the voice of Duty, her promise to the people of Morevi, drowning out the voice of her heart. *A lifetime of duty begins now.*

She stared at herself in the mirror. There seemed no purpose for this action. She did not adjust her hair, she did not add to her court paint design, she did not pull a fold of her clothes into place or pick at a crease. She simply looked at herself. The reflection of a queen stared back at her. *Do it now and do it quickly.* The voice in her mind was cold. Emotionless, as was her tone with him. "I thank you for the gift, Captain." She would not call him "privateer". For his service to her, he deserved a certain amount of respect. "But perhaps it is inappropriate."

The ring slipped off her finger awkwardly. It did not wish to leave her, but she was determined to remove it, even if it meant sacrificing a digit.

"Inappropriate? Askana, what is troubling you?"

She watched him walk up behind her in the mirror. The ru-yilei was worn in proper Morevian fashion across his back. She wondered when Kubi-Sogi had shown him this, or if it was something he picked up in watching the other soldiers of her Guard. The wolf-head of the pommel winked a ruby eye maliciously at her. The red tassels tied around the hilt for good fortune swayed gently.

"Rafe, what do you foresee in your future?"

"My future?" He laughed flippantly, leaning into her. The mirror created a portrait of a breathtaking couple. Askana did not start, but it was an unsettling image before her. Rafe smiled brightly, "I would entertain a future at your side for as long as God or Nadinath, or both, will allow. Together, we destroyed a seaport, charmed the reigning monarch of England, and led the unlikeliest of allies against an overwhelming enemy and won. In my eyes, that is a match I wish to keep."

"If we were to wed, would you stay with me? Give up your life on the sea? The *Defiant*? England?"

"Wed?" he asked with surprise. So much for slow and easy. "Askana, I had no idea you felt so—" The smile on his face widened, "I would be most honoured. I would miss the sea, but there is adventure to be found here by your side."

Her voice grew colder with every word. "No, Rafe, you misunderstand. Under the law of Morevi as set by her Queen, you would fulfil the position of Consort. The male version of a concubine. If I remember correctly, you used to make a career of holding that position with other women." The Queen grinned and gave a gentle nod, "Furthermore, you told me your mother was something similar to a consort in your realm. It is, no doubt, in your blood. At least with me you would have a status of minor nobility to add to that."

The carefully chosen words cut him deeply. "Askana?" Rafe quickly regained his composure as he sat by her side, "What is the matter? Share your heart with me."

"My heart?" Her laugh sounded light, amused. "Are you certain a man of your base station would understand the heart of a queen?"

The silence spoke more than a thousand words. Rafe knew that laugh. He knew it too well.

"You have served your Queen and Morevi well, Captain. Above and beyond the agreed-upon arrangement." Askana lightly touched up her court makeup as she spoke, her voice the definition of control. "You have not only assisted in revealing a conspiracy to the Crown, you have restored the Queen of Morevi." Askana took a deep breath as she casually looked over the array of colours in her makeup palette, "If your seed does find good earth within me, you may have even provided a potential heir to the Realm, provided the child is a girl. For this, you have the Crown's eternal gratitude. Your payment will reflect as much. An extra five thousand crowns? I believe that will suffice for your services here in my bedchambers."

"That will not be necessary." There was no shock in his voice. No sorrow. It was even. Still.

"Very well then." Askana no longer regarded his reflection but focused on her own. "You may collect your payment from Kubi-Sogi."

The jungle sounds continued their music while Rafe stood behind her, paralysed. The chiding. The laugh. *No, not you, Askana, not you.* Rafe needed certainty. "Your Majesty, are you dismissing me?"

She laughed again. Brittle. Hard. "Oh, my dear Captain, you thought what we shared was something more than a mere night's pleasure? Love? A quaint notion. A children's saying comes to mind:

> *'Whether for a mouse, whether for a louse,*
> *Or a fine lady's hunting hound.*
> *About a thief's neck,*
> *The hangman's noose will still go round.'*

"I do think for a feared outlaw of the oceans, you surrender your heart too easily." For her words to catch she had to look at him. "I am most certain your Baroness would understand my mind in this matter."

"I am most certain of that," he said, his voice cloaked in resign.

"The Queen of Morevi and its people thank you for your services, but We desire that you do not overstay your welcome, nor do We wish for you to impose on Us any longer."

She watched him in the mirror. *By the Goddess*, Askana thought as she closed her eyes, *it is done*.

The ring of the ru-yilei drawn from its scabbard drowned out the sounds of the Morevian jungle. The morning sun caught a reflection off the fine blade over her head. She did not move. The look in Rafe's eyes was an unbridled fury but his blade did not seek her for an attack. The metal swung wildly, the sounds of the blade slicing through the air coupled with his own wails of anger and frustration. Vases shattered. Curtains entangled themselves about the blade as they were torn free of their rings. His screams and actions sent birds confined in cages into a maddened and futile flight to escape nowhere.

The shirai preluded Elunear's entrance as guards and servants burst through the doorway of the chambers to protect their Queen. Rafe's sword stopped just underneath the Queen's chin. The servants gasped, and even Elunear's rage dimmed in comparison to her shock. For a moment, no one moved.

"Rise." Rafe hissed.

She followed his lead to the window. The curtains now gathered into crumpled heaps. He had cut them down in one smooth turn before the blade even reached her. The sunlight poured in and the beauty of the Morevian landscape lay spread out before them.

"Look at it, Askana. *LOOK AT IT!* It is merely jungle, wild animals, and earth. Nothing more." Rafe's weapon lowered, but no one moved on him. They were given a hint of his ability. Anyone so much as attempting a play for the privateer would fall. "Well, by the grace of God, you can have it! If this is what you desire and if it is all you desire then *so be it*. You are more than welcome to it!"

"How dare you mock me, and mock what you cannot even begin to understand," Askana said in a tone matching his own ferocity. "You have no idea under the Goddess of what you speak. Jungle and wild animals? Is that what you see? This is my land, Rafe! My dream realised. It is as tied to me as my own flesh, and I am its guardian. You see before you not Askana, not the Black Widow, not the High Priestess, but the Queen! As Queen, I have bestowed my pardon and have granted you safe passage. Do not try me further!"

"All I wanted was for us to have a life together, an alliance of sorts the way we worked so well together." The blade, now seeming too heavy for the privateer to hold in challenge, struck against the floor, giving a light ring as it did. "I desired a partnership, perhaps. Something shared. Is that so difficult? Is that so wrong? I know that somewhere inside that Morevian heart of yours, you do deny yourself what could be the grandest adventure you and I could take." She remained unmoved by his words. His voice hardened. "If you let Telmrant in, why not me?"

It was a well-dealt strike, particularly in view of all her subjects. "He could have been a king." Her voice cracked lightly, then she took control once more. "He was a King's brother. I am a Queen, and Queen of a land of women. You forget we have no real love of men. They are there when we want them, as you were. It was enjoyable, Rafe. I will not deny that fact. You provided a pleasant diversion."

"Then I will no longer trouble you, Your Grace. I leave with the tide." Rafe sheathed the fine weapon and gave a bow peppered with a mock flourish that caused the servants to gasp, "As hired saviour to this God-forsaken land, I do leave you to your precious Kingdom and Council. Play your sick little games to wile away the hours in between your bed-warming distractions, be it Jermal or some other poor sot. And take heart, Your Grace, any dalliance from this day forward will not cost your treasury one coin."

Taking in one last look of the Queen, Rafe went to leave. Servants and Guard kept silent, not out of respect but stunned at the audacity and insubordination of this Otherworlder. Askana was willing to tolerate his jibes in the past. There was no reason for it now. *Not here,* Askana raged, *not before my subjects. I will not be spoken to in such a fashion!*

"Privateer—"

"CAPTAIN!" Rafe turned sharply back upon her, his hand grabbing the collar of her morning robes, "Captain Rafael Stringfellow Rafton, if you please, Your Grace." She could feel spittle hit her face as he drew her closer. "With everything I *endured* under your employment, I have earned that much from you."

Elunear sprang towards them. Her shirai moved with blade forward to break his hold on her, and perhaps slit his throat.

The mirror's reflection warned him of Elunear's brave offensive. He moved so swiftly that no one saw him remove the shirai from her grasp.

The punch shocked everyone.

"If you ever raise this weapon at me again, girl," Rafe said, the Guard's shirai in his grasp. His ferocity was gone for the moment, but everyone noted the white-knuckled grip he kept around the weapon. "you had better be certain." Rafe tossed the shirai to another attending Guard, his eyes warning, if not daring, them to advance. "The Queen has given me my leave and I do embrace it as I did her and many others of her ilk!" He grabbed Askana by the shoulders and forced her to look at the panoramic view of Morevi, "This is your dream, Askana Moldarin, and yours alone."

A chill pervaded her where a moment ago there was blazing heat.

He did not slam the doors on his exit. There was no need for it. For a moment, nothing except their breathing and the joyous sounds of celebration in the city streets far off in the distance remained. It mocked her.

"Peiria," Askana's clear, too-calm voice broke the stillness. "Take Elunear outside and tend to her. The rest of you, leave your Queen in peace."

"Your Majesty," protested a young servant, "He cannot be allowed such insolence against—"

"OUT!" her voice sounded in the manner of a cracking whip.

Everyone flinched. It was the first time Askana had ever lost dignity enough to shout at her attendants. Swiftly, the room emptied.

The Black Widow was alone at last. In echoing emptiness, She sank down slowly onto her knees, eyes closed, head bowed. The sunlight streamed in on her, catching the silks and making her skin gleam, her hair shined with a dark lustre. Under the painted lids, a wetness was gathering. The wetness pooled and mixed with the reddish powder the maids had so carefully applied. In a haunting, silent wail that sounded more like a draft of wind escaping from a small slit in a corridor wall, the Queen crawled to her vanity. Another voice drove her to it. *Look upon the water, and see the face of the one who has wakened me in thee.*

Askana looked through the blurring vision of tears at her own reflection. In her court makeup, her skin appeared smooth and placid as that of a statue. Two crimson tears streaked down the still, white cheeks. The statue was crying tears of blood.

The morning had begun as the previous one. The day before was nothing more than a vague memory, but her body would not so easily forget the Captain's departure. She ached from head to toe and felt completely drained of life. The Queen was relieved the court makeup concealed her pallid look of exhaustion. She could not recollect if she had cried herself to sleep or not, but neither could she recall retiring for the night.

Their footfalls gently sounded throughout the corridors as they proceeded to the Raising of the Consort, a ceremony that needed to be performed properly now that Askana was in attendance. Those Houses loyal to Askana Moldarin and those desiring advancement remained to make their presence known. It would be made official, written in the Golden Books that Jermal would be the Chosen Companion and Provider to the Throne.

Her morning served as a strange echo as she tended to responsibilities shunned the previous day. The signature and seal of Moldarin graced decree upon decree. Most of them were compensations to performers and vendors for their services to celebrations still lingering in the streets that day. The continuing revels for their victory along with the Raising of the Consort would later call for her presence. *What a beloved change*, Askana thought with a smile, *to be needed as Queen to attend a celebration of peace.*

If only she felt like celebrating.

"As for the treasury, taxes may need to be raised, Your Majesty," sighed Kubi-Sogi.

Now Duty reared its ugly head. Taxation. Regardless of it being war or peace, each had a sum needing to be paid. *I will not bleed my beloved realm dry*, she thought softly. "What is your suggestion, *Sen-sheru?*"

He could not help but smile at this new title she bestowed on him. In some dialects, "sen-sheru" meant "old teacher" but he knew the address as "little father". It was a smile he needed as they spoke of such a grim matter. "I know you do not wish to tax your people any more, but in the matter of Captain Rafton and the cost of his services, it will put a strain upon the Royal Treasury."

The name made her want to flinch, but she was not a trembling maid. It would truly be a day of celebration when his name faded from the air.

It was obvious in Kubi-Sogi's tone he was not privy to yesterday's events. He did not see her reaction as he shook his head, his eyes in disbelief at the numbers. "I understand, Your Grace, the need, but to agree to such a price?"

"I agree, his sum was lofty. But tell me, Sen-sheru, what price you would place on the salvation and tranquillity of Morevi?" She paused in the sunlit path of the great corridors. "I did what had to be done. For the greater good of Morevi."

Against her will and discipline, her mind conjured up a tormenting image of the brash privateer standing before her in the dimly lit room, his voice caressing her senses as his touch once had.

"You confess to pillaging my ships, you eye me like some paramour with no regard to my standing, and now you dare make such a financial demand upon the Morevian treasury? You insult me with such an offer!"

"Perhaps I do, your Majesty, but my price is non-negotiable."

"By the Grace of the Goddess, I wonder if his price was so inflated as to serve his pride." she scoffed, continuing to the Great Hall. "Regardless, his actions speak for him. Fifteen thousand crowns is adequate compensation."

"Fifteen thousand?" Kubi-Sogi shook his head quickly with a surprised laugh, "Forgive me, Your Majesty, but you are mistaken."

"How much did you pay him?"

"Five," he shrugged. "He accepted five thousand crowns from the Royal Treasury. He mentioned that four would go to his crew and the remaining thousand would be distributed freely amongst the people of Morevi in honour of his fallen First Officer. From the reports I received, he did just that."

"Five?" she asked dazedly.

"And your share?"

"The Sea Wolf would return to his den and disappear. With ten thousand, I could find a small manor of my own, purchase myself a proper crest, and enjoy the status of a gentleman."

Her words trembled as she asked her adviser, "What of his share?"

"He made no mention of it. I thought it no matter to us for the five thousand would do ample damage against the Royal Coffer."

"She again extended the payment to me. I took the money. She knew me all too well, and turned my weaknesses against me. There is no pain more cruel than that."

The doors of the Great Hall towered before them. Kubi-Sogi gave a gentle sigh, "We can discuss the matter in more detail later. Duty awaits as do the Ladies of the Blood. You must now be Queen and be joined your Consort before the Council." He smiled as he held her hand, "May Nadinath bless you, Your Majesty."

"Thank you," she said involuntarily. "Do not raise the taxes. I have plans in mind."

The truth was she had nothing in mind. She was, for the time being, lost. It would pass. Once her pain became a distant memory, as her nature dictated, she would think of something. She always did.

So it was a very preoccupied Askana Moldarin who entered the Great Hall, a long red carpet cutting over the great seal of House Moldarin, leading the way to a lifetime of duty. At the end of her walk down this deep crimson path awaited her Consort as she had promised the people of Morevi. The sounds of harps, tambours, and tiny flutes provided a haunting melody for her lone procession from doorway to throne. She felt their eyes upon her. Some proud. Others relieved. A few rewriting the rules of the Great Game. They all rose in honourable deference to the First Queen of Morevi, the whispers and chatter now coming to a halt for the moment. Her presence commanded respect. Those who once took faith in the words of Min-Lu lowered their heads in shame as Askana's love for this realm was apparent. In this ceremony, down to a simple action as an entrance, it would be known that her right to the throne would never be challenged or questioned. Under her rule shall Morevi prosper.

"This is your dream, Askana Moldarin, and yours alone."

Her pace slowed for a moment. His voice was so clear. She wanted to look for him, perhaps hidden within the Collected Houses, but her gaze remained focused on Jermal. His face was so alive. This would be his day as well as hers. Perhaps it was not what she expected but his loyalty was apparent. Moments of survivalist instincts aside.

"The core of it is this...he shall be linked to you. You shall feel one another's pain. The effect may last a few months, a few years, perhaps forever. This meddling with the Fates is very unpredictable. You both will share immortality, of a sort. One of you cannot die without the other."

Linked. One soul. The Caillech had warned her of the cost. Perhaps the privateer's reckless lifestyle or occasional tryst would haunt her now and then. No matter.

She felt her breath escape her. It was the same pain again that she felt on board his ship. She had dismissed it then as the chill of the open sea, but Askana found it difficult to breathe in the spacious hall. Was the throne any closer? Her eyes began to play tricks upon her. The throne seemed to be slipping further away from her. Her feet grew heavier and the pain in her chest pierced her once more.

"Sometimes I do wonder—this sacrifice for a country—is it truly worth it? Does this band of gold, velvet, and jewels that I wear across my brow truly merit the sacrifice? As King, I believed the world would be mine for the taking, and yet I find myself denied of the simplest things that would make me...complete."

His words were not so far from her own. Good King Hal. She would not admit it to any other soul, but she wished to see him again. The tightness in her chest awakened once more, but her walk never faltered.

"I assure you, your brother is an ally I cannot afford to lose. He is not of the same nature as the men I have known. Granted, he is an outlaw. He is also a scoundrel. But his heart is noble. Above all this he is a good man, and that is rare."

This time, Askana hesitated. She could hear the voices of the dignitaries rise in a slight din, but she merely closed her eyes and breathed through the piercing sensation deep within her chest. Had she said that? It was her voice. They were her words. In a brief moment her mind returned to the previous day. He was rare. In her land and in his own.

It was wild abandon. A moment of ecstasy, nothing more. Duty to her realm must prevail. To extend beyond the desires and pleasures of the flesh. Morevi must come first.

Her walking began once more.

"Pull Me out of the stone, My child."

That was merely a dream, Askana's thoughts screamed. It was not possible for there to be a fourth figure within the stone. The Order of Nadinath never spoke of such a thing. A dream cannot alter an Order with such deep roots as the Temple of Nadinath.

He saw her, though.

A trick of light and shadows on black stone. The privateer was correct in that. She finally sensed under her feet the steps leading to the throne.

"Pull Me out of the stone, My child."

Why did the Goddess call to her now? What torture was this? Does Nadinath not show mercy? Askana turned to face her Court. She had it all now. The crown. The realm. Peace. Morevi now entered its Golden Age. The Golden Age of Peace and Prosperity under her rule.

"This is your dream, Askana Moldarin, and yours alone."

Her eyes closed. These voices would fade eventually and the name of Rafe Rafton reduced to nothing more than just a name recorded in the Golden Books. The privateer would soon forget her as well. She breathed through the stinging pain in her chest, cresting once more as the ocean's waves would do against his ship.

"You shall feel one another's pain..."

Askana had her kingdom. It was worth the price.

"And yet I find myself denied of the simplest things that would make me...complete."

She could hear the voices of Priest and Priestess but they sounded distant, more dream-like than the echoes that now maddened her in this state of meditation. She tried to focus on the Priest of El-Baz and his blessings upon the Consort, his words echoing the ideals of the Old Regime. Now came the Priestess of Nadinath bestowing her blessings upon the Queen, appealing to the Goddess for health and bliss upon Askana Moldarin.

"Pull Me out of the stone, My child."

May Nadinath bless the New Age of Morevi! Now will they respect and follow the Moldarin Dynasty.

"This is your dream, Askana Moldarin, and yours alone."

The Queen heard Jermal speak softly into her ear. "A penny for your thoughts."

Askana's eyes flicked open, her breath catching in her throat as she turned sharply to look at him, "What did you say, Jermal?"

"I asked 'Are we to secure my office?'." Jermal's gold veil shimmered lightly as he whispered underneath the blessings of Nadinath. "I am a little lost here, Askana. All the ceremonies are beginning to look and sound alike."

Askana stared at him blankly. She had seen Markuna in him at one time. Perhaps she could find it within him again. It would be an exercise in patience, but perhaps she could.

"It is this ceremony that preludes our bonding. Once we consent to the bonding of our bloodlines, you will officially be raised to the title of Consort."

"But what of the ceremony that happened in your absence?"

"We need to follow the protocol established by my ascension. In my absence, the Council turned to the Ancient Laws established by men. The time you occupied the throne will be regarded as if it never happened." Askana returned her gaze to the Priest and Priestess, "Know this. You did well in my absence. I am pleased with you, Jermal."

"Ah, I see. *'Pleased'*," Jermal noted, "not *'happy'*. There is a difference, Askana."

"Jermal, do not be impertinent," she spoke gently as they knelt before the Priest and Priestess. *I will find Markuna in him again,* she assured herself. "We will speak on this matter another time."

"Before or after we talk about the pirate and your behaviour with him?" Jermal snapped, loud enough only for Askana and the attending clerics who glanced to one another as they heard words meant only for the Queen's ears.

"Jermal!" hissed Askana as a long band of gold fabric was presented for blessings from the Priest and Priestess. It was to symbolise their bonding. "Do not challenge your Queen so openly! We will discuss all matters later."

"Something I look forward to," he huffed.

The gold band was held aloft by the Priest, then by the Priestess, accompanied by a light applause from the witnesses. Jermal extended his hand, Askana placed hers above his own. The band slipped elegantly around his wrist.

On the feel of it touching her skin, Askana's hand recoiled as if the fabric burned her. *No,* cried a voice once silenced by Duty, *you will not do this!* She held her hand in this position for a moment, dumbfounded at the curious reflex to a ceremony she knew she was ready to undergo. Voices slowly rose in speculation. *Silence, all of you,* cried her Heart, *you do not know the pain of your Queen!*

Then came another voice heard only by her, a cold voice that surprised her for a moment. "Damn you, Askana Moldarin, place your hand on mine and let us finish this once and for all," whispered Jermal sharply. "After all I endured in the past, in your absence, and in your return, *you owe me.*"

The surprise was only for a moment. A brief, fleeting moment.

Askana's growl filled the Great Hall as she grabbed Jermal by his brilliant ceremonial robes. The Priest and Priestess were knocked clear, the golden band, braziers and bowls of Holy Oil all falling to the floor, as the Queen threw her Consort across the vast marble space. Screams and gasps replaced the musicians' notes as Askana approached the would-be King slowly. A complete rage overwhelmed her as she picked up the stunned Jermal by the scruff of his robes and drew her hand back as if to mercilessly pound his face until he were dead.

She hesitated, her fist suspended behind her head as she gnashed her teeth together. Her breathing was laboured, a painful wheezing that was now the only sound in the Great Hall. Then came his voice, heard only by Askana. *"I have just seen a woman very different from what the stories do tell,"* he had said to her. It would not please him if she were to take Jermal's life. It was not his style. He did not think it was hers either.

"I OWE YOU?!" Askana screamed at Jermal with all the rage of the Destroyer behind her, "Tell me, thief, who owes the Queen?!" She was blind with anguish. She released his robes, dropping him on the floor. Jermal was too petrified to crawl away from her. She just stood over him. In her eyes a storm was merely beginning. Her powerful voice then filled the Great Hall as she now addressed the Ladies of the Blood. "Tell me who owes the First Queen of Morevi?! Was it you, Lady Radna, who fended off assassins and took the lives of her own subjects to root out the conspiracy against the realm? Or perhaps it was the High Lady Miarad who risked her life in crossing The Rift in search of allies, allies who fought bravely and died for a country that was not their own so that you all may enjoy the benefits of power, free of its responsibilities? Was I mistaken in thinking it was, in fact, High Lady Pira and her sister Pura who led you all in the War of the Fan and Slipper?"

When Askana's eyes fell on Dirare, the High Regent flinched. This was something newly awakened. Something she had never seen before. The fear she felt in being hunted by the Morev'ar was pale in the presence of Askana's madness. For the first time in their relationship, Dirare had no clue what her opponent was to say or do next. That terrified her.

"Is this what I owe to you, High Lady Dirare? For my service to you, the High Council, and to Morevi?" She was sobbing now, looking at her High Regent with imploring eyes. "Do you not see? He did not take the money this time." Dirare could only stare at her, not understanding the significance of what the Queen was saying. As she wept, a laugh—a hearty, bravado laugh—welled in her as Askana went from face to face around her in the Great Hall, repeated again and again, "He did not take the money this time."

She now was standing alone under the eyes of the assembled Blood and Council, but no one moved. The players of the Great Game were at a loss for Askana played a most impressive stratagem. She spoke her heart. The members of the High Council looked to one another. Askana had named them all, making it clear to the remaining Houses this sudden outburst was, somehow, their doing. A few scornful glances also fell upon Lady Dirare who could not believe this display before her. The eyes upon the First Queen of Morevi were now in complete awe. In this moment of weakness, Askana had never appeared more powerful.

Her laugh subsided. In silence, she took a long, slow look around the Great Hall, as if it were her last. She did not know what would unfold after this, but she had spoken her heart. Now it was time to follow it.

If she rode fast enough, perhaps she could catch his ship before it left Arathelle.

"Cap'n? We are across The Rift, sir."

The Sea Wolf stood with arms crossed before the grand bay windows of his quarters. His eyes were still looking at The Rift as they crossed through it to their own world. He smiled at the song filtering from the decks above him. A sweet, charming melody of returning to missed loved ones, fields covered with heather, and mist-covered mountains. In a few days, he would be home.

He took a place in the aftercastle at the beginning of their voyage home, his eyes still fixed on Iomer. He was in plain view.

When the Ports of Arathelle were out of sight, he remained there, his eyes still fixed on the lands of Naruihm.

When the land disappeared from view, Captain Rafton retired to his quarters and still kept his eyes where Naruihm was. It was as if he intended to look across The Rift itself.

"I know, Mister Bayliss. You have successfully brought us across." Rafe smiled and gave a gentle nod, "Well done. You will make a formidable First Officer."

Bayliss shrugged, "I am no Mister Nassir, sir."

Rafe's head lowered for a moment, the voice of his friend and comrade still lingering in his mind. The pain in his heart, however, was not for him. With a last look at his signet ring—the wolf's head over an intertwined rose and Turi flower—he took in a long, deep breath and stepped away from the window. Turning to Bayliss, Rafe gave him a playful wink, "No, you are no Nassir. But you are a wonderful Bayliss, Mister Bayliss. Take us home."

Answers of the Higher Power

Lines snapped taut and winches groaned under the weight of cargo as men struggled on the other end of ropes. Shouts rose and fell. Horses that were being unloaded from holds whinnied, kicking feebly as they were lifted in slings over the water and onto the dock. Seagulls wheeled on sea breezes and cried to one another, always quick to grab a crust or discarded scrap of food. Taighar still remained the bustling capital of commerce for the Eyriener nation, even in its continuing rebuilding since the Great Dock Fire.

Trade was still brisk, though many merchants were speculating on a sudden recession following the fiasco in Morevi. Representatives to the Royal Treasury in Iambourgh were doing their best to quell such doubts. They were still in a state of disarray since the fall of the Merchants' Circle. Evidence of unaccounted income and corruption in the royal offices was now coming to the surface, leading to tribunals and swift executions for this "financial treason" to the Crown. This, followed by their defeat, left Eyrie in a state of economic turmoil. The nation desperately needed money, therefore trade was paramount. It was essential for their survival. The few remaining ships of the once invincible Eyriener Navy patrolled the waters, stopping and checking every vessel as an assurance of safety to its people.

The *Cimmaron*, however, was a ship not inconvenienced by the routine boarding. There was nothing unique in her make that warranted this exemption. She was a handsome vessel, sleek and quick across the sea. Her main function of ferrying wealthy passengers had not earned the deference of the Eyriener Navy. It was the smaller banner, a starburst surrounded by smaller stars neatly arranged in two circles against a field of deep purple, flying underneath the *Cimmaron's* banner that granted her an uninterrupted voyage.

Men and women of privilege now descended the ship's gangplank, turning their noses up at the sailors and labourers sweating in the cool of early spring. These gruff men of the sea, in return, had their fun by shouting ribald jests as they would pass. When the passenger wearing the distinctive cloak of deepest blue and a pendant matching the small banner that flew on the *Cimmaron* stepped into view, the jests faltered and died. Men quickly returned to their tasks of unloading the ship's hold. His fellow passengers gave him a wide berth, the men herding their women close behind them. The Eyriener females turned their heads, as if to hide behind their wimples. Not out of modesty or reverence, but out of fear.

He smiled to himself. Eyriener women were not to his taste. Then again, women in general held little interest for him. Apart from vessels of procreation, something he would not have to consider for several decades, they were a distraction. To rise in the circles he wished to enter, one's whole life must be dedicated to one pursuit, and one only.

He was a tall man, slender, in a finely embroidered coat of exquisite cut, breeches and shining boots, all of the darkest colours, much like his cloak. From his outward appearance, he could have passed for a noble or rich merchant wearing only a modest amount of jewellery, all of the same stone. This was before passers-by caught his eyes. They were not grey, brown, or black. They were not of any *one* colour. They were fractured gems that shone with a whole rainbow of hues that changed depending on the quality of light. They dispelled any notion that he was an ordinary man and gave him an unsettling, inhuman quality.

The coach of lacquered black, the Royal Crest of Goradan in gold on its doors, was waiting for him. He stepped in without a word. He did not need to tell the driver where to take him. Everything was as it had been arranged. The coachman clicked his tongue at his horses and the carriage moved smoothly out into the crowded street, heading for the Palace.

King Cedric Ballir Goradan the IV had been flipping through a book of treatises with not much interest when the visitor was announced. His strong, thick fingers clenched on the book's spine so hard that its backing split and leather cover creased inwards. When the attendant left, he threw the book into a corner furiously. One of the large hounds asleep before the hearth raised its head to look at its master inquiringly as he strode to the desk and rested his palms on it, thinking. Rows of books lined the cedar shelves of this room, and more stood on stands and small tables. He was not a man of books. His hound returned his head back to the luxuriant black bearskin where he and his two brothers slept. Other hunting trophies adorned the walls beside tapestries and coats of arms. Three full suits of armour stood on wooden dummies ranged against one wall, and racks held decorative weapons.

The books had belonged to his father. The weapons were his.

He lifted his head and the long mirror on the opposite wall threw his reflection back at him. The King of Eyrie had been practising in the yard with his favoured knights earlier that morning. He had not bothered to change out of his chain mail shirt and leather breeches. His servants persuaded him to add a clean surcoat of red and gold embroidery, clean boots, and finally a band of gold studded with diamonds and bloodstones around his head. A far cry from the ridiculously ornamented, flamboyant robes considered fashionable in Court. He felt more at ease in his mail, particularly with this visitor. He pondered briefly whether it would be possible to issue a royal decree banning traditional Court attire. In his eyes, Eyriener robes of ceremony and formality resembled the woodcuts he had seen of the First Queen and past Kings of Morevi. With their defeat at the hands of those harpies, he wanted his realm purged of any mementoes from that cursed realm. The view from his window, however, made that impossible. The reconstruction of Taighar seemed to have no end in sight.

A breeze from outside caught one of the loose pages of the book he had thrown across the room. It flitted across the stone floor of his chambers and then was swept into the hearth. He watched the page crumple on itself in the fire, and a smile crossed his face. A fitting tribute to his nature. He was not a scholar like his father. He was a soldier and a campaigner. That was his art, and that was what he understood supremely well. As such, he had a dream. A dream of an empire that would reach across Naruihm. He would return Eyrie to the times when his ancestors ruled completely, unchallenged. This dream was to begin with The Silken Box.

It was a true pity High Lord Coumiran had perished in Morevi. Cedric still relished the idea of grinding the man to powder himself.

The campaign had failed, and he must face the consequences of this military disaster. The most unwelcome and unsettling of those now entered his chambers. At the sound of the doors, his hounds leapt up, a rumble beginning in their throats. They were large enough to stand at waist height of the visitor. When his eyes looked in their direction, their growls were reduced to quick, panicked whimpers. The cloaked man merely placed a finger to his lips, and the hounds returned to their deep slumber before the hearth.

At least they had sent a man. Not an Elf or a Shandarei. Or a woman, for that matter. The Fellowship of the Jewels had too many women in positions of high power for his taste. Women were never made for leadership. Quickly, he tried to clear his mind of fleeting, idle thoughts. It was never good to entertain them since the magicians of the Fellowship all had distinct talents. Some possessed the power to move objects without touching them. Others could bend steel with a thought. It was the mind readers that Cedric loathed.

The magician bowed to him. Just low enough to be polite, no more. Cedric gritted his teeth. Those possessing power always had equal arrogance to match.

The man appeared older than him, but it was always impossible to tell. His jewels, five rings and a pendant, were brilliant lapis set in aged silver. Not the full ten, no ear-studs, no collar. This told Cedric that he was still far from any appointments or official titles in the Fellowship. He was a simple emissary. Still, a simple emissary was enough for concern. It was unknown the last time any Eyriener set eyes on *any* member of the Fellowship.

"Greetings, Magister," the King smiled at the man. "Was your journey fine?"

"I did not come to partake in social pleasantries, Your Majesty," spoke the man in a clipped, short tone. He did not even try to mask his annoyance. "You launched an unprovoked attack on Morevi."

No pleasantries. No formalities. Cedric could see that dealing with him—*a King*—was beneath this Magister. *For the glory of my father and Eyrie,* he thought proudly before raising his voice. "Yes, that I did."

"Why?" The man was clearly not one to waste words.

Cedric did not relish the thought of servants present to listen and whisper, let alone recount how he placated this sorcerer. With a loud, dry *"snap"* of his fingers, they disappeared.

"Reasons are not that simple when it comes to politics," the King replied, pouring a chalice of wine. He never liked the magicians. He did not trust the immaterial and the elusive, preferring things one could see and feel, like the feel of a good sword and the powerful rise of a horse beneath him. Cedric added spices from waiting dishes to enhance the hearty flavour of the vintage, then offered the goblet with a civil smile. "Wine?"

Only a magician could enjoy the privilege of having a king pour wine for him. "Reasons are very simple when it comes to politics if one comes to the point," said the magician as he took the cup into his hand. He gave an exaggerated sigh, shaking his head. "I remind you, Your Majesty, that only courtiers and nobles appreciate the frivolity of court embellishment. I am here for the plain truth. Now give it to me."

Cedric gripped his own chalice tightly. The wine was smooth, almost thick with age and redolent with flavours of oak and grape. It calmed him before he answered. "The attack was not totally unprovoked, Magister—may I know your name?"

"Adrian." The tall man waved at him to continue.

Given only a surname as a reply. His voice was level in light of this wizard's impertinence. "Morevi has undergone a rather drastic change of values. I am sure the Fellowship is not ignorant of this. As we are their neighbour, you can hardly expect us to be unworried by their social upheaval."

"Arathelle is their closest neighbour and controls their access to the sea. If you are worried of an attack, Your Majesty, you should lay your fears to rest. Arathelle would seem the obvious and more profitable prize."

"These savages are far more familiar with the jungles and mountains than my people are," Cedric pointed out, stepping over to a large map on the wall. "They could use the Sleeping Dragons as their front and launch offensives against our lands, our people. And from what my soldiers told me, those savages possess armies that are vast in numbers. Vast!" He darted a look at Adrian, trying to gauge his opinions. Personal bias could be a handy lever.

There was no change of expression. Strange, multi-coloured eyes remained fixed on him.

"They worship a warlike Goddess, and in their civil war they slaughtered the men. In one stroke they changed the natural order of things. In this bitter hatred for men, what do you think their opinions of our culture would be, Magister? We stick to the old and proper ways, with the male ruling over family and home and the woman answering and accepting, unconditionally and unquestionably. As it has always been. Of recent years, since this reversal of dominance in Morevi, we have lost many of our women. They have abandoned their responsibilities here to follow this woman's religion called Nadinath. What is to say this new queen will not lead her devotees on a holy crusade against us?"

"We do not dictate social mores and rules, Your Majesty. The War of the Fan and Slipper was an isolated war that held no bearing or sway on Eyrie. People are free to decide whom they will worship. Askana Moldarin is a strong, capable Queen, which is further proven by the fact that she was able to repel your attack, Your Majesty." Cedric was now white with anger. Without so much as an acknowledgement of the King's displeasure, Adrian continued, "This is not why the Fellowship has sent me. Our concern was your enlisting of the one called Coumiran, or the 'Dark Merchant' as he was called by your people. A practitioner of the Dark Arts. Morevi did not attack your Kingdom, Your Majesty. Rather, you enlisted a renegade warlock into your service and struck first, placing Arathelle at risk."

"We struck before they could strike us! Askana Moldarin allied herself with another kingdom from beyond The Rift. A realm of which we know nothing, neither their wants nor their desires!"

King Cedric fought back his smile of satisfaction. He had Magister Adrian on this point. The Rift was a sensitive issue with the Fellowship. Travel across it was expressly forbidden. Only the Elves were exempt from their laws for reasons shared only between them and the Fellowship. Rumour also told there was an uneasy alliance between them, the conditions of it vague and uncertain. Perhaps not a "treaty" so much as an understood tolerance of one another.

"Indeed." The magician put down his wine. "Tell me, would this unknown realm be the same realm of corsairs that plague our oceans? These same corsairs that were commissioned by the Merchants' Circle to plunder ships bearing Morevian marks? If I do recall, there was one in particular that you yourself held in high regard. You call him 'The Sea Wolf'."

His ears turned red as he pointed a finger at the magician, the destruction still fresh in his mind, "That Otherworlder in the company of the Whore-Queen of Morevi single-handedly destroyed half of Taighar and slaughtered the Merchants' Circle!"

"So, you covertly hire this pirate to plunder Queen Askana's ships. Then Queen Askana hires this same pirate to aid her. Under her employment, he destroys a port of Eyrie." Adrian smiled pleasantly, tracing the rim of the fine silver goblet with the tip of his index finger. "In the eyes of the Fellowship, that would be considered poetic justice. Would you not agree?"

King Cedric went to speak but merely lowered his hand. An eye for an eye. It maddened him further that he, at one time, extended to that bastard Rafe Rafton a standing invitation to sit with him at his table for royal repast!

"I see that you were easily manipulated by this renegade Coumiran. Whether you were completely under his control, allied with him, or simply focused on your own gain remains to be seen. That will be for me to judge.

"As far as The Rift is concerned, that is our matter, Your Majesty. We control it. Never forget that. Fail to honour the Treaty of Naruihm signed by your forefathers and you will pay." Somehow, without changing his voice or manner, Adrian's tone turned menacing. "Do you understand?"

Cedric understood, as did the rest of Naruihm. The Fellowship of the Jewels was created centuries ago to control the practice of magic. They would only judge matters between kingdoms and countries if it affected the well-being of Naruihm or if magic was involved. To maintain this control over magic, it meant that all nations were under their supervision. This did not mean they had free reign over the world. By the Treaty of Naruihm, it was not permissible for a magician to commit murder. There were, however, other things they could do. More painful things. In some situations the Fellowship would actually approve.

Under his chain mail King Cedric broke into a sweat.

Magister Adrian kept his gaze on Cedric, his eyes glittering unnaturally in the light from the windows. "The balance must be kept and peace must be ensured. You upset that balance when you enlisted the warlock. Therefore, I shall watch and learn. You will teach. Do you understand what I am saying?"

"Yes," he said tersely.

"Excellent," Adrian nodded, his rings flashing gaily as he picked up his goblet. "You serve very fine wine, Your Majesty. I hope your estate offers rooms of the same quality."

The young King knew that this was, in fact, a dismissal.

The siege lasted four days. On the fourth day the gates were broken to splinters and the invaders swept in like Kir'shia on a scent-trail.

The message reached the Astarkhan on the day before the Raising of the Consort. The Queen had commanded that the gates of The Retreat be opened and the Holy Record surrendered to the Council. The Astarkhan was to present himself immediately to explain this serious breach of security that allowed a full one-third of the Servants of the Kingdom to engage in acts of high treason. What was not written, but what everyone understood, was that the days of power had come to an end for the Morev'ar. Weighing heavily in the precise, graceful hand of the court-scribe was Askana's decree. The Morev'ar would answer directly to the monarch, never again holding their favoured position—exemption from any law but their own.

The letter was burned. The Astarkhan never went to the Palace.

Soldiers arrived the next day, carrying out the orders of the Queen, even as she sped towards the ports of Arathelle.

Now the tranquil beauty of the grounds was torn and ravaged. Green lawns were expanses of mud-churned and fire-scorched ground. The water of the streams and fountains were tinged with blood. The smell of smoke and ash made the air harsh. Half-burned buildings sagged on their foundations. Broken glass and pottery littered the ground. Turi gardens The Retreat were famous for were cut down and trampled, those close to the buildings sacrificed to the fire.

The battle came to an end when soldiers broke past the last line of defence and invaded the *shokirya*, the inner sanctum where the Astarkhan had lived. The Palace Guard now dragged away bodies while the few captives were being herded onto rude carts. For their defiance, they traded the grand, lavish courtyards and gardens of The Retreat for prisons where they would stay until they stood trial for treason.

Losan lay on his back on the raised wood walk that led to the shokirya. On either side of him, small fountains spouted fans of shimmering water into the air. The goldfish were just beginning to swim around again, though the red colour all around them must have puzzled their poor, foolish brains. Three Morev'ar were sprawled in the water, their throats cut. He knew he was dying. Air sped from the small wound in his chest every time he breathed. Sometimes a bloody froth of bubbles rose just above the skin so he could see it if he tilted his head. If anyone were to have asked him in that moment, he would have said with immeasurable pride that the battle and his death were worth it all.

The Astarkhan and the elders were incensed by the treachery in their ranks as well, but the audacity of this new Queen and her collection of elevated handmaids would not be tolerated. Matters had been arranged quickly. Losan attended to some of them himself. The lands, of course, were forfeit, but the Holy Books that dated back to the time of the Morev'ar's foundation would not be so easily captured. Losan could still in his fleeting moments feel the elation when the Astarkhan disappeared over the horizon. They had won this battle before these children arrived.

He could hear the curses of the soldiers and the sound of crashing and breaking coming from within the shokirya. *Sacrilege*, Losan thought harshly, *but what did it matter now. They would all answer for it one day!*

He was feeling just the slightest pain when he breathed. He hoped Death would claim him soon. He was not afraid. None of them were.

Heavy footsteps sounded on the walk. Someone knelt beside his head with a click of plate. There were soldiers standing around him. "Where is the Astarkhan?" There were three of them. Young, but men, not boys. Their green armour was dented and scratched, covered with gore.

"Probably hiding in some hole somewhere," muttered one of his companions, grinding his sword into the glossy wooden plank tiredly, resting his hands on its hilt.

Losan opened his mouth but it was hard to speak. A gauntleted hand covered the fatal wound to keep the air from rushing out. The Guard's fingers became slick with Morev'ar blood as Losan spoke with a strained, raspy breath. His last. "Search to the far corners of oblivion, you will never find him, you dogs!"

Losan's other hand shot out, grasping the handle of the knife in the soldier's belt. With an oath and a final burst of strength, he lunged at the soldier. The man flung himself backwards so the blade rang harmlessly across his breastplate instead of gouging his eye out as the attack intended. The dying Morev'ar toppled back. His head cracked against the smooth steps leading to the shokirya and his vision filled with light.

The dagger fell to the boards with a clatter as the breath rattled in Losan's throat. Then everything was still. In the fountains, the goldfish fanned their veil-like tails as they swam in aimless circles.

Music thrummed over the natural rhythms of the jungle. Thousands of flowers floated on the surface of the water, swirling in the falls and eddying slowly downstream away from the Temple of Nadinath. Great pillars of carved and coloured sandalwood depicting dragons, birds, and fabulous creatures smouldered at all the bridges, sending clouds of perfume into the air.

When the High Priestess set foot on the first bridge, hundreds of voices lifted into the air joyously and white doves fluttered skyward, thrown from cages into freedom, to soar in the skies forever as frail symbols of peace, love, and purity. They were celebrating the homecoming of the Goddess' Chosen.

Extravagantly costumed and masked dancers whirled to the beat of the drums, the bones, and the cymbals. In the braziers, fires burned and torches glowed. On the slender towers, Priestesses angled huge mirrors down into the courtyards so the Temple blazed with light stolen from the sun.

Petals that rained down on Askana Moldarin crushed beneath her feet as she walked. Perfumed water sprinkled on her along with ceremonial oils. She drank cupful after cupful of blessed wine at each door of the Temple as custom demanded. Mixed into this wine were herbs and spices that would open her mind, heighten her awareness, and carry her closer to the Beloved Mother. The wine flowed freely among the devotees as the procession moved to the great central chamber where the huge, three-faced statue of the Goddess stood.

The drumbeats increased, and the music of the flutes rose in a frenzy along with the sharper sound of pipes. The High Priestess danced barefoot with the others, flowers in her hair and garlands around her neck, taken by the spirit of the Goddess. She whirled in the crush of dancing bodies, to forget, to abate the sorrow she had carried since her ride, to return to the Love and Guidance of Nadinath.

In the warmth, she felt the embrace of her sister, Lubria. Then came the welcome of a simple washerwoman. Another, a young Lady of a noble house. Yet another, a former prostitute. It did not matter. She let them wind their arms around her and pull her into the crush. There was nothing but the array of colours around her, the music, and her body moving of its own accord to the demanding rhythm. Then it came to her, a Love so pure that none could doubt it. A Love that gave everything and asked for nothing, that burned and healed her soul of all wounds.

From noise, heat, and the warmth of the living, she receded at last into the void of her wine-induced euphoria, the darkness and cold clarity that meant she had reached the inner goal at last. The Love was still all around her. An unconditional Love. Love that was free and unafraid.

Yet you are afraid.

Askana answered, *I have not found myself. I do not know myself, or what I do.*

It is in you. You know who you are meant to be, and what you must do, but fear clouds your mind.

I fear aloneness. I fear emptiness. I fear that none but You love me, and that I have failed. In this great abyss, Askana hung her head low, sinking to her knees.

You feel empty when a feast lies before you. You are alone when the crowd is around you. You fear shame and the loss of false honour. The Goddess' voices rose as thunder in a storm. *You fear ME.*

Why would I fear You? Askana implored, her arms reaching out into the darkness. *You who love all.*

You fear me because of your own guilt. You have not done as I asked of you.

I am afraid to do it. She could feel herself begin to wither. Lost. Alone. *I do not know how.*

Trust in Me. My hand will guide you.

She opened eyes that had not closed, and saw her Sisters all around her. Priestesses in red, black, and white, dancers in their costumes, women in plain robes dancing ecstatically with loose hair and half-closed eyes.

Askana reached out and touched one of the women on the forehead. The girl swooned and fell to the floor.

She recoiled at once. *I am afraid.*

Do as I command you. It is I who moves your limbs. It is I who touched that girl. Do not fear.

This is Chaos, Askana thought wildly in her delirium.

There is no such thing as Chaos. It is a higher level of order, from which I created the world and all the living.

She reached out and touched a Priestess this time, an older woman in red. The woman's eyelashes fluttered and she sank peacefully.

Askana reached out and touched them all, one after the other, every one within her reach with quick, feather-light brushes. They fell before her as others fell in battle. They went not to the jaws of Death but the embrace of sleep.

In this sleep, they dreamed. Nadinath was with them. She and Askana guided them.

The morning's light had barely broken the cover of night when Priestesses and Devotees led by their High Priestess went deep into the jungles, searching for the signs that their collected dream showed them. They descended deep into the jungles of the Sleeping Dragons, the outside world of Naruihm merely a fading memory as they continued into the sea of green. It was Askana's hand that uncovered it, encompassed in winding vines, leaves, and roots. Many wept. Some with joy, some with fear.

In the loving embrace of the High Priestess of Nadinath, the child-sized four-faced statue was brought back to the Temple with great ceremony.

The Queen of Morevi spent more and more time at the docks of Arathelle in the Royal Guesthouse built early in her reign. The official reason was to improve the relations between the respective kingdoms, to pay homage to both Arathellian monarchs and their involvement in restoring her to the throne. Her tensions between the Elven King and Queen softened as this gratitude served as a link. Still, with so much cause to rejoice, the road Askana travelled in her healing reached far into the distance, perhaps across The Rift itself. Members of her retinue who accompanied her to Arathelle often remarked on her love for the evening breezes from the sea. In the evenings and early mornings before dawn, the Queen liked to sit out on the balcony looking out to sea. Her eyes on the horizon as if looking for something to appear.

She had taken interest in a decree passed by the Fellowship of the Jewels concerning The Rift. No ships were allowed to pass through the portal. Otherworlder ships had always been few, most lost at sea, and as time passed their numbers dwindled even further until it appeared that most had forgotten about The Rift's existence, save for the ships belonging to the Fellowship that constantly patrolled the waters around it.

Their patrols, however, could not catch *all* ships that crossed.

Reports came to her that would bestow on her face a smile more radiant than the most brilliant of sunsets. She would hear of her ships attacked on the open waters of Naruihm by Eyriener marauders. Armed with the Otherworlder weapons, they would attempt to pillage her ships for their cargo of emeralds, tea, and chocha or sink them to avenge their own lost in their siege against Morevi. A few were claimed by these barbarians, but many returned home safely. All with the same story.

A grand ship, larger than any of Eyriener make, carrying the same weapons only threefold, would appear from nowhere. In a blaze of fire and deafening roar of thunder, this vessel would allow her ships to escape. It would then disappear in the smoke of battle, only reappearing if the ships flying the banner of the Turi flower were threatened.

And somewhere in the oceans...

The thunder of cannon fire.

The clash of steel.

The black banner of a wolf's head over an intertwined rose and Turi flower flying proudly in the warm sea air.

The Snow of Devon

The little girl's face creased in concentration as she rested her elbows on the table. Then, pushing back the embroidered sleeve of her cherry-pink linen robe, she reached across the par-stern board and picked out a piece with chubby fingers. "Check."

Sunlight dappled the courtyard where these two strategists sat. The sweet sound of birdsong filled their ears, but that was not why the fair-haired child smiled a bit. Across from her, the regal woman in a flowered morning robe tapped her cup on the polished black surface of the ebony table, frowning as if perplexed, "Are you sure of that, Ashtari?"

Big black eyes under blonde brows looked at her. "Yes. You're not bluffing me this time, Auntie. I am much too smart for you because I am almost five now. Kubi-Sogi says I can't have piggy-back rides with him any more because I am too big."

A wry smile perked the corner of the woman's mouth at picturing the Blademaster bearing this rambunctious bundle of youthful energy on his old back. "That's right. You'd give him a terrible backache." She turned back her sleeve with a whisper of cloth and replaced the white sword with the green marble samsagi. "Checkmate."

The girl's face fell so dramatically that the champion had to laugh. "My sweetling, you are being far too hard on yourself. You kept me on the defensive all this time. You have the mind and the heart of a skilled tactician. Some truly brilliant strategies you had in this game. You are the smartest child I know." A smile passed across the woman's face as she whispered in confidence, "When you play with Kalea, this time you will beat her. Be sure to wager on the game."

A mischievous smile dawned on the small face with its rosy cheeks, a strange, unique blush coming to her golden-coloured skin. Still charming and sweet. "The loser has to get on hands and knees, and jump all around the courtyard like a frog. They have to make croaking noises," she said conspiratorially. "And eat a fly."

The woman threw back her head and laughed. "You little imp! How are you going to catch a fly?"

"Mama can do it." Then the small face grew pensive. "But Mama's not here." She looked up at her playmate. "Can you do it like Mama does, Auntie?"

Dirare went silent at the sight of the girl's dark eyes. Contrition. She did not mean to remind the child that her mother was gone. "I will get Kubi-Sogi to catch one with his tongue like a real frog." The woman slid away from the table and beckoned the young girl to her, arms stretched wide, giving her the appearance of an eagle proudly displaying her wingspan. "Come here, sweetling."

She never felt as happy as she did when holding this little girl in her arms. At first, her birth seemed like Askana's revenge on her. Dirare herself was childless, incapable of bearing. Her House might die unless she took someone in as her successor, which she would surely be forced to do. She could not have imagined the pain that night, when the screams of a woman rent the air of the Palace soon to be joined by the wailing of a new-born child. She watched, full of this pain and envy as the child waved her little feet and hands in the cradle. A baby was a miracle no deity could rival. A miracle denied to her. How bitter and angry she had been.

Without Arnese her life seemed aimless, empty. For the first time she realised how lonely she was. Askana seemed to have everything. The outburst in the Great Hall, however, was contrary evidence to that. She would hear the jealous voices of the new Blood ridicule and criticise the Queen in private, only to hush their voices with a silent look, a disarming smile of civility. They had not seen their Queen that afternoon in the Great Hall.

No, she did not have everything, Dirare thought ashamedly. *I saw to that.*

In the Queen's bedchambers, she viewed it as her greatest political victory. Now, even when rocking this sweet girl back and forth in her arms, she questioned her true intentions that night. Perhaps she had not been as neutral and logical as she thought. Perhaps she had been motivated by jealousy.

"Auntie?" The girl's ebony eyes looked up to her, a question of honesty only a child would dare ask.

"Yes, sweeting?"

"Is Mama going to come back?"

Dirare gave a slight gasp as she looked at the girl askance, "Of course she will, my light, little princess!" That was Askana's pet name for her when she would pick up the child and spin her about make her laugh. Such a delightful laugh, full of life and spirit. "She told you she would come back and your mother is not one to break an oath. Why would you ask such a question?"

Ashtari looked up at her dubiously. "Uncle Jermal went away and never came back."

It jarred her. Truth did indeed come from the mouths of babes, whether one wished to hear it or not. For once in her life, Dirare found it difficult deciding what to say. From what she understood, this brute honesty was a trait of her father's.

At that moment, a light ringing of bells announced the entrance of a young Maiden of the Temple. She made obeisance formally.

Dirare watched out of the corner of her eye as she and Ashtari bowed in turn. She was pleased to see that the child performed with such grace and ease. As Princess, she must know the elaborate rituals and ceremony, ingrained into her in preparation for life at Court when often she would have to make lightning quick decisions when performing these gestures.

"High Regent, it is time for the Princess' morning exercises if it so pleases you," said the Maiden, eyes respectfully downcast.

Dirare nodded her head, "You have my consent." The serenity was interrupted by a most unladylike *"whoop"* as the Princess danced around the Maiden, who was trying hard to suppress a smile. Exasperated but amused, she clicked her tongue, "What in the world has possessed you, child!"

Ashtari barely paused in her hopping, "Lubria promised to take me into the Wood today to visit the Caillech. Part of my training."

The Southern Wood?! She opened her mouth to protest but Ashtari darted up and kissed her with a cheery "Goodbye, Auntie!"

The energetic girl pulled the Maiden unceremoniously out of the room. Dirare could hear her shouting *"Piggyback, piggyback!"* all the way down the hall.

If it were my child…

Dirare caught her thought and just stood in the doorway of her chambers, clinging to the girl's vibrancy as it reverberated through the Palace corridors. Then came a delightful, piercing shriek of joy and play. It seemed that the Princess was granted her piggyback ride.

Lubria. She did not like the creature, and the feeling was mutual. It was clear that the creature was not welcome at the Palace, but it was also clear not to push Askana further. Dirare took comfort in that her rooms were forbidden to the creature. It was more of a precautionary measure as the creature preferred to spend her time at the Temple and in the Southern Wood. She thanked El'Baz often for that little mercy. If only Ashtari were not so attached to her.

She was so like her mother in how her words could leave an impression. She mentioned his name so innocently. Now the man's image was fresh in Dirare's mind. She could still see him, loaded as a pack mule, preparing for what seemed to be a journey with no end. Jermal had not left without a word. He had come to see her.

"Perhaps you were right from the beginning, High Lady. There is no place for me here."

She had become too used to the man being there like a millstone around her neck. This was why his intention to leave stunned her, yet she understood. *"Where will you go?"*

He had smiled a little sadly. *"To see the rest of this strange new world, I suppose. There are so many other lands I have yet to visit. I am a drifter, Lady. Always have been. I never had a home or strong ties in my world. I suppose this is my lot in life."*

"Do you have enough provisions?"

"You're joking, right? Look at me!" He laughed incredulously. *"The Queen was very generous."* He paused for a moment. There was no bitterness in his voice. He knew the Queen's heart during the ceremony. He never lost her love, never truly having it in the first place. *"In any case I've not used my true skills for a while. It is time I started again before I lose my touch."* He then turned to look beyond the horizon as if his heart had already left for distant shores. *"With everything I've gone through, Morevi has never looked so beautiful as it does now. I've experienced things some people never see in several lifetimes. I'm a different person than when I got here. I owe a lot to this place."*

"You wish to convey this to Her Majesty?"

He then turned to her with a strange, slanting smile. *"I don't feel this solely for her."*

She had thought that she was beyond blushing. People flirted at Court. It was the way of it. *"You will be coming back?"*

"Maybe. When I am ready. Or maybe I will find my fortune elsewhere. Time will tell the tale, Dirare." As if addressing her by name had not been "improper" enough, he brazenly touched her lips with his own. Softly, briefly. *"Take care, High Regent. Thank you."*

Time would, indeed, tell the tale, especially in the Palace of a Thousand Suns. Askana had every right to hate her, but she had sacrificed even the luxury of that emotion. This anger, along with the other emotions she denied herself, was channelled back into Morevi. New trade routes were established. Expansion of cities and villages was booming. Two new cities were established, Haramal and Jalhammad. With the help of the Elves, they built these new cities as well as roads and pathways linking the far reaches of the Kingdom without destroying too much of the surrounding jungle and natural resources. Their latest project was the Aerial Bridge. Dirare could not help but smile in pride of it. The bridge was supported by cables in the treetops and slender pillars from the ground hundreds of feet below and would remain rock-steady even in a storm, stretching from the Kinessa Plains south of Songkusai, then onward to link Haramal and Lahsa. In the Arathelle shipyards, Morevi began construction of their own navy. The treasuries and granaries were full.

In the Hall of Dawn, she pledged to serve her Queen with unquestioned loyalty and devotion, and she did. With Dirare at her side, Askana ruled the Kingdom well, yet she remained spiritless.

It had taken the birth of Ashtari for life to return slowly to the Palace. What could have led Askana to her door that day?

"You are a supreme player of par-stern, High Regent. Would you be interested in imparting some of your knowledge to my daughter?"

Askana had subtly emphasised the word *"knowledge"* and then led the laughing, chubby toddler into her Royal Apartments with herself simply staring at the Queen. Dirare originally thought it was yet another strategy in the Great Game, but Askana no longer enjoyed playing it. She now resorted instead to a blunt honesty and dispensing of words to bring to light the truth. In a strange way, she had become the strongest player in the Great Game without knowing it. The child was too young at that time for any such teaching, but the meaning of the request was clear enough. Askana must have seen her longing. As attached as she was now to Ashtari, she would never menace the Royal Line and would, indeed, pour all her energies into securing the position of House Moldarin and build a legacy unparalleled for its future Queens.

Ashtari was their link, heralding their new beginning as ruler and adviser. Not close friends, not enemies, but forced to rely on each other on more than one occasion. Forced to live in such close proximity. The High Regent would never be a friend in the same manner as the Anjara or the Blademaster, but there was no longer the rivalry between them that the Old Blood of Council would make reference to in social and political circles. A steely gaze from the Royal Adviser would remind them that her understood truce with Askana did not, in any way, diminish her power as the House of Jarahd.

The strong survive and carry on to live and see greater things than ever imagined. Askana was strong enough to survive more than this, but nothing is without a price.

Rumours had reached her, floating in with the tide like pieces of driftwood. The Queen was having trouble sleeping. Then she was sleeping too much. She was not eating. Then suddenly she was driving the cooks mad with demands for banquet-foods at odd hours. She rode every horse in the stables in one week, returning after dark so tired she could barely stagger back to her bedchamber and collapse into her bed. She drifted off during audiences when she was supposed to be listening to the grievances of the people and making judgements. The midwives thought another child might be on the way, but that was sheer nonsense since Askana had no consort or lover of any sort. From innocent comments spoken by Ashtari, Dirare could tell the Queen was plagued by dreams, dreams of a most bizarre nature. Dreams that provided her with a lost solace. These dreams were the place she longed to be. These dreams also terrified her so that she did not wish to sleep.

Dirare was ready for this day. It surprised her Askana took so long a time before summoning her to the Queen's Chambers in the middle of the night.

"I shall be leaving Morevi for a time." The Queen seemed very calm, as if some weight were removed from her shoulders. She sat on a tasselled cushion before the three large mirrors in front of her wardrobe as two maidservants attended to her hair. *"You shall take over governance in my absence."*

Dirare bowed her head. *"Might I inquire as to how long Your Majesty's absence shall be?"*

"I am not sure."

She knew the answer. Asking this was merely a formality. *"Might I ask then, the reason for Your Majesty's absence?"*

Askana gently dismissed her maids, waiting for the sound of doors to close before she moved. When the Queen turned, Dirare was driven to gasp, flinch. The Queen's eyes were no longer calm. Their look was calculating like that of a predator trying to estimate the distance between her claws and her prey. It reminded Dirare too much of that creature Lubria. The mask of her court paint made her appear as a statue come to life.

"You know why, Dirare. Let us not play games. We have known each other too long for that." With a rustle of silk, she rose, stepping leisurely across to one of her mirrors. She stood there, tilting the mirror so she could see both their reflections. It was a new tactic of Askana's that Dirare had to admit was very effective. *"I am sure your spies have already informed you of it. You know the tradition. Ashtari's fifth birthday will be in two months' time."*

It was an excuse. A strong one, but an excuse nonetheless. *"Your Majesty—"*

"Dirare, nothing you can say or do frightens me any longer. None of the earlier risks that forced my hand can menace me now. Morevi is mine," Askana spoke calmly, stating fact. *"I gave it everything and now it is time for my realm to give me something in return."* She turned from the mirror in a swirl of white and green, *"Therefore, permit me this dalliance if that is how you look upon it."* The Regent moved to speak but Askana did not yield or even raise her hand to cut her off. Askana spoke with a tone as graceful and as quick as his ivory-handled rapier had been. *"Do not stir the old arguments, My Regent, for this time what I do is for Askana, and though it shall pain me and Ashtari, I shall not hesitate to cut you down if you stand against me in this."*

It was not an empty threat, but a clear decision from the First Queen. She would not be challenged on this.

Dirare could not help but smile. This would truly be a pleasure, perhaps even atonement for what she had done years ago.

"Your Majesty, you did not permit me to finish. One of my ships is leaving the harbour in four days time. It is, if I may presume to say so, the fastest that we have. Captain Tamashi is quite cunning, skilled in evasion tactics and navigation. You will need that when facing Fellowship patrols and The Rift itself. It bears enough supplies for two months voyage without stops. If you intend to leave, Your Majesty, you had best take that ship. I have already made arrangements with the captain."

It was the first time in a long time she had ever seen Askana taken aback. Dirare's smile widened at the memory, the same smile she wore then.

"How long ago were these preparations made?" Askana had asked her.

"One week ago, my Queen."

Perhaps time had, in fact, mellowed them both. Perhaps they were growing into two old spinsters who would spend their old age knitting and snapping at each other.

Perish the thought!

Now, as she stepped out into the warmth of the morning sun, Dirare thought pensively of the woman who was her Queen, her partner in governance, and the mother of the child she loved. Where was she? Would she return successful? Would she return at all?

"May El'Baz and Nadinath both grant you strength once more, my Queen," whispered Dirare as she looked out from her window.

Her words expected no answer. They merely floated out over Morevi. Across the Sleeping Dragons. Over the oceans of Naruihm. And across The Rift...

She pulled the skins closer. They provided some warmth and a bit of protection from the elements, but her exposed skin could not have prepared her for the sensation of what collected across the deck of the *Dragon's Wing*. She watched in fascination as the intricate pattern of ice touched her skin only to melt instantly, forming a solitary drop upon her wrist. A moment's chill and then it was gone. The sailors watched with an almost childish glee at how it collected on their coats while the captain covered her charts to avoid the frost and moisture from claiming the ink.

Snow. This was snow.

A single white flake landed gently on the luxuriant sable hairs of a fur, and more out of curiosity than anything else, she lifted it to her eyes. It appeared in its brief, momentary existence as the finest lace, intricate and pearlescent. Its beauty touched her heart, then it melted into a drop of water as did the others. So beautiful and so fragile. This was the lesson of the snowflake—that beautiful things never lasted. Yet here she was chasing this lost dream, to restore one beautiful, fragile night and make it last forever.

"The port is in view," Captain Tamashi spoke gently in her ear.

She turned to the female captain, muffled in furs so that her face remained hidden from the crew. Only Tamashi and the accompanying Guard needed to know her identity. "Then drop anchor here, and have a boat take me into town. I desire no disturbance. No one should notice us as we are not of this world."

Tamashi bowed, shivering slightly in the snow, and retreated. Anchors were dropped into the cold waters with a pair of soft splashes. Then, a single boat left the ship, heading for the docks of Plymouth.

It had been a number of years since her eyes fell upon this land within King Henry's realm. Devon. Instead of slipping away in the cover of night, she approached it in full light of day, only to remain in concealment of her cloak. It was far from the ports of London, but it bustled with activity. She could see wooden skeletons of ships in the middle of construction. Barges unloaded their cargo holds. The voices of sailors and tradesman echoed into the cold, transparent veil of winter. She knew this port also served as a gateway to the landmass called Europe. So like King Henry to refer to a body of water between his own realm and his rival's as The *English* Channel. She smiled softly, *Dear Hal.*

The rhythm of the boat, the relaxing sounds that cut through the water, resurrected memories that occupied her thoughts whenever she looked on her daughter. It was her eyes. Ashtari had his brilliance in her eyes. When they looked into her own, she was forced to embrace the memories of their time. His bravado. His touch.

His fury.

Now, once again, she found herself approaching another seaport. Dreams brought her across The Rift to a kingdom she swore never to set foot in again. Leads and instincts took her to a country called Wales, then to an Emerald Island farther west still warm and green in the grip of winter, and now here. The seaport she recalled from her adventure.

She always approached a battle with a sense of the enemy. Before the first move in the Game of War, she would know ten moves ahead of what the opponent would attempt against her. This is what made her queen—knowing the enemy. This opponent she knew once, but that was six years ago. Who was he now? Did he heed her hidden wish and cast her aside, reducing her to a distant memory?

If so, then why those dreams? Countless dreams. Such glorious dreams...

She was facing an unknown. It would be a Game of Chance today, but did he not call it something else?

"A leap of faith," she whispered aloud as their dinghy slipped amongst the grander vessels of war and modest fishing boats.

The smell of salt-water, fish, and wood pervaded the air. The coarse shouts of sailors and fishermen sounded eerily like those of the Eyriener ports, except that the words were thick with a uniquely English sound. Some cast glances at the tiny boat and its occupants, particularly at their furs. It was obvious that the four men were soldiers of some sort, or hired blades judging from the glimpses of steel their heavy cloaks afforded. Rope ladders were tossed down from above, and slowly they climbed up onto the docks. They were strangers to their port, but their charge walked through the streets as if she had been there before.

The tavern's sign swayed in the breeze. "Wait here," she said to the detail.

The soldiers looked at each other uncertainly, but they knew not to question her word. With a nod from their commander, they took a place by the pub's doorway as their mistress slipped inside.

She had come full circle. A thought in the back of her mind wondered if his sister would be present today. After all, this was her pub. It reflected her zeal and lust for life. The Boar and The Bull was obviously a place where mischief and merriment were to be found upon a regular basis. Unlike the eclectic mix of races and creeds at The Barrier Reef, they were all the subjects of King Henry. The odd drunkard or two were asleep, either at the table or the bar. The brilliance of snow was replaced by the dim shadows of this place. The sudden change gave her a moment's pause but she could still take in the sights and sounds of the people around her.

"Now here is a lovely one." His breath was rank. Straight from the fires of Xorinok. He struggled to remain standing as he slurred his words, "I have travelled the world an' back again," He gave a grotesque belch and then continued, not missing a single stride in his thoughts, "but I never did see such beauty as you, lass."

"Indeed," her voice matched the chill of the outside weather. "Is that for me? Or for all three of us who sway before your drunken gaze?"

"Three?" The drunk gave a good laugh, making her wrinkle her nose under her hood. "Can you not see, wench, there be *four* of you here." He turned to an empty space to the right of her. His head bobbled back and forth as if he was shaking his head ruefully, "Now do not fuss, lass. She did not forget you. I did notice you an' you are pretty too." His drunken stare returned to her, "But not as pretty as *you*. Go on, give us a kiss."

Powerful hands grabbed the slob from behind and pulled him away from the woman's presence, "All right now, Jack, that is more than enough from you! Is your *wife* not expecting you?" The poor drunk stumbled out of the pub and down the street, presumably for home. The barkeep shook his head, "That sot! To be drunk at such a time."

The small knife slowly returned to her gauntlet. She took in the face of this large man before her, reading his soft, kindly eyes. She was in no danger. "Why is this not a time for such behaviours?"

"Indeed, miss, 'tis Christmastide. Scant days before the birth of our Saviour. Do you not know this?"

"I am not familiar with this realm." Her voice softened, "I am a visitor from a far-off land."

She heard his voice in a moment. Her introduction to the monarch of England. *"Her Majesty, Askana Moldarin, comes from the lands in the Far East. The extremely Far East."* It brought a smile to her face. Her heart skipped, a momentary reflex.

Please, Goddess, she prayed silently, *let my journey end here.*

The burly man scratched his chin doubtfully. "Don't get many visitors from 'far-off', and none that speak like you, miss," he shrugged. "Might you be wanting a room for the night then?"

"No, thank you. Some warmed spiced wine, perhaps, and a seat near the hearth?"

The big man nodded, and she followed him to the other side of the room, her black eyes searching through the dimness. She passed by a pair of men well into their drink, and one bravely reached out for her sleeve, apparently to bless his lap with a visit. She felt the touch on her cloak, and her reaction was merely a reflex. She continued past the table, leaving the man choking as if struck in the throat.

Colin's eyes watched this one. Her attack was so quick that no one saw it in the faint lighting of the pub. He saw it though, and did not appreciate this stranger causing problems. He grabbed the steaming cup from a passing barmaid's tray and placed the wassail before her. The stream rose from it slowly to disappear before it could pass her hood.

"There you are, my lady. A bit of wassail to temper your disposition." He grunted with little sincerity, "A joyous Christmas to you."

"Stay a moment, barkeep." Even in the gentleness she had given her voice, there still rang the air of royalty within it, causing the man to pause. "I am in need of a blade. Lethal in the ways of combat. A man of courage and bravery. I have heard talk of such a man. A privateer. He captains a vessel christened *Defiant.*"

The silence swept across the tables of The Boar and The Bull. Heads slowly turned to this figure cloaked in furs and skins, the face still not revealed but lost in the shadows of her cowl. The pause was for a brief moment before a chorus of "Wassail, Wassail" rose from one of the tables.

Most of the pub returned to their repast and merriment. Others watched. All they needed was a word. A look. Then it would happen.

"If memory serves me right, his name is Rafe Rafton," the woman asked. "Do you know of him?"

"Rafe Rafton?" Colin said with a manner of searching through his vast memory of captains, softly repeating the name again and again. Then, he shook his head. "I know many a sea captain in these parts and no one answers to that name here." Colin called out to all in the pub, "Lads, do you know of any that captains a ship called the *Defiant?*"

The stillness returned. Askana could now feel a tension rising. She also noticed something about this barkeep and these sailors. Not only were they offensive in every way, they were horrible liars.

And they were clumsy. Extremely clumsy.

Her chair flew from under her, but it was the reverse kick that sent it up into the man attempting to jump her from behind. Another sailor managed to grab her arm, but from what seemed to be the very darkness itself came gloved leather hands that twisted his arm back. The other struck his elbow. A blood curdling crunch could be heard, immediately followed by his horrific scream. The sailor with a welt now burning across his neck charged for her. He was stopped by a dart that shot from her wrist and landed deep into his shoulder.

Before Colin could reach for his dagger, a blade of the finest silver, as brilliant as the snow now collecting outside, slipped from her wrist and rested against his neck.

"Is this how you celebrate your Messiah's birth in England?" The blade scratched gently at his throat, stretching the skin as though trying to shave him. There was movement from other sailors, but the blade pressed harder against Colin, keeping them in their seats. The cloaked woman bent his spine backward, causing him to let out a small grunt in pain, "I shall ask only one more time—where is Rafe Rafton?"

"Here is Rafe Rafton," said a voice from the stairwell behind her, causing everyone in the room save for Colin and the woman to turn their heads. "What do you want with me?"

For a moment no one moved, and the silence was absolute.

"Who are you?" spoke his voice.

His familiar voice. She did not dream now. He was there. She closed her eyes, a fear consuming her like wildfire. *Turn to face him, Askana,* implored her Heart. She heard the creak of wooden steps as he descended to the tavern.

"Why do you have a knife at Colin's throat? Release him for you have my attentions, my Lady. What do you want?"

Her eyes opened again, the memory of a moment's passion returning to her. *"Tell me what you want. Not what the Queen commands, but what you, Askana, want."*

It was time to face this fear of six years.

"What do I want?" Soft as it was, her voice stopped him in mid-step. She threw the bartender aside and turned to face him. "There is a novel question." Slowly she reached up with her free hand, and slipped back her hood.

The firelight gleamed in hair so black it looked as if it had been lacquered. Ornaments of gold and jade decorated thick braids wound into a crown upon a head that needed no crown to make it regal. Time had been more than kind to her but was it a trick of light that caused her hair to have the odd strand of white? Age still refused to mar the beauty she carried. His heart did cease for a moment when he saw her, then he felt himself calm. *Why should my heart cease for you,* he thought bitterly, *when yours did nothing for me so many years ago?*

Askana did not recognise him for a moment. A thin moustache hugging his top lip and a tuft of blonde, brown, and red hair upon his chin gave him a very different look. Less of a braggart or a reckless swashbuckler. It gave him refinement, subduing the youthful face he possessed. No one would dare disturb the tranquillity of this moment.

The *"click-click"* of pistols from above his head and behind the bar made them both blink.

The woman from the balcony above the stairwell was a professional, but a professional *what* remained uncertain for the moment. She came from the room Rafe apparently occupied, wearing only a sheet haphazardly wrapped around her body. In her other hand was a pistol, the hammer pulled back in a ready position and now aimed at Askana's head. The bartender held a double-barrelled wheel-lock pistol of his own. He held it hard against his chest as if to steady it. He was still visibly shaken from having the knife upon his throat.

"Captain, she did mention the *Defiant*, the name of your former ship! She be one of them assassins from that place you did speak of—Eyrie, was it?"

"Easy, Colin. I know her." Rafe held a hand upward and both pistols lowered slowly. Rafe's eyes never left Askana as he motioned to the pistol-wielding woman, "You can leave."

The woman shot glances at both Rafe and the cloaked foreigner. For a moment, she wondered if she should spend the bullet on this strange woman or on the Privateer Captain.

The stranger merely lifted her wrist to reveal the array of darts. "I believe you were told to leave."

The wench slowly returned the pistol's hammer back. The stranger's words struck her hard, driving her back into the room. It was not a threat she made. It was a command.

Rafe walked up to her slowly. She could reach out to touch him. She did not dare. His voice remained flat, "Well met, Askana Moldarin, Black Widow of Morevi." The same words he spoke to her when they met. Only this time, his voice was sharp, jaded. "You appear in the most damned of places!"

"You were never one to waste time." Her black eyes slid sharply to him. "I am surprised there was only one girl in that room." *But is that not what you wished, Askana?* chided her Heart. *You wanted him to forget, did you not?*

"Well, what with the holiday, I kept my passions in check," he quipped. "There would be a touch of blasphemy in enjoying a menagerie of maids, would you not agree?"

His bitterness suddenly abated at the sound of a man's legs kicking spasmodically. He joined Colin holding down the fallen sailor, helpless, never seeing a fit like this. Rafe braced his knee against the sailor's chest, turning his eyes to her. "It seems I am not the only one continuing bad habits," Rafe said as he removed the dart from the Englishman's shoulder. "As we have waited six years, we can wait a little longer. This man cannot. Give him the remedy, Your Grace."

A glimmer of the man who put his crew before his own wants and needs. "Why should I?" Askana spat, her eyes seeing the knife by the man's hand. A knife meant for her. "He has little time left. My poisons have not weakened with time."

"Askana, I beg this boon of you. You do not take life unnecessarily."

Hearing him speak her name unsettled her, but only for a moment. "Do I not? I take life when I wish." Her cold words were contradicted by her actions as she dropped to Rafe's side, taking out a tiny glass vial and a single dart from her wrist gauntlet. "The poison moves too fast. This will have to go in a vein."

She dipped the dart into the vial, rose her arm high, and then drove it hard into the man's neck. The sailor's back arched sharply, struggling against Rafe and the wide-eyed Colin, then his body slowly eased back to the stone floor. Rafe closed his eyes in relief as the man's breathing was shallow but calming with each breath, his body flinching only when Askana removed the dart from his neck. He gave Colin a nod who, in turn, motioned for the fallen sailor to be carried up to a vacant room.

For a moment, they remained kneeling on the floor, the Queen and the Pirate, taking the sight of one another. Together, once more. Already in their brief time reunited, they were disrupting the holiday merriment of his sister's pub. *The things we could have done, Askana,* he lamented silently. *We heard the chimes at midnight, challenged the darkness, and won a kingdom together. The sights we could have beheld.*

The din of the pub resumed, a touch of nervousness now in the air. Askana picked herself up off the floor and returned to her table by the hearth. She waited. For what, she was uncertain. She was lost in a storm of emotions, the prevailing one being outrage. These common sailors with their awkward attacks and lewd advances were insulting enough. The woman coming from his room, unforgivable.

So were your words six years ago, whispered her Heart. *You now look upon what you created in that moment. Well done, Askana, well done.*

"So what brings you to Devon? Did you come for the wassail? A drink not found in your beloved realm? Well then, let us try this again." Rafe slammed his palm against the small table, causing Askana to jump. "Colin, two cups of wassail for myself and Her Majesty, Askana Moldarin of Morevi."

They remained in silence waiting on the Christmastide libation. Rafe's eyes fixed on her, Askana's on the worn, wooden table surface. The wassail finally came as did the question she knew had to be first and foremost in his mind.

"Why are you here? After all this time?" He did not want to conceal anything from her. He wanted her to know. He wanted her to hear the anger and irritation in his voice. "Do you have another task for me?"

He had felt her sometimes in the past years. Physical pain. Unexplained euphoria. Flashes that had connected them both and left him bereft when they passed.

Askana could not tell him right away. It had to be a slow, arduous process, or did it? She needed Kubi-Sogi by her side. Her teacher. Her sen-sheru. Or perhaps she needed her sister, Lubria. Strength. Cunning. This was needed now more than ever.

"How is your good King?" Askana asked as if to avoid his question, "Still married to the child-queen, Kathryn Howard?"

Rafe smiled lightly and shook his head, "Oh, Askana, although I have kept a watchful eye from the shadows, you have not been keeping tabs on your ally from across The Rift. King Henry had sweet little Kathryn beheaded on charges of infidelity and treason. Our Queen is a good and virtuous lady named Katherine Parr. She tends to our King in His twilight time."

He looked at her for a moment, his mind silently continuing his words to her. *Whenever a bullet did hit me or a blade tried to end my life, I asked for your forgiveness. Did you grant it to me, Askana? Did you know that whenever I spilt my blood I prayed for your well-being? Forgive me, my light, little queen.*

Askana nodded, hardly surprised by the child-queen's demise. She wondered if Henry could accept Kathryn's fate better than his confidant's, Thomas More. The way the child died did not raise comment in her mind. Such punishments were accepted. She folded her fingers on the table as she thought of what to say. "I sealed myself off from England, from everything that reminded me of you."

Her own thoughts continued as his did. *Did you know that during the war, when an Eyriener arrow sank deep into my leg, I prayed that the pain would not hurt you too badly? The tears I let fall were not for me, they were for the pain I knew I would be causing you. And did you feel the pain of the birth? Did you for one moment guess what caused that?*

"I see. Now, six years of isolation brings you here? For what?" Rafe leaned forward, his eyes attempting to find her own, "You have done so well in keeping me nothing more than a pleasant diversion, I believe you called me? What brings the Black Widow all this way, across The Rift?"

"Rafe, shortly after you left, do you remember anything that ever disturbed your sleep? Pain. A terrible, tearing pain that came and went like the swinging of a pendulum, that felt like you were being ripped and torn in two?"

Reluctantly, outwardly bothered by the question, Rafe sifted through his memories, memories of their adventure together and the hard, cold time that followed. Then his brow cleared. "I thought that was a nightmare of mine." Worry creased his skin. Rafe's hands reached across the table and rested lightly over hers, still encased in chestnut-brown leather gloves. His hands clenched lightly around hers. Warm, protective. "Was it real, Askana? What happened?"

Her mind reeled when he touched her. Her nerves were frayed, and she could feel herself begin to tremble. She hated this feeling. Even in battle she had always been calm because she knew what was to come, and what to do. Here, all she knew was that she had to fight. But fight for what and how?

Then, in the tempest of her fear, the hearth's firelight caught the glint of his signet ring. The wolf's head, rose, and Turi flower. It was the right time. She could feel it in his grasp. He wanted to heal the pain, perhaps take revenge against the force that caused her such pain. *My protector*, she thought in passing, with a slight smile. *It was not a mighty empire or even a vengeful enemy, but a sweet little soul.*

"Rafe, I should have told you this earlier, but I was too afraid, too proud. Too foolish, perhaps." She looked him in the eye then. "I have a daughter."

He felt his blood chill. His hands released her as he sat back, appalled at the audacity of this woman. Perhaps complete disregard for the emotions of others was a luxury of royalty. "This is what brings you across The Rift? An apology for putting me through pains of labour?" Rafe laughed incredulously, loud enough to catch the attention of the surrounding patrons. His voice boomed loudly, as if he intended to pull everyone into their private conversation. "Yes, Your Grace, I do remember that dream. I thought it was a case of bad mutton. Nearly killed the ship's cook!" He leaned forward, his voice as bitter as his world's December winter. "How very kind of you. Well then, I accept your apology and concern, and commend you for giving birth to your heir of the regime. My *sincerest* congratulations to you and Jermal. How proud you must be of your selection in breeding stock."

She jerked up in her seat as if slapped. For a long, tense moment they stared at each other, anger roiling with other emotions just as strong. "I did not marry Jermal!" she snapped. "We never shared my bed since—" Her voice caught in her throat. She took her gaze to the fire in the hearth, finding a strange calm before looking at Rafe again. "The girl's name is Ashtari. She is five years old."

In the light of the fire, his face went pale. It all registered in moments, but he refused to be taken again for a fool. He surrendered so much to her in that one night. Now he readied himself for her deception, her "Great Game" that she was so apt at playing.

"Askana, do not toy with me as you did once before."

"I never..." Her words trailed off again. How was she to explain? Did she deserve forgiveness in any case? Sitting across from him, Askana was at a loss.